The Collected Supernatural and Weird Fiction of Fitz-James O'Brien

The Collected Supernatural and Weird Fiction of Fitz-James O'Brien

Thirty-Seven Short Stories of the Strange and Unusual Including 'From Hand to Mouth', 'The Legend of Barlagh Cave', 'The Other Night', and Eight Poems Including 'The Ghost', 'Sir Brasil's Falcon' and 'The Lost Steamship'

Fitz-James O'Brien

LEONAUR

The Collected
Supernatural and Weird
Fiction of
Fitz-James O'Brien
Thirty-Seven Short Stories of the Strange and Unusual Including 'From Hand to Mouth', 'The Legend of Barlagh Cave', 'The Other Night', and Eight Poems Including 'The Ghost', 'Sir Brasil's Falcon' and 'The Lost Steamship'

by Fitz-James O'Brien

FIRST EDITION

Leonaur is an imprint of Oakpast Ltd

Copyright in this form © 2017 Oakpast Ltd

ISBN: 978-1-78282-662-0 (hardcover)
ISBN: 978-1-78282-663-7 (softcover)

http://www.leonaur.com

Publisher's Notes

The views expressed in this book are not necessarily those of the publisher.

Contents

The Wondersmith

1: Golosh Street and Its People.

A small lane, the name of which I have forgotten, or do not choose to remember, slants suddenly off from Chatham Street, (before that headlong thoroughfare rushes into the park,) and retreats suddenly down towards the East River, as if it were disgusted with the smell of old clothes, and had determined to wash itself clean. This excellent intention it has, however, evidently contributed towards the making of that imaginary pavement mentioned in the old adage; for it is still emphatically a dirty street. It has never been able to shake off the Hebraic taint of filth which it inherits from the ancestral thoroughfare. It is slushy and greasy, as if it were twin brother of the Roman Ghetto.

I like a dirty slum; not because I am naturally unclean,—I have not a drop of Neapolitan blood in my veins,—but because I generally find a certain sediment of philosophy precipitated in its gutters. A clean street is terribly prosaic. There is no food for thought in carefully swept pavements, barren kennels, and vulgarly spotless houses. But when I go down a street which has been left so long to itself that it has acquired a distinct outward character, I find plenty to think about. The scraps of sodden letters lying in the ash-barrel have their meaning: desperate appeals, perhaps, from Tom, the baker's assistant, to Amelin, the daughter of the dry-goods retailer, who is always selling at a sacrifice in consequence of the late fire.

That may be Tom himself who is now passing me in a white apron, and I look up at the windows of the house (which does not, however, give any signs of a recent conflagration) and almost hope to see Amelia wave a white pocket-handkerchief. The bit of orange-peel lying on the sidewalk inspires thought. Who will fall over it? who but the industrious mother of six children, the youngest of which is only nine months old, all of whom are dependent on her exertions for support?

I see her slip and tumble. I see the pale face convulsed with agony, and the vain struggle to get up; the pitying crowd closing her off from all air; the anxious young doctor who happened to be passing by; the manipulation of the broken limb, the shake of the head, the moan of the victim, the litter borne on men's shoulders, the gates of the New York Hospital unclosing, the subscription taken up on the spot.

There is some food for speculation in that three-year-old, tattered child, masked with dirt, who is throwing a brick at another three-year-old, tattered child, masked with dirt. It is not difficult to perceive that he is destined to lurk, as it were, through life. His bad, flat face—or, at least, what can be seen of it—does not look as if it were made for the light of day. The mire in which he wallows now is but a type of the moral mire in which he will wallow hereafter. The feeble little hand lifted at this instant to smite his companion, half in earnest, half in jest, will be raised against his fellow-beings forevermore.

Golosh Street—as I will call this nameless lane before alluded to—is an interesting locality. All the oddities of trade seemed to have found their way thither and made an eccentric mercantile settlement. There is a bird-shop at one corner wainscoted with little cages containing linnets, waxwings, canaries, blackbirds, Mino-birds, with a hundred other varieties, known only to naturalists. Immediately opposite is an establishment where they sell nothing but ornaments made out of the tinted leaves of autumn, varnished and gummed into various forms. Further down is a second-hand book-stall, which looks like a sentry-box mangled out flat, and which is remarkable for not containing a complete set of any work.

There is a small chink between two ordinary-sized houses, in which a little Frenchman makes and sells artificial eyes, specimens of which, ranged on a black velvet cushion, stare at you unwinkingly through the window as you pass, until you shudder and hurry on, thinking how awful the world would be if everyone went about without eyelids. There are junk-shops in Golosh Street that seem to have got hold of all the old nails in the ark and all the old brass of Corinth. Madame Filomel, the fortune-teller, lives at No. 12 Golosh Street, second storey front, pull the bell on the left-hand side. Next door to *Madame* is the shop of Herr Hippe, commonly called the Wondersmith.

Herr Hippo's shop is the largest in Golosh Street, and to all appearance is furnished with the smallest stock. Beyond a few packing-cases, a turner's lathe, and a shelf laden with dissected maps of Europe, the interior of the shop is entirely unfurnished. The window, which is lofty and wide, but much begrimed with dirt, contains the only pleasant object in the place. This is a beautiful little miniature theatre,—that is to say, the orchestra and stage. It is fitted with charmingly painted scenery and all the appliances for scenic changes. There are tiny traps, and delicately constructed "lifts," and real footlights fed with burning-fluid, and in the orchestra sits a diminutive conductor before his desk, surrounded by musical manikins, all provided with the smallest of violoncellos, flutes, oboes, drums, and such like.

There are characters also on the stage. A Templar in a white cloak is dragging a fainting female form to the parapet of a ruined bridge, while behind a great black rock on the left one can see a man concealed, who, kneeling, levels an arquebuse at the knight's heart. But the orchestra is silent; the conductor never beats the time; the musicians never play a note; the Templar never drags his victim an inch nearer to the bridge; the masked avenger takes an eternal aim with his weapon. This repose appears unnatural; for so admirably are the figures executed that they seem replete with life. One is almost led to believe, in looking on them, that they are resting beneath some spell which hinders their motion. One expects every moment to hear the loud explosion of the arquebuse,—to see the blue smoke curling, the Templar falling,—to hear the orchestra playing the requiem of the guilty.

Few people knew what Herr Hippo's business or trade really was. That he worked at something was evident; else why the shop? Some people inclined to the belief that he was an inventor, or mechanician. His workshop was in the rear of the store, and into that sanctuary no one but himself had admission. He arrived in Golosh Street eight or ten years ago, and one fine morning, the neighbours, taking down their shutters, observed that No. 13 had got a tenant. A tall, thin, sallow-faced man stood on a ladder outside the shop entrance, nailing up a large board, on which "Herr Hippe, Wondersmith," was painted in black letters on a yellow ground. The little theatre stood in the window, where it stood ever after, and Herr Hippe was established.

But what was a Wondersmith? people asked each other. No one could reply. Madame Filomel was consulted; but she looked grave, and said that it was none of her business. Mr. Pippel, the bird-fancier, who was a German, and ought to know best, thought it was the English for some singular Teutonic profession; but his replies were so vague that Golosh Street was as unsatisfied as ever. Solon, the little humpback, who kept the odd-volume book-stall at the lowest corner, could throw no light upon it. And at length people had to come to the

9

conclusion that Herr Hippe was either a coiner or a magician, and opinions were divided.

2: A Bottleful of Souls.

It was a dull December evening. There was little trade doing in Golosh Street, and the shutters were up at most of the shops. Hippe's store had been closed at least an hour, and the Mino-birds and Bohemian waxwings at Mr. Pippel's had their heads tucked under their wings in their first sleep.

Herr Hippe sat in his parlour, which was lit by a pleasant wood-fire. There were no candles in the room, and the flickering blaze played fantastic tricks on the pale grey walls. It seemed the festival of shadows. Processions of shapes, obscure and indistinct, passed across the leaden-hued panels and vanished in the dusk corners. Every fresh blaze flung up by the wayward logs created new images. Now it was a funeral throng, with the bowed figures of mourners, the shrouded coffin, the plumes that waved like extinguished torches; now a knightly cavalcade with flags and lances, and weird horses, that rushed silently along until they met the angle of the room, when they pranced through the wall and vanished.

On a table close to where Herr Hippe sat was placed a large square box of some, dark wood, while over it was spread a casing of steel, so elaborately wrought in an open arabesque pattern that it seemed like a shining blue lace which was lightly stretched over its surface.

Herr Hippe lay luxuriously in his arm-chair, looking meditatively into the fire. He was tall and thin, and his skin was of a dull saffron hue. Long, straight hair, sharply cut, regular features, a long, thin moustache, that curled like a dark asp around his mouth, the expression of which was so bitter and cruel that it seemed to distil the venom of the ideal serpent, and a bony, muscular form, were the prominent characteristics of the Wondersmith.

The profound silence that reigned in the chamber was broken by a peculiar scratching at the panel of the door, like that which at the French court was formerly substituted for the ordinary knock, when it was necessary to demand admission to the royal apartments. Herr Hippe started, raised his head, which vibrated on his long neck like the head of a cobra when about to strike, and after a moment's silence uttered a strange guttural sound. The door unclosed, and a squat, broad-shouldered woman, with large, wild, oriental eyes, entered softly.

"Ah! Filomel, you are come!" said the Wondersmith, sinking back in his chair. "Where are the rest of them?"

"They will be here presently," answered Madame Filomel, seating herself in an armchair much too narrow for a person of her proportions, and over the sides of which she bulged like a pudding.

"Have you brought the souls?" asked the Wondersmith.

"They are here," said the fortune-teller, drawing a large pot-bellied black bottle from under her cloak. "Ah! I have had such trouble with them!"

"Are they of the right brand,—wild, tearing, dark, devilish fellows"? We want no essence of milk and honey, you know. None but souls bitter as hemlock or scorching as lightning will suit our purpose."

"You will see, you will see, Grand Duke of Egypt! They are ethereal demons, every one of them. They are the pick of a thousand births. Do you think that I, old midwife that I am, don't know the squall of the demon child from that of the angel child, the very moment they are delivered? Ask a musician how he knows, even in the dark, a note struck by Thalberg from one struck by Listz!"

"I long to test them," cried the Wondersmith, rubbing his hands joyfully. "I long to see how the little devils will behave when I give them their shapes. Ah! it will be a proud day for us when we let them loose upon the cursed Christian children! Through the length and breadth of the land they will go; wherever our wandering people set foot, and wherever they are, the children of the Christians shall die. Then we, the despised Bohemians, the gypsies, as they call us, will be once more lords of the earth, as we were in the days when the accursed things called cities did not exist, and men lived in the free woods and hunted the game of the forest. Toys indeed! Ay, ay, we will give the little dears toys! toys that all day will sleep calmly in their boxes, seemingly stiff and wooden and without life,—but at night, when the souls enter them, will arise and surround the cots of the sleeping children, and pierce their hearts with their keen, envenomed blades! Toys indeed! O, yes! I will sell them toys!"

And the Wondersmith laughed horribly, while the snaky moustache on his upper lip writhed as if it had truly a serpent's power and could sting.

"Have you got your first batch, Herr Hippe?" asked Madame Filomel. "Are they all ready?"

"O, ay! they are ready," answered the Wondersmith with gusto,—opening, as he spoke, the box covered with the blue steel lacework;

"they are here."

The box contained a quantity of exquisitely carved wooden manikins of both sexes, painted with great dexterity so as to present a miniature resemblance to nature. They were, in fact, nothing more than admirable specimens of those toys which children delight in placing in various positions on the table,—in regiments, or sitting at meals, or grouped under the stiff green trees which always accompany them in the boxes in which they are sold at the toy-shops.

The peculiarity, however, about the manikins of Herr Hippe was not alone the artistic truth with which the limbs and the features were gifted; but on the countenance of each little puppet the carver's art had wrought an expression of wickedness that was appalling. Every tiny face had its special stamp of ferocity. The lips were thin and brimfull of malice; the small black bead-like eyes glittered with the fire of a universal hate. There was not one of the manikins, male or female, that did not hold in his or her hand some miniature weapon. The little men, scowling like demons, clasped in their wooden fingers swords delicate as a housewife's needle. The women, whose countenances expressed treachery and cruelty, clutched infinitesimal daggers, with which they seemed about to take some terrible vengeance.

"Good!" said Madame Filomel, taking one of the manikins out of the box and examining it attentively; "you work well, Duke Balthazar! These little ones are of the right stamp; they look as if they had mischief in them. Ah! here come our brothers."

At this moment, the same scratching that preceded the entrance of Madame Filomel was heard at the door, and Herr Hippe replied with a hoarse, guttural cry. The next moment two men entered. The first was a small man with very brilliant eyes. He was wrapt in a long shabby cloak, and wore a strange nondescript species of cap on his head, such a cap as one sees only in the low billiard-rooms in Paris. His companion was tall, long-limbed, and slender; and his dress, although of the ordinary cut, either from the disposition of colours, or from the careless, graceful attitudes of the wearer, assumed a certain air of picturesqueness. Both the men possessed the same marked oriental type of countenance which distinguished the Wondersmith and Madame Filomel. True gypsies they seemed, who would not have been out of place telling fortunes, or stealing chickens in the green lanes of England, or wandering with their wild music and their sleight-of-hand tricks through Bohemian villages.

"Welcome, brothers!" said the Wondersmith; "you are in time. Sister Filomel has brought the souls, and we are about to test them. Monsieur Kerplonne, take off your cloak. Brother Oaksmith, take a chair. I promise you some amusement this evening; so make yourselves comfortable. Here is something to aid you."

And while the Frenchman Kerplonne, and his tall companion, Oaksmith, were obeying Hippe's invitation, he reached over to a little closet let into the wall, and took thence a squat bottle and some glasses, which he placed on the table.

"Drink, brothers! "he said; "it is not Christian blood, but good stout wine of Oporto. It goes right to the heart, and warms one like the sunshine of the south."

"It is good," said Kerplonne, smacking his lips with enthusiasm.

"Why don't you keep brandy? Hang wine!" cried Oaksmith, after having swallowed two bumpers in rapid succession.

"Bah! Brandy has been the ruin of our race. It has made us sots and thieves. It shall never cross my threshold," cried the Wondersmith, with a sombre indignation.

"A little of it is not bad, though, Duke," said the fortune-teller. "It consoles us for oar misfortunes; it gives us the crowns we once wore; it restores to us the power we once wielded; it carries us back, as if by magic, to that land of the sun from which fate has driven us; it darkens the memory of all the evils that we have for centuries suffered."

"It is a devil; may it be cursed! "cried Herr Hippe, passionately. "It is a demon that stole from me my son, the finest youth in all Courland. Yes! my son, the son of the Waywode Balthazar, Grand Duke of Lower Egypt, died raving in a gutter, with an empty brandy bottle in his hands. Were it not that the plant is a sacred one to our race, I would curse the grape and the vine that bore it."

This outburst was delivered with such energy that the three gypsies kept silence. Oaksmith helped himself to another glass of port, and the fortune-teller rocked to and fro in her chair, too much overawed by the Wondersmith's vehemence of manner to reply. The little Frenchman, Kerplonne, took no part in the discussion, but seemed lost in admiration of the manikins, which he took from the box in which they lay, handling them with the greatest care.

After the silence had lasted for about a minute, Herr Hippe broke it with the sudden question, "How does your eye get on, Kerplonne?"

"Excellently, Duke. It is finished. I have it here." And the little Frenchman put his hand into his breeches pocket and pulled out a large artificial human eye. Its great size was the only thing in this eye

13

that would lead anyone to suspect its artificiality. It was at least twice the size of life; but there was a fearful speculative light in its iris, which seemed to expand and contract like the eye of a living being, that rendered it a horrible staring paradox. It looked like the naked eye of the Cyclops, torn from his forehead, and still burning with wrath and the desire for vengeance.

The little Frenchman laughed pleasantly as he held the eye in his hand, and gazed down on that huge, dark pupil, that stared back at him, it seemed, with an air of defiance and mistrust.

"It is a devil of an eye," said the little man, wiping the enamelled surface with an old silk pocket-handkerchief; "it reads like a demon. My niece—the unhappy one—has a wretch of a lover, and I have a long time feared that she would run away with him. I could not read her correspondence, for she kept her writing-desk closely locked. But I asked her yesterday to keep this eye in some very safe place for me. She put it, as I knew she would, into her desk, and by its aid I read every one of her letters. She was to run away next Monday, the ungrateful! but she will find herself disappointed."

And the little man laughed heartily at the success of his stratagem, and polished and fondled the great eye until that optic seemed to grow sore with rubbing.

"And you have been at work, too, I see, Herr Hippe. Your manikins are excellent. But where are the souls?"

"In that bottle," answered the Wondersmith, pointing to the pot-bellied black bottle that Madame Filomel had brought with her. "Yes, Monsieur Kerplonne," he continued, "my manikins are well made. I invoked the aid of Abigor, the demon of soldiery, and he inspired me. The little fellows will be famous assassins when they are animated. We will try them tonight."

"Good!" cried Kerplonne, rubbing his hands joyously. "It is close upon New Year's Day. We will fabricate millions of the little murderers by New Year's Eve, and sell them in large quantities; and when the households are all asleep, and the Christian children are waiting for Santa Claus to come, the small ones will troop from their boxes, and the Christian children will die. It is famous! Health to Abigor!"

"Let us try them at once," said Oaksmith. "Is your daughter, Zoné-la, in bed, Herr Hippe? Are we secure from intrusion?"

"No one is stirring about the house," replied the Wondersmith, gloomily.

Filomel leaned over to Oaksmith, and said in an undertone, "Why

14

do you mention his daughter? You know he does not like to have her spoken about."

"I will take care that we are not disturbed," said Kerplonne, rising. "I will put my eye outside the door, to watch."

He went to the door and placed his great eye upon the floor with tender care. As he did so, a dark form, unseen by him or his second vision, glided along the passage noiselessly, and was lost in the darkness.

"Now for it!" exclaimed Madame Filomel, taking up her fat black bottle. "Herr Hippe, prepare your manikins!"

The "Wondersmith took the little dolls out, one by one, and set them upon the table. Such an array of villainous countenances was never seen. An army of Italian bravoes, seen through the wrong end of a telescope, or a band of prisoners at the galleys in Liliput, will give some faint idea of the appearance they presented. While Madame Filomel uncorked the black bottle, Herr Hippe covered the dolls with a species of linen tent, which he took also from the box. This done, the fortune-teller held the mouth of the bottle to the door of the tent, gathering the loose cloth closely round the glass neck. Immediately tiny noises were heard inside the tent. Madame Filomel removed the bottle, and the Wondersmith lifted the covering in which he had enveloped his little people.

A wonderful transformation had taken place. Wooden and inflexible no longer, the crowd of manikins were now in full motion. The bead-like eyes turned, glittering, on all sides; the thin, wicked lips quivered with bad passions; the tiny hands sheathed and unsheathed the little swords and daggers. Episodes, common to life, were taking place in every direction. Here two martial manikins paid court to a pretty, sly-faced female, who smiled on each alternately, but gave her hand to be kissed to a third manikin, an ugly little scoundrel, who crouched behind her. There a pair of friendly dolls walked arm in arm, apparently on the best terms, while, all the time, one was watching his opportunity to stab the other in the back.

"I think they'll do," said the Wondersmith, chuckling as he watched these various incidents. "Treacherous, cruel, bloodthirsty. All goes marvellously well. But stay! I will put the grand test to them."

So saying, he drew a gold dollar from his pocket, and let it fall on the table, in the very midst of the throng of manikins. It had hardly touched the table when there was a pause on all sides. Every head was turned towards the dollar. Then about twenty of the little creatures rushed towards the glittering coin. One, fleeter than the rest, leaped

15

upon it and drew his sword. The entire crowd of little people had now gathered round this new centre of attraction. Men and women struggled and shoved to get nearer to the piece of gold. Hardly had the first Lilliputian mounted upon the treasure, when a hundred blades flashed back a defiant answer to his, and a dozen men, sword in hand, leaped upon the yellow platform and drove him off at the sword's point. Then commenced a general battle. The miniature faces were convulsed with rage and avarice. Each furious doll tried to plunge dagger or sword into his or her neighbour, and the women seemed possessed by a thousand devils.

"They will break themselves into atoms," cried Filomel, as she watched with eagerness this savage *mêlée*. "You had better gather them up, Herr Hippe. I will exhaust my bottle and suck all the souls back from them."

"O, they are perfect devils! they are magnificent little demons!" cried the Frenchman, with enthusiasm. "Hippe, you are a wonderful man. Brother Oaksmith, you have no such man as Hippe among your English gypsies."

"Not exactly," answered Oaksmith, rather sullenly, "not exactly. But we have men there who can make a twelve-year-old horse look like a four-year-old,—and who can take you and Herr Hippe up with one hand, and throw you over their shoulders."

"The good God forbid!" said the little Frenchman. "I do not love such play. It is incommodious."

While Oaksmith and Kerplonne were talking, the Wondersmith had placed the linen tent over the struggling dolls, and Madame Filomel, who had been performing some mysterious manipulations with her black bottle, put the mouth once more to the door of the tent. In an instant, the confused murmur within ceased. Madame Filomel corked the bottle quickly. The Wondersmith withdrew the tent, and, lo! the furious dolls were once more wooden-jointed, and inflexible; and the old sinister look was again frozen on their faces.

"They must have blood, though," said Herr Hippe, as he gathered them up and put them into their box. "Mr. Pippel, the bird-fancier, is asleep. I have a key that opens his door. We will let them loose among the birds; it will be rare fun."

"Magnificent! "cried Kerplonne. "Let us go on the instant. But first let me gather up my eye."

The Frenchman pocketed his eye, after having given it a polish with the silk handkerchief; Herr Hippe extinguished the lamp; Oaksmith took a last bumper of port; and the four gypsies departed for Mr. Pippel's, carrying the box of manikins with them.

3: SOLON.

The shadow that glided along the dark corridor, at the moment that Monsieur Kerplonne deposited his sentinel eye outside the door of the Wondersmith's apartment, sped swiftly through the passage and ascended the stairs to the attic. Here the shadow stopped at the entrance to one of the chambers and knocked at the door. There was no reply.

"Zonéla, are you asleep?" said the shadow, softly.

"O, Solon, is it you?" replied a sweet low voice from within. "I thought it was Herr Hippe. Come in."

The shadow opened the door and entered. There were neither candles nor lamp in the room; but through the projecting window, which is open, there came the faint gleams of the starlight, by which one could distinguish a female figure seated on a low stool in the middle of the floor.

"Has he left you without light again, Zonéla? "asked the shadow, closing the door of the apartment. "I have brought my little lantern with me, though."

"Thank you, Solon," answered she called Zonéla; "you are a good fellow. He never gives me any light of an evening, but bids me go to bed. I like to sit sometimes and look at the moon and the stars,—the stars more than all; for they seem all the time to look right back into my face, very sadly, as if they would say, 'We see you, and pity you, and would help you, if we could.' But it is so mournful to be always looking at such myriads of melancholy eyes! and I long so to read those nice books that you lend me, Solon!"

By this time the shadow had lit the lantern and was a shadow no longer. A large head, covered with a profusion of long blonde hair, which was cut after that fashion known as *à l'enfants d'Edouard*; a beautiful pale face, lit with wide, blue, dreamy eyes; long arms and slender hands, attenuated legs, and—an enormous hump;—such was Solon, the shadow. As soon as the humpback had lit the lamp, Zonéla arose from the low stool on which she had been seated, and took Solon's hand affectionately in hers.

Zonéla was surely not of gypsy blood. That rich auburn hair, that looked almost black in the lamp-light, that pale, transparent skin, tinged with an under-glow of warm rich blood, the hazel eyes, large

17

and soft as those of a fawn, were never begotten of a Zingaro. Zonéla was seemingly about sixteen; her figure, although somewhat thin and angular, was full of the unconscious grace of youth. She was dressed in an old cotton print, which had been once of an exceedingly boisterous pattern, but was now a mere suggestion of former splendour; while round her head was twisted, in fantastic fashion, a silk handkerchief of green ground spotted with bright crimson. This strange head-dress gave her an elfish appearance.

"I have been out all day with the organ, and I am so tired, Solon!—not sleepy, but weary, I mean. Poor Furbelow was sleepy, though, and he's gone to bed."

"I'm weary, too, Zonéla;—not weary as you are, though, for I sit in my little book-stall all day long, and do not drag round an organ and a monkey and play old tunes for pennies,—but weary of myself, of life, of the load that I carry on my shoulders"; and, as he said this, the poor humpback glanced sideways, as if to call attention to his deformed person.

"Well, but you ought not to be melancholy amidst your books, Solon. Gracious! If I could only sit in the sun and read as you do, how happy I should be! But it's very tiresome to trudge round all day with that nasty organ, and look up at the houses, and know that you are annoying the people inside; and then the boys play such bad tricks on poor Furbelow, throwing him hot pennies to pick up, and burning his poor little hands; and oh! sometimes, Solon, the men in the street make me so afraid,—they speak to me and look at me so oddly!—I'd a great deal rather sit in your bookstall and read."

"I have nothing but odd volumes in my stall," answered the humpback. "Perhaps that's right, though; for, after all, I'm nothing but an odd volume myself."

"Come, don't be melancholy, Solon. Sit down and tell me a story, I'll bring Furbelow to listen."

So saying, she went to a dusk corner of the cheerless attic room, and returned with a little Brazilian monkey in her arms,—a poor, mild, drowsy thing, that looked as if it had cried itself to sleep. She sat down on her little stool, with Furbelow in her lap, and nodded her head to Solon, as much as to say, "Go on; we are attentive."

"You want a story, do you?" said the humpback, with a mournful smile. "Well, I'll tell you one. Only what will your father say, if he catches me here?"

"Herr Hippe is not my father," cried Zonéla, indignantly. "He's

18

a gypsy, and I know I'm stolen; and I'd run away from him, if I only knew where to run to. If I were his child, do you think that he would treat me as he does? make me trudge round the city, all day long, with a barrel-organ and a monkey,—though I love poor, dear little Furbelow,—and keep me up in a garret, and give me ever so little to eat? I know I'm not his child, for he hates me."

"Listen to my story, Zonéla, and we'll talk of that afterwards. Let me sit at your feet";—and, having coiled himself up at the little maiden's feet, he commenced:—

"There once lived in a great city, just like this city of New York, a poor little hunchback. He kept a second-hand book-stall, where he made barely enough money to keep body and soul together. He was very sad at times, because he knew scarce anyone, and those that he did know did not love him. He had passed a sickly, secluded youth. The children of his neighbourhood would not play with him, for he was not made like them; and the people in the streets stared at him with pity, or scoffed at him when he went by. Ah! Zonéla, how his poor heart was wrung with bitterness when he beheld the procession of shapely men and fine women that every day passed him by in the thoroughfares of the great city! How he repined and cursed his fate as the torrent of fleet-footed firemen dashed past him to the toll of the bells, magnificent in their overflowing vitality and strength!

"But there was one consolation left him,—one drop of honey in the jar of gall, so sweet that it ameliorated all the bitterness of life. God had given him a deformed body, but his mind was straight and healthy. So, the poor hunchback shut himself into the world of books, and was, if not happy, at least contented. He kept company with courteous *paladins*, and romantic heroes, and beautiful women; and this society was of such excellent breeding that it never so much as once noticed his poor crooked back or his lame walk. The love of books grew upon him with his years. He was remarked for his studious habits; and when, one day the obscure people that he called father and mother—parents only in name—died, a compassionate book-vender gave him enough stock in trade to set up a little stall of his own.

"Here, in his bookstall, he sat in the sun all day, waiting for the customers that seldom came, and reading the fine deeds of the people of the ancient time, or the beautiful thoughts of the poets that had warmed millions of hearts before that hour, and still glowed for him with undiminished fire. One day, when he was reading some book, that, small as it was, was big enough to shut the whole world out

19

from him, he heard some music in the street. Looking up from his book, he saw a little girl, with large eyes, playing an organ, while a monkey begged for alms from a crowd of idlers who had nothing in their pockets but their hands. The girl was playing, but she was also weeping. The merry notes of the polka were ground out to a silent accompaniment of tears. She looked very sad, this organ-girl, and her monkey seemed to have caught the infection, for his large brown eyes were moist, as if he also wept.

"The poor hunchback was struck with pity, and called the little girl over to give her a penny,—not, dear Zonéla, because he wished to bestow alms, but because he wanted to speak with her. She came, and they talked together. She came the next day,—for it turned out that they were neighbours,—and the next, and, in short, every day. They became friends. They were both lonely and afflicted, with this difference, that she was beautiful, and he—was a hunchback."

"Why, Solon," cried Zonéla, "that's the very way you and I met!"

"It was then," continued Solon, with a faint smile, "that life seemed to have its music. A great harmony seemed to the poor cripple to fill the world. The carts that took the flour-barrels from the wharves to the storehouses seemed to emit joyous melodies from their wheels. The hum of the great business streets sounded like grand symphonies of triumph. As one who has been travelling through a barren country without much heed feels with singular force the sterility of the lands he has passed through when he reaches the fertile plains that lie at the end of his journey, so the humpback, after his vision had been freshened with this blooming flower, remembered for the first time the misery of the life that he had led. But he did not allow himself to dwell upon the past. The present was so delightful that it occupied all his thoughts. Zonéla, he was in love with the organ-girl."

"O, that's so nice!" said Zonéla, innocently,—pinching poor Furbelow, as she spoke, in order to dispel a very evident snooze that was creeping over him. "It's going to be a love-story."

"Ah! but, Zonéla, he did not know whether she loved him in return. You forget that he was deformed."

"But," answered the girl gravely, "he was good."

A light like the flash of an aurora illuminated Solon's face for an instant. He put out his hand suddenly, as if to take Zonéla's and press it to his heart; but an unaccountable timidity seemed to arrest the impulse, and he only stroked Furbelow's head,—upon which that individual opened one large brown eye to the extent of the eighth of an inch, and, seeing that it was only Solon, instantly closed it again, and resumed his dream of a city where there were no organs and all the copper coin of the realm was iced.

"He hoped and feared," continued Solon, in a low, mournful voice; "but at times he was very miserable, because he did not think it possible that so much happiness was reserved for him as the love of this beautiful, innocent girl. At night, when he was in bed, and all the world was dreaming, he lay awake looking up at the old books against the walls, thinking how he could bring about the charming of her heart. One night, when he was thinking of this, with his eyes fixed upon the mouldy backs of the odd volumes that lay on their shelves, and looked back at him wistfully, as if they would say, 'We also are like you, and wait to be completed,' it seemed as if he heard a rustle of leaves.

"Then, one by one, the books came down from their places to the floor, as if shifted by invisible hands, opened their worm-eaten covers, and from between the pages of each the hunchback saw issue forth a curious throng of little people that danced here and there through the apartment. Each one of these little creatures was shaped so as to bear resemblance to. some one of the letters of the alphabet. One tall, long-legged fellow seemed like the letter A; a burly fellow, with a big head and a paunch, was the model of B; another leering little chap might have passed for a Q; and so on through the whole. These fairies—for fairies they were—climbed upon the hunchback's bed, and clustered thick as bees upon his pillow. 'Come!' they cried to him, 'we will lead you into fairy-land.'

"So saying, they seized his hand, and he suddenly found himself in a beautiful country, where the light did not come from sun or moon or stars, but floated round and over and in everything like the atmosphere. On all sides, he heard mysterious melodies sung by strangely musical voices. None of the features of the landscape was definite; yet when he looked on the vague harmonies of colour that melted one into another before his sight he was filled with a sense of inexplicable beauty. On every side of him flattered radiant bodies, which darted to and fro through the illumined space. They were not birds, yet they flew like birds; and as each one crossed the path of his vision he felt a strange delight flash through his brain, and straightway an interior voice seemed to sing beneath the vaulted dome of his temples a verse containing some beautiful thought.

"The little fairies were all this time dancing and fluttering around him, perching on his head, on his shoulders, or balancing themselves on his fingertips. 'Where am?' he asked, at last, of his friends, the fairies. 'Ah, Solon!' he heard them whisper, in tones that sounded like the distant tinkling of silver bells, 'this land is nameless; but those whom we lead hither, who tread its soil, and breathe its air, and gaze on its floating sparks of light, are poets forevermore.' Having said this, they vanished, and with them the beautiful indefinite land, and the flashing lights, and the illumined air; and the hunchback found himself again in bed, with the moonlight quivering on the floor, and the dusty books on their shelves, grim and mouldy as ever."

"You have betrayed yourself You called yourself Solon," cried Zonéla. "Was it a dream?"

"I do not know," answered Solon; "but since that night I have been a poet."

"A poet?" screamed the little organ girl,—"a real poet, who makes verses which everyone reads and everyone talks of?"

"The people call me a poet," answered Solon, with a sad smile. "They do not know me by the name of Solon, for I write under an assumed title; but they praise me, and repeat my songs. But, Zonéla, I can't sing this load off of my back, can I?"

"O, bother the hump!" said Zonula, jumping up suddenly. "You 're a poet, and that's enough, isn't it? I'm so glad you're a poet, Solon! You must repeat all your best things to me, won't you?"

Solon nodded assent.

"You don't ask me," he said, "who was the little girl that the hunchback loved."

Zonéla's face flushed crimson. She turned suddenly away, and ran into a dark corner of the room. In a moment, she returned with an old hand-organ in her arms.

"Play, Solon, play!" she cried. "I am so glad that I want to dance. Furbelow, come and dance in honour of Solon the Poet."

It was her confession. Solon's eyes flamed, as if his brain had suddenly ignited. He said nothing; but a triumphant smile broke over his countenance. Zonéla, the twilight of whose cheeks was still rosy with the setting blush, caught the lazy Furbelow by his little paws; Solon turned the crank of the organ, which wheezed out as merry a polka as its asthma would allow, and the girl and the monkey commenced their fantastic dance. They had taken but a few steps when the door suddenly opened, and the tall figure of the Wondersmith appeared on the threshold. His face was convulsed with rage, and the black snake

22

that quivered on his upper lip seemed to rear itself as if about to spring upon the hunchback.

4: THE MANIKINS AND THE MINO.

The four gypsies left Herr Hippe's house cautiously, and directed their steps towards Mr. Pippel's bird-shop. Golosh Street was asleep. Nothing was stirring in that tenebrous slum, save a dog that savagely gnawed a bone which lay on a dust-heap, tantalizing him with the flavour of food without its substance. As the gypsies moved stealthily along in the darkness they had a sinister and murderous air that would not have failed to attract the attention of the policeman of the quarter, if that worthy had not at the moment been comfortably ensconced in the neighbouring "Rainbow" bar-room, listening to the improvisations of that talented vocalist, Mr. Harrison, who was making impromptu verses on every possible subject, to the accompaniment of a *cithern* which was played by a sad little Italian in a large cloak, to whom the host of the "Rainbow" gave so many toddies and a dollar for his nightly performance.

Mr. Pippel's shop was but a short distance from the Wondersmith's house. A few moments, therefore, brought the gypsy party to the door, when, by the aid of a key which Herr Hippe produced, they silently slipped into the entry. Here the Wondersmith took a dark-lantern from under his cloak, removed the cap that shrouded the light, and led the way into the shop, which was separated from the entry only by a glass door, that yielded, like the outer one, to a key which Hippe took from his pocket. The four gypsies now entered the shop and closed the door behind them.

It was a little world of birds. On every side, whether in large or small cages, one beheld balls of various-coloured feathers standing on one leg and breathing peacefully. Love-birds, nestling shoulder to shoulder, with their heads tucked under their wings and all their feathers puffed out, so that they looked like globes of malachite; English bullfinches, with ashen-coloured backs, in which their black heads were buried, and corselets of a rosy down; Java sparrows, fat and sleek and cleanly; *troupials*, so glossy and splendid in plumage that they looked as if they were dressed in the celebrated armour of the Black Prince, which was jet, richly damascened with gold; a cock of the rock, gleaming, a ball of tawny fire, like a setting sun; the *campanero* of Brazil, white as snow, with his dilatable tolling-tube hanging from his head, placid and silent;—these, with a humbler crowd of linnets, canaries, robins, mocking-birds, and phoebes, slumbered calmly in their little cages, that were hung so thickly on the wall as not to leave an inch of it visible.

"Splendid little morsels, all of them!" exclaimed Monsieur Kerplonne. "Ah, we are going to have a rare beating!"

"So Pippel does not sleep in his shop," said the English gypsy, Oaksmith.

"No. The fellow lives somewhere up one of the avenues," answered Madame Filomel. "He came, the other evening, to consult me about his fortune. I did not tell him," she added with a laugh, "that he was going to have so distinguished a sporting party on his premises."

"Come," said the Wondersmith, producing the box of manikins, "get ready with souls, Madame Filomel. I am impatient to see my little men letting out lives for the first time. Just at the moment that the Wondersmith uttered this sentence, the four gypsies were startled by a hoarse voice issuing from a corner of the room, and propounding in the most guttural tones the intemperate query of "What'll you take?" This sottish invitation had scarce been given, when a second extremely thick voice replied from an opposite corner, in accents so rough that they seemed to issue from a throat torn and furrowed by the liquid lava of many bar-rooms, "Brandy and water."

"Hollo! Who's here?" muttered Herr Hippe, flashing the light of his lantern round the shop.

Oaksmith turned up his coat-cuffs, as if to be ready for a fight; Madame Filomel glided, or rather rolled, towards the door; while Kerplonne put his hand into his pocket, as if to assure himself that his supernumerary optic was all right.

"What'll you take?" croaked the voice in the corner, once more.

"Brandy and water," rapidly replied the second voice in the other corner. And then, as if by a concerted movement, a series of bibular invitations and acceptances were rolled backwards and forwards with a volubility of utterance that threw Patter *versus* Clatter into the shade.

"What the devil can it be?" muttered the Wondersmith, flashing his lantern here and there. "Ah! it is those Minos."

So saying, he stopped under one of the wicker cages that hung high up on the wall, and raised the lantern above his head, so as to throw the light upon that particular cage. The hospitable individual who had been extending all these hoarse invitations to partake of intoxicating beverages was an inhabitant of the cage. It was a large Mino-bird, who now stood perched on his crossbar, with his yellowish-orange bill sloped slightly over his shoulder, and his white eye cocked knowingly upon the Wondersmith. The respondent voice in the other corner came from another Mino-bird, who sat in the dusk in a similar cage, also attentively watching the Wondersmith. These Mino-birds have a singular aptitude for acquiring phrases.

"What'll you take?" repeated the Mino, cocking his other eye upon Herr Hippe.

"*Mon Dieu!* what a bird!" exclaimed the little Frenchman. "He is, in truth, polite."

"I don't know what I'll take," said Hippe, as if replying to the Mino-bird; "but I know what you'll get, old fellow! Filomel, open the cage-doors, and give me the bottle."

Filomel opened, one after another, the doors of the numberless little cages, thereby arousing from slumber their feathered occupants, who opened their beaks, and stretched their claws, and stared with great surprise at the lantern and the midnight visitors.

By this time the Wondersmith had performed the mysterious ma-nipulations with the bottle, and the manikins were once more in full motion, swarming out of their box, sword and dagger in hand, with their little black eyes glittering fiercely, and their white teeth shining. The little creatures seemed to scent their prey. The gypsies stood in the centre of the shop, watching the proceedings eagerly, while the Lil-liputians made in a body towards the wall and commenced climbing from cage to cage. Then was heard a tremendous fluttering of wings, and faint, despairing "quirks" echoed on all sides. In almost every cage there was a fierce manikin thrusting his sword or dagger vigorously into the body of some unhappy bird. It recalled the antique legend of the battles of the Pygmies and the Cranes.

The poor love-birds lay with their emerald feathers dabbled in their heart's blood, shoulder to shoulder in death as in life. Canar-ies gasped at the bottom of their cages, while the water in their little glass fountains ran red. The bullfinches wore an unnatural crimson on their breasts. The mockingbird lay on his back, kicking spasmodically, in the last agonies, with a tiny sword-thrust cleaving his melodious throat in twain, so that from the instrument which used to gush with wondrous music only scarlet drops of blood now trickled. The mani-kins were ruthless. Their faces were ten times wickeder than ever, as they roamed from cage to cage, slaughtering with a fury that seemed entirely unappeasable.

Presently the feathery rustlings became fewer and fainter, and the little pipings of despair died away; and in every cage lay a poor murdered minstrel, with the song that abode within him forever quenched;—in every cage but two, and those two were high up on the wall; and in each glared a pair of wild, white eyes; and an orange beak, tough as steel, pointed threateningly down. With the needles which they grasped as swords all wet and warm with blood, and their beadlike eyes flashing in the light of the lantern, the Lilliputian assassins swarmed up the cages in two separate bodies, until they reached the wickets of the habitations in which the Minos abode. Mino saw them coming,—had listened attentively to the many death-struggles of his comrades, and had, in fact, smelt a rat.

Accordingly he was ready for the manikins. There he stood at the barbican of his castle, with formidable beak couched like a lance. The manikins made a gallant charge. "What'll you take?" was rattled out by the Mino, in a deep bass, as with one plunge of his sharp bill he scattered the ranks of the enemy, and sent three of them flying to the floor, where they lay with broken limbs. But the manikins were brave automata, and again they closed and charged the gallant Mino. Again, the wicked white eyes of the bird gleamed, and again the orange bill dealt destruction.

Everything seemed to be going on swimmingly for Mino, when he found himself attacked in the rear by two treacherous manikins, who had stolen upon him from behind, through the latticework of the cage. Quick as lightning the Mino turned to repel this assault, but all too late; two slender, quivering threads of steel crossed in his poor body, and he staggered into a corner of the cage. His white eyes closed, then opened; a shiver passed over his body, beginning at his shoulder-tips and dying off in the extreme tips of the wings; he gasped as if for air, and then, with a convulsive shudder, which ruffled all his feathers, croaked out feebly his little speech, "What'll you take?" Instantly from the opposite corner came the old response, still feebler than the question,—a mere gurgle, as it were, of "Brandy and water." Then all was silent. The Mino-birds were dead.

"They spill blood like Christians," said the Wondersmith, gazing fondly on the manikins. "They will be famous assassins."

5: TIED UP

Herr Hippe stood in the doorway, scowling. His eyes seemed to scorch the poor hunchback, whose form, physically inferior, crouched before that baneful, blazing glance, while its head, mentally brave,

26

reared itself as if to redeem the cowardice of the frame to which it belonged. So, the attitude of the serpent: the body pliant, yielding, supple; but the crest thrown aloft, erect, and threatening. As for Zonéla, she was frozen in the attitude of motion;—a dancing nymph in coloured marble; agility stunned; elasticity petrified.

Furbelow, astonished at this sudden change, and catching, with all the mysterious rapidity of instinct peculiar to the lower animals, at the enigmatical character of the situation, turned his pleading, melancholy eyes from one to another of the motionless three, as if begging that his humble intellect (pardon me, naturalists, for the use of this word "intellect" in the matter of a monkey!) should be enlightened as speedily as possible. Not receiving the desired information, he, after the manner of trained animals, returned to his muttons; in other words, he conceived that this unusual entrance, and consequent dramatic tableau, meant "shop." He therefore dropped Zonéla's hand, and pattered on his velvety little feet over towards the grim figure of the Wondersmith, holding out his poor little paw for the customary copper. He had but one idea drilled into him,—soulless creature that he was,—and that was alms.

But I have seen creatures that professed to have souls, and that would have been indignant if you had denied them immortality, who took to the soliciting of alms as naturally as if beggary had been the original sin, and was regularly born with them, and never baptized out of them. I will give these Bandits of the Order of Charity this credit, however, that they knew the best highways and the richest founts of benevolence,—unlike to Furbelow, who, unreasoning and undiscriminating, begged from the first person that was near. Furbelow, owing to this intellectual inferiority to the before-mentioned Alsatians, frequently got more kicks than coppers, and the present supplication which he indulged in towards the Wondersmith was a terrible confirmation of the rule.

The reply to the extended pleading paw was what might be called a double-barrelled kick,—a kick to be represented by the power of two when the foot touched the object, multiplied by four when the entire leg formed an angle of 45° with the spinal column. The long, nervous leg of the Wondersmith caught the little creature in the centre of the body, doubled up his brown, hairy form, till he looked like a fur driving-glove, and sent him whizzing across the room into a fur corner, where he dropped senseless and flaccid.

This vengeance which Herr Hippe executed upon Furbelow

seemed to have operated as a sort of escape-valve, and he found voice. He hissed out the question, "Who are you?" to the hunchback; and in listening to that essence of sibilation it really seemed as if it proceeded from the serpent that curled upon his upper lip.

"Who are you? Deformed dog, who are you? What do you here?"

"My name is Solon," answered the fearless head of the hunchback, while the frail, cowardly body shivered and trembled inch by inch into a corner.

"So, you come to visit my daughter in the night-time, when I am away?" continued the Wondersmith, with a sneering tone that dropped from his snake-wreathed mouth like poison. "You are a brave and gallant lover, are you not? Where did you win that Order of the Curse of God that decorates your shoulders? The women turn their heads and look after you in the street, when you pass, do they not? lost in admiration of that symmetrical figure, those graceful limbs, that neck pliant as the stem that moors the lotus! Elegant, conquering, Christian cripple, what do you here in my daughter's room?"

Can you imagine Jove, limitless in power and wrath, hurling from his vast grasp mountain after mountain upon the straggling Encela-dus,—and picture the Titan sinking, sinking, deeper and deeper into the earth, crushed and dying, with nothing visible through the super-incumbent masses of Pelion and Ossa but a gigantic head and two flaming eyes, that, despite the death which is creeping through each vein, still flash back defiance to the divine enemy? Well, Solon and Herr Hippe presented such a picture, seen through the wrong end of a telescope,—reduced in proportion, but alike in action. Solon's fee-ble body seemed to sink into utter annihilation beneath the horrible taunts that his enemy hurled at him, while the large, brave brow and unconquered eyes still sent forth a magnetic resistance.

Suddenly the poor hunchback felt his arm grasped. A thrill seemed to run through his entire body. A warm atmosphere, invigorating and full of delicious odour, surrounded him. It appeared as if invisible band-ages were twisted all about his limbs, giving him a strange strength. His sinking legs straightened. His powerless arms were braced. As-tonished, he glanced round for an instant, and beheld Zonéla, with a world of love burning in her large lambent eyes, wreathing her round white arms about his humped shoulders. Then the poet knew the great sustaining power of love. Solon reared himself boldly.

"Sneer at my poor form," he cried, in strong vibrating tones, fling-ing out one long arm and one thin finger at the Wondersmith, as if he would have impaled him like a beetle. "Humiliate me if you can. I care not. You are a wretch, and I am honest and pure. This girl is not your daughter. You are like one of those demons in the fairy tales that held beauty and purity locked in infernal spells. I do not fear you, Herr Hippe. There are stories abroad about you in the neighbourhood, and when you pass people say that they feel evil and blight hovering over their thresholds. You persecute this girl. You are her tyrant. You hate her. I am a cripple. Providence has cast this lump upon my shoulders. But that is nothing. The camel, that is the salvation of the children of the desert, has been given his hump in order that he might bear his human burden better. This girl, who is homeless as the Arab, is my appointed load in life, and, please God, I will carry her on this back, hunched though it may be. I have come to see her because I love her,—because she loves me. You have no claim on her; so I will take her from you."

Quick as lightning the Wondersmith had stridden a few paces, and grasped the poor cripple, who was yet quivering with the departing thunder of his passion. He seized him in his bony, muscular grasp, as he would have seized a puppet, and held him at arm's length, gasping and powerless; while Zonéla, pale, breathless, entreating, sank half-kneeling on the floor.

"Your skeleton will be interesting to science when you are dead, Mr. Solon," hissed the Wondersmith. "But before I have the pleasure of reducing you to an anatomy, which I will assuredly do, I wish to compliment you on your power of penetration, or sources of information; for I know not if you have derived your knowledge from your own mental research or the efforts of others.

"You are perfectly correct in your statement that this charming young person, who day after day parades the streets with a barrel-organ and a monkey,—the last unhappily indisposed at present,—listening to the degrading jokes of ribald boys and depraved men,—you are quite correct, sir, in stating that she is not my daughter. On the contrary, she is the daughter of an Hungarian nobleman who had the misfortune to incur my displeasure. I had a son, crooked spawn of a Christian!—a son, not like you, cankered, gnarled stump of life that you are,—but a youth tall and fair and noble in aspect, as became a child of one whose lineage makes Pharaoh modern,—a youth whose foot in the dance was as swift and beautiful to look at as the golden sandals of the sun when he dances upon the sea in summer.

"This youth was virtuous and good; and being of good race, and dwelling in a country where his rank, gypsy as he was, was recognised, he mixed with the proudest of the land. One day he fell in with this accursed Hungarian, a fierce drinker of that devil's blood called brandy. My child until that hour had avoided this bane of our race. Generous wine he drank, because the soul of the sun, our ancestor, palpitated in its purple waves. But brandy, which is fallen and accursed wine, as devils are fallen and accursed angels, had never crossed his lips, until in an evil hour he was seduced by this Christian hog, and from that day forth his life was one fiery debauch, which set only in the black waves of death.

"I vowed vengeance on the destroyer of my child, and I kept my word. I have destroyed *his* child,—not compassed her death, but blighted her life, steeped her in misery and poverty, and now, thanks to the thousand devils, I have discovered a new torture for her heart. She thought to solace her life with a love-episode! Sweet little epicure that she was! She shall have her little crooked lover, sha'n't she? O, yes! she shall have him, cold and stark and livid, with that great, black, heavy hunch, which no back, however broad, can bear, Death, sitting between his shoulders!"

There was something so awful and demoniac in this entire speech and the manner in which it was delivered, that it petrified Zonéla into a mere inanimate figure, whose eyes seemed unalterably fixed on the fierce, cruel face of the Wondersmith. As for Solon, he was paralyzed in the grasp of his foe. He heard, but could not reply. His large eyes, dilated with horror to far beyond their ordinary size, expressed unutterable agony.

The last sentence had hardly been hissed out by the gypsy when he took from his pocket a long, thin coil of whip-cord, which he entangled in a complicated mesh around the cripple's body. It was not the ordinary binding of a prisoner. The slender lash passed and repassed in a thousand intricate folds over the powerless limbs of the poor humpback. When the operation was completed, he looked as if he had been sewed from head to foot in some singularly ingenious species of network.

"Now, my pretty lop-sided little lover," laughed Herr Hippe, flinging Solon over his shoulder as a fisherman might fling a netful of fish, "we will proceed to put you into your little cage until your little coffin is quite ready. Meanwhile we will lock up your darling beggar-girl to mourn over your untimely end."

So saying, he stepped from the room with his captive, and securely locked the door behind him.

When he had disappeared, the frozen Zonéla thawed, and with a shriek of anguish flung herself on the inanimate body of Furbelow.

6: THE POISONING OF THE SWORDS.

It was New Year's Eve, and eleven o'clock at night. All over this great land, and in every great city in the land, curly heads were lying on white pillows, dreaming of the coming of the generous Santa Claus. Innumerable stockings hung by countless bedsides. Visions of beautiful toys, passing in splendid pageantry through myriads of dimly lit dormitories, made millions of little hearts palpitate in sleep. Ah! what heavenly toys those were that the children of this soil beheld, that mystic night, in their dreams! Painted cars with orchestral wheels, making music more delicious than the roll of planets. Agile men, of cylindrical figure, who sprang unexpectedly out of meek-looking boxes, with a supernatural fierceness in their crimson cheeks and fur-whiskers.

Herds of marvellous sheep, with fleeces as impossible as the one that Jason sailed after; animals entirely indifferent to grass and water and "rot" and "ticks." Horses spotted with an astounding regularity, and furnished with the most ingenious methods of locomotion. Slender foreigners, attired in painfully short tunics, whose existence passed in continually turning heels over head down a steep flight of steps, at the bottom of which they lay in an exhausted condition with dislocated limbs, until they were restored to their former elevation, when they went at it again as if nothing had happened. Stately swans, that seemed to have a touch of the ostrich in them; for they swam continually after a piece of iron which was held before them, as if consumed with a ferruginous hunger.

Whole farmyards of roosters, whose tails curled the wrong way,— a slight defect, that was, however, amply atoned for by the size and brilliancy of their scarlet combs, which, it would appear, Providence had intended for pen-wipers. Pears, that, when applied to youthful lips, gave forth sweet and inspiring sounds. Regiments of soldiers, that performed neat but limited evolutions on cross-jointed contractile battlefields. All these things, idealised, transfigured, and illuminated by the powers and atmosphere and coloured lamps of dream-land, did the millions of dear sleeping children behold, the night of the New Year's Eve of which I speak.

It was on this night, when Time was preparing to shed his skin, and come out young and golden and glossy as ever,—when, in the vast chambers of the universe, silent and infallible preparations were making for the wonderful birth of the coming year,—when mystic dews were secreted for his baptism, and mystic instruments were tuned in space to welcome him,—it was at this holy and solemn hour that the Wondersmith and his three gypsy companions sat in close conclave in the little parlour before mentioned.

There was a fire roaring in the grate. On a table, nearly in the centre of the room, stood a huge decanter of port wine, that glowed in the blaze which lit the chamber like a flask of crimson fire. On every side, piled in heaps, inanimate, but scowling with the same old wondrous scowl, lay myriads of the manikins, all clutching in their wooden hands their tiny weapons. The Wondersmith held in one hand a small silver bowl filled with a green, glutinous substance, which he was delicately applying, with the aid of a camel's-hair brush, to the tips of tiny swords and daggers. A horrible smile wandered over his sallow face,—a smile as unwholesome in appearance as the sickly light that plays above reeking graveyards.

"Let us drink great draughts, brothers," he cried, leaving off his strange anointment for a while, to lift a great glass, filled with sparkling liquor, to his lips. "Let us drink to our approaching triumph. Let us drink to the great poison, Macousha. Subtle seed of Death,—swift hurricane that sweeps away Life,—vast hammer that crushes brain and heart and artery with its resistless weight,—I drink to it."

"It is a noble decoction, Duke Balthazar," said the old fortune-teller and midwife, Madame Filomel, nodding in her chair as she swallowed her wine in great gulps. "Where did you obtain it?"

"It is made," said the Wondersmith, swallowing another great draught of wine ere he replied, "in the wild woods of Guiana, in silence and in mystery. But one tribe of Indians, the Macoushi Indians, know the secret. It is simmered over fires built of strange woods, and the maker of it dies in the making. The place, for a mile around the spot where it is fabricated, is shunned as accursed. Devils hover over the pot in which it stews; and the birds of the air, scenting the smallest breath of its vapor from far away, drop to earth with paralyzed wings, cold and dead."

"It kills, then, fast?" asked Kerplonne, the artificial-eye maker,—his own eyes gleaming, under the influence of the wine, with a sinister lustre, as if they had been fresh from the factory, and were yet untarnished by use.

"Kills?" echoed the Wondersmith, derisively; "it is swifter than thunderbolts, stronger than lightning. But you shall see it proved before we let forth our army on the city accursed. You shall see a wretch die, as if smitten by a falling fragment of the sun."

"What? Do you mean Solon?" asked Oaksmith and the fortune-teller together.

"Ah! you mean the young man who makes the commerce with books?" echoed Kerplonne. "It is well. His agonies will instruct us."

"Yes! Solon," answered Hippe, with a savage accent.

"I hate him, and he shall die this horrid death. Ah! how the little fellows will leap upon him, when I bring him in, bound and helpless, and give their beautiful wicked souls to them! How they will pierce him in ten thousand spots with their poisoned weapons, until his skin turns blue and violet and crimson, and his form swells with the venom,—until his hump is lost in shapeless flesh! He hears what I say, every word of it. He is in the closet next door, and is listening. How comfortable he feels! How the sweat of terror rolls on his brow! How he tries to loosen his bonds, and curses all earth and heaven when he finds that he cannot! Ho! ho! Handsome lover of Zonéla, will she kiss you when you are livid and swollen? Brothers, let us drink again,—drink always. Here, Oaksmith, take these brushes,—and you, Filomel,—and finish the anointing of these swords. This wine is grand. This poison is grand. It is fine to have good wine to drink, and good poison to kill with; is it not?"—and, with flushed face and rolling eyes, the Wondersmith continued to drink and use his brush alternately.

The others hastened to follow his example. It was a horrible scene: those four wicked faces; those myriads of tiny faces, just as wicked; the certain unearthly air that pervaded the apartment; the red, unwholesome glare cast by the fire; the wild, and reckless way in which the weird company drank the red-illumined wine.

The anointing of the swords went on rapidly, and the wine went as rapidly down the throats of the four poisoners. Their faces grew more and more inflamed each instant; their eyes shone like rolling fireballs; their hair was moist and dishevelled. The old fortune-teller rocked to and fro in her chair, like those legless plaster figures that sway upon convex loaded bottoms. All four began to mutter incoherent sentences, and babble unintelligible wickednesses. Still the anointing of the swords went on.

"I see the faces of millions of young corpses," babbled Herr Hippe, gazing, with swimming eyes, into the silver bowl that contained the

Macousha poison,—"all young, all Christians,—and the little fellows dancing, dancing, and stabbing, stabbing. Filomel, Filomel, I say!"

"Well, Grand Duke," snored the old woman, giving a violent lurch.

"Where's the bottle of souls?"

"In my right-hand pocket, Herr Hippe";—and she felt, so as to assure herself that it was there. She half drew out the black bottle, before described in this narrative, and let it slide again into her pocket,—let it slide again, but it did not completely regain its former place. Caught by some accident, it hung half out, swaying over the edge of the pocket, as the fat midwife rolled backwards and forwards in her drunken efforts at equilibrium.

"All right," said Herr Hippe, "perfectly right! Let's drink."

He reached out his hand for his glass, and, with a dull sigh, dropped on the table, in the instantaneous slumber of intoxication. Oaksmith soon fell back in his chair, breathing heavily. Kerplonne followed. And the heavy, stertorous breathing of Filomel told that she slumbered also; but still her chair retained its rocking motion, and still the bottle of souls balanced itself on the edge of her pocket.

7: Let Loose.

Sure enough, Solon heard every word of the fiendish talk of the Wondersmith. For how many days he had been shut up, bound in the terrible net, in that dark closet, he did not know; but now he felt that his last hour was come. His little strength was completely worn out in efforts to disentangle himself. Once a day a door opened, and Herr Hippe placed a crust of bread and a cup of water within his reach. On this meagre fare he had subsisted. It was a hard life; but, bad as it was, it was better than the horrible death that menaced him. His brain reeled with terror at the prospect of it. Then, where was Zonéla? Why did she not come to his rescue? But she was, perhaps, dead.

The darkness, too, appalled him. A faint light, when the moon was bright, came at night through a chink far up in the wall; and the only other hole in the chamber was an aperture through which, at some former time, a stove-pipe had been passed. Even if he were free, there would have been small hope of escape; but, laced as it were in a network of steel, what was to be done? He groaned and writhed upon the floor, and tore at the boards with his hands, which were free from the wrists down. All else was as solidly laced up as an Indian *papoose*. Nothing but pride kept him from shrieking aloud, when, on the night of New Year's Eve, he heard the fiendish Hippe recite the programme of his murder.

While he was thus wailing and gnashing his teeth in darkness and torture, he heard a faint noise above his head. Then something seemed to leap from the ceiling and alight softly on the floor. He shuddered with terror. Was it some new torture of the Wondersmith's invention? The next moment, he felt some small animal crawling over his body, and a soft, silky paw was pushed timidly across his face. His heart leaped with joy.

"It is Furbelow!" he cried. "Zonéla has sent him. He came through the stove-pipe hole."

It was Furbelow, indeed, restored to life by Zonéla's care, and who had come down a narrow tube, that no human being could have threaded, to console the poor captive. The monkey nestled closely into the hunchback's bosom, and, as he did so, Solon felt something cold and hard hanging from his neck. He touched it! It was sharp. By the dim light that struggled through the aperture high up in the wall, he discovered a knife suspended by a bit of cord. Ah! how the blood came rushing through the veins that crossed over and through his heart, when life and liberty came to him in this bit of rusty steel!

With his manacled hands he loosened the heaven-sent weapon; a few cuts were rapidly made in the cunning network of cord that enveloped his limbs, and m a few seconds he was free!—cramped and faint with hunger, but free! free to move, to use the limbs that God had given him for his preservation,—free to fight,—to die fighting, perhaps,—but still to die free. He ran to the door. The bolt was a weak one, for the Wondersmith had calculated more surely on his prison of cords than on any jail of stone, and more; and with a few efforts the door opened. He went cautiously out into the darkness, with Furbelow perched on his shoulder, pressing his cold muzzle against his cheek. He had made but a few steps when a trembling hand was put into his, and in another moment Zonéla's palpitating heart was pressed against his own.

One long kiss, an embrace, a few whispered words, and the hunchback and the girl stole softly towards the door of the chamber in which the four gypsies slept. All seemed still; nothing but the hard breathing of the sleepers and the monotonous rocking of Madame Filomel's chair broke the silence. Solon stooped down and put his eye to the keyhole, through which a red bar of light streamed into the entry. As he did so, his foot crushed some brittle substance that lay just outside the door; at the same moment, a howl of agony was heard to issue from the room within. Solon started; nor did he know that at that instant he had crashed into dust Monsieur Kerplonne's supernumerary eye, and the owner, though wrapt in a drunken sleep, felt the pang quiver through his brain.

While Solon peeped through the keyhole, all in the room was motionless. He had not gazed, however, for many seconds, when the chair of the fortune-teller gave a sudden lurch, and the black bottle, already hanging half out of her wide pocket, slipped entirely from its resting-place, and, falling heavily to the ground, shivered into fragments.

Then took place an astonishing spectacle. The myriads of armed dolls, that lay in piles about the room, became suddenly imbued with motion. They stood up straight, their tiny limbs moved, their black eyes flashed with wicked purposes, their thread-like swords gleamed as they waved them to and fro. The villainous souls imprisoned in the bottle began to work within them. Like the Lilliputians, when they found the giant Gulliver asleep, they scaled in swarms the burly sides of the four sleeping gypsies. At every step they took, they drove their thin swords and quivering daggers into the flesh of the drunken authors of their being. To stab and kill was their mission, and they stabbed and killed with incredible fury. They clustered on the Wondersmith's sallow cheeks and sinewy throat, piercing every portion with their diminutive poisoned blades. Filomel's fat carcass was alive with them. They blackened the spare body of Monsieur Kerplonne. They covered Oaksmith's huge form like a cluster of insects.

Overcome completely with the fumes of wine, these tiny wounds did not for a few moments awaken the sleeping victims. But the swift and deadly poison Macousha, with which the weapons had been so fiendishly anointed, began to work. Herr Hippe, stung into sudden life, leaped to his feet, with a dwarf army clinging to his clothes and his hands,—always stabbing, stabbing, stabbing. For an instant, a look of stupid bewilderment clouded his face; then the horrible truth burst upon him. He gave a shriek like that which a horse utters when he finds himself fettered and surrounded by fire,—a shriek that curdled the air for miles and miles.

"Oaksmith! Kerplonne! Filomel! Awake! awake! We are lost! The souls have got loose! We are dead! poisoned! accursed ones! demons, ye are slaying me! Ah! fiends of hell!"

Aroused by these frightful howls, the three gypsies sprang also to their feet, to find themselves stung to death by the manikins. They raved, they shrieked, they swore. They staggered round the chamber.

Blinded in the eyes by the ever-stabbing weapons,—with the poison already burning in their veins like red-hot lead,—their forms swelling and discolouring visibly every moment,—their howls and attitudes and furious gestures made the scene look like a chamber in hell.

Maddened beyond endurance, the Wondersmith, half-blind and choking with the venom that had congested all the blood-vessels of his body, seized dozens of the manikins and dashed them into the fire, trampling them down with his feet.

"Ye shall die too, if I die," he cried, with a roar like that of a tiger. "Ye shall burn, if I burn. I gave ye life,—I give ye death. Down!—down!—burn!—flame! Fiends that ye are, to slay us! Help me, brothers! Before we die, let us have our revenge!"

On this, the other gypsies, themselves maddened by approaching death, began hurling manikins, by handfuls, into the fire. The little creatures, being wooden of body, quickly caught the flames, and an awful struggle for life took place in miniature in the grate. Some of them escaped from between the bars and ran about the room, blazing, writhing in agony, and igniting the curtains and other draperies that hung around. Others fought and stabbed one another in the very core of the fire, like combating salamanders. Meantime, the motions of the gypsies grew more languid and slow, and their curses were uttered in choked guttural tones. The faces of all four were spotted with red and green and violet, like so many egg-plants. Their bodies were swollen to a frightful size, and at last they dropped on the floor, like over-ripe fruit shaken from the boughs by the winds of autumn.

The chamber was now a sheet of fire. The flames roared round and round, as if seeking for escape, licking every projecting cornice and sill with greedy tongues, as the serpent licks his prey before he swallows it. A hot, putrid breath came through the keyhole, and smote Solon and Zonéla like a wind of death. They clasped each other's hands with a moan of terror, and fled from the house.

Next morning, when the young year was just unclosing its eyes, and the happy children all over the great city were peeping from their beds into the myriads of stockings hanging nearby, the blue skies of heaven shone through a black network of stone and charred rafters. These were all that remained of the habitation of Herr Hippe, the Wondersmith.

From Hand to Mouth

1: How I Fell in with Count Goloptious

The evening of the 8th of November, in the present year, was distinguished by the occurrence of two sufficiently remarkable events. On that evening Mr. Ullman produced Meyerbeer's opera of *The Huguenots*, for the first time in this country, and we were unexpectedly visited by a snow-storm. Winter and the great lyrical dramatist made their debut together. Winter opened with a slow movement of heavy snowflakes,—an andante, soft and melancholy, and breathing of polar drowsiness.

The echoing streets were muffled, and the racket and din of the thoroughfares sounded like the roar of a far-off ocean. The large flakes fell sleepily through the dim blue air, like soft white birds that had been stricken with cold in the upper skies, and were sinking benumbed to earth. The trees and lamp-posts, decorated with snowy powder, gave the city the air of being laid out for a grand supper-party, with ornamental confectionery embellishing the long white table. Through the hoar drifts that lay along the streets peeped the black tips of building-stones and mud-piles in front of half-finished houses, until Broadway looked as if it was enveloped in an ermine robe, dotted with the black tails with which cunning furriers ornament that skin.

Despite the snow, I sallied forth with my friend Cobra, the musical critic of the *New York Daily Cockchafer*, to hear Meyerbeer's masterpiece. We entered a mute omnibus with a frozen driver, whose congealed hands could scarcely close upon our fares,—which accounted perhaps for a slight error in the change he gave us,—and so rolled up silently to Union Square, whence we floundered into the Academy. I listened to that wonderful picture of one of France's anniversaries of massacre, with bloody copies of which that "God-protected country" (*vide* speech from the throne on any public occasion) is continually

39

furnishing the civilized world.

The roar of Catholic cannon,—the whistle of Huguenot bullets,—the stealthy tread of conspiring priests,—the mournful wailing of women whose hearts foretell evil before it comes,—the sudden outburst of the treacherous, bloodthirsty Romish tiger,—the flight and shrieks of men and women about to die, the valiant, despairing fighting of the stern Protestants,—the voice of the devilish French king, shouting from his balcony to his assassins the remorseless command, "*Tuez! tuez!*"—the ominous trickling of the red streams that sprung from cloven Lutheran hearts, and rolled slowly through the kennels;—all this arose before me vital and real, as the music of that sombre opera smote the air. Cobra, whose business it was—being a critic—not to attend to the performance, languidly surveyed the house, or availed himself of the intermission between the acts to fortify himself with certain refreshing but stimulating beverages.

The opera being concluded, we proceeded to Pilgarlik's,—Pilgarlik keeps a charming private restaurant at the upper end of Broadway,—and there, over a few reed-birds and a bottle of Burgundy, Cobra concocted his criticism on *The Huguenots*,—in which he talked learnedly of dominants, sub-dominants, ascending by thirds, and descending by twenty-thirds, and such like, while I, with nothing more weighty on my mind than paying for the supper, smoked my cigar and sipped my concluding cup of black coffee in a state of divine repose.

The snow was deep, when, at about one o'clock, a.m., Cobra and myself parted at the corner of Eighth Street and Broadway, each bound for his respective home. Cobra lived in Fourth Avenue,—I live, or lived, in Bleecker Street. The snow was deep, and the city quite still, as I half ran, half floundered down the sidewalk, thinking what a nice hot brandy-toddy I would make myself when I got home, and the pleasure I would have in boiling the water over my gas-light on a lately invented apparatus which I had acquired, and in which I took much pride; I also recollected with a thrill of pleasure that I had purchased a fresh supply of lemons that morning, so that nothing was needed for the scientific concoction of a nightcap.

I turned down Bleecker Street and reached my door. I was singing a snatch of Pierre Dupont's song of *La Vigne*, as I pulled out my night-key and inserted it in that orifice so perplexing to young men who have been to a late supper. One vigorous twist, and I was at home. The half-uttered triumphal chant of the Frenchman, who dilates with metrical malice on the fact that the vine does not flourish in England, died on my lips. The key turned, but the door, usually so yielding to the members of our family, obstinately refused to open. A horrible thought flashed across my mind. They had locked me out! A new servant had perhaps arrived, and cautiously barricaded the entrance; or the landlady—to whom, at the moment, I was under some slight pecuniary responsibility—had taken this cruel means of recalling me to a sense of my position.

But it could not be. There was some mistake. There was fluff in my key,—yes, that was it,—there was fluff in the barrel of my night-key. I instantly proceeded to make a Pandean pipe of that instrument, and blew into the tube until my face resembled that queer picture of the wind in Æsop's fables, as it is represented in the act of endeavouring to make the traveller take off his cloak. A hopelessly shrill sound responded to my efforts. The key was clear as a flute. Was it the wrong key? I felt in every pocket, vaguely expecting a supernumerary one to turn up, but in vain. While thus occupied, the conviction forced itself on my mind that I had no money.

Locked out, with a foot of snow on the ground, and nothing but a three-cent piece and two new cents—so painfully bright that they presented illusory resemblances to half-eagles—in my pocket!

I knew well that an appeal to the bell was hopeless. I had tried it once before for three hours at a stretch, without the slightest avail. It is my private conviction that every member of that household, who slept at all within hearing of the bell, carefully stuffed his or her ears with cotton before retiring for the night, so as to be out of the reach of temptation to answer it. Every inmate of that establishment, after a certain hour, determinedly rehearsed the part of Ulysses when he was passing the Sirens. They were deaf to the melody of the bell. I once knew a physician who, to keep up appearances, had a night-bell affixed to his door. The initiated alone knew that he regularly took the tongue out before he went to bed. His conscience was satisfied, and he slept calmly. I might just as well have been pulling his bell.

Break the windows! Why not? Excellent idea; but, as I before stated, my pecuniary position scarcely allowed of such liberties. What was I to do? I could not walk up and down the city all night. I would freeze to death, and there would be a horrible paragraph in the morning papers about the sad death of a destitute author. I ran over rapidly in my mind every hotel in the city with which I was at all acquainted, in order to see if there was in any one of them a night-porter who knew me. Alas! Night-porters knew me not.

Why had I not a watch or a diamond ring? I resolved on the instant to purchase both as soon as I got ten or twelve hundred dollars. I began to wonder where the news-boys' depot was, and recollected there was a warm spot somewhere over the *Herald* press-room, on which I had seen ragged urchins huddling as I passed by late of night. I was ruminating gravely over the awful position in which I was placed, when a loud but somewhat buttery voice disturbed me by shouting from the sidewalk: "Ha, ha! Capital joke! Locked out, eh? You'll never get in."

A stranger! perhaps benevolent, thought I. If so, I am indeed saved. To rush down the steps, place my hand upon his shoulder, and gaze into his face with the most winning expression I was capable of assuming, was but the work of several minutes,—which, however, included two tumbles on the stoop.

"Can it—can it be," I said, "that you have a night-key?"

"A night-key!" he answered with a jolly laugh, and speaking as if his mouth was full of turtle,—"a night-key! What the deuce should I do with a night-key? I never go home until morning."

"Sir," said I, sadly, "do not jest with the misery of a fellow-creature. I conjure you by the sanctity of your fireside to lend me your night-key."

"You've got one in your hand; why don't you use that?"

I had. In the excitement of the moment I had quite overlooked the fact that, if I had fifty night-keys, I would still have found myself on the wrong side of the door.

"The fact is—pardon me—but I forgot that the door was locked on the inside."

"Well, you can't get in, and you can't stay out," said the stranger, chuckling over a large mouthful of turtle. "What are you going to do?"

"Heaven only knows, unless you are in a position to lend me a dollar, which, sir, I assure you, shall be returned in the morning."

"Nonsense. I never lend money. But if you like, you shall come to my hotel and spend the night there, free of charge."

"What hotel?"

"The *Hotel de Coup d'Œil*, in Broadway."

"I never heard of such an establishment."

"Perhaps. Nevertheless, it is what is called a first-class hotel."

"Well, but who are you, sir?" I inquired; for, in truth, my suspicions began to be slightly excited by this time. My interlocutor was rather a singular-looking person, as well as I could make out his features in the dusk. Middle height, broad shoulders, and a square, pale face, the upper part of which seemed literally covered with a pair of huge blue spectacles, while the lower portion was hidden in a frizzly beard. A small space on either cheek was all that was uncovered, and that shone white and cold as the snow that lay on the streets. "Who are you, sir?"

"I—I am Count Goloptious, Literary Man, *Bon vivant*, Foreign Nobleman, Linguist, Duellist, Dramatist, and Philanthropist."

"Rather contradictory pursuits, sir," I said, rather puzzled by the man's manner, and wishing to say something.

"Of course. Every man is a mass of contradictions in his present social state."

"But I never heard your name mentioned in the literary world," I remarked. "What have you written?"

"What have I not written? Gory essays upon Kansas for the *New York Tribune*. Smashing personal articles for the *Herald*. Carefully constructed non-committal double-reflex-action with escape-movement leaders for the *Daily Times*; sensation dramas for the Phantom Theatre. Boisterous practical joke comedies for Mr. Behemoth the low comedian; and so on *ad infinitum*."

"Then as a *bon vivant*—?"

"I have been immensely distinguished. When Brillat Savarin was in this country, I invented a dish which nearly killed him. I called it *Surprise des Singes avec petite verole*."

"Linguist?"

"I speak seventeen languages, sir."

"Duellist?"

"I was elected a Member of Congress for South Carolina."

"Philanthropist?"

"Am I not offering to you, a stranger, the hospitality of the *Hotel de Coup d'Œil?*"

"Enough, sir," I cried; "I accept your offer. I thank you for your timely assistance."

"Then let us go," answered the Count Goloptious, offering me his arm.

2: THE HOTEL DE COUP D'ŒIL.

The count led me out of Bleecker Street into Broadway. We trudged a few blocks in silence, but whether towards Union Square or the Battery I could not for the life of me tell. It seemed as if I had lost all my old landmarks. The remarkable corners and signposts of the great thoroughfare seemed to have vanished.

We stopped at length before a large edifice, built of what seemed at first glance to be a species of variegated marble; on examining more closely, I perceived that every stone in the front of the building was a mosaic, in which was represented one of the four chief organs of the body. The stones were arranged in the form of a cross, with these designs depicted on them.

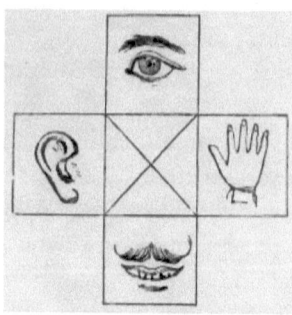

The effect of the entire front of this huge building, staring at you with a myriad painted eyes, listening to you with a myriad painted ears, beckoning to you with a myriad painted hands, and grinning at you with a myriad painted mouths, was inconceivably strange and bewildering.

"This is the hotel," said Count Goloptious. "Let us enter." We passed under a gigantic portal towards two gleaming doors of plate-glass, which voluntarily unclosed as we approached. A magnificent hall lay before us. The pavement was of tessellated marble, on every square of which the strange emblems which decorated the front of the establishment were repeated. From the centre of this vast chamber a spiral staircase arose, from each coil of which small bridges of delicate gilt iron work branched off, and led into what seemed to be the corridors of the building. At one end of the hall stood a curious Oriental-looking structure, within which, seated upon a sort of throne, I beheld a portly bearded personage whose breast was festooned with gold chains, and whose fingers were covered with rings.

"That is the night clerk," whispered the count to me, pointing to this person. "Go and enter your name on the book."

I approached the Oriental temple, and, finding a hotel register with leaves of vellum and bound in silver and mother-of-pearl, open on a shelf close by, took up a pen and wrote down my name. The clerk did not even condescend to glance at me, while doing this.

"Would you like some supper?" asked the count.

"No, no," I answered; "I want only to go to bed." The truth is, the whole scene so bewildered me, that I began to fear that I had gone mad.

"Very well. I will call for your candle." So saying the count approached a large model of a human ear, which was fixed in the wall of the Oriental temple, and putting his lips to it called out, "A bedroom light for 746."

In an instant, a continuous murmur seemed to fill the hall and ascend towards the roof of the building. It appeared to me that ten thousand voices took up the words, "A bedroom light for 746," one after the other, until the sentence rolled along like the fire of a line of infantry. I turned, startled, towards the direction from which those echoes proceeded, and on casting my eyes upon the great spiral staircase beheld the cause.

3: EYE, EAR, HAND, AND MOUTH.

The balustrades of the staircase on either side, and the sides of the different galleries branching off, were all decorated with two of the mystical emblems I had before seen so often repeated in this strange hotel. On the one side a line of human mouths ran up the edges of the staircase, while on the other a line of human hands occupied a corresponding position. There was, however, this difference between them and the symbols occupying the front of the establishment. They were all modelled in high relief. The balustrades seemed as if they had been decorated with the pillage of numberless anatomical museums. As I turned suddenly and glanced towards the staircase, I saw the lips of those ten thousand mouths moving, and whispering softly but distinctly the words, "A bedroom light for 746."

I had scarcely recovered from the astonishment with which this sight overwhelmed me, and the rolling whisper had hardly died away in the domed roof of the hall, when my attention was attracted by a speck of light which appeared far away up on the staircase, and seemed to be travelling slowly down the huge spiral. I watched it with a sort of stupid interest, and when it came nearer discovered that it was nothing less than a chamber wax-light in a silver candlestick, which the ten thousand hands that lined the edge of the balustrade opposite to the balustrade of the mouths were carefully passing from one to the other. In a few moments it reached the bottom, where the last hand, a huge muscular-looking fist, held it.

"There is your light," said the count; "follow it upstairs, and it will lead you to your room. I will, for the present, wish you a goodnight, as I have to go and take my before-morning walk."

I confusedly wished my strange friend goodnight, and walked towards the hand that held my candle. As I approached, the hand passed it to the hand next above, and the candle so began to ascend the stairs. I followed. After toiling up an interminable number of steps, the hands suddenly took the candle off into one of the side galleries, in which at last it stopped before a huge polished door, on the upper panels of which were painted again a huge eye and an equally gigantic ear. I could not help noticing that the eye had a demoniac expression.

I pushed the door open, and, taking the candle from the attendant hand, was about to enter the room, when my attention was attracted by that member giving my coat a gentle twitch. I turned, and there beheld the hand stretched out with an expression—if ever hand had an expression—which was inexpressibly pleading. I was puzzled. What could it want? I would follow the example of my friend Count Goloptious, and speak to the ear. Approaching my lips to the ear painted over my door, I put the question, "What does this amiable hand want?"

In an instant, a fusillade of whispers came rolling up the line of mouths, answering, "He wants a quarter for his trouble." My heart sank,—I had only five cents.

"Pshaw!" said I, trying to bluff the thing off, "I can't attend to it now"; and so saying, stepped towards my room. As I entered and hurriedly closed the door, I beheld every hand down the long coil of stairs simultaneously double up and shake at me in menace, while a horrid sardonic laugh ran down the line of mouths. I never beheld anything more devilish than that spiral smile of scorn.

On closing the door of my room, I was not a little annoyed to find that the eye and the ear, which were on the outside, were on the inside also, so exactly alike that they seemed to have come through for the purpose of watching me, and listening to my sleep-talk. I felt wretchedly uncomfortable at the idea of undressing before that eye. It was fixed on me wherever I moved in the room. I tried to pin a handkerchief over it, but the wood of the door was too hard and the pins would not stick. As the handkerchief fell to the ground, I beheld the horrid eye wink at me with a devilish expression of derision.

Determined not to be overlooked, I put out the light and undressed in the dark, when I tumbled into bed in a state of confusion of mind not easily described. I had scarcely laid my head on the pillow, when I heard a distinct knock at my door. Cursing the intrusion, and not without some tremor, being uncertain what new enchantment might be brewing, I opened it. There was the hand outstretched, and pleading for its infernal quarter. The abominable member was evidently determined to keep me awake all night. There was but one thing to be done,—to bribe him with a promise. I put my lips to the ear and said: "If the hand does not disturb me, I will put a gold ring on his finger tomorrow."

The ten thousand mouths repeated with tones of approval, "He will put a gold ring on his finger tomorrow," and the ten thousand hands waved their thanks. I shut my door, congratulating myself on my escape, and, flinging myself on the bed, soon fell fast

4: DR. KITCHENER IN A DREAM

A horrible heat seemed to surround my head. I suffered in tolerable agony. Count Goloptious had unscrewed my caput just at the point known to anatomists as the condyles, and deliberately placed it in the centre of a ring of burning brands which he had laid on the floor. The Philanthropic Duellist then drew a volume from his pocket, which, even in my excited condition, I could not help recognizing as Doctor Kitchener's cookery-book, and commenced deliberately to read aloud the recipe for roasting a goose alive, which is contained in that immortal work. I now perceived with unutterable indignation that he intended to cook my head after Kitchener's inhuman instructions.

The flames leaped higher and higher around my blistering cheeks. My whiskers—whiskers on which countless barbers had exhausted the resources of their art—shrivelled into ashy nothings. My eyeballs protruded, my lips cracked; my tongue, hard and wooden, beat against the roof of my mouth. I uttered a half-inarticulate cry for water. The count laughed a devilish laugh, and consulted his book.

"True," he said, "the worthy doctor says, that when the goose thirsteth let her be fed with water, so that the flesh shall be tender when cooked. Let us give the poor head a drink."

So saying, he reached towards my parched lips a pannikin fixed on the end of a long handle. I quaffed eagerly the liquor which it contained. Ah! how grateful was that draught of brandy and water! I drained the cup to the bottom. But the bliss was short lived. The flames hissed and crackled. My hair caught fire, and my poor head blazed like a Frenchman's "*ponch-bol.*" The sparkles from the burning brands flew against my forehead and into my eyes, scorching and blinding me. My brain simmered in the arched cells of my skull. My anguish was insufferable, and as a last desperate resource I cried out to the count: "Take me from the fire,—take me from the fire,—I am overdone!"

The count answered to this: "Patience, patience, head of a heathen! You are roasting beautifully. A few minutes more, and I will pour some Worcestershire sauce over you."

Worcestershire sauce! That essence of every peppery condiment known to civilized man! Worcestershire sauce, the delight of East Indian officers on half-pay, and the horror of French men who encounter it in London restaurants, and return to *La Belle* with excoriated palates; this biting, inflammatory stuff to be poured over a wretched head, whose scalp was cracking like the skin of a roasted apple,—it was too much to endure, so I gave vent to my feelings in one unearthly shriek of agony—and awoke.

My head was hot, but, thank Heaven, it was not roasting. It was lying on a tumbled pillow across which a stream of the morning sunlight was pouring in a golden tide. There was no Count Goloptious,—no circle of firebrands,—no Worcestershire sauce,—I was in bed, and alone in the *Hotel de Coup d'Œil.*

So soon as I had sufficiently recovered from the effects of my horrible dream, I sat up in bed, and inspected my apartment. It was large and lofty and sumptuously furnished. A touching attention to my necessities was visible as I glanced round the room. By my bedside, on a small Buhl table, stood a large tumbler containing a creaming champagne cocktail. I drained it as a libation to the God of Morning. It was an appropriate sacrifice. The early sunlight itself seemed to flash through its amber globules. The white foam of dawn creamed in its effervescence. The tonic flavour of the fresh air that blows over the awaking earth was represented by the few drops of Boker's bitters with which it was tinctured. The immediate glow which it sent through every limb typified the healthy circulation produced by morning exercise.

I lay back on my pillow and began to speculate on the strange series of incidents which had befallen me. Who was Count Goloptious? What weird hotel was this, of which I had become an inmate? Were the days of enchantment indeed revived? or did I merely dream of those myriads of beseeching hands and whispering mouths and ever-wakeful eyes?

I glanced involuntarily to the door at this juncture, and lo! there I beheld the eye which seemed set in the panel of my door. A full flood of the sunlight that poured across my bed struck across that side of my room, and I saw the eye winking drowsily in the blaze,—drowsily, but yet wakefully, like one who is accustomed to watch between sleeping and waking; a sentinel which was never entirely somnolent.

The eye was watching me, despite the sleepy film with which it was overspread. Did I make any abrupt movement in the bed, its half-closed lid suddenly opened, and stared at me with appalling vigilance. There was no avoiding it. It commanded every corner of the room.

How was I to rise and attire myself, with so unpleasant a super vision? I had no longer the resource of extinguishing the light. The sun was beyond the reach of such a process. I meditated for a while, and at length hit upon the idea of constructing a species of wigwam out of the bedclothes, and dressing myself under its shelter. This I accomplished all the more easily, as I had laid my clothes, on retiring to rest, within easy reach of the bed; and as I constructed my impromptu tent, I thought I could discern an expression of drowsy disappointment shooting from underneath the half-closed lid of the Sentinel Eye.

5: How I Magnetized My Eye

Having finished my toilet sufficiently to justify my stepping from my bed, I was proceeding with my ablutions, when I heard a few chords struck upon a piano, in what seemed to be the next apartment. The moment after, a rich, luxurious *contralto* voice commenced to sing Schubert's beautiful serenade. I listened entranced. It seemed as if Alboni herself were singing. Those showers of rich, round notes falling in rhythmical sequence; that *sostenuto*, that, when first uttered, seemed a sound too weak to live, but growing and swelling every moment until it filled all the air with delicious sound, and then lessening and lessening till it almost died away, like distant music heard across the sea at night; those firm accentuations; the precision of those vocal descents, when the voice seemed to leap from the pinnacles of the gamut with the surety and fearlessness of a chamois-hunter leaping from Alpine peaks;—all told me that I was listening to a queen of song.

I ran to the window of my room, and, opening it, thrust my head forth. There was a window next to mine, but I could see nothing. The blinds were down, but I could feel the glass panes vibrating with that wondrous tide of song.

A woman,—a great singer,—the greatest I had ever heard, lived next to me. What was she like? That heavenly voice could never come from a lean and withered chest, from a skeleton throat. She must be young, must be lovely. I determined on the instant to form her acquaintance.

But there was the Sentinel Eye! How to evade the vigilance of that abominable optic? Its horrible magnetic gaze followed me in every motion that I made. Magnetic gaze! There was an idea. It was doubtless an enchanted eye; but was there any enchantment that could stand against the human will? I was strong, body and soul. My magnetic power I had frequently proved to be of the highest force; why not exercise it on my sentinel? I resolved to attempt to magnetize The Eye!

I shut the window, and, taking a chair, seated myself opposite the demoniac optic. I fixed my eyes upon it, and, concentrating all the will of which I was master, sent a powerful magnetic current straight to the centre of the glaring pupil. It would be a desperate struggle, I knew, but I was determined not to succumb. The Eye became uneasy. It glanced hither and thither, and seemed to wish to avoid my gaze. The painted eyelids drooped; the devilish pupil contracted and dilated, but still the orb always had to return and meet mine.

Presently the glaze of a magnetic sleep began to overspread it. The scintillating lights that played within grew dim. The lid drooped, and, after lifting once or twice, I beheld the long, dark lashes fall, and slumber veiled my sentinel.

6: Fair Rosamond

No sooner was the Sentinel Eye fairly magnetized than I hastened to the window and flung it open. I possess a tolerable tenor voice, and as I thought vocalism was the simplest way of attracting the attention of the fair unknown, I sang the first verse of the charming serenade in the *Knight of Arva*; a melody full of grace and passion, for which Mr. Glover never obtained sufficient commendation. I had hardly concluded the first verse when I heard the neighbouring window unclose. Unable to restrain my curiosity, I thrust my head out of my casement. Almost at the same instant a lovely face emerged from the window on the right. I had just time to get a flash of a glorious blond head, when the apparition disappeared. My head went in also. I waited a few moments, then cautiously, and after the manner of a turtle, protruded my caput once more. The Blond Head was out, but went in again like a flash. I remained with outstretched neck. After a brief pause I saw a gleam of fair curls. Then a white forehead, then a nose *retroussé*, then an entire face. I instantly withdrew into my shell.

The Blond Head was timid, and I wished to encourage it.

Have you ever seen those philosophical toys which are constructed for the purpose of telling whether the day will be rainy or shiny? No. Then I will describe one to you.

There is a rustic house with two portals, one on either side. In the portal on the right a little man is concealed; in the portal on the left, a woman. They are both connected with a vertical coil of catgut, which runs from the base to the roof of the house, between the two. In dry weather the catgut relaxes, and the little man, by the action of such relaxation, is swung out of his portal into the open air. In wet weather the catgut contracts, and the woman enjoys the atmosphere. This toy has two advantages.

One is, that it is infallible in its predictions, as it never announces fine weather until the weather is already fine; the other, that it affords an admirable illustration of the present social state of woman. When the day of storm arrives, in goes the man to his comfortable shelter, and out comes the woman to brave the elements. How many households does this typify! In sunshine and summer weather the husband is a charming fellow, and flaunts abroad in all his splendour; but when the clouds gather, when the fire goes out on the hearth for want of fuel, and duns are at the door, then poor woman is sent out to meet them, while the lord of creation hides in the cellar. I commend the toy to the consideration of Miss Lucy Stone.

Well, the Blond Head and myself played at weather-telling for five minutes. No sooner was one in than the other was out. It was a game of "tee to—tottering" performed after a new fashion. I resolved to put an end to it.

I gave three distinct hems.

There is a good deal of expression in a "hem." There is the hem of alarm, such as Alexis gives to Corydon, who is flirting in the garden with Phillis, when that young lady's mother is approaching. There is the hem of importance, such as that with which old Beeswax, the merchant, who is "worth his million, sir," prefaces a remark: the hem of confusion,—the hem of derision or unbelief,—the hem of satisfaction,—the hem of disappointment,—in short, a whole circle or hemmysphere of hems, each expressive in its way of a peculiar emotion. My hem was the hem of interrogation.

It was answered, and the next moment the Blond Head hovered, as it were, on the window-sill. It looked like a bird whose cage door has been opened after years of captivity, and who flutters on the threshold, not daring to advance into the free air.

I advanced my head boldly, and caught the Blond Head on the wing. It was retreating after the usual fashion, and with the usual rapidity, when I shot it with the word,—

"Stay!"

It fluttered for an instant, and then remained still.

"We are neighbours," I remarked to the Blond Head. It was a truism, I know, but still it was a remark. After all, what does it matter what you say to most women, so that what you say is a remark?

"So, I perceive," answered the Head, still fluttering a little.

"May I have the honour of knowing—" I commenced.

"Certainly," interrupted the Blond Head, "I am Rosamond."

"The fair Rosamond, I see," I interposed, in my gallantest manner.

"Yes," replied Rosamond, with wonderful *naïvéte*, "fair perhaps, but very unhappy."

"Unhappy! How? Can I relieve you,—be of any service?"

A glance of suspicion was shot at me from a pair of large, lustrous blue eyes.

"Are you not one of his satellites?" asked the Blond Head.

"I a satellite?" I answered indignantly,—"I am no one's satellite, unless indeed it be yours," I added; "for I would gladly revolve round so fair a planet."

"Then you are not a friend of Count Goloptious?"

"No. I never saw him until last night. He brought me to this hotel, where I have been bewildered by enchantments."

"All my doing! all my doing!" cried Rosamond, wringing her hands.

"How your doing?" I inquired, with some astonishment.

"I am the artist,—the fatal, the accursed artist. It was I who painted, I who modelled."

"Painted, modelled what?"

"Hush! you can save me, perhaps. I will see you again today. Is not the Eye watching you?"

"I have magnetized it."

"Good! you are a clever fellow," and Rosamond's eyes sparkled. "You must help me to escape."

"From what?"

"I will tell you—but quick! shut your window. Count Goloptious is coming."

The Blond Head gave me a sweet smile, and retreated. I did likewise, and closed my window. The next moment my door opened, and Count Goloptious entered.

7: THREE COLUMNS A DAY.

Count Goloptious entered. He seemed somewhat agitated, and banged the door to loudly. The shock dispelled the magnetic slumber of the Sentinel Eye, which suddenly opened its heavy lid and glared around with an expression which seemed to say, "I'd like to catch anybody saying that I have been asleep!"

"Sir," said the count, "you have been misconducting yourself."

"I? Misconducting myself! What do you mean, Count Goloptious?"

"You have been singing love-songs, sir. In a tenor voice, too. If you were a bass I would not so much care, but to sing tenor,—it's infamous!"

The blue goggles of the count seemed to scintillate with anger as he glared at me.

"What the devil is the meaning of all this mystery?" I demanded angrily, for I really was getting savage at the incomprehensibility of everything that surrounded me. "What do your infernal eyes and hands and ears and mouths mean? If you are a nightmare, why don't you say so, and let me wake up? Why can't I sing love-songs if I like,—and in a tenor voice, if I like? I'll sing alto if I choose, Count Goloptious."

"It is not for you to penetrate the mysteries of the *Hotel de Coup d'Œil*, sir," answered the count. "You have enjoyed its hospitalities, and you can go. You have sung tenor songs, sir. You know, as well as I, the influence of the tenor voice upon the female heart. You are familiar with the history of the opera, sir. You have beheld penniless Italians, with curled moustaches, and with no earthly attraction except a peculiar formation of the windpipe, wreck the peace of the loveliest of our females. There is a female in this vicinity, sir. A poor, weak-minded girl, who has been placed under my guardianship, and who is crazy on the subject of music. You have been singing to her, sir. Yes, with that accursed mellifluous voice of yours,—that vocal honey in which you tenors administer the poison of your love,—with that voice, sir, you are endeavouring to destroy the peace of mind of my ward. You have slept here, sir. You can go now."

"I have not the slightest intention of going now, Count Goloptious. This hotel suits me admirably well. It has certain little drawbacks to be sure. It is not pleasant to be always overlooked and overheard in one's privacy." Here I pointed to the Ear and the Eye. "But still one can grow accustomed to that, I suppose. By the way, I should like some breakfast."

My coolness took the count completely by surprise. He stared at me without being able to utter a word. The fact was, that the Blond Head had bewitched me. Those clouds of golden hair that enfolded the wondrous oval of her face like a continual sunset had set my heart on fire. Never, never would I quit that hotel, unless I bore her with me. She had hinted at misfortune in our brief interview. She was a captive,—a captive of the false count, who now pretended that he was her guardian. Meshed in the countless spells and enchantments that surrounded her, she was helpless as those fair creatures we read of in the *Arabian Nights*. I would be her rescuer. I would discover the charm before which the bonds should melt. It was Andromache and Perseus and the sea-monster over again, in the year 1858. The count, it is needless to say, was the monster. I had no Medusan shield, it is true, but I felt powerful as Perseus, for all that. My blond Andromache should be saved.

"So, you won't go, eh?" said Goloptious, after a long silence.

"No."

"You had better."

"This is a hotel. I have a right to accommodation here as long as I pay for it. Hotels belong to the public, when the public has money."

"I know I can't force you to go, but I don't think, young sir, that you will be able to pay for your board."

"How much do you charge here, by the day?"

"Three columns a day."

"Three what?"

"Three columns a day."

"I have heard of pillar dollars, but hang me if I ever heard of money that was called columns."

"We don't take money in pay at the *Hotel de Coup d'Œil*. Brain is the only currency that passes here. You must write me three columns of the best literary matter every day; those are our terms for this room. We have rooms higher up which rent for less. Some go as low as a paragraph. This is a four-column room usually, but you can have it for three."

Was the fellow laughing at me? His countenance was perfectly serious the whole time he was speaking. He talked as deliberately as if he had been a simple hotel clerk talking to a traveller, who was about pricing rooms. The whole thing struck me so comically that I could not refrain from a smile. I determined to carry the thing out in the count's own vein.

"Meals are of course included?" I said inquiringly.

"Certainly, and served in your own room."

"I don't think the apartment dear," I continued, inspecting my chamber with a critical eye. "I'll take it."

"Very good"; and I saw a gleam of gratified malice shoot through the count's great blue goggles.

"Now," said I, "perhaps you will inform me, Count Goloptious, why a few moments since you were so anxious to get rid of me, and why now you so tranquilly consent to my remaining an inmate of the *Hotel de Coup d'Œil?*"

"I have my reasons," said the count, mysteriously. "You have now taken a room in the *Hotel de Coup d'Œil;* you will never quit it unless with my consent. The Eye shall watch you, the Ear shall hear you, the Hands shall detain you, the Mouths shall betray you; work is henceforth your portion. Your brain is my property; you shall spin it out as the spider his web, until you spin out your life with it I have a lien on your intellect. There is one of my professions which I omitted in the catalogue which I gave you on our first meeting,—I am a publisher!"

8: THE BLOND HEAD.

This last speech of the count's, I confess, stunned me. He was then a publisher. I, who for years had been anxiously keeping my individuality as an author intact, who had been strenuously avoiding the vortex of the literary whirlpool of which the publisher is the centre, who had resisted, successfully, the absorbing process by which that profession succeeds in sucking the vitals out of the literary man, now suddenly found myself on the outer edge of the maelstrom, slowly but surely revolving towards the central funnel which was to swallow me.

An anticipation of unknown misfortunes seemed to overwhelm me. There was something sternly prophetic in the last tones of Goloptious's voice. He seemed to have had no turtle in his throat for several days. He was harsh and strident.

I determined to consult with the Blond Head in my extremity. It would, at least, be a consolation to me to gaze into those wondrous blue eyes, to bask in the sunshine of that luminous hair.

I raised my window, and hummed a bar of *Com'e Gentil*. In a moment, the adjoining window was raised, and out came the Blond

Head. The likeness to the weather-toy existed no longer: both our heads were out together.

"You have seen Goloptious," said the Blond Head. "What did he say?"

"Excuse me from continuing the conversation just at this moment," I replied. "I have forgotten something."

I had. The Ear and the Eye were in full play,—one watching, the other listening. Such witnesses must be disposed of, if I was to hold any secret conversation with Rosamond. I retired therefore into my chamber again, and set to work to deliberately magnetize the eye. That organ did not seem to relish the operation at all, but it had no resource. In a few moments, the film over spread it, and it closed. But what was to be done with the ear? I could not magnetize that. If, like the king in Hamlet, I had only a little poison to pour into it, I might deafen it forever. Or, like the sailors of Ulysses, when passing the island of the Sirens—ah! Ulysses!—that was the idea. Stop up the ear with wax! My bedroom candle was not all burned out. To appropriate a portion of that luminary, soften it in my hands, and plaster it over the auricular organ on my door was the work of a few moments. It was a triumph of strategy. Both my enchanted guardians, completely entrapped, and by what simple means!

I now resumed my out-of-window conversation with Rosamond with a feeling of perfect security.

"I have seen Goloptious," I said, in reply to her previous question, "and am now a boarder in the *Hotel de Coup d'Œil.*"

"Great heavens, then you are lost!" exclaimed Rosamond, shaking her cloudy curls at me.

"Lost! How so?"

"Simply that you are the slave of Goloptious. He will live on your brains, until every fibre is dried up. You will become a mental atrophy,—and, alas! worse."

"What do you mean? Explain, for Heaven's sake. You mystify me."

"I cannot explain. But we must endeavour to escape. You are ingenious and bold. I saw that by the manner in which you overcame the Sentinel Eye by magnetism. This hotel is a den of enchantments. I have been confined here for over a year. My profession is that of a sculptor, and I have been forced to model all those demon hands and mouths and ears with which the building is so thickly sown. Those weird glances that strike through the countless corridors from the myriad eyes are of my painting. Those ten thousand lips that fill this place with unearthly murmurs are born of my fingers. It is I, who, under the relentless sway of Goloptious, have erected those enchanted symbols of which you are the victim. I knew not what I did, when I made those things. But you can evade them all. We can escape, if you will only set your ingenuity to work."

"But, really, I see nothing to prevent our walking downstairs."

"There is everything. You cannot move in this house without each motion being telegraphed. The Hands that line the staircase would clutch your skirts and hold you firm prisoner, were you to attempt to leave."

"The Hands—be dished!" I exclaimed.

At this moment, there came a knock. I hastily drew my head in, and opened my door. I beheld the Hand of the night before, pleadingly extended; and at the same moment a running fire of murmurs from the Mouths informed me that he wanted the gold ring I had promised him. It was evident that this infernal hand would dun me to all eternity, unless he was paid.

I rushed to the window in my despair.

"Rosamond! fair Rosamond!" I shouted. "Have you got a gold ring?"

"Certainly," answered the Blond Head, appearing.

"Stretch as far as you can out of your window and hand it to me."

"Alas, I cannot stretch out of the window."

"Why not?"

"Do not ask me,—oh! do not ask me," answered the Blond Head, with so much anguish in her tones that I inwardly cursed myself for putting so beautiful a creature to pain.

"But," I continued, "if I reach over to you with a pair of tongs, will you give it to me?"

"O, with pleasure!" and the Blond Head smiled a seraphic smile.

A pair of tongs being adjacent, a plain gold ring was quickly transferred from Rosamond's slender finger to my hand. With much ceremony, I proceeded to place it on the smallest finger of the Hand, not being able, however, to get it farther than the first joint. Even this partial decoration seemed however to meet with approval, for the ten thousand hands commenced applauding vigorously, so much so that for a moment I fancied myself at the opera.

"Good heavens!" I thought, "what a *claque* these hands would make!"

There was one thing, however, that puzzled me much as I re-entered my room.

Why was it that Fair Rosamond could not lean out of the window? There was some mystery about it, I felt certain. I little thought in what manner or how soon that mystery was to be solved.

9: ROSAMOND MAKES A GREEN BIRD

No sooner was my debt to the Hand thus satisfactorily acquitted, than, in the elation of the moment at having for the first time in my life paid a debt on the appointed day, I immediately applied my lips to the Ear on the inside, and communicated my desire for some pens, ink, and paper. In an incredibly short space of time, the Hands, doubtless stimulated by the magnificence of my reward, passed a quantity of writing materials up the stairs, and in a few moments, I was at work on my three columns, being determined from that time not to fall into arrears for my board.

"It is of the utmost importance," I thought, "that I should be unfettered by pecuniary liabilities, if I would rescue Rosamond from the clutches of this vile count. I feel convinced of being able to baffle all his enchantments. Yes, Hands, ye may close, Ears, ye may listen, Eyes, ye may watch, Mouths, ye may scream the alarm, but I will deceive ye all! There is no magician who can out- conjure the imagination of man."

Having mentally got rid of this fine sentence, I set myself regularly to work, and in a short space of time dashed off a stunning article on the hotel system of England as contrasted with that of America. If that paper was ever printed, it must have astonished the reader; for written as it was, under the influence of the enchantments of the *Hotel de Coup d'Œil*, it mixed up the real and the ideal in so inextricable a manner, that it read somewhat like a fusion of alternate passages from Murray's guide-book and the *Arabian Nights' Entertainments*. Such as it was, however, it being finished, I folded it up and sent it by the Hand, with my compliments to Count Goloptious, begging that he should at the same time be informed that I was hungry, and wanted my breakfast. My message whirred along the ten thousand Mouths, and faded away down into the hall below.

I had scarcely re-entered my apartment when I heard the Blond Head open the window, and commence singing a strange wild sort of recitative, evidently with the view of attracting my attention. I listened, and found that it ran thus:—

Rosamond sings: "I have a bird, a bright green bird, who was born today.

"Today the sunshine entered him through his eyes; his glittering wings rustled in the breath of the warm noon, and he began to live.

"He is merry and bold and wise, and is versed in the mysteries that are sung by the Unseen Spirits.

"Yet he knows not the mystical joys of the silently growing forests.

"No egg ever contained him.

"No down, white and silken, ever sheltered him from the cold.

"No anxious, bright-eyed mother ever brought him the oily grain of the millet to eat, or sat on the neighbouring tree-tops, singing the holy hymns of maternal love.

"He never heard the sonorous melodies of the trees, when the wind with rushing fingers strikes the various notes of the forest, and Ash and Oak, Alder and Pine, are blent in the symphonic chords of the storm.

"Ten white fingers made him.

"The great sun—too far away to know what it was doing—hatched him into life, and in the supreme moment when his little heart just commenced to beat, and his magical blood to ebb and flow through the mystic cells of his frame, his maker cast from her lips, through his gaping golden bill, a stream of song, and gifted him with voice.

"This is the bird, bold and merry and wise, who will shake my salvation from his wings.

"Ah! until the hour of my delivery arrives, he shall be fed daintily on preserved butterflies, and shall scrape his bill on a shell of pearl! "

I opened my window as the last words of this strange song died away, and I had scarcely done so when a bright green bird, with an orange bill and cinnamon-coloured legs, flew from Rosamond's window into my room, and perched on the table. It was a charming bird. Its shape was somewhat like that of the mocking-bird,—long, slender body, piquant head, and sweeping tail. Its colour was of the most dazzling green, and its feathers shone like satin.

"Good morning, pretty bird," said I, holding out my finger to my visitor, who immediately flew to my hand and established himself there.

"Good morning," answered the Green Bird, in a voice so like Rosamond's that I was startled; "I am come to breakfast with you."

As the Green Bird spoke, a small bright feather dropped from its wing and fell slowly to the ground.

"I am delighted to have your society," I replied, with the utmost courtesy, "but I fear that I shall not be able to offer you any preserved butterflies. Nay, I have not as much as a beetle in pickle."

"Don't mention it," said the bird, with an off-hand flirt of his tail; "I can put up with anything. Besides, you know, one can always fall back on eggs."

To my surprise another bright green feather disengaged itself from the bird's plumage, and floated softly towards the carpet.

"Why, you'll lose all your feathers," said I. "Are you moulting?"

"No," answered the bird, "but I am gifted with speech on the condition that I shall lose a feather every time I use the faculty. When I lose all my feathers, which I calculate will not take place for about a year, I shall invent some artificial ornithological covering."

"Gracious! "I exclaimed, "what a figure—of speech you will be!"

At this moment, the usual knock was heard at my door, on opening which I discovered a large tray covered with a snowy cloth, on which were placed a number of small porcelain covers, some bottles of red and white wine, a silver coffee-service, in short, everything necessary for a good breakfast.

10: Breakfast, Ornithologically Considered.

In a few moments, my repast was arranged on the table, at which I seated myself, the Green Bird perching on the edge of a pretty dish of scarlet fruits at which he pecked, occasionally moistening his golden bill in the slender glass of *Barsac* which I placed near him.

"Breakfast," said the bird, looking at me with a glance of undisguised contempt while I was devouring a plate of *rognons au vin de champagne*,—"breakfast is a meal utterly misinterpreted by human beings. What can be more unhealthy or more savage than the English or American breakfast? The latter is a miracle of indigestibility. The elastic, hot cakes. The tough, over-cooked meats. The half-boiled, muddy coffee. The half-baked, alum-tempered bread. Breakfast should be a light meal, invigorating, yet not overloading,—fruits to purify the palate and the physical system, and a little red wine to afford nourishment to the frame, and enable it to go through the work of the day. In the morning man arises refreshed, not exhausted; his frame needs but little support; it is only when the animal vitality has been used up by a hard day's labour, that the meal of succulent and carbonised food is required. The French make their breakfast too elaborate; the English too heavy; the Americans too indigestible."

"Am I to understand, then," I asked, "that birds breakfast more sensibly than men?"

"Certainly," replied the Green Bird. "What is more delicate, and at the same time more easy of digestion, than the mucilaginous caterpillar? The dragonfly, when carefully stripped of its corselet, is the lobster of the Insectivora. The green *acarus* is a dainty morsel, and the yellow roses sigh with relief when we gobble up their indolent enemy. The *coccinella*, or ladybird, is our turtle: with what dexterity is he stript of his upper shell and eaten palpitating!

"But the chief hygienic feature about the breakfast of us birds is, that we exercise in order that we may eat. Supposing the blackbird, on withdrawing his head from under his crimson epaulet in the early morning, were merely to yawn, and stretch his wings, and, hopping lazily down branch by branch to the pool at the bottom of the tree on which he roosts, take his bath. That finished, we will suppose him retreating to his covert, when he rings a bell made of the blue campanula, and, being answered by an attendant Tom Tit, commands breakfast to be served. Tom Tit disappears, and after the usual absence returns with a meal of beetles, caterpillars, ripe cherries, and wild honey, neatly served on a satiny leaf of the Maple.

"Blackbird falls to and gorges himself. What an unhealthy bird he would be, compared with the Blackbird as he really is, stretching his wings at the first light of dawn, and setting off on a foraging expedition through the woods and fields! What glorious exercise and excitement there are in this chase after a breakfast! How all the physical powers are cultivated!

"The sight is sharpened. There is not a cranny in the bark of a tree, or a crevice in the earth, that the eye of the hungry bird does not penetrate. The extremist tip of the tail of a burrowing worm cannot remain undiscovered; he is whipped out and eaten in a moment. Then the long flight through the fresh air; the delicious draught of cool dew taken from time to time; the——"

"But," said I, interrupting the Green Bird, who I began to perceive was an interminable talker, "how is it possible for men to have the opportunity of pursuing their meals in the manner you describe? It would indeed present rather a ridiculous appearance, if at six o'clock in the morning I were to sally out, and run all over the fields turning up stones in order to find fried smelts, and diving into a rabbit burrow in the hope of discovering mutton chops *en papillotes*."

"If I were a man," said the Green Bird, sententiously, "I would have my meals carefully concealed by the servants in various places, and then set to work to hunt them out. It would be twice as healthy as the present indolent method."

Here he took another sip at the *Barsac*, and looked at me so queerly that I began to have a shrewd suspicion that he was drunk.

A brilliant idea here flashed across my mind. I would intoxicate the Green Bird, and worm out of him the reason why it was that the Blond Head was never able to stretch farther out of her window than the shoulders. The comicality of a drunken bird also made me favourable to the idea.

"As far as eating goes," said I, "I think that you are perhaps right; but as to drinking, you surely will not compare your insipid dew to a drink like this! "and, as I spoke, I poured out a glass of *Richebourg*, and handed it to the bird.

He dipped his bill gravely in it, and took one or two swallows.

"It is a fine wine," he said sententiously, "but it has a strong body. I prefer the *Barsac*. The red wine seems to glow with the fires of earth, but the white wine seems illumined by the sunlight of heaven."

And the Green Bird returned to his *Barsac*.

11: Leg-Bail.

"So, the fair Rosamond made you," I said carelessly.

"Yes, from *terra-cotta*," answered the Green Bird; "and, having been baked and coloured, I came to life in the sun. I love this white wine, because the sun, who is my father, is in it"; and he took another deep draught.

"What induced her to construct you? "I asked.

"Why, with a view of escaping from this place, of course."

"O, then you are to assist her to escape?"

"Not at all,—you are to assist her. I will furnish her with the means."

"What means?"

"With the wings."

"The what?" I asked, somewhat astonished.

"The wings!"

"What the deuce does she want of wings? She is not going to escape by the window, is she?"

"Ha, ha, ha! Ho, ho, ho! He asks what Rosamond wants of wings!" And the bird, overcome with laughter at the ludicrousness of some esoteric jest, tumbled into his glass of *Barsac*, from which I rescued him draggled and dripping, all the more draggled as during our conversation he had been continually shedding his feathers.

"Well, what does she want of wings?" I asked, rather angrily, because a man does not like to see people laughing at a joke into the secret of which he is not admitted.

"To fly with," replied the Green Bird, nearly choking with the involuntary draught of white wine he had swallowed during his immersion.

"But why does she want to fly?"

"Because she has no legs,—that's the reason she wants to fly," said the bird, a little crossly.

"No legs!" I repeated, appalled at this awful intelligence,—"no legs! O, nonsense! you must be joking."

"No, I'm choking," answered the Green Bird.

"Why, she is like Miss Biffin, then, born without legs. Heavens! what a pity that so lovely a head shouldn't have a leg to stand on!"

"She wasn't born without legs," replied the Bird. "Her legs are downstairs."

"You don't mean to say that they have been amputated?"

"No. Count Goloptious was afraid she would escape; and as he wanted only her bust, that is, her brain, hands, and arms, he just took her legs away and put them in the store-room. He'll take your legs away some day, too, you'll find. He wants nothing but heads in this hotel."

"Never!" I exclaimed, horror-stricken at the idea. "Sooner than part with my legs, I'd—"

"Take arms against him I suppose. Well, *nous verrons.* Gracious! what a lot of feathers I have shed!" suddenly continued the Bird, looking down at a whole pile of green feathers that lay on the floor. "I'm talking too much. I shan't have a feather left soon if I go on at this rate. By the way, where is your mirror? I must reproduce myself."

12: Holding the Mirror up to Nature.

I handed the Green Bird a small dressing-glass which lay on the bureau,—I mean, I placed it before him, for the impossibility of *handing* a bird anything will strike even the most uncultivated mind,—and seated myself to watch his proceedings with a considerable amount of curiosity.

I wish, before proceeding any further, to make a few random re marks on the looking-glass in America.

I take a certain natural pride in my personal appearance. It is of no consequence if my nose is a trifle too long, my chin too retreating, or my head too angular. I flatter myself that the elegance of a man's appearance does not depend on his individual traits, but upon his *tout ensemble*. I feel, when regarding myself in a well-constituted mirror, that, in spite of any trifling defects in detail, my figure on the whole is rather *distingué*.

In the matter of mirrors, I have suffered. The hotel and boarding-housekeepers of this country—actuated doubtless by a whole some desire to crush that pet fly called "vanity," with which the Devil angles for human souls—have, I am convinced, entered into a combination against the admiration of the human face divine by its owner.

Like Proteus, I find myself changing my shape wherever I go. At the Bunkum House, I am a fat boy. At the St. Bobolink, a living skeleton. Once I was seriously alarmed on inspecting myself for the first time in the glass,—on an occasion when I had just taken possession of a new boarding-house,—at discovering that one of my eyebrows was in the middle of my forehead. I had been informed by a medical student,—since plucked,—from whom I derived most of my chirurgical information, that paralysis not unfrequently produced such effects. I descended in some trepidation to the parlour, where I had an interesting interview with my landlady, who succeeded in removing the unpleasant impression from my mind that I was a victim to that unbecoming disease.

The glass was not, however, changed, and I never looked in it and beheld that eyebrow in the middle of my forehead, without the disagreeable sensation that in the end I should die a Cyclops.

The glass which I placed before the Green Bird possessed, I regret to say, certain defects in the plane of its surface, which rendered self-contemplation by its aid anything but an agreeable occupation. I know no man egotist enough to—as the novels say—"spend hours before" such a mirror.

The Green Bird, as soon as he beheld himself in this abominable mirror, uttered a scream of disgust. I must say, that, on looking over his shoulder, the image formed by him in the glass was not a graceful one. He was humped, one leg was shorter than the other, and his neck looked as if it had just been wrung by a schoolboy.

What attracted my attention most, however, were certain peculiarities in the reflected image itself. It scarcely seemed a reflection. It was semi-substantial, and stood out from the surface of the glass in a sort of half-relief, that grew more and more positive every moment. In a few seconds more, the so-called image detached itself from the mirror, and hopped out on the table, a perfect counterpart of the Green Bird, only humped, with one leg shorter than the other, and a wry neck. It was an ornithological caricature.

The Green Bird itself now sidled away from its position before the mirror, and the Caricature Bird took his place. If the image cast by the former was distorted, no words can convey the deformity of the image cast by the latter. It was a feathered cripple. It was all hump. It stood on one long attenuated leg. Its neck was tortuous as the wall of Troy.

This rickety, ornithological image produced itself in the mirror, in precisely the same fashion as did its predecessor, and, after gradually growing into substance, detached itself from the polished sur face, and came out upon the table, taking its position before the mirror, vice the first humpback resigned.

What the image cast by the third bird was like I cannot at all attempt to portray. It was a chaos of neck and humps and feathers. The reproduction, nevertheless, went on, and the prolific mirror kept sending forth a stream of green abortions, that after a little while were no longer recognisable as belonging to any species of animal in the earth below, or the heavens above, or the caverns that lie under the earth. They filled my room. Swarms of limping, wall-eyed, one-legged, green-feathered things hustled each other on the floor. My bed was alive with a plumed mass of deformity. They filled the air, making lame efforts at flight, and blindly falling to the floor, where they tumbled about in inextricable confusion. The whole atmosphere seemed thick with green feathers. Myriads of squinting eyes glittered before me. Quintillions of paralytic yellow bills crookedly gaped at me.

I felt myself treading on a thick carpet of soft, formless life. The fluttering of embryonic wings, the twittering of sickly voices, the ruffling of lustreless plumages, produced a continuous and vague sound that filled me with horror. I was knee-deep in the creatures. From out the distorting mirror they poured in a constant stream, like a procession of nightmares, and the tide-mark of this sea of plumage rose higher and higher every instant. I felt as if I was about to be suffocated,—as if I was drowning in an ocean of Green Birds. They were on my shoulders.

Nestling in my hair. Crooning their loathsome notes into my ear. Filling my pockets, and brushing with their warm fuzzy breasts against my cheek. I grew wild with terror, and, making one desperate effort, struggled through the thick mass of life that pressed like a wall around me to the window, and, flinging it open, cried in a despairing voice: "Rosamond! Rosamond! Save me, Rosamond!"

13: A Stupid Chapter, and I Know It

"What's the matter?" cried the Blond Head, appearing at her window, with all her curls in a flurry.

"Your Green Bird," I answered, "has been misconducting himself in the most abominable manner. He—"

"You surely have not let him get at a mirror?" screamed Rosamond.

"Unfortunately, I have; and pretty things he has been doing with it. My room is full of Green Birds. If you don't call them away, or tell me how to get rid of them, I shall be killed, as the persons suspected of hydrophobia were formerly killed in Ireland, that is, I shall be smothered by a feather-bed."

"What a wretch of a bird to waste himself in such a foolish way, when he was so particularly wanted! But rest a moment. I will rid you of your unpleasant company."

So saying, Rosamond withdrew her head from the window, and in a second or two afterwards a long shrill whistle came from her room, wild and penetrating as the highest notes of the oboe. The instant the Green Birds heard it, they all commenced jostling and crushing towards the open window, out of which they tumbled in a continual stream. As scarcely any of them could fly, only a few succeeded in reaching the sill of Rosamond's casement,—the goal towards which they all struggled. The rest fell like a green cataract on the hard flags with which the yard underneath my window was paved. In this narrow enclosure they hustled, and crawled, and limped, and writhed, till the place, filled with such a mass of feathered decrepitude, resembled an ornithological *Cour des Miracles*.

So soon as my room was cleared of the bird multitude, I commenced sweeping up the mass of green feathers which lay on the floor, and which had been shed by the original Green Bird, during his conversation with me at breakfast. While engaged in this task, I heard a laugh which seemed to come from my immediate neighbourhood. I turned, and there sat the Green Bird on the mantel piece, arranging what feathers he had left with his bill.

"What," I said, "are *you* there? Why, I thought you had gone with the rest of them!"

"Go with such *canaille* as that set!" answered the Green Bird, indignantly. "Catch me at it! I don't associate with such creatures."

"Then, may I ask, why the deuce did you produce all this *canaille* in my room, Green Bird?"

"It was your own fault. I intended to produce a few respectable and well-informed Green Birds, who would have been most entertaining society for you in your solitude, and materially aided you in your projects against Count Goloptious. But you presented me with a crooked mirror, and, instead of shapely and well-behaved Green Birds, I gave birth to a crowd of deformed and ill-mannered things, of no earthly use to themselves or anyone else. The worst of it is, they will build nests in the yard underneath, and bring forth myriads of callow deformities, so that unless they are instantly destroyed you will have no peace from them."

"I'll shoot them."

"Where's your gun?"

"Well, then, I'll fish for them with a rod, line, and hook, as the Chinese fish for swallows, and then wring their necks."

"Pooh! that won't do. They'll breed faster than you can catch them. However, you need not trouble yourself about them; when the time comes I'll rid you of them. I owe you something for having caused this trouble; besides, your *Barsac* was very good."

"Will you take another glass?" I said.

"No, thank you," politely replied the Green Bird. "I have drank enough already. About those feathers (I had just swept the green feathers up into a little heap),—what are you going to do with them?"

"To burn them, of course. I can't have them littering my room."

"My dear sir," said the Green Bird, "those feathers are immensely valuable. They will be needed to make Rosamond's wings. Put them into one of the drawers of the bureau, until they are wanted."

I obeyed.

14: On the Advantages of Marrying a Witch.

"Now," continued the bird, "what are your plans for escape?"

"I haven't any, except a general idea of throttling Goloptious the next time he comes in here, gagging the Mouths, handcuffing the Hands, and bunging up all the Eyes, and then bolting somewhere or other with the Blond Head,—that is, if we can recover her legs,—say to Grace Church, where, with the blessing of Brown, we can become man and wife."

"Are you not afraid to marry a sorceress?"

"Why should I be? Haven't I been continually calling every woman with whom I have been in love an enchantress; and writing lots of verses about the 'spells' with which she encompassed me; and the magic of her glance, and the witchery of her smile? I'm not at all sorry, if the truth must be confessed, to meet an enchantress at last. She will afford me continual amusement. I need never go to see Professor Wyman, or Herr Dobler, or Robert Houdin. I can get up a little Parlour Magic whenever I choose. Fancy the pleasure of having *Genii* for servants, just like Aladdin!

"No Irish Biddies, to over-roast your beef, and under-boil your potatoes; to 'fix' her mop of capillary brushwood with your private, particular hairbrush; to drink your brandy and then malign the cat; to go out on Sunday evenings, 'to see his Reverence Father McCarthy,' touching some matter connected with the confessional, and come home towards midnight drunk as an owl; to introduce at two in the morning, through the convenient postern of the basement, huge 'cousins,' whose size prevents you from ejecting them with the speed they merit, and who impudently finish their toddies before they obey your orders to quit. *Genii* have no cousins, I believe. Happy were the people in the days of Haroun Al Raschid.

"On these grounds, I esteem it a privilege to marry a witch. If you want dinner, all you have got to do is to notify your wife. She does something or other, kills a black hen, or draws a circle in chalk, and lo! an attendant *Genius*, who lived four years in his last place, appears, and immediately produces an exquisite repast, obtained by some inscrutable means, known only to the *Genii*, and you dine, without having the slightest care as to marketing, or butcher's or baker's bills.

"Then again, if your wife knits you a purse, what more easy for her than to construct it after the pattern of Fortunatus's? If she embroiders you a pair of slippers, they can just as well as not be made on the last of the seven-league boots. Your smoking-cap can possess the power of conferring invisibility like that of Fortunio.

"You can have money when you want. You can dress better at church than any of her acquaintances, because all the treasures of Solomon are at her disposal, to say nothing of those belonging to Jamshid. You can travel faster than any locomotive. You can amuse yourself with inspecting the private lives of your friends. You can win at cards when you desire it. You can at any moment take up your drawing-room carpet, and make it sail away with you and all your earthly possessions to Minnesota, if you please. You can buy a block on Fifth

Avenue, and build a palace in a night, and, in short, be always young, handsome, wealthy, happy, and respected. Marry an enchantress! why, it's even more profitable than marrying a Spirit Medium!"

"So you intend to marry Rosamond," remarked the Green Bird, with the slightest sneer in the world.

"Certainly. Why not?"

"I don't see how you're to do it. She has not got any legs, and may not be able to get away from here. You won't have any legs in a day or two. You are both in the power of Count Goloptious; and, even if you were to escape from your rooms, you would not be able to find the way out of the *Hotel de Coup d'Œil*."

"If I were forced to walk on my hands, I would bear Rosamond away from this cursed den of enchantment."

"An excellent speech for Ravel to make," replied the Green Bird, "but I fancy that your education as an acrobat has been neglected."

"I think I see at what you are aiming," I answered. "You want to make terms. How much do you want to assist Rosamond and myself to escape? I learn from her song that you know the ropes."

"I know the stairs and the doors," said the Green Bird, indignantly, "and that is more to the purpose."

"Well, if you show us the way to get free, I will give you a golden cage."

"Good."

"You shall have as much hemp-seed as you can eat."

"Excellent."

"And as much *Barsac* as you can drink."

"No," here the Green Bird shook his head; "I won't drink any more of your wine, but I want every morning a saffron cocktail."

"A what?"

"A saffron cocktail. Saffron is our delight, not only of a shiny night, but also of a shiny morning, in all seasons of the year. It is the Congress Water of birds."

"Well, you shall have a saffron cocktail."

"And fresh groundsel every day."

"Agreed."

"Then I am yours. I will give my plot."

The Green Bird Makes a Plot Which Differs from All Other Contemporary Plots in Being Short and Sweet

"Sir," said the Green Bird, "you wish to escape."

"Undoubtedly."

"The chief enemies which you have at present to fear are the Hands that clutch, and the Mouths that betray."

"I am aware of that fact."

"It is necessary that you should visit Rosamond's room."

"I would give my life to accomplish such a call."

"All you want to enable you to accomplish it is a couple of lead-pencils and a paper of pins."

"Well?"

"Well, that's my plot. Order them at the Ear, and when you get them I will show you how to use them"; and the Green Bird ruffled out his feathers and gave himself airs of mystery.

I immediately went to the Ear, and, removing the wax with which I had deafened it, ordered the articles as prescribed. I confess, however, that I was rather puzzled to know how with the aid of two lead-pencils and a paper of pins I was to baffle the spells of Goloptious.

15: Preparations for Flight.

While awaiting the arrival of the desired articles, I heard Rosamond calling me through the window. I immediately obeyed the summons.

"An idea has just struck me," said the Blond Head. "I am exceedingly anxious, as you know, to get away from here, and I have no doubt with your aid might succeed in doing so, but how am I to take my trunks?"

"Your what?"

"Trunks. You did not suppose, surely, that I was staying here without a change of dress."

"I always thought that imprisoned heroines contrived in some miraculous manner to get along without fresh linen. I have known, in the early days of my novel-reading, a young lady run through six volumes, in the course of which she was lost in forests, immersed in lakes, and imprisoned in dungeons, in a single white skirt and nothing on her head. I often thought what a colour that white skirt must have been at the end of the novel."

"O," said Rosamond, "I have quite a wardrobe here."

"Well, I'm afraid you'll have to leave it behind."

"What! leave all those ducks of dresses behind! Why, I'd rather stay here forever than part with them. It's so like a man to say, in the coolest manner in the world, 'Leave them behind.'" And the Blond Head here agitated her curls with a certain tremulous motion, indicative of some indignation.

"My dear, you need not be angry," I said soothingly. "Perhaps, after all, we can manage to get your trunks away also. How much luggage have you got?"

"'I' will read you the list I made of it," answered Rosamond.

This is her list,—I jotted it down at the time in pencil. The remarks are my own:—

One large trunk, banded with iron, and containing my evening dresses.

One large square trunk containing my bonnets, two dozen. (The excusable vanity of an individual having nothing but a head.)

One cedar chest containing my furs. (At this point I ventured a joke about a cedar chest being a great deal too good for such minkses. I was promptly suppressed by the dignified statement that they were sables.)

One circular box for carrying the incompressible skirt. (Doubtless an expansive package.)

A bird-cage.

A case for artificial flowers.

A feather case. (Containing the last feather which is supposed to be fatal to the Camel.)

A willow basket for bonnets. (More bonnets!)

Three large trunks. (Contents not stated,—suspicious circumstance.)

Four small trunks. (What male who has ever travelled with a lady does not remember with terror her small parcels? The big ones gravitate naturally to the baggage-car; but you are requested to see after the little ones yourself. You carry them in your arms, tenderly, as if they were so many babies. What lamentations if they slip,—and they are always doing it,—and fall in the street! Something very precious must be inside. In the cars, you have to stow them away under the seat so that you have no room for your legs. Woe to you if one is lost or mislaid. It always contains the very thing of all others which the owner would not have lost for worlds.)

A bandbox. (The bandbox is the most terrible apparatus connected with the locomotion of females. It refuses utterly to accommodate itself to travel. Its lid comes off. It will fit into no shaped vehicle. Of its own accord, it seems to place itself in positions favourable to its being sat upon. When crushed or in any way injured, it is capable of greater shabbiness of appearance than any other article of luggage.)

A dressing-case.

A portable bath.

An easel. (Easily carried.)

Three boxes of books. (A porter who was once removing my luggage called my attention to the weight of the box in which I had packed my books. They were certainly very heavy, and yet I had selected them with the greatest care.)

Here Rosamond stopped, and then proposed going over the list again, as she was sure she had forgotten something.

I respectfully declined the repetition, but asked her by what possible means she expected to transport such a quantity of luggage out of the *Hotel de Coup d'Œil.*

"You and the Green Bird can manage it, I suppose," she answered; "and I wish you would make haste, for I am getting very weary of not being able to walk. I shall enjoy so having my legs back again."

"Have you any idea where Count Goloptious put them?"

"O yes. They are in some cellar or other in a bin, with a number of other legs."

"Are the bins numbered?"

"Certainly."

"Do you know the number of your bin?"

"No. How should I?"

"It strikes me as rather awkward that you do not. For supposing that the Green Bird and myself succeed in getting down stairs in search of your legs, if we don't know the number of the bin we shall have some difficulty in finding the right ones, and it would be very disagreeable if you had to walk off with another person's legs."

"I never thought of that," said Rosamond, gravely. "A misfit would be horribly uncomfortable."

16: A THRILLING CHAPTER

We were certainly in a very unpleasant fix. To go downstairs on a wild-goose chase among the bins in search of the legs of the Blond Head would be anything but agreeable.

"Can you not make any pair do for the present?" I asked.

"Any pair? Certainly not. Could you get along with any other head but your own? "

The question rather took me aback. I confessed that such a change was not at all to be desired.

"Then go," said the Blond Head, "and search for them."

"Faint heart," etc.; a musty adage came into my head, and I answered, "I will do so." Turning to the Green Bird, I asked, "Will you come to the cellars?"

"Yes, at once," was the answer.

"Lead the way, then; you must be better acquainted here than I am."

The Green Bird led the way down the stairs, with all the hands before us; but not one moved now. Down! down! at least an hundred flights, then through a hall, and into a vast chamber black as midnight.

"How are we to find the legs in this plutonian darkness?" I asked.

"Silence!" said the Green Bird, and a falling feather aroused an echo that sounded like the beating of an hundred drums; "speak not if you would succeed!"

In silence, I followed on through the cavernous chamber with its pitchy walls,—on, still on. At last a small blue light appeared burning in the distance like the eye of a tiger. As we approached, it gradually increased in size, until, at last, as we neared it, it became magnified into an opening some sixty feet wide. Beyond, burned a lake of deadly blue sulphur, shedding a pale unearthly light. As we passed through the opening, a figure suddenly appeared before us. It was that of an old man. He carried a stick in his right hand, and walked with a feeble gait, but, what struck me as rather peculiar, his head, instead of being on his shoulders, he carried under his left arm.

"Who are you?" he asked, speaking from the head under his arm.

"I am an author," I replied.

"Look there?" he said, as he pointed to the burning lake.

I looked, and beheld what I had not before noticed. It was inhabited. Hundreds of poor wretches were there, burning and writhing in the seething flame.

"Who are those wretched beings?" I queried, in terror.

"Ha! ha! ha!" laughed the old man. "Those are authors!"

"Why doomed to a residence here?"

"Because, when on the earth beyond, they failed to fulfil their mission. They lost sight of their goal. They digressed from the path of honour. They—"

"I see. They went it blind."

"Exactly."

"There," and he pointed to a floating head near the edge of the lake,—"there is a plagiarist. His is the A No. 1 degree. There," and he pointed to another, "is one who published and edited a newspaper."

"His offence? "I asked.

"Blackmailing. There is one who wrote flash novels."

"Jack Sheppard. The Bhoys," I muttered.

"Ay; you be wise; avoid the broad path; keep faith; be true. And now what seek you here?"

I told him my errand.

"And you hope to find the legs?"

"I do."

"Come, then, with me. Here, carry my head."

I took the head, and, with the Green Bird by my side, followed the singular old man. He led us round by the lake, so close that, at times, the heat seemed to scorch my clothing. Presently he stopped opposite a great door of blue veined marble. Pushing that open, we entered a large and brilliantly lighted apartment. Here, upon every side, countless legs protruded from the wall. As we entered, the legs all at once commenced kicking as though they would eject us from their abode.

The old man took his head from us, and, putting it under his arm, commanded the legs to desist from their threatening attitudes. In an instant, they all fell dormant.

"Here," he said, "are the legs of all who have ever slept in the *Hotel de Coup d'Œil*, and here you will find those of the Blond Head."

"But how am I to know them?" I said.

"That I cannot tell you."

"I can tell them," said the Green Bird, now speaking for the first time since we left the darkness; and it flew around the room, stopping to look at now one pair of legs, now another. At last it stopped opposite a remarkably crooked pair of limbs. "Here they are," he said.

"Nonsense! it cannot be. Such a beauty as the Blond Head never propelled on such pedals as those."

"It is true," answered the bird. "Take them down, and see."

I seized the legs, and with a sudden jerk pulled them from their place. What was my surprise on finding Count Goloptious before me. The legs were his.

"Ha!" he exclaimed, "you would trick me, but I have watched you. The Blond Head is safe."

"Safe!" I echoed.

"Ay, safe, safe in my stronghold, the *Hotel de Coup d'Œil.*"

"'Tis false!" cried the Green Bird. "She is here!" As it spoke, it flew to a small door in the wall which I had not before noticed. Tapping with its beak against it, it opened instantly, and, looking in, I beheld the Blond Head complete. Never did I be hold a being so beautiful as she seemed to me at that glance. Grace, beauty, voluptuousness,—well, imagine all the extensive descriptions of female loveliness you have ever read in two-shilling novels, put them all altogether, and pile on as much more, and then you have her description.

"Fair Rosamond," I exclaimed, as I started forward to gain her,—"Fair Rosamond, you shall be saved."

"Never!" cried Count Goloptious,—"never! Beware, rash youth! You have dared to criticise Italian opera, you have dared write political leaders, you have dared theatrical managers, you have dared a fickle public,—all this you have done, but brave not me. If you would be safe, if you value your life, go, depart in peace!"

As he spoke, I felt the chivalric blood fast coursing through my veins. Go, and leave the fair being I loved in the power of a monster? No, I resolved upon the instant that I would die with her, or I would have her free.

"Count," I exclaimed in passionate tones, "I defy thee. I will never forsake yon wretched lady."

"Then your doom is sealed." He stamped three times upon the floor, and instantly the Green Bird disappeared. The place was wrapped in darkness. I felt myself borne through the murky, foul air of the cavern through which we had first passed, with the rapidity of a cannon-ball. Emerging from it, I found myself in the arms of the count; by his side stood the old man with his head under his arm.

"Here," cried the count, "is the nine hundred and twentieth. Eighty more, and we are free."

A demoniacal laugh burst from the old man as he took me, unable to resist him, from Goloptious. "Go, go to your brother authors, to the blue lake of oblivion. Go," he exclaimed with a sardonic bitterness, as he pitched me from him into the burning lake.

A wild shriek. The burning sulphur entered my ears, my eyes, my mouth. My senses were going, when suddenly a great body, moving near, struck me. The liquid opened, and closed over me. I found myself going down, down. At last, I struck the bottom. One long scream of agony, and—

17: How It All Happened.

"Good gracious! is that you? Why, how came you there?"

"Dunno."

"Bless me, you've almost frozen. Come, up with you."

"What! Bunkler, that you? Where's the Blond Head?"

"Blond what? You 've been drinking."

"Where's Count Goloptious?"

"Count the deuce; you're crazy."

"Where's the Green Bird?"

"You're a Green Bird, or you wouldn't lie there in the snow. Come, get up."

In an instant, I was awake. I saw it all. "What's the time?" I asked.

"Just two!"

Could all that have happened in an hour! Yes. The *Hotel de Coup d'Œil*. The Blond Head. The Green Bird. The Count. The Blue Lake. The Hands. The Legs. The Eyes, the everything singular, were the creations of Pilgarlik's Burgundy. I had slipped in the snow at the door, and was dreaming.

The cold had revived me, and I was now shivering. I arose. My friend and fellow-boarder, Dick Bunkler, who had been tripping it on the light fantastic toe at a ball in the Apollo, was before me; and lucky it was for me that he had gone to that ball, for had I lain there all night, the probability is Coroner Connery would have made a V off my body, next day.

"How came you to lie there *outside* the door? "asked Dick.

"The door is fast; my night-key wouldn't work."

"Night-key! ha! ha! night-key!"

I looked at my hand, and beheld what? My silver pencil-case,—the only piece of jewellery I ever possessed.

Dick opened the door, and in a very short time was engaged in manufacturing the "Nightcap" which I had promised myself an hour before. Over it I told my dream in the snow, and we enjoyed a hearty laugh at the effect of the bottle of Burgundy which passed from *Hand to Mouth*.

A Dead Secret

In what manner, I became acquainted with that which follows, and from whom I had it, it serves not to relate here. It is enough that he was hanged, and that this is his story:

"And how came you," I asked, "to be—" I did not like to say hanged, for fear of wounding his delicacy, but I hinted my meaning by an expressive gesture.

"How came I to be hanged!" he echoed, in a tone of strident hoarseness. "You would like to know all about it—wouldn't you?"

He was sitting opposite to me at the end of the walnut-tree table in his shirt and trowsers, his bare feet on the bare polished oak floor. There was a dark bistre ring round each of his eyes; and they—being spherical rather than oval, with the pupils fixed and coldly shining in the centre of the orbits—were more like those of some wild animal than of a man. The hue of his forehead, too, was ghastly and dingy; blue, violet, and yellow, like a bruise that is five days old.

There was a clammy sweat on his beard and under the lobes of his ears; and the sea-breeze coming gently through the open Venetians (for the night was very sultry), fanned his long locks of coarse, dark hair until you might almost fancy you saw the serpents of the Furies writhing in them. The fingers of his lean hands were slightly crooked inward, owing to some involuntary muscular rigidity, and I noticed that his whole frame was pervaded by a nervous trembling, less spasmodic than regular, and resembling that which shakes a man afflicted with *delirium tremens*.

I had given him a cigar. After moistening the end of it in his mouth, he said, bending his eyes toward me, but still more on the wall behind my chair than on my face:

"It's no use. You may torture me, scourge me. Flay me alive. You may rasp me with rusty files, and seethe me in vinegar, and rub my eyes with gunpowder—but I can't tell you where the child is. I don't know—I never knew. How am I to make you believe that I don't know—that I never knew!"

"My good friend," I remarked, "you do not seem to be aware that, so far from wishing you to tell me where the child you allude to is, I am not actuated by the slightest curiosity to know anything about any child whatever. Permit me to observe that I cannot see the smallest connection between a child and your being hanged."

"No connection!" retorted my companion, with vehemence, "It is the connection—the cause. But for that child I should never have been hanged."

He went on muttering and panting about this child; and I pushed toward him a bottle of thin claret. (Being liable to be called up at all hours of the night, I find it lighter drinking than any other wine.) He filled a large tumbler—which he emptied into himself, rather than drank—and I observed that his lips were so dry and smooth with parchedness, that the liquid formed little globules of moisture on them, like drops of water on an oil-cloth. Then he began, he said:

"I had the misery to be born about seven-and-thirty years ago. I was the offspring of a double misery, for my mother was a newly-made widow when I was born, and she died in giving me birth. What my name was before I assumed the counterfeit that has blasted my life, I shall not tell you. But it was no patrician, high-sounding title, for my father was a petty tradesman, and my mother had been a domestic servant. Two kinsmen succoured me in my orphanage. They were both uncles; one by my father's, one by my mother's side. The former was a retired sailor, rich, and a bachelor. The latter was a grocer, still in business. He was a widower, with one daughter, and not very well to do in the world. They hated each other with the sort of cold, fixed, and watchful aversion that a savage cat has for a dog too large for her to worry.

"These two uncles played a miserable game of battledore and shuttlecock with me for nearly fourteen years. I was bandied about from one to the other, and equally maltreated by both. Now, it was my Uncle Collerer who discovered that I was starved by my Uncle Morbus, and took me under his protection. Now, my Uncle Morbus was indignant at my Uncle Collerer for beating me, and insisted that I should return to his roof. I was beaten and starved by one, and starved and beaten by the other. I endeavoured—with that cunning which brutal treatment will teach the dullest child—to trim my sails to please both uncles. I could only succeed by ministering to the hatred they mutually had one for the other. I could only propitiate Collerer by abusing Morbus: the only road to Morbus's short-lived favour was by defaming Collerer. Nor do I think I did either of them much injustice; for they were both wicked-minded old men. I believe either of them would have allowed me to starve in the gutter; only each thought that, appearing to protect me, would naturally spite the other.

"When I was about fifteen years old, it occurred to me, that I should make an election for good and all between my uncle's; else, between these two knotty, crabbed stools I might fall to the ground. Naturally enough I chose the rich uncle—the retired sailor, Collerer; and although I dare say he knew I only clove to him for the sake of his money, he seemed perfectly satisfied with my hearty abuse of my Uncle Morbus, and my total abnegation of his society; for, for three years I never went near his house, and when he met me in the street I gave him the breadth of the pavement, and recked nothing for his shaking his fist at me. and calling me an ungrateful hound.

"My Uncle Collerer, although retired from the sea, had not left off making money. He lent it at usury on mortgages, and in numberless other crawling; ways. I soon became his right hand, and assisted him in grinding the needy, in selling up poor tradesmen, and in buckling on the spurs of spendthrifts when they started for the race, the end of which was to be the jail. My uncle was pleased with me; and although he was miserably parsimonious in his housekeeping and in his allowance to me, I had hopes and lived on; but very much in the fashion of a rat in a hole.

"I had known Mary Morbus, the grocer's daughter, years before. She was a sickly, delicate child, and I had often teased and struck and robbed her of her playthings, in my evil childhood. But she grew up a surpassingly beautiful creature, and I loved her. We met by stealth in the park outside her father's door while he was asleep in church on Sundays; and I fancied she began to love me. There was little in my mind or person, in my white face, elf-locks, and dull speech to captivate a girl; but her heart was full of love, and its brightness gilded my miserable clay. I felt my heart newly opened. I hoped for something more than my uncle's moneybags. We interchanged all the flighty vows of everlasting affection and constancy common to boys and girls; and although we knew the two fierce hatreds that stood betwixt us and happiness, we left the accomplishment of our wishes to time and fortune, and went on hoping and loving.

"One evening, at supper-time—for which meal we had the heel of a Dutch cheese, a loaf of seconds bread, and a pint of small beer—I noticed that my Uncle Collerer looked more malignant and sullen than usual. He spoke little, and bit his food as if he had a spite against it. When supper was over, he went to an old worm-eaten bureau in which he was wont to keep documents of value; and, taking out a bundle of papers, untied and began to read them. I took little heed of that; for his favourite course of evening reading was bonds and mortgage deeds; and on every eve of bills of exchange falling due he would spend hours in poring over the acceptances and endorsements, and even in bed he would lie awake half the night moaning and crooning lest the bills should not be paid on the morrow. After carefully reading and sorting these papers, he tossed them over to me, and left the room without a word. Then I heard him going upstairs to the top of the house, where my room was.

"I opened the packet with trembling hands and a beating heart. I found every single letter I had written to Mary Morbus. The room seemed to turn round. The white sheet I held and the black letters dancing on it were all I could see. All beyond—the room, the house, the world—was one black unutterable gulf of darkness. I tried to read a line—a line I had known by heart for months; but, to my scared senses, it might as well have been Chaldee. Then my uncle's heavy step was heard on the stairs.

"He entered the room, dragging after him a small black portmanteau in which I kept all that I was able to call my own.

"'I happened to have a key that opens this,' he said, 'and I have read every one of the fine love-letters that silly girl has sent you. But I have been much more edified by the perusal of yours, which I only received from your good Uncle Morbus—strangle him!—last night. I'm a covetous hunk, am I? You live in hopes, do you? Hope told a flattering tale, my young friend. I've only two words to say to you,' continued my uncle, after a few minutes' composed silence on his part, and of blank consternation on mine. 'All your rags are in that trunk. Either give up Mary Morbus—now and forever, and write a letter to her here in my presence to that effect—or turn out into the street and never show your face here again. Make up your mind quickly, and for good.' He then filled his pipe and lighted it.

While he sat composedly smoking his pipe, I was employed in making up my wretched mind. Love, fear, interest, avarice—cursed avarice—alternately gained ascendency within me. At length, there came a craven inspiration that I might temporise; that by pretending to renounce Mary, and yet secretly assuring her of my constancy, I might play a double game, and yet live in hopes of succeeding to my uncle's wealth. To my shame and confusion, I caught at this coward expedient, and signified my willingness to do as my uncle desired.

"'Write then,' he resumed, flinging me a sheet of letter-paper and a pen. 'I will dictate.'

"I took the pen; and following his dictation wrote, I scarcely can tell what now; but I suppose some abject words to Mary, saying that I resigned all claim to her hand.

"'That'll do very nicely, nephew,' said my uncle, when I had finished. 'We needn't fold it, or seal it, or post it, because—he, he, he!—we can deliver it upon the spot.'

"We were in the front parlour, which was separated from the back room by a pair of folding-doors. My uncle got up, opened one of these; and with a mock bow ushered in my Uncle Morbus and my Cousin Mary.

"'A letter for you, my dear,' grinned the old wretch; 'a letter from your *true love*. Though I dare say you'll have no occasion to read it, for you must have heard it. I speak plain enough, though I am asthmatic, and can't last long—can't last long—eh, nephew?' This was a quotation from one of my own letters.

"When Mary took the letter from my uncle, her hand shook as with the palsy. But, when I besought her to look at me, and passionately adjured her to believe that I was yet true to her, she turned on me a glance of scornful incredulity; and, crushing the miserable paper in her hand, cast it contemptuously from her.

"'*You* marry my daughter,' my Uncle Morbus piped forth—'you? Your father couldn't pay two-and-twopence in the pound. He owed me money, he owes me money to this day. Why ain't there laws to make sons pay their fathers' debts? You marry my daughter? Do you think I'd have your father's son—do you think I'd have your uncle's nephew for my son-in-law?'

"I could see that the temporary bond of union between my two uncles was already beginning to loosen; and a wretched hope sprang up within me.

"'Get out of my house, you and your daughter, too!' cried my Uncle Collerer 'You've served my turn, and I've served yours. Now, go!'

"I could hear the two old men fiercely, yet feebly, quarrelling in the passage, and Mary weeping piteously without saying a word. Then the great street door was banged to, and my uncle came in, muttering and panting. 'I hope you are satisfied now, uncle,' I said.

"'Satisfied!" he cried with a sort of shriek, catching up the great earthen jar, with the leaden top, in which he kept his tobacco, as though he meant to fling it at me. 'Satisfied!—I'll satisfy you: go. Go! and never let me see your hang-dog face again!'

"'You surely do not intend to turn me out of doors, uncle,' I said.

"'March, bag and baggage. If you are here a minute longer, I'll call the police. Go!' And he pointed to the door.

"'But where am I to go?' I asked.

"'Go and beg,' said my uncle; 'go and cringe to your dear Uncle Morbus. Go and rot!'

"So saying he opened the door, kicked my trunk into the hall, thrust me out of the room and into the street, and pushed my portmanteau after me, without my making the slightest resistance. He slammed the door in my face, and left me in the open street, at twelve o'clock at night.

"I slept that night at a coffee-shop. I had a few shillings in my pocket and, next morning, I look a lodging at, I think, four shillings a week, in a court, somewhere up a back street between Gray's Inn and Leather Lane, Holborn. My room was at the top of the house. The court below swarmed with dirty, ragged children. My lodging was a back garret; and when I opened the window, I could only see a narrow strip of sky, and a foul heap of sooty roofs, chimneypots and leads, with the great dingy brick tower of a church towering above all. Where the body of the church was I never knew.

"I wrote letter after letter to my uncles and to Mary, but never received a line in answer. I wandered about the streets all day, feeding on saveloys and penny loaves. I went to my wretched bed by daylight, and groaned for darkness to come; then groaned that it might grow light again. I knew no one to whom I could apply for employment, and knew no means by which I could obtain it. The house I lived in and the neighbourhood were full of foreign refugees and street mountebanks, whose jargon I could not understand.

"My little stock of money slowly dwindled away; and, in ten days, my mind was ripe for suicide. You must serve an apprenticeship to acquire that ripeness. Crowded streets, utter desolation and friendlessness in them, scanty food, and the knowledge that when you have spent all your money and sold your coat and waistcoat yon must starve, are the best masters. They produce that frame of mind which coroners' juries call temporary insanity. I determined to die. I expended my last coin in purchasing laudanum at different chemists' shops—a pennyworth at each; which, I said, I wanted for the toothache; for I knew they would not supply a large quantity to a stranger. I took my dozen vials home, and poured their contents into a broken mug that stood on my wash-handstand. I locked the door, sat down on my fatal black portmanteau, and tried to pray; but I could not.

"It was about nine in the evening, in the summer time, and the room was in that state of semi-obscurity you call 'between the lights.' While I sat on my black portmanteau, I heard through my garret window, which was wide open, a loud noise, a confusion of angry voices, in which I could not distinguish one word I could comprehend. The noise was followed by a pistol-shot. I hear it now, as distinctly as I heard it twenty years ago; and then another. As I looked out of the window I saw a pair of hands covered with blood, clutching the sill, and I heard a voice imploring help for God's sake!

"Scarcely knowing what I did, I drew up from the leads below and into the room the body of a man, whose face was one mass of blood-like a crimson mask. He stood upright on the floor when I had helped him in; his face glaring at me like the spot one sees after gazing too long at the sun. Then he began to stagger, and went reeling about the room, catching at the window curtain, the table, the wall, and leaving traces of his blood wherever he went—I following him in an agony—until he fell face foremost on the bed.

"I lit a candle as well as I could. He was quite dead, his features were so scorched and mangled, and drenched, that not one trait was to be distinguished. The pistol must have been discharged full in his face, for some of his long black hair was burnt off. He held, clasped in his left hand, a pistol which evidently had been recently discharged.

"I sat by the side of this horrible object twenty minutes or more, waiting for the alarm which I thought must necessarily follow, and resolving what I should do. But all was as silent as the grave. No one in the house seemed to have heard the pistol-shot, and no one without seemed to have heeded it. I looked from the window, but the dingy mass of roofs and chimneys had grown black with night, and I could perceive nothing moving. Only, as I held my candle out of the window it mirrored itself dully in a pool of blood on the leads below.

"I began to think I might be accused of the murder of this unknown man. I, who had so lately courted a violent death, began to fear it, and to shake like an aspen at the thought of the gallows. Then

I tried to persuade myself that it was all a horrible dream; but there, on the bed, was the dreadful dead man in his blood, and all about the room were the marks of his gory fingers,

"I began to examine the body more minutely. The dead man was almost exactly of my height and stoutness. Of his age, I could not judge. His hair was long and black like mine. In one of his pockets I found a pocket-book, containing a mass of closely-written sheets of very thin paper, in a character utterly incomprehensible to me; moreover, there was a roll of English banknotes to a very considerable amount. In his waistcoat pocket was a gold watch; and in a silken girdle round his waist, were two hundred English sovereigns and *louis d'ors*.

"What fiend stood at my elbow while I made this examination I know not. The plan I fixed upon was not long revolved in my mind. It seemed to start up matured, like Minerva, from the head of Jupiter. I was resolved. The dead should be alive, and the live man dead. In less time than it takes to tell, I had stripped the body, dressed it in my own clothes, assumed the dead man's garments, and secured the pocket-book, the watch, and the money about my person. Then I overturned the lighted candle on to the bed, slouched my hat over my eyes, and stole downstairs. No one met me on the stairs, and I emerged into the court.

"No man pursued me, and I gained the open street. It was only an hour after perhaps, as I crossed Holborn toward St. Andrew's Chinch, that I saw fire-engines come rattling along; and, asking unconcernedly where the fire was, heard that if was 'somewhere off Gray's Inn Lane.'

"I slept nowhere that night. I scarcely remember what I did; but I have an indistinct remembrance of flinging sovereigns about in blazing gas-lit taverns. It is a marvel to me now that I did not become senseless with liquor, unaccustomed as I was to dissipation. The next morning I read the following paragraph in a newspaper:

AWFUL SUICIDE AND FIRE NEAR GRAY'S INN LANE. Last night the inhabitants of Cragg's Court, Hustle Street, Gray's Inn Lane, were alarmed by volumes of smoke issuing from the windows of number five in that court, occupied as a lodging-house. On Mr. Plose, the landlord, entering a garret on the third floor, it was found that its tenant, Mr. ——, had committed suicide by blowing his brains out with a pistol, which was found tightly clenched in the wretched man's hand. Either from the ignition of the wadding, or from some other cause, the fire had communicated to the bedclothes; all of which, with the bed and a portion of the furniture, were consumed. The engines of the North of England Fire Brigade were promptly on the spot; and the fire was with it difficulty at last successfully extinguished; little beyond the room occupied by the deceased being injured. The body and face of the miserable suicide were frightfully mutilated; but sufficient evidence was afforded from his clothes and papers to establish his identity.

No cause is assigned for the rash act; and it is even stated that he had prolonged his existence a few hours later, he would have come into possession of a fortune of thirty thousand pounds, his uncle, Cripple Collerer, Esq., of Raglan Street, Clerkenwell, having died only two days before, and having constituted him his sole heir and legatee. That active and intelligent parish officer, Mr. Pybus, immediately forwarded the necessary intimation to the coroner, and the inquest will be held this evening at the Kiddy's Arms, Hustle Street.

"I had lost all—name, existence, thirty thousand pounds, everything—for about four hundred pounds in gold and notes.

"So I suppose," I said, as he who was hanged paused, "that you gave yourself up with a view of re-establishing your identity; and, failing to do that, you were hanged for murder or arson?"

I waited for a reply. He had lit another cigar, and sat smoking it. Seeing that he was calm, I judged it best not to excite or aggravate him in further questioning, but staid his pleasure. I had not to wait long.

"Not so," he resumed; "what I became that night I have remained ever since, and am now; that is, it I am anything at all. The very day on which that paragraph appeared, I set off by the coach. my only wish was to get as far from London and from England as I possibly could; and, in due time, we came to Hull. Hearing that Hamburg was the nearest foreign port, to Hamburg I went. I lived there for six months in an hotel, frugally and in solitude, and endeavouring to learn German; for, on narrower examination of the papers in the pocket-book, I guessed some portions of them to be written in that language. I was a dull scholar; but at the end of six months, I had scraped together enough German to know that the dead man's name was Müller; that he had been in Russia, in France, and in America.

"I managed to translate portions of a diary he had kept while in this latter country; but they only related to his impressions of the towns he had visited. He often alluded, too, casually to his 'secret' and his 'charge;' but what that secret and that charge were, I could not discover. There were also hints about a 'shepherdess,' and 'antelope,' and a 'blue tiger'—fictitious names, I presumed, for some persons with whom he was connected. The great mass of the documents was in a cipher utterly inexplicable to my most strenuous ingenuity and research. I went by the name of Müller; but I found that there were hundreds more Müllers in Hamburg, and no man sought me out.

"I was in the habit of going every evening to a lager-beer house outside the town, to smoke my pipe. There generally sat at the same table with me a little fat man in a grey great-coat, who smoked and drank beer incessantly. I was suspicious and shy of strangers; but, between this little man and me there gradually grew up a quiet kind of tavern acquaintance.

"One evening, when we had had a rather liberal potation of pipes and beer, he asked me if I had ever tasted the famous Baierische or Bavarian beer, adding that it threw all other German beers into the shade, and liberally offering to pay for a flask of it. I was in rather merry humour, and assented. We had one bottle of Bavarian beer; then another, and another, till, what with the beer and the pipes and the wrangling of the domino-players, my head swam.

"'I tell you what,' said my companion, "'we will just have one *chopine* of brandy. I always take it after Baierischer beer. We will not have it here, but at the *Grüne Gans* hard by; which is an honest house, kept by Max Rombach, who is a widow's son.'

"I was in that state when a man having already had too much is sure to want more, and I followed the man in the grey coat. How many *chopines* of brandy I had at the *Grüne Gans* I know not; but I found myself in bed next morning with an intolerable thirst and a racking headache. My first action was to spring out of bed, and search in the pocket of my coat for my pocketbook. It was gone. The waiters and the landlord were summoned; but no one knew anything about it. I had been brought home in a carriage, very inebriated, by a stout man in a grey great-coat, who said he was my friend, helped me upstairs, and assisted me to undress. The investigation ended with a conviction that the man in the grey coat was the thief. He had, manifestly, been tempted to the robbery by no pecuniary motive; for the whole of my remaining stock of banknotes, which I always kept in the pocketbook,

I found in my waistcoat-pocket neatly rolled up.

"That evening I walked down to the beer-house where I usually met my friend—not with the remotest idea of seeing him, but with the hope of eliciting some information as to who and what he was.

"To my surprise he was sitting at his accustomed table, smoking and drinking as usual; and, to my stern salutation, replied with a good-humoured hope that my head was not any worse for the *branntwein* overnight.

"'I want a word with you,' said I.

"'With pleasure,' he returned. Whereupon he put on his broad-brimmed hat and followed me into the garden behind the house, with an alacrity that was quite surprising.

"'I was drunk last night,' I commenced.

"'*Zo*,' he replied, with an unmoved countenance.

"'And while drunk,' I continued, 'I was robbed of my pocketbook.'

"'*Zo*,' he repeated with equal composure.

"'And I venture to assert that you are the person who stole it.'

"'*Zo*. You are quite right, my son,' he returned, with the most astonishing coolness. 'I did take your pocketbook; I have it here. See.'

"He tapped the breast of his grey great-coat; and, I could clearly distinguish, through the cloth, the square form of my pocketbook, with its great clasp in the middle. I sprang at him immediately, with the intention of wrenching it from him; but he eluded my grasp nimbly, and, stepping aside, drew forth a small silver whistle, on which he blew a shrill note. In an instant, a cloak or sheet was thrown over my head. I felt my hands muffled with soft but strong ligatures; and, before I had time to make one effort in self-defence, I was lifted off my feet and swiftly conveyed away, in total darkness. Presently we stopped, and I was lifted still higher, was placed on a seat; a door was slammed to; and the rumbling motion of wheels convinced me that I was in a carriage.

"My journey must have lasted some hours. We stopped from time to time; to change horses, I suppose. At the commencement of the journey I made frantic efforts to disengage myself and to cry out. But I was so well gagged, and bound, and muffled, that in sheer weariness and despair, I desisted. We halted at last for good. I was lifted out, and again carried swiftly along for upward of ten minutes. Then, from a difficulty of respiration, I concluded that I had entered a house, and was, perhaps, being borne along some underground passage. We ascended and descended staircases. I heard doors locked and unlocked.

Finally, I was thrown violently down on a hard surface. The gag was removed from my mouth, and the mufflers from my hands; I heard a heavy door clang to, and I was at liberty to speak and to move.

"My first care was to disengage myself from the mantle, whose folds still clung around me. I was in total darkness—darkness so black, that at first, I concluded some internal device had been made use of to blind me. But, after straining my eyes in every direction, I was able to discern high above me a small circular orifice, through which permeated a minute thread of light. Then I became sensible that I was not blind, but in some subterranean dungeon. The surface on which I was lying was hard and cold—a stone pavement. I crawled about, feeling with my hands, endeavouring to define the limits of my prison. Nothing was palpable to the touch, but the bare smooth pavement, and the bare smooth walls. I tried for hours to find the door, but could not. I shouted for help; but no man came near me.

"I must have lain in this den two days and two nights—at least the pangs of hunger and thirst made me suppose that length of time to have elapsed. Then the terrible thought possessed me that I was imprisoned there to be starved to death. In the middle of the third day, as it seemed to me, however, I heard a rattling of keys; one grated in the lock; a door opened, a flood of light broke in upon me; and a well-remembered voice cried, 'Come out!' as one might do to a beast in a cage.

"The light was so dazzling that I could not at first distinguish anything. But I crawled to the door; and then standing up, found I was in a small courtyard, and that opposite to me was my enemy, the man of the grey coat.

"In a grey coat no longer, however. He was dressed in a scarlet jacket, richly laced with gold; which fitted him so tightly with the short tails sticking out behind, that, under any other circumstances, he would have seemed to me inconceivably ridiculous. He took no more notice of me than if he had never seen me before in his life; but, merely motioning to two servants in scarlet liveries to take hold of me under the arms waddled on before.

"We went in and out of half a dozen doors, and traversed as many small courtyards. The buildings surrounding them were all in a handsome style of architecture; and in one of them I could discern, through the open grated windows on the ground floor, several men in white caps and jackets. A distant row of copper stew-pans and a delicious odour made me conjecture that we were close to the kitchen. We stopped some moments in this neighbourhood; whether from previous orders, or from pure malignity toward me, I was unable then to tell. He glanced over his shoulder with an expression of such infinite malice, that, what with hunger and rage, I struggled violently but unsuccessfully to burst from my guards. At last we ascended a narrow but handsomely carpeted staircase; and, after traversing a splendid picture gallery, entered an apartment luxuriously furnished; half library and half drawing-room.

"A cheerful wood fire crackled on the dogs in the fireplace; and, with his back toward it, stood a tall elderly man, his thin grey hair carefully brushed over his forehead. He was dressed in black, had a stiff, white neckcloth, and a parti-coloured ribbon al his buttonhole. A few feet from him was a table, covered with books and papers; and sitting thereat in a large armchair, was an old man, immensely corpulent, swathed in a richly furred dressing-gown, with a sort of jockey cap on his head of black velvet, to which was attached a hideous green shade. The servants brought me to the foot of this table, still holding my arms.

"'Monsieur Müller,' said the man in black, politely, and in excellent English. 'How do you feel?'

"'I replied, indignantly, that the stale of my health was not the point in question. I demanded to know why I had been trepanned, robbed, and starved.

"'Monsieur Müller,' returned the man in black, with immovable politeness. 'You must excuse the apparently discourteous manner in which you have been treated. The truth is, our house was built, not for a prison, but for a palace; and, for want of proper dungeon accommodation, we were compelled to utilise, for the moment, an apartment which I believe was formerly a wine-cellar. I hope you did not find it damp.'

"The man with the green shade shook his fat shoulders, as if in silent laughter.

"'In the first instance, *Monsieur*,' resumed the other, politely motioning me to be silent; for I was about to speak, 'we deemed that the possession of the papers in your pocketbook" (he touched that fatal book as he spoke) 'would have been sufficient for the accomplishment of the object we have in view. But finding that a portion of the correspondence is in a cipher of which you alone have the key, we judged the pleasure of your company absolutely indispensable.'

"'I know no more about the cipher, and its key than you do,' I ejaculated, 'and, before heaven, no secret that can concern you is in my keeping.'

"'You must be hungry, Monsieur Müller,' pursued the man in black, taking no more notice of what I had said than it I had not spoken at all. 'Carol, bring in lunch.'

"He, lately of the grey-coat, now addressed as Carol, bowed, retired, and presently returned with a tray covered with smoking viands and two flasks of wine. The servants halt loosened their hold; my heart leaped within me, and I was about to rush toward the viands, when the man in black raised his hand.

"'One moment, Monsieur Müller,' he said, 'before you recruit your strength. Will you oblige me by answering one question, Where is the child?'

"'*Ja*, where is the child?' echoed the man in the green shade.

"'I do not know,' I replied, passionately; 'on my honour I do not know. If you were to ask me for a hundred years, I could not tell you.'

"'Carol,' said the man in black, with an unmoved countenance, 'take away the tray. Monsieur Müller has no appetite. Unless,' he added, turning to me, 'you will be so good as to answer that little question.'

"'I cannot,' I repeated; 'I don't know; I never knew.'

"'Carol,' said my questioner, taking up a newspaper, and turning his back upon me, 'take away the things. Monsieur Müller, good-morning.'

"In spite of my cries and struggles, I was dragged away. We traversed the picture gallery; but, instead of descending the staircase, entered another suite of apartments. We were crossing a long vestibule lighted with lamps, and one of my guards had stopped to unlock a door while the other lagged a few paces behind (they had loosened their hold of me. and Carol was not with us), when a panel in the wainscot opened, and a lady in black perhaps thirty years of age and beautiful—bent forward through the aperture.

"'I heard all,' she said, in a rapid whisper. 'You have acted nobly. Be proof against their temptations, and Heaven will reward your devotedness.'

"I had no time to reply, for the door was closed immediately. I was hurried forward through room after room; until al last we entered a small bed-chamber, simply but cleanly furnished. Here I was left, and the door was locked and barred on the outside. On the table were a small loaf of black bread, and a pitcher of water. Both of these I consumed ravenously.

"I was left without further food for another entire day and night. From my window, which was heavily grated, I could see that my room overlooked the courtyard where the kitchen was, and the sight of the cooks, and the smell of the hot meat drove me almost mad.

"On the second day, I was again ushered into the presence of the man in black, and the man with the green shade. Again, the infernal drama was played. Again, I was tempted with rich food. Again, on my expressing my inability to answer the question, it was ordered to be removed.

"'Stop!' I cried desperately, as Carol was about to remove the food, and thinking I might satisfy them with a falsehood; 'I will confess. I will tell all.'

"'Speak,' said the man in black, eagerly, 'where is the child?'

"'In Amsterdam,' I replied at random.

"'Amsterdam—nonsense!' said the man in the green shade impatiently, 'what has Amsterdam to do with the Blue Tiger?'

"'I need not remind you,' said the man in black, sarcastically, 'that the name of any town or country is no answer to the question. You know as well as I do that the key to the whereabouts of the child is *there*,' and he pointed to the pocketbook.

"'Yes; *there*,' echoed the man in the green shade. And he struck it.

"'But, sir—' I urged.

"The answer was simply, 'Good-morning, Monsieur Müller.'

"Again, was I conducted back to my prison; again, I met the lady in black, who administered to me the barren consolation that Heaven would reward my devotedness. Again, I found the black loaf and the pitcher of water, and again I was left a day and a night in semi-starvation, to be again brought forth, tantalised, and questioned, and sent back again.

"'Perhaps,' remarked the man in black, at the fifth of these interviews, 'it is gold that Monsieur Müller requires. See.' As he spoke, he opened a bureau crammed with bags of money, and bade me help myself.

"In vain I protested that all the gold in the world could not extort from me a secret which I did not possess. In vain I exclaimed that my name was not Müller; in vain I disclosed the ghastly deceit I had practiced. The man in black only shook his head, smiled incredulously, and told me—while complimenting me for my powers of invention—that my statement confirmed his conviction that I knew where the child was.

"After the next interview, as I was returning to my starvation meal of bread and water, the lady in black again met me.

"'Take courage,' she whispered. 'Your deliverance is at hand. You are to be removed tonight to a lunatic asylum.'

"How my translation to a madhouse could accomplish my deliverance, or better my prospects, did not appear very clear to me; but that very night I was gagged, my arms were confined in a strait waistcoat, and placed in a carriage, which immediately set off at a rapid pace. We travelled all night; and, in the early morning, arrived at a large stone building. Here I was stripped, examined, placed in a bath, and dressed in a suit of coarse grey cloth. I asked where I was. I was told in the Alienation Refuge of the Grand Duchy of Sachs-Pfeiffiger.

"'Can I see the head-keeper?' I asked.

"The *Herr Ober-Direktor* was a little man with a shiny bald head and very white teeth. When I entered his cabinet he received me politely, and asked me what he could do for me? I told him my real name, my history, my wrongs; that I was a British subject, and demanded my liberty. He smiled, and simply called—'Where is Kraus?'

"'Here, *Herr*,' answered the keeper.

"'What number is *Monsieur?*'

"'Number ninety-two.'

"'Ninety-two,' repeated the *Herr Direktor*, leisurely writing. 'Cataplasms on the soles of the led. Worsted blister behind the ears, a mustard plaster on the chest, and ice on the head. Let it be Baltic ice.'

"The abominable instructions thus ordered were all applied. The villain Kraus tortured me in every imaginable way; and in the midst of his tortures, would repeat, 'Tell me where the child is, Müller, and you shall have your liberty in half an hour.'

"I was in the madhouse for six months. If I complained to the doctor of Kraus's ill-treatment and temptations, he immediately began to order cataplasms and Baltic ice. The bruises I had to show were ascribed to injuries I had myself inflicted in fits of frenzy. The maniacs with whom I was caged declared, like all other maniacs, that I was outrageously mad.

"One evening, as I lay groaning on my bed, Kraus entered my cell. 'Get up,' he said, 'you are at liberty. I was bribed, by you know who, with ten thousand Prussian *thalers* to get your secret from you, if I could; but I have been bribed with twenty thousand Austrian *florins* (which is really a sum worth having) to set you free. I shall lose my place, and have to fly; but I will open an hotel at Frankfort for the Englanders, and make my fortune. Come!' He led me downstairs, let me out of a private door in the garden; and, placing a bundle of clothes and a purse in my hand, bade me goodnight.

"I dressed myself, threw away the madman's livery, and kept walking along until morning, when I came to the custom-house barrier of another Grand Duchy. I had a passport ready provided for me in the pocket of my coat, which was found to be perfectly *en régle,* and I passed unquestioned. I went that morning to the coach-office of the town, and engaged a place in the *Eilwagen* to some German town, the name of which I forget; and, at the end of four days' weary traveling, I reached Brussels.

"I was very thin and weak with confinement and privation; but I soon recovered my health and strength. I must say that I made up by good living for my former compulsory abstinence; and both in Brussels and in Paris, to which I next directed my steps, I lived on the best. One evening I entered one of the magnificent restaurants in the Palais Royal to dine. I had ordered my meal from the *carte,* when my attention was roused by a small piece of paper which had been slipped between its leaves. It ran thus:

> Feign to eat, but eat no fish. Remain the usual time at your dinner, to disarm suspicion, but immediately afterwards make your way to England. Be sure, in passing through London, to call on Hildeburger.

"I had ordered a *sole au gratin;* but when it arrived, managed to throw it piece by piece under the table. When I had discussed the rest of my dinner, I summoned the *garçon,* and asked for my bill.

"'You will pay the head waiter, it you please, *Monsieur,*' said he.

"The head waiter came. If he had been a centaur or a sphinx I could not have stared at him with more horror and astonishment than I did; for there, in a waiter's dress, with a napkin over his arm, was Carol, the man of the grey coat.

"'Müller,' he said, coolly, bending over the table. 'Your sole was poisoned. Tell me where the child is, and here is an antidote, and four hundred thousand *francs.*'

"For reply I seized the heavy water decanter, and dashed it with all the force I could command, full in the old ruffian's face. He fell like a stone, amid the screams of women, the oaths of men, and cries of à la Garde! *À la Garde!* I slipped out of the restaurant and into one of the passages or outlets which abound in the Palais Royal. Whether the man died or not, or whether I was pursued, I never knew. I gained my lodgings unmolested, packed up my luggage, and started the next morning by the diligence, for Boulogne.

"I arrived in due time in London; but I did not call on 'Hildeburger' because I did not know who or where Hildeburger was. I started the very evening of my arrival in London for Liverpool, being determined to go to America. I was fearful of remaining in England, not only on account of my persecutors, but because I was pursued everywhere by the spectre of the real Müller.

"I took my passage to New York in a steamer which was to sail from the docks in a week's time. It was to start on a Monday; and on the Friday preceding I was walking about the Exchange, congratulating myself that I should soon have the Atlantic between myself and my pursuers. All at once I heard the name of Müller pronounced in a loud tone close behind me. I turned, and met the gaze of a tall, thin, young man with a downy moustache, who was dressed in the extreme of fashion, and was sucking the end of an ebony stick.

"'Monsieur Müller,' he said, nodding to me easily.

"'My name is not Müller,' I answered, boldly.

"'You have not yet called on Hildeburger!' he added, slightly elevating his eyebrows at my denial.

"I fell a cold shiver pass over me, and stammered, 'N—n—no!'

"'We had considerable difficulty in learning your whereabouts," he went on with great composure. 'The lady was obstinate. The screw and the water were tried in vain; but at length, by a judicious use of the cord and pulleys, we succeeded.'

"I shuddered again.

"'Will you call on Hildeburger now!' he resumed quickly and sharply. 'He is here—close by.'

"'Not now, not now.' I faltered. 'Some other time.'

"'The day after tomorrow?'

"'Yes, yes,' I answered eagerly, 'the day after tomorrow.'

"'Well, Saturday be it. You will meet me here, at four in the afternoon! Good! Do not forget. Au revoir, Monsieur Müller.'

He had no sooner uttered these words than he turned and disappeared among the crowd of merchants on 'Change.

I could not doubt, by his naming Saturday, as the day for our meeting, that he had some inkling of my intended departure. Although I had paid my passage to New York, I determined to forfeit it, and to change my course so as to evade my persecutors. I entered a shipping-office, and learned that a good steamer would leave George's Dock at ten that same night, for Glasgow. And to Glasgow for the present I made up my mind to go.

"At a quarter before ten I was at the dock with my luggage. It was raining heavily, and there was a dense fog.

"This way for the Glasgow steamer—this way,' cried a man in a Guernsey shirt, 'this way, your honour. I'll carry your trunk!'

"He took up my trunk as he spoke, and led the way down a ladder, across the decks of two or three steamers, and to the gangway of a fourth, where a man stood with dark bushy whiskers, dressed in a pea-coat, and holding a lighted lantern.

"'Is this the Glasgow steamer?' I asked.

"'All right!' answered the man with the lantern. 'Look sharp, the bell's a-going to ring.'

"'Remember poor Jack, your honour,' said the man in the Guernsey, who had carried my trunk. I gave him sixpence and stepped on board. A bell began to ring, and there was great confusion on board with hauling of ropes and stowing of luggage. The steamer seemed to me to be intolerably dirty and crowded with goods; and, to avoid the crush, I stepped aft to the wheel. In due time, we had worked out of the dock and were steaming down the Mersey.

"'How long will the run to Glasgow take, think you my man?' I asked of the man at the wheel, he stared at me as it he did not understand me, and muttered some unintelligible words. I repeated the question.

"'He does not speak English,' said a voice at my elbow, 'nor can any soul on board this vessel, except you and I, Monsieur Müller.'

"I turned round, and saw to my horror the young man with the ebony cane and the downy moustache.

"'I am kidnapped!' I cried. 'Let me have a boat. Where is the captain?'

"'Here is the captain,' said the young man, as a fiercely bearded man came up the companion-ladder. 'Captain Miloschvich of the Imperial Russian ship *Pyroscaphe*, bound to St. Petersburg, M. Müller. As Captain Miloschvich speaks no English you will permit me to act as interpreter.'

"Although I feared from his very presence that my case was already hopeless, I entreated him to explain to the captain that there was a mistake; that I was bound for Glasgow, and that I desired to be set on shore directly.

"'Captain Miloschvich,'" said the young man, when he had translated my speech, and received the captain's answer, 'begs you to understand that there is no mistake; that you are not bound for Glasgow, but
for St. Petersburg; and that it is quite impossible for him to set you on
shore here, seeing that he has positive instructions to set you on shore
in Cronstadt. Furthermore, he feels it his duty to add that should you,
by any words or actions, attempt to annoy or disturb the crew or passengers, he will be compelled to put you in irons, and place you at the
bottom of the hold.'

"The captain frequently nodded during these remarks, as if he perfectly understood their purport, although unable to express them; and,
to intimate his entire coincidence, he touched his wrists and ankles.

"If I had not been a fool I should have resigned myself to my fate.
But I was so maddened with misfortune, that I sprang on the young
man, hoping to kill him, or to be killed myself, and to be thrown into
the sea. But I was chained, beaten, and thrown into the hold. There,
among tarred ropes, the stench of tallow-casks, and the most appalling
seasickness, I lay for days, fed with mouldy biscuit and putrid water. At
length, we arrived at Cronstadt.

"All I can tell you, or I know of Russia is, that somewhere in it
there is a river, and on that river a fortress, and in that fortress a cell,
and in that cell a knout. Seven years of my existence were passed in
that cell, under the lashes of that knout, with the one horrible question dinning in my ears, 'Where is the child?'

"How I escaped to incur worse tortures, it is bootless to tell you.
I have swept the streets of Palermo as a convict, in a hideous yellow
dress. I have pined in the Inquisition at Rome. I have been caged
in the madhouse at Constantinople, with the rabble to throw stones
and mud at me through the bars. I have been branded in the back in
the *bagnes* of Toulon and Rochefort; and everywhere I have been offered liberty and gold if I would answer the question, 'Where is the
child?' At last, having been accused of a crime I did not commit, I was
condemned to death

"Upon the scaffold they asked me, 'Where is the child?' Of course,
there could be no answer, and I was—"

Just then, Margery, my servant, who never will have the discrimination to deny me to importunate visitors, knocked at the door, and
told me that I was wanted in the surgery. I went downstairs, and found
Mrs. Walkinshaw, Johnny Walkinshaw's wife, who told me that her
"master" was "took all over like," and quite "stroaken of a heap." John-

ny Walkinshaw is a member of the ancient order of Sylvan Brothers; and, as I am club-doctor to the Sylvan Brothers, he has a right to my medical attendance for the sum of four shillings a year. Whenever he has taken an overdose of rough cider he is apt to he "stroaken all of a heap," and to send for me.

I was the more annoyed at being obliged to walk to Johnny Walkenshaw's cottage at two in the morning, because the wretched man had been cut short in his story just as he was about to explain the curious surgical problem of how he was resuscitated. When I returned he was gone, and I never saw him more. Whether he was mad and had hanged himself, or whether he was sane and had been hanged according to law, or whether he had ever been hanged, or never been hanged, are points I have never quite adjusted in my mind.

Jubal, the Ringer

1

High in the brown belfry of the old Church of Saint Fantasmos sat Jubal the Ringer, looking over the huge town that lay spread below. A great black network of streets stretched far away on every side—the sombre web of intertwisted human passions and interests, in which, year after year, many thousand souls had been captured and destroyed.

Sleeping hills with clear-cut edges rose all about the dark town, which seemed to be lying at the bottom of a vast purple goblet, whose rim, touched with the whiteness of approaching day, looked as if they were brimming with the foam of some celestial wine. Deep in the distance rolled a long river, musical through the night, and shaking back the moonbeams from its bosom as if in play.

It was an old belfry, the belfry of Saint Fantasmos. it sprang from a vaulted arch with four groinings, which hung directly over the altar, so that one above in the bell-room could see, through the cracks in the stone ceiling, the silver lamps that lit the shrine, the altar-railings, the priest, the penitents below. Old flat mosses clung to the weather-beaten sides of the belfry, and the winds went in and out through it wheresoever they willed, from the very summit, which was pointed, there arose a tall iron rod, on which stood a golden cock, with head erect to catch the morning breeze, with feathers spread to bask in the morning sun. A golden cock, I said: alas! golden no longer. Wind and weather had used him badly, and he had moulted all his splendour. Battered, and grey, and rusty, with draggled tail and broken beak, he was no more the brave cock that he had been of yore. He had a ma-levolent and diabolical aspect. He looked as if he had made a compact with the demons of the night.

How blame him, if he had ceased to be an amiable cock? For years he had done his duty bravely to the town in all weathers, telling the points of the wind with unerring sagacity. The winds furious at having their secrets betrayed, would often steal softly down upon him in the disguise of a delicate breeze, and then burst upon him with the roar of a lion, in the hope of tumbling him from his sentinel's post. But they never caught him, for he was then young and agile, and he glided round at the slightest breath, so that the winds never could succeed in coming upon his broadside, but went off howling with anger to sea, where they wrecked ships, and buried them under the waves.

But the town neglected the poor cock, and he was never regilded or repaired, so that in time his pivots grew rusty, and he could no longer move with his former agility. Then the storms persecuted him, and the Equinox came down on him savagely twice a year, and buffeted him so that he thought his last hour was come; and those who passed by Saint Fantasmos on those tempestuous nights heard him shrieking with rage, through the wild aerial combats, till thinking it the voice of a demon high up in the clouds, they crossed themselves, and hurried home to bed.

So, the cock, and the belfry, and Jubal the Ringer grew old together; but Jubal was the oldest of all, for the human heart ages more quickly than stone or copper, and the storms that assail it are fiercer and sharper than the winds or the rains.

2

Jubal sat in the window of the belfry, looking over the black town, and moaning to himself. The day had not yet risen, but was near at hand.

"This morn," he said, shaking his long hair, which was already sprinkled with grey, "this morn she will be wed. This morn she will stand in front of the altar below, the light from the silver lamps shining on her white forehead, that I love better than the moon; and her lover will put the gold ring upon her finger, and the priest will bless her with lifted hands, while I, through the cracks in the vaulted ceiling, will behold all this: I, who adore her: I who have loved her for years, and followed her with my eyes as she wandered through the fields in May, toying with the hawthorn hedges, herself more fragrant, whiter, purer than the blossoms which she gathered.

"I, who used to spend the early dawn traversing the woods, gathering the red wild strawberries while the silver dews still lay upon them, in order that I might place them secretly at her door! Ah! she never knew how in the cold winter nights I sat in the fork of the apple-tree outside her chamber-window, watching her light, and gazing on her shadow as it fell upon the blind. Sometimes the shadow would seem to lengthen, and come across the walk and climb the tree, and I would strive to fold it in my arms, as if it was my beloved in person; but it would suddenly recoil and elude me, and I could do nothing but kiss the branches where it had fallen, with my cold lips.

"One day, she went to gather while and yellow water-lilies, that swam on the surface of a pond. She held a long crook in her hand, with which she reached out and endeavoured to bring them to shore. But they were cunning and slippery, and did not wish to be captured, by even so fair a maid as she; so when her crook touched them, they ducked their pearly and golden crests under the waters and escaped, coming up again all dripping and shining, and seeming to laugh at the eager girl.

"Being vexed at this, she stretched out her crook still farther, when the treacherous bank gave way, and my Agatha went down into the deep pond. I was near—I was always near her, though she knew it not—and I plunged in, and sought her amid the loathsome weeds. I brought her to shore, and chafed her fair forehead, and revived her. Then when she had recovered, I said to her: 'I am Jubal, the Ringer: I love you Agatha: will you make my lonely life happy forever? With a look of wild horror, she broke from me, and fled to her home.

"And I am despised, and she weds another. While the blessings are being given, and the church is white with orange-wreaths, and the poor wait in the porch for the nuptial bounty, I, who adore her, must sit aloft in this old belfry, and ring out jubilant chimes for the wedded pair.

"Aha! they know not Jubal, the Ringer. I can work the spells my mother worked, and I know the formulas that compel spirits. Agatha, thou false one, and thou, smooth-checked lover, who dreamst perhaps of her now, and thou, sacred priest, who givest away to another that which belongs to me, beware, for ye shall perish!"

Then Jubal laughed horribly, and spread his arms out as it he would embrace the night, and muttered certain strange sentences that were terrible to hear.

As he muttered, there came from the west a huge cloud of bats, that fastened themselves against the sides of the old belfry, and there was one for every stone, they were so numerous. And presently a ceaseless clicking re-sounded through the turret, as if myriads of tiny labourers were plying their pick-axes; a hail of falling fragments of mortar tinkled continually on the tin roofing of the Church of St. Fantasmos; and the bats seemed to eat into the crevices of the old belfry, as it they were about to sleep forever in its walls.

Presently the day rose. The sunbeams poured over the edges of the hills as the molten gold pours from the caldron of a worker in metals. The streets began to pulse with the last throbs of life, and Jubal, the Ringer, laughed aloud, for not a single bat was visible. The entire multitude had buried themselves in the walls of the belfry.

3

The street leading to the Church of St. Fantasmos was by nine o'clock as gay as the enamelled pages of a pope's missal. The road was strewn with flowers, and the people crushed the tender lily of the valley and the blue campanula and the spiced carnation under their feet. In and out between the throng of loiterers ran persons bearing boughs of the yellow laburnum in full blossom, until the way seemed arabesqued with gold. The windows on either side were filled with smiling faces, that pressed against the panes, like flowers pressing toward the light against conservatory casements. The linen of the maidens' caps was white as snow, and then cheeks were rose-red; and each jostled the other so as better to see the wedding procession of the fair Agatha and her gallant lover on its way to the altar of St. Fantasmos Presently the marriage cavalcade came by. It was like a page from a painted book. Agatha was so fair and modest; the bridegroom was so manly; the parents were so venerable with their white locks, and their faces lit with the beautiful sunset of departing life.

As the procession passed beneath the windows, bunches of ribbons and flowers and bits of gay-coloured paper, on which amorous devices were written, were flung to the bride and bridegroom by the bystanders; and a long murmur swelled along the street, of "God protect them, for they are beautiful and good!" And this lasted until they entered the gates of the church, where it was taken up by the poor people of the town who awaited them there. So, with benedictions falling upon them thick as the falling leaves of autumn, they passed into the Church of St. Fantasmos; but as they gained the threshold the bride looked up to the belfry, and there she fancied she beheld a man's head glaring at her with two fiery eyes, so that she shuddered and looked away. The next instant she looked up again, but the head was gone.

The people who were not invited to the ceremony loitered in the yard without, intending to accompany the bride home when the sacred rite was concluded, and cheer her by the way with songs composed in her honour. While they waited, the chimes in the belfry began to peal.

"How now!" cried one. "It is too soon for the chimes to peal. The couple arc not yet married."

"What can Jubal be dreaming of?" said a second.

"Listen," cried a third; "did you ever hear such discords. Those are not wedding chimes. it is the music of devils."

A terrible fear suddenly fell over the multitude as they listened. Louder and louder swelled the colossal discords of the bells. The clouds were torn with these awful dissonances; the skies were curdled with the groans, the shrieks, the unnatural thunders that issued from the belfry.

The people below crossed themselves, and muttered to one another that there was a devil in the turret.

There was a devil in the turret, for Jubal was no longer man. With his eyes fixed on the crack in the vaulted ceiling, through which he saw the marriage ceremony proceeding, and his sinewy arms working with superhuman strength the machinery that moved the bells, he seemed the incarnation of a malevolent fiend. His hair stood erect; his eyes burned like fire-balls; and a white foam rose continually to his lips, and breaking into flakes, floated to the ground.

Still the terrible peals went on. The tortured bells swung now this way, now that, yelled forth a frightful diapason of sound that shook the very earth. Faster and faster Jubal tolled their iron tongues. Louder and louder grew the brazen clamour. The huge beams that supported the chimes cracked and groaned. The air, beaten with these violent sounds, swelled into waves that became billows, that in turn became mountains, and surged with irresistible force against the walls of the turret. The cock on the summit shivered and shrieked, as it the equinoxes of ten thousand years had been let loose on him at the same moment. The stones in the walls trembled, and from between their crevices vomited forth dust and mortar. The whole turret shook from base to apex.

Suddenly the people below beheld a vast cloud of bats issue from between the stones of the belfry and fly toward the west.

Then it appeared as if the bells spent their last strength in one vast accumulated brazen howl, that seemed to split the skies. The turret rocked twice, then toppled. Down through the vaulted arch, crushing it in as if it had been glass; down through the incensed air that filled the aisle, on priest and bride and bridegroom and parents and friends, came a white blinding mass of stone and mortar, and the next instant there was nothing but a cloud of dust slowly rising, a splash of blood here and there, that the dry stones soaked in, and one battered human head with long hair, half-visible through the mass of ruin. it was Jubal dead, but also Jubal avenged.

When on the ensuing October the wild equinoxes came like a horde of Cossacks over the hills, to make their last assault upon the golden cock, they found neither bird nor belfry, and the mischief they did that night at sea, out of mere spite, was, the legend says, incredible.

A Daydream

Dimes came to me the other night and suggested to me in a mysterious kind of way, that we should visit the Five Points together. I am constitutionally prudent, and I demurred.

"There is a good deal of murder knocking about the streets nowadays, my dear Dimes," said I. "Society is unsafe. A respectable man cannot even keep a quiet, orderly house, under the supervision of a middle-aged female of irreproachable morals, but he is found hacked to pieces in his room one fine morning. The corners of the streets are rounded off into gangs of ruffians ready to garrotte any passenger who has a three-cent-piece on his person. The police are everywhere but where they ought to be; and, as a general thing, take more interest in elections than in assassinations. On the whole, my dear Dimes, I don't think I will go."

"But," said Dimes, "there's no danger. We will go with Captain Currycomb of the 150th ward, as efficient an officer, let me tell you, Sir, as any in the city of New York. He will show us everything, and I'd like to see the man that would touch us while under his protection. Besides, look here."

Whereupon, Dimes pulled out an exquisite revolver, mounted in ivory and silver, and no larger than some night-keys that I have seen young men who live in cheap boarding-houses carry. It was a seducing weapon. Murderously enticing. I held it in my hand for a few moments, felt the silky lock, passed my fingers over the polished stock, and looked along the delicate barrel, on whose blue mirror-like surface the light played as on a lake. I found myself speculating suddenly on what would occur if I were to shoot Dimes. I saw the precise spot in his temple—a little above the left eyebrow—where the bullet would enter. I saw the sudden spasm—almost invisible, so slight was it—that convulsed his frame as the ball struck him. I saw the rapid flash of the eye on me—so rapid that we have no term to measure it with—one glance of terror, reproach, amazement, and then his legs bent, and, doubling up under him as if the bones had been suddenly withdrawn, he rolled on the floor.

I found myself remarking as I stood over him, that the murdered man had fallen in a strange altitude. He lay on the floor with his body bent forward, his forehead touching the earth, and his arms extended in front. I was reminded instantly of the pictures of a Moslem at prayer with his head toward the Holy City; and then my memory almost instantly recalled a large book bound in Russia leather, called the *Oriental Annual*, which I had read when a child, and which contained the picture of a Turk at his devotions.

I then busied myself again with Dimes. He lay still in the same position, dead. He had died almost instantly. That last fleeting look he gave me was the flash of his passing soul. The carpet on which he lay was a white ground with a pattern of ivy leaves hailing across it. Plainly discernible on this white carpet was a small red stream that slowly, slowly flowed from Dimes's temple, until it reached a bunch of ivy leaves, where it spread into a little round pool. I recollect very well the whimsical thought suggesting itself to me that this round patch of blood nestling among the ivy leaves bore a rude resemblance to a cluster of the scarlet berries of the plant itself.

I had hardly conceived this idea, when, as if by the sudden loosing of some cord, a huge blackness fell upon me, and I awoke to the awful responsibility of murder. Up to that time I had looked curiously at the incident, but now I became agitated. My heart beat. My temples were bedewed with a cold sweat. The dead man seemed no longer like the praying Moslem in the picture, but rather like some dark fiend about to lift himself from the earth and destroy me. I ran here and there, and hastily made preparations for flight. Somehow, whatever I did, I seemed to stumble against the corpse. I saw with horror that my boots left tracks of blood on the carpet. I tried to take them off, but they seemed glued to my feet.

I raved and blasphemed, and ran to the fireplace, where I scraped the soles upon the ashes—but the blood would not dry; it still left wet prints on the floor wherever I moved. I felt my brain whirling. Then came a knocking at the door. Should I answer, or remain silent? What to do? The knocking grew louder—the door shook. They were bursting it open! I ran to the window—it was fifty feet from the ground! I rushed back to the yielding door, set my back firmly against it—but in vain; some unseen, irresistible force urged it inward. I strained every muscle—life and death were on it—I could not any longer—

"Here, Dimes," said I, "take your pistol. I should be afraid to carry such things about me. I'm afraid I have a dash of the assassin in my blood. Nevertheless, I'll avail myself of Captain Currycomb, and go with you to the Five Points."

"Do you know, my dear fellow," said Dimes, "that just now when you were cocking that pistol, you looked quite wild about the eyes!"

I laughed and said nothing. Dimes would have distrusted me for evermore if he knew that I had contemplated his murder even in a daydream.

What Was It?

It is, I confess, with considerable diffidence that I approach the strange narrative which I am about to relate. The events which I purpose detailing are of so extraordinary a character that I am quite prepared to meet with an unusual amount of incredulity and scorn. I accept all such beforehand. I have, I trust, the literary courage to face unbelief. I have, after mature consideration, resolved to narrate, in as simple and straightforward a manner as I can compass, some facts that passed under my observation, in the month of July last, and which, in the annals of the mysteries of physical science, are wholly unparalleled.

I live at No.—Twenty-Sixth Street, in New York. The house is in some respects a curious one. It has enjoyed for the last two years the reputation of being haunted. It is a large and stately residence, surrounded by what was once a garden, but which is now only a green enclosure used for bleaching clothes. The dry basin of what has been a fountain, and a few fruit-trees ragged and unpruned, indicate that this spot in past days was a pleasant, shady retreat, filled with fruits and flowers and the sweet murmur of waters.

The house is very spacious. A hall of noble size leads to a large spiral staircase winding through its centre, while the various apartments are of imposing dimensions. It was built some fifteen or twenty years since by Mr. A——, the well-known New York merchant, who five years ago threw the commercial world into convulsions by a stupendous bank fraud. Mr. A—— , as everyone knows, escaped to Europe, and died not long after, of a broken heart. Almost immediately after the news of his decease reached this country and was verified, the report spread in Twenty-Sixth Street that No.—was haunted. Legal measures had dispossessed the widow of its former owner, and it was inhabited merely by a caretaker and his wife, placed there by the house-agent into whose hands it had passed for purposes of renting or sale.

These people declared that they were troubled with unnatural noises. Doors were opened without any visible agency. The remnants of furniture scattered through the various rooms were, during the night, piled one upon the other by unknown hands. Invisible feet passed up and down the stairs in broad daylight, accompanied by the rustle of unseen silk dresses, and the gliding of viewless hands along the massive balusters. The caretaker and his wife declared they would live there no longer. The house-agent laughed, dismissed them, and put others in their place. The noises and supernatural manifestations continued. The neighbourhood caught up the story, and the house remained untenanted for three years. Several persons negotiated for it; but, somehow, always before the bargain was closed they heard the unpleasant rumours and declined to treat any further.

It was in this state of things that my landlady, who at that time kept a boarding-house in Bleecker Street, and who wished to move further up town, conceived the bold idea of renting No. —, Twenty-Sixth Street. Happening to have in her house rather a plucky and philosophical set of boarders, she laid her scheme before us, stating candidly everything she had heard respecting the ghostly qualities of the establishment to which she wished to remove us. With the exception of two timid persons,—a sea-captain and a returned Californian, who immediately gave notice that they would leave,—all of Mrs. Moffat's guests declared that they would accompany her in her chivalric incursion into the abode of spirits.

Our removal was effected in the month of May, and we were charmed with our new residence. The portion of Twenty-Sixth Street where our house is situated, between Seventh and Eighth Avenues, is one of the pleasantest localities in New York. The gardens back of the houses, running down nearly to the Hudson, form, in the summer time, a perfect avenue of verdure. The air is pure and invigorating, sweeping, as it does, straight across the river from the Weehawken heights, and even the ragged garden which surrounded the house, although displaying on washing days rather too much clothes-line, still gave us a piece of greensward to look at, and a cool retreat in the summer evenings, where we smoked our cigars in the dusk, and watched the fire-flies flashing their dark-lanterns in the long grass.

Of course, we had no sooner established ourselves at No. — than we began to expect the ghosts. We absolutely awaited their advent with eagerness. Our dinner conversation was supernatural. One of the boarders, who had purchased Mrs. Crowe's *Night Side of Nature* for his own private delectation, was regarded as a public enemy by the entire household for not having bought twenty copies. The man led a life, of supreme wretchedness while he was reading this volume. A system of espionage was established, of which he was the victim. If he incautiously laid the book down for an instant and left the room, it was immediately seized and read aloud in secret places to a select few. I found myself a person of immense importance, it having leaked out that I was tolerably well versed in the history of supernaturalism, and had once written a story the foundation of which was a ghost. If a table or a wainscot panel happened to warp when we were assembled in the large drawing-room, there was an instant silence, and everyone was prepared for an immediate clanking of chains and a spectral form.

After a month of psychological excitement, it was with the utmost dissatisfaction that we were forced to acknowledge that nothing in the remotest degree approaching the supernatural had manifested itself. Once the black butler asseverated that his candle had been blown out by some invisible agency while he was undressing himself for the night; but as I had more than once discovered this coloured gentleman in a condition when one candle must have appeared to him like two, I thought it possible that, by going a step further in his potations, he might have reversed this phenomenon, and seen no candle at all where he ought to have beheld one.

Things were in this state when an incident took place so awful and inexplicable in its character that my reason fairly reels at the bare memory of the occurrence. It was the tenth of July. After dinner was over I repaired, with my friend Dr. Hammond, to the garden to smoke my evening pipe. Independent of certain mental sympathies which existed between the Doctor and myself, we were linked together by a vice. We both smoked opium. We knew each other's secret, and respected it. We enjoyed together that wonderful expansion of thought, that marvellous intensifying of the perceptive faculties, that boundless feeling of existence when we seem to have points of contact with the whole universe,—in short, that unimaginable spiritual bliss, which I would not surrender for a throne, and which I hope you, reader, will never—never taste.

Those hours of opium happiness which the Doctor and I spent together in secret were regulated with a scientific accuracy. We did not blindly smoke the drug of paradise, and leave our dreams to chance. While smoking, we carefully steered our conversation through the brightest and calmest channels of thought. We talked of the East, and endeavoured to recall the magical panorama of its glowing scenery. We criticised the most sensuous poets,—those who painted life ruddy with health, brimming with passion, happy in the possession of youth and strength and beauty. If we talked of Shakespeare's *Tempest*, we lingered over Ariel, and avoided Caliban. Like the Guebers, we turned our faces to the east, and saw only the sunny side of the world.

This skilful colouring of our train of thought produced in our subsequent visions a corresponding tone. The splendours of Arabian fairyland dyed our dreams. We paced that narrow strip of grass with the tread and port of kings. The song of the *rana arborea*, while he clung to the bark of the ragged plum-tree, sounded like the strains of divine musicians. Houses, walls, and streets melted like rain-clouds, and *vistas* of unimaginable glory stretched away before us. It was a rapturous companionship. We enjoyed the vast delight more perfectly because, even in our most ecstatic moments, we were conscious of each other's presence. Our pleasures, while individual, were still twin, vibrating and moving in musical accord.

On the evening in question, the tenth of July, the Doctor and myself drifted into an unusually metaphysical mood. We lit our large *meerschaums*, filled with fine Turkish tobacco, in the core of which burned a little black nut of opium, that, like the nut in the fairy tale, held within its narrow limits wonders beyond the reach of kings; we paced to and fro, conversing. A strange perversity dominated the currents of our thought. They would not flow through the sun-lit channels into which we strove to divert them. For some unaccountable reason, they constantly diverged into dark and lonesome beds, where a continual gloom brooded. It was in vain that, after our old fashion, we flung ourselves on the shores of the East, and talked of its gay bazaars, of the splendours of the time of Haroun, of *harems* and golden palaces.

Black *afreets* continually arose from the depths of our talk, and expanded, like the one the fisherman released from the copper vessel, until they blotted everything bright from our vision. Insensibly, we yielded to the occult force that swayed us, and indulged in gloomy speculation. We had talked some time upon the proneness of the human mind to mysticism, and the almost universal love of the terrible, when Hammond suddenly said to me, "What do you consider to be the greatest element of terror?"

The question puzzled me. That many things were terrible, I knew. Stumbling over a corpse in the dark; beholding, as I once did, a woman floating down a deep and rapid river, with wildly lifted arms, and awful, upturned face, uttering, as she drifted, shrieks that rent one's heart, while we, the spectators, stood frozen at a window which overhung the river at a height of sixty feet, unable to make the slightest effort to save her, but dumbly watching her last supreme agony and her disappearance. A shattered wreck, with no life visible, encountered floating listlessly on the ocean, is a terrible object, for it suggests a huge terror, the proportions of which are veiled. But it now struck me, for the first time, that there must be one great and ruling embodiment of fear,—a King of Terrors, to which all others must succumb. What might it be? To what train of circumstances would it owe its existence?

"I confess, Hammond," I replied to my friend, "I never considered the subject before. That there must be one Something more terrible than any other thing, I feel. I cannot attempt, however, even the most vague definition."

"I am somewhat like you, Harry," he answered. "I feel my capacity to experience a terror greater than anything yet conceived by the human mind;—something combining in fearful and unnatural amalgamation hitherto supposed incompatible elements. The calling of the voices in Brockden Brown's novel of *Wieland* is awful; so is the picture of the Dweller of the Threshold, in Bulwer's *Zanoni;* but," he added, shaking his head gloomily, "there is something more horrible still than these."

"Look here, Hammond," I rejoined, "let us drop this kind of talk, for heaven's sake! We shall suffer for it, depend on it."

"I don't know what's the matter with me tonight," he replied, "but my brain is running upon all sorts of weird and awful thoughts. I feel as if I could write a story like Hoffman, tonight, if I were only master of a literary style."

"Well, if we are going to be Hoffmanesque in our talk, I'm off to bed. Opium and nightmares should never be brought together. How sultry it is! Goodnight, Hammond."

"Goodnight, Harry. Pleasant dreams to you."

"To you, gloomy wretch, *afreets*, ghouls, and enchanters."

We parted, and each sought his respective chamber. I undressed quickly and got into bed, taking with me, according to my usual custom, a book, over which I generally read myself to sleep. I opened the volume as soon as I had laid my head upon the pillow, and instantly flung it to the other side of the room. It was Goudon's *History of Monsters,*—a curious French work, which I had lately imported from

Paris, but which, in the state of mind I had then reached, was anything but an agreeable companion. I resolved to go to sleep at once; so, turning down my gas until nothing but a little blue point of light glimmered on the top of the tube, I composed myself to rest.

The room was in total darkness. The atom of gas that still remained alight did not illuminate a distance of three inches round the burner. I desperately drew my arm across my eyes, as if to shut out even the darkness, and tried to think of nothing. It was in vain. The confounded themes touched on by Hammond in the garden kept obtruding themselves on my brain. I battled against them. I erected ramparts of would-be blankness of intellect to keep them out. They still crowded upon me. While I was lying still as a corpse, hoping that by a perfect physical inaction I should hasten mental repose, an awful incident occurred. A Something dropped, as it seemed, from the ceiling, plumb upon my chest, and the next instant I felt two bony hands encircling my throat, endeavouring to choke me.

I am no coward, and am possessed of considerable physical strength. The suddenness of the attack, instead of stunning me strung every nerve to its highest tension. My body acted from instinct, before my brain had time to realize the terrors of my position. In an instant, I wound two muscular arms around the creature, and squeezed it, with all the strength of despair, against my chest; In a few seconds, the bony hands that had fastened on my throat loosened their hold, and I was free to breathe once more.

Then commenced a struggle of awful intensity. Immersed in the most profound darkness, totally ignorant of the nature of the Thing by which I was so suddenly attacked, finding my grasp slipping every moment, by reason, it seemed to me, of the entire nakedness of my assailant, bitten with sharp teeth in the shoulder, neck, and chest, having every moment to protect my throat against a pair of sinewy, agile hands, which my utmost efforts could not confine,—these were a combination of circumstances to combat which required all the strength, skill, and courage that I possessed.

At last, after a silent, deadly, exhausting struggle, I got my assailant under by a series of incredible efforts of strength. Once pinned, with my knee on what I made out to be its chest, I knew that I was victor. I rested for a moment to breathe. I heard the creature beneath me panting in the darkness, and felt the violent throbbing of a heart. It was apparently as exhausted as I was; that was one comfort. At this moment, I remembered that I usually placed under my pillow, before going to bed, a large yellow silk pocket-handkerchief. I felt for it instantly; it was there. In a few seconds more I had, after a fashion, pinioned the creature's arms.

I now felt tolerably secure. There was nothing more to be done but to turn on the gas, and, having first seen what my midnight assailant was like, arouse the household. I will confess to being actuated by a certain pride in not giving the alarm before; I wished to make the capture alone and unaided.

Never losing my hold for an instant, I slipped from the bed to the floor, dragging my captive with me. I had but a few steps to make to reach the gas-burner; these I made with the greatest caution, holding the creature in a grip like a vice. At last I got within arm's-length of the tiny speck of blue light which told me where the gas-burner lay. Quick as lightning I released my grasp with one hand and let on the full flood of light. Then I turned to look at my captive.

I cannot even attempt to give any definition of my sensations the instant after I turned on the gas. I suppose I must have shrieked with terror, for in less than a minute afterward my room was crowded with the inmates of the house.

I shudder now as I think of that awful moment. *I saw nothing!* Yes; I had one arm firmly clasped round a breathing, panting, corporeal shape, my other hand gripped with all its strength a throat as warm, and apparently fleshly, as my own; and yet, with this living substance in my grasp, with its body pressed against my own, and all in the bright glare of a large jet of gas, I absolutely beheld nothing! Not even an outline,—a vapor!

I do not, even at this hour, realize the situation in which I found myself. I cannot recall the astounding incident thoroughly. Imagination in vain tries to compass the awful paradox.

It breathed. I felt its warm breath upon my cheek. It struggled fiercely. It had hands. They clutched me. Its skin was smooth, like my own. There it lay, pressed close up against me, solid as stone,—and yet utterly invisible!

I wonder that I did not faint or go mad on the instant. Some wonderful instinct must have sustained me; for, absolutely, in place of loosening my hold on the terrible Enigma, I seemed to gain an additional strength in my moment of horror, and tightened my grasp with such wonderful force that I felt the creature shivering with agony.

Just then Hammond entered my room at the head of the household. As soon as he beheld my face—which, I suppose, must have been an awful sight to look at—he hastened forward, crying, "Great heaven, Harry! what has happened?"

"Hammond! Hammond!" I cried, "come here. O, this is awful! I have been attacked in bed by something or other, which I have hold of; but I can't see it,—I can't see it!"

Hammond, doubtless struck by the unfeigned horror expressed in my countenance, made one or two steps forward with an anxious yet puzzled expression. A very audible titter burst from the remainder of my visitors. This suppressed laughter made me furious. To laugh at a human being in my position! It was the worst species of cruelty. *Now*, I can understand why the appearance of a man struggling violently, as it would seem, with an airy nothing, and calling for assistance against a vision, should have appeared ludicrous. *Then*, so great was my rage against the mocking crowd that had I the power I would have stricken them dead where they stood.

"Hammond! Hammond!" I cried again, despairingly, "for God's sake come to me. I can hold the—the thing but a short while longer. It is overpowering me. Help me! Help me!"

"Harry," whispered Hammond, approaching me, "you have been smoking too much opium."

"I swear to you, Hammond, that this is no vision," I answered, in the same low tone. "Don't you see how it shakes my whole frame with its struggles? If you don't believe me, convince yourself. Feel it,—touch it."

Hammond advanced and laid his hand in the spot I indicated. A wild cry of horror burst from him. He had felt it!

In a moment, he had discovered somewhere in my room a long piece of cord, and was the next instant winding it and knotting it about the body of the unseen being that I clasped in my arms.

"Harry," he said, in a hoarse, agitated voice, for, though he preserved his presence of mind, he was deeply moved, "Harry, it's all safe now. You may let go, old fellow, if you're tired. The Thing can't move."

I was utterly exhausted, and I gladly loosed my hold.

Hammond stood holding the ends of the cord that bound the Invisible, twisted round his hand, while before him, self-supporting as it were, he beheld a rope laced and interlaced, and stretching tightly around a vacant space. I never saw a man look so thoroughly stricken with awe. Nevertheless, his face expressed all the courage and determination which I knew him to possess. His lips, although white, were set firmly, and one could perceive at a glance that, although stricken

116

with fear, he was not daunted.

The confusion that ensued among the guests of the house who were witnesses of this extraordinary scene between Hammond and myself,—who beheld the pantomime of binding this struggling Something,—who beheld me almost sinking from physical exhaustion when my task of jailer was over,—the confusion and terror that took possession of the bystanders, when they saw all this, was beyond description. The weaker ones fled from the apartment. The few who remained clustered near the door and could not be induced to approach Hammond and his Charge. Still incredulity broke out through their terror. They had not the courage to satisfy themselves, and yet they doubted. It was in vain that I begged of some of the men to come near and convince themselves by touch of the existence in that room of a living being which was invisible. They were incredulous, but did not dare to undeceive themselves. How could a solid, living, breathing body be invisible, they asked. My reply was this. I gave a sign to Hammond, and both of us—conquering our fearful repugnance to touch the invisible creature—lifted it from the ground, manacled as it was, and took it to my bed. Its weight was about that of a boy of fourteen.

"Now, my friends," I said, as Hammond and myself held the creature suspended over the bed, "I can give you self-evident proof that here is a solid, ponderable body, which, nevertheless, you cannot see. Be good enough to watch the surface of the bed attentively."

I was astonished at my own courage in treating this strange event so calmly; but I had recovered from my first terror, and felt a sort of scientific pride in the affair, which dominated every other feeling.

The eyes of the bystanders were immediately fixed on my bed. At a given signal Hammond and I let the creature fall. There was the dull sound of a heavy body alighting on a soft mass. The timbers of the bed creaked. A deep impression marked itself distinctly on the pillow, and on the bed, itself. The crowd who witnessed this gave a low cry, and rushed from the room. Hammond and I were left alone with our Mystery.

We remained silent for some time, listening to the low, irregular breathing of the creature on the bed, and watching the rustle of the bedclothes as it impotently struggled to free itself from confinement. Then Hammond spoke.

"Harry, this is awful."

"Ay, awful."

"But not unaccountable."

"Not unaccountable! What do you mean? Such a thing has never occurred since the birth of the world. I know not what to think, Hammond. God grant that I am not mad, and that this is not an insane fantasy! "

"Let us reason a little, Harry. Here is a solid body which we touch, but which we cannot see. The fact is so unusual that it strikes us with terror. Is there no parallel, though, for such a phenomenon? Take a piece of pure glass. It is tangible and transparent. A certain chemical coarseness is all that prevents its being so entirely transparent as to be totally invisible. It is not *theoretically impossible*, mind you, to make a glass which shall not reflect a single ray of light,—a glass so pure and homogeneous in its atoms that the rays from the sun will pass through it as they do through the air, refracted but not reflected. We do not see the air, and yet we feel it."

"That's all very well, Hammond, but these are inanimate substances. Glass does not breathe, air does not breathe. *This* thing has a heart that palpitates,—a will that moves it,—lungs that play, and inspire and respire."

"You forget the phenomena of which we have so often heard of late," answered the Doctor, gravely. "At the meetings called 'spirit circles,' invisible hands have been thrust into the hands of those persons round the table,—warm, fleshly hands that seemed to pulsate with mortal life."

"What? Do you think, then, that this thing is—"

"I don't know what it is," was the solemn reply; "but please the gods I will, with your assistance, thoroughly investigate it."

We watched together, smoking many pipes, all night long, by the bedside of the unearthly being that tossed and panted until it was apparently wearied out. Then we learned by the low, regular breathing that it slept.

The next morning the house was all astir. The boarders congregated on the landing outside my room, and Hammond and myself were lions. We had to answer a thousand questions as to the state of our extraordinary prisoner, for as yet not one person in the house except ourselves could be induced to set foot in the apartment.

The creature was awake. This was evidenced by the convulsive manner in which the bed-clothes were moved in its efforts to escape. There was something truly terrible in beholding, as it were, those second-hand indications of the terrible writhings and agonized struggles for liberty which themselves were invisible.

Hammond and myself had racked our brains during the long night to discover some means by which we might realise the shape and general appearance of the Enigma. As well as we could make out by passing our hands over the creature's form, its outlines and lineaments were human. There was a mouth; a round, smooth head without hair; a nose, which, however, was little elevated above the cheeks; and its hands and feet felt like those of a boy. At first, we thought of placing the being on a smooth surface and tracing its outline with chalk, as shoemakers trace the outline of the foot. This plan was given up as being of no value. Such an outline would give not the slightest idea of its conformation.

A happy thought struck me. We would take a cast of it in plaster of Paris. This would give us the solid figure, and satisfy all our wishes. But how to do it? The movements of the creature would disturb the setting of the plastic covering, and distort the mould. Another thought. Why not give it chloroform? It had respiratory organs,—that was evident by its breathing. Once reduced to a state of insensibility, we could do with it what we would. Doctor X—— was sent for; and after the worthy physician had recovered from the first shock of amazement, he proceeded to administer the chloroform.

In three minutes afterward, we were enabled to remove the fetters from the creature's body, and a modeller was busily engaged in covering the invisible form with the moist clay. In five minutes more, we had a mould, and before evening a rough facsimile of the Mystery. It was shaped like a man,—distorted, uncouth, and horrible, but still a man. It was small, not over four feet and some inches in height, and its limbs revealed a muscular development that was unparalleled. Its face surpassed in hideousness anything I had ever seen. Gustavo Doré, or Callot, or Tony Johannot, never conceived anything so horrible. There is a face in one of the latter's illustrations to *Un Voyage où il vous plaira*, which somewhat approaches the countenance of this creature, but does not equal it. It was the physiognomy of what I should fancy a ghoul might be. It looked as if it was capable of feeding on human flesh.

Having satisfied our curiosity, and bound everyone in the house to secrecy, it became a question what was to be done with our Enigma? It was impossible that we should keep such a horror in our house; it was equally impossible that such an awful being should be let loose upon the world. I confess that I would have gladly voted for the creature's destruction. But who would shoulder the responsibility? Who would undertake the execution of this horrible semblance of a human being? Day after day this question was deliberated gravely.

The boarders all left the house. Mrs. Moffat was in despair, and threatened Hammond and myself with all sorts of legal penalties if we did not remove the Horror. Our answer was, "We will go if you like, but we decline taking this creature with us. Remove it yourself if you please. It appeared in your house. On you the responsibility rests." To this there was, of course, no answer. Mrs. Moffat could not obtain for love or money a person who would even approach the Mystery.

The most singular part of the affair was that we were entirely ignorant of what the creature habitually fed on. Everything in the way of nutriment that we could think of was placed before it, but was never touched. It was awful to stand by, day after day, and see the clothes toss, and hear the hard breathing, and know that it was starving.

Ten, twelve days, a fortnight passed, and it still lived. The pulsations of the heart, however, were daily growing fainter, and had now nearly ceased. It was evident that the creature was dying for want of sustenance. While this terrible life-struggle was going on, I felt miserable. I could not sleep. Horrible as the creature was, it was pitiful to think of the pangs it was suffering.

At last it died. Hammond and I found it cold and stiff one morning in the bed. The heart had ceased to beat, the lungs to inspire. We hastened to bury it in the garden. It was a strange funeral, the dropping of that viewless corpse into the damp hole. The cast of its form I gave to Doctor X—— , who keeps it in his museum in Tenth Street.

As I am on the eve of a long journey from which I may not return, I have drawn up this narrative of an event the most singular that has ever come to my knowledge.

Harry Escott

Note: It is rumoured that the proprietors of a well-known museum in this city have made arrangements with Dr. X—— to exhibit to the public the singular cast which Mr. Escott deposited with him. So extraordinary a history cannot fail to attract universal attention.

The Other Night

The other night we had a dream. We had been pouring all day over Adam Eagle's volumes, laboriously deciphering a quaint essay on the moral principles of annuals, in which the writer endeavoured to prove that beasts possessed conscientiousness, and performed their various avocations as much from a sense of duty as from instinct. The writing was queer and cramped, and pained the eyes to read it. The pages were so soiled with mould and damp as to be entirely illegible in some places, and some idle urchin had been busy pricking architectural designs on the paper, some of which, though very ingenious in themselves, sadly interfered with the perusal of the manuscript. We grew very weary; yes, Adam! we absolutely grew drowsy over thy hallowed volumes!

A sensation of cobwebs overspread our frame; a species of impalpable but tenacious thread-work seemed to encompass each limb, and weave itself around our long hair. It appeared as though a thousand busy little sprites were engaged in hanging a liny leaden weight to each particular hair of our eyelashes. Little balls of sand were apparently stuffed into the corners of our eyes, making us blink terribly. We found our flingers constantly wandering over our eyelids, and poking themselves into all corners of our face. Our moustache suffered considerable persecution. We were fidgety, and twirled the ends into watchsprings over and over again. The room was certainly too hot! No; it is the dressing-gown! Off goes the offending garment, and we luxuriate in shirt-sleeves. What hideously tight shoes these are! Where are our slippers? Of course, we never can find anything when we want it. The slippers are not to be seen. A short search after them enlivens us a little.

We then feel a sudden disposition to be reflective. Our head rests frequently on one hand, and we assume a pensive altitude. It is not that we arc sleepy! oh, no; *that* has gone off long ago. We merely wish to—wish—to—in—to—to—Pshaw! this is really too absurd; dozing at this hour of night, with so much work before us. Nonsense! we will make an effort. A basin of cold water and a sponge will do it, and we shall be as brisk as a bee. We perform an ablution, and enter the study, endeavouring with faint success to look lively, as we pass the looking-glass. It is, however, a dreary effort. We notice that we look pale, and that our hair has a limp and tired aspect. There is work to be done, however, and we hasten our mental fangs into it furiously.

It is very interesting, at least we try hard to persuade ourselves of the fact, and we devour it. Our eyebrows, however, annoy us a little, we do not very well know why; but we keep plucking at them, and passing our finger absently along our temples. But we still read on, read firmly and systematically. The words have sometimes an unaccountable inclination to fraternise, the tail of one intertwining itself with the head of another, and the effect is rather confusing, as thus: "Thenightwas-chillandcoldand-rain," etc. It does not matter much, though. A little patience, and they will settle themselves down again in their proper places. The lamp is very annoying. One moment it looks bright and clear, the next it is as dull as a New-York gas-lamp on a dark night, or the City-Hall clock on every night.

Thinking it may be something in ourselves, we keep our eyes wide open, and stare at it; but the sprites are again busy hanging then little weights on our eyelashes, and we feel our lids gradually dropping. We catch ourselves nodding, with a convulsive jerk, and hem and blow our nose audibly, in order to drown conscience. The noise has the effect of terrifying a mouse, who, emboldened by the silence, had come out from his hole, and was amusing himself with eating a corner off of *The Pilgrim's Progress*. We feel pleased at inspiring such terror. The reflective mood comes on again; the chin drops into the hollow of the hand, and we pretend to be speculating on the origin of fear. But nod—nod—nod. There seems to be a swaying of the universe. Room, bookshelves, lamp, furniture, all rock and nod, and we alone maintain a just equilibrium.

All things get cloudy; but whether this arises from the atmosphere, or from our hair falling into our eyes, we cannot tell. Mist is everywhere; we seem to be sitting in mist; no, it is a sea; it looks like mist, it is so smooth and blue: we are sitting in an armchair, with brass nails, on a smooth blue sea. That is, it is very like a sea; but it can't be one exactly, for a sea has rocks, and all the rocks here are books—great, rugged folios, over which the waves of vapor burst and foam.

Presently this ocean mist divides, and the book-rocks clang then huge covers with a noise like seashore thunder, and an aged figure emerges from the sea. It is the Solitary. It is Adam Eagle himself. Adam Anadoymene! He is clad in an old linsey-woolsey dressing-gown. There are *papooshes* on his feet, and his right hand, all thin and withered, is stained to the bone with ink. His countenance is noble and mild, with traces of suffering marked upon it. And the white hair falls back in rich masses from his forehead, like a cataract of snow. But his eyes are strange. They seem to behold nothing material. They do not even see me, the adorer, the worshipper of the seven volumes. Their gaze is illimitable. They seem to be striving even to pierce beyond the farthest beyond. They know no clouds or intervening mists. They spiritually tunnel mountains, and speed unheeding through the valleys lar away. Were we standing on the outer edge of the disc of Neptune, straight in the local line of those eyes, we would feel convinced that they saw not us, but were piercing through us into backward space.

While we were watching the Solitary intently, a strange murmuring noise, like that which one makes when one springs a number of book-pages, keeping the thumb pressed against the edges, rustled around us, and again the smooth blue sea-mist divided, and straight in Adam Eagle's path an angelic form, of sculptured vapor, rose and floated buoyantly. Never did mortal eyes behold a fairer thing, boy or woman, spirit or etherealised matter—we knew not which it was. Its beauty was not of sex or form, and lay not within lines. It was boundless and universal grace.

It had scarce hovered an instant in the air, when the Solitary beheld it. That he did see it, could only be inferred from the sudden flaming of his eyes; for in all other respects, his gaze seemed to be as distant as before. But his eyeballs burned suddenly, and light seemed to scintillate from them, and make prismatic bows against the vapoury outlines of the apparition. His lips moved as it in inward speech, and he extended his long, thin, transparent hand, as though he would magnetise and compel the spirit. Then the latter seemed to smile all over, and laugh even in the very folds of its impalpable drapery; and began with a slow even motion to describe a great circle.

As if drawn by some viewless magnetic relation, the Solitary glided over the smooth, blue sea-mist, and followed its track. With extended hand, he glided after it in the great circle, burning with eagerness to increase his speed and overtake it, but restrained by some invisible law which regulated his motion. When the beautiful spirit had described the great circle, it commenced another of less diameter than the first, and moved with a slightly increased velocity, which communicated itself to Adam Eagle. The next circle was smaller still, and the velocity heightened. And still the disembodied Grace floated on before with its universal smile, and still the Solitary pursued it with imprisoned eagerness. Smaller and smaller grew the circles, swifter and swifter grew the pursuit, until al last both narrowed into a furious whirl.

Adam's long white hair streamed back, as if some good spirit were trying to tear him from his vain pursuit, and his large reflective eyes were starting from their sockets, as though they would leap out and fasten themselves upon the vapor-shape. But always, even in the last swift eddies of the chase when all features were confused into a dim outline, the Shape maintained the same unvarying and universal smile, that lightened its very drapery. Swift, swift; round and round. The circles must end in a centre, where all motion ceases. Adam gasps for breath, as his transparent fingers almost touch the object of his pursuit—another whirl, and they are spinning on one pivot. A sudden stoppage. The Solitary opens wide his arms to grasp the Shape. The universal smile in which it is clothed deepens into a sun-burst of laughter; all is brightly dim for an instant; and then, Adam Eagle is alone!

A moan breaks from his lips, as down from the upper sky there fall upon his beating temples a few gentle snowflakes; his head drops upon his breast; the smooth, blue sea-mist divides again, and he sinks slowly, leaving behind him painted on my heart a picture of unutterable anguish. Then the rustling sound breaks forth again, the book-rocks clang their covers like sea-shore thunder, and I commence sailing over the blue sea-mist in my brass-nailed armchair. The voyage is pleasant enough, but somehow or other, owing to my steering improperly with a paper-cutter, we run ashore upon a reef of book-rocks. We feel that our last moment is come; the vapor of the sea-mist foams up about us, and our armchair is gradually sinking. We fire guns of distress with a gold pencil-case, and prepare a raft.

But to our horror we discover that the blue sea-mist will support nothing but brass-nailed armchairs. We are slowly settling down; the sea-mist is on a level with our chin; another moment, and we are lost; when, oh! joy, an albatross comes floating by. We seize one of his wide wings, and are suddenly up-borne into the highest heaven, and then dashed as suddenly against the earth. On recovering from the shock, we find that we have upset the ink-bottle, and are lying on the floor, embracing a folio edition of Vertol's *Knights of Malta*

A Terrible Night

"By Jove! Dick, I'm nearly done up."

"So am I. Did anyone ever see such a confounded forest, Charley?"

"I am not alone weak, but hungry. Oh, for a steak of moose, with a bottle of old red wine to wash it down!"

"Charley! beware, take care how you conjure up such visions in my mind. I am already nearly starving, and if you increase my appetite much more it will go hard with me if I don't dine off of you. You are young, and Bertha says you're tender—"

"Hearted, she meant. Well, so I am, if loving Bertha be any proof of it. Do you know, Dick, I have often wondered that you, who love your sister so passionately, were not jealous of her attachment to me."

"So, I was, my dear fellow, at first—furiously jealous. But then I reflected that Bertha must one day or the other marry, and I must lose my sister, so I thought it better that she should marry my old college chum and early friend, Charley Costarre, than anyone else. So, you see there was a little selfishness in my calculations, Charley."

"Dick, we were friends at school, and friends at college, and I thought at both those places that nothing could shorten the link that bound us together, but I was mistaken. Since my love for, and engagement to your sister, I felt as if you were fifty times the friend that you were before. Dick, we three will never part!"

"So, he married the king's daughter, and they all lived together as happy as the days are long," shouted Dick with a laugh, quoting from nursery tale.

The foregoing is a slice of the conversation with which Dick Linton and myself endeavoured to beguile the way, as we tramped through one of the forests of Northern New York. Dick was an artist, and I was a sportsman, so when one fine autumn day he announced his intention going into the woods for a week to study Nature, it

125

seemed to me an excellent opportunity for me to exercise my legs and my trigger finger at the same time. Dick had some backwoods friend who lived in a log-hut on the shores of Eckford Lake, and there we determined to take up our quarters. Dick, who said he knew the forest thoroughly, was to be the guide, and we accordingly, with our guns on our shoulders, started on foot from Root's, a tavern known to tourists, and situated on the boundaries of Essex and Warren counties. It was a desperate walk; but as we started by daybreak, and had great faith in our pedestrian qualities, we expected to reach the nearest of the Eckford lakes by nightfall.

The forest through which we travelled was of the densest description. Overhead the branches of spruce and pine shut out the day, while beneath our feet lay a frightful soil, composed principally of jagged shingle, cunningly concealed in an almost impenetrable brush. As the day wore on, our hopes of reaching our destination grew fainter and fainter, and I could almost fancy, from the anxious glances that Dick cast around him, that in spite of his boasted knowledge of the woods he had lost his way. It was not, however, until night actually fell, and that we were both sinking from hunger and exhaustion, that I could get him to acknowledge it.

"We're in a nice pickle. Master Dick," said I, rather crossly, for an empty stomach does much to destroy a man's natural amiability. "Confound your assurance that led you to set up as a guide. Of all men painters are the most conceited."

"Come. Charley," answered Dick, good-humouredly, "there's no use in growling so loudly. You'll bring the bears and panthers on us if you do. We must make the best of a bad job, and sleep in a tree."

"It's easy to talk, my good fellow. I'm not a partridge, and don't know how to roost on a bough."

"Well, you'll have to learn then; for if you sleep on the ground, the chances are ten to one but you will have the wolves nibbling at your toes before daylight."

"I'm hanged if I'll do either!" said I, desperately. "I'm going to walk all night, and I'll drop before I'll lie down."

"Come, come, Charley, don't be a fool!"

"I was fool only when I consented to let you assume the role of guide."

"Well, Charley, if you are determined to go on, let it be so. We'll go together. After all, it's only an adventure."

"I say, Dick, don't you see a light?"

"By Jove, so there is! Come, you see Providence intervenes between us and wolves and hunger. That must be some squatter's hut."

The light to which I had so suddenly called Dicks attention was very faint, and seemed to be about half a mile distant. if glimmered through the dark branches of the hemlock and spruce trees, and weak as the light was I hailed it as a mariner without a compass hails the star by which he steers. We instantly set out in the direction of our beacon. In a moment, it seemed as if all fatigue had vanished, and we walked as if our muscles were as tense as iron, and our joints oily as a piston-shaft.

We soon arrived at what in the dusk seemed to be a clearing of about five acres, but it may have been larger, for the tall forest rising up around if must have diminished its apparent size, giving if the appearance of a square pit rather than a farm. Toward one corner of the clearing we discerned the dusky outline of a log-hut, through whose single end window a faint light was streaming. With a sigh of relief, we hastened to the door and knocked. It was opened immediately, and a man appeared on the threshold. We explained our condition, and were instantly invited to walk in and make ourselves at home. All our host said he could offer us were some cold Indian corn cakes, and a slice of dried deer's-flesh, to all of which we were heartily welcome. These viands in our starving condition were luxuries to us, and we literally revelled in anticipation of a full meal.

The hut into which we had so unceremoniously entered was of the most poverty-stricken order. if consisted of but one room, with a rude brick fireplace at one end. Some deer-skins and old blankets stretched out by way of a bed at the other extremity of the apartment, and the only seats visible were two sections of a large pine trunk that stood close to the fireplace. There was no vestige of a table, and the rest of the furniture was embodied in a long Tennessee rifle that hung close to the rough wall.

If the hut was remarkable, its proprietor was still more so. He was, I think, the most villainous looking man I ever beheld. About six feet two inches in height, proportionately broad across the shoulders, and with a hand large enough to pick up a fifty-six pound shot, he seemed to be a combination of extraordinary strength and agility. His head was narrow, and oblong in shape. His straight Indian-like hair fell smoothly over his low forehead as if it had been plastered with soap. And his black, bead-like eyes were set obliquely, and slanted downward toward his nose, giving him a mingled expression of ferocity and cunning. As I examined his features attentively, in which I thought I could trace almost every bad passion, I confess I experienced a certain feeling of apprehension and distrust that I could not shake off.

While he was getting us the promised food, we tried, by questioning him to draw him into conversation. He seemed very taciturn and reserved. He said he lived entirely alone, and had cleared the spot he occupied with his own hands. He said his name was Joel; but when we hinted that he must have some other name, he pretended not to hear us, though I saw his brows knit, and his small black eyes flash angrily.

My suspicions of this man were further aroused by observing a pair of shoes lying in a corner of the hut. These shoes were at least three sizes smaller than those that our gigantic host wore, and yet he had distinctly replied that he lived entirely alone. If those shoes were not his, whose were they? The more I reflected on this circumstance the more uneasy I felt, and apprehensions were still further aroused, when Joel, as he called himself, took both our fowling-pieces, and, in order to have them out of the way, as he said, hung them on crooks from the wall, at a height that neither Dick or I could reach without getting on a stool.

I smiled inwardly, however, as I felt the smooth barrel of my revolver that was slung in the hollow of my back, by its leathern belt, and thought to myself, if this fellow has any bad designs, the more unprotected he thinks us the more incautious he will be, so I made no effort to retain our guns. Dick also had a revolver, and was one of those men who I knew would use it well when the time came.

My suspicions of our host grew at last to such a pitch that I determined to communicate them to Dick. Nothing would be easier than for this villainous half-breed—for I felt convinced he had Indian blood in him—nothing would be easier than, with the aid of an accomplice, to cut our throats or shoot us while we were asleep, and so get our guns, watches, and whatever money we carried. Who, in those lonely woods, would hear the shot, or hear our cries for help? What emissary of the law, however sharp, could point out our graves in those wild woods, or bring the murder home to those who committed it? Linton at first laughed; then grew serious; and gradually became a convert to my apprehensions. We hurriedly agreed that, while one slept, the other should watch, and so take it in turns through the night.

Joel had surrendered to us his couch of deer-skin and his blanket; he himself said he could sleep quite as well on the floor, near the fire. As Dick and I were both very tired, we were anxious to get our rest as soon as possible. So after a hearty meal of deer-steak and tough cakes, washed down by a good draught from our brandy flask, I, being the youngest, got the first hour's sleep, and flung myself on the conch of skins. As my eyes gradually closed, I saw a dim picture of Dick seated sternly watching by the fire, and the long shape of the half-breed stretching out like a huge shadow upon the floor.

After what I could have sworn to be only a three-minute doze, Dick woke me, and informed me that my hour was out; and turning me out of my warm nest, lay down without any ceremony, and in a few seconds, was heavily snoring. I rubbed my eves, felt for my revolver, and seating myself on one of the pine-slumps, commenced my watch. The half-breed appeared to be buried in a profound slumber, and in the half-weird light cast by the wood embers, his enormous figure seemed almost Titanic in its proportions.

I confess I felt that in a struggle for life he was more than a match for Dick and myself. I then looked at the fire, and began a favourite amusement of mine—shaping forms in the embers. All sorts of figures defined themselves before me. Battles, tempests at sea, familiar faces, and above all shone, ever returning, the dear features of Bertha Linton, my affianced bride. She seemed to me to smile at me through a burning haze, and I could almost fancy I heard her say, "While you are watching in the lonely forest I am thinking of you, and praying for your safely."

A slight movement on the part of the slumbering half-breed here recalled me from those sweet dreams. He turned on his side, lifted himself slowly on his elbow, and gazed attentively at me. I did not stir. Still retaining my stooping attitude, I half closed my eyes, and remained motionless. Doubtless he thought I was asleep, for in a moment or two he rose noiselessly, and creeping with a stealthy step across the floor, passed out of the hut. I listened—Oh, how eagerly! It seemed to me that, through the imperfectly-joined crevices of the log-walls, I could plainly hear voices whispering.

I would have given worlds to have crept nearer to listen, but I was fearful of disturbing the fancied security of our host, who I now felt certain had sinister designs upon us. So, I remained perfectly still. The whispering suddenly ceased. The half-breed re-entered the hut in the same stealthy way in which he had quitted it, and after giving a scrutinising glance at me, once more stretched himself upon the floor and affected to sleep. In a few moments, I pretended to awake—yawned, looked at my watch, and finding that my hour had more than expired, proceeded to wake Dick. As I turned him out of bed I whispered in his ear, "Don't take your eyes off that fellow, Dick. He has accomplices outside; be careful!" Dick gave a meaning glance, carelessly touched his revolver, as much as to say, "Here's something to interfere with his little arrangements," and took his seat on the pine-stump, in such a position as to command a view of the sleeping half-breed and the doorway at the same time.

This time, though horribly tired, I could not sleep. A horrible-load seemed pressing on my chest, and every five minutes I would start up to see if Dick was keeping his watch faithfully. My nerves were strung to a frightful pitch of tensity; my heart beat at every sound, and my head seemed to throb until I thought my temples would burst. The more I reflected on the conduct of the half-breed, the more assured I was that he intended murder. Full of this idea, I look my revolver from its sling, and held it in my hand, ready to shoot him down at the first movement that appeared at all dangerous. A haze seemed now to pass across my eyes. Fatigued with long watching and excitement, I passed into that semiconscious state, in which I seemed perfectly aware of everything that passed, although objects were dim and dull in outline, and did not appear so sharply defined as in one's waking moments.

I was apparently roused from this state by a slight crackling sound. I started, and raised myself on my elbow. My heart almost ceased to beat at what I saw. The half-breed had lit some species of dried herb, which sent out a strong aromatic odour as if burned. This herb he was holding directly under Dick's nostrils, who I now perceived, to my horror, was wrapped in a profound slumber. The smoke of this mysterious herb appeared to deprive him of all consciousness, for he rolled gently off of the pine-log, and lay stretched upon the floor.

The half-breed now stole to the door, and opened if gently. Three sinister heads peered in out of the gloom. I saw the long barrels of rifles, and the huge brawny hands that clasped them. The half-breed pointed significantly to where I lay with his long bony finger, then drawing a large, thirsty-looking knife from his breast, moved toward me. The time was come. My blood stopped—my heart ceased to beat. The half-breed was within a foot of my bed; the knife was raised; another instant and if would have been buried in my heart, when, with a hand as cold as ice, I lifted my revolver, look deadly aim, and fired!

A stunning report, a dull groan, a huge cloud of smoke furling around me, and I found myself standing upright, with a dark mass lying at my feet.

"Great God! what have you done, Sir?" cried the half-breed, rushing toward me. "You have killed him! He was just about to wake you."

I staggered against the wall. My senses, until then immersed in sleep, suddenly recovered their activity. The frightful truth burst upon me in a flash. I had shot Dick Linton while under the influence of a nightmare! Then everything seemed to fade away, and I remember no more.

There was a trial, I believe. The lawyers were learned, and proved by physicians that it was a case of what is called *Sominolentia,* or sleep-drunkenness; but of the proceedings I took no heed. One form haunted me, lying black and heavy on the hut floor; and one pale face was ever present—a face I saw once after the terrible catastrophe, and never saw again—the wild, despairing face of Bertha Linton, my promised bride!

Mother of Pearl

1

I met her in India, when, during an eccentric course of travel, I visited the land of *palanquins* and *hookahs*. She was a slender, pale, spiritual-looking girl. Her figure swayed to and fro when she walked, like some delicate plant brushed by a very gentle wind. Her face betokened a rare susceptibility of nervous organisation. Large, dark-grey eyes, spanned by slender arches of black eyebrows; irregular and mobile features; a mouth large and singularly expressive, and conveying vague hints of a sensual nature whenever she smiled.

The paleness of her skin could hardly be called paleness; it was rather a beautiful transparency of texture, through the whiteness of which one beheld the underglow of life, as one sees the fires of a lamp hazily revealed through the white ground-glass shade that envelops it. Her motions were full of a strange and subtle grace. It positively sent a thrill of an indefinable nature through me to watch her moving across a room. It was perhaps a pleasurable sensation at beholding her perform so ordinary an act in so unusual a manner.

Every wanderer in the fields has been struck with delight on beholding a tuft of thistle-down floating calmly through the still atmosphere of a summer day. She possessed in the most perfect degree this aerial serenity of motion. With all the attributes of body, she seemed to move as if disembodied. It was a singular and paradoxical combination of the real and ideal, and therein I think lay the charm.

Then her voice. It was like no voice that I ever heard before. It was low and sweet; but how many hundreds of voices have I heard that were as low and just as sweet! The charm lay in something else. Each word was uttered with a sort of dovelike "*coo*,"—pray do not laugh at the image, for I am striving to express what after all is perhaps inexpressible. However, I mean to say that the harsh gutturals and hissing dentals of our English tongue were enveloped by her in a species of vocal plumage, so that they flew from her lips, not like pebbles or snakes, as they do from mine and yours, but like humming-birds, soft and round, and imbued with a strange fascination of sound.

We fell in love, married, and Minnie agreed to share my travel for a year, after which we were to repair to my native place in Maine, and settle down into a calm, loving country life.

It was during this year that our little daughter Pearl was born. The way in which she came to be named Pearl was this.

We were cruising in the Bay of Condatchy, on the west coast of Ceylon, in a small vessel which I had hired for a month's trip, to go where I listed. I had always a singular desire to make myself acquainted with the details of the pearl fishery, and I thought this would be a good opportunity; so with my wife and servants and little nameless child,— she was only three months old,—on whom, however, we showered daily a thousand unwritable love-titles, I set sail for the grounds of a celebrated pearl fishery.

It was a great although an idle pleasure to sit in one of the small coasting-boats in that cloudless and serene climate, floating on an un-ruffled sea, and watch the tawny natives, naked, with the exception of a small strip of cotton cloth wound around their loins, plunge into the marvellously clear waters, and after having shot down far beyond sight, as if they had been lead instead of flesh and blood, suddenly break above the surface after what seemed an age of immersion, hold-ing in their hands a basket filled with long, uncouthly shaped bivalves, any of which might contain a treasure great as that which Cleopatra wasted in her goblet. The oysters being flung into the boat, a brief breathing-spell was taken, and then once more the dark-skinned diver darted down like some agile fish, to recommence his search. For the pearl oyster is by no means to be found in the prodigal profusion in which his less aristocratic brethren, the millponds and blue-points and *chinkopins*, exist. He is rare and exclusive, and does not bestow himself liberally. He, like all high-born castes, is not prolific.

Sometimes a fearful moment of excitement would overtake us. While two or three of the pearl-divers were under water, the calm, glassy surface of the sea would be cleft by what seemed the thin blade of a sharp knife, cutting through the water with a slow, even, deadly motion. This we knew to be the dorsal fin of the man-eating shark. Nothing can give an idea of the horrible symbolism of that back fin. To a person utterly unacquainted with the habits of the monster, the

134

silent, stealthy, resistless way in which that membranous blade divided the water would inevitably suggest a cruelty swift, unappeasable, relentless.

This may seem exaggerated to anyone who has not seen the spectacle I speak of. Every seafaring man will admit its truth. When this ominous apparition became visible, all on board the fishing-boats were instantly in a state of excitement. The water was beaten with oars until it foamed. The natives shouted aloud with the most unearthly yells; missiles of all kinds were flung at this Seeva of the ocean, and a relentless attack was kept up on him until the poor fellows groping below showed their mahogany faces above the surface.

We were so fortunate as not to have been the spectators of any tragedy, but we knew from hearsay that it often happened that the shark—a fish, by the way, possessed of a rare intelligence—quietly bided his time until the moment the diver broke water, when there would be a lightning-like rush, a flash of the white belly as the brute turned on his side to snap, a faint cry of agony from the victim, and then the mahogany face would sink convulsed, never to rise again, while a great crimson clot of blood would hang suspended in the calm ocean, the red memorial of a sudden and awful fatality.

One breathless day we were floating in our little boat at the pearl fishery, watching the diving. "We" means my wife, myself, and our little daughter, who was nestled in the arms of her "*ayah*," or coloured nurse. It was one of those tropical mornings the glory of which is indescribable. The sea was so transparent that the boat in which we lay, shielded from the sun by awnings, seemed to hang suspended in air. The tufts of pink and white coral that studded the bed of the ocean beneath were as distinct as if they were growing at our feet. We seemed to be gazing upon a beautiful *parterre* of variegated candytuft. The shores, fringed with palms and patches of a gigantic species of cactus, which was then in bloom, were as still and serene as if they had been painted on glass.

Indeed, the whole landscape looked like a beautiful scene beheld through a glorified stereoscope;—eminently real as far as detail went, but fixed and motionless as death. Nothing broke the silence save the occasional plunge of the divers into the water, or the noise of the large oysters falling into the bottom of the boats. In the distance, on a small, narrow point of land, a strange crowd of human beings was visible. Oriental pearl merchants. *Fakirs* selling amulets. Brahmins in their dirty white robes, all attracted to the spot by the prospect of gain (as fish collect round a handful of bait flung into a pond), bargaining, cheating, and strangely mingling religion and lucre. My wife and I lay back on the cushions that lined the after part of our little skiff, languidly gazing on the sea and the sky by turns. Suddenly our attention was aroused by a great shout, which was followed by a volley of shrill cries from the pearl-fishing boats.

On turning in that direction, the greatest excitement was visible among the different crews. Hands were pointed, white teeth glittered in the sun, and every dusky form was gesticulating violently. Then two or three negroes seized some long poles and commenced beating the water violently. Others flung gourds and calabashes and odd pieces of wood and stones in the direction of a particular spot that lay between the nearest fishing-boat and ourselves. The only thing visible in this spot was a black, sharp blade, thin as the blade of a pen-knife, that appeared, slowly and evenly cutting through the still water.

No surgical instrument ever glided through human flesh with a more silent, cruel calm. It needed not the cry of "Shark! shark!" to tell us what it was. In a moment, we had a vivid picture of that unseen monster, with his small, watchful eyes, and his huge mouth with its double row of fangs, presented to our mental vision. There were three divers under water at this moment, while directly above them hung suspended this remorseless incarnation of death. My wife clasped my hand convulsively, and became deathly pale. I stretched out the other hand instinctively, and grasped a revolver which lay beside me. I was in the act of cocking it when a shriek of unutterable agony from the *ayah* burst on our ears. I turned my head quick as a flash of lightning, and beheld her, with empty arms, hanging over the gunwale of the boat, while down in the calm sea I saw a tiny little face, swathed in white, sinking—sinking—sinking!

What are words to paint such a crisis? What pen, however vigorous, could depict the pallid, convulsed face of my wife, my own agonised countenance, the awful despair that settled on the dark face of the *ayah*, as we three beheld the love of our lives serenely receding from us forever in that impassable, transparent ocean? My pistol fell from my grasp. I, who rejoiced in a vigour of manhood such as few attain, was struck dumb and helpless. My brain whirled in its dome.

Every outward object vanished from my sight, and all I saw was a vast, translucent sea and one sweet face, rosy as a sea-shell, shining in its depths,—shining with a vague smile that seemed to bid me a mute farewell as it floated away to death! I was roused from a trance of anguish by the flitting of a dark form through the clear water, cleaving its way swiftly toward that darling little shape, that grew dimmer and dimmer every second as it settled in the sea. We all saw it, and the same thought struck us all. That terrible, deadly back fin was the key of our sudden terror. The shark! A simultaneous shriek burst from our lips.

I tried to jump overboard, but was withheld by someone. Little use had I done so, for I could not swim a stroke. The dark shape glided on like a flash of light. It reached our treasure. In an instant, all we loved on earth was blotted from our sight! My heart stood still. My breath ceased; life trembled on my lips. The next moment a dusky head shot out of the water close to our boat,—a dusky head whose parted lips gasped for breath, but whose eyes shone with the brightness of a superhuman joy. The second after, two tawny hands held a dripping white mass above water, and the dark head shouted to the boatmen. Another second, and the brave pearl-diver had clambered in and laid my little daughter at her mother's feet. This was the shark! This the man-eater! This hero in sun-burned hide, who, with his quick, aquatic sight, had seen our dear one sinking through the sea, and had brought her up to us again, pale and dripping, but still alive!

What tears and what laughter fell on us three by turns as we named our gem rescued from the ocean "Little Pearl!"

2

I had been about a year settled at my pleasant homestead in Maine, when the great misfortune of my life fell upon me.

My, existence was almost exceptional in its happiness. Independent in circumstances; master of a beautiful place, the natural charms of which were carefully seconded by art; married to a woman whose refined and cultivated mind seemed to be in perfect accord with my own; and the father of the loveliest little maiden that ever tottered upon tiny feet,—what more could I wish for? In the summer-time we varied the pleasant monotony of our rustic life by flying visits to Newport and Nahant. In the winter, a month or six weeks spent in New York, party-going and theatre-going, surfeited us with the rapid life of a metropolis, but gave us food for conversation for months to come. The intervals were well filled up with farming, reading, and the social intercourse into which we naturally fell with the old residents around us.

I said a moment ago that I was perfectly happy at this time. I was wrong. I was happy, but not perfectly happy. A vague grief overshadowed me. My wife's health gave me at times great concern. Charming and *spirituelle* as she was on most occasions, there were times when she seemed a prey to a brooding melancholy. She would sit for hours in the twilight, in what appeared to be a state of mental apathy, and at such times it was almost impossible to rouse her into even a moderate state of conversational activity.

When I addressed her, she would languidly turn her eyes on me, droop the eyelids over the eyeballs, and gaze at me with a strange expression that, I knew not why, sent a shudder through my limbs. It was in vain that I questioned her to ascertain if she suffered. She was perfectly well, she said, but weary. I consulted my old friend and neighbour, Doctor Melony, but, after a careful study of her constitution, he proclaimed her, after his own fashion, to be "Sound as a bell, sir! sound as a bell!"

To me, however, there was a funereal tone in this bell. If it did not toll of death, it at least proclaimed disaster. I cannot say why those dismal forebodings should have possessed me. Let who will explain the many presentiments of good and bad fortune which waylay men in the road of life, as the witches used to waylay the traveller of old, and rise up in his path prognosticating or cursing.

At times, though, Minnie, as if to cheat speculation, displayed a gayety and cheerfulness beyond all expectation. She would propose little excursions to noted places in our neighbourhood, and no eyes in the party would be brighter, no laugh more ringing than hers. Yet these bright spots were but checkers on a life of gloom;—days passed in moodiness and silence; nights of restless tossing on the couch; and ever and anon that strange, furtive look following me as I went to and fro!

As the year slowly sailed through the green banks of summer into the flaming scenery of the fall, I resolved to make some attempt to dissipate this melancholy under which my wife so obviously laboured.

"Minnie," I said to her, one day, "I feel rather dull. Let us go to New York for a few weeks."

"What for?" she answered, turning her face around slowly until her eyes rested on mine,—eyes still filled with that inexplicable expression! "What for? To amuse ourselves? My dear Gerald, how can New York amuse you? We live in a hotel, each room of which is a stereotyped copy of the other. We get the same bill of fare—with a fresh date—every day for dinner. We go to parties that are a repetition of the parties we went to last year. The same thin-legged young man leads 'the German,' and one could almost imagine that the stewed terrapin which you got for supper had been kept over since the previous winter. There is no novelty,—no nothing."

"There is a novelty, my dear," I said, although I could not help smiling at her languid dissection of a New York season. "You love the stage, and a new, and, as I am told, a great actress, has appeared there. I, for my part, want to see her."

"Who is she? But, before you answer, I know perfectly well what a great American dramatic novelty is. She has been gifted by nature with fine eyes, a good figure, and a voice which has a tolerable scale of notes. Someone, or something, puts it into her head that she was born into this world for the special purpose of interpreting Shakespeare. She begins by reciting to her friends in a little village, and, owing to their encouragement, determines to take lessons from some broken-down actor, who ekes out an insufficient salary by giving lessons in elocution. Under his tuition—as she would under the instruction of any professor of that abominable art known as 'elocution'—she learns how to display her voice at the expense of the sense of the author.

"She thinks of nothing but rising and falling inflections, swimming entrances and graceful exits. Her idea of great emotion is hysterics, and her acme of by-play is to roll her eyes at the audience. You listen in vain for a natural intonation of the voice. You look in vain on the painted—over-painted—face for a single reflex of the emotions depicted by the dramatist;—emotions that, I am sure, when he was registering them on paper, flitted over his countenance, and thrilled his whole being as the auroral lights shimmer over the heavens, and send a vibration through all nature! My dear husband, I am tired of your great American actress. Please go and buy me half a dozen dolls."

I laughed. She was in her cynical mood, and none could be more sarcastic than she. But I was determined to gain my point.

"But," I resumed, "the actress I am anxious to see is the very reverse of the too truthful picture you have painted. I want to see Matilda Heron."

"And who is Matilda Heron?"

"Well, I can't very well answer your question definitely, Minnie; but this I know, that she has come from somewhere, and fallen like a bombshell in New York. The metaphor is not too pronounced. Her appearance has been an explosion. Now, you *blasé* critic of actresses, here is a chance for a sensation! Will you go?"

"Of course, I will, dear Gerald. But if I am disappointed, call on the gods to help you. I will punish you, if you mislead me, in some awful manner. I'll—write a play, or—go on the stage myself."

"Minnie," said I, kissing her smooth white forehead, "if you go on the stage, you will make a most miserable failure."

3

We went to New York. Matilda Heron was then playing her first engagement at Wallack's Theatre. The day after I arrived I secured a couple of orchestra seats, and before the curtain rose Minnie and I were installed in our places,—I full of anticipation, she, as all prejudging critics are, determined to be terribly severe if she got a chance.

We were too well bred, too well brought up, too well educated, and too cosmopolitan, to feel any qualms about the morality of the play. We had read it in the French under the title of *La Dame aux Camélias,* and it was now produced in dramatic form under the title of *Camille.*

If my wife did not get a chance for criticism, she at least got a sensation. Miss Heron's first entrance was wonderfully unconventional. The woman dared to come in upon that painted scene as if it really was the home apartment it was represented to be. She did not slide in with her face to the audience, and wait for the mockery that is called "a reception." She walked in easily, naturally, unwitting of any outside eyes. The petulant manner in which she took off her shawl, the commonplace conversational tone in which she spoke to her servant, were revelations to Minnie and myself. Here was a daring reality. Here was a woman who, sacrificing for the moment all conventional prejudices, dared to play the lorette as the lorette herself plays her dramatic life, with all her whims, her passion, her fearlessness of consequences, her occasional vulgarities, her impertinence, her tenderness and self-sacrifice!

It was not that we did not see faults. Occasionally Miss Heron's accent was bad, and had a savour of Celtic origin. But what mattered accent, or what mattered elocution, when we felt ourselves in the presence of an inspired woman!

Miss Heron's *Camille* electrified both Minnie and myself. My wife was particularly *bouleversée.* The artist we were beholding had not in a very marked manner any of those physical advantages which Minnie had predicated in her onslaught on the dramatic stars. It is true that Miss Heron's figure was commanding, and there was a certain powerful light in her eyes that startled and thrilled; but there was not the beauty of the "favourite actress." The conquest that she achieved was purely intellectual and magnetic.

Of course, we were present at the next performance. It was *Medea*. We then beheld the great actress under a new phase. In *Camille*, she died for love; in *Medea* she killed for love. I never saw a human being so *rocked* by emotion as was my wife during the progress of this tragedy. Her countenance was a mirror of every incident and passion. She swayed to and fro under those gusts of indignant love that the actress sent forth from time to time, and which swept the house like a storm. When the curtain fell she sat trembling,—vibrating still with those thunders of passion that the swift lightnings of genius had awakened. She seemed almost in a dream, as I took her to the carriage, and during the drive to our hotel she was moody and silent. It was in vain that I tried to get her to converse about the play. That the actress was great, she acknowledged in the briefest possible sentence. Then she leaned back and seemed to fall into a reverie from which nothing would arouse her.

I ordered supper into our sitting-room, and made Minnie drink a couple of glasses of champagne in the hope that it would rouse her into some state of mental activity. All my efforts, however, were without avail. She was silent and strange, and occasionally shivered as if penetrated with a sudden chill. Shortly after, she pleaded weariness and retired for the night, leaving me puzzled more than ever by the strangeness of her case.

An hour or two afterward, when I went to bed, I found Minnie apparently asleep. Never had she seemed more beautiful. Her lips were like a bursting rosebud about to blow under the influence of a perfumed wind, just parted as they were by the gentle breath that came and went. The long, dark lashes that swept over her cheek gave a pensive charm to her countenance, which was heightened by a rich stray of nutty hair that swept loosely across her bosom, tossed in the restlessness of slumber. I printed a light kiss upon her forehead, and, with an unuttered prayer for her welfare, lay down to rest.

I know not how long I had been asleep when I was awakened from a profound slumber by one of those indescribable sensations of mortal peril which seem to sweep over the soul, and with as it were the thrill of its passage call louder than a trumpet. Awake! arouse! your life hangs by a hair! That this strange physical warning is in all cases the result of a magnetic phenomenon I have not the slightest doubt. To prove it, steal softly, ever so softly, to the bedside of a sleeper, and, although no noise betrays your presence, the slumberer will almost invariably awaken, aroused by a magnetic perception of your proximity.

How much more powerfully must the stealthy approach of one who harbours sinister designs affect the slumbering victim! An antagonistic magnetism hovers near; the whole of the subtile currents that course through the electrical machine known as man are shocked with a powerful repulsion, and the sentinel mind whose guard has just been relieved, and which is slumbering in its quarters, suddenly hears the rappel beaten and leaps to arms.

In the midst of my deep sleep I sprang with a sudden bound upright, with every faculty alert. By one of those unaccountable mysteries of our being, I realised, before my eyes could be by any possibility alive to external objects, the presence of a great horror. Simultaneously with this conviction, or following it so quickly as to be almost twin with it, I beheld the vivid flash of a knife, and felt an acute pain in my shoulder. The next instant all was plain, as if the scene, instead of passing in a half-illuminated bedroom, had occurred in the full sunlight of the orient. My wife was standing by my bedside, her hands firmly pinioned in mine, while on the white coverlet lay a sharp table-knife red with the blood which was pouring from a deep wound in my shoulder. I had escaped death by a miracle. Another instant and the long blade would have been driven through my heart.

I never was so perfectly self-possessed as on that terrible occasion. I forced Minnie to sit on the bed, while I looked calmly into her face. She returned my gaze with a sort of serene defiance.

"Minnie," I said, "I loved you dearly. Why did you do this?"

"I was weary of you," she answered, in a cold, even voice,—a voice so level that it seemed to be spoken on ruled lines,—"that is my reason."

Great heavens! I was not prepared for this sanguinary calm. I had looked for perhaps some indication of somnambulism; I had vaguely hoped even for the incoherence or vehemence of speech which would have betokened a sudden insanity,—anything, everything but this awful avowal of a deliberate design to murder a man who loved her better than the life she sought! Still I clung to hope. I could not believe that this gentle, refined creature could deliberately quit my side at midnight, possess herself of the very knife which had been used at the table, across which I lavished a thousand fond attentions, and remorselessly endeavour to stab me to the heart. It must be the act of one insane, or labouring under some momentary hallucination. I determined to test her further. I adopted a tone of vehement reproach, hoping, if insanity was smouldering in her brain, to fan the embers to such a flame as would leave no doubt on my mind. I would rather she should be mad than feel that she hated me.

"Woman! "I thundered fiercely, "you must have the mind of a fiend to repay my love in this manner. Beware of my vengeance. Your punishment shall be terrible."

"Punish me," she answered; and oh! how serene and distant her voice sounded!—"punish me how and when you will. It will not matter much." The tones were calm, assured, and fearless. The manner perfectly coherent. A terrible suspicion shot across my mind.

"Have I a rival?" I asked; "is it a guilty love that has prompted you to plan my death? If so, I am sorry you did not kill me."

"I do not know any other man whom I love. I cannot tell why it is that I do not love you. You are very kind and considerate, but your presence wearies me. I sometimes see vaguely, as in a dream, my ideal of a husband, but he has no existence save in my soul, and I suppose I shall never meet him."

"Minnie, you are mad!" I cried, despairingly.

"Am I?" she answered, with a faint, sad smile slowly overspreading her pale face, like the dawn breaking imperceptibly over a cold grey lake. "Well, you can think so if you will. It is all one to me."

I never beheld such apathy,—such stoical indifference. Had she exhibited fierce rage, disappointment at her failure, a mad thirst for my life-blood, I should have preferred it to this awful stagnation of sensibility, this frozen stillness of the heart. I felt all my nature harden suddenly toward her. It seemed to me as if my face became fixed and stern as a bronze head.

"You are an inexplicable monster," I said, in tones that startled myself, they were so cold and metallic; "and I shall not try to decipher you. I will use every endeavour to ascertain, however, whether it is some species of insanity that has thus afflicted you, or whether you are ruled by the most vicious soul that ever inhabited a human body. You shall return to my house tomorrow, when I will place you under the charge of Doctor Melony. You will live in the strictest seclusion. I need not tell you that, after what has happened, you must henceforth be a stranger to your daughter. Hands crimsoned with her father's blood are not those that I would see caressing her."

"Very well. It is all one to me where I am, or how I live."

"Go to bed."

She went, calmly as a well-taught child, coolly turning over the pillow on which was sprinkled the blood from the wound in my shoulder, so as to present the underside for her beautiful, guilty head to repose on; gently removed the murderous knife, which was still lying on the coverlet, and placed it on a little table by the side of the bed, and then without a word calmly composed herself to sleep.

It was inexplicable. I stanched my wound and sat down to think.

What was the meaning of it all? I had visited many lunatic asylums, and had, as one of the various items in my course of study, read much on the phenomena of insanity, which had always been exceedingly interesting to me for this reason: I thought it might be that only through the aberrated intellect can we approach the secrets of the normal mind. The castle, fortified and garrisoned at every angle and loophole, guards its interior mysteries; it is only when the fortress crumbles that we can force our way inside, and detect the secret of its masonry, its form, and the theory of its construction.

But in all my researches I had never met with any symptoms of a diseased mind similar to these my wife exhibited. There was a uniform coherence that completely puzzled me. Her answers to my questions were complete and determinate,—that is, they left no room for what is called "cross-examination." No man ever spent such a night of utter despair as I did, watching in that dimly lit chamber until dawn, while she, my would-be murderess, lay plunged in so profound and calm a slumber that she might have been a wearied angel rather than a self-possessed demon. The mystery of her guilt was maddening; and I sat hour after hour in my easy-chair, seeking in vain for a clew, until the dawn, spectral and grey, arose over the city. Then I packed up all our luggage, and wandered restlessly over the house until the usual hour for rising had struck.

On returning to my room I found my wife just completing her toilet. To my consternation and horror, she flung herself into my arms as I entered.

"Gerald!" she cried, "I have been so frightened. What has brought all this blood on the pillow and the sheets? Where have you been? When I awoke and missed you and discovered these stains, I knew not what to think. Are you hurt? What is the matter?"

I stared at her. There was not a trace of conscious guilt in her countenance. It was the most consummate acting. Its very perfection made me the more relentless.

"There is no necessity for this hypocrisy," I said; "it will not alter my resolve. We depart for home today. Our luggage is packed, the bills are all paid. Speak to me, I pray you, as little as possible."

"What is it? Am I dreaming? Gerald, my darling! what have I done, or what has come over you?" She almost shrieked these queries.

"You know as well as I do, you fair-faced monster. You tried to murder me last night, when I was asleep. There's your mark on my shoulder. A loving signature, is it not?"

I bared my shoulder as I spoke, and exposed the wound. She gazed wildly in my face for a moment, then tottered and fell. I lifted her up and placed her on the bed. She did not faint, and had strength enough left to ask me to leave her alone for a few moments. I quitted her with a glance of contempt, and went downstairs to make arrangements for our journey. After an absence of about an hour I returned to our apartments. I found her sitting placidly in an easy-chair, looking out of the window. She scarcely noticed my entrance, and the same old, distant look was on her face.

"We start at three o'clock. Are you ready?" I said to her.

"Yes. I need no preparation." Evenly, calmly uttered, without even turning her head to look at me.

"You have recovered your memory, it seems," I said. "You wasted your histrionic talents this morning."

"Did I?" She smiled with the most perfect serenity, arranged herself more easily in her chair, and leaned back as if in a reverie. I was enraged beyond endurance, and left the room abruptly.

That evening saw us on our way home. Throughout the journey she maintained the same apathetic air. We scarcely exchanged a word. The instant we reached our house I assigned apartments to her, strictly forbidding her to move from them, and despatched a messenger for Doctor Melony. Minnie, on her part, took possession of her prison without a word. She did not even ask to see our darling little Pearl, who was a thousand times more beautiful and engaging than ever.

Melony arrived, and I laid the awful facts before him. The poor man was terribly shocked.

"Depend on it, it's opium," he said. "Let me see her."

An hour afterward he came to me.

"It's not opium, and it's not insanity," he said; "it must be somnambulism. I find symptoms, however, that puzzle me beyond all calculation. That she is not in her normal condition of mind is evident; but I cannot discover the cause of this unnatural excitement. She is coherent, logical, but perfectly apathetic to all outward influences. At first, I was certain that she was a victim of opium. Now I feel convinced that I was entirely wrong. It must be somnambulism. I will reside for a time in the house, and trust me to discover this mystery. Meanwhile she must be carefully watched."

Melony was as good as his word. He watched her incessantly, and reported to me her condition. The poor man was dreadfully puzzled. The strictest surveillance failed to elicit the slightest evidence of her taking any stimulants, although she remained almost all the time in the apathetic state which was so terrible to behold. The doctor endeavoured to arouse her by reproaches for her attempt on my life. She, in return, only smiled, and replied that it was a matter in which she had no further interest. Not a trace of any somnambulistic habit could be discovered. I was thoroughly wretched.

I secluded myself from all society but that of Melony; and had it not been for him and my darling little Pearl I am certain that I should have gone mad. The most of my days I spent wandering in the great woods which lay in the neighbourhood of my farm, and my evenings I endeavoured to divert with reading or a chat with the good doctor. Yet, talk of what we might, the conversation would always return to the same melancholy topic. It was a maze of sorrow in which we invariably, no matter in what direction we wandered, brought up at the same spot.

4

The doctor and myself were sitting one evening, late, in my library, talking gloomily enough over my domestic tragedy. He was endeavouring to persuade me to look more brightly on the future; to dismiss as far as possible from my mind the accursed horror that dwelt in my home, and to remember that I had still a dear object left on which to centre my affections. This allusion to little Pearl, in such a mood as I was then in, only served to heighten my agony. I began immediately to revolve the chances that, were my wife's disease really insanity, it would be perpetuated in my dear child. Melony, of course, poohpoohed the idea; but with the obstinacy of grief I clung to it.

Suddenly a pause took place in the argument, and the dreary sounds that fill the air in the last nights of autumn swept around the house. The wind soughed through the tree-tops, which were now almost bare, as if moaning at being deprived of its leafy playmates. Inexplicable noises passed to and fro without the windows. Dead leaves rustled along the piazza, like the rustle of the garments of ghosts. Chilly draughts came from unseen crevices, blowing on back and cheek till one felt as if some invisible lips were close behind, pouring malignant breaths on face and shoulder. Suddenly the pause in our conversation was filled by a noise that we knew came neither from air nor dry leaf. We heard sounding through the night the muffled tread of footsteps. I knew that, except ourselves, the household had long since retired to bed.

By a simultaneous action we both sprang to our feet and rushed to a door which opened into a long corridor leading to the nursery, and which communicated, by a series of rambling passages, with the main body of the house. As we flung back the door a light appeared at the further end advancing slowly toward us. It was borne by a tall, white figure. It was my wife! Calm and stately, and with her wonderful serene step, she approached. My heart was frozen when I saw spots of blood on her hands and night-robe. I gave a wild cry, and rushed past her. In another instant, I was in baby's room. The night light was burning dimly; the coloured nurse was sleeping calmly in her bed; while, in a little cot in another part of the room, I saw—Ah! how tell it?—I cannot! Well, little Pearl was murdered,—murdered! My darling lay—

It was I now who was insane. I rushed back into the corridor to slay the fiend who had done this horrible deed. I had no mercy for her then. I would have killed her a thousand times over. Great Heaven! She was leaning against the wall conversing as calmly with the doctor as if nothing had happened; smoothing her hair with her reddened fingers, nonchalant as if at an evening party. I ran at her to crush her. Melony leaped between us.

"Stop," he cried. "The secret is out";—and as he spoke he held up a little silver box containing what seemed to be a greenish paste. "It is *hasheesh*, and she is confessing!"

Her statement was the most awful thing I ever listened to. It was as deliberate as a lawyer's brief. She had contracted this habit in the East, she said, long before I knew her, and could not break it off. It wound her nature in chains of steel; by degrees it grew upon her, until it became her very life. Her existence lay as it were in a nut-shell, but that shell was to her a universe. One night, she continued, when she was under the influence of the drug, she went with me to see a play in which the wife abhors her husband and murders her children. It was *Medea*. From that instant murder became glorified in her sight, through the medium of the spell-working drug. Her soul became rapt in the contemplation of the spilling of blood. I was to have been her first victim, Pearl her second. She ended by saying, with an ineffable smile, that the delight of the taking away of life was beyond imagination.

I suppose I must have fainted, for when I awoke from what seemed oblivion I found myself in bed, with Dr. Melony by my side. He laid his finger on his lip, and whispered to me that I had been very ill, and must not talk. But I could not restrain myself.

"Where is she?" I muttered.

"Where she ought to be," he answered; and then I caught faintly the words, "Private madhouse."

★★★★★★

O *hasheesh!* demon of a new paradise, spiritual whirlwind, I know you now! You blackened my life, you robbed me of all I held dear; but you have since consoled me. You thought, wicked enchanter, that you had destroyed my peace forever. But I have won, through you yourself, the bliss you once blotted out. Vanish past! Hence present! Out upon actuality! Hand in hand, I walk with the conqueror of time, and space, and suffering. Bend, all who hear me, to his worship!

Uncle and Nephew

1

I am sure you must have passed twenty times by the establishment of Doctor Auvray without suspecting that miracles are performed there. It is a modest building, almost hidden from the street; even the yellow-lettered inscription, *Maison de Santé*, ordinarily displayed above the entrance of such establishments, is not to be seen here. It is situated toward the southwestern extremity of the Avenue Montaigne, between the Gothic palace of Prince Soltykoff and Triat's gymnasium. An iron gate, painted in imitation of bronze, opens on a little garden stocked with lilacs and roses. The porter's lodge is at the right; the pavilion to the left is occupied by the doctor's office and the apartments of his family, which is composed of a wife and daughter. The main building is at the rear of the garden, and fronts to the southeast, all its windows looking on to a small *parc* well planted with horse-chestnuts and lindens. it is there that the doctor takes care of and often heals persons afflicted with insanity.

I would not introduce you to the house if there were danger of meeting all sorts of insanity there; but do not hesitate, you will not be pained by the spectacle of hopeless imbecility or of raving madness, or even of any complete wreck of mind. M. Auvray has made a specialty of monomania. He is an excellent man, full of knowledge and of intelligence, half physician, hall philosopher, a disciple of Esquirol and of Laromiguière. If you should ever chance to meet him with his bald head, his smooth-shaved chin, his black clothes, and his fatherly look, you would not know whether to set him down for a physician, a professor, or a priest. When he opens his thick lips, you fancy he is going to say, "My child," to you.

The vocation of M. Auvray was decided while he was an assistant at the Salpêtrière. He studiously applied himself there to the observation of monomania, that curious disease of the menial faculty which is rarely explicable by a physical cause, which corresponds with no visible lesion of the nervous system, and which is healed, it at all, by moral treatment. He was aided in his observations by a young nurse of the division Pinel, who was rather pretty and very well bred. He fell in love with her, and, as soon as he had passed doctor, married her.

It was starting in life modestly. However, he had a little property which he spent in founding the establishment we are speaking of. With a little charlatanism, he might have made a fortune by it; he preferred to cover his annual expenses by it. He is not fond of noise, and, when he has effected a wonderful cure, does not go to the housetops to proclaim it. His reputation has grown up of itself, quietly as it were, without his knowledge. To give you a proof of it. His treatise on *La Monomonie*, published by Bailliere in 1812, is now in its sixth edition, though the author never sent a copy of it to the newspapers.

Modesty is surely a good thing in itself, but it ought not be pushed to excess. Mademoiselle Auvray has not more than twenty thousand *francs* for her dowry, and she will be twenty-two on the 30th of April.

About two weeks ago (I think it was Thursday, December 1) a *coupé de louage* stopped before the iron gate of M. Auvray. The gate opened at the coachman's *"Porte, s'il vous plait!"* the carriage drove on to the pavilion, when two men alighted and hurried into the doctor's office. The domestic offered them chairs, and begged them to wait till her master had finished his morning round among the patients. it was ten o'clock.

One of the two visitors was a man of fifty, tall, black hair, sanguine complexion; large projecting ears, thick clumsy hands, enormous thumbs; a coarsely organised man—not made of the finer clay. This was M. Morlot.

His nephew, François Thomas, is a young man of twenty-three. The description of his person is difficult, for it has no salient points, he is neither tall nor short, handsome nor ugly; he has not the proportions of Hercules nor the contour of a dandy. He is non-eccentric, modest from head to foot. The colour of his hair and of his coat was a sort of *neutral* brown; the turn of his features and mind what the passports would call "medium." When he entered the office he seemed much agitated; he walked to and fro with a sort of violence in his movements, never standing still, looking at twenty things at once, all of which he would have taken hold of with his hands if they had not been bound.

"Try to be quiet now," said his uncle; "what I am doing is for your good. You will be happy here, and the doctor is going to cure you."

"I am not ill. What have you tied my hands for?'"

"Because you would have thrown me out of the window it I had not. You have lost your reason, my poor François; M. Auvray will restore it."

"Uncle, I reason as well as you do, and I do not understand what you mean. I have a sound mind, a calm judgment, and an excellent memory. Shall I recite some verses to you, or translate a Latin sentence? There is a Tacitus in the bookcase. If you want other kinds of proof, I will solve you a problem in arithmetic or geometry. You shake your head? Well, then, let me tell you what we have done this morning. You came at eight o'clock—not to wake me, for I was not asleep, but to force me out of bed. I dressed myself without the help of Germain; you urged me to go with you to Doctor Auvray's, and I refused; you insisted, I became angry, and you bound my hands with the assistance of Germain. I will dismiss him this evening. I owe him thirteen days' wages, that is thirteen *francs*, for I hired him at thirty *francs* a month. You will owe him something, for it is through you that he loses his New Year's present. There, does that hold together? is that rational? And you still think you can make me pass for an insane man? Ah! my dear uncle, treat me better than this! remember that my mother was your sister! What would my poor mother say it she could see me here? I am not angry with you; the matter can be arranged without quarrel. You have a daughter, Mademoiselle Claire Morlot."

"Hah! I have caught you now. you see yourself that you have lost your wits. I have a daughter—I? Why, I am a bachelor—very, even!"

"You have a daughter," repeated François, mechanically.

"My poor nephew! Come now, just pay attention. Have you a cousin?"

"A cousin? No, I have no cousin. Oh, you will not catch me tripping. I have no cousin, male or female."

"I am your uncle, am I not?"

"Yes, you are my uncle; although you have not behaved like one this morning."

"If I had a daughter, she would be your cousin; but you have no cousin, then I have not a daughter."

"You are quite right. I had the pleasure of seeing her this summer at Ems with her mother. I love her; I have reason to think that I am not indifferent to her, and I have the honour of asking you for her hand."

"Whose hand?"

"The hand of *mademoiselle*, your daughter."

"Really," said Uncle Morlot to himself, "M. Auvray must be skilful, indeed, if he cures him. I shall pay six thousand *francs* for the yearly board out of my nephew's income. Six out of thirty leaves twenty-four. I shall be rich. Poor François!"

He sat down and opened the first book that came under his hand.

"Take that chair," he said to François; "I am going to read to you. Try to listen; that will quiet you."

He began:

"Monomania is the persistence of one idea, the exclusive dominion of one passion. Its seat is in the emotional part of our nature, it is there where we must seek it and cure it. Its causes are love, fear, vanity, ambition, remorse. it reveals itself by the same symptoms as the passion; sometimes by joy, gayety, boldness, and noise; sometimes by timidity, sadness, and silence." While the reading was going on, François seemed to grow calm and fall into a doze. The room was warm.

"Bravo!" said M. Morlot to himself. "Here is a wonder performed by medicine already; it puts a man to sleep who is neither hungry nor drowsy."

François was not asleep, but he imitated the appearances of it to perfection. He gradually sank his head, and regulated his respiration with mathematical monotony. The uncle was completely deceived. He continued his reading for a while in a low tone, then he yawned, then he stopped, then he let the book slip out of his hands, then closed his eyes, then fell away into a *bona fide* slumber, to the great satisfaction of his nephew, who was maliciously watching him from under his eyelashes.

François now began by moving his chair. M. Morlot remained quiet as a post. François walked a little, making his boots creak on the polished floor: M. Morlot fell to snoring. The lunatic then went to the doctor's desk, where he found a knife, the handle of which he managed to push fast into a corner, and then rubbing the cord against the blade, soon severed it.

On recovering the use of his hands, he was tempted to utter a cry of joy; but restraining himself, he softly approached his uncle. In two minutes M. Morlot was effectively manacled; but with such delicacy was the operation performed that his slumbers were not disturbed.

After admiring his work, François picked up the book that had fallen on the floor. it was the last edition of the *Monomanie Raisonnante*. He took a seat in a corner of the room, and fell to reading like a sage while awaiting the arrival of the doctor.

2

It is proper that you should know something of the previous life of François and his uncle. François was the only son of a toy-merchant of the Passage Saumur, named Thomas. The toy-trade is a good business: there is a hundred *per cent*, profit on almost all the articles.

After the death of his father, François enjoyed a clean income—doubtless so called because it saves one from dirty actions—of thirty thousand *francs* a year.

His tastes, as I have already intimated, I believe, were very simple. He preferred whatever was not striking, and naturally chose his gloves, waistcoats, and *paletots* within that range of quiet colours which lies between maroon and black. Even in his tenderest infancy he had no recollection of having dreamed of military uniforms, and those honorary ribbons, for which most of us are so ambitious, never disturbed his slumbers. He did not wear a quizzing-glass, because, he said, his eyesight was good; nor a pin in his cravat, because his cravat kept its place very well without one; but the real cause was that he was afraid of attracting observation. His varnished leather boots dazzled him. He would have been sorely troubled if the accident of birth had imposed upon him a remarkable name. If, to complete it, he had been christened Améric or Fernand, he would never in the world have signed in full. Happily, his names were as unpretentious as if he had chosen them himself.

His timidity prevented him from entering into any profession. After having passed the threshold of the *baccalaureate*, he stopped at the great door which opens on active life, where he remained contemplating the seven or eight roads that lay before him. The bar seemed to him too noisy, medicine too bustling, a professorship too imposing, commerce too complicated, an administrative career too confining. As for the army, it was not to be thought of—not that he was afraid of the enemy, but he trembled at the idea of a uniform. He kept, then, to his first trade, not because it was the easiest, but because it was the quickest: he lived on his income.

As he had not earned his own money, he readily lent it. In reward of so rare a virtue, Heaven sent him many friends. He loved them all sincerely, and cheerfully yielded to their wishes. When he met one of them on the *Boulevard*, he always suffered himself to be taken by the arm, turned about, and followed the route that was proposed. Do not understand that he was stupid, or weak, or ill-informed. He knew three or four living languages, with as much of Latin and Greek, and other branches of knowledge, as are studied at school; he had certain notions about commerce, manufactures, agriculture, and literature, and could pass a sound judgment upon a book it nobody was by to bear him.

But his weakness appeared in all its strength in his relations with the better sex. He needed to be always in love with some of their number, and if on waking he had not some object of love for his thoughts to turn to, he rose dispirited, and was seen to put on his stockings wrong side out. If he went to a concert or to the theatre, the first thing was to look over the house in search of a face to please him; if he found one, he fell in love with it, and the concert was charming, the play admirable; if he was unsuccessful in his search, then everyone sang out of tune, and the actors murdered their parts. His heart had such an abhorrence of vacuum, that in presence of a moderate beauty he went to extravagant expense of imagination to perfect her charms. As you might guess without my saying it, this universal tenderness was absolutely innocent. He was in love with all the women without avowing it to them, for he had never dared to speak to a single one. He was the purest, the most harmless of *debauchees*; a Don Juan, if you choose, but before Donna Julia.

When he was in love, he was always editing to himself bold declarations which he could never get his lips to publish. And so, he would compose his whole courtship; reveal the inmost sentiments of his breast; carry on long conversations for which he furnished both questions and answers; devise speeches so touching, so ardent, they might have softened rocks and melted ice. But no woman gratefully recognised these mute aspirations. "*Faint heart never won fair lady.*" There is a great difference between wishing and willing—

However, last August, four months before tying his uncle's hands, he dared to love openly. At Ems he met, this summer, a young lady almost as shy as himself, whose sensitive timidity gave him courage. She was a Parisian, frail, delicate, and pale as fruit ripened in the shade. You could see the blood flow through the blue veins under her transparent skin. She was there as companion for her mother, whom a chronic malady (I think it was some affliction of the throat) led to use the waters of Ems. Mother and daughter seemed to have lived little in the world, to judge from the wondering looks they cast upon the noisy crowd of guests at the Springs.

François was presented to them one day, without ceremony, by a friend who was on his way to Italy. He saw them constantly for a month, and was, so to speak, their only society. For sensitive temperaments, a crowd is a great solitude, and the more noise the world makes around them, the more they incline to withdraw into a corner to whisper with each other. The young Parisian and her mother entered into full possession of François' heart at the outset, and were not displeased with their quarters. Like the first navigator who set foot in America, they explored with delight this virgin and mysterious country, and every day discovered new treasure's there. They never inquired whether he were rich or poor. it was enough for them to know that he was good, and no treasure they could have found would have been more precious for them than that of this heart of gold.

On his side, François was delighted with his metamorphosis. You have heard or read how the spring breaks out in the gardens of Russia. Yesterday everything was covered with snow; today comes a sunbeam that puts winter to flight. At noon, the trees are in blow; at night, they are thick with leaves; on the morrow, almost, they bear fruits. So, did François's love bloom and fructify. His coldness of exterior and his awkwardness were carried away like ice-cakes by a flood. The embarrassed, shamefaced boy became a man in the course of a few weeks. I do not know which one of the party first uttered the word *marriage*. But what does that matter? it is always understood when two pure natures talk of love.

François was of age and his own master, but the object of his affections could not dispose of her hand without first asking and obtaining the consent of her father. And here the timidity of the unfortunate youth regained the upper hand. it was in vain that Claire said to him: "Write frankly; my father has already been informed of the nature of our relations; you will receive his consent by return mail." He wrote and rewrote his letter a hundred times, but could not muster resolution to send it.

And yet the task was an easy one, which the most commonplace mind would have accomplished successfully. He knew the name, position, fortune, and even the disposition of his future father-in-law. He had been let into all the secrets of the family; he was almost become a member of it. He had only to write in two words what he was, and what he had; there could be no doubt about the answer. He hesitated, however, so long, that at the end of a month Claire and her mother could not repress some rising doubts. Still, they might have patiently waited a fortnight longer, had it not been for paternal prudence. If Claire was in love, and if her lover was not ready to declare his intentions officially, the only course to pursue was to put her, as soon as possible, in a place of safety at Paris. Then, perhaps, M. François Thomas would make up his mind to come and ask her hand in marriage; he would know where to find her.

One morning when François called for the ladies to take them to walk, the hotel-keeper informed him that they had left for Paris. Their apartment was already occupied by an English family. So rude a blow falling suddenly on so weak a head disturbed his reason. He left the hotel in a state verging on frenzy, and went looking for Claire in all the places where he used to walk with her. On coming back to his room, he had a violent headache, which he treated in the most violent manner. He was bled, he took scalding hot baths, he wrapped his feet in great sinapisms. He would avenge his moral sufferings on his body. When he thought himself cured he set out for France, determined to demand the hand of Claire immediately on arriving at Paris; he would not stop even to change his coat. On reaching the city, he hurried out of the rail-car, leaving his baggage to take care of itself, jumped into a *fiacre,* and cried out to the coachman,

"To *her* house, at a gallop!"

"And where is that, Sir?"

"She is at her father's, Monsieur ——, Rue ——. Ah! I can't think now."

He had forgotten both name and address.

"I must go to my room," he said to himself; "I shall recover Claire's name when this agitation is over."

He handed his card to the coachman, and was driven home.

His *concierge,* a childless old man; named Emmanuel, came out to meet him. François made a profound bow, and addressed him as follows: 'Sir, you have a daughter, Mademoiselle Claire Emmanuel. I wished to ask her hand of you by letter, but I thought it would be more proper to make this request in person."

It was evident that his brain was turned, and his Uncle Morlot, of the Faubourg St. Antoine, was sent for with all speed.

This Uncle Morlot was the honestest man in the Rue de Charonne, which is one of the longest streets in Paris. He manufactured antique furniture with ordinary skill and extraordinary conscientiousness. He never sold stained pear-tree wood for ebony, nor a chest-of-drawers of his own make for a relic of the Middle Ages. He possessed the art of imitating venerable cracks and worm-holes in new wood as well as any of his brethren of the trade; but with him it was a principle and a law to do wrong to no one. From a spirit of moderation that seems almost absurd in trades that serve the calls of luxury only, he limited his net profits to five *per cent*. He had consequently gained more esteem than money in the exercise of his trade. He never made out a bill that he did not add up the items three times over, such was his fear of committing an error to his own advantage.

Alter being in business thirty years, he was hardly better off in worldly goods than when he completed his term of apprenticeship. He had earned his living like the humblest of his workmen, and he used to ask himself, with a little jealousy of his brother-in-law, how the latter had gone to work to amass his wealth; If M. Thomas assumed toward him a certain air of superiority, such as accords with the vanity of a *parvenu*, he in turn took an air of yet higher superiority, such as accords with the pride of a man who is above using certain means of success. He gloried in his very mediocrity of fortune. "At least," he would say, "it is honestly earned, and is all my own."

Man is a strange animal. I do not claim the observation as original. This worthy M. Morlot, whose scrupulous honesty was the jest of the whole faubourg, felt at the bottom of his heart a something like an agreeable titillating sensation when he was told of the malady of his nephew. He heard a soft, insinuating little voice that whispered: "If François is insane, you will be his guardian." Probity immediately replied: "We shall be none the richer for that." "What!" returned the voice; "the board and lodging of a lunatic does not cost thirty thousand *francs* a year. And besides, we shall be put to a deal of trouble; shall be obliged to neglect our own affairs; we deserve some compensation for all that, and there we wrong no one." "But," resumed Disinterestedness, "one should give his services *gratis* to one's own family."

"Really!" grumbled the voice. "Then, why has our family never done anything for us? We have seen hard times; notes coming due, and bills not paid; but neither nephew François, nor his father before him, ever thought of lending a helping hand." "Poh!" cried Good Nature, "all this will come to nothing; it is a false alarm. François will be well, we hope, before the week is over." "But, perhaps," continued the obstinate little voice, "the disease will kill the patient, and we shall receive the inheritance without doing any one wrong. We have worked hard these thirty years, and here we are. Who knows but an accident at last may make our fortune?"

The good man stopped his ears, but they were so large, so ample, they flared out so grandly like great sea-shells, that the subtle, persevering little voice still found entrance in spite of him. He left the establishment in the Rue de Charonne in charge of the foreman, and took up his winter quarters in the handsome apartments of his nephew. He slept in a good bed, and found himself the better for it. He sat at an excellent table, and was suddenly cured of the cramps in his stomach with which he had been troubled for a number of years. He soon accustomed himself to the services of Germain, his nephew's valet. Gradually he reconciled himself with the condition of François; he accepted the notion that perhaps he would never be cured. Occasionally, indeed, as if to pay a debt to conscience, he would repeat to himself, "In any case, I am not harming anyone."

By the end of three months he grew tired of having a crazy man in the house; for he had come to consider himself at home there. François's senseless talk, and his mania of demanding Claire in marriage of everyone he met, became quite insupportable. He resolved to clear the house of him, and send him for treatment to Dr. Auvray. "After all," thought he, "my nephew will be better cared for, and I shall be more at my ease. Science tells us that change of scene is beneficial to the insane. I must do my duty."

With such thoughts passing through his mind he had fallen asleep, when François conceived the idea of binding his hands.

3

The d
octor entered, making his excuses. François rose, laid aside his book, and explained the affair with extreme volubility, as he walked up and down the room.

"Sir," said he, "I have brought here my maternal uncle to commit to your care. You see he is a man between forty-five and fifty, hardened by manual labour and the trials of a laborious life. He was born of healthy parents, in a family where there has never before been a case of mental alienation. So, you will not have an hereditary insanity to struggle with. His malady is, perhaps, one of the most curious monomanias that your wide experience has ever observed. He passes, with an incredible rapidity, from the extreme of cheerfulness to the extreme of sadness; it is a strange mixture of monomania, properly so called, and of melancholy."

"He has not, then, entirely lost his mind?"

"No, Sir; he is mad only on one point, and belongs properly to your specialty."

"What is the character of his malady?"

"Alas! Sir, it is the character of our times—cupidity! The poor man is truly a type of his age. After having laboured from childhood up, he finds himself without fortune. My father, beginning when he did, left me a handsome estate. My dear uncle began by being envious; then he thought that, being my only relative, he would become my heir in case of my death, and my guardian in case of insanity; and as a feeble mind easily believes what it desires, the unhappy man persuaded himself that I had lost my senses. He said so to everyone—he will tell you so. In the carriage, on our way here, though his hands were tied, he thought it was he who was bringing me to you."

"When was he first taken?"

"About three months ago. He came into my porter's lodge and said to him, with a wild air, 'M. Emmanuel, you have a daughter—leave her in the lodge and come help me bind my nephew.'"

"Does he at all comprehend his condition? Does he know that he is in an unsound state?"

"No, Sir; and I think that is a good sign. I should also tell you that his physical functions are somewhat deranged, that he has lost his appetite, and is subject to wakefulness."

"So much the better! An insane person who sleeps and eats regularly is nearly incurable. Permit me to waken him."

M. Auvray gently shook the shoulder of the sleeper, who started to his feet. His first movement was to rub his eyes. When he found that his hands were bound he guessed what had passed during his sleep, and broke out into loud laughter, exclaiming, "This is a good joke!"

"You see," said François, in a whisper, to the doctor; "in five minutes he will be furious."

"I will manage him," replied the doctor; and smiling on the patient as it he had been a child that he wished to amuse, he said,

"My friend, you awake betimes; have you had pleasant dreams?"

"I! I have not dreamed at all. I was laughing to see myself tied—tied up like a fagot of kindling-wood. One would say that I was the madman."

"You see!" said François.

"Have the kindness to relieve me, Doctor; I can explain better when I am at my ease."

"I will unbind you, my friend; but then you must promise to be quiet?"

"Really, now, Doctor, do you take me for a crazy man?"

"Not at all; but you are not well. We will nurse you and cure you. There, your hands are free, but do not do any mischief."

"What the devil do you mean? I brought you my nephew—"

"Yes, yes," said the doctor, "we will talk about that presently. I found you asleep; do you often sleep in the daytime?"

"Never! it is that stupid book—"

Aha! thought the author, the case is a grave one. "And so, you think your nephew is insane!'"

"To be sure he is, Sir; and the proof of it is that I had to tie his hands with this cord."

"But it is you who had your hands tied. Don't you remember that I released you this very minute?"

"That was I! 'Twas he! Ah, let me explain the whole matter."

"Softly, my friend, you are getting excited, you are very red; I don't want to fatigue you. Only answer my questions. You say your nephew is diseased?"

"Insane, crazy, mad."

"And you are content to see him mad?"

"What, I?"

"Answer me frankly. You don't want he should get well, do you'?"

"Why not?"

"So that his fortune may remain in your hands. You want to be rich, do you not? You are tired with working for a whole lifetime without making a fortune, are you not? And you think your time has come at last, eh?"

M. Morlot made no answer. His eyes were fixed on the floor. He asked himself whether he were dreaming an ugly dream; and he was confused with the binding of hands, and the questioning, and this inquisitor, who seemed to read in his conscience as an open book.

"Does he hear voices?" asked the doctor of the nephew. The poor uncle felt his hair rise on end. He recalled that obstinate voice that whispered in his ear, and answered mechanically,

"Sometimes."

"Ah! it is a case of hallucination."

"No, no, I am not mad. For Heaven's sake let me go out; I shall lose my sense's here. Ask any of my friends, they will tell you that I am of sound mind. Feel my pulse; you will see that I have no fever."

"My poor uncle!" said François. "He does not know that insanity is a delirium without fever."

"If, Sir," added the doctor, "we could give our patients a fever, we could heal the whole of them."

M. Morlot threw himself in a sort of desperation on the sofa.

"M. Auvray," said François, always keeping up his rapid march across the room, "I am profoundly pained with the misfortune of my uncle, but it is a great consolation for me to commit him to the care of a person like yourself. I have read your admirable work *La Monomanie Raisonnante;* nothing equal to it has been written since the admirable *Traité des Maladies Mentales* of the great Esquirol. Some days ago, I breakfasted with the *internes* at the Salpêtrière. One of them is an old college friend, M. Ravin. You may know him."

"I have heard of him as a young physician of extraordinary promise."

"They all told me that if my uncle could be cured, it would be by you, Sir. I know your kindness for your patients, and will not offend you by a special recommendation to your attention of my uncle. As for the price of his board, I leave that entirely with you;" and here François quietly drew a bank-note for a thousand *francs* from his pocket-book and laid it on the mantelpiece. "I shall have the honour of calling here in the course of next week. At what hour is it permitted to visit the patients?"

"From twelve to two o'clock. For myself, I am always at home. Good-day Sir."

"Stop him!" cried the uncle; "don't you let him go! It is he that is crazy. I'll tell you all about his insanity."

"Pray be quick, my dear uncle," said François, retiring; "I leave you in the hands of M. Auvray; he will take the best care of you."

M. Morlot started to run after his nephew, but was stopped by the doctor.

"The deuce is in it," exclaimed the poor uncle; "was there ever such luck! He won't say the first bit of nonsense! If he would only once begin, you would see that it is not I who am the madman."

François already had his hand on the door-handle. Suddenly he turned as it he had forgotten something, and coming straight up to the doctor, said: "Sir, the malady of my uncle is not the sole cause of my visit."

"Aha!" murmured M. Morlot, who saw a ray of hope in the speech.

The young man continued. "You have a daughter."

Here the poor uncle could no longer contain himself; "You hear what he says: you have a daughter!"

The doctor replying to François: "Yes, Sir; but please tell me how—"

"You have a daughter, Mlle, Claire Auvray."

"There! there! I told you so," exclaimed the uncle.

"Yes, Sir," said the doctor.

"She was at Ems three months ago with her mother."

"Bravo! bravo!" shouted M. Morlot.

"Yes, Sir," replied M. Auvray.

M. Morlot ran up to the doctor and said, "You are not the doctor; you are one of the patients of the house."

"My friend," replied the doctor, "if you are not quiet, we shall have to give you a *douche*."

M. Morlot retired in alarm. His nephew continued. "Sir, I love *mademoiselle*, your daughter. I have some reason to hope that the sentiment is reciprocated, and if her sentiments have not changed since the month of September last, I have the honour of asking her hand from you."

The doctor replied, "It is, then, M. François Thomas to whom I have the honour of speaking!"

"The same, Sir; I should have given you my name at the outset."

"Permit me to remark, Sir, that you have been somewhat dilatory in your movements."

At this moment, the attention of the doctor was attracted by M. Morlot, who was rubbing his hands with a sort of fury. "What is the matter, my friend;'" he asked with his mild, fatherly voice.

"Oh, nothing, nothing! I was rubbing my hands."

"And what are you rubbing your hands for?"

"There is something sticks to them."

"Show me; I do not see anything."

"You do not see! Why, there, there, between the fingers; I see it plain enough!"

"What do you see?"

"My nephew's fortune, take it off, Doctor. I am an honest man; I wish ill to no one."

While the doctor was listening attentively to the wild talk of M. Morlot, a strange revolution was going on in the person of François, he grew pale, he trembled, his teeth chattered. M. Auvray turned toward him to ask what was the matter.

"Nothing," he replied; "she is coming, I hear her, it is the delight—, but it is too much for me. Happiness falls on me like the snow. it will be a hard winter for lovers. Pray see, Doctor, what I have in my head."

M. Morlot ran up to him, crying out: "That's enough! Don't go on in that way! I do not want you should be mad any longer. They would say that it is I who have robbed you of your reason. I am an honest man. Doctor, look at my hands; feel in my pockets; send to my house in the Rue de Charonne, Faubourg St. Antoine; open all the drawers; you will see that I have nothing belonging to other people."

The doctor was becoming embarrassed between his two patients, when a door opened, and Claire came to tell her father that breakfast was on the table.

François started toward her with a convulsive movement. But his physical forces seemed to fail the purposes of his will, he fell back heavily into an armchair, and could hardly stammer out, "Claire, it is I; I love you. Will you —"

He passed his hand over his forehead. His pale face flushed hot and red. His temples beat violently, he felt a strange compression in the head. Claire, almost beside herself with contending emotions, took his hands in hers; his skin was dry, and the pulse beat so violently as to alarm the poor girl. It was not thus that she had hoped to meet him. In a few minute's the symptoms of a violent bilious fever showed themselves. "What a pity," said Doctor Auvray, "that this fever had not attacked his uncle; it would have cured him!"

He rang; a servant came and Madame Auvray entered, whom François hardly recognised, so much was he overcome by the fever. it was necessary to put him to bed without delay. Claire offered her chamber. it was a pretty little room, with a bed with while curtains, and a few simple ornaments; on the mantlepiece was an onyx vase, the only present that Claire had accepted from her lover.

While they were giving the first cares to François, his uncle in a high state of excitement bustled about in the room, embracing his nephew, seizing Madame Auvray by the hand, and crying out at the top of his voice, "Save him, save him, quick! I do not want he should die. I shall make objections to his death; I am his guardian; I have the right to protest; I am his uncle, his guardian! If you don't cure him, they will say it is I that have killed him. But I take you to witness that I do not ask for his inheritance. I give all his estate to the poor. A glass of water, if you please, to wash my hands!"

They transferred him to the Infirmary. Here he became so violent that it was necessary to put on the strait waistcoat.

Madame Auvray and her daughter devoted themselves to the care of François. you may tell me if you will, that these two women saw in him, the one a son-in-law, the other a husband, but I believe that if he had been a stranger, he would have been nursed with equal care. St. Vincent de Paul only invented a uniform; there are sisters of charity in all ranks and all ages of women.

Seated night and day in the sick room, mother and daughter gave their spare moments to whispered conversation on their recollections and their hopes. They could not explain either the long silence of François, nor his sudden return, nor the occasion that had led him to the Avenue Montaigne. If he loved Claire, why had he waited three months? Did he need the malady of his uncle to introduce himself to M. Auvray? If he had forgotten his love, however, why not take his uncle to some other physician? There are enough of them at Paris. Perhaps he thought himself healed of his passion until it was revived by the sight of Claire—but no; for he had asked her hand in marriage before seeing her.

To all their questions François in his delirium gave answer. Claire, hanging over his lips, gathered up his least words; she commented upon them with her mother and with the doctor, who soon began to see the true state of the case. For a man practiced in unravelling the most confused ideas, and reading in the minds of insane persons as in a blotted book, the ravings of a feverish brain are an intelligible language. He comprehended how his patient had lost in part his reason, and how he had been the innocent cause of the insanity of his uncle.

Then began for Mademoiselle Auvray a new series of fears. François had been insane. Would the crisis that she had unconsciously provoked heal the patient? The doctor declared that the fever had the privilege of judging, that is, exterminating insanity: there are, however, no rules without exception; above all, in medicine. And supposing him fully recovered, were not relapses to be feared? Would M. Auvray consent to give his daughter to one of his patients?

"For myself," said Claire, smiling sadly, "I am not afraid: I would take the risk. It is I who have caused all his misfortunes—ought I not to console him? After all, the sum of his madness consisted in asking for my hand—he will have nothing to ask for the day when I shall be his wife—then we shall have nothing to fear. The poor boy was sick only from an excess of love: cure him of that, dear father, but not entirely. Let him remain mad enough to love me as I love him!"

"We shall see," replied M. Auvray. "Wait till the fever is over. If he is ashamed or vexed at having been ill; if I see him sad or melancholy after his recovery, I will not answer for him. If, on the contrary, he recollects his malady without shame or regret, if he speaks of it calmly, if he feels no repugnance at the sight of those who attended upon him during his illness, then I have no fear of relapses."

"And why, dear father, should he be ashamed of having loved to excess? it is a noble and generous frenzy that never enters into little souls. And why should he feel repugnance at the sight of those who nursed him during his illness? It is mother and I who have nursed him."

Alter six days of delirium, an abundant perspiration carried off the fever, and the patient entered on his convalescence. When he discovered himself in a strange chamber, between Madame and Mademoiselle Auvray, his first idea was that he was at the hotel of the *Quatre Saisons* in the main street of Ems. His weakness, his emaciation, and the presence of the doctor corrected the first impression: he recollected himself, but vaguely. The doctor came to his assistance. He administered to him the truth, but with prudence, as he would have measured out corporeal nourishment to an enfeebled body.

François commenced by listening to his own story as to a romance in which he played no part; he was another man, an entirely new man, and he came out from his fever as from a tomb. Gradually the gaps in his memory filled up. His brain was full of empty cases, which one by one seemed to receive their appropriate contents. Soon he became master of his mind, and entered into possession of the past. This cure was a work of science, and, more than that, of patience. Here was the admirable quality of M. Auvray's paternal cares. The excellent man had the very genius of greatness. The twenty-fifth of December, François, sitting up in bed, propped by a chicken broth and the half of an egg, related clearly, distinctly, without wandering, and without embarrassment, with no other emotion than that of a tranquil joy, his story for the past three months. Claire and Madame Auvray wept as they listened. The doctor pretended to be taking notes, but something else than ink fell upon the paper.

When the story was finished, the convalescent added, by way of conclusion: "Today, December 25, at three o'clock in the afternoon, I said to my excellent Doctor, my honoured father, M. Auvray, whose street and number I shall never again forget, 'Sir, you have a daughter.

Mademoiselle Claire Auvray. I met her this summer at Ems with her mother: I love her—she has given me proof that she loves me; and, if you are not afraid that I should again become insane, I have the honour of asking her hand from you."

The doctor nodded slightly, but Claire put her arms round the sick man's neck, and kissed him on the forehead. The same day M. Morlot, growing more calm, and freed from his strait waistcoat, rose at eight o'clock in the morning. On getting out of bed, he took his slippers, turned them inside out, examined them carefully, and then passed them over to the attendant, begging him to see if they did not contain thirty thousand *francs* of yearly income. It was only after receiving an assurance in the negative that he would consent to put them on. He combed himself during a full hall hour, constantly repeating that he did not wish it should be said that his nephew's fortune had passed upon his head. He then shook every article of clothing out of the window, having first carefully searched all the pockets before he would put it on. Being finally dressed, he asked for a piece of chalk, with which he wrote in capital letters on the walls of his room:

THOU SHALT NOT COVET THY NEIGHBOUR'S GOODS

Then he began to rub his hands with incredible vivacity, to convince himself that the property of François had not stuck to them. He then carefully scratched his fingers, counting them from the first to the tenth, for fear he should forget one of them. When M. Auvray made him his daily visit, he thought he was before a magistrate, and immediately requested to be searched. The doctor informed him that François was cured. The poor man asked if the money had been found. "If my nephew is going to leave the house, he will want his money. Where is it? I have not got it, unless it is in my bed!" And forthwith he turned his bed upside down before anyone could stop him. The doctor shook him by the hand as he went out. This hand he rubbed with scrupulous care. When they brought him his breakfast, he began by examining the napkin, the glass, the knife, the plate, constantly repeating that he did not want to eat up his nephew's estate. When he finished his meal, he washed his hands with care. "The fork was silver," he said; "I do not want any of that sticking to my hands."

M. Auvray, however, does not despair of curing him with time. Such maladies are most apt to yield to the efforts of science in the summer and autumnal months.

A Voyage in My Bed

I could not sleep. Hour after hour of intolerable weariness wore away, and found me still watchful and restless. My hands grew hot, and fever seemed to fill my veins as I tossed upon my bed. The very silence of the street seemed to assume a certain vacant monotony, and struck upon my senses with the apparent regularity of a tune. I grew maddened at this void of sound, and wished fervently for even the slightest noise to break the stillness. Then my brain began seeking for occupation. I endeavoured, with an earnestness and depth of thought worthy of a better aim, to define amid the surrounding darkness the limits of my room, and by that to regulate my own position.

Curiously enough, I had lost all perception, or rather remembrance of the exact position of my bed. I could not tell which was the head or which was the foot; and though I recollected distinctly all the features of the room, and knew in what direction the bed usually lay, I felt now as it I had suddenly been thrust into the chamber amid utter darkness, without the slightest clue to its shape or limits.

If I had had no recollection of the features of my room, I should not have been so puzzled. I should simply have considered myself as inhabiting for the moment a dark space of which I knew neither the shape nor boundaries. But the perfect and distinct image which was painted on my brain of each article of furniture which the room contained, and its precise locality as regarded every other article in that room, thrust itself so pertinaciously upon me that I could not avoid attempting to realise it.

Here, thought I, is the dressing-table, with two scent-bottles, one on either side—a silver shaving pot in the centre, and the razors and brushes lying on the end next to the window; there is the little bookshelf hanging at the further end of the room by red cords against the—But stay; where *is* the wall? How far off is it from me at this moment? Does it lie at a right or obtuse angle with my body as I am now placed?

Pshaw! the more; I try to reach that confounded wall, the more bewildered I become. It seems to be continually shifting its position; and when I think I have it firmly fixed in a certain position—lo! it suddenly strikes me that I am quite wrong, and that it lies in precisely an opposite direction. Well! Let that pass. Suppose we proceed with our inventory. Now I am quite positive as to the exact spot which is covered by that small round table with the books on it. When I arranged it this evening before getting into bed, I put it right between my bed and the window, and I recollect remarking at the time that it must be in the middle of the room, because its claw covered precisely the red medallion which forms the very centre of my Turkish carpet. Let me see—the carpet—carpet—hang it! where *is* the carpet? Why, as I live I cannot tell for my very life which is the ceiling or which is the floor; whether the carpet is above or below me!

Where am I? How am I? Have I been turned upside down, or has the world been suddenly reversed? Where is the floor? where the walls? where the window? I feel like Mahomet's coffin suspended in mid-air, and as if I was every moment about to be let go. How am I King? If I put my foot out of bed, what side will it be on? I try by feeling the posts of my bedstead to discover which is the head, but they are all four alike, and I can feel nothing but smooth sticks of wood. What am I to do? I shall go mad—stark staring mad—it I endeavour to solve these mysteries any longer.

There is but one resource left, and that is to make a grand effort, and—get up. Ay! but how? It is easy to say get up, but if one does not know where the floor is, how is one—Besides, there is such a weight on my chest that drags me back when I attempt to rise; and a most extraordinary fear has suddenly come over me, so that I do not think worlds would tempt me to get out of bed into the dark, fathomless void which encompasses me. it seems to me like making up one's mind to step off the edge of the world into space.

Ugh! what an effort! one leg out of bed and dangling over the dark void in which my couch is suspended. Shall I go on? Shall I trust myself any further? Ha! What's this? A carpet—the floor—what joy! My brain is suddenly revulsed with returning consciousness of locality, and I walk firmly across the dark room, scramble hastily into my clothes, and cramming my hat over my eyes, wander out through the door and down the stairs, with a sort of indistinct idea pervading my mind that a walk will do me good.

Do you know that I have lived in this house for four years, and it never before struck me that the balusters that line the stairs are made of rope—thick, twisted cables? but now for the first time I am conscious of the fact, and they quiver in my grasp as I go fumbling down the staircase.

How very cold the hall-door feels as I open it. How smooth and polished too. Why, it is marble—pure, white marble! I did not know that we were so luxurious. Pooh! nonsense; how stupid of me! To be sure it is marble—always was marble. Don't I recollect a year ago, when the pet monkey tried to scramble up the front, and failed because it was so smooth and slippery?

At last I am in the street. The cool fresh air blows over my temples, and fills me with a luxurious sense of languid pleasure. It must be near morning, for the stars are growing pale, and the eastern brim of the sky seems covered with the white leprosy of dawn. The city is as yet, however, still and silent as a desert, and my footsteps sound—no, by the by, it has just struck me that they do not sound. I feel as it I was walking upon some dull, elastic substance, and on looking down I discover for the first time that the streets are paved with India-rubber. What a great improvement this is! No more noise—no more rattling of carts, or trampling of horses; all living things will fleet by as swiftly and silently as a dream.

Three o'clock! tolled by the iron pulse of that old cathedral. How picturesque it looks half wrapped in shadow and jutting out its great stone elbows halfway across the narrow street. But the deuce! now that I think of it, I don't recollect ever seeing that cathedral before, though I suppose I have traversed this street five times a day for the last four years. How very strange! There is something very peculiar, too, about the aspect of all the other houses. I remember them well enough, but somehow, they don't feel quite the same. Oh! I suppose it is the twilight that deceives me; I have never been out so early before, and the shadows that precede the dawn are mocking me with mysteries. I will defy them; I will leave them soon behind. Rapidly, rapidly do the streets fleet by as I run along; bridges, churches, houses are past, and the country comes near. On still I run with unfailing breath and firm step, and milestone after milestone passes me by, until at last I stop. I am out of breath, and this seems a sweet place to rest in.

I see a road. it is cool and shady; the autumn tints are hovering half timidly upon the green threshold of summer, and the glossy leaves of the beech trees that line the path are beginning to look brown about the edges. There is no dust: a cool rain has fallen overnight, and the morning sun has not yet had time to swallow up the glittering drops that tremble on the leaves. The last primroses of the year blossom hardily amid the grassy banks that bound the highway, and seem as if they were determined to see the summer out. There is a fresh and delicate fragrance on the air; it is like the perfumed breath of some young virgin.

The road is still and silent; not a footprint is to be traced in the yielding soil which forms its surface. No one has passed this way yet; but there are indications that cannot be mistaken of someone's approach.

The sparrows suddenly whirr out of the hedge just where the road makes an angle; that rabbit, who has been for the last half hour coolly devouring his breakfast of rib-leaf by the roadside, erects his long ears—sits up on his haunches—listens attentively for a second or two, and then scampers off to his hole as if a weasel was at his heels. A moment more, and the dull echo of footsteps sounds along the damp soil; the next two persons turn the angle of the road and walk forward beneath the shadow of the trees. One is a girl, the other a man. The man, who walks first, is a tall, athletic fellow, with a thick neck and a bad scowling countenance. He is dressed in a loose fustian suit, and has a soiled red silk handkerchief knotted carelessly around his throat. He swings a short, heavy stick in his hand, and lounges on with the heavy, reluctant gait of the confirmed vagabond.

The girl follows him, her slender, delicate form bending beneath the weight of a heavy bag which she carries on her back. She must be either daughter or sister of the big, hulking fellow who walks before her, for though her face is beautiful and womanly, and it would be difficult to trace in those fair, patient features and deep-blue eyes any of the coarse sensuality which breathes in the face of her companion, yet there is an indescribable tone of resemblance spread over her entire form—a likeness if you will, but newly incarnated, elevated, purified.

Heavens! how one's blood boils to see that fair, delicate creature panting, struggling, sinking, under that cruel burden, while her huge gladiator of a father walks onward lazily, looking up at the sun-gleams that struggle through the trees, whistling indolently to himself snatches of old tunes, knocking off the heads of the roadside flowers as he passes with his heavy stick! By Saint Denis, if that silk-worm playing amid the leaves had not wound his delicate cords around me and fettered my limbs, I would seize the fellow by the throat, and choke the sluggish life out of him!

Poor girl! thou art faint indeed. Thy supple back is bent and bruised beneath thy cruel load. Thy knees tremble, and the round proportions of thy face are contracted into harsh painful lines with muscular exertion. She stops an instant to recruit her shattered strength. She leans her burden, still on her shoulders, against the green bank that hems in the road, while her thin hand wanders mournfully amid the cool grass and the primroses that blossom by her side. The wretch who accompanies her detects this movement by the sudden cessation of her light footsteps on the road. He turns round with a savage scowl.

"Curse you," he says, "what ails you now? Why don't you come on?"

"I am very faint and tired, father; indeed I am. Let me rest for a moment, and I will be quite ready."

O voice of woman! whether thou art laden with accents of anger, supplication, or pity; whether thou fallest on man's ear garmented with that deep scorn that riots secretly in thy nature, and which only *one* wrong can ever thoroughly arouse; or whether thou art robed in those low, mild words of consolation that rob charity of all its sting, and makes pity light to be borne; or whether thou comest fire-winged with passion, and clad in sighs that burn, yet do not kill; thou art the only music in nature that can satisfy the cravings of the soul—the only harmony that can move the rocks of man's being and deity his dreams!

As the girl uttered her excuse, she looked wistfully at the man, and made a motion of entreaty with her hand; but he was soulless—a savage that no melody could charm—and the sweet plaintive tones of her voice fell unheeded on his ear. He moved a step or two towards her, and raised his stick threateningly.

"Come, no shamming now, my lady; I'm not going to stand any of your nonsense; you ought to know me well enough by this time, I think. Get up this moment and come after me, or by — I'll—"

"What?"

The fellow started. His syllable was pronounced in a clear sonorous voice, that rang like the thrill of glass through the pure air, and for a moment it was a matter of doubt where it came from. The mystery, however, was solved the next instant, by the parting of the hedge that topped the bank behind, and the apparition of a young man in the gap.

He was very young, not more than nineteen; but there was fire in

171

his blue eyes, and determination in his full muscular lip.

"What?"

The syllable still seemed to linger on the air, and the brutal pedestrian still stood irresolutely in the centre of the road, with one foot advanced towards his daughter, the short stick poised threateningly in his hand, and his face turned with an air of vulgar astonishment and stupid wonder to the spot from which this sudden interruption had proceeded. And the girl was a picture. Lying against the dark green bank, her heavy load tottering and half-supported by her fragile shoulder; one delicate hand grasping a tuft of damp grass lightly, while her face was upturned to the stranger with a mingled look of wonder, fear, and admiration. Youth gazing upon youth! it was a harmony of life; and there in the pathway, with frowning brow and clenched hand, stood the Discord that made it beautiful!

"What I like," said the man at last, in a rough brutal voice, and slamming his hat over his eyes with what was meant to be an independent bang. "She's my daughter, and I'd like to see the man that would step between me and her."

With a look of ineffable disdain, the youth turned to the girl, and said, in a low, sweet voice:

"You are very weary. Let me carry that load for you until you are rested."

Then did the pair stare indeed at the stranger; but with what different eyes. To hear a gentleman—for such his dress and air betrayed him to be—offering to carry a filthy sack for a common beggar girl! Why, it was like the *Arabian Nights* acted in broad daylight, and on a country road!

The girl did not reply; but she looked at the stranger with one of those deep, wondering, grateful looks, which men seldom see more than once in a lifetime, and then she turned to her father.

"Come! none of this nonsense; the girl's able to do for herself, and if she isn't, it's time for her to learn. Here, Nan, you slut, get up at once; I'm in a hurry."

The girl rose from the bank with a deep sigh and an air of patient grief, and tried to walk onwards; but she had not tottered three steps, when, with a single bound, the stranger cleared the hedge, and stood in the road between father and daughter.

"The girl is faint with fatigue!" he cried, earnestly. "You cannot be so cruel as to insist upon her proceeding."

"Come, come, my chicken, I ain't going to stand any of your nonsense. You just leave my girl alone, will you?"

"But you will kill her! Have you no pity for your daughter? Look! I will send a servant with you, wherever you are going, it you will only let him carry that load."

"She shall carry it, by G—d!" said the man, with a sudden outburst of fun. "Out of the way, you whelp!"

The young man planted his feel firmly on the ground, looked full in the speaker's face with a clear and unwavering glance, and said simply:

"She shan't."

Then did the savage nature of the vagabond break out in all its power. The muscles of his face contracted; his throat swelled, and his veins grew almost black with passion. He took a step forward, and said, in a tone somewhat between a hiss and a growl:

"You'd better leave this place."

The young man smiled slightly, but did not move. Then, without another syllable being uttered by either, the struggle commenced. The girl laid down her load by the roadside, and knelt in the long grass to watch. Not a word was spoken; all was so silent that the birds in the boughs above scarce turned their heads to look at the deadly combat taking place beneath. It was a strange scene. So early in the morning, in that quiet country road, where one would expect to meet nothing but mild shepherdesses and their swains, to see two men battling silently for life; and in the long grass that lined the roadside, a fair girl kneeling, watching, fainting, praying, as the fight went on!

The youth was slender and lightly formed; but there was plenty of muscle in his round limbs, and his movements were as elastic and wary as those of a young panther. His antagonist was powerful, but heavy; and with greater strength, possessed less agility. The pair were well matched; and the struggle was intensely interesting, because it was equal.

With arms locked, and set teeth, through which the short gasping breath hissed as it went and came, the combatants struggled silently. Nothing was heard but the crunching of the gravelly soil as their feet dug into it in the effort, as it were, to grasp the earth. Several times the large man lifted the youth from off his feet, and swung him round with immense strength; but each time he preserved his balance with wonderful skill, and landed again on his legs, light and unshaken by the shock. He did not attempt for an instant to throw his antagonist, but evidently acted on the defensive, trusting to his own power of endurance to weary the other out.

And the large man did soon begin to show symptoms of fatigue. His efforts became each moment more rapid and convulsive, and his throat seemed to swell and his mouth to open with incipient exhaustion. His large hands appeared to be slipping now and then from their hold, though the next instant they tightened with fresh energy. But he cannot last. His breathing is thick, and his limbs are failing him. Now, youth, that championest the young! athlete in the arena of mercy! now, put forth all the strength that nature and thy cause can lend thee, and hurl the scoundrel to the earth! A grinding of feet into the loose gravel, a moment of terrible, infernal contest, and—Bravo! well done, young hero; thy opponent lies stunned, motionless, and bleeding on the path; and thou, fresh from victory, art bending over the fainting girl and whispering tenderly!

A few moments' interval, and the conquered man recovers his senses. He lifts his head slowly from the ground and looks round with an air of stupid bewilderment; he scarce knows where he is. Suddenly his eye lights upon the pair talking by the roadside—the youth and maiden. A scowl of intense hatred flits over his face, but it is mingled with fear. His coward nature, once subdued, dare not rise again against the victor. He strives to get up. Oh! if this cursed silkworm had not wound his impalpable fetters so inextricably around me, I would rush upon him and complete what the youth has only begun; but I am powerless as a slave.

The man arose and stood erect, with a scowl upon his face. The blood streamed across his cheek from a broad jagged cut in his temple, and he had the look of a demon who had been wounded by a god. He made a sign to the girl, savage and imperative, to follow him. She turned pale, and looked up into her protector's face. He told her to stay where she was, and not obey her father. But it seemed as if the latter held some invisible chain by which he dragged her to his side; for as he signed to her, she lifted up the heavy sack and commenced tottering towards him, despite the entreaties of the youth. She evidently walked against her will, for her eyes continually turned towards her champion with a sad, regretful glance.

Then as the young man saw her gradually, and step by step, drawn away from him, a change came over his whole bearing. His eye became preternaturally piercing and his form grew straighter and seemed to expand. He held out his arm, and pointed with his gathered fingers straight at the man's eyes. Then, as if by magic, the progress of the girl suddenly ceased. At the same instant, her father's form became rigid and motionless as a statue, while his eyes were gradually glazed over with a sort of lifeless him. After pausing for an instant to observe the effect of his spell, the youth seized the trembling girl in his arms, and parting the green screen of the hedge with one hand, bounded through the gap. The elastic branches, rustling, closed again; but between the fading blossoms of the laurels I could see two forms, with clasping arms, tread the green distance of a summer glade. The sunlight fell upon their hair, and trembled round them like a net of gold. Their eyes were turned on each other; their lips met. Oh! what would I not give to follow them beyond those dark shadows; but this silkworm!

The man stood straight before me in the road—a horrible effigy. He was frozen into stone, and every line of his garments seemed as hard and sharp as if it had been but freshly chiselled from the block. He looked as solid as the great Pyramid; staring, staring right into my heart with his cold lifeless eyes. Oh, it was horrible to be obliged to bear it! If I could only have moved. If I could only have touched him with the very tip of my little finger. but the chains of the silkworm were woven above, around, beneath me, and had twisted themselves into an iron lattice-work about my tongue.

I could not endure it any longer. I strained every muscle of my body to bursting; the foam gathered on my lips, and my eyes stood out in their sockets, burning and bloodshot; and yet, not a motion. Again, again I tried, and—yes; O joy! I heard the yellow fetters crack. They stretched, they glistened in the sun. In another moment, I should be able to dash that cursed stone man to the earth. One more effort; it was done. The wondrous filaments flew asunder with a sound like thunder, and I darted from my silken prison on the frozen effigy. I raised my hand to strike—

Oh-h-h! bless my soul! What's this? How I've hurt my hand! But where am I? Why this is my bed. And the Stone Man? There's the broad sunlight, too, gushing in at my windows. I suppose I was dreaming; yes, I must have dreamed something or other, but I don't know exactly what. But it's very late. I must make haste, or I shall be late for business. Betty-y-y!

175

Tommatoo

1: THE HOUSE BY THE STONE-YARD.

A fairy that had lost the power of vanishing, and was obliged to remain ever present, doing continual good; a cricket on the hearth, chirping through heat and cold; an animated amulet, sovereign against misfortune; a Santa Claus, without the wrinkles, but young and beautiful, choosing the darkest moments to leap right into one's heart, and drop there the prettiest moral playthings to gladden and make gay,— such, in my humble opinion, was Tommatoo.

As yet I do not ask the reader to agree with me; for over him I have this one great advantage,—I know who Tommatoo is. When, however, he makes her acquaintance also, hears her twitter round the house, beholds the flash of her large dusky-grey eyes, is wonder-struck at the marvellous twinkling of her ever-dancing little feet, he can take his choice of all the personifications with which I began this story, and I feel convinced that he will select the most beautiful to enrobe Tommatoo.

There is (or rather was, six years ago, when the incidents to be narrated took place,—but I shall narrate them in the present tense) a vast flat of land stretching along the New York shore of the North River, close to where Thirty-Second Street vanishes into a swamp, in which unborn avenues are supposed to be slowly maturing. Although yet in embryo, they are already christened, and city engineers have imaginative ground-plans hanging on their walls, where Twelfth and Thirteenth Avenues are boldly represented, with as much minuteness as Fifth or Sixth. Should, however, any sanguine person be led by those delusive maps to seek for such mythical thoroughfares, Ponce de Leon, after his pursuit of the Fountain of Youth, would not offer a more striking example of ill-success. On reaching the spot where imagination depicted the long perspective of rails, with crowded and

177

hurrying cars gliding smoothly to and fro, he would behold this vision of civic activity replaced by the dreary and mysterious waste I have spoken of, without even a sign-post pointing to the splendid future reserved for it by city surveyors.

This tract of land is perhaps the most melancholy and mysterious spot in the whole city. The different streets that cross the island pull up, as it were, suddenly on reaching this dreary place, seemingly afraid to trust themselves any further. The buildings that approach nearest to its confines are long, low ranges of fetid slaughter-houses, where on Sundays bloated butcher-boys lounge against the walls; and on week-days one hears through the closed doors the muffled blow, the heavy fall of the oxen within; the groan, and the hard-drawn breath; and then a red, sluggish stream trickles out from under the doorway and flows into the gutter, where hungry dogs wait impatiently to lap it up. The murderous atmosphere, these smells of blood, seem appropriate enough as one approaches this desolate locality.

A great plain of red, swampy clay is covered here and there with numberless huge, helpless beams of timber,—some floating like dead rafts in the stream, and chained to the bank; others high and dry, black-ening in the sun, and shadowing criminal-looking dogs that skulk in and out among them all day long. One or two immature piers jut out into the river here and there, and grimy sloops that seem to have no particular trade, unless it is to rot calmly at their moorings, lie along-side, and grate and chafe lazily against the slimy logs. A few homeless boys, with smeared faces and thin, starved arms, who seem to have dressed themselves in the rags and kite-tails that flutter on telegraph-wires, lie on the sunny sides of the timber piles sleeping away hunger, or sometimes sit on the edges of the green piers languidly fishing for something which they never catch.

Cinders most unaccountably prevail all over the place; they crackle under the feet, and the dogs gather round occasional piles of them, growling over a burned bone lying in the ashes: where they come from is not to be known. There are no houses, no factories, and the rotting sloops are so damp and (slimy) that it would be a mockery to suppose a fire had ever been lit in any one of them. Nevertheless, the cinders prevail; and at certain hours in the day two or three crouching creatures wander slowly among the heaps, picking mysterious objects, with hands that seem themselves to have been burned into coke.

The place is also a species of morgue for dead dogs. Every cur that the Hudson drowns floats inevitably to this spot and is swept up on the swampy bank,—when the outlawed mongrels that skulk between the timber logs crowd around it, and perhaps identify the corpse. On Sundays, you see a few low-browed, soap-locked loafers strolling among the piles, pitching stones into the water, and, if it is summer, stripping off their tattered shirts to have a swim; but on week-days the place is entirely dead. The starved boys and the shadowy rag-pickers flitting here and there give no air of life; they seem very thin and impalpable, and haunt the place like ghosts.

Further on this dreary swamp changes somewhat its character. The great balks of timber disappear, and a few shingle huts—so loosely built that the wind whistles through their walls with a shriek of triumph—are scattered here and there. Large masses of stone lie about, hewn into square blocks for house-fronts, and in the daytime the monotonous click of the stone-cutter's chisel shrills continually from the shingle huts. This straggling stone-yard, for such it is, is perhaps less desolate than the swamp further down, but at night—when the moon streams on the huge white blocks that lie there so cold and dead, and the huts are deserted by the workmen, and nothing moves but a shadowy dog that flits by, seen for an instant against the pallid stones—the place is inexpressibly weird and lonely.

Just on the confines of this stone-yard, in a rutty, half-made road that is bounded on both sides by burned-looking building-lots, where nothing hides the scalded earth but some unhealthy boulders, and occasional remnants of old shoes that are black and pulpy with decay, stands a small house built of unpainted shingles. It is two-storeyed, with a basement, and a somewhat imposing flight of steps up to the door; yet it wears a reckless and despairing aspect. I have no doubt when this house was built it had many youthful hopes of establishing a neighbourhood and becoming a dwelling of respectability. It promised itself, perhaps, a coat or two of paint, and had visions of being the ancestor of a street. But year after year wore away, and it found itself still naked as when it was born.

No companion dwelling lifted its head to cheer the solitude. On all sides, the bleak river-winds tousled and smote its bare walls until its windows chattered with the cold. It grew weary of waiting for the neighbourhood that never was to come, and seemed to care no longer what became of it. It let beardy mosses grow all over its haggard face. Its edges were chipped and ragged; its chimneys, no longer spruce and tapering, bulged and tottered to one side, like the crushed hat of a confirmed drunkard. It buttoned itself up no more about the

179

chest with its snug, comfortable doors, but let them hang loose on one hinge, and flap about in the wind. It was evident to anyone who saw it that the house near the stone-yard had gone to the bad.

Forlorn and seedy as it looked, this house was inhabited. The shivering, shrunken windows gleamed with lights by night, yet not cheerfully, but with a wild glare, like that which streams from the eyes of those about to die. If the skulking men that prowled in summer evenings among the sheds of the stone-yard, whistling mysteriously to each other, had any taste for music, the house would have been to them a source of great wonder. Sometimes for hours together a wild and mellow music would stream upon the air, soaring over the dreary yard, wailing sadly along the waste river-grounds and by the rotting sloops until it reached the water, when it would float triumphally along, as if it knew that it was leaving the desolate place behind it, and bury itself deep in the sleeping groves that nodded on the distant Weehawken heights. The character of these melodious sounds was entirely mystical and strange. They were not born of violin or bugle, and yet seemed to have the souls of both instruments intermingling with another distinctly their own;—another soul, not merely instrumental, but human, passionate, luxuriant, as if all the utterances of a great Italian love—desire, entreaty, and triumph—were translated into aerial harmonies.

To you and I, reader, there need be no mystery in either house or music. That despairing-looking *chateau* was inhabited but by three people,—an old man, a young girl, and a youth of about twenty-one. As age is entitled to its traditional homage of precedence, I will first introduce to you the elder of the trio. I beg to present to your notice the maestro, Baioccho.

You could not possibly conceive a man made up with less waste of material than Signor Baioccho. Nature, when she formed him, must have been terribly short of stuff. There was too little of everything in his physical composition. He was abbreviated in every limb and feature. This, nevertheless, was fortunate, for had he been on a large scale he would have been insupportably ugly; he was too small, however, to be repulsive, and so was only queer. But how queer he was, with his withered, pinched-up face, his sparse, stiff beard, which looked like a thin growth of thorns, and his quaint, convulsed figure, that gave one the idea that all inside of him was catgut and wheels, and that something was continually breaking in his machinery! Yet, with all this likeness to a comic toy, how inexpressibly mournful was the countenance of Signor Baioccho! what terrible sorrow was hopelessly shut up in that wretched little frame!

Baioccho had been a musician, and was now a cook. Years ago, when opera was young in New York, Baioccho came here from Italy with a company, set up an opera-house, was instantly successful, and made a fortune. Music was his religion, the lyric stage his temple, the conductor's desk his altar, the overture his mass. But he became a fanatic in his faith. He enlarged his house; he spent thousands of dollars on the production of new operas, and, as a matter of course, he became bankrupt. For the opera is like a Parisian mistress, the most charming, fascinating, bewildering of all creations, and invariably leaves you without a shilling at last. For many years poor Baioccho struggled to keep his feet. He led orchestras at second-rate theatres; he gave lessons on the piano and violin, always hoping, always dreaming of one day grasping again the magical baton, the sceptre of his world.

It was a vain struggle, however; other **maestri** came over from Italy with still more wondrous and expensive singers than those Baioccho brought, and they built opera-houses, and bought newspaper puffs, and covered the dead walls with huge announcements of colossal successes; and the world, rushing on the heels of novelty, swept over the ancestor of American opera, and poor Baioccho found himself trampled on, bruised, and left to die. It were too sad a task to enumerate the various steps which led Baioccho from Parnassus to the kitchen. An accomplishment of which in his palmy days he had been not a little proud, was now brought into requisition to save him from starvation; the hand that was too weak to hold the baton found itself still able to brandish the ladle.

Those gay Italian tenors, those majestic *bassos*, little thought when, round his elegant supper-table long ago, they used to applaud his amateur cookery, delicious mayonnaises, harmonious salads, that the day would arrive when the poor conductor would don the white apron and cotton cap very seriously, and sweat all day in a restaurant kitchen through an eternal round of soups and roasts and *entrees* ever the same. But so, it was. Those who frequented Calcar's Restaurant would now and then behold a wizened little man stealing quietly from some mysterious passage leading to the kitchen, and sneaking up to the bar, where he would hastily swallow a potent draught of raw brandy, and shuffle back guiltily to the place whence he came. And they would see one or two old New-Yorkers looking pitifully after him, and saying to each other that they remembered poor Baioccho when he drove his carriage. He now trudged home every night on foot; and it was sad to see the old fellow, unsteady with drink, staggering down the rutty road to the house near the stone-yard, where the faithful Tommatoo kept watch until she heard his stumbling footstep, when, tripping to the door, she tenderly helped him up to bed.

So! we have come at last to Tommatoo. I have been longing to get to her for some time past, but it would have been unkind to have deserted old Baioccho now that he is so poor. Salutation to his misfortunes!

Tommatoo was Baioccho's only child. In some quaint old Italian chapel, it may be by the shores of Sorrento, a smiling babe was one sunny day christened by the stout old *padre*, and the name bestowed was Tomasina. Melodious as was this pretty name, the little girl that bore it, as soon as she reached lisping age, obstinately refused to be known by any cognomen but that of Tommatoo. This sounded awfully heathenish to old Baioccho, but she was apparently determined, and in time her imperious infant will had its effect on the family. She became Tommatoo to all intents and purposes, as far as household experience went, and even when she grew up to the age of reason did not seem anxious to reclaim her original appellation.

Tommatoo was one of those lovely, fair-haired Italians that one sees so seldom, but which once seen are never forgotten. At some antique period, when Alaric was king, some of the blood of his blonde race must have mingled with the olive-skinned Roman Baiocchi, and after centuries of rest suddenly bloomed in Tommatoo. Her eyes were a dark liquid grey, like a twilight lake. Her face was pale, yet not cold, for a southern fire seemed to smoulder beneath the skin, with a beautiful, subdued glow. Her mouth, small and moist and rosy, pouted over pearly teeth, half seen, and the curves of her smooth cheeks swept into a wickedly dimpled chin, that aided and abetted with all its might the criminal beauty of her bewildering lips. This sweet virginal face was set in a golden frame of luxuriant hair, that one of Raphael's saints might have envied.

Yet why speak of Tommatoo's beauty so rapturously? I shall have no enthusiasm left for that bright and joyous nature that burst from her as the sun bursts from a golden cloud, shedding its own lustre on everything, and infusing into all a portion of its own innate warmth. Everyone has felt at times, when wandering through the fields, the intense joy experienced from the twittering of the birds amidst the branches and the glancing of their tiny forms through the leaves.

Some such pure and healthy influence did Tommatoo exercise over the little household. She twittered and sung, and, as it were, fluttered lightly through the rooms, until one could swear that the sun shone wherever she went. All day, while old Baioccho was absent attending to his culinary duties, compounding wondrous soups, and moving amidst the thick steams of the kitchen like an elf in some incantation scene, Tommatoo was putting the old house in order; sweeping up the little sitting-room, displaying its scanty furniture to the best advantage, and occasionally darting like a swallow into Mr. Gustavo Beaumont's sanctum sanctorum.

It must be confessed that this was one of the household occupations that Tommatoo performed with the greatest willingness; for Mr. Gustavo Beaumont was young, handsome, and played the most delightful melodies on his great instrument, invented by himself, entitled the Pancorno. The Pancorno was a singular piece of mechanism, hideously suggestive, in appearance, of some nameless instrument of torture from the dungeons of the Inquisition, yet in reality capable of soothing the most agonizing pains by the sweetness of its notes. By aid of some interior arrangement of tubes, the vibrations of the horn portion acted in turn upon what must have been a series of wires also concealed, and which seemed to give the effect of a trio between flute, violin, and French-horn. It was from the Pancorno that the seraphic strains heard at night across the stone-yard floated so harmoniously, giving to the old house an air of being one of those enchanted abodes frequent in fairy tales, in which dwelt some spellbound prince, who thus summoned in music his faithful knights to his rescue.

Gustave was a clever young Frenchman, with an extraordinary passion for music, whom old Baioccho had known ever since he was a child. He was the son of the *bassoon* in one of the orchestras which the *maestro* had conducted in his palmy days; but one night the bassoon died in the middle of a rapid passage, and the little Gustave was left without a father, and but one friend, Baioccho. The old Italian took the *bassoon's* son home, brought him up as his own child along with Tommatoo; and when his fall came Gustave still shared his scanty means. To do the young fellow justice, he wanted to work, but the old man would not have it. "You are a genius, Gustave," he would say, "and, please the Virgin, you shall do something great."

So, Gustave did nothing great or small save the invention of the Pancorno, out of which he expected to reap a fortune, and he continued to live at the house by the stone-yard, having first scrupulously bargained with his entertainer to pay three dollars a week, which, as he did nothing but play on the Pancorno and make love to Tommatoo, it is needless to say he never earned and never paid. It quieted his conscience, however, and he used to say to himself that when he sold his invention for one hundred thousand dollars, that being the least he would take for it, old Baioccho should live like a prince.

And this is the last of the inmates of the house by the stone-yard.

2: A Family Group

"Is that you, father?"

"Ah, the little Tommatoo! So, you maintain the watch for the poor old father? Bless you, little angel!"

"Take care of the step, father. Take care."

"Put yourself easy, my child. I will be remindful of the step. I am very steadfast on my feet this evening."

And, as if to falsify his testimony, poor old Baioccho staggered up the steps leading to the hall-door, and would have fallen if Tommatoo had not caught one of his thin arms and held him up.

"It is nothing; it is nothing!" he exclaimed, as he tottered through the hall into the little parlour. "I can walk myself well enough. But it is the kitchen,—that dam kitchen! It has got into my head, my child. Where is the cognac?"

"Do you think it would do you any good, father?" asked Tommatoo, sorrowfully; "won't it make your head bad?"

"Ah, little dove! It does not comprehend. My child, the cognac is the life to me. When I stew and form dishes and mingle soups all day long in that dam kitchen, it gets into my head; and sometimes, *mon Dieu!* when I stand over the *ragout*, and try to forget the place where I have found myself for a moment, the old times return upon me and I become very sad and sorrowful, so that I have to walk myself out to the bar and drink the cognac; and then, *per baccho!* I remember myself not, and I go back to my kitchen quite raised. Give me one little glass of cognac, my child?—one glass for the poor old father!"

Tommatoo fluttered over to a little cupboard that stood on one side of the room, and brought out a bottle and a wine-glass, and, pouring out some brandy, handed it to the old man.

He raised it tremulously to his mouth, and quaffed it off' at a single draught; then, smacking his lips, he muttered, "Ah! the cognac is the soul to the old men like me!"

There was nothing disgusting in Baioccho's intoxication. The in-

184

ebriety of the old musician was as cleanly as the tipsiness of a toy-man—had such been possible. His little eyes only twinkled the bright-er, and his nose seemed longer and sharper and thinner, and his lips moved more rapidly; but that was all. His speech was not thick, nor were his ideas clouded. It was drunkenness idealised.

"What has my child to tell me of the day?" asked the old man, invigorated as it were by the *petit verre de cognac*.

Tommatoo drooped her eyelids, coloured a little, and did not reply for a moment.

"Someone has been here," she said, at last.

"Which was it, little one?"

"It was—it was—" And the little one faltered.

"*Diable!*" cried the old man, leaping like an enraged cat from his chair, as if an idea had flashed upon him suddenly. "Ten millions of devils! was it not that brute Giuseppe?"

"It was, father," answered Tommatoo, soothingly. "Pray, don't fly into a rage. I could not help it."

"The wretch! the abandoned-by-God miserable fellow!" shouted old Baioccho, growing more and more excited each moment. "So, he must place himself near my child, my angel, to steal her away from me! But we will see! What did he say to you?" he added, turning almost fiercely to Tommatoo.

"O, nothing more than what he has said to you. He said he loved me very much, and if I would marry him that he would take us all back to Italy, and that you should end your days in comfort."

"O, the serpent! His mother and his grandfather were snakes! You know not that man, Tommatoo! He is capable of roasting his father on a spit!"

"But, dear father, you know I hate him. I will never marry anyone but Gustave, and not that until you wish it. I laughed at Giuseppe, and told him to go away." And Tommatoo made an ineffectual attempt to give some idea of her stern manner to Giuseppe; but if the reality was at all like the representation, I don't think that the descendant of snakes was very much crushed.

"Ah, child! you are as innocent as the flower that grows under our feet!" and Baioccho looked down, but, finding no flowers, continued: "He will perform some mischief to us. I feel it in—in the air!" and the sharp eyes seemed to pierce into the depths of the gloomy room, and fasten on some spectral misfortune. "Now Gustave is a good boy. He will be a great man. His Pancorno shall be played in many universal cities, and the good fortune shall come to him. Thou shalt be the wife of Gustave, my small pet child!"

"But," said Tommatoo, with a half-smile, "I think he loves his Pancorno better than he does me."

"It is the love of the artist, *mignonne*. He loves it with his soul, but his heart—ah, that is thine!"

"Hark! there he is!" cried Tommatoo, hushing her father into silence as the liquid, delicious notes of the Pancorno stole through the house.

"Yes, let us listen. heaven, how beautiful!" exclaimed the old musician, rapturously; then in a half-whisper added, "One little glass more of the cognac, *ma biche*."

And there they sat in the dusk of the room, the old man warming his veins with the cognac, the young girl dreaming of her lover, and both listening to the music that bore them far away, out of the old house by the stone-yard, into a delicious land, where the sea lay like a mistress on the broad breast of the beaches, and the breath of the orange groves wandered like unheard music through the slopes and valleys.

"I think so of my home," murmured the old *maestro*, and I know that a tear fell through the twilight as he spoke,—"of my dear, dear home when I hear the music. Ah! why does not my brother—the brother of my youth—replace me in my dear Italy? He is more rich than a great many of Jews, and yet he will not spare his poor brother one *scudo*, Tommatoo. O, if I were the rich Pietro, and he the poor cook Giulio Baioccho, I would not count my *zechins* until he had what he wanted. If he would only promise to leave my little Tommatoo something when he died, I would not care for myself. Ah, the bad brother! *Mignonne*, one other little *verre de cognac* for the poor old cook."

"Shall I go and tell Gustave that you have come home?" asked Tommatoo. "We must have supper soon, you know, father."

"Do, my beloved. Sweet as are the notes of the Pancorno, thy voice is sweeter still. Go and gladden the good Gustave with its music."

Tommatoo tripped to the door, perched for a moment on the threshold like a little bird hovering on the edge of its cage, then, after looking back into the dusky room with a radiant smile that seemed to illuminate the twilight, she vanished, and in a few moments the notes of the Pancorno ceased, and there were light, pattering footsteps heard in its stead.

The old musician, when she was gone, buried his head in his hands, and seemed lost in meditation ;—so lost that he neither heard nor saw anything around him ;—neither the footsteps that came softly toward him through the gloom, nor the tall cloaked form that stood beside him, until a hand laid on his shoulder startled him from his reverie, and he looked up.

"Who is that?" he asked, with a sort of astonished abruptness, as he in vain tried to distinguish the newcomer's features through the darkness.

"It is I,—Giuseppe," answered the figure in a very calm voice, and in Italian.

"What dost thou here again, outcast?" cried the old *maestro*, starting from his seat hurriedly and in great agitation. "I tell thee that thou shalt never wed my daughter. I know thee well. I know of thy prison life. I know of that bloody affair, in Venice, when even the sacred stole of the priest could not shield his heart from thy accursed hand. Begone! or I will call for help, and have thee lodged in the jail."

"Come, come, Baioccho, no need of all this bad language. You wrong me, I swear you wrong me. I am not the man you take me for, nor do I wish to press my suit with Tommatoo. I come for other ends. I bear great tidings to thee. I bring thee great riches."

"Ah, boaster, you will not cajole me with your fine words!" cried the old cook, mockingly.

"If I do, may I forget my mother's grave!" exclaimed Giuseppe, earnestly. "Walk with me for ten minutes along the road, and if I prove not my words thou shalt never see my face again."

In spite of his detestation of his fellow-countryman Baioccho could not prevent his heart from leaping to his mouth at the mention of wealth. In a moment, he saw himself emancipated from the accursed kitchen, his Tommatoo clad as became her beauty, Gustave's Pancorno brought before the public, and all three living happily in the dear Italy, making a music out of life itself.

"Well," said he, "I will go and walk with you. But why not tell it here?"

"Because houses are less safe to speak in than the universe," said Giuseppe. "You forget that I was once a conspirator, and am cautious."

"I remember it well enough," muttered Baioccho, as both left the house, "and the police of Venice remember it better."

They walked slowly toward the stone-yard. Neither spoke,—Baioccho disdaining to show any impatience, Giuseppe remaining silent for some motive of his own. So on through the stone-yard; amidst the white blocks that loomed like dim ghosts through the darkness; by the shingle huts that, with their jagged corners and irregular roofs, seemed in the darkness to crouch like strange animals, squatting upon the dreary earth; over rough masses of unhewn stone, through deep ruts left by cart-wheels in the soft clay, until they reached the river.

"Well," said Baioccho, at last, "how long am I to wait for this wondrous intelligence?"

"Your brother is dead," answered Giuseppe.

"What!" almost shrieked the old cook, "and—and—he left—"

"You everything."

"Holy Virgin be praised!" ejaculated the poor old fellow, clasping his hands and kneeling in the damp, oozy earth. "My dear Tommatoo will be rich,"

"I have just arrived from Italy," continued Giuseppe. "I saw your brother. I found him dying. I spoke to him about you, and induced him to will to you the fortune which he was going to leave to the Church. Do you not think I deserve some reward for all this?"

"You shall have it. I swear it!" cried the old musician, fervently. "You shall name your own reward."

"Good. I want your daughter."

"Ah, traitor! that is what you demand!" cried the excitable old man in his shrill voice. "Never! never! never! No; you shall have money, but no Tommatoo,—no Tommatoo."

"Tommatoo is your heir at law when you die," remarked Giuseppe.

"Certainly. I know why you want to wed with her, you fellow!"

"She will inherit very soon."

"Eh!" The old man did not exactly seem to comprehend, but peered up into Giuseppe's face.

"She will come into possession in ten minutes," added Giuseppe, and rapidly as lightning he passed a sort of handkerchief across Baioccho's mouth, stifling all utterance. The old man, though thin, possessed a great tenacity of muscle, and he struggled long and vigorously against his assailant. He twined about his legs, he crawled up his huge chest, he dug his bony fingers into his throat, all the while uttering through the gag upon his mouth terrible muffled cries of agony that were more dreadful from their being so suppressed. The youth and strength of Giuseppe told at last. The old man grew faint and almost ceased to struggle. In an instant Giuseppe seized him by the waist, lifted him clear off the ground, and swung him into the river. He watched him sink. "I think that Tommatoo is mine now," he muttered, as he turned and fled rapidly back through the stone-yard.

Baioccho sank, but speedily came to the surface. Instinctively he stretched out his hands, and suddenly one of them came in contact with some floating substance. He grasped it, and found it a drifting beam of timber that had become loosed from its moorings to the bank and was travelling with the stream. With some difficulty, he got astride of it and removed his gag. His first impulse was to shout for help, for he could not swim, and he was already some distance from the bank, and he put all his strength into a furious cry. The sound of his own voice echoing over that desolate shore seemed to tell him how little chance he had of obtaining assistance in that way, and, after shouting until his lungs were sore, he gave it up, and clung to the hope of being picked up by some boat.

The tide was running out rapidly, and a wind was blowing downstream, so that Baioccho could tell from the rippling of the waves around the beam that he was floating fast with the current. It was very dark. On either side of the bank he could see the faint lights in the houses, and now and then the black spectral hull of some sloop or schooner would suddenly appear to him as he floated past, and then vanish. All on the river seemed dead. There was not a sound of life. There did not seem a hope for the old musician.

Still he floated fast. Past the dreary black wharves, round which vessels made palisades of masts seen dimly against the dull sky. Past the shadowy groves of the Elysian Fields, that now, alas it seemed like the banks of Acheron. Past the cheerful Atlantic Gardens, where lights gleamed on the water, and people were making merry, while the poor old musician was floating to his death. Past the great hive of the city, that in the gloom seemed to lie upon the water exhausted with its day's labour. And so, on out into the broad bay. Then for the first time Baioccho felt that he would be swept out to sea. He had not recoiled from his fate up to this time, for he was brave, and, after all, drowning was only death. But starvation—ah! that thought was too horrible, and for the first time a groan escaped from the poor musician. He then thought of Tommatoo, of Gustave, of their agony at his never returning,—their vague sorrow for his fate, which would never be known. Then he prayed to God that the murderer, Giuseppe, would be baffled in his designs on his dear child,— and then—

A dull, roaring sound along the water. A hissing of the air and of the sea. A red glare from what seemed like a fierce angry eye moving over the waves. A sparkle of foam, seen white through the gloom, and Baioccho saw the ferry-boat bearing right down on him. He shouted; he tried to stand upright on the timber log, but it slipped and turned; he took off his coat and flung it high in the air,—all to attract attention. But in vain. Closer, closer came the fiery eye. With what seemed to the old musician ever-increasing speed the sharp prow cut through the water. The funnel gave out short puffs of triumph, the wheels beat their paddles madly on the water, as if they knew what work they had to do, then a sudden, awful shriek from Baioccho. The projecting ledge of the boat shot over him. He touched it for an instant with his hand, and then went under.

3: THE GRANDSON OF SNAKES.

"Father, Gustave will be down in a few minutes, and we will have supper!" cried Tommatoo, fluttering into the dark room like some pretty little nocturnal bird. "Father! why don't you answer? Why, where can he be? Ah, that cognac! He has perhaps taken too much while I was away,—poor father!" and Tommatoo hastily lit, with a lucifer match, a little fluid lamp, and held it high above her head while her eyes everywhere sought the expected recumbent form of the old musician.

"Why, he is not here!" she cried, in a tone half of astonishment, half of alarm. "O, where has he gone? Not out into this dark, dark night. God forbid! I will call Gustave";—and she ran toward the door of the apartment. But ere she quite reached it she stopped and drew back, for a tall, dark figure filled the little doorway, and a pair of bright sinister eyes reflected back the lamplight.

"Ah, pretty one! you did not expect to see me again today, did you?" said the newcomer, in a half-mocking tone, and in Italian; "but you see how it is: I am fascinated, and haunt the spot where I will find you."

"Signor Giuseppe, my father does not wish you to come here; you know what I think, and yet you come. That I think is wrong";—and Tommatoo looked like a moralist of the Middle Ages, if one could imagine such a personage with beautiful blond hair, large dark-grey eyes, and the neatest little waist in the world.

"Ah! none of you appreciate me," answered Giuseppe, advancing into the chamber. "Your father is a good man, but full of prejudices. I am progressive, and he does not understand progress,—that is all. But I am a good fellow, *signorina*,—a capital fellow for all that."

He looked at this moment, standing close to the door and un-clasping his heavy cloak, with his pale, unhealthy skin shining in the lamplight, and his eyes glistening with a furtive meaning, so truly the reverse of a good fellow that I am not surprised at the faint frown that perched for a moment on Tommatoo's forehead, and then suddenly slid off her smooth temples and was lost.

"I am going, Signor Giuseppe," she said, making a movement to-ward the door, between which and her the Italian was standing. "I wish you good evening."

"Stay a moment!" he cried, interposing. "Where is the worthy Baioccho?"

"He is not here. I do not know where he is. Let me pass, *signor*. I am going to search for him."

"Perhaps he has taken too much of the delightful cognac of which he is so fond," said Giuseppe, sneeringly.

"My father is a good man, *Signor!*" cried Tommatoo, indignantly, "and his weaknesses should be respected. Let me pass, sir!"

"Not just yet, little one. I have something to say to you. You know that I love you. I told you so three months ago, before I went to Italy. I tell you so now that I have returned."

"I do not want to hear your confession, *signor*. I wish to go and seek my father."

"Listen to me, Tommatoo,"—and he stretched his long arm across her till it fell like a great bar between her and the door. "Listen. If you become my wife, this is what I will do for you. I will take you to Italy, and you shall have a villa that the Prince Borghese might envy. We will have much money,—I shall be very rich indeed,—and all Italy shall not contain finer horses, carriages, servants, than ours. I will be mag-nificent, Tommatoo, gorgeous, princely. Perhaps, too, I will purchase a patent of nobility,—it is to be done; there's the banker Torlonia. And how would my Tommatoo like to sit in state and be called Princi-pezza? Ah! it would be glorious, would it not?"

So excited was he with the visions he had himself conjured up that Giuseppe stretched forth his arms, and, enclosing Tommatoo between them, drew her toward him, while a devilish glitter shone in his dark eyes.

"We are alone, sweet dove," he said, in a soft voice; "none in this silent house to watch us. Will you not vow to be my bride,—the bride of Giuseppe that loves you so, and who will make you a little coun-tess? Ah! the little one is not so cruel after all."

But he mistook Tommatoo's terrified immobility for a timid though undemonstrative assent. To his utter astonishment, after a moment's silence, that young lady opened her mouth and shrieked, "Gustave! Hasten! Gustave, I am in danger!" with all the power of an excellent set of lungs,

"Whew! who the devil is Gustave?" muttered Giuseppe, astounded. "I thought that none lived in the house but those two. Who the devil is this Gustave?" And as he spoke he thrust his hand inside his coat as if feeling for some weapon.

There was an immediate response to Tommatoo's call, in the shape of the descent of a pair of boots four stairs at a time. In a few seconds, the boots had reached the door, and Gustave Beaumont, who stood in them, suddenly appeared on the scene of action.

"*Diavolo!*" ground Giuseppe between his teeth, as he beheld this new apparition. Then, taking a stride backward, he seemed like some wild animal preparing for a spring.

"*Qu'est ce que c'est? Qu'est ce que ce Monsieur la?*" rapidly demanded Monsieur Gustave, looking rather ominously at Giuseppe, who, not understanding a word of French, preserved a grim silence.

"Gustave! this man persecutes me. Protect me from him!" cried Tommatoo, bounding toward the young Frenchman and taking shelter as it were under his wing.

"*Soyez tranquille, enfant!*" said Gustave, fondly enfolding her little form with his arm. "What the devil you do here, sare," he continued, in English, seeing that Giuseppe had not replied to his previous interrogatories in French. "For why do you bring the fright to this young girl, sare? Who you are, sare? I demand to know. *Moi!* Gustavo Beaumont!"

"I reply myself not, sir, to your interrogations, when they put themselves to me in a manner so insolent," answered Giuseppe, haughtily, his eyes flashing through the gloom of the half-lit chamber.

"Ask him about our dear father, Gustave," cried Tommatoo, earnestly, nestling up to the young musician's side. "I left him here a few moments since, and he has disappeared. I feel sure that this bad man knows something of him. Ask him, dear Gustave."

"One cannot know about all the world," answered Giuseppe, before Gustave had time to interrogate him. "My business is not with the old man. Look in the cellar where the strong waters are kept. He will be there."

With a mocking laugh the Italian folded his cloak around him and strode toward the door. Gustave removed his arm from Tommatoo's waist, round which it had stolen, and placed himself resolutely between Giuseppe and the door, and barred his passage.

"You shall not depart from here until we know about Signor Baioccho. You are suspected a great deal."

"Let me pass away from here," cried Giuseppe, advancing savagely, "or, by the head of the Virgin, you will meet with misfortune!" And placing his hand in his breast he half drew a small poniard.

Gustave saw the motion, and quick as thought sprang on the Italian, weaving his young, sinewy arms around his waist, and pressing his chin against his antagonist's breast until he fairly howled with pain. Tommatoo, with one faint moan, sank on her knees on the ground, and one might see, by the clasped hands and the murmuring lips, dimly shown in the imperfect lamp-light, that the little one was offering up her prayers to heaven.

The pair now struggling were evenly matched as far as youth and size. But in point of endurance the Italian had decidedly the advantage. The sedentary life which the young Frenchman led had relaxed his naturally powerful muscular system; and consequently, although capable of a vast momentary effort, he was entirely unable to sustain a prolonged contest. For the space of two minutes nothing was heard in the room but the hard breathing of the struggling men; the slipping of the feet on the uncarpeted floor; the sudden stamp, as one sought an advantage which the other as quickly frustrated. Gustave's main object seemed to be to keep the Italian from using his poniard, and this he sought to effect by pressing him so closely in his arms as to render it an impossibility to use his hands.

For some time, he was successful in this; but presently his want of tenacity of muscle showed itself in the relaxation of his grip and the quick recurrence of his breaths, almost amounting to panting. Inch by inch Giuseppe loosened his arm from the Frenchman's grasp, and inch by inch his hand moved toward his breast where the poniard lay, his eyes all the while flashing with a light that seemed to announce his approaching vengeance. In vain did Gustavo strain every nerve to hold his own. The large drops of sweat gathered on his forehead; the blood flowed from between his lips, bitten in the agony of exertion; and his knees fairly shook with the power of a will that far exceeded the strength of the frame on which it was exercised. He could not last much longer. Giuseppe, in proportion as he beheld his adversary sinking, seemed to gain additional force. He at length extricated his arm.

At length, he grasped the poniard and plucked it from its sheath. Held aloft an instant over Gustave's head, it quivered in its descent; when, with a dull, heavy thud, some enormous weight fell on the back part of the Italian's head, the dagger was dashed from his hand, and he fell stunned and senseless on the floor.

"Sweet child, my life owes itself to you!" said Gustavo, as he stood over the prostrate form of his antagonist, while he gazed with intense astonishment on Tommatoo, who, revealed to him by the Italian's fall, exhibited herself as the agent of that lucky event, assisted by an enormous bludgeon which she held in her hand.

"It was an inspiration of heaven, I think," said she simply. "I was praying to the Virgin, when I recollected that papa's big stick was in the corner; so I stole toward it, lifted it up, and struck that bad fellow with it,—only I did not think I could strike him so hard. I hope he is not very much hurt." And she looked pityingly down on the villain whom a moment before she would have gladly seen perish.

"*Cré nom de Dieu!* He moves himself!" cried Gustavo, beholding a slight indication of returning animation in the body of the Italian. "Quick, Tommatoo! ropes to bind him up! Bring me great, strong twines, for he is very dangerous, this fellow. Ha, rascal! you are there! You lie very low now, brigand! We will trouble ourselves with your care, sir. Yes, we will have the honour to conduct you to the bureau of the Chief of the Police, and there we will demand of you that you shall let us know all your villainies. Quick, child,—the twines! The fellow will get himself up very presently."

And so, chattering a sort of mingled monologue of reproach, triumph, and sarcasm, Gustave passed the rope which Tommatoo brought him around Giuseppe's body in so scientific and elaborate a manner that the wretched man was as incapable of motion as an Indian *papoose* strapped to its board, and lay on the floor with nothing but the winking of his large, dark, villainous eyes to tell of his being animate.

Now came the great question, who was to go for the police. If Gustave went, Tommatoo would be left alone in that terrible house, with that terrible man, who might unloose that wonderful network of bonds in which Gustave had enlaced him. If Tommatoo went, she would have to thread her way alone through that dreary, dangerous locality; and she confessed she had not the courage to make the attempt. If they both went, who was to take care of the captive? So they, perforce, came to the conclusion that they must wait until morning; and accordingly Gustave, determined not to lose sight of his prize, lifted him on his shoulder as one would a bale of goods, and, carrying him up to his own room,—the room in which the Pancorno resided,—threw him into a corner. Then he and Tommatoo sat down gloomily to speculate and wonder over Baioccho's disappearance. It was in vain that they interrogated Giuseppe. That individual glared at them from his corner like a coil of ropes with a pair of large eyes hidden somewhere in it, but would condescend to no reply. And so, the hours passed, as they gloomily watched for the day.

Weary with speculation, and heart-sore enough with pondering over the fate of old Baioccho, Gustave, as the small hours wore on, could no longer resist his inclination to invoke the genius of the Pancorno to disperse the sad thoughts that hung like black clouds around him and Tommatoo; so he sat down to that mysteriously constructed instrument, and poured forth those wild improvisations that seemed to interpret some love-passage in the history of young Æolus. And when the sun broke faintly over the dreary stone-yard, and its first rays fell on the livid face of the Italian lying bound in the corner, it floated upward through the sky, buoyed by those harmonies that seemed to seek their native heaven.

4: THE PÆN OF THE PANCORNO.

The ——th Ward Station-House. It was the early hour of the morning, before the overnight prisoners had departed to be judged by the immaculate justices presiding in the neighbouring district police court, and the poor, sleepless-looking, blear-eyed people were emerging from the "lock-up "in the basement, still heavy with the poison of bad liquor and spotted all over the face with the bites of mosquitoes that abound in all police stations. Along the walls of the general room hung rows of glazed fire-caps and locust-wood clubs, while, stretched in rank and file on the floor beneath, one saw a quantity of India rubber overshoes, splashed with the mud gathered in the weary night-tramp on the heels of crime. What stories of city vice spoke in those dirty, flexible shoes!

One saw the burglar at work with file and centre-bit, and accomplice keeping watch with pricked-up ears. The file grates and the centre-bit cuts, and the confederate strains his hearing as the grasshopper leaps from the wall; but none sees the dark shadows creeping round the corner, and the pavement yields no echo to the muffled feet; and the silent overshoes steal on until, with one quick leap and one heavy blow with the club, the burglar and confederate lie powerless on the ground.

The ——th Ward Station-House was a dreary-looking establishment. The police captain in plain clothes, with a presentation watch in his pocket, attached to a presentation chain, and a presentation diamond ring on his finger, and a presentation pin in his shirt front, which having buttons did not seem to require it, sat on a high chair behind a high counter on which he measured out justice by the yard. Two or three sly-looking men, in plain clothes also, with a furtive glance in the eyes, and an air of always seeming to be looking round a corner that bespoke the detective, or "shadow," lounging on the stout chairs, picking their teeth and watching everybody, even the police captain, as if they were ready at any moment to detect anybody in something illegal.

A pleasant-looking chain of handcuffs hung on the wall, some ten or twelve pair linked together,—cold, brutal-looking loops of iron that seemed to regret it was wrists and not necks that it was their duty to clasp. Sitting on the sill of the deep window, which opened into the street, were two little children crying lustily. They had been lost or had run away, and in the face of the boy, a large-eyed French lad, some six years old, one could see the determination working that made him preserve, when questioned, a sullen silence as to his name and home. The other, a little girl,—thanks to the philoprogenitive organ of one of the police,—was munching a jam tart amidst all her grief, and slobbering the unwholesome pastry with her tears.

But chief of all the figures in that melancholy room were three persons who had, in the charge of a policeman, arrived at early dawn. Deep in one corner, the farthest from the door, sat Giuseppe, now carefully uncorded but still scowling out of his cloak, as if he might dart poisoned poniards out of his eyes; while before the high counter on which the prize police captain measured out his two-pennyworth of justice, stood Gustavo and Tommatoo, who was weeping bitterly.

"You say that you left your father for but a few moments, and on your return, he had disappeared?" inquired the prize captain, solemnly.

"Yes, sir!" sobbed Tommatoo. "My dear, dear father! What has become of him? O, that bad man!"—a wicked glance at Giuseppe in the corner.

"And when you returned you found the prisoner in the room where you had left your father?"

"Yes, sir; and I know that he knows where my father is,—I see it in his eyes. O, sir, make him tell,—make him tell. Pinch him until he tells,—beat him until he tells!"

The prize captain smiled, condescendingly.

"Lieutenant!" he said, "telegraph a description of this Baioccho to the chief's office, with inquiries."

Immediately a thin policeman commenced working the telegraph that lay in one comer of the room, but the monotonous click of the instrument was but little consolation to the aching bosom of Tommatoo.

A half-hour passed—an hour—during which Tommatoo related over and over again the details of her little story to the prize captain. The subordinates of the office began to take an interest in her, and gathered round her as she sat nestling close to Gustave, who was completely amazed by the novelty of his situation, and each had a kind word for the little maiden.

An hour passed. Ah, how dreary! dreary to Giuseppe scowling in his cloak, carefully watched by two stalwart policemen; dreary to Gustave, who wondered how policemen could live without music; dreary to little Tommatoo, who, with swollen eyes, and heavy, sad heart, sorrowed for the old musician.

Presently there was a bustle. A carriage drove up to the door with policemen on the box, and Tommatoo's heart fluttered. The door of the vehicle opened, and out tottered Baioccho, feebly singing, crowing, dancing, with his old eyes twinkling with cognac, and a suit of gigantic clothes on, out of which he seemed to be endeavouring to scramble. In another instant Tommatoo was in his arms.

"Ah, *mon enfant, ma fille bien aimé!* the old father has brought himself back. *Per baccho!* brought himself back with the joy in his heart. The assassin failed in his work. Ha! "

This last exclamation was caused by a sudden rush for the door which Giuseppe had made the moment the old musician appeared. His attempt at escape was vain, however, for before he had made two steps he was collared, and a pair of handcuffs magically slipped over his wrists. He sat down again sullenly, but with a face white with terror.

"Ha! serpent that thou art!" cried Baioccho, placing himself before Giuseppe and shaking his withered old fist at him. "Thy time has arrived. Thou wilt hang for this. So, you thought to drown the poor old *maestro* who never harmed you? But no! the God above is good, and when waves lifted themselves up to engulf me, and the boat of the passage came to knock me on the head, a heaven-descended rope put itself into my hand, and a blessed sailor pulled me up to the deck. O, no! I am not dead yet, and the sweet dove that you covet will find some other nest than thine!"

Then turning to the prize captain, the old man, still with one arm round his daughter, poured forth his voluble tale ;—how Giuseppe had flung him into the river; how he was floating out to sea when the ferry-boat had come down on him; and how, just in the nick of time, someone on board had discerned him in the water and flung him a rope;—all this mixed up in his extraordinary English, and interlarded with French and Italian imprecations on the head of Giuseppe, so that the prize captain was entirely bewildered, and all that he could do was to order the assassin into the lock-up, and bind over the old *maestro* to appear in evidence. This done, he and Gustave and Tommatoo, now chirping like a bird, went home together.

I would not like to count all the *petits verres de cognac* that the old musician took that night; but I know that Baioccho on that occasion danced the most singular dances, and sang the most eccentric songs, and told Tommatoo and Gustave at least fifty times the wondrous story of his adventures, and how his brother was, he believed, dead, and had left him all his wealth; and so, the night closed on jubilation in the old house by the stone-yard.

Strange to say, Baioccho's brother was dead and had left him his heir. This, it was supposed, Giuseppe had learned in Italy, and had hastened home with the intention of profiting by an information of which he was the earliest recipient. Chance, however, frustrated his plans, and after a trial, in which Baioccho's eccentric evidence was a feature, the gates of the State prison closed over the assassin.

In time Baioccho realized his inheritance and bade farewell to the kitchen. The Pancorno was brought before the public, and everyone remembers the sensation it created that winter at the Antique Concerts given at Niblo's. Women, while listening to its wonderful strains, could not help noticing how handsome was the young Frenchman who played on it; yet none saw the lovely face that every night gazed from the front row on the performer; but I know that Gustavo Beaumont played all the better because he knew that Tommatoo, otherwise Madame Beaumont, was looking at him. Madame Beaumont! Tommatoo as a *madame!* Can you realise it? I can't.

An Arabian Nightmare

It came to pass, some years ago, that I went to the fair of Nishin, Novogorod, which is in the land of the Muscovites, who are unbelievers, and worship the pictures of created things. And, lo! I took to the fair fur caps and cloaks from Tibet, and woollen garments from Cashmere, and also the dates of Bokhara. And our Lord the Prophet, whose tomb I have visited (and whose name is blessed), gave me a ready sale for my merchandise, so that I had soon a girdle full of *roubles*, which are coins of the Muscovites.

And, behold! I made acquaintance with one of the unbelievers, whose name was Demski, and who had brought to the fair garments of white fur and garments of seal-skin. And, of a truth, before the fair was over, I was greatly troubled in my body by reason of the noise and the crowd, and the anxieties of buying and selling; and also by reason of the unwholesome food, wherewith the Muscovites (may God enlighten them!) are wont to fill themselves.

And I was afflicted with a great trembling of the limbs, so that walking fatigued me—although I am one who had journeyed to Mecca (the riches of which place may God increase). And whereas, when I was in Khiva, my girdle caused a shortness of the breath, and a constriction of the ribs: it would now have fallen over my waist, if the good *roubles*, whereof our Lord the Prophet had permitted me to despoil the Muscovites, had not kept it in its place. And when Demski saw that I walked with difficulty, and was even as a peeled wand for thinness, he said:

"Verily, oh Hamet! the way to Khiva is long, and the motion of camels, I have heard, is an affliction to the limbs: it were better for thee to go with me and my merchandise unto Berezow, which is a town on the River Obb, in the province of Tobolsk; for though the winter is long and cold; yet, when we roll thee up in furs, and give thee the warmest corner of the stove, and cause the pores of thy skin to be opened by means of the sweating house, thou will not think of the snow or of the long night."

And I said, "Of a truth, oh my friend! the words of the poet are exemplified in thee, saying:

In a brother, I have found no love,
But a stranger hath shown me affection.
And a stranger has been to me more
Than the son of my mother."

But he answered:

"These are foolish words! When I come to Khiva, thou wilt prepare the *kabobs* and the *pilaff* for me. And now, oh Hamet, make ready thy goods; for on the second day we shall harness the horse to the sledge."

And on the second day Demski loaded his sledge with merchandise, even with dried meal and fish, and with brandy, and with stewed pears (may *Allah* confound them and exterminate them!), for of such things do the Muscovites eat. And he spread fur cloaks upon the merchandise, and we sat thereon, and he struck the horse with a whip having three lashes, and we went like the horses of the Kurds, and like the camels of the Bedawee.

And, lo, the journey was long; but the novelty thereof sustained me, for from my youth up, I have loved to see strange places, and to hear of the people who dwell therein. And when we came to Berezow, we found there Petrovna, the wife of Demski, and Alexandrovitch, their little son, and I gave to her a handkerchief of bright colours, and to him a *tarboosh* of red cloth; so that they were glad to see me, and I abode with them during the winter. And, verily, I saw a strange thing; for the sun appeared not for the space of five months. And when I saw this, I said, "Of a truth this is a land forsaken of God. And it is because the people thereof worship the pictures of created things."

And I abode much in the house, going only from the stove to the sweating-house, and from the sweating-house to the stove. And in the sweating-house they took from me my clothes, and set me on warm stones, and poured water on stones heated in the fire, until the house was filled with the steam thereof, and beat my body gently with the twigs of birch, until the perspiration ran from me; and indeed, this is of great convenience in so cold a land. And in the house, we talked of the countries we had seen, and of the wonderful works of God: and

Demski taught me the game of chess, and I taught him that of Ahama, which I had learned of an Osruanlee when I journeyed to Mecca, (which may God establish!).

And, lo! one evening noticed that Alexandrovitch, the son of Demski, was cutting out the bits of bone wherewith the game of chess is played, and fashioning them into the images of created things. And I saw that the bone wherefrom he was cutting them was that of a large animal; and I said, "Oh Demski! Whence is that bone for I have seen here no animals whose bones are of such a bigness, but only a few hares and foxes, with white fur. For in this accursed land, God has withdrawn the light of his countenance from the animals, and there is no colour in them."

And Demski told me that the bone was found in the ice; and that also whole animals were found therein, with the hair and flesh on them; and that amongst them were the bones of the elephant, and even entire elephants, which are animals that I have seen in the land of the Mogul, where the inhabitants (may *Allah* instruct them!) worship cows. And I said, "Oh Demski! how came these animals in the ice? for they are animals that inhabit hot countries, and could not live in this cold place, which causeth the blood to stand still, and maketh the fingers like those of dead men."

And he said:

"Thy question is that of a man of understanding; and verily there was a learned man here, whom the *Czar* (whom God preserve!) sent to us, a man of the nation of Franks, who examined these bones, and looked at the creatures as they lay in the ice, and said to me and to others, that this land had once been warmer and fit for such creatures, and that these frozen rivers and seas had once flowed like the great rivers and the ocean which thou hast seen."

And I said:

"Oh Demski! this is but foolishness; and God will confound these *Feringees*, who pry into the origin of things. For these are works of Eblis and of the *Jan*, and these creatures are shut up here by enchantment, even as Gog and Magog were shut up by Iskandar, in the mountains near the Caspian Sea. And Gog and Magog are always digging through the mountain to get out; but cannot, by reason of the strong enchantment wherewith they are enchanted; nor shall they, because they cannot say, '*Inshallah!*' which means 'God willing.' But one day there shall be a boy amongst them, called '*Inshallah*;' and one of them shall say to him, '*Inshallah*, I will dig through the rock;' and straightway they shall dig through the rock, and overspread the world, and Deijal shall come forth to lead them. And who knows but these creatures are shut up here by like enchantment, and will one day come forth."

And Demski and Petrovna, and Alexandrovitch, then son, allowed that I had spoken wisely, and praised me much; so that when supper came I was elated, and eat of the dried meat and of fish, and of stewed pears, which I had never before tasted (may *Allah* confound them!); and drank of the brandy until I shouted and sang, as one should not shout and sing who has travelled to Mecca—(may God establish it and maintain it!) And, behold, when I lay down on the stone to sleep, was much pleased that I had spoken so wisely about Eblis and the *Jan*, and Gog and Magog, and Iskandar; for it beseemeth a *schereef* to instruct the ignorant, and one who hath wisdom to impart it to one who hath not. So, I slept.

But about the middle of the night I felt a heavy hand upon my breast, and I awoke; and, lo! when one of the evil one's stood by me, even a *Jin*, having the face of a bull, and a hand like the foot of an elephant, and his hand was upon my breast.

And he said, "Oh Hamet, arise and go with me!"

And I answered, "Oh Bull face! Whither?"

And he said, "Unto the shores of the Frozen Sea, and to the palace of Eblis, and to the abode of the enchanted creatures of whom thou spakcst before supper."

Then said I, "Now are the words of the poet accomplished, for he said:—

Speak no evil of the Jan, for they are always about thee,
And one of them shall carry thy words to the rest in the palace of
Elbis.'"

And the Bull Face grinned. And I arose, and went with him out of the house; and he took me by the hand, and we ran swiftly, like the Mahry, on which the Tonarick rides forth to plunder. And when I saw that he meddled not with Demski, nor with Petrovna, his wife, neither with any of the people of Berezow, I said, "See, now! what it is to worship the pictures of created things; for the *Jan* regard these people as brothers." And the Bull Face snorted.

And by this time, we had come to the shores of the Frozen Sea; but the ice was not all of equal strength, nor was the sea covered by it; but great shapes of ice sailed down it, which were of a blue colour, by reason of the moon. And the *Jin* would have carried me over: but when he essayed it, was too heavy for him; so that he said, "Of a truth, this wretch must have some holy thing about him, that cannot lift him." And I remembered with joy that I had on my heart a piece of cloth wherewith I had touched the Holy Stone at Mecca, and repeated the verses:—

Keep holy things about thee, and gird thee with sacred spells: that thy wickedness may be forgiven for the sake of that thou wearest.

And the *Jin* struck the ice with a stone, and made it crack; and, lo! I heard it cracking and splitting all across the sea, until the sound thereof was louder than that of thunder. And the *Jan* who were in the palace of Eblis heard it; and straightway three of them, having the faces of hawks and the claws of eagles, came flying to us. And the Bull Face said:

"Oh, Hook Noses! Eblis sent me to bring this wretch to him, but he is too heavy for me, by reason of some holy thing which he hath about him. Help me to carry him." And they took me in their arms, and flew. And when I felt the swiftness of our motion through the air, and reflected that the evil ones might let me fall on the ice, or into the cold sea, I resolved to entreat them courteously; and said to one of the Hook Noses who bore up my right shoulder, "Wherefore, oh my *aga!* doth my lord Eblis abide in this desolate place with creatures forsaken of God?"

And he said: "Not choice, but necessity, brought us hither, thou abandoned one; for Eblis was once lord of the morning star, and God had given him a brightness well-nigh equal to that of the sun, and permitted his star to be seen of men, even till the third hour of the day; but Eblis wished that his light might be greater, and that his star might be seen of men all the day long; wherefore God banished him from the morning star, and shut him up here with forsaken creatures; and as for us, we are even as he is."

And the Bull Face and the Hook Noses howled for grief, and I was sorry that I had questioned them, for I thought, they have a sore burden to bear, and I have reminded them of it. And now they flew down to the land, whereon the palace of Eblis stands; and, verily, it is a land of ice, for there are neither trees nor plants in it, nor any living herb, nor any running water, but only great rocks and columns of ice; even pillars like those of Tadmor, which Solomon built in the desert. And in these columns, I saw what will scarce be believed; for I saw all manner of animals, entire and perfect, even elephants bigger than any that I ever saw in the land of the Mogul, and great deer, and crocodiles, such as live by the Nile. These were all shut up in the ice, as flies and straws are enclosed in the amber of the merchants; and the expression of their countenances was that of animals which have died in pain.

And I said to them who were with me, "Oh *Jan!* how came these creatures here?"

And one of them said, "Of a truth, this was once a land with rivers of water, and with trees and plants, both great and small, and these creatures lived therein; but when God sent Eblis hither, he caused the sun to shine on other parts of the world and not on this so that these creatures were all frozen up here, and the breath went out of them."

Then thought I, "Lo! now this is what the Frank said to Demski and to others. Surely God has cursed these Franks, for they speak like the *Jans.*" But though there was no sun in this land, there was light, such as I never saw before or since; for it proceeded from no visible cause, but resembled the reflection of a lamp upon a wall; and verily the ice was luminous, and I saw pale flames on the top of every rock and pillar of ice, and they resembled the mist which surrounds the moon when rain is about to be sent. And the flames were everywhere, even in the ground whereon I walked, and in the air which I breathed; but there was no heat in the flame.

And, lo! we came into the hall where Eblis sat, and it was all of luminous ice, and the inhabitants thereof were of ice also; and as I looked at the *Jan* who had brought me, behold! they were all of ice, and pale flames were around all their heads, and at the ends of all their fingers, and their bodies were luminous, so that I could see their hearts beat. And Eblis sat on a frozen throne, and his body looked like a pure opal without flaw, and his face was like unto a milk-white cornelian. And there was no light in the palace, or in all that land, but that which came from the ice, and from the inhabitants thereof.

And they set me in the midst. And Eblis said, "What present has my servant Hamet brought to his lord?"

And I answered, "Nay, my *Sultan*; I was taken in the night, and have brought nothing, and, moreover, I am not the servant of my *Sultan*; but if he will send me back to Berezow, to the house of Demski, I will give him, as a present, fur caps of Thibet, and woollen garments of Cashmere, inasmuch as he needeth them sorely."

And thereat the men of ice laughed, until their joints cracked horribly. And Eblis said, "Yea! but thou hast served me often; even at the fair of Novogorod, when thou didst sell fur caps for two *roubles*, that were not worth one; and again, no later than last night, when thou didst drink brandy and eat stewed pears."

And I said, "Of a truth, the fur caps were not good, and the stewed pears are an accursed food; but I am a poor man, and my *Sultan* will take a small present from me."

And he answered, "Yea! I will take even what thou hast with thee;" and turning to a blue *Jin*, who stood near him, he said, "Take from him the girdle of *roubles* which is about his waist." And when I heard this, I thought, "It were better for me to die than to let these accursed ones have my *roubles*; as man can only die once, but poverty is an abiding affliction."

So, I look courage, and cried, "Oh! Frozen Ones, accursed are your mothers and your sisters; but my *roubles* ye shall not have." And I held up my garments and ran; and the men of ice ran too, and slid round about me on the ice and caught at me with their slippery hands, and chilled me with their icy breath. And the rocks, and the pillars, and the frozen ground, shot out pale flames at me as I passed; and the creatures in the pillars, the expression of whose countenance was that of creatures which had died in pain, writhed themselves in the ice, and grinned at me horribly.

And all the men of ice shouted, "Hamet! Stop, Hamet! Thy *roubles*, Hamet! Thy *roubles*!" And their words struck against the rocks, and ran along the frozen ground, and along the surface of the sea, until all that desolate place repeated "Hamet! Stop, Hamet! Thy *roubles*, Hamet! Thy *roubles!*" and my foot slipped. And as I strove to save myself from falling, behold! I was on my back on the stove in the house of Demski, and he and his wife and their son were shouting to me. And they said that I had slept long: but how I escaped from those frozen ones, I know not but I suppose the bit of cloth, with which I had touched the Holy Stone, redeemed me from them, even from the power of the *Jan*; by which one may see that it is good to go to Mecca, and that Mohammed is the Prophet of God.

And when the spring came I departed from Demski and his wife, and returned to Khiva, both I and my *roubles*, wherof those evil one's had wished to rob me.

Three of a Trade; or Red Little Kris Kringle

The city was muffled in snow, and looked as calm and pale and stately as a queen in her ermine robes. It was night, and the tinkling of innumerable sleigh-bells made the frosty air musical. The sleighs themselves sped silently through the streets, painted blackly against the white snow as they passed, like so many phantoms winging their way to a festival on the Bracken Mountains.

It was late, for the corner groceries were shut. The last draught of poison had been drained over the counter. The last victim had staggered home to his trembling wife. The red, unwholesome light that flared over the door had been extinguished, and the bar-keeper was snoring in his bed behind the flour-barrels.

In the bleak shelter afforded by the projecting wooden awning of one of the corner groceries in Greenwich Street, close to where that thoroughfare nears the river, and huddled up against the side of the large coal-bin that stood hasped and padlocked on one side of the entrance, two little figures were visible in the dim glimmer of the night. Two little children they were, sitting with their cold arms embracing each other, their chill cheeks pressed together, and their large, weary eyes looking out hungrily into the blank street.

Down by the wharves they saw the tall, slender masts of ships piercing the sky like the serried lances of some band of gigantic Cossacks. Among the black hulls, a few late lights still shone, and the air rang occasionally with the voice of a drunken sailor, who, from some friendly doorstep, where he had involuntarily cast anchor, chanted his experiences of a young West Indian lady of colour, who rejoiced in the horticultural name of Nancy Banana.

Presently a mystic music seemed to fall from the arched skies upon the city. It was the chimes from old Trinity ringing the Old Year out and the New Year in. The thrilling notes of the changes following each other in measured flow, vibrated through the air like music made by the feet of marching angels. They jubilantly seemed to scale the slope of heaven. The wild melodious clangour floated over the great silent city. Myriads of aerial Moors, clashing their cymbals, seemed to march over the housetops. The clock was trembling on the stroke of twelve, and Time had one foot already in the territories of the New Year.

"Tip, listen to the bells," said one of the two children, that were huddled beneath the grocery awning, speaking in a faint, though clear voice, like a bell heard in a fog, "listen. It is time for Kriss Kringle to come."

Tip's cold little lips opened, and nothing issued therefrom but a low, plaintive "I'm hungry, Binnie."

"So am I," said Binnie, with a sort of far-off cheeriness, as if his heart was at a considerable distance, and could communicate only very faintly. "But, let us wait. Perhaps Kriss Kringle will bring us something nice. What would you like most, Tip?"

"Coffee and cakes wouldn't be bad," said Tip, hesitatingly, as if rather afraid of the consequences if he allowed his imagination to run away with him.

"Or a plate of roast beef, rare, with potatoes and peach pie," suggested the more reckless Binnie, "just such as mother used to give us on Sunday. Poor mother!"

"What are we going to do tomorrow, Binnie, to get some money?"

"Shovel snow off the stoops," answered Binnie, resolutely. "We'll go into Union Square early, and ask all around at the houses whether they want the sidewalk cleared. Some of 'em are sure to give us a quarter; we might make fifty cents, and then wouldn't we have a time!"

"When we were living in the country with mother what fun we used to have on New Year's," said poor little Tip, creeping up closer to Binnie, with a shiver, for the night was gelling very cold, and a few large snowflakes commenced falling straight down from the fleecy sky, white as the manna that fell in the desert, but alas! not so nutritious.

"O golly! yes. What a good mother she was to us, and what things we used to find in the old stocking that she gave us to hang up! Kriss Kringle don't come to us any more now that she's dead. I wonder if he really used to come down the chimney, Tip, or if 'twas only make believe."

"I don't know," said Tip, "I watched ever so many nights, but somehow I always fell asleep just before he came, and then the things got into the slocking. I used to dream, though, that I saw him. A little man with a red coat all covered with gold lace, and a long feather in his cap and a little sword by his side. And he used to smile at me, and say, 'Tip, will you be a good boy if I put something into the stocking for you? and then I used to promise, and when I had promised I used to hear music sounding all through the house, a great deal finer than the music we heard when we went to the circus, Binnie; and then Kriss Kringle would take off his hat to me, and make a jump, and go clean up the chimney out of sight, like a red cricket. Ah! how cold it is, Binnie, and how hungry I am. Tell us a story."

The wind arose in the north, and came down upon the city with a savage howl. The heavy snowflakes fled before him into every angle and nook, like terrified white birds trying to hide themselves from some vast-winged, screaming falcon. They thrust themselves into the crevices of the windows, and between the slats of the window-blinds; they got under the sills of the doors. They left the centre of the streets, and flew madly into the gutters; they huddled themselves into the dark corner where Tip and Binnie were cowering, ran up the legs of their ragged trousers and slid down between their frail shirt-collars and their cold little necks. It was a fierce, biting, scratching wind of prey, and poor Binnie and Tip felt his talons digging into their flesh.

Just as the pair of vagrants had drawn closer together, and Binnie was trying to stop his teeth—which began to chatter—from biting in two the thread of the story that the patient little fellow was about to tell his brother, they heard a faint cry, something between a moan and a whistle, sounding close to them. Looking out into the dim twilight they beheld a dwarfish figure standing on the sidewalk, moaning and waving its arms. It seemed to be a little man about two feet high, clad in a red coat, covered with gold lace, and wearing a little cap, in which was stuck a long feather, that was bent nearly horizontal by the wind. A tiny sword, about the length of a lead-pencil, dangled at his side.

"O, Binnie," whispered Tip, "it's Kriss Kringle come again. I know him. He used to look exactly like that in my dream. I ain't afraid of him. Are you?"

"Not a bit," answered Binnie. "He looks a nice little chap. I hope he has brought us something."

The little man on the sidewalk seemed very uneasy, he waved his long arms continually, look off his little cap every now and then with a quick jerk, as if he were making a series of abbreviated bows to the two little vagrants, and then hopped about, moaning the same shrill and extraordinary moan.

"Binnie, I think he's cold; let us ask him to come and lie down with us and warm himself," said Tip. "You know, in all the fairy books, if you treat a fairy well, he's sure to give you three wishes."

Whatever Binnie may have thought of the suggestion of warming anything by putting it close to two such little icicles as himself and his brother, the latter part of the speech seemed to strike him as containing a felicitous idea. So, bracing his chattering teeth as well as he could, he said,—

"Kriss Kringle, will you come and lie down with us, and we will warm you?"

The little red-coated man made no reply to this hospitable invitation, but danced, and shivered, and moaned, and doffed his tiny cap many times in succession.

"Come, Kriss Kringle," continued Binnie, beckoning to the dwarf, "come in out of the snow."

"Maybe he don't speak English, Binnie," suggested the imaginative Tip.

This was a new view of the case, and Binnie began to consider within himself whether, by some inspiration of the moment, he might not suddenly master the particular foreign tongue with which their new friend was acquainted, when, suddenly, the little man made a swift leap and landed right in Tip's lap.

"Why, Binnie!" cried Tip, "it's not Kriss Kringle after all, it's only a monkey!"

Sure enough it was a monkey: a poor shivering little Brazilian, with pleading eyes and soft, silky hands, and a countenance that seemed to tell of a life of sorrow. A bit of broken chain dangling from a belt round his waist told his story. The eternal organ in the street; the black-bearded, heartless Italian; the little switch that scored his back at home; the cruel pinches to induce politeness, when wondering schoolboys proffered their hoarded coppers; the melancholy panto-mime of sprightly gratitude which was taught with blows, and per-formed in fear and trembling. Poor little runaway! Poor little vagrant! He seemed to know that he had found brothers in misfortune when he thrust his timid, silky paw in Binnie's hand, and laid his little hairy face against Tip's bosom.

The children vied with each other in attentions to the poor little wanderer. I do believe that if Tip had an apple or a chestnut at that moment, hungry as he was, he would have given it to his red little Kriss Kringle. The boys placed him between them, and tried to snuggle him up in their tattered clothes. He clung to them as if he really loved them. His little hand found its way into Tip's shirt-bosom,—if that collection of discoloured tatters which he wore beneath his jacket could be called a shirt,—and laid just over his heart. The poor vagrants kissed and fondled their pet; and, God help them! were almost happy for the time.

Meanwhile the snow drifted and drifted right under the shed where the vagrants lay. It began to pile itself up about them on all sides, and it clung to every projection of their persons. The air grew colder and colder. The wind swooped at them under the shed—still, like the wide-winged, shrieking falcon,—as if it would take them up in its talons and bear them away to its bleak nest to feed its unfledged tempests. Closer and closer the three houseless creatures drew together, until a great drowsiness fell upon them, and the sough of the storm sounded farther and farther off, and sleep and snow covered them.

Then a dream came to Binnie and Tip. Red little Kriss Kringle jumped up suddenly from his rest in their bosom, clad in the brightest finery. A wondrous while egret's plume waved in his cap, and he wore a breastplate of diamonds. His red coat was redder than the blossoms of the wild Lobelia, and his sword was filled with gold. Then he said to the boys, "Boys, ye have been very kind to me, and sheltered me when it was cold, so now ye shall come with me to the sweet land of the South, where ye shall idle in the sunshine for ever and ever!"

Then he led them down to the wharf nearby, where, moored among the black hulls of the ships, they found a beautiful golden boat, so bright with main-coloured flags that it seemed as if her tall masts had swept the rainbows from the sky. Fairy music sounded as the sails were set, and they sailed and sailed and sailed until they landed on the sweet Southern shore.

There they found strange trees with leaves of satin and fruits of gold. Wonderful birds shot like stars from bough to bough. The rivers sang like musical instruments. From the limbs of the trees trailed brilliant tapestries of orchideous flowers, which, with their roots in the air, sucked the sunlight into their secret veins, until their blossoms were covered with the splendour of Day.

Here red little Kriss Kringle led them to the foot of a huge tree covered with white flowers, and made them lie down while he fed them with fruits of a magical flavor. The sun shone cheerfully on their heads. The birds sang their pleasant songs. The huge tree rained its white blossoms on them, as they dropped off to sleep, weary with delight, until they reposed beneath a coverlet of scented snow.

When the first day of the New Year dawned, and the grocer's boy came from his bed behind the flour-barrels to take down the shutters, he saw a mound of snow close by the side of the coal-bin, he brought the shovel to take it away, and the first stroke disclosed the three little vagrants lying stark and still, enfolded in each other's arms.

Broadway Bedevilled

After five years of restless wandering up and down the earth, gathering no moss, trying every soil and taking root in none, a scandalously unproductive man, of no use to myself or my fellows, bound to them by no lies of common sympathy or service, I found myself home again, where there was no home. My father's house had no place for me; my father repudiated and ignored me; my mother's children turned their faces from me.

My old friends passed by on the other side, and looked at me askance, astonished at the seeming bravado which could permit me to thrust myself in their way, or stand where they might meet me. Intemperate, possessed of a devil of drink—thirst, eternal thirst, from my rising up to my lying down—mad, irresponsible to God or man—never premeditating, never foreseeing the result of any word I might utter, any deed I might commit—liable at any time to say or do that which would invoke me and others in a common ruin—I rushed madly along through life, like a mad ox in a crowded street, only by some strange providence seeming mercifully to avoid the crash which all expected.

My resources of an almost desperate character—precarious, wholly accidental, derived at the moment, from the place where I might happen to be—my powers, by a sort of convulsive struggle, exercised to procure the absolute requirements of the moment, the necessities of food, and drink, and sleep, no more-—making no provision for the future, hoping nothing from the next day, and caring as little what evil thing the next day might bring forth—I found myself alone in New York—truly, in its most actual and painful sense, alone.

My family had agreed not to pronounce my name among them. A large and influential circle of friends, who had once hoped for at least good things of me, shrugged their shoulders and shook their heads, kindly content to give me up, only thinking I should be grateful that they did no more. Educated in a profession which requires the exercise of the coolest sagacity in emergencies, and at all times well-braced nerves and a steady head and hand, I had been compelled to throw away that resource—too glad that it was in my power to avoid the constantly recurring risk of sacrificing human life in the devilish mania, which so often possessed me, that I dreaded even the sight of the operating knife, and turned away from the possibility of my services being required, as from the chance of committing some dreadful crime.

Still, always strangely believing, even in my maddest moments, that I should not die soon—still, always possessed of invincible faith in some mysterious power that would surely be exerted, in good time, in my behalf—still convinced through all my being that I should not die until I had redeemed myself—even looking death, starvation, prisons, and self-destruction straight in the face from moment to moment, yet never fearing either: a feeling which was so entirely superstitious that it hung about me like an atmosphere, and accompanied me like an angel; that became an essence, an aroma, which I was continually breathing, of which I was always sensible, which I took with me into all places and all companies—the sufficing sense of a supernatural protection. I never ceased to believe that I should one day, by its help, conquer myself, and assert my manhood.

This was no operation of reason. It was superstition—it was fatalism—it was even spiritualism, it you choose to call it so. It may have been, for aught I know (and, without any tendency to spiritualistic notions, I am content to believe it was), the actual presence and attendance, always, of someone who had loved me, and was now dead. I should be happy to believe that it was my mother. But there it ever was; and I never saw the moment, however hopeless, however mad, however lost, when that feeling was not at hand, coming to succour, to save me. it was that which kept my hands from my throat; it was that which enabled me to look bravely in the face of men and women who were overwhelming me with indignant reproaches.

"Wait a little; wait a little!"

That was my cry from morning till night, to myself, and to all I could get to listen to me.

Such a man was I, when, one evening, I set out about dusk to loaf—that is the word—to kill time, to run amok down the narrow lane of a day—having all day drank fire in one scalding stream.

I reached Madison square. As I walked, the scene around me whirling, upside down, in the same jumbled condition as my own mind, scarcely knowing whither my steps were tending, nor caring much—strange and alarming sensations took possession of me; yet not altogether strange, for I had had premonitions of the kind before, but never so forcibly.

I knew that my mind was wandering. I was conscious only now and then of where I was. Especially had I an overpowering dread of danger—of danger holding the way in front of me, following closely behind me, and near me on either side. The nature of this danger was undefined. I could not explain it to myself. It took no dimensions which I could measure or count, no shape which I could describe; but it was none the less there.

I quickened my step, as I turned my face toward the Battery, with the intention of returning to my hotel, where I had been staying for several days, and where I was well known. Although the proprietors of this house were my friends, and had been kind to me, I was yet aware of my liability to be dismissed, on account of the insanity of my actions and language, and the danger from my presence.

As I walked, men walked by my side; or I encountered them as they stood in knots on the corners; or they crossed over from the opposite side of the street, always eying me suspiciously, threateningly—men whose aspect was dangerous, who had more or less of the cutthroat in their air—"roughs" and fighting men, who seemed to have some cause of quarrel with me, some insult or outrage which I had committed, and they would resent.

As they stood, by twos or threes, on the pavement, I could distinctly hear them say, "That's our man"—"keep your eye upon him." Occasionally they would cross the street, and, meeting others there, would interchange communications with them, all the while keeping their attention upon me, and frequently repeating my name; still they followed me—some on either side, others before, others behind me, and some even in the middle of the street. Again, and again, I could hear them say, "Don't let him be out of your sight for a moment." Not seldom they dispersed themselves, mingling with the throng of passers in a manner to avoid observation by any but myself—myself painfully, intensely aware of their presence, having marked every man afar off.

I employed many of the tricks to which men resort in dangerous straits. Sometimes, I stopped for a moment, but they also stopped. When I would seem to be examining the windows of shops, they would stand at a little distance, watching me from the corners of their eyes, and whispering mysteriously to each other. When I turned back, they, also, turned back. If I passed into a shop, under pretence of purchasing something, when I returned to the door I still found them waiting for me, as before. I did not, for a moment, miss one of them, nor did I doubt that I was the object of their conspiracy.

Frequently they drew nearer to me, so near, indeed, that I could plainly hear them consulting together, and laying their plan of action. Then I pressed steadily on, thinking it best to feign ignorance of their pursuit. My pace was not hurried; I aimed to keep as much as possible in the crowd, and in the glare of light from shop windows, carefully avoiding all dark places, and always crossing the street whenever I had to pass a spot where unoccupied houses, or buildings in the course of erection, made a deep shadow in the midst of the general brightness. I was careful to mingle with knots and throngs of pedestrians, and specially did I aim to keep within the neighbourhood of women, pitifully mindful of the protection of their company.

At last I hailed an omnibus, and entered it, at once two of my pursuers entered with me, whilst the rest took another, which immediately followed us. Seated opposite me, in the stage, were an old gentleman, a lady, seemingly his wife, a little boy, and my two enemies. But they made no open demonstration toward me, of threat or otherwise; though frequently they whispered to each other, eying me closely the while with that same deadly glance, which, at last, wrought me up to so high a pitch of fear that I could have screamed. Yet this fear was strangely soothed by a desire to penetrate the mystery, and to learn what it was I had done, that they should seek my life; for, that it was my life they sought, had been to me, from the first, most apparent. Indeed, that could not have been plainer it I had been conscious of some damning crime, for which I was thus chased.

What may here seem incoherent or maudlin in my story, was to me the most circumstantial of events. Presently the two men stopped the omnibus and alighted, but immediately entered the other in which their companions were, charging the driver, at the same time, to follow closely behind my stage, and not to lose sight of it.

I recollect all the horrors of that journey. I recall the unutterable anguish, the bursting torture, that might, had I been madder, have relieved itself with screams. I remember how I drew as near as decency would permit, to a lady who sat next me, as it were to shield myself with her innocence, all the while silently imploring that protection which, as a gentleman, I could not supplicate in words. Indeed, to the inmates of that omnibus, I, perhaps, appeared a little agitated, though otherwise a quiet and respectable passenger. I had, I hope, the bearing of a gentleman.

Since that experience, I have often thought whether it could not be possible for a certain magnetic influence, passing from a man so intensely charged as I was at that moment, to another of a highly susceptible and sympathetic organisation, to impart to the latter a suspicion of the other's case, and of his almost paralysing fear. it seems to me, now, that I could not sit for twenty minutes in a vehicle with a man possessed of such a devil, without discovering his secret and following up my discovery with efforts to soothe and assist him.

As we rode on, I still preserved a quiet demeanour, seeking to be apparently indifferent to the shapes that chased me. We passed some companies of soldiers with bands of music, and threaded our way through throngs of vehicles and people, amid bewildering confusion, and the mingling of voices, and forms undefined in the darkness; for I am near-sighted, and the mystery of the occasion was much increased by that fact. As we proceeded, I felt myself approaching nearer and nearer to my doom. And yet I would not speak; I would not implore help; I would not throw myself upon the protection of the police. I was resolved either to escape by my own unaided sagacity or strength of arm, or to take the worst that could befall me. I felt that the fiends that followed me were sent by God, and that I must abide the issue. I scorned to seek an asylum at that moment.

I am now going to describe phantasms which, although they were the tricks of madness, I as vividly recall at this hour as though they were the realities of yesterday.

At last we reached the Astor House. Only the old gentleman and the lady I have mentioned were with me in the stage. Then, for the first time, my fear became so great that, for a moment, my insane firmness failed me. I asked the gentleman, with an air of indifference as good as I could command, whether he was going as far as Wall Street? He replied no; that he was about to get out there. Accordingly, he stopped the omnibus, and descended with the lady. Fearing to be left alone in the vehicle, lest I should be taken at a disadvantage, I also alighted, and would have followed them. Immediately the other stages topped, and my bloodhounds, numbering about a dozen, followed me.

As usual, the space in front of the Astor House was brilliantly illuminated by the lights of the hotel and those of Barnum's Museum.

To avoid the shade of St. Paul's church, I crossed Broadway diagonally; but my pursuers were close upon me, with hurried commands and ejaculations, such as: "keep close-"—"stand by"—"take care to head him off"—"if he attempt to go into a house, down with him." As I advanced, they became more compact, and all were near me. At length, we were within two doors of a hotel. Its front was brightly lighted, and knots of guests and other persons were seated or standing at the doors and windows. I resolved to take refuge there. I braced myself up with the intention of rushing in.

My pursuers suspected my purpose; for I heard them cry, "don't let him enter there"—"knock him down!" But I determined to take that chance, and bring down upon my head, there and immediately, the worst that could happen. I carried in my hand a small whalebone switch, having at the top a round leaden knob, covered with a sort of whipcord. I grasped this about halfway down, but continued to walk steadily forward, turning my face neither to the right nor to the left, to scrutinise the men who pressed close to my sides, not quickening my pace nor behaving the slightest alarm or anxiety, till I came upon a stream of light that fell toward me from the street-lamps before the hotel entrance. As I turned composedly to enter there, as one accustomed to the place, one of my devils cried, "Now, boys, close up, quick!" Hardly were the words uttered, when I flung myself upon the man who was nearest me, and, with all my force, dashed the heavy leaden head of the cane in his face, and struck him squarely between the eyes.

No time to be lost. I rushed through the vestibule. Fairly leaping over men seated at the door, over piles of baggage, over the office-counter, I ran through a small door and up some stairs, crying, "Stop them! Save me!" and at last found myself on the floor of a servants' room at the very top of the house, with servants, clerks, and guests around me, giving me water, bathing my temples, and rendering me such assistance as they could, whilst blood flowed copiously from my mouth and nose, and stained my clothing and the floor.

This was *Delirium Tremens*. All that I have here related, of the pursuit and conflict, was but an accusing vision. My abused brain had conjured up that horrid warning. And yet, that very night, walking the floor with my kind friends, I told them the story as circumstantially as I tell it now; as clearly aware, too, as I am at this moment, that my foes were spectres.

Since that day, the doctrine of universal salvation has had arguments as well as charms for me. So much of hell as was compressed into that stage-trip from Madison Square to Barnum's Museum, has saved me from believing in an eternity of it.

The Pot of Tulips

Twenty-eight years ago, I went to spend the summer at an old Dutch villa which then lifted its head from the wild country that, in present days, has been tamed down into a site for a Crystal Palace. Madison Square was then a wilderness of fields and scrub oak, here and there diversified with tall and stately elms. Worthy citizens who could afford two establishments rusticated in the groves that then flourished where ranks of brown-stone porticos now form the landscape; and the locality of Fortieth Street, where my summer palace stood, was justly looked upon as at an enterprising distance from the city.

I had an imperious desire to live in this house ever since I can remember. I had often seen it when a boy, and its cool verandas and quaint garden seemed, whenever I passed, to attract me irresistibly. In after years, when I grew up to man's estate, I was not sorry, therefore, when one summer, fatigued with the labours of my business, I beheld a notice in the papers intimating that it was to be let furnished. I hastened to my dear friend, Jaspar Joye, painted the delights of this rural retreat in the most glowing colours, easily obtained his assent to share the enjoyments and the expense with me, and a month afterward we were taking our ease in this new paradise.

Independent of early associations, other interests attached me to this house. It was somewhat historical, and had given shelter to George Washington on the occasion of one of his visits to the city. Furthermore, I knew the descendants of the family to whom it had originally belonged. Their history was strange and mournful, and it seemed to me as if their individuality was somehow shared by the edifice. It had been built by a Mr. Van Koeren, a gentleman of Holland, the younger son of a rich mercantile firm at The Hague, who had emigrated to this country in order to establish a branch of his father's business in New York, which even then gave indications of the prosperity it has since reached with such marvellous rapidity. He had brought with him a fair young Belgian wife; a loving girl, if I may believe her portrait, with soft brown eyes, chestnut hair, and a deep, placid contentment spreading over her fresh and innocent features.

Her son, Alain Van Koeren, had her picture—an old miniature in a red gold frame—as well as that of his father; and in truth, when looking on the two, one could not conceive a greater contrast than must have existed between husband and wife. Mr. Van Koeren must have been a man of terrible will and gloomy temperament. His face—in the picture—is dark and austere, his eyes deep-sunken, and burning as if with a slow, inward fire. The lips are thin and compressed, with much determination of purpose; and his chin, boldly salient, is brimful of power and resolution. When first I saw those two pictures I sighed inwardly and thought, "Poor child! you must often have sighed for the sunny meadows of Brussels, in the long, gloomy nights spent in the company of that terrible man!"

I was not far wrong, as I afterward discovered. Mr. and Mrs. Van Koeren were very unhappy. Jealousy was his monomania, and he had scarcely been married before his girl-wife began to feel the oppression of a gloomy and ceaseless tyranny. Every man under fifty, whose hair was not white and whose form was erect, was an object of suspicion to this Dutch Bluebeard. Not that he was vulgarly jealous. He did not frown at his wife before strangers, or attack her with reproaches in the midst of her festivities. He was too well-bred a man to bare his private woes to the world. But at night, when the guests had departed and the dull light of the quaint old Flemish lamps but half illuminated the nuptial chamber, then it was that with monotonous invective Mr. Van Koeren crushed his wife. And Marie, weeping and silent, would sit on the edge of the bed listening to the cold, trenchant irony of her husband, who, pacing up and down the room, would now and then stop in his walk to gaze with his burning eyes upon the pallid face of his victim.

Even the evidences that Marie gave of becoming a mother did not check him. He saw in that coming event, which most husbands anticipate with mingled joy and fear, only an approaching incarnation of his dishonour. He watched with a horrible refinement of suspicion for the arrival of that being in whose features he madly believed he should but too surely trace the evidences of his wife's crime.

Whether it was that these ceaseless attacks wore out her strength, or that Providence wished to add another chastening misery to her burden of woe, I dare not speculate; but it is certain that one luckless night Mr. Van Koeren learned with fury that he had become a father two months before the allotted time. During his first paroxysm of rage, on the receipt of intelligence which seemed to confirm all his previous suspicions, it was, I believe, with difficulty that he was prevented from slaying both the innocent causes of his resentment. The caution of his race and the presence of the physicians induced him, however, to put a curb upon his furious will until reflection suggested quite as criminal, if not as dangerous, a vengeance.

As soon as his poor wife had recovered from her illness, unnaturally prolonged by the delicacy of constitution induced by previous mental suffering, she was astonished to find, instead of increasing his persecutions, that her husband had changed his tactics and treated her with studied neglect. He rarely spoke to her except on occasions when the decencies of society demanded that he should address her. He avoided her presence, and no longer inhabited the same apartments. He seemed, in short, to strive as much as possible to forget her existence. But if she did not suffer from personal ill-treatment it was because a punishment more acute was in store for her. If Mr. Van Koeren had chosen to affect to consider her beneath his vengeance, it was because his hate had taken another direction, and seemed to have derived increased intensity from the alteration. It was upon the unhappy boy, the cause of all this misery, that the father lavished a terrible hatred.

Mr. Van Koeren seemed determined, that, if this child sprang from other loins than his, the mournful destiny which he forced upon him should amply avenge his own existence and the infidelity of his mother. While the child was an infant his plan seemed to have been formed. Ignorance and neglect were the two deadly influences with which he sought to assassinate the moral nature of this boy; and his terrible campaign against the virtue of his own son was, as he grew up, carried into execution with the most consummate generalship. He gave him money, but debarred him from education.

He allowed him liberty of action, but withheld advice. It was in vain that his mother, who foresaw the frightful consequences of such a training, sought in secret by every means in her power to nullify her husband's attempts. She strove in vain to seduce her son into an ambition to be educated. She beheld with horror all her agonized efforts frustrated, and saw her son and only child becoming, even in his youth, a drunkard and a libertine. In the end, it proved too much for her strength; she sickened, and went home to her sunny Belgian plains. There she lingered for a few months in a calm but rapid decay, whose calmness was broken but by the one grief; until one autumn day, when the leaves were falling from the limes, she made a little prayer for her son to the good God, and died. Vain orison! Spendthrift, gamester, libertine, and drunkard by turns, Alain Van Koeren's earthly destiny was unchangeable. The father, who should have been his guide, looked on each fresh depravity of his son's with a species of grim delight. Even the death of his wronged wife had no effect upon his fatal purpose. He still permitted the young man to run blindly to destruction by the course into which he himself had led him.

As years rolled by, and Mr. Van Koeren himself approached to that time of life when he might soon expect to follow his persecuted wife, he relieved himself of the hateful presence of his son altogether. Even the link of a systematic vengeance, which had hitherto united them, was severed, and Alain was cast adrift without either money or principle. The occasion of this final separation between father and son was the marriage of the latter with a girl of humble, though honest extraction. This was a good excuse for the remorseless Van Koeren, so he availed himself of it by turning his son out of doors.

From that time forth they never met. Alain lived a life of meagre dissipation, and soon died, leaving behind him one child, a daughter. By a coincidence natural enough, Mr. Van Koeren's death followed his son's almost immediately. He died as he had lived, sternly. But those who were around his couch in his last moments mentioned some singular facts connected with the manner of his death. A few moments before he expired, he raised himself in the bed, and seemed as if conversing with some person invisible to the spectators. His lips moved as if in speech, and immediately afterward he sank back, bathed in a flood of tears. "Wrong! wrong!" he was heard to mutter, feebly; then he implored passionately the forgiveness of someone who, he said, was present.

The death struggle ensued almost immediately, and in the midst of his agony he seemed wrestling for speech. All that could be heard, however, were a few broken words. "I was wrong. My—unfounded— For God's sake look in—You will find—" Having uttered these fragmentary sentences, he seemed to feel that the power of speech had passed away forever. He fixed his eyes piteously on those around him, and, with a great sigh of grief, expired. I gathered these facts from his granddaughter and Alain's daughter, Alice Van Koeren, who had been summoned by some friend to her grandfather's dying couch when it was too late. It was the first time she had seen him, and then she saw him die.

The results of Mr. Van Koeren's death were a nine days' wonder to all the merchants in New York. Beyond a small sum in the bank, and the house in which he lived, which was mortgaged for its full value, Mr. Van Koeren had died a pauper! To those who knew him and knew his affairs, this seemed inexplicable. Five or six years before his death he had retired from business with a fortune of several hundred thousand dollars. He had lived quietly since then,—was known not to have speculated, and could not have gambled. The question then was, where had his wealth vanished to. Search was made in every secretary, in every bureau, for some document which might throw a light on the mysterious disposition that he had made of his property. None was found. Neither will, nor certificates of stock, nor title deeds, nor bank accounts, were anywhere discernible.

Inquiries were made at the offices of companies in which Mr. Van Koeren was known to be largely interested; he had sold out his stock years ago. Real estate that had been believed to be his was found on investigation to have passed into other hands. There could be no doubt that for some years past Mr. Van Koeren had been steadily converting all his property into money, and what he had done with that money no one knew. Alice Van Koeren and her mother, who at the old gentleman's death were at first looked on as millionaires, discovered, when all was over, that they were no better off than before. It was evident that the old man, determined that one whom, though bearing his name, he believed not to be of his blood, should never inherit his wealth or any share of it, had made away with his fortune before his death,—a posthumous vengeance which was the only one by which the laws of the State of New York relative to inheritance could be successfully evaded.

I took a peculiar interest in the case, and even helped to make some researches for the lost property, not so much, I confess, from a spirit of general philanthropy, as from certain feelings which I experienced toward Alice Van Koeren, the heir to this invisible estate. I had long known both her and her mother, when they were living in honest poverty and earning a scanty subsistence by their own labour; Mrs. Van Koeren working as an embroideress, and Alice turning to account, as a preparatory governess, the education which her good mother, spite of her limited means, had bestowed on her.

In a few words, then, I loved Alice Van Koeren, and was deter-

225

mined to make her my wife as soon as my means would allow me to support a fitting establishment. My passion had never been declared. I was content for the time with the secret consciousness of my own love, and the no less grateful certainty that Alice returned it, all unuttered as it was. I had, therefore, a double interest in passing the summer at the old Dutch villa, for I felt it to be connected somehow with Alice, and I could not forget the singular desire to inhabit it which I had so often experienced as a boy.

It was a lovely day in June when Jasper Joye and myself took up our abode in our new residence; and as we smoked our cigars on the *piazza* in the evening we felt for the first time the unalloyed pleasure with which a townsman breathes the pure air of the country.

The house and grounds had a quaint sort of beauty that to me was eminently pleasing. Landscape gardening, in the modern acceptation of the term, was then almost unknown in this country, and the "laying out" of the garden that surrounded our new home would doubtless have shocked Mr. Loudon, the late Mr. Downing, or Sir Thomas Dick Lauder. It was formal and artificial to the last degree. The beds were cut into long parallelograms, rigid and severe of aspect, and edged with prim rows of stiff dwarf box. The walks, of course, crossed always at right angles, and the laurel and cypress trees that grew here and there were dipped into cones, and spheres, and rhomboids.

It is true that, at the time my friend and I hired the house, years of neglect had restored to this formal garden somewhat of the raggedness of nature. The box edgings were rank and wild. The clipped trees, forgetful of geometric propriety, flourished into unauthorised boughs and rebel offshoots. The walks were green with moss, and the beds of Dutch tulips, which had been planted in the shape of certain gorgeous birds, whose colours were represented by masses of blossoms, each of a single hue, had transgressed their limits, and the purple of a parrot's wings might have been seen running recklessly into the crimson of his head; while, as bulbs, however well-bred, will create other bulbs, the flower-birds of this queer old Dutch garden became in time abominably distorted in shape;—flamingos with humps, golden pheasants with legs preternaturally elongated, macaws afflicted with hydrocephalus,—each species of deformity being proportioned to the rapidity with which the roots had spread in some particular direction.

Still, this strange mixture of raggedness and formality, this conglomerate of nature and art, had its charms. It was pleasant to watch the struggle, as it were, between the opposing elements, and to see nature triumphing by degrees in every direction.

The house itself was pleasant and commodious. Rooms that, though not lofty, were spacious; wide windows, and cool *piazzas* extending over the four sides of the building; and a collection of antique carved furniture, some of which, from its elaborateness, might well have come from the chisel of Master Grinling Gibbons. There was a mantel-piece in the dining-room, with which I remember being very much struck when first I came to take possession. It was a singular and fantastical piece of carving. It was a perfect tropical garden, menagerie, and aviary, in one. Birds, beasts, and flowers were sculptured on the wood with exquisite correctness of detail, and painted with the hues of nature.

The Dutch taste for colour was here fully gratified. Parrots, love-birds, scarlet lories, blue-faced baboons, crocodiles, passion-flowers, tigers, Egyptian lilies, and Brazilian butterflies, were all mixed in gorgeous confusion. The artist, whoever he was, must have been an admirable naturalist, for the ease and freedom of his carving were only equalled by the wonderful accuracy with which the different animals were represented. Altogether it was one of those oddities of Dutch conception, whose strangeness was in this instance redeemed by the excellence of the execution.

Such was the establishment that Jasper Joye and myself were to inhabit for the summer months.

"What a strange thing it was," said Jasper, as we lounged on the *piazza* together the night of our arrival, "that old Van Koeren's property should never have turned up!"

"It is a question with some people whether he had any at his death," I answered.

"Pshaw! everyone knows that he did not or could not have lost that with which he retired from business."

"It is strange," said I, thoughtfully; "yet every possible search has been made for documents that might throw light on the mystery. I have myself sought in every quarter for traces of this lost wealth, but in vain."

"Perhaps he buried it," suggested Jasper, laughing; "if so, we may find it here in a hole one fine morning."

"I think it much more likely that he destroyed it," I replied. "You know he never could be got to believe that Alain Van Koeren was his son, and I believe him quite capable of having flung all his money into the sea in order to prevent those whom he considered not of his blood inheriting it, which they must have done under our laws."

"I am sorry that Alice did not become an heiress, both for your sake and hers. She is a charming girl."

Jasper, from whom I concealed nothing, knew of my love.

"As to that," I answered, "it is little matter. I shall in a year or two be independent enough to marry, and can afford to let Mr. Van Koeren's cherished gold sleep wherever he has concealed it."

"Well, I'm off to bed," said Jasper, yawning. "This country air makes one sleepy early. Be on the lookout for trap-doors and all that sort of thing, old fellow. Who knows but the old chap's dollars will turn up. Goodnight!"

"Goodnight, Jasper!"

So, we parted for the night. He to his room, which lay on the west side of the building; I to mine on the east, situated at the end of a long corridor and exactly opposite to Jasper's.

The night was very still and warm. The clearness with which I heard the song of the katydid and the croak of the bull-frog seemed to make the silence more distinct. The air was dense and breathless, and, although longing to throw wide my windows, I dared not; for, outside, the ominous trumpetings of an army of mosquitoes sounded threateningly.

I tossed on my bed oppressed with the heat; kicked the sheets into every spot where they ought not to be; turned my pillow every two minutes in the hope of finding a cool side;—in short, did everything that a man does when he lies awake on a very hot night and cannot open his window.

Suddenly, in the midst of my miseries, and when I had made up my mind to fling open the casement in spite of the legion of mosquitoes that I knew were hungrily waiting outside, I felt a continuous stream of cold air blowing upon my face. Luxurious as the sensation was, I could not help starting as I felt it. Where could this draught come from? The door was closed; so were the windows. It did not come from the direction of the fireplace, and, even if it did, the air without was too still to produce so strong a current. I rose in my bed and gazed round the room, the whole of which, though only lit by a dim twilight, was still sufficiently visible. I thought at first it was a trick of Jasper's, who might have provided himself with a bellows or a long tube; but a careful investigation of the apartment convinced me that no one was present.

Besides, I had locked the door, and it was not likely that anyone had been concealed in the room before I entered it. It was exceedingly strange; but still the draught of cool wind blew on my face and chest, every now and then changing its direction,—sometimes on one side, sometimes on the other. I am not constitutionally nervous, and had been too long accustomed to reflect on philosophical subjects to become the prey of fear in the presence of mysterious phenomena. I had devoted much time to the investigation of what are popularly called supernatural matters, by those who have not reflected or examined sufficiently to discover that none of these apparent miracles are Supernatural, but all, however singular, directly dependent on certain natural laws. I became speedily convinced, therefore, as I sat up in my bed peering into the dim recesses of my chamber, that this mysterious wind was the effect or forerunner of a supernatural visitation, and I mentally determined to investigate it, as it developed itself, with a philosophical calmness.

"Is anyone in this room?" I asked, as distinctly as I could. No reply; while the cool wind still swept over my cheek. I knew, in the case of Elizabeth Eslinger, who was visited by an apparition while in the Weinsberg jail, and whose singular and apparently authentic experiences were made the subject of a book by Dr. Kerner, that the manifestation of the spirit was invariably accompanied by such a breezy sensation as I now experienced. I therefore gathered my will, as it were, into a focus, and endeavoured, as much as lay in my power, to put myself in accord with the disembodied spirit, if such there were, knowing that on such conditions alone would it be enabled to manifest itself to me.

Presently it seemed as if a luminous cloud was gathering in one corner of the room,—a sort of dim phosphoric vapor, shadowy and ill-defined. It changed its position frequently, sometimes coming nearer and at others retreating to the furthest end of the room. As it grew intenser and more radiant, I observed a sickening and corpse-like odour diffuse itself through the chamber, and, despite my anxiety to witness this phenomenon undisturbed, I could with difficulty conquer a feeling of faintness which oppressed me.

The luminous cloud now began to grow brighter and brighter as I gazed. The horrible odour of which I have spoken did not cease to oppress me, and gradually I could discover certain lines making themselves visible in the midst of this lambent radiance. These lines took the form of a human figure,—a tall man, clothed in a long dressing-robe, with a pale countenance, burning eyes, and a very bold and prominent chin. At a glance, I recognised the original of the picture of old Van Koeren that I had seen with Alice. My interest was now aroused to the highest point; I felt that I stood face to face with a spirit, and doubted not that I should learn the fate of the old man's mysteriously concealed wealth.

The spirit presented a very strange appearance. He himself was not luminous, except some tongues of fire that seemed to proceed from the tips of his fingers, but was completely surrounded by a thin gauze of light, so to speak, through which his outlines were visible. His head was bare, and his white hair fell in huge masses around his stern, saturnine face. As he moved on the floor, I distinctly heard a strange crackling sound, such as one hears when a substance has been overcharged with electricity. But the circumstance that seemed to me most incomprehensible connected with the apparition was that Van Koeren held in both hands a curiously painted flower-pot, out of which sprang a number of the most beautiful tulips in full blossom.

He seemed very uneasy and agitated, and moved about the room as if in pain, frequently bending over the pot of tulips as if to inhale their odour, then holding it out to me, seemingly in the hope of attracting my attention to it. I was, I confess, very much puzzled. I knew that Mr. Van Koeren had in his lifetime devoted much of his leisure to the cultivation of flowers, importing from Holland the most expensive and rarest bulbs; but how this innocent fancy could trouble him after death I could not imagine. I felt assured, however, that some important reason lay at the bottom of this spectral eccentricity, and determined to fathom it if I could.

"What brings you here?" I asked audibly; directing mentally, however, at the same time, the question to the spirit with all the power of my will. He did not seem to hear me, but still kept moving uneasily about, with the crackling noise I have mentioned, and holding the pot of tulips toward me.

"It is evident," I said to myself, "that I am not sufficiently in accord with this spirit for him to make himself understood by speech. He has, therefore, recourse to symbols. The pot of tulips is a symbol. But of what?"

Thus, reflecting on these things, I continued to gaze upon the spirit. While observing him attentively, he approached my bedside by a rapid movement, and laid one hand on my arm. The touch was icy cold, and pained me at the moment. Next morning my arm was swollen, and marked with a round blue spot. Then, passing to my bedroom-door, the spirit opened it and went out, shutting it behind him. Catching for a moment at the idea that I was the dupe of a trick, I jumped out of bed and ran to the door. It was locked with the key on the inside, and a brass safety-bolt, which lay above the lock, shot safely home. All was as I had left it on going to bed. Yet I declare most solemnly, that, as the ghost made his exit, I not only saw the door open, but *I saw the corridor outside, and distinctly observed a large picture of William of Orange that hung just opposite to my room.*

This to me was the most curious portion of the phenomena I had witnessed. Either the door had been opened by the ghost, and the resistance of physical obstacles overcome in some amazing manner,— because in this case the bolts must have been replaced when the ghost was outside the door,—or he must have had a sufficient magnetic accord with my mind to impress upon it the belief that the door was opened, and also to conjure up in my brain the vision of the corridor and the picture, features that I should have seen if the door had been opened by any ordinary physical agency.

The next morning at breakfast I suppose my manner must have betrayed me, for Jasper said to me, after staring at me for some time, "Why, Harry Escott, what's the matter with you? You look as if you had seen a ghost!"

"So, I have, Jasper."

Jasper, of course, burst into laughter, and said he'd shave my head and give me a shower-bath.

"Well, you may laugh," I answered; "but you shall see it tonight, Jasper."

He became serious in a moment,—I suppose there was something earnest in my manner that convinced him that my words were not idle,—and asked me to explain. I described my interview as accurately as I could.

"How did you know that it was old Van Koeren?" he asked.

"Because I have seen his picture a hundred times with Alice," I answered, "and this apparition was as like it as it was possible for a ghost to be like a miniature."

"You must not think I'm laughing at you, Harry, he continued, "but I wish you would answer this. We have all heard of ghosts,— ghosts of men, women, children, dogs, horses, in fact every living animal; but hang me if ever I heard of the ghost of a flower-pot before."

"My dear Jasper, you would have heard of such things if you had studied such branches of learning. All the phenomena I witnessed last night are supportable by well-authenticated facts. The cool wind has attended the appearance of more than one ghost, and Baron Reichenbach asserts that his patients, who you know are for the most part sensitive to apparitions, invariably feel this wind when a magnet is brought close to their bodies. With regard to the flower-pot about which you make so merry, it is to me the least wonderful portion of the apparition.

"When a ghost is unable to find a person of sufficient receptivity, in order to communicate with him by speech it is obliged to have recourse to symbols to express its wishes. These it either creates by some mysterious power out of the surrounding atmosphere, or it impresses, by magnetic force on the mind of the person it visits, the form of the symbol it is anxious to have represented. There is an instance mentioned by Jung Stilling of a student at Brunswick, who appeared to a professor of his college, with a picture in his hands, which picture had a hole in it that the ghost thrust his head through.

"For a long time this symbol was a mystery; but the student was persevering, and appeared every night with his head through the picture, until at last it was discovered that, before he died, he had got some painted slides for a magic lantern from a shopkeeper in the town, which had not been paid for at his death; and when the debt had been discharged, he and his picture vanished forevermore. Now here was a symbol distinctly bearing on the question at issue. This poor student could find no better way of expressing his uneasiness at the debt for the painted slides than by thrusting his head through a picture. How he conjured up the picture I cannot pretend to explain, but that it was used as a symbol is evident."

"Then you think the flower-pot of old Van Koeren is a symbol?"

"Most assuredly, the pot of tulips he held was intended to express that which he could not speak. I think it must have had some reference to his missing property, and it is our business to discover in what manner."

"Let us go and dig up all the tulip beds," said Jasper, "who knows but he may have buried his money in one of them?"

I grieve to say that I assented to Jasper's proposition, and on that eventful day every tulip in that quaint old garden was ruthlessly uprooted. The gorgeous macaws, and ragged parrots, and long-legged pheasants, so cunningly formed by those brilliant flowers, were that day exterminated. Jasper and I had a regular battue amidst this floral preserve, and many a splendid bird fell before our unerring spades.

We, however, dug in vain. No secret coffer turned up out of the deep mould of the flower-beds. We evidently were not on the right scent. Our researches for that day terminated, and Jasper and myself waited impatiently for the night.

It was arranged that Jasper should sleep in my room. I had a bed rigged up for him near my own, and I was to have the additional assistance of his senses in the investigation of the phenomena that we so confidently expected to appear.

The night came. We retired to our respective couches, after carefully bolting the doors, and subjecting the entire apartment to the strictest scrutiny, rendering it totally impossible that a secret entrance should exist unknown to us. We then put out the lights, and awaited the apparition.

We did not remain in suspense long. About twenty minutes after we retired to bed, Jasper called out, "Harry, I feel the cool wind!"

"So, do I," I answered, for at that moment a light breeze seemed to play across my temples.

"Look, look, Harry!" continued Jasper in a tone of painful eagerness, "I see a light—there in the corner!"

It was the phantom. As before, the luminous cloud appeared to gather in the room, growing more and more intense each minute. Presently the dark lines mapped themselves out, as it were, in the midst of this pale, radiant vapor, and there stood Mr. Van Koeren, ghastly and mournful as ever, with the pot of tulips in his hands.

"Do you see it?" I asked Jasper.

"My God! yes," said Jasper, in a low voice. "How terrible he looks!"

"Can you speak to me, tonight?" I said, addressing the apparition, and again concentrating my will upon my question. "If so, unburden yourself. We will assist you, if we can."

There was no reply. The ghost preserved the same sad, impassive countenance; he had heard me not. He seemed in great distress on this occasion, moving up and down, and holding out the pot of tulips imploringly toward me, each motion of his being accompanied by the crackling noise and the corpse-like odour. I felt sorely troubled myself to see this poor spirit torn by an endless grief,—so anxious to communicate to me what lay on his soul, and yet debarred by some occult power from the privilege.

"Why, Harry," cried Jasper after a silence, during which we both watched the motions of the ghost intently, "why, Harry, my boy, there are *two* of them!"

233

Astonished by his words, I looked around, and became immediately aware of the presence of a second luminous cloud, in the midst of which I could distinctly trace the figure of a pale but lovely woman. I needed no second glance to assure me that it was the unfortunate wife of Van Koeren.

"It is his wife, Jasper," I replied; "I recognise her, as I have recognised her husband, by the portrait."

"How sad she looks!" exclaimed Jasper in a low voice.

She did indeed look sad. Her face, pale and mournful, did not, however, seem convulsed with sorrow, as was her husband's. She seemed to be oppressed with a calm grief, and gazed with a look of interest that was painful in its intensity, on Van Koeren. It struck me, from his air, that, though she saw him, he did not see her. His whole attention was concentrated on the pot of tulips, while Mrs. Van Koeren, who floated at an elevation of about three feet from the floor, and thus overtopped her husband, seemed equally absorbed in the contemplation of his slightest movement. Occasionally she would turn her eyes on me, as if to call my attention to her companion, and then, returning, gaze on him with a sad, womanly, half-eager smile, that to me was inexpressibly mournful.

There was something exceedingly touching in this strange sight;— these two spirits so near, yet so distant. The sinful husband torn with grief and weighed down with some terrible secret, and so blinded by the grossness of his being as to be unable to see the wife-angel who was watching over him; while she, forgetting all her wrongs, and attracted to earth by perhaps the same human sympathies, watched from a greater spiritual height, and with a tender interest, the struggles of her suffering spouse.

"By Jove!" exclaimed Jasper, jumping from his bed, "I know what it means now."

"What does it mean?" I asked, as eager to know as he was to communicate.

"Well, that flower-pot that the old chap is holding—" Jasper, I grieve to say, was rather profane.

"Well, what of that flower-pot?"

"Observe the pattern. It has two handles made of red snakes, whose tails twist round the top and form a rim. It contains tulips of three colours, yellow, red, and purple."

"I see all that as well as you do. Let us have the solution."

"Well, Harry, my boy! don't you remember that there is just such a flower-pot, tulips, snakes and all, carved on the queer old painted mantel-piece in the dining-room."

"So, there is!" and a gleam of hope shot across my brain, and my heart beat quicker.

"Now as sure as you are alive, Harry, the old fellow has concealed something important behind that mantel-piece."

"Jasper, if ever I am Emperor of France, I will make you chief of police; your inductive reasoning is magnificent."

Actuated by the same impulse, and without another word, we both sprang out of bed and lit a candle. The apparitions, if they remained, were no longer visible in the light. Hastily throwing on some clothes, we rushed down stairs to the dining-room, determined to have the old mantel-piece down without loss of time. We had scarce entered the room when we felt the cool wind blowing on our faces.

"Jasper," said I, "they are here!"

"Well," answered Jasper, "that only confirms my suspicions that we are on the right track this time. Let us go to work. See! Here's the pot of tulips."

This pot of tulips occupied the centre of the mantelpiece, and served as a nucleus round which all the fantastic animals sculptured elsewhere might be said to gather. It was carved on a species of raised shield, or boss, of wood, that projected some inches beyond the plane of the remainder of the mantel-piece. The pot itself was painted a brick colour. The snakes were of bronze colour, gilt, and the tulips—yellow, red, and purple—were painted after nature with the most exquisite accuracy.

For some time, Jasper and myself tugged away at this projection without any avail. We were convinced that it was a movable panel of some kind, but yet were totally unable to move it. Suddenly it struck me that we had not yet twisted it. I immediately proceeded to apply all my strength, and after a few seconds of vigorous exertion I had the satisfaction of finding it move slowly round. After giving it half a dozen turns, to my astonishment the long upper panel of the mantel-piece fell out toward us, apparently on concealed hinges, after the manner of the portion of escritoires that is used as a writing-table. Within were several square cavities sunk in the wall, and lined with wood. In one of these was a bundle of papers.

We seized these papers with avidity, and hastily glanced over them. They proved to be documents vouching for property to the amount of several hundred thousand dollars, invested in the name of Mr. Van

Koeren in a certain firm at Bremen, who, no doubt, thought by this time that the money would remain unclaimed forever. The desires of these poor troubled spirits were accomplished. Justice to the child had been given through the instrumentality of the erring father.

The formulas necessary to prove Alice and her mother sole heirs to Mr. Van Koeren's estate were briefly gone through, and the poor governess passed suddenly from the task of teaching stupid children to the envied position of a great heiress. I had ample reason afterward for thinking that her heart did not change with her fortunes.

That Mr. Van Koeren became aware of his wife's innocence, just before he died, I have no doubt. How this was manifested I cannot of course say, but I think it highly probably that his poor wife herself was enabled at the critical moment of dissolution, when the link that binds body and soul together is attenuated to the last thread, to put herself in accord with her unhappy husband. Hence his sudden starting up in his bed, his apparent conversation with some invisible being, and his fragmentary disclosures, too broken, however, to be comprehended.

The question of apparitions has been so often discussed that I feel no inclination to enter here upon the truth or fallacy of the ghostly theory. I myself believe in ghosts. Alice—my wife—believes in them firmly; and if it suited me to do so I could overwhelm you with a scientific theory of my own on the subject, reconciling ghosts and natural phenomena.

Duke Humphrey's Dinner

"Have we no more coal, Agnes?"

"No more."

"What the deuce are we going to do for fire?"

"I haven't the slightest idea, Dick. You're clever. Why don't you invent some way of warming one's self without the aid of fire?"

"If you were a man I could box with you," said Dick, looking meditatively at his wife as if wondering whether she could stand a round or two. "Boxing warms one up famously; but then we have no gloves."

"No," said Agnes, with a laugh, "and we shall have no shoes either in a very short time,"—and she pushed out, as she spoke, a little foot with a dilapidated slipper on it.

"What a funny thing it is to have no money, Agnes!" said Dick, gazing at a very small fire which smouldered in the grate, with a rather contemplative air. "Do you know that, if it wasn't so confoundedly cold, I'd rather enjoy poverty. Now in summer-time there must be something very *piquant* in misery."

"Only to think," answered Agnes, "of the thousands of dollars that I've thrown away on follies, when a tenth part of the sum would be a perfect dream of happiness now."

"At present five dollars would present as magnificent an appearance as the English national debt in gold sovereigns."

"Do you remember the ball at which you first proposed to me, Dick?"

"Don't I?"

"The large, lofty rooms, glowing with burnished gold and soft lights;—the carpets, with their elastic, mossy pile, into which one's feet sank so far and so pleasantly that they became loath to leave their nests, making one lounge lazily instead of walking;—the conservatory, dimly lit with coloured lamps, where tropical leaves nodded heavily, as if bathed in Eastern dreams, and the rich scent of the tuberoses wandered through the trees like the souls of dead flowers roaming in search of some bloomy paradise;—the music streaming through the wide doors of the dancing-rooms, and quivering off into the distance; the rustle of rich silks; the murmur of the thousand voices; the light; the perfume; the glory of youth and joy spreading over everything like an atmosphere of human sunshine in which myriads of gay and splendid butterflies floated. Don't you remember, Dick?"

"I do," answered Dick, with rather a sad smile, and a glance round the wretched room in which they were sitting. "I remember well the glories of the life in which you were born, and the contrast, strange enough, with the life to which I have brought you. You have described the past; let me describe the present. A fourth-storey room in a tumble-down tenement-house in the filthiest part of Mulberry Street. German shoemakers and Irish washerwomen above and below us. No furniture, save a table and a pallet-bed. A couple of old wineboxes to sit on, in place of chairs. Two feet of snow on the ground, and no coal; an exceedingly healthy and promising hunger gnawing at both of us, and no money to buy food. All our available goods sold or pawned long ago. Repudiated by our relatives because we chose to marry each other on the ridiculous basis of mutual affection.

"All our efforts to obtain work being constantly frustrated by either Providence or his Satanic Majesty. Just enough of inconvenient pride left in us to prevent us from begging. And I think, my dear Agnes, you have as pretty a case for suicide as ever came up in evidence before a Paris police court. Don't you feel like a pan of charcoal and a last embrace? or a dose of strychnine and a despairing letter to our friends? I would offer you a pair of pistols and a mutual shooting arrangement, but at present my account at the Merchants' Bank is rather confused, and I do not like to draw a check for any amount until it is settled."

And the young husband laughed as heartily as if the whole thing were a sort of comedy which he was rehearsing, and which he thought he was doing exceedingly well.

"Dick," said his wife, very earnestly, coming round to where her husband sat, and kissing him gently on the forehead,—"Dick, you are jesting, are you not? You have no such ideas, I trust?"

"Jesting? Of course, I am, you dear little puss! Of all the unphilosophical things a man can do, killing himself is about the most unphilosophical. To kill another man is unphilosophical, because the chances are ten to one that the murder will be discovered, and the perpetrator hanged. Therefore, murder is only a devious way of committing suicide, with the additional disadvantage of having killed a fellow-creature. But, as far as regards the individual, suicide is still more unphilosophical than murder, for you do not allow yourself even a chance of escape. We may have to die of starvation, my dear little Mentor, though I think it unlikely. If we have, however, the best thing we can do is to use all the means in our power to avert the unpleasant occurrence, and, if it comes, meet it manfully,—you may say womanfully, if you choose.

"But if we were to kill ourselves by poison in order to avoid dying twenty hours later of starvation, don't you think we should be doing rather an absurd thing? Particularly if, after we were dead, our spirits discovered that Providence would have sent us, at the nineteenth hour, some guardian angel, in shape of a friend, who would have relieved us from all our misery. No, my dear, we won't have any prussic acid, or French exits from life. When we are too weak to stand up, we will lie down side by side; and when we are too exhausted to live, we will clasp our hands together, bless God with our last breath, and die like the babes In the wood. Perhaps, after we are dead, that Irish washerwoman who lives in the fifth storey may come in, like the robin in the legend, and cover us with leaves. She isn't very like a robin, certainly," continued Dick, with an air of mock meditation, "for she swears frightfully, and, I regret to say, smells of whiskey."

This struck the pair as so very comic an idea that they simultaneously clapped their hands, and burst into peals of laughter. To hear those shrieks of merriment one would have thought this young couple the blithest and most careless creatures in the world.

Their history was a simple romance. They were both orphans, the only difference being that Agnes Grey was an orphan with rich relatives, and Richard Burdoon an orphan with no relatives at all. Agnes had been adopted by her uncle, an old bachelor, who lived in Boston,—a selfish old man, who, once he took possession of the poor girl, looked on her as his personal property, and regarded all who would seek to deprive him of her as atrocious burglars, worthy of the extremest penalties of the law. He petted her, then, as Caligula petted his favourite horse. She was clothed in purple and fine linen, and had her gilded stable.

Agnes Grey had but to express a desire, and every luxury that wealth could purchase dropped at her feet from the hands of the abominable old fairy, her uncle. She gave balls and *matinées*, and rode on Arab steeds. Her jewels were the newest and the most wonderful, her dresses unimaginably well-fitting. Having wealth, beauty, and an indulgent guardian, this charming young girl wanted but one thing,— a lover. It is a curious dispensation of Providence, that, while some young ladies are all their lives waiting for lovers, that commodity never arrives, whereas others have scarce begun to feel the vague desire, when lo! it rains and hails and snows any quantity of adoring young gentlemen.

Agnes Grey, then, had scarcely conjured up the youngest of desires in her most secret heart, when the wall opened, and Mr. Richard Burdoon, stepping out, proclaimed himself her lover. I don't mean to say that the wall opened in reality, but it is a metaphorical way I have of expressing that he arrived in the nick of time. They met at a party. Mr. Burdoon, having been left a few thousand dollars just one year previously by the death of his only surviving relative, set off for Europe to spend them. He succeeded to admiration, and, at the time I speak of, had just returned with an immense deal of useless experience, and just three hundred and fifty dollars. Considering, very properly, that so enormous a capital justified any folly, he ran off with Miss Agnes Grey, without consulting her avuncular dragon.

That jealous old relative, wounded in his tenderest spot, raged like a fury, disowned his unhappy niece, and swore a solemn oath that he would let her die of starvation ere he would assist her. At first, Agnes and her husband mentally whistled at his threats. Had they not three hundred and fifty dollars? Armed with so incalculable a sum, what cared they for poverty? They came to New York. Ah! how quickly did the scenes in the panorama succeed each other! Metropolitan Hotel and fine apartments; then boarding-house, and sudden departure therefrom owing to bills unpaid; then cheap lodgings and visits to the pawnbroker; then appealing letters to old uncle,—all of which were returned unopened. Lastly, in the miserable tenement in Mulberry Street, we find them without sixpence, laughing in the face of starvation.

What wonders will not youth and hope work! What horrible witches fly affrighted at its merry laugh, piercing as the clarion of the cock! Midas should have been the god of youth, for he turned everything to gold!

After a pause in the merry talk of this young couple, which I took advantage of in order to relate all I knew of their history, Dick said suddenly, as if the conviction forced itself on him for the first time, "Do you know, Agnes, that I feel absolutely hungry?"

"No! Do you, though?" said Agnes, with the most comic air of surprise. "Let us hasten up dinner."

"Certainly," answered Dick, falling instinctively in with her humour. "This cook of ours is confoundedly slow today. I shall give her warning";—and he made a feint of looking at his watch.

"I will ring the bell, and tell John to hurry her," said Agnes, pulling an imaginary bell-rope. "John," she continued, after a pause sufficient to allow the mythical John to mount the stairs,—"John, tell the cook to send up the dinner instantly. Master is very angry at the delay."

"Yes, mum," replied a gruff voice, which Agnes, of course, did not affect to consider as proceeding from the bottom of Dick's chest. Then Agnes and her husband talked of indifferent matters for a moment or two, as if beguiling the weary time before dinner. After a proper period of delay, John's gruff voice announced dinner in the same mysterious manner as before. Then Dick made a great show of giving Agnes his arm, and leading her in state into the dining-room. This solemn procession, however, consisted in marching round the naked chamber a couple of times, and bringing up before the old deal table, which was supposed to be loaded with all the delicacies of the season. Dick was agreeably surprised at the splendour of the repast.

"What!" he exclaimed, seating himself on the old wine-box, and glancing over the bare table,—"what a sumptuous feast! Ha! I shall enjoy it. My appetite is splendid. John, remove the cover from the soup. This is *potage à la reine*, my dear. Excellent, if I may judge by the odour. Shall I send you some?"

"Thank you, dear," answered Agnes, receiving a supposititious soup-plate from the mythical John. "It is delicious! But oh! I declare, I have burned my mouth, it is so hot!" and Agnes went through all the spasms of a person suffering from a spoonful of hot soup.

"As I live, a salmon!" exclaimed Dick, starting into an attitude of surprise. "It is early in the season for such fish."

"It was sent from Scotland, in ice," replied Agnes.

"It is a noble animal!" said Dick, using an aerial fish-knife with wonderful dexterity. "There is no sport more magnificent than that of salmon-fishing, particularly on the Scotch and Irish rivers. The noble scenery, the rapid river, the long, lithe rod, the whizzing line that drops the gorgeous fly into the deep pool, where the silver-sided rascals lurk.

Then the strike; the quick whirring of the wheel; the flashing leaps of the captive; the moments of agony when the line slackens as he runs up stream; the joy when he pulls again; the breathless anxiety when the gaff is thrust under him as he swims; the deep sigh of relief when he is hauled, flapping, shining, bleeding, dying, into the boat;—all this is—"

"Very eloquent, no doubt," says Agnes; "but your salmon is cooling all this time, my dear husband."

"Ah! true," cries Dick, with a sudden start, and applying himself with instant vigour to the discussion of a supposed cut of rosy flesh, with mealy flakes of white lying in the crevices of the meat. "What a delicious salmon! We are indebted to our noble friend in Scotland."

"You will find this *turban de volaille aux truffes* very excellent," said Agnes, peering with the air of a connoisseur at the ideal dish before her. "François's last master says that he is celebrated for it."

"Hum! we will see," muttered Dick, pursing up his lips, and leaning back as far as he could on the wine-box, with a critical importance. "Good heavens, Agnes!" he exclaimed, the moment after, with an air of horror, "how could you recommend this? Why, the fellow has not put a single cock's-comb in it! Pshaw! Here, John, take this away, and tell François, if he sends up a dish of that kind again, I will condemn him to eat it."

"Fortunately, there are some delicious *cotelettes à la financiere* left, so that we can dispense with the *volaille*," says Agnes.

"They are indeed excellent," answers Dick, making believe that his mouth is full of the succulent meat of the *cotelettes*.

So on through the whole of this strange repast. Delicacy after delicacy was announced,—some relished, others criticised, more dismissed indignantly. The unlucky François came in for many severe rebukes, transmitted through the mythical John. The game was pronounced overdone, and an English pheasant—a present from an illustrious British friend—was condemned as having been utterly spoiled in the dressing. The dessert, however, consisted of a *soufflet*, and a delicious confection, called *gâteaux Egyptienne*, was solemnly pronounced to be perfect, and John was commissioned to convey a flattering compliment to François, as a salve for the rebukes given during the previous courses. Two children, playing at "feasting," could not have conducted this visionary repast more earnestly. The correct wines were drunk at the correct moment, and all the little ceremonies of a formal dinner scrupulously performed.

When all was over,—when the coffee had been served and drunk, when the table had been cleared away, and John had respectfully retired,—the eyes of the young couple met, and a flash of laughter sprang from the encounter. Casting aside the elegant formality of the great lady *en grand tenue,* Agnes ran to her husband, and, clasping him round the neck, fairly sobbed out her laughter on his breast.

"Do you know, dear," said Dick, after a little while, "it may entail on me the reputation of being a glutton, of having a wolf in my stomach, of being a vampire, or a thousand other unpleasant report, but I nevertheless cannot help confessing that I feel rather more hungry than I did before I commenced that exquisite dinner, which, in spite of some failures, does François infinite credit."

"Would you like to dine over again, Dick?" inquired his wife, with a grave air. "Nothing is easier, you know."

"Certainly," answered Dick, dubiously, "nothing is easier; but—but I'm rather afraid that my tastes are becoming somewhat coarse. I am really ashamed of the very idea; but the fact is that at this very moment I have an intense longing for a piece of roast beef."

"That is singular," said Agnes, with an air of surprise. "However, nature sometimes avenges itself on luxury, by afflicting her votaries with homely tastes. I really pity you, Dick. For my part, nothing less delicate than a reed-bird,—tender, succulent, melting,—an epitome, in fact, of perfume, nourishment, and flavour,—nothing less than this could possibly tempt my pampered appetite."

"I declare, Agnes," cried Dick, "I have a fancy just now to behave like a poor devil who hasn't got a penny. Yes! you may shrug your shoulders, but I really wish to divest myself of my splendour, and commit an act that contradicts the magnificence with which we are surrounded."

"Explain yourself."

"You remember that magnificent edition of Erasmus which my old friend, Harry Waters, gave me when I was going abroad. Well, I cherish that book dearly, for the sake of him, and the few affectionate lines he has written on the fly-leaf. Now, if a very poor man had that book he would sell it, if he had nothing else to dispose of, for it is clasped with silver, and is worth something; so I, who wish, merely for a freak, to experience the sensations of a poor man, have an idea of going out and selling that book,—merely for the sake of the illusion, you know. Nothing more, on my honour."

"You always had queer fancies, dear," answered Agnes, as unconcernedly as if she had millions in her purse; but one might see beneath all that careless gayety a sudden flash of hope sparkle for an instant. One could see very plainly that this book—which, doubtless, had till then been forgotten—gave her a new lease of life; one could see very plainly how bravely she had been smiling in the face of hunger and of death.

"Let me perform the last act of the millionaire before I play the part of a beggar," said Dick, rising joyously from his wine-box. "Sardanapalus burned his furniture; why should not I consume my chairs? The fire is going out in a most unaccountable manner; let us see how this *fauteuil* will blaze." So saying, he broke the wine-box into fragments, and cast it into the almost fireless grate.

The wine-box blazed. A lofty, ruddy flame sprang up in the fireplace, and shed a glow over the cold, naked room. It seemed as if the purple Burgundy that once had lain between those few boards had left some portion of its fiery heart behind it. Who knows but that a bottle of that glowing wine was at that very moment sparkling on some splendid table,—that in some other hemisphere the curtains were drawn close, and the wax-lights blazing, and a party of jolly fellows, with legs well stretched under the shining mahogany, were toasting beautiful women, while the case which held the precious juice they were quaffing, the shell from which the soul that they were inhaling had fled, was burning in a rusty grate, and making a bonfire to scare away the wehrwolf, death?

"The blaze is really quite cheerful," said Agnes, warming her hands, while a faint glow of pleasure spread itself over her face. "Do you know that I think a wood-fire preferable to all others?"

"It recalls the feudal times," answered Dick. "We are in a vast baronial hall. The roof is solid with ribs of blackened oak, and antlers hang from the walls, to each horn of which cling a thousand memories of the chase. The floor is of solid stone. Old, tattered banners droop from the walls, and wave heavily, as if too weak with age to shake off the thickening dust that soils their historic splendour. No modern garments shroud our limbs. You, dearest, are clad in a lustrous Cramoisie velvet, with peaked stomacher, and stately train sweeping on the ground. A cavalier's hat, with its trailing feather, droops over my temples. My sword clangs against the pavement, and I assume a picturesque and haughty attitude, as I stand with my back to the wide fireplace, where huge logs of oak, supported by iron 'dogs,' spit and blaze, and send streams of sparkles up the huge chimney. I am at present meditating whether Hubert the *seneschal* shall be beheaded or not. Shall I order his instant execution, or—"

"Sell the book?" interrupted Agnes; "please yourself."

"By Jove, I forgot!" said Dick, forgetting in a moment all his splendour and feudality. "Agnes, I'll be back in five minutes. Tell John to prepare tea, and let us have the Sevres service";—and he bolted down the crazy stairs, reaching the bottom in a few bounds.

Agnes smiled sorrowfully as she crouched over the rapidly-sinking fire. The wine-box was fast losing its fiery spirit and degenerating into a dull mass of blackening embers. Now that her joyous young husband was away she had no one with whom she could laugh at misery. It takes two to fight that crawling, cruel monster. The moment the echoes of Dick's footsteps had died away the horror laid its cold hand upon her heart. It was in vain that she tried to sing, to laugh, to conjure up those comical visions which she and Dick had used so often before as an exorcism. She felt a black wall, as it were, closing gradually round her; the air became too thick to breathe; the last bit of sky was gradually being shut off,—then—then a quick foot on the stairs, a merry cricket-like voice, a half-sung carol, and Dick burst into the room, performing a species of triumphal dance. A piece of paper fluttered in his hand.

"Two dollars! "he cried, executing an indescribable figure. "Going for two dollars! This splendid, magnificent, delicious, succulent book, with silver facings, like a militia officer, going for two dollars! Who'll bid? Only two dollars! Gone at two dollars!"

"You don't mean to say—" said Agnes, rising eagerly.

"I do. I absolutely got two dollars for the book. It was worth fifteen; but then you know we must not be too nice. Isn't it splendid?" and he waved the two-dollar bill as a young ensign waves his standard in the battle. "I brought it home, Agnes dear, because I think you are the best person to spend it. These wretches of tradespeople would certainly cheat me if I attempted to buy any eatables. What shall it be?"

"What do you think of sausages?" said Agnes, suggesting rather timidly. "They are cheap and—"

"Excellent!" cried Dick, with a new pirouette, "charming! I adore the sausage. Sausage, with some nice white bread, a pat of butter, and a few apples, and we shall feast in dazzling splendour!"

"Not forgetting a cigar for Dick," whispered Agnes, looking up lovingly in his face. "I know that you long for a cigar."

"Angel!" cried Dick, clasping her in his arms, and waltzing round the room with her. "There are no soundings to the depth of woman's love!"

"I'm off to the market, love," said Agnes, giving him a kiss; but this chaste salute was suddenly interrupted by a knock at the door. Both hearts leaped. Who could it be? A new misfortune? The bookseller, where Dick sold the book, seemed suspicious about his being in possession of such property. Heaven grant that nothing unpleasant threatened, was the prayer of the young couple.

"Does Mr. Burdoon live here?" said a very deep, gruff voice.

"Yes," said Dick, boldly, "come in."

A short, thick-set man in a great-coat entered, and stood near the door. It was a dusky twilight in the room. The Assyrian bonfire of the wine-box had just expired in a few convulsive sparkles, and it was in vain that Dick tried to see the stranger's countenance.

"Are you Mr. Burdoon?" asked the visitor.

"I am," answered Dick; "what is your business, sir? I would ask you to be seated, but, unfortunately, all my furniture is packed up."

"Never mind," answered the man, gruffly. "You sold a book a short time since at Mr. Marbell's bookstore, did you not?"

"I really am not aware, sir," said Dick, haughtily, "that this is any one's business but my own."

"Softly, softly, my friend," answered the newcomer. "No need of quarrelling. How did that book come into your possession?"

"Are you a police-officer?" inquired Dick, in a menacing tone.

"Never mind," said the man, "answer my question first."

"When I have answered it, I shall kick you downstairs, my friend."

"I'll run the risk," said the fellow, with a short laugh.

"Well, then, it was given to me by a friend," answered Dick, making an ominous step toward the intruder.

"Wait a moment,—don't kick me down stairs just yet. Why did you part with that book?"

"Curse you, that's none of your business," cried Dick, savagely. "If you value your bones you'll leave me."

"I don't value my bones, so I'll stay until you have answered me," said the man, very quietly. Dick could not help smiling at this audacity.

"Every question I answer," said he, "I shall give you an additional kick for. You know the terms,—ask away."

"Why did you part with that book?"

"Because I was starving. Because I saw my wife fainting, and dying of cold and hunger before my eyes, all the time with a brave smile upon her lips. Because I have sought for work and could not get it. Because there was neither food, nor fire, nor furniture in this wretched hole. Because starvation was flapping his wings like a vulture, hoping each moment to plunge his beak into our vitals. For these reasons, I sold the book that dear old Harry Waters gave me, and for none other would I have profaned his gift. Now I have exposed my misery to you, sir, whoever you are, and you shall pay dearly for it. I will break every bone in your body," and he sprang like a tiger at the short, thick-set man, who stood in the gloom. He felt himself suddenly seized by the shoulder, and rooted to the earth, as if he had been in the grip of an enormous vise.

"Dick Burdoon," said the thick-set man, and this time his voice was sweet and soft as a woman's, "you are not going to kick me, Dick Burdoon; for many a star-lit night, in the silent fields, you have lain with my arms around you, and your head upon my bosom, while we talked of the splendid things we would achieve when we two went out into life hand in hand."

Dick trembled like a leaf, and said not a word.

"You will not kick me, Dick Burdoon," went on the thick-set man, loosening his grasp of Dick's shoulder, and drawing closer as he spoke, "because one day, when the sun was pitiless, and the river cool, a young, weak boy, tempted by the clear waters, ventured into a deep part, and went down. And then his friend, older and stronger than himself, plunged in, determined to rescue that fair boy or perish with him. And he dived into the deep waters twice, and the second time he found him, clasped in the meshes of loathsome weeds, with the merciless river sweeping away his young life. The elder boy struggled with him to land, and when they reached the shore people could scarce tell the saver from the saved. But when both recovered their strength and speech, the younger boy swore eternal gratitude to his preserver, and they vowed to be friends forevermore."

"I remember! I remember!" cried Dick sobbingly.

"Since that time," continued the thick-set man, "their paths in life have lain asunder; but I know that in the hearts of both the old friendship lives still, and that, if one of the twain were frowned on by the world, the other would pour out his life in smiles to make it sunshine with him again. That is why I know that you will not kick me, Dick Burdoon."

"Harry! Harry Waters,—my dear, dear old boy!" cried Dick through his tears, and flinging himself into the visitor's arms. "God

247

bless you for coming, Harry, for I needed you sorely."

"I saw you, my boy," said Harry, folding him in an embrace so gentle that one would imagine he was fondling a child,—"I saw you the moment you entered the shop. You know I was always famous for poking in old bookstores, and I am glad I have such tastes. I saw you selling the old Erasmus, my boy, and knew that something must be wrong with you. I followed you here, and now we three are joined, thank God, for a long time to come." And the kind fellow took poor, timid Agnes's hand and drew her close till all three were united in one fond trinity of love.

Need I tell how Harry Waters, the rich bachelor, carried Agnes and Dick off that evening to his house, and made much of them there? Need I say how they lived with him until Dick got employment, from which he has gradually raised himself to be a great merchant? Need I tell about that solemn christening, whereat Dick's firstborn was named, with much ceremony, Harry Waters Burdoon? A hint of all those happy days will, I am sure, be enough for the warm-hearted reader, who has long since, I know, wished the young couple a full meal. One thing I must relate, however,—an incident that occurred on the evening after the sale of the Erasmus. When the sobbings and the embraces were all over, Harry Waters, by way of saying something general, said to Dick, "By the way, have you dined yet?"

Dick turned to his wife, who smiled.

"O, yes, we dined sumptuously an hour ago," said Dick.

"Ah! indeed!" said Harry, rather surprised.

"Yes! we dined with Duke Humphrey!"

The Old Boy

Every man is double. He is what he knows himself to be, and what others think of him. The two men—the outward and the visible, and the inward and invisible man—are often very different sorts of people.

Perhaps this thesis was never more forcibly illustrated than in my own case. I had the misfortune, when scarcely fifteen years of age, to dream a most rare and ominous dream. So distinct was the vision in all its details, that it rather resembled a visit to another world, or a *clairvoyant* projection of the soul into the future, than an ordinary dream. Its most astounding peculiarity was its apparent duration. Everybody almost is familiar with the fact, that in a dream a few moments are often so prodigiously crowded with images and sensations that they appear as many hours. But I doubt whether there are many dreamers living who can boast of having condensed ten years of life into a single night. Such, however, was precisely my case. I awoke ten years older in mind than when I fell asleep the night before. I awoke with a distinct remembrance of ten years of active experience. I had the clearest recollection of thoughts and events during the whole period.

During these ten years of dreaming, I had left school, studied at a university, travelled, loved, fought, and written works which had obtained for me a great literary reputation. In a word, I had become a great and distinguished man, accustomed to receive the consideration due to my position. I had possessed fortune, power, a host of admirers, and, above all, the consciousness of power and manhood. I awoke a mere child in the eyes of the world; a delusive phenomenon, an anachronism, a living paradox; a schoolboy ten years older than himself; an experienced man ten years younger than his ideas.

Al first I could scarcely realise the absurd fact of my youth. I was inclined to take truth for vision, and vision for truth. But finding myself soon driven to fall back on metaphysics, and on such notions as that life is itself a dream, and that ideas and events differ only in a trifling degree, I thought it wisest to avoid becoming insane by taking a more practical view of my position. I certainly had dreamed myself into a most unboyish state of intellect and feelings. I certainly had awakened to a most unmanlike appearance of juvenility, and a most inconsistent state of boyish thraldom. I was at an English boarding-school—the Rev. Doctor Whopham's classical academy! What a ridiculous misfortune for the author of books, the politician, the man of the world, of my dream memory!

I was just revolving these contradictions in my mind when the school-bell rang for the boys to get up. It was six o'clock in the morning. For the last five or six years of my life (in the internal dream) I had been accustomed to lie in bed in the morning and muse on the composition of my works. On the present occasion, I continued to ponder lazily over my mysterious vision, when I was suddenly roused from my reverie by one of the boys in the room calling out in a shrill tone:

"Hollo! Darkman, do you mean to get up today, or wait till tomorrow?"

At the same moment another of the boys thought it a capital joke to throw a bolster at me, which, descending precisely on my face, for the moment half smothered me, and so irritated my temper in the anomalous condition of my mind, that forgetting my boyhood for the nonce, I sprang out of bed, seized the offender roughly by the shoulder, and administered a couple of boxes on the ear, with such lusty goodwill, that the whole room rung with their vibration.

"Take that, you insolent young monkey!" I cried in a stern, contemptuous tone, which amazed the offender, who was as nearly of my own size and age as might be.

"I say," retorted the boy angrily, "none of that girl's play with me; if you please, come on and fight like a man, if you can!" and the boy doubled his fists and threw himself into a very orthodox pugilistic altitude.

This brought me to my senses, and recalled me to a consciousness of my absurd position. However, there was, of course, no retreat, and I prepared for the inevitable contest. He had told me to fight like a man. Little did he imagine how much of a man I was. Ten years of adventures had given me a self-possession and courage very different from the mere effervescence of boyish audacity. Confidence is strength. I looked upon my antagonist as a child. My manly pride almost disdained such an enemy. He had scarcely returned my blow when I assailed him with such decisive resolution, that in a few moments he was grovelling on the floor at my feet, bleeding and vanquished.

The other boys applauded me admiringly, as I strode scornfully back to my bedside and began to dress in silence.

It was the first time they had witnessed anything of the kind on my part. Though not by any means weak or small for my age, I was of an extremely effeminate appearance. My complexion was singularly fair and delicate; my hair soft, light, and wavy; whilst previous to the change wrought in my character by the dream, I had been remarkable for the gentleness of my manners, and though not timid, had always avoided quarrelling and fighting as much as possible. But now I had acquired all the stern combativeness which ten years of arduous struggles rarely fail to impart to the human disposition. Accordingly, when on descending to the schoolroom Dr. Whopham severely reprimanded me for my violence, I showed no manner of contrition for the offense, but looked coldly and indifferently at the doctor, who in my eyes was now no more than a vulgar pedagogue, very much my inferior in acquirements and talents.

"Do you hear, sir?" said the doctor; "I say that I will make an example of you."

"You had better not," said I sarcastically, thinking of a repartee I had made to Washington Irving a year or two before (in the dream;) "I should make a bad example to a certainty."

"You shall be flogged, sir," said the doctor, losing all patience. "By G—, I'll not be bearded by any boy in my school. I will flog you this very day."

"I think you will not, sir," said I with affected politeness.

"Why not," thundered Whopham, growing purple in the face with rage, "you poisonous young viper:'"

"Because it you attempted such a thing, or effected it by force, I would infallibly kill you."

"Kill me!" cried the doctor; "the young wretch, the unprincipled, immoral young monster—he threatens to murder me!"

"Yes; it you lay hands on me, I do," was my deliberate answer.

"Why, what's the matter with the boy?" said the head usher, coming up; "is he mad? He used to be the most peaceable and gentle boy in the whole school, and look at him now; his face is like a Satan's."

"Wicked, but angelic," said I, laughing. "Mr. Polyglot, I thank you for the compliment."

"Does the devil possess the boy?" exclaimed Dr. Whopham, looking at my erect attitude of defiance with a mysterious feeling of dismay, and perhaps imagining that I relied upon the rank of my relatives, who were of wealth and distinction, to bear me out in my rebellious conduct.

"Hark you, you couple of old fools!" said I, with an indescribable pleasure in their utter confusion, "we have had enough of this. I meant to run away, but perhaps you may as we'll expel me. At all hazards, here we part; so, goodbye forever. Boys, goodbye."

As I spoke, I made a dash at the nearest schoolroom window, which was open to admit the fresh air, vaulted over the windowsill, and manfully took to my heels. In a few hours, I had distanced all my pursuers, for I was the best runner at the school, and I did not spare my legs. For several days after I could scarcely walk. Meanwhile I had taken the rail to London. I was sale. I was free. I was to all intents and purposes the man of my dream, without his position, his fortune, or his fame; at least, so I fondly fancied.

And now what was to be my course? At all hazards, I was resolved not to return to my relations. How could I explain to them the change that had taken place in my being? They would have confined me as a lunatic, or sent me back to school as a culprit. My first resolution, then, was to preserve my personal liberty at all costs. Anything was better than the slavery of a school-life—even starvation; but that I did not apprehend. I had a gold watch of which I could nearly guess the value. I raised ten pounds (fifty dollars) upon it the next day. Half that sum, judiciously invested, supplied me with clothes suitable to the appearance of a man several years older than myself, which I had resolved to assume. A pair of spectacles lilted with green glasses, a stiff cravat and shirt collar, and a rather clerical suit of black, were my whole means of disguise. Being nearly as tall as the average run of men, I was thus enabled to conceal my extreme youth, and to enter upon the career which I had proposed to myself as the source of my future income. This career was literature. Nor need it be wondered at that I adopted the pursuit which, in my dreamlife, I had already rained to such a successful issue.

In a few days, by assiduous labour, I had dashed off one of those strange, wild, improbable, plausible, and supernaturally interesting stones of which the literature of all nations scarcely furnishes a dozen examples. I knew, however, by my old dream experience, what a new aspirant for literary lame had to expect from publishers. I also knew how to deal with this despicable race of moral Jews, who discount thought and devour the mental wealth of genius precisely as their prototypes eat up the fortunes of the members of rich and noble families. Accordingly, I look excellent precautions against their ignorance on one hand, and their impertinence on the other.

I introduced myself to the firm of Grey, Brown, Yellowboy & Co. as the private secretary of a young gentleman of fortune, who indulged in literary ambition. I spoke with sincere admiration of my own genius, that is, of my imaginary master's; finally, I presented the MS. of my story as a work which had been produced under the most singular auspices. It was, in fact, I said, a translation and completion of a fragment never printed, which the illustrious Theodore Amadeus Hoffman had left behind him, and which, by incredible labour, my young employer had succeeded in deciphering and translating.

The publisher was extremely anxious to see the author, whom I did not forget to make the cousin of a duke, and a man of noble name and family. But I told him that, until after the publication of the work, such an interview would be impossible, as Mr. Percy Egremont (my supposed master) had even then started for Rome on a secret mission born the home government. The publisher, who could not penetrate my grave demeanour and green spectacles, treated me with distinguished politeness—not the less that I alluded to my own prospects of a diplomatic career under the patronage of Mr. Egremont.

He purchased the copyright of the work; and had good cause to rejoice in his speculation, for it ran through five editions in the space of as many months, and I found myself both famous and, comparatively speaking, rich. The publisher happened to be one of the most honest of his tribe, and I had received for each edition of my little book—which, by the way, was expensively printed and illustrated—the sum of thirty guineas, in all one hundred and fifty, or about eight hundred dollars.

Thus, I had achieved at a bound what, in my dream, and too often in the real lives of authors of the highest merit, was the result only of years of toil and drudgery—a position. I had a name, and the command of a publisher. I could draw money in advance, it I required it, on my mere promise of an unwritten book. At fifteen years of age I was one of the happy few whom success stamps with the mark of the most exclusive of all nobilities, acknowledged superiority. But I had the memory of ten years of battle in my heart. In secret, I tell all the sadness which poets are prone to who weep the miseries of humanity—all the weariness of life which a varied experience of its pleasures and its cares produces in the mind of the earnest thinker. Meanwhile other sensations natural to my age, and stimulated by my unnatural extension of experience, began to exercise an empire over my soul which neither reason nor prudence could contend against. The beauty of fair and gentle women haunted my dreams. The melody of angel voices, heard in poetic reveries, resolved themselves into the musical accents of silken-haired and blue-eyed girls. I had slid imperceptibly into society through the agency of my publisher and the literary men to whom he had introduced me, since, on the undeniable success of my book, I had laughingly thrown off my mask and declared myself to be Percy Egremont in person.

And as Percy Egremont, I was everywhere welcome. My extreme youth—for, though none suspected my real age, I could not be supposed to be more than nineteen or twenty at the very farthest—my fame echoed by every newspaper and review throughout the kingdom, my girlish face and gentle manners, all contributed to make me a sort of general pet lion. Even my brother authors loved and spoke well of me. How could they suspect, beneath my effeminate aspect, the iron will and hardened heart of a man practised in all the wiles and stratagems, inured to all the tempests and convulsions of a worldly and insatiable ambition!

If, with all this, I felt at times that my life was after all a sort of protracted imposture, a kind of sublimely methodical madness, what mattered? I was the last person in the world to underrate the value of a dream. So, I dreamed on, and took no thought for the morrow.

I had made the acquaintance, amongst other young men of literary tastes, of Lord Arthur Carisbrook, and by him had been introduced to his mother, the dowager Lady Carisbrook, and his sister, Lady Rosina, a girl of eighteen, who had just been presented at court, and was in all probability destined to be the recognised beauty of the season.

The moment her dark-blue, languishing eyes fell upon me, a flood of new-born vitality streamed through my frame. My chest seemed to expand, every fibre of my body to dilate with an ecstatic sensation of power. I felt myself a man indeed, and capable of contending with men. But, alas! I was still at least ten years older than I looked!

"What a pretty boy!" I overheard the countess say to her son as I turned to speak to Rosina.

"Yes, Mamma," replied the young Lord, "you would hardly imagine that he was the author of *Nairad*."

"Why, dress him in Rosina's clothes," said the countess, "and he would look more girlish than your sister."

I bit my lips with vexation. But the expression of Rosina's eyes, which, as she was tall, were precisely on a level with my own, soon distracted my thoughts from this mortifying remark. Rosina was, in truth, a girl worthy of a poet's love. She was full of animation, yet free from *coquetry*; she appreciated all, she enjoyed nature, she adored beauty. She had only one fault—an intense fear of ridicule. She had a soul brave and lofty enough to have defied menace, and dared persecution; but her courage faded before a sarcasm; a sneer descended on her resolutions like a blight upon the nectarines. This peculiarity of her character I discovered at our first interview, thanks to my supernatural knowledge of the intricacies of human fancies and motives.

At the same time, I conceived for her one of those insane, unspeakable, delicious passions which can only come into existence under rare and extraordinary circumstances. Such passions know no middle path; they bring with them either supreme happiness or intolerable misery. In my case, it required the most careful policy and perfect self-restraint, to give even the hope of a happy result. I do not allude to social difficulties. The love of Rosina secured, an elopement was a cardinal remedy for all such obstacles. But to be loved, and loved as madly as I myself loved, by Rosina, it was absolutely necessary that I should avoid ridicule. My weak point was my youth. Feeling that any affectation of disguising it would only render me absurd, I resolved, with the policy of a due politician, to annihilate its weakness by making it a tower of strength.

Accordingly, I assumed the part of a gay, careless boy-poet. I made no pretence to the dignity of maturity. I took liberties with everybody, and allowed everybody to treat me as a precocious youth, who had no idea of appearing otherwise than he was. Lady Carisbrook took a great liking to me—she little thought what exquisite art I had employed to ingratiate myself—and I was invited to join a large party of fashionable people at her country mansion.

It was on this occasion, that I hoped to bring my schemings to a happy climax. By my boyish vivacity and unassuming manners, I acquired the affections of nearly all the guests assembled. My subtle jests passed for random flashes of humour. Sayings, which Talleyrand might have been proud of, were repeated as happy blunders of a prattling youth. My authorship of *Nairad*, which might have opened the eyes of any one of ordinary perspicacity, was for the time forgotten.

It was only when alone with Rosina, that my tone and manner

underwent a total transformation. To her, I discoursed naturally and freely, with all the gravity of a philosopher, and enthusiasm of an ambitious genius. For her ear, I reserved the stores of my mysteriously acquired knowledge, all the wonders of my daring projects and aspirations. I made her my confidant and friend. I never said a word of love. I even forced myself to look at her without betraying my passion. I had but one object—to teach her to respect me. In the presence of third parties I avoided showing even the most shadowy indication of the love that consumed my soul. Thus, I escaped the ridicule of rival suitors, the odious comparison with their robust forms and whiskered faces; thus, in short, I convinced Rosina of my superiority, before she had even dreamed of comparing me with others.

All went well. My policy was triumphant, and at length the crisis was brought on, which was either to establish my complete success, or utter failure.

"How is it," said Rosina, as we stood talking, before dinner, in a conservatory of exotic plants, to which we had retreated from an instinctive wish to enjoy one another's society undisturbed—"How is it, Percy, that you are so different when alone with me, from what you are in company?"

"It is because, my dear Lady Rosina, the mass of mankind are not worth talking sense to, as they are barely capable of understanding nonsense. Besides, I am a mere boy, comparatively speaking, and it would be bad taste to show myself wiser or cleverer than older people. I have also the misfortune to look much younger even than I am; my face is—"

"More like a pretty girl's than a man's," said Rosina, laughing, with a wickedly puzzling expression.

I did not blush, as I should probably have done, had anyone else said the same thing. It was not the wounded vanity of a child, it was the baffled passion of a man, that caused me to turn pale, to feel my knees almost sink beneath me, and to contract my brows with an expression of pain that no self-command could conceal.

But my agony was of brief duration. Rosina took my hand in hers, and pressing it in a way that caused me the most delicious thrill of enjoyment, said, in a very different tone, and with a look that penetrated through all my artificial panoply: "Percy, I think Alcibiades, at your age, must have been what you are now, a combination of the beauty of a woman and the soul of a hero!"

Scarcely had Rosina uttered these perilously flattering words, than

I had clasped her lovely form to my heart in an embrace of frantic delight, and pressed upon her lips a kiss that caused me to turn faint with rapture. In another instant, I was at her feet. I looked up. She was trembling from head to foot. Her eyes were swimming in tears. She said nothing, she raised me gently; one more passionate embrace, and at the sound of the dinner bell, we hastened to put on an indifferent aspect, and join the assembled guests in the drawing-room. Henceforth our eyes might have served us as telegraphs.

And now, laugh who will at what follows. Years of peril, vicissitude, and wild adventure lie between me and that hour. I yet shudder to recall its eventful moments. On entering the drawing-room I met face to face a newly arrived guest. Almost petrified with horror, I recognised—Doctor Whopham. I saw, too, with the same glance, that he too. had recognised me. Exposure was inevitable. Nevertheless, I did not lose my presence of mind. I tried the only chance I had.

"Doctor," said I, shaking him by the hand, and speaking in an under tone, "silence!—silence at any price—at *any* price!"

But the schoolmaster either would not or could not understand me; probably the latter, as he was a man of heavy and obtuse intellect. He stared at me for a moment in stupid amazement; then burst out in a tone that was audible from one end of the room to the other:

"What! you here? So, I've caught you at last, Master Darkman, have I? Your relations have been half crazy about you. Don't frown at me, you young villain! Ha, ha! gentlemen and ladies, would you believe it? this is one of my boys who ran away, some six or seven months ago, from my school. Well! this is a *dies fortunata!* His relations have offered all sorts of rewards for his recovery. Excuse me, your lordship, but how, in the name of Scylla and Charybdis, did this boy come here!"

I did not regard the supercilious smiles and broad grins of the faces that surrounded me, all radiant with infernal curiosity and enjoyment of the ridiculous scene. I turned, crushed as I was in soul, with a proud and calm air, towards Rosina. She was laughing—yes, laughing aloud at my hideous discomfiture! As her eyes encountered my look of eternal reproach, she burst into a yet more extravagant fit of laughter.

We were always a fierce and violent race, we of the Darkman family. A man darkened by a fearful crime was its legendary founder. And now all the blackness of Helll seemed concentrated in my heart.

"Dog!—idiot!" I cried savagely, "what is the meaning of this farce— this incomprehensible insolence. Apologise at once, and choose other subjects for your jests in future."

"Oh, indeed!" said the schoolmaster. "Oh, indeed! you call me dog and idiot, do you? Wait till I see your father, or till I get you back to school, and have you flogged as you deserve. Only let me—"

At this moment, the coarse speaker was interrupted in his diatribe by a blow on the head from the pedestal of a massive bronze lamp, which in my fury I had seized and wielded as if it had been a mere bamboo cane. Amid a general cry of horror, the doctor fell senseless to the ground, and a stream of blood from his fractured skull began to form an ominous pool upon the carpet. I was only restrained from repeating the blow by the united efforts of the bystanders.

The next day I awoke in the county gaol.

Some weeks elapsed. The schoolmaster did not die. He only became a lunatic, which, to a man who was born a fool, was perhaps no great misfortune. I myself was liberated, on the ground of temporary insanity, which my incoherent ravings in the delirium of a fever that had supervened on the last-named events not a little encouraged. Pale, wasted, and broken-spirited, I, some months later, being on a visit to an aunt in London, ventured to knock at Lord Carisbrook's door. My former friend received me, to my amazement, with more than his usual cordiality.

"Are you prepared," said I, "to hear a story which vulgar minds would call incredible?"

"I assure you that I am burning with curiosity to hear the explanation of your mystery."

I told him all—even to my interview with his sister, and her terrible laughter.

"And now," said he, "I will tell you something, since it appears after all that you are a man of an honourable family. Rosina did not join in the brutal laugh at your misfortune. She loved you too well, to take a pleasure in your ridicule."

"How, you would persuade me to disbelieve my senses?'"

"Yes; but if you would save Rosina another *fit of hysterics*, you will leave me and join her in the next room."

In another instant, my future bride was in my arms. To real love its object can never be ridiculous. Two years later the marriage of the only son of Sir Lionel Darkman to Lady Rosina Carisbrook was announced in the papers.

And strange to say, the memory of that dream never faded, but remained, as it were, an integral part of my life. When other subjects failed us, it was a constant resource for conversation; and Rosina, smoothing my hair with her white hand, would say, gently smiling, "Now tell me some of your adventures in dreamland."

And when ten years were elapsed, the two memories, of the visioned and the real life, remained strangely distinct; and I perceived that the latter was, indeed, but a continuation of the former. Indeed, Rosina often whispered—what my own vanity would have scarcely ventured to suggest—that I had become at last a greater man even than the man of my vision. Perhaps this flattering fancy was but a dream, like the other. At any rate, I doubt whether I shall ever dream again half so pleasantly!

Thus, I owe my fame, my bride, and my happiness, to a dream.

How I Overcame My Gravity

I have all my life been dallying with science. I have coquetted with electricity, and had a serious flirtation with pneumatics. I have never discovered anything, nevertheless I am continually experimentalising. My chambers are like the Hall of Physics in a University. Air-pumps, pendulums, prisms, galvanic batteries, horseshoe magnets with big weights continually suspended to them: in short, all the paraphernalia of a modern man of science are strewn here and there, or stowed away on shelves, much to the disgust of the maid-servant, who on cleaning-day longs to enter the sanctuary, yet dare not trust her broom amidst such brittle furniture.

To survey my rooms; you would infallibly set me down as a cross between Faraday and Professor Morse. I dabble in all branches of Natural Philosophy. I am continually decomposing water with electricity, and combining gases until they emit the most horrible-odours. I have had four serious explosions in my laboratory, and have received various warnings from the Fire Marshal. The last was occasioned by the obstinacy of an Irish maid-servant, who, happening to behold a large mass of phosphorus in the dark, would insist on "putting it out" with a pail of water. The consequence was, of course, a conflagration that was near destroying the entire establishment. My friends visit me with fear and trembling. They are never certain that the bell-pull may not be the pole of an electro-magnetic battery, and when they seat themselves in a chair seem to expect some unwonted phenomenon to exhibit itself.

You will at once perceive, therefore, that I am an enthusiast. People when they pass me in the street point, me out to their friends, and whisper, "Very clever man, but *so* eccentric!" I have gotten an immense reputation for ability, yet I don't believe that my best friend would trust me with the management of the most trivial business matter. Nor am I so much surprised at this. I will confess that I am continually suffering losses on my own little properly, and it would seem my late to form relations with all the bankrupts and swindlers in the United States. These drains on my estate I always hoped to make good by an invention. I am a very worldly fellow at bottom, let me tell you, notwithstanding all my scientific pranks. I keep an eye out for the main chance; and I always held the hope that even when my affairs were going most to ruin I would eventually light upon some lucky discovery which would make everything right again. There's Professor Morse. He lit upon an invention, and see what's the result? Why, he's asked over to Moscow by the Emperor of Russia to be present at his coronation, and is given a palace to live in, with a whole Ukraine of horses and Cossacks at his disposal!

For a long time, I had turned my attention to solving the problem of aerial locomotion. I fancy even now that I hit the white when I enunciated my grand principle of progression by means of atmospheric inclined planes; and at the time I made a model of a machine which illustrated my theory very fairly, but I had not capital enough for experiments on a large scale; and so great was the prejudice against all kinds of ballooning among moneyed men that I could not find the means to exploit what is incontestably a great physical truth.

One day as I was walking down Mercer Street, in the neighbourhood of Bleecker, I came opposite to the establishment of Chilton, the chemist, which stood on the corner. Revolving a thousand formless projects in my brain, my eyes, wandering like my mind, happened to light on the open door of the chemist's store. There, on a table placed a little way inside the entrance, I beheld a number of brass instruments lying, the shape and construction of which I was unfamiliar with. Idly and half-mechanically I crossed over and entered the store for the purpose of examining them. The young man in attendance advanced to meet me—for I am known as a sort of amateur *savant*—and asked how he could serve me.

"What is this?" I asked, taking one of the instruments that had attracted my attention from the table. "It seems to me to be some novelty."

"It is truly a novelty," said my friend, the budding chemist. "It is a trifle—an ingenious trifle, certainly—discovered by a Connecticut genius, and its operations have as yet been entirely unaccounted for."

"Ah!" I cried, becoming suddenly interested, "let us look."

The machine which I held in my hand may be thus briefly described. Imagine a brass globe, some three inches in diameter, having its axis playing in a narrow but tolerably thick rim of brass, just as a terrestrial globe revolves in its horizon. The only difference being that the globe was not central in the rim, or horizon; one of its poles being nearer to the end of its axis than the other. This peculiarity, I afterward discovered, was not essential to its working, being merely a matter of convenience. The remainder of the apparatus consisted of an upright steel rod, fixed in a heavy wooden platform, candlestick fashion, and pointed like an electrical conductor.

"How does it work," I asked, after examining it attentively, "and what principle does it illustrate?"

"It overthrows an established principle," answered my young friend, "and I am not clear as to what one it gives in place of it."

"Let us see it."

"Willingly."

So saying the young man took the globe, which revolved with little friction in its brass horizon, and winding a siring round that portion of the axis which occupied the greatest space between the globe and ring, held the latter against his breast, and pulling the string violently, as boys pull the string of a humming-top, caused the globe to revolve with marvellous swiftness on its axis. The globe being thus in a rapid state of revolution in its horizon, he now showed me on the under surface of the last, and in a right line with the poles of the axis, a small cavity drilled, which admitted of the machine being placed on the upright pointed steel rod, without any chance of slipping. This cavity was *not a hole,* only an indentation in which the point of the upright rod fitted, just as the axle of a watch wheel is received into the jewel.

When this pivot, so to speak, was placed by the young chemist on the steel pointed rod, the globe and its horizon, to my utter astonishment, proceeded to revolve in a plane at right angles to the revolution of the globe! There was a weight of some six pounds supporting itself in the air, and revolving with a regular motion! If my reader will take a long wedge of iron, heavier at one end than the other, and place the light end on the point of a rod stuck into the earth, and at right angles with it, and then conceive that wedge of iron revolving around the point where it touches the upright rod, he will have a pretty clear idea of the marvel which I witnessed at Mr. Chilton's.

The attraction of gravitation then was overcome! In the same position in which I saw it maintaining itself, if the resolution of the brass globe was checked the whole apparatus would instantly tumble to the earth. Why, then, did the simple centrifugal force of the globe enable it to thus marvellously poise itself in air? I was bewildered, and though my brain, from habit of dealing with problems, instantly groped for a reason, it could find non satisfactory.

"Has no explanation been offered of this wonder?" I asked the chemist.

"None, Sir," was the reply; "at least none that were in the least logical or conclusive. Several people have sent us elaborate explanations, but when all have been divested of their scientific phraseology, they amount but to one arbitrary assertion of the fact that it revolves contradictorily to the laws of gravitation."

I bought one of the toys and went home. I was lost in wonder. What became of Newton's famous apple now? It was rotten to its core. Had the wind or some other subtle power impressed upon it such a force as to cause it to revolve with immense rapidity it would never have fallen, and Newton would never have discovered the so-called principle of the attraction of gravitation.

The more I pondered the more the marvel grew upon me. I spun the toy for hours, and was never weary of beholding it move in its appointed circle, self-sustaining and mysterious. After all, I considered it as only wonderful to me, because I have been so long in the habit of accepting the theory of gravitation as an established fact. This new force, whatever it is that supports this toy in air, is not a whit more mysterious than the assumed force which is said to draw all things toward the centre of the earth, and keep the planets in their places. Ask what it is, and people tell you "the attraction of gravitation." Ask them what "the attraction of gravitation" is, and they will tell you "the force which draws matter to the centre of the earth," and so the game of science runs. Arbitrary names are forced on you as facts. From battledore to battledore the shuttlecock is sent flying. The result becomes the definition and the explanation.

It was in one of those moods of mind in which a man sometimes finds himself, groping for day through a horrible and oppressive darkness, yet certain that the chink through which it will flow lies somewhere within reach, that I suddenly lit upon the conviction that in this new discovery I held the secret of aerial locomotion!

I argued in this way: If a violent rotary motion is sufficient to overcome the gravitating tendency of brass, it surely is that of human flesh. Neither is it at all necessary that the body of the person wishing to soar aloft should itself revolve. That would be fatal to life. But here, in this toy, I see the revolution of a brass globe supporting a heavy brass horizon, and if I were to put another weight, say a cent, on that brass horizon, it would still be supported; therefore, if a machine on the same principle, and proportionately large, be constructed, it will support a man as this supports a cent. I had lit upon the truth that "a body revolving on its own axis with sufficient velocity becomes sell-supporting, and can be impressed with a force that shall impel it in any given direction!"

With all the fever of a man of science and an enthusiast I set to work. My machine cost me long nights of labour and brainwork. I will endeavour to describe it.

It was a copper globe of vast dimensions, hollow inside, and traversed by a huge axis, which buried its poles into an enormous horizon of iron. In the interior of this globe, parallel with the axis and a little above it, ran a false axis, also of iron, but playing loosely in holes bored in the globe itself, so that when the globe revolved this axis did not turn. On this bar of iron was placed a seal, which was intended for my own accommodation. This arrangement, it will be perceived, insured to any person placed on the seat an equilibrium, no matter how quickly the globe by which he was surrounded revolved. It was, in fact, the same principle on which ships' lamps are suspended. There the lamp always remains horizontal, no matter how heavily the vessel rolls.

The machinery by which the globe was caused to revolve on its axis is much too complicated to admit of any description unaccompanied with diagrams; suffice it to say, that it was so powerful as to insure a revolution of this enormous copper sphere at the rate of sixty times in a second. A vast iron pillar, answering to the upright steel rod of the toy, I had also constructed. This was destined to receive and sustain the brass horizon. A machine constructed after the manner of the ancient catapult was also arranged for the purpose of launching the globe into air so soon as it had attained the necessary revolutionary velocity. The power of this catapult was cunningly graduated to certain distances.

Assuming that the globe while revolving possessed no weight, it would with a slight push travel forever through space unless the resistance of the atmosphere lessened and conquered its motion. But the globe would only revolve for a certain time, and in proportion as the velocity of revolution decreased so would its tendencies to the earth return; thus, knowing precisely how long this velocity would last, and in what ratio it would decrease, I was enabled to calculate to a pound what force to impress upon it by the aid of the catapult, in order to send it any given distance.

Everything being complete, and having invited a few friends to witness the experiment, I took my seat on the false axis with a beating heart, and gave the signal by which the attendants were to set the globe in motion. In an instant, the copper sphere was whirling around me with a velocity that I could not measure, but could only guess at from the humming noise that to me in the interior sounded like the thunder of a thousand skies. The interior of the globe was lit by pieces of massive flint glass set firmly in a belt form round the centre. These windows, from the rapidity of motion, blended together in a zone of light that flashed continually before my sight. My seat on the axis, poised in the midst of this terrible whirl, remained steady and unaltered. Suddenly I felt a jerk, a singular sensation quivered through my frame, and, rather by instinct than sensation, I knew that the catapult had launched me into space.

I had calculated my distance for St. Paul's, Minnesota, and had accordingly set the catapult to the scale of force necessary to cast the globe that distance, making the proper allowance for the decrease of velocity. Would I succeed? I confess at this moment I felt grave doubts. A thousand things might happen. The theory was perfect, but how many perfect theories had failed in practice! My elevation might be improperly calculated, and the machine be dashed to pieces against some intervening mountain. A few seconds would, however, decide all, as I had calculated that the journey would not consume more than four minutes and a half.

While occupied with these considerations I chanced to glance at the belt of light formed by the quickly-revolving windows. it seemed to me to have changed its shape strangely. Instead of its previous regularity of form, it had become, as it were, ragged and uneven. On looking closer, and examining it as narrowly as I could examine anything passing in such rapid revolution, I fancied that I saw it widen gradually before my eyes. And, as if to confirm my suspicions, a blast of cold air fell on my cheek, and immediately after a hollow roaring filled the globe.

The horrid truth burst upon me. I had forgotten to make the solidity of the copper globe more than equal to the centrifugal force, and the machine was bursting to pieces when I was at my highest elevation.

My brain seemed to whirl with the globe on making this discovery, and with staring eyes I glared at the awful rent that was so rapidly increasing. A hurly-burly like that of the infernal regions filled my ears. It was the air rushing into the globe. Then came a crash and a horrid splitting sound. Instinctively I grasped the immovable axis on which I was seated. Another crash, and I saw dimly the huge mass of copper surrounding me fly into a thousand vast fragments, and I knew that I was falling.

I gave one wild shriek, and—

"Mr. Wisp! Mr. Wisp! What are you doing? Let the tea-urn alone, Mr. Wisp!"

I looked up from the carpet on which I was lying, and saw my wife, Mrs. William Wisp, extricating the silver tea-urn—fortunately not filled—from my embraces. I was never able to explain to the good woman why I abstracted that article of plate from the side-table during my dream; and for the first time in the history of science an inventor was to be found congratulating himself that his invention had not succeeded.

The Mezzo-Matti

1

"Good morning to you, Beppo. I have come after my shoes," cried a voice, in the happiest of tones, outside the lattice.

"Your shoes.'" answered the cobbler, from inside, with a mingled expression of anger and amazement, as he hammered away at his work.

"Why, yes, certainly, I want my shoes; are they not finished?"

"Not even on the lasts," replied Beppo, in the most indifferent of tones.

"Oh! Say you are joking. For heaven's sake do not play upon my feelings! Not finished: Why, I ordered them ten days ago, and I had your most solemn promise—which the saints have recorded—that they should be ready today at noon. Alas! Oheme! What shall I do? I cannot go to church with Idiletta without my shoes; and today, at noon precisely, I am to be married!"

"I cannot help that, Tito, my prince of bridegrooms. Put off your wedding; you and your Idiletta can wait a spell."

"But just consider, Beppo—the marriage-guests are invited, the maccaroni is already on the boil, and I must have those shoes."

"Now," thought Beppo, "I have long had a grudge against this Tito; his shoes are almost ready, and maybe I will get a *carlin* more for them by holding them back:" and, not answering a word, he went on with his work.

"Look, now," said Tito, and he unbound the scarf that encircled his waist, "here are the ten *carlins* for them." Beppo leaned his head out of the lattice, and saw a gold *ducal* among the silver pieces. His cupidity was instantly aroused. Tito wenl on: "I am a richer man than I was yesterday, and I have no objection to add a *carlin* more, just for the pleasure of seeing my new buckles on them."

"A richer man! So, I see, Tito. Eleven *carlins* is not half what they are worth."

"Beppo, listen: in addition, when the fruit-season comes, you shall have a basket of melons, and just as many figs as you can carry; and as to mulberries, why—"

"Goodness gracious! How you promise!" interrupted the cobbler, with a smile of derision. "Whose garden is to suffer, or has Tito, the vagabond, become governor of the province?"

"Most skilful and greatest of shoemakers, I have had a stroke of good fortune; the biggest prize in the lottery is nothing to my luck. Just listen to how I, Tito, am going to be a man pretty well-to-do in the world. My mother—as all the village knows—when I was an infant, went to Naples, and there became muse to a noble family. Last night, as I was deeply immersed in thought, calculating whether I could afford cheese with my today's maccaroni, a great lackey, all bedecked with gold, calls me by name, and says his master anxiously awaits my coming at the hotel, and begs me to follow him.

"I was dumb with surprise, but in I went. In the handsomest room in the house, I found a host of gentlemen, all equipped for the chase; and one of them, nobler and finer than the rest, with a royal decoration in his buttonhole, suddenly rises, seizes me around the neck, and introduces me to the company as his foster-brother. He asks questions about me and my poor mother, and shed tears when he heard of her death, and, giving me a piece of gold, bade me have masses said for the repose of her soul. I told him that I was going to be married, and that Idiletta was the dearest—prettiest—sweetest—"

"Exactly, you ass! Just so," savagely interrupted Beppo. "Was there ever such a born fool! I suppose you would like this troop of huntsmen to give your Idiletta the chase. These Neapolitans are Famous huntsmen—" and here Beppo maliciously gave quite an artistic representation of the cries of a woman, with the hulloah and noise of the hunt in the distance.

"Out on you, Beppo, for a foul-mouthed cobbler!" roared Tito, in a rage. "Why, you wicked creature, they have purposely postponed their hunt today, in order to witness my marriage."

"Hmph!" enviously replied Beppo, jerking his shoulders on a level with his ears. "And so, ended the affair?"

"No," joyfully sang out Tito, slinging his cap up in the air. "My foster-brother, beside a handful of gold, gave me a broad slice of land, just over the hill there. Hurra! *viva!* I shall grow my own figs and melons, and won't I build me a house, and have a long-eared donkey, blessed be all the saints! And now," here Tito held up for want of breath, "Nothing is wanting to complete my happiness but those shoes; but if I do not have them in an hour," here, with fine Italian versatility of character, Tito's voice and face were plunged into the deepest abyss of melancholy, "I shall be the most wretched of men."

Beppo was silent, and thus he mused: "Twenty minutes will finish Tito's shoes. This foster-brother has so overwhelmed this beggar, Tito, with joy, that the little wit the dog had has all left him. He is going to have a donkey and a wife! This rascally Tito is to be raised to the very tip-top of happiness—is he? Well, he must afford to pay for his marriage-shoes. This cursed foster-brother has done all this for Tito. Now, I. Beppo, am nothing more than a poor cobbler, and can, by no means, pretend to have the power of this foster-brother—oh no! not in the least—but still, if, in my small way, I, Beppo, can do anything to make him miserable, I, too, will have shown some power, though of rather a different sort. A basket of figs, and a *carlin* more! the mean rascal! Tell him say ten *carlins* more, five baskets of figs, and, perhaps, I will let him have them; for I have him at my mercy now."

"Well, Beppo? Answer quickly," gasped out Tito, as if life and death were at stake.

"You may, perhaps, have them today; they are commenced, and I might, perhaps, finish them, provided I was properly paid for them. I am overrun with business. I am now mending Padre Alessandrino's shoes."

"Why, Padre Alessandrino is to marry us."

"Exactly. Now, if I should work at your shoe's, the good *Padre's* would not be finished, and the church," here the hypocrite crossed himself, "the blessed church calls for first obedience. Now, Tito, would you have his holiness go to mass with his toe out, or his heel run down? Would you, you sacrilegious dog.'"

Here was a quandary for Tito; there was logic in it.

"But," added Beppo, "if you will give me ten *carlins* more, and ten baskets of figs, why then, perhaps—"

"I cannot afford it, O, what shall I do?"

"Wear your old ones," tauntingly said Beppo.

"Why poke fun at me? You know I have gone barefoot ever since I was born!"

"Cannot help that, *signor* landholder: if you have gone so long in natural silk stockings, hop about so a trifle longer. My terms are ten *carlins* more, and in a half hour I shall ask twenty; so make up your mind, and, if you have nothing better to offer, the sooner you get out of my sunlight the better," and with this Beppo closed the lattice with a slam, through which Tito's handsome face had been peering like a Titian in a rustic frame. Tito's steps were heard slowly moving away, and Beppo resumed his hammer, and, in an audible tone, thus talked to himself:

"Curse his luck! why should this Tito swim in a sea of gold? This Idiletta! who does she take me for, to turn up her nose at Beppo and jump at Tito? It is true, I never demeaned myself by asking her to have me. She is comely, but not a copper in the world. I do not care about her, though she might have waited, if only through politeness, to see what my intentions were, and whether I had made a choice. To the evil one with my trade. If I could only leave a sharp nail in the heel of every shoe I cobbled, how I would glory in it; it is a satisfaction, however, to know that the leather I put in them is not worth a straw. Tito will give me no more? We shall see. The sun has already passed my window, and it must be noon, and Tito will have to make a higher bid—fifteen *carlins* more at the very lowest—he can afford it. Even suppose they do not get married today, they will have tomorrow or the next day, and this time a year hence they will not perceive it; for, may I be hanged if he gets his shoes today, without well paying for them."

Just then a supplicating knock was heard at the window. "Ah," said Beppo, never budging. "I thought as much, he will pay for them, let him knock again."

"Beppo it is Tito; open! open!" Beppo, with feigned amazement, opened the window, and there stood Tito, the picture of despondency. "In the name of all the saints, my shoes!" he said.

"I told you, an hour ago, that you must pay for them. I want fifteen *carlins* now."

"Let me implore you."

"Fifteen *carlins!*"

"I can give nothing more."

"Well, then, off with you."

"But you promised me the shoes!"

"I do not care a wax-end if I did; circumstances alter cases. He! He! Wear one of your Idiletta's, her feet are big enough; for she probably will stand in yours, beside wearing something else, which I am too polite to mention."

"I am not to have the shoes, then?"

"No; if you want them today at noon, and it wants just twenty minutes of it, I must be paid a *carlin* the minute. Perhaps somebody else in the village will make 'em in time." Beppo relied on being the only shoemaker in the place.

"Mother of mercies, what shall I do—o—o!" blubbered Tito in a paroxysm of grid.

"Stop your bellowing, you sucking calf, and hand over the money, or do without them."

"Well, then," suddenly answered Tito, with a smile, and as cool as an iced-lemonade, "I will not want them at all, not even for a *gill*."

"*Diavolo!*" said Beppo, between his teeth. "Well, do without them, they shall shoe your betters."

"I have not the least doubt of it," added Tito very quietly, as he drew from under his jacket a pair of dancing pumps, on which sparkled the biggest possible kind of buckles. "See, look, Beppo, how these fit!" and he put one on; "they fit like the skin to a grape, and you could not make such to save your soul. Now *addio, addio*, I bear no malice. Come to the wedding and welcome—we are going to have such a dance—here is a new step in the *tarentella*," and here Tito cut a pigeon-wing, one foot bare and the other elegantly shod. "By the way, just think of it; we spend tomorrow at Naples, the first day of the honeymoon—won't we go into the Ravioli, lighten the wine-flask, and see Polichinello! I am mad with joy—*addio! addio!*" and away he bounded like a deer.

Beppo stood stock still. He was improvising a chaste Neapolitan oath. Presently, having duly considered the subject, he let it out——. It was something individual, yet generic; microscopic, yet Cyclopean; diffused, yet searching; generally sending all people, animals included, to the infernal regions, and Tito most particularly.

"This foster-brother has given him a pair of his cast-off slippers; may they give him the gout—" Here he brought down his hammer on his thumb with an awful whack, and, with another curse, threw it from him. The implement described a summerset or so, pitched into the middle of his water-vase, shivering it to pieces, and then, with a ricochet, went smashing through the lattice. "To Satan with my luck! They are going to Naples, Tito and Idiletta, are they? May Vesuvius spit lava on them! By the holy St. Crispin, I will go there, too, yes, with his very shoes, and just for spite I'll work at them this very minute, not that the *Padre's* (I sincerely pray that someone may just want the *Padre* for the last sacrament about their wedding-time) are finished," and saying this, he went to work, and presently Tito's shoes were done.

Beppo's surprise about Tito's shoes was correct. Tito, chagrined at the idea of being married without shoes, had sought his patron, who instantly presented him with a pair of his own.

Tito told the story of his distress, and the cupidity of the cobbler, with inimitable skill. His story was listened to, by all the gentlemen, with exceeding gravity. Now it happened that Tito's patron was president, and the rest of the company members, of a celebrated club that then existed in Naples, and what they did will form the subject of the next chapter.

2

By sunrise next morning, Beppo took his shoes, tied the thongs together, slung them over his stick, and trudged away towards Naples.

The village was just getting hid behind a vine-clad hill, when past flew the happy Tito with the blushing Idiletta in a *curricolo,* racing away as fast as the horse could tear. Tito's arm encircled Idiletta's taper waist, and, to steady himself, he had planted his feet, adorned with his new shoes and buckles, against the dasher of the vehicle. As they galloped past, a ray of sunshine threw a spark from the buckle right into Beppo's eyes, so that he blinked. They lovingly kissed their hands to him, threw him a flower, and, in a moment were lost in a cloud of dust.

"*Maladetta,*" howled out Beppo after them, as he ground the flower in the dust, "May the axle-tree split, and may you break your necks in the ditch! No matter, it is but ten miles to Naples, and I shall get there as soon as they. Curse them, who are they, that they should ride, when their betters walk? In Naples, I shall sell these shoes, and, let me see, I will have a Polenta, and a flask of Capri."

"Hulloah!" sang out a labourer, engaged in making a ditch by the roadside. "I say, my young man, who are those two pretty people driving past so pleasantly?"

"Who? A stupid fellow, with his wife, and she, between you and I, is no better than she should be—may they be jolted to jelly."

"Ah?" said the man, digging away.

"Yes, added Beppo, his mouth full of venom, "She is a slattern—a loose creature—but a proper match for a thief like her husband."

"Well, appearances are deceptive, one never can tell what people really are. Now, you," went on to say the labourer, as he rested on his spade, "look like a shoemaker, though, from what is hanging from your stick there, one might think—"

274

"What?" inquired Beppo.

"Why, you see, if you take my advice, you won't expose yourself in that way; the game-laws, you know, are very strict—"

"What, under heavens, are you gathering?"

"Why, you see," said the man, with a cunning look, "a pair of birds like those, I know, are tempting. What elegant fellows—Only take care the gamekeepers don't ask you where you got them."

"You are mad!" cried Beppo, giving him a look of disdain, as he marched along, with his shoes dangling from his stick.

On he went a mile, until he met a man leading an ass, who bore huge baskets full of chickens and turkeys. With a loud "woah!" the man stopped the beast, and thus accosted the astonished Beppo.

"I say, friend, have you a mind to sell those birds there? I'll give you the pick of a turkey or a pair of fat chickens for them. You are a lucky fellow to have the first of the season: take 'em to the palace, and offer them to the cook of the palace, and you will get your own price for them—they always buy the first birds. If I was going to Naples, I should not mind giving you forty *carlins* for that pair. Success to you," and, with this, jerking the ass, he went on his way.

Stock still stood Beppo in amazement, his mouth wide open. "Strange!—wonderful! To meet two crazy people, one after the other, what can it portend! Oh, St. Jeromio keep the evil eye from me!"

On he went, until the road descended to the bottom of a pleasant valley. At the base of the hill, Beppo saw a traveling carriage, which two stout horses were slowly dragging up the hill. As they came leisurely by, Beppo saw two gentlemen inside, and when they were almost opposite, he heard one of them say to the other, "There now, talk to me about your bustards or your mallards, nonsense! There is a pair of pheasants worth more than all the *beccaficos* and *ortolans* in the world. Give me one of those well larded, and basted with oil, and done brown to a turn, and I declare it to be a morsel fit for a king. Hulloah! Postillion, stop your horses! Young man, what do you want for those pheasants?"

Beppo heard no more, but, taking to his heels, ran down the hill as if the devil was after him; a big stone caught his fool, and he rolled on the ground. "*Sangre de dio!*" roared the cobbler, looking around, as he gave a sidelong glance at his shoes. "Can I be bewitched, or am I drunk? Everybody calls my shoes pheasants! Am I sunstruck?" Here he paused, rubbed his eyes, and gazed affrighted at his shoe's. "It is impossible, and yet everybody says so!" He bathed his head in the running brook, and, recovering from his bruises, went slowly along, but by no means comfortably. A latent, unaccountable uneasiness had hold of him. Gradually his pace slackened, his knees trembled, and great drops of perspiration streamed down his face.

"Pheasants!" he exclaimed, "are they pheasants? Am I Beppo, or somebody else?" He looked anxiously around for someone to testify to his identity. "St. Jeromio help me—I wear your medal round my neck!" and he felt for it in his breast. It was there, and he mechanically repeated an *ave*, looking sacredly all about him. He started. A hundred feet further on, under an olive-tree, lay a little child, sound asleep, he walked treacherously towards it, his *ave* half finished. Suddenly, with one of those strange mental efforts, his mind was made up—the child must determine the subject. With a cross face and flashing eye, he sprang at the child, gave it a brutal shake, and, holding in one hand the shoes, and in the other his uplifted stick, he roared out—"You beggarly lillle imp, what are these? Tell me truly, or I will break every bone in your body."

The child rubbed its sleepy eyes—then shouted, without a moment's hesitation, "Pheasants, pheasants!"

"Heavens!" exclaimed Beppo, "is the saying true, that children and fools speak the truth?" and instantly, from a state of suspense, he sprang, at one bound, to the extreme of certainty. To Beppo it was an incontrovertible fact, that his shoes were pheasants.

"They are pheasants—rather of the black breed, but pheasants they must be."

"Of course they are," cried the child. "I set traps, and nets, and bird-lime for them, and a fine pair of birds I never saw."

"What are they worth?'"

"Seventy-five *carlins* to the poorest country huckster, and in Naples he could sell them at double that price."

"You are a clever little fellow," sweetly replied Beppo; "and now, little dear, go on with your nap."

"*Viva!*" exultingly cried the cobbler, as he took the high road. "Luck has come to more people than to Tito. There must be some saint who has taken me under his special protection. Here am I, possessor of an elegant pair of pheasants, (how I can't exactly say), worth one hundred and fifty *carlins*, at the lowest estimation."

Just then a setter-dog bounded across the road, and a sportsman emerged from a neighbouring thicket. "Here, Fido! here," cried the hunter, and in ran the dog. "Down charge," said the master, and the animal crouched at his feet.

"I say, countryman, where on earth did you get those golden pheasants? What a brace! Here have I been beating this cover ever since sunrise, and without a single shot. I have to go home with an empty game-bag, and if you have a mind to sell, say the word. Will two hundred *carlins* buy them?"

"No," answered Beppo, "I have been offered two hundred and fifty for them."

"Well, they are dirt cheap at that; at Naples you may get twice that for them. What a brace of birds!—what splendid tails!" and here he stroked down the shoes; his dog commenced a series of eccentric jumps at them. "Look, now, at that dog; there is a nose for you; knows them right off. Well, good-day to you; I am sorry I have not money enough about me to buy them; goodbye; I wish you luck!" and away went hunter and dog.

"*Per Bacco!* who does this fellow take me for, with his offer; my birds are not for such poor mouths as his. Strange how the dog knew them; why shouldn't he? it is his nature, Zounds! how heavy they are! but thank gracious, there is Naples, and in five minutes I shall be in the market-place." With this he hurried on, never heeding a priest, a soldier, and a water-carrier, who all stopped, and admired his golden pheasants.

He soon was in the suburbs, elbowing his way through the motley crowd, but, was somewhat surprised that no one took any notice of his precious game. "Ah," said he, "these poor devils don't know a golden pheasant from a goose; wait until I get on the *plaza*." Passing through a narrow street, Beppo heard the sound of a tambourine, and a merry laugh chiming to it. Presently two people, arm-in-arm, leant over the balcony, and kissed their hands to him; it was Tito and Idiletta. "Come up, come up," cried Tito; "this is the place; we are just going to have a dance; up with you here, Beppo, and we will drink a glass together to your good luck!"

"To the evil one with you," answered Beppo, "crow of a Tito, and cat of an Idiletta. I suppose you are the only ones who can enjoy themselves in Naples. See! look! I have here," and he shook his stick, with the shoes dangling on them, "what will let me buy you and your Idiletta."

"They are only a pair of —" Here the speech was interrupted by Tito's pretty wife, who, giving him a loud kiss, playfully pulled him in at the window; and Beppo turned his back on them, and went round the corner.

He got to the grand *plaza*, which was thronged, for it was market-day. He looked around for a place, and spying an empty spot between a fish-woman and a vegetable-vender, insinuated himself into the vacant space. Taking the shoes from off his stick, and carefully blowing off the dust from them, he exposed them to view. No one as much as took notice of him; he was slightly disappointed; so, crowding before his two neighbours, he commenced yelling at the top of his voice, "Pheasants—golden pheasants! who will buy? who wants 'em?"

"Stop your noise!" growled the fish-woman.

"Stop my noise? I had better stop my nose, for your fish smell most confoundedly. Pheasants! pheasants!"

"I say, you fool, what on earth are you howling? where do you see any pheasants?" inquired the cabbage-seller.

"Pheasants!" roared out Beppo, not heeding her.

Some boys came up, who stared in amazement at Beppo, holding his shoes high over their heads. "Pepe! Pepe! a lark! a man with an old pair of shoes, who says they are pheasants. I say, Aunty Cabbage, is not he—?" and here the urchin made that particular Italian sign, which consists in touching the forehead with the forefinger, and giving the hand a wag or so, which is the Neapolitan for crazy.

"Pheasants! golden, golden!" kept on Beppo.

"Shoes! an old pair of shoes!" interposed the cabbage-woman. "Zerlina, that man is a lunatic."

"You lie, you scorpion! it is you who are mad," retorted Beppo.

"Liar yourself," responded Zerlina, throwing a slice of tunny-fish at him.

"A fight! a row! a crazy man!" sang out the assembled crowd. Somebody threw a rotten melon, and a bombardment of spoiled vegetables followed. Beppo, foaming with rage, laid about him with his stick; the two women closed with him, and in a twinkling, he was soused in the fountain.

"Police! police!" cried the crowd; "a crazy man, just broken loose from the mad-house! help! murder! down with him!"

Poor Beppo was in the water; every time his head appeared, as quickly was it pushed under again. Up came the *sbirri*. "What does all this mean, you blackguard, kicking up a fuss in the market-place? This is no place to sell shoes!" and the police pulled the cobbler out of the water by the ears.

"I was selling my pheasants," cried Beppo—his mouth full of

slime—not a bit cooled by the immersion.

"*Signor* policemen, he is mad—crazy as a hare," cried the women.

"Off with him," yelled the people. Beppo was kicked and pummelled by everyone who could get a chance at him, and at last, more dead than alive, was lugged to the guard-house.

That night his head was shaved, and he was copiously bled. Next morning, the head magistrate was on the point of sending him to the mad-house, when, in the nick of time, came a note to the committing magistrate, which read as follows:

"*Excellenza*, etc., etc., etc.:

"The club, of which you were once a most useful member, send you the following, which please notice. Beppo, the shoe-maker, broke his word with his customer, through envy and jealousy, at the same time with the desire of extorting money from him. The club, happening to hear of the circumstance, determined to punish Beppo, and so arranged it that everyone from Beppo's village to Naples swore his shoes were pheasants, and Beppo believed them. We regret that Beppo was a greater fool than we took him for. Enclosed please find ten *carlins*, which present to Beppo on our part as the original price for his shoes.

"We are, *Excellenza*,

"With much respect,

"The Mezzo-Matti."

Beppo was sent home, a wiser man. His disposition was much sweetened, though the villagers declared that for a long time he was quite shaken as to his understanding.

Milly Dove

It was the quaintest of imaginable rooms. It was deep and dark in the corners, where the very spirit of mystery itself seemed to hide away, while there lay from end to end of the crazy old floor a long bar of golden light, that had poured in through the single window, seeming like a luminous pathway which, if followed, would take one straight out through the diamonded casement, and so on to heaven. The walls were dim, and deeply panelled with some dark, melancholy wood, and in the chinks of every panel active spiders lived a toilsome life, passing their days in the construction of suspension-bridges from their houses to the ceiling,—which works were apparently undertaken from a purely scientific motive, as they were never seen to traverse them after they were finished.

Three chairs lurked in the corners of this half-lit chamber. One of them—old-fashioned, with a high back and crooked arms—seemed to repose in the twilight of the place, like some high-shouldered old *beau* of the last century, silently reflecting, as it were, on the habits of the present generation. This old fellow was not, however, always in retreat. He was many a time during the day dragged forth into the centre of the stream of golden light that poured through the deep window, where he seemed to blink and shrink from the unwonted glare, while a small, bright figure nestled into his comfortable angles, and pierced his bent and padded old arms with cruel pins, to which divers endless cotton threads were fastened. And then, as the sunlight poured splendidly through the diamond panes, powdering the air with golden dust and playing on the carvings of the ceiling, there was not a prettier picture in the world—not even in your grand foreign galleries beyond the sea—than Milly Dove, sitting in her sumptuous old chair.

She was very, very pretty, this little Milly Dove. Her eyes were so dark and blue, and the light that shone in them seemed to be so far off behind, that one saw it shining, shining miles and miles away, like the lights of a distant city across the sea! Then her hair was of such a rich brown,—golden-hued where the light struck it,—and her rosy, clover mouth was so fresh and dewy, that, if I were a painter, I would not have tried to paint Milly Dove for the world.—I would only have dreamed of her.

Milly sat the greater part of the day in that highbacked chair, right in the sunny stream, working at her embroidery or knitting. I said before—prettily enough too, I think—that the light, as it poured in, seemed like a path to heaven. If it were so, who that saw this little maiden seated in its radiance would not say that she was an angel made to tread it?

She did not tread it, however, or even dream of any such proceeding as marching out through the window on a pavement of sunbeams, and wandering off into problematical regions. Not that Milly Dove did not wish to go to heaven; but she had so many things to do down below here that she never would have thought of such a journey, unless it pleased God to take her.

She had much to do, that little thing, though you would not think it to look at her. Milly Dove kept a shop. Yes! absolutely kept a shop. Directly opposite to that old-fashioned window which lit the little room, a small glass door stood always half open, through which one could catch a glimpse of a small counter and small shelves, and a varied assortment of the smallest merchandise it was possible to keep. Tiny drums for infants of a military turn of mind; scanty bundles of cotton and muslin stuffs, large enough, perhaps, to furnish dolls' dresses; infinitesimal brooches; ridiculously reduced thimbles; stunted whips; dwarf rakes and spades, and baby wheelbarrows, together with a hundred such like articles, useful or ornamental, lay on the shelves, were hidden away in secret places under the counter, or depended in bunches from the low ceiling.

It seemed exceedingly odd to be obliged to regard Milly Dove as the owner of all this magnificent and varied property. Her childish figure had nothing of the rigidity of a proprietor; she did not look as if she had any pockets to keep her money in; nor did she possess in the faintest degree the air of being arithmetical. No one would believe, to look into those clear, unworldly eyes, that she could buy or sell anything to the slightest advantage,—unless, indeed, it were eggs, that commodity having been, as everyone knows who has read storybooks, intrusted from time immemorial to pretty little girls to convey to market. Now, in spite of all this, Milly Dove was a famous hand at a bargain.

It was excellent to see her standing behind her small counter, insisting pertinaciously on the price of some article which she was selling; explaining with much gravity, to the cunning clown who wished to purchase, its various merits and positive value; declaring that, if she gave it a cent cheaper, it would be a dead loss to her,—and how were folks to live if they did not make some profit on their goods? Then all this with such a sweet and gentle firmness, such a mixture of innocence and shrewdness, that it must be a hard customer indeed who could find the heart to beat her down.

That house,—a small, old-fashioned New England tenement, smelling of the Mayflower,—together with the shop and its stock of goods, was all that Milly Dove possessed in this wide world. Her parents were dead, and this old roof, with a scanty supply of merchandise, was all they had to bequeath to their only child. And she managed her inheritance wonderfully well, let me tell you! By the aid of her little shop, she made nearly two hundred and fifty dollars in the year; and she had a tenant for the upper part of the house, in the person of a Mr. Josiah Compton, who paid her probably as much more; so that this little proprietor of sixteen, although somewhat forlorn, was not very poor, and was able to lay something by every year in a savings bank at Boston.

Mr. Josiah Compton was Milly's only friend. He was a gnarled bachelor of fifty-six; odd, kind-hearted, passionately attached to flowers and music, and loving dearly everything old and quaint, and which did not smell, as he said, of the modern varnish. He had lived in this house a very long time. Indeed, he had been living there for many a year before Milly was born, and loved the place for the air of quiet antiquity with which it was haunted. There was a curious old garden at the back of the house, which Mr. Josiah Compton had with his own hands brought to a high state of floral culture. He had laboured at it for years, and had written the history of his toil in flowers.

The ground glowed with tulips and ranunculuses; fiery lychnises and rich-blossomed roses flaunted in the deep borders; trumpet honeysuckles thrust the golden lips of their horns through a tented drapery of glossy leaves, as if about to sound a challenge to the blue convolvulus; dahlias, drunk with dew, nodded their heavy heads; the campanulas, with their bells of intense blue, grew in close ranks around the edges of the beds, like a tiny army guarding the borders of this kingdom of flowers. Colour and perfume floated like a spell through the entire place. The brilliant plants, trained into no formality, sprang up to heaven with a splendid freedom. The walks were paved with the blossoms that they shed, and the heavens were fragrant with the odours that they breathed

On this garden Mr. Compton's window opened; and he would sit in the summer time at his piano, with the casement flung wide, the rich perfume of the flowers floating in upon the languid air, and the rich music he awakened surging over and under and through all, and mingling itself inextricably with the warm breath of the blossoming roses.

Mr. Compton's playing—and he played beautifully—was a source of intense pleasure to Hilly, as she sat in her old-fashioned parlour underneath, and watched the shop through the half-open door. Poor child! of music as an art she was profoundly ignorant. Dominants, subdominants, fifths and sevenths, intervals, *contrapunta*, and such like, were mysteries unknown to her by name. She had never heard any other performer than Mr. Compton; but those wild voluntaries that he played pleased her mightily,—those sad, harmonious wailings, that poured all day long through the open window, until toward the close of day, when the sun was setting, they would burst into some triumphal melody that would sweep her soul up along the path of golden light striking heavenward, until it reached a goal so dazzlingly beautiful that she grew blinded with its glories.

She was very happy sitting there in the sunshine, knitting and listening to the music. Occasionally some villager, in need of a ball of twine or a pair of scissors, would enter the shop, and then Milly, jumping nimbly from her perch, would glide behind the small counter, looking intensely business-like. Or mayhap it would be some great boy who had just come into possession of wealth unlimited in the shape of a quarter-dollar, and who tremblingly entered Milly's little shop, determined, yet scarce knowing how, to spend it. And to all such Milly Dove was beautifully kind and patient; showing them, with perfect good humour, all the expensive toys to which they pointed, although perfectly aware all the time of the extent of their means, which were generally displayed in their hands with the most confiding simplicity. Her little sales over, she would again retreat to her parlour, to knit, or, it may be, to take a good long peep at her panorama.

Milly Dove had a panorama. Not a panorama ever so many miles long, professing to exhibit the entire world in the most satisfactory manner possible in an hour and twenty-five minutes. No; Milly's panorama was, I must confess, limited in extent, but it possessed endless variety for her, and I do believe that she was never tired of looking at it.

The panorama was by no means complicated. Its exhibition was not encumbered with huge pulleys, and impossibly heavy weights and windlasses and cog-wheels to keep it moving. But, in spite of this insignificance when compared with a "seven-mile mirror," Milly's panorama was for her a splendid pastime. It was an endless round of enjoyment, a garden of perpetual delights.

This work of art consisted of a large wooden box supported on four long, diverging, attenuated legs. It contained a few coloured prints hung on hinges from the top, one hiding the other, each capable of being lifted into a horizontal position, so as to disclose the next picture in succession, by a series of little pulleys of a primitive character fixed on the exterior of the box. These pictures, when viewed through the double convex lens which was fixed in the front of the box at a proper focal distance, were magnified and glorified in so wonderful and splendid a manner, that to Milly they presented the aspect of illimitable paintings, unsurpassable in beauty of design or brilliancy of colour. How this treasure of art had come into her family the little maiden was altogether ignorant. Her mother was possessed of it long before Milly made her appearance in the world, and when dying had left no tradition of its history. The probability was, that some wandering exhibitor may have left it with Mrs. Dove in pledge for unpaid board, and had never redeemed it, poor fellow!

But there it was, and when Milly was left alone in the world it became hers,—and proud enough of it she was, I can assure you. It afforded the dear child wondrous delight to look through the peephole, and draw up the paintings one after the other. She knew nothing of history,—I don't like her a bit the less for that,—and the subjects of these splendid illustrations would have remained mysteries to her forever, had it not been for the kindness of Mr. Compton, who would pull the strings as she peeped, and, assuming the air and manner of a veritable showman, explain each cartoon as it appeared. That gentleman, however, was not always quite certain himself as to what scenes were really depicted in this splendid gallery; but then he never hesitated on account of any want of knowledge, but assigned to each picture the most probable explanation and title he could think of.

I have seen many grand battle-pieces in great galleries across the sea that might just as well have been called the Battle of Pavia as the Battle of Agincourt, and have looked at many a heathen goddess painted by some great old artist, who might quite as well have been put down as Moll Flanders in the catalogue, and no one would have questioned the propriety of the title. So, I do not blame Mr. Compton in the least for his impromptu style of nomenclature. It satisfied Milly perfectly, and he had no other object.

These explanations did not, however, tax Mr. Compton's inventive faculties very largely. There were the Pyramids of Ghizeh, which he could not very well mistake, and which afforded him an opportunity of delivering a very learned discourse on the manners and customs of the ancient Egyptians, all carefully extracted from an encyclopaedia; and there was the Battle of Waterloo, which the Duke of Wellington's nose and Napoleon's coat identified sufficiently; but, again, there arose a fiery painting with flames, and soldiers, and much killing, and falling horses, with agonized mothers of large families in the fourth stories, which, having no better name for it, Mr. Compton christened the Battle of Prague; and when he afterward performed the piece of music of that name on the piano, and came to the part called by the composer in an explanatory note "the cries of the wounded," there remained no shadow of doubt on Milly's mind that the picture was indeed a faithful representation of that terrible combat, and that Mr. Compton was the best-informed historian in the world.

Of late, somehow, Milly, poor child, was not quite so interested in her panorama, or so attentive to her shop as was her wont. She had not peeped through that magical hole for many days; her knitting was, I regret to say, of an unusually spasmodic character; when she sat in the sunshine it seemed almost too gay for her; and her pretty little face seemed to have a cloud of sadness covering it. But she welcomed the music with more pleasure than ever; and the more melancholy it was, the better she liked it; for it seemed then to speak to her in a language which she understood, yet could not interpret,—harmoniously talking of strange things which she thought she felt, and still was unable to comprehend. So she sat all day and listened to Mr. Compton's wild improvisations, as they floated over the flowers, till perfume and harmony seemed to be mingling, and she grew so abstracted in her habits that she had to be called thrice by Mrs. Barberry, who wanted to buy a flour-dredge, before she thought of answering.

It was singular, but no less true, that just at this time I had the privilege of peeping into that pure little maiden's mind, and observing, in secret, all its innocent little operations. It was a rare privilege, I know, but I hope I love honour, beauty, and virtue too much not to look upon the prerogative as holy. You will hear, therefore, from me only such things as are necessary to the conduct of the story I am endeavouring to relate.

I saw, at my very first peep, what it was that induced Milly to forget her panorama, and pay such little heed to old Mrs. Barberry. The cause of all this distraction was a certain person, of whom you shall know more before I have done with you.

About a week previous to the time I am speaking of a stranger had made his appearance in the little town of Blossomdale, in which Milly lived; and just about the same time Milly, who had heard of the stranger's arrival—as one hears everything in a village—but had not seen him, observed a man of singular aspect passing her shop frequently. Coupling the two facts together she came to the conclusion that this person and the strange arrival were one; which at least proves that Milly Dove was capable of inductive reasoning.

He was a remarkable man, this stranger. Not very tall, but rather powerfully built; he always walked rapidly, with his frame stooped forward from the hips, as if his mind were in advance of his body. His face was somewhat narrow, and delicately featured. A thin moustache curled around a small mouth, and his hair was profuse, though not long. But it was in his eyes that his individuality chiefly resided,—eyes that seemed to gaze at nothing, and yet see everything. They did not look, they absorbed, those great dark eyes, and shed from out their own darkness a shadow over the whole face. They were eyes truly delightful to look at,—as it is delightful to look down into a calm sea,—and hard to be forgotten.

Milly did not easily forget them, I promise you. They haunted her as she sat alone in the little half-lit parlour, and seemed to glow with a strange light in the dim corners where the spiders dwelt. She looked at them, and they looked at her all the livelong day, and this was why she forgot her panorama.

Now Milly Dove told Mr. Compton everything. He was her only friend. He stood to her in the place of a parent, and loved her as a daughter. Confidence existed between them as a matter of course, and she talked to him as the stream flows. So, she soon told him about this stranger: how she had seen him; how his face haunted her continually; how she kept thinking about him all day long; how she watched for him at the hour when it was usual for him to pass her door, and felt a sort of dim, indistinct pleasure when he passed. All this she told her old friend simply, truly, naturally, without even the remotest idea of the nature or origin of her feelings; for Milly was at that happy age when people are not learned in the mysteries of themselves, and do not possess the mournful knowledge which enables them to anatomize their own hearts.

Mr. Compton at first looked rather sad at hearing this naive confession; but after a moment he laughed and kissed her fair forehead, saying that she would soon forget this wonderful stranger. Then he sat down at his piano and played so wild and wonderful a strain, fraught with such depths of pure and unconscious passion, that Milly lay statue-like near him, and dreamed so perfectly that she dreamed no more.

2

It was a pleasant June day. Through the open window in Milly's little room a mingled stream of sunshine and the breath of flowers rolled in, filling the chamber with light and perfume. The spiders dozed in the crevices of the panelled walls, while their aerial webs shone like delicate threads of silver. The high-shouldered chairs sidled off into the corners, as if they were ashamed of their age, and the great panorama, which stood on one side of the door, glared with its huge, eye-like lens at the green window, like a species of four-legged Cyclops. Milly, as usual, was sitting in the sun. Nestled into that great, high-backed chair, which was a world too large for her, she worked absently at some intricate feminine fabric,—a fabric it was that I believe would have driven me crazy if I had been set down to learn its mysteries. There were dozens of strings pinned to various portions of the unhappy old chair.

More strings trailed on the floor, whose courses, if followed, would be found to terminate in numberless little balls, that kept continually rolling off into the corners and disturbing the spiders that lived on the first floors of the panels. Then each string had to be unpinned every second minute, and juggled with after some wondrous fashion, until, having been thrust, by a species of magic known only to Milly, through an interminable perspective of loops, it was solemnly repinned to the chair, and then the whole process began again.

Whether it was owing to the complication of this terrible web, or to the preoccupation of her own thoughts, no Penelope ever made so many blunders as Milly Dove, on that June morning. Every now and then the web would come to a sudden stand-still; a minute investigation of certain curious knots would result in the discovery of some heart-rending error. Then the vagrant balls would have to be hunted up in the corners, and the pin would have to come out, and with a pettish toss of the head and a little pouting of the under lip, the child would tediously unravel all the false work and begin again.

Sometimes she would let it drop altogether, and gaze absently through the open window, as if she were watching the humming-birds that hung before the golden-lipped tubes of the trumpet-honey-suckle; or she would turn toward the desolate panorama, that seemed to gaze reproachfully at her with its single eye, and ponder over the propriety of taking another peep at that bloody Battle of Prague, or the extraordinary representation of the Israelites gathering the manna in the desert,—which said manna seemed to have been made into very respectable and well-baked quartern loaves before it fell.

Milly's reveries, whatever they were, were interrupted by the entrance of Master Dick Boby, the eldest son of Judge Boby, who was the richest and greatest man in the village. Master Boby had acquired—probably by inheritance—the sum of half a dollar, and immediately upon coming into possession of his property had set off for Milly's shop, uncertain as to whether he would purchase her entire stock or simply confine himself to the acquisition of a stick of molasses candy. Milly, with her pleasant smile, was behind the counter in an instant, awaiting the commands of the young squire.

"What's them guns apiece. Miss Milly?" inquired Master Boby, pointing to a couple of flimsy fowling-pieces that stood in the corner.

"Six dollars apiece, sir."

"I guess you'd take half-price for them if a body was to buy both?" said the young millionaire, half inquiringly, as if he had only to put his hand in his pocket and pull out the money.

"Well," said Milly, "I didn't buy them; they were here when father died, and as they've been so long on my hands, I'd be glad to sell them cheap. You can have them both for seven dollars and fifty cents, if you want them, Master Dick."

"O, I don't want them; only father might, if his own gun was to burst. What's the price of them skates, Miss Milly?"

"A dollar fifty, sir. They are capital skates, and came all the way from York. But what do you want of skates this weather, Master Dick?"

"O, I didn't know but I might lose my own skates next winter, you know, so I thought I'd ask. Are you going to the circus show this evening, Miss Milly? for if you'd like to go, I can get tickets from father, and I'll take you." And Master Dick looked admiringly at the pretty little maiden.

"Thank you kindly, sir; but I don't think Mr. Compton would like me to go. He says the circus is a bad place."

"He don't know nothing," answered Master Dick, surlily; "but if you won't go, I know one who will. Give me an ounce of molasses candy, and half an ounce of peppermint, Miss Milly."

Milly had just opened the drawer containing the confections demanded by Master Dick, and was about measuring out the required quantity of molasses and peppermint, when she saw something through the window that made her suddenly stop. A gentleman was marching slowly down the street. He appeared to be lost in reverie, for his head was thrown back, and his eyes were fixed on vacancy, while he moved on apparently unconscious of the existence of everybody, himself included. He was a pleasant gentleman, too, and seemed to be occupied with pleasing thoughts, for a sort of half-born smile played around his thin lips, seeming always on the point of becoming a laugh but never fulfilling its promise.

This gentleman had just arrived opposite to Milly's door, when his reverie was suddenly and most unexpectedly interrupted by a big stone. This big stone was a stone of infamous habits. It lurked under a specious coating of clay, seemingly soft and elastic in its nature, but all the while turning up one sharp and treacherous edge, that to the foot of the tight-booted and unwary pedestrian caused unutterable tortures. It was a Tartuffe among stones,—hypocritical, velvety, inducing confidence,—but woe to the toe that lit upon its venomous edge!

Well, of course this thoughtful gentleman marched straight upon this assassin of a stone. *Tschut!* A terrible "thud" of toes against the treacherous edge, a wild flinging out of arms in a vain attempt at equilibrium, a convulsive ejaculation which I hope nobody heard, and our pedestrian measured his length in the dust. He rose in a moment, looked reproachfully at the stone as if to upbraid it for its misconduct, then, recalled probably by some unusual sensation, he looked down at his legs. Alas! across his left knee there was a great gaping split in his trousers, through which a wide vista of linen was visible. The poor gentleman gazed ruefully at this scene of destruction; looked around, and then again at his knee; then tried to walk a step or two; stopped, looked at his knee once more, and seemed to meditate profoundly on his position.

While rapt in this painful reverie, the victim of that abominable stone was startled by a very sweet little voice at his elbow. This voice, belonging to Milly Dove, said, "Please, sir, if you will step into the shop, I will mend it for you."

The gentleman turned round, and gave a rapid glance at the sunny, girlish face that looked up into his with such a frank, easy expression, as if it was the most natural thing in the world that he should fall, and that she should come out and offer to mend his trousers.

"Thank you, child!" said he, simply. "I am very much obliged to you. What is your name?"

"Milly Dove, sir."

"And this is your father's shop, I suppose?" And the stranger glanced round as he entered, with a half-smile at the varied assortment of goods that it contained. It was quite deserted; for Master Dick Boby, left alone with the candy, had, I regret to say, helped himself and departed.

"No, sir; it's mine!" answered Milly, poking in her pocket for her needle-box.

"Yours! why, you are young to be at the head of an establishment."

"I was sixteen my last birthday, sir. Will you come into the inside room, if you please, so that you may put your foot upon a chair?"

The stranger did as he was bidden, and Milly's nimble fingers were soon busily drawing together the jagged edges of that gaping rent in his injured trousers. He looked down upon her with a wondering gaze.

"I suppose some of your relatives live with you here?" he said, after a pause, during which he had been studying her features intently.

"No, sir; I am alone."

"Alone!"

"No; that is—not exactly alone. Mr. Compton lodges upstairs."

"Mr. Compton?" said the stranger, a sort of dark shadow falling across his face like a veil. "Who is Mr. Compton? A young man?"

"A friend of my mother's, sir. He lives here all the year round, and is a dear, pleasant gentleman. He's quite young, too; not more than fifty-six."

"Ah!" and the Knight of the Rueful Breeches seemed to breathe more freely. "That is young indeed! How long have you been keeping shop?"

"Two years, sir. My mother died about that time, and the neighbours were all very good to me when I began. I think it will do now, sir!"

"Thanks! thanks!" replied the stranger, scarce giving a glance at the neat seam across his knee. "You are an excellent little workwoman." And as he spoke he seated himself deliberately in Milly's high-backed chair, much to that young lady's surprise. "You have a pretty room here," he continued, looking round him approvingly,—"a very pretty room! The sunlight gushing in through that window, and parting, as it were to make good its entrance, the honeysuckles that wave before it, has a charming effect. Is it you who take care of the flowers out there?"

"O, there's not much to do now," said Milly, modestly. "Mr. Compton made the garden, and now I help him a little. They grow there so nicely, the flowers do! And in the spring I freshen up the beds a little, and weed the walks, and clip off the dead branches, and I think the sun and the rain do the rest."

"Hum! That's prettily said!"

Poor Milly grew scarlet at the tone of easy assurance in which this approbation was uttered. This gentleman seemed to have an air of the world about him that somehow alarmed her, she knew not why,—his walk, his way of speech, his manner, were all so different from those of the loutish villagers to whom she had been accustomed.

He was even unlike Mr. Compton, who to Milly, until then, had been the highest type of human perfection.

"I'd like to live in a room like this!" muttered the stranger half aloud, gazing round him with evident pleasure. "It has a sweet, thoughtful air; and that garden outside would fill me with poetry. I'd like very much indeed to live here!"

"Then why don't you come?" was on the tip of Milly 's tongue; but she suddenly recollected herself in time, and so was silent.

"Do you ever read. Miss Milly Dove?" was the next question, as the visitor turned abruptly to the young maiden.

"No—yes—that is—sometimes," was the alarmed reply.

"Which means that you do not read at all?" said the stranger, gravely.

Milly looked as if she was immediately about to tuck the end of her little apron into her eyes, and weep herself away.

"Well," continued he, "that can be remedied; but Mr. Compton should have given you books."

"Sir," said Milly stoutly, quick to espouse her friend's cause, though unable to defend her own,—"Sir, Mr. Compton knows a great deal more, in fact, than anyone I ever saw, and everything that he does is right."

The stranger laughed. "You are a chivalrous but illogical little maiden," said he, in a tone of insufferable patronage.

"I may not read much," said Milly, flushing up, "but I have a panorama."

"O, you have a panorama? A panorama of what? Let us see this wonder that supplies the place of books."

"Shall I show it to you, sir?" asked Milly timidly.

"Certainly; but before profiting by your kindness, I must introduce myself formally. I am Mr. Alexander Winthrop, a poor gentleman, with enough for his appetites, and too little for his desires. I am fond of travelling, books, and thinking. I am only twenty-five years old, although I look thirty. I live close to New York, and am at present at Blossomdale on business. Now, you know all that I intend you to know about me; so, we will go on with our panorama."

This off-hand introduction was delivered with such gravity that poor Milly did not know what to make of it. At first, she thought he was laughing at her, but on looking at his eyes she could not detect the slightest twinkle of merriment; so, she nodded her little head to Mr. Alexander Winthrop, as if to say, "All right, I know you," and then proceeded to introduce him to the panorama.

"This," said Milly in a solemn voice, as she made him put his eye to the peep-hole, and proceeded to pull the strings that lifted the pictures, "this is the invasion of Mexico by the Spaniards. The man in the big boat is Cortes, a very cruel man indeed; and the man on the shore is Montezuma, the king of Mexico, who may be known by his red skin."

"Hem!" coughed Mr. Alexander. "How do you know that this is the invasion of Mexico?"

"Mr. Compton told me, sir."

"O, Mr. Compton told you! Then it's all right, of course. But," he continued, muttering to himself, "if Mr, Compton is right, Cortes dressed exceedingly like William Penn; and Montezuma would make a capital North American Indian."

"This picture," continued Milly, pulling another string, "represents the great Pyramids of Egypt, built by various kings to serve for their tombs. The ancient Egyptians were far advanced in civilization, while the rest of the globe was plunged in the obscurity of ignorance. Their chief god was Osiris, and the priesthood was so powerful that the government, in truth, was an ecclesiastical one. The ancient Egyptians were in the habit of placing a skeleton at the head of the table when they feasted, for the purpose of reminding them of their mortality, and it is believed that from them first sprang the art of embalming bodies. They were a highly commercial people, and found large markets for the products of their industry and art, in the ancient cities of Greece and Rome."

"Why, child, where did you learn this?" exclaimed Mr. Alexander, gazing with astonishment on the little maiden, who ran off this *farrago* of learning with the glibness of a lecturer on ancient history, looking all the while exceedingly proud of her knowledge.

"Mr. Compton told me," she answered proudly.

Mr. Alexander could no longer contain himself, but burst into a shout of laughter that made Milly's ears tingle. Her round cheeks flushed, and the tears rose to her eyes. Poor little thing! She thought this Mr. Alexander Winthrop exceedingly rude, and yet she could not feel angry with him.

"Well, what's the next picture?" he asked, as soon as he had recovered from his mirth, and without making the slightest apology for his improper behaviour.

"It's the Battle of the Nile," answered Milly, rather sullenly, for she did not exactly like the merciless laugh of her new friend.

"I was there all the while," chimed in Mr. Alexander.

"You couldn't. It happened ever so long ago," answered Milly quickly, delighted at finding Mr. Alexander out in a fib.

That gentleman was on the point of going off into another fit of merriment, when a wild prelude on a piano wavered harmoniously through the window. After wandering up and down the keys for a short time, striking out fragments of melodies, and fluttering uncertainly from one to the other, as a butterfly roams from bud to bud, not knowing which to choose, the performer at length struck on a theme that seemed to satisfy him, and then poured out his entire soul. That it was a voluntary, one could discern in an instant, from the occasional irregularity of the rhythm, and lack of proper sequence between the parts; but it was so wild, so original, so mournful, so full of broken utterances of passion, that one might have imagined it the wail of a lost angel, outside the gates of that paradise which he saw but could not enjoy.

"That is a great performer," said Mr. Alexander, rising. "I must go and see him."

"It's Mr. Compton," cried Milly, eagerly; "he does not like to be disturbed. You must not go now."

"I don't care," said Mr. Alexander, very coolly. "Where's the stairs? O, here!—all right!" And before she could detain him, he had bounded up the stairs, and was gone.

"I make no apology for coming in here in this way," said Mr. Alexander, as he pushed open Mr. Compton's door, "because, if you don't want people to rush in on you unannounced, you should not play so well, nor improvise such original themes."

"You are an artist, then?" said Mr. Compton, rising in some surprise at this sudden intrusion. "All such have a right to enter here."

"Enough of an artist to comprehend you," said the young man, bluntly. "You are an artist, Mr. Compton, and have never done anything but toy with art. More shame for you!"

"Who is my lecturer?" said Mr. Compton, rather sternly.

"My name is Alexander Winthrop."

"What! he who—"

"Hush!" cried the young man, lifting his finger; for at that moment Milly appeared, with flushed cheeks, on the threshold of the door. "I am only Alexander Winthrop I tore my trousers by a fall opposite to this house. This little fairy," pointing to Milly, "mended them for me. I heard you playing; I ran upstairs. Now you know all about me."

"Then you must be the stranger of whom Milly has so often spoken to me, as passing the door every day," said Mr Compton, with a bland ignorance of the incautiousness of his remark, and totally heedless of Milly's agonised telegraphings to make him stop.

"O, then, the little fairy knew me before!" exclaimed Mr. Alexander, eagerly. "So, we were old acquaintances, Miss Milly?"

Milly said nothing, but appeared to have suddenly remembered that her shop had been left unprotected, and disappeared as if by magic.

"I want to have a talk with you, Mr. Compton, said Mr. Alexander, looking after her.

Mr. Compton sighed. "Let us go into the garden," he said; and they went out together.

3

Two months after this, Milly Dove sat in her little room, reading. Those wondrous fabrics on which she used to labour with such patience were gone. There was dust on the panorama; its single eye was dim and melancholy. No more balls disturbed the repose of the fat old spiders in the panels; the very shop itself seemed to have an uncared-for look.

The reason of all this was that Milly Dove had become a student,—a hard, close, unwearying student,—and the books that she read were given to her by Mr. Alexander. One author in particular pleased her mightily. A man named Ivan Thorle had lately astonished the world with an alternate succession of works of philosophy and fiction. In both paths did he seem to be equally at home. His novels were tender, impassioned, truthful, and always breathing the sublimest scorn for everything mean and unholy. His philosophy was still more wonderful, because it was so clear. The progress of man was always his theme. The gradual amalgamation of races; the universal equalization of climate from the cultivation of the entire globe; the disappearance of poverty from the earth before the influence of machinery, which laboured for all; the consequent improvement of the physical condition of our race; the abolishment of crime ;—in short, the apogee of the world.

On all this he expatiated with a profundity of thought and simplicity of expression that made him at once the deepest and clearest of writers. Ivan Thorle, then, opened a new world for Milly. For the first time she comprehended the true beauty of life, and experienced those delicious sensations which one experiences when beginning to observe,—an epoch, let me tell you, that comes much later than one imagines. Thus a trinity of genius and goodness reigned supreme in Milly Dove's little heart,—Mr. Compton, Mr. Alexander, and Ivan Thorle,—and although her reason placed Mr. Compton first, as being the oldest friend, and Ivan Thorle next, as being the greatest genius, yet I doubt much if that little maiden's heart did not put Mr. Alexander Winthrop, her affianced lover, high above all.

There was one thing that grieved this dear child, and it was so strange a grief for her to have had at that period that it seems a mystery to me how she ever could have had it. It was that Mr. Alexander was not a great writer. She loved him very dearly, and she knew that Mr. Compton loved him, and they talked very learnedly together for hours at a time. He was very clever, this Mr. Alexander Winthrop; but oh! if he would only write books like Ivan Thorle! If he would create those dear stories,—so pure, so good, and so true!

If he would make those splendid books that made everyone love his fellow-men better when he had read them, and which were so purely written that a child might understand them! If he would only do this, she told him many times, as she clung to his breast, she would be as happy as the humming-birds that lived outside, forever in the sunshine! And Mr. Alexander would stroke her brown hair, and kiss her white forehead, and, smiling mysteriously, say, "Some time, per-haps—" But he did not write books, and Milly Dove was sad.

Her sadness was now, however, for the moment lost in the perusal of Ivan Thorle's last book, *The Ladder of Stars*,—a strange mixture of romance and philosophy; and Milly pored over it in her high-backed chair, while the humming-birds outside looked in at her with their sharp, cunning eyes, and said to themselves, as they saw her rosy lips, "Bless us! where there are flowers there must be loads of honey. Let us go in and get it!" But now and then these rosy flowers had a strange way of opening with a laughing sound, and showing rows of white seed inside, in a manner unlike any flower ever before seen; so that the humming-birds thought they might be dangerous flowers, and did not go in.

Milly was reading one of the most beautiful passages in the *Ladder of Stars*, when she heard a step behind her. She turned, and beheld one of the most beautiful ladies she had ever seen, standing in the doorway. A tall, proud-looking lady she was, with bright eyes and fierce lip, and the smallest hands in the world. And such dress! So rich and elegant and flowing! Milly thought she was a fairy. Being naturally polite, however, even to fairies, the little maiden rose and advanced timidly to this *sultana*. The lady did not keep her long in suspense.

"Your name is Milly Dove?" she said, in a commanding voice.

"Yes, ma'am," said Milly, half frightened at the tone of the question.

"You are going to marry a man calling himself Alexander Win-throp. Is it not so?"

"Yes, ma'am." Milly's limbs began to tremble at this point.

"You must not marry him."

"Why, ma'am?" Milly's strength began to come back a little.

"Because he would make you unhappy."

"How do you know, ma'am?" O Milly Dove! Milly Dove! where did you pick up the Socratic mode of reasoning?

"Because I know it," said the *sultana*, stamping her foot. "You can-not marry him. He loves me. I know he does!" she continued pas-sionately.

"He loves me better!" said Milly, quietly. "I know it, for he told me so."

"You! love you better! Listen, child. You do not know this man. He is proud, wealthy, learned, a genius, and courted by all the world. His sphere in life rolls through another orbit than yours. His genius, his tastes, his friendships, will all separate him from you. He thinks he loves you now; well, in three months he will be disenchanted. He will neglect you,—ill-treat you, perhaps,—laugh at your ill-breeding, sport with your ignorance, and break your heart. Be warned in time. Here! I am rich. You shall have money, as much money as you wish, if you fly this place and promise never to see Alexander Winthrop again. I will make you wealthy, happy, everything you wish, only leave me my love! leave me my love!" She held out a purse to Milly as she spoke, and her splendid form literally shook with passion.

Poor Milly was thunderstruck; she knew not what to do. O, how she wished for either Alexander or Mr. Compton!

"Ma'am," said she at last, "I don't want money. I never knew that Mr. Alexander was rich; but it makes no matter to me whether he is or not. I know he loves me; for he said so, and he never tells a lie. Therefore, I cannot do as you wish me. I am sorry, ma'am, that you should love Mr. Alexander too."

"But you must, I tell you,—you must, girl! You shall not wed him! He is mine! Do you not know—"

"She does *not* know. Miss Helen De Rham," said Mr. Alexander himself, stepping, at this juncture, out of the shop, and putting his arm around Milly's waist.

"O, you are here, sir!" said Miss De Rham, with a scornful curl of her upper lip. "Enjoying love in a cottage, which, no doubt, you taste merely as a literary experience to be made serviceable in your next book. It is a pretty idyll."

"Madam," said Alexander, "let me hear no unworthy sneers against a love so pure that you could not understand it. Milly, as this lady has thought fit to intrude herself on my privacy and yours, it is fit that you should learn the history of our association."

"Tell it, sir, by all means," said Miss De Rham, seating herself in a chair; "you are accustomed to weave romances."

"I tell the truth, madam, always; and if I did not this pure mind here is too true a touchstone not to detect the falsehood. Milly, that handsome lady there was once my friend. I believe I loved her, for she was beautiful and gifted. We were much together, and I understand that she expressed admiration for my talents. I thought her honest, and I loved her for her honesty; for she was one of those who could talk with that frank bluntness that so well simulates sincerity. Well, she was ambitious; she wanted to be a goddess, when she was only a woman; she wished to write, when God had only given her the power to appreciate.

"She came to me one day with a poem,—a beautiful poem, which she said she had written. I got it published for her; it was admired everywhere. On the strength of it she rose to the reputation of a woman of genius. Well, Milly, it was all a lie!—an acted, a spoken, a perpetuated lie!—the poem was not hers. It was written for her by a *protégé* of hers, who betrayed her trust, and the deception was discovered. I left Miss De Rham, Milly Dove, to the shame which, if she had a heart, ought to have eaten it out."

"And you could not discover the difference between an innocent piece of vanity and a crime! Ivan Thorle, in spite of all your knowledge you know not the world!"

"I do not wish to know it better. Miss De Rham. Leave me and my bride in ignorance and peace. Go, madam, back to your town luxury and refined atmosphere, where pretty names are given to bad deeds. I wish to remain unmolested with that pure love which will ever be a mystery to you. Go! "

"What name did she call you?" cried Milly Dove, breathlessly, as the proud lady swept scornfully out through the little shop.

"Milly, you may now know what I have long concealed. I am Ivan Thorle!"

"You? You? O, I am so glad—so glad—so glad! Dear Alexander, I have now nothing to wish for."

"But I have, dear Milly!"

Those who have read Alexander Winthrop's latest and best novel, *The Village Bride*, will see there how happily he and Milly and Mr. Compton lived together; and they will recognise in the lecturer on Woman's Rights the portrait of Miss De Rham.

The Man Without a Shadow (A New Version)

Fortunate fellow that I am! I have lost my shadow!

But do not imagine that, like the poor Peter Schlemihl, I have sold it to the Devil! Heaven forbid that any Devil should be stupid or extravagant enough to buy such a Shadow!

No; as it came, so it has departed, a thing of mystery, an awful bore.

It is not my natural shadow I speak of; but an unnatural, an impertinent Shadow, which of late attached itself to my person, and could not be shaken off whether in the glare of sunshine or the pale moonlight, in the rays of volatile gas or of explosive camphene.

I first observed it about six weeks ago. I knew it was a shadow, for I never could detect anything real or true about it; nevertheless, to look at it, one would have taken it for a man, or, at the least, a monkey. I have had my doubts in the latter point. But no! I will not insult monkeydom by the suspicion. It was only a Shadow—no more.

When I first observed it at a friend's house, I tried to find out what it was; but my friend knew as little as myself. it had followed him from another friend's, and that friend said it had followed him from somewhere else. Of its origin, nothing was known. Like all Shadows, its nature was involved in obscurity. At any attempt to throw light upon it, it disappeared entirely—like other Shadows.

Still it was a very troublesome Shadow, and very different from my own dear aboriginal Shadow which so closely resembled me in outline, that no one would fail to detect my relationship; but this new strange Shadow was not a bit like me. it was my opposite in every respect even at dinner. And it was not only a troublesome, but an expensive Shadow; for when I dined, it dined with me, and when the bill came, the waiter charged for the Shadow as if for a human being—and truly it had a most astonishing semblance of eating and drinking about it! Whatever I took it took, when I drank wine it drank wine—nay, it drank even more than I drank myself, for Shadows are generally larger than the objects which shun them.

I should almost have questioned whether it was a Shadow, had it not in all respects aped my movements and reflections. If I said it was a hot day, the Shadow said it was a hot day, or I fancied it said so. If I wiped my forehead, the Shadow seemed to do the same. If I put my hand in my pocket to pay for cigars, the Shadow did the same—only being a Shadow, it never brought out any money to pay for them, which is a peculiarity of Shadows.

When I praised anything the Shadow praised, and when I condemned the Shadow condemned—at least so its altitude seemed to imply. When I was going uptown the Shadow was going uptown, and when I inclined towards the Battery the Shadow was likewise attracted thither. Wherever I went, the Shadow went too. What I did, the Shadow did. What I thought the Shadow thought, and what I swore the Shadow swore. Of its Shadowy nature, there could be no question.

It is now a whole week since it left me. When I last saw it, I was dressing to go out, and the Shadow, of course, had precisely at that epoch occasion to dress too; so, it put on one of my clean shirts (as I did myself), and went out with me. At the door, it borrowed a five-dollar bill, and—vanished. It is the nature of Shadows to vanish. I have since heard that the same Shadow has vanished from more than one boarding house in the most shadowy manner.

May the reader never be haunted by Shadows!

I have a scientific theory, by the way, with reference to these visitors from Shadowland. it is, that they are the spiritual manifestations of departed (*i.e.* emigrated) Dodos. I mean to suggest the idea at the next meeting of the Royal Society, in London.

Mr. Grubbe's Night with Menmon

In the far west of London—preserving main traces of its original characteristics, amidst the wide expanse of architectural innovations which are continually springing up around it—there is a sober and antiquated, but withal respectable, locality, known to those travellers whose enterprise has led them thus far into the occidental suburbs, as Brompton. it is a district principally inhabited by theatricals, *literati,* and small annuitants; and is much esteemed on account of the salubrity of its climate, the mildness of its society, and the economy of its house-hold arrangements. Its chief natural curiosities are tea-parties and old ladies; and its overland journey to London is performed by omnibuses, unless the route by water is preferred. But this is somewhat circuitous—Cadogan pier, which is the nearest port, standing in the same relation to Brampton as Civita Vecchia does to Rome.

Mr. Withers Grubbe, who was an old inhabitant of this pleasant village, resided in a modest tenement, situated at the edge of the great Fulham road, this establishment comprised himself and his house-keeper—a staid woman, of matronly appearance—from which circumstance it may be fairly presumed that he was either a widower or a bachelor; but the uncertainty as to which of these two orders of single life he came under will be quite removed, when we state that he was an antiquary, an entomologist, and a general natural philosopher, somewhat resembling a cocoa-nut—being shrivelled in external appearance, but possessing a good heart or kernel, and not entirely destitute of the milk of human kindness.

As his favourite pursuits had been, from time immemorial, at variance with matrimony, he had never taken unto himself a wife. Once, and once only, did his friends speak of his falling in love. it was in the park, one bright frosty morning, when he saw a lady whose cloak somewhat resembled the delicate tintings of the privet moth; but this lepidopterous attachment was very transient, and the next chrysalis of the *Sphynx Atropos,* or number of the *Gentleman's Magazine,* that came to hand, immediately banished it from his mind.

And he was an occasional correspondent to the afore-named humorous publication. He had sent them a drawing of the old key of his dustbin, and a dissertation upon several wornout brass button-tops he had from time to time picked up in his walks, believing them to be ancient coins; as well as a plan of the Roman encampment on the Birmingham railway, and other interesting articles, the majority of which were "declined with thanks," by the venerable and undying Mr. Urban.

He belonged also to most of the learned and scientific bodies, to all of whom he read the rejected contributions, so that his time was pretty well occupied, and more especially in the spring; for then his *larvae* and *aureliae* broke forth into a new life, and there was such a buzzing, and fluttering, and pinning, and labelling all over the house, with intrusive butterflies getting into the bedrooms, and strange caterpillars walking up and downstairs, that people of ordinary nerves and uninterested in insect architecture were afraid to go into the house.

But he cherished all his living things with singular affection, even to the moths which had fastened upon his waistcoats, and the cockroaches which ran about his kitchen; although Mrs. Weston, the housekeeper, could never understand that the former insects only did any mischief in their first stage of existence, and that the latter were to be looked upon as sacred things, from the high veneration they were held in amongst the ancient Egyptians. The poor, ignorant woman, in the darkness of her intellect, classed them all as "warmint."

The great aim of Mr. Grubbe's labours was to get up some paper that should produce a striking sensation in the learned world, by the novel facts that it might disclose-—a consummation which had never yet arrived, for his most interesting discoveries had always been forestalled. To this great end did he consume his midnight patent stearin; for this did he burn holes in all his carpets with the contents of his galvanic battery, and get phosphorus under his nails, or take all the colour from his table-covers; in prosecuting this endeavour, by rubbing his buffer of black lead over cartridge-paper, laid upon engraved stones and brass tablets, to take the impression, was he three times apprehended for Swing, and once for sacrilege.

But hitherto he had never produced any extraordinary impression beyond that which his appearance created with the rustics; and although he was a walking catalogue of the British Museum—far more copious and elaborate than those lured by country visitors at contiguous fishmongers, and public-houses—he found every object therein had been so often and so minutely described, that nothing fresh was left to dilate upon. And this opinion for a time subdued his energy, until one evening he was present at the unrolling of a mummy. He listened with intense attention to the remarks of the lecturer, and envied him the proud position he was for a time placed in, as the descriptive link between the present and the long-past epochs.

But when the ceremony was finished, and Mr. Grubbe found, upon reviewing the lecture, that our acquaintance with the ancient Egyptians extended just far enough to show that we knew nothing at all about them, a fresh chain of research presented itself to his mind, and from that time every other pursuit was merged in the depths of the Great Pyramid, or perched upon the edge of Belzoni's sarcophagus. He made a mummy of his favourite cat; called his abode Sphynxcottage; and allowed the kitchen to swarm with cockroaches—which he called *scarabaei*, and Mrs. Weston black beadles—more than ever.

Things stood thus, when, one sultry July morning, a learned friend called to beg his company in a visit to the Docks, to view some wonderful organic remains, not yet landed, which a ship had brought from a distant country. Mr. Grubbe immediately prepared for the excursion; and, after having drawn an odd pair of boots upon the wrong legs in his absence of mind, as well as omitted to take off his duffel dressing-gown, he gave himself up to the care of Mrs. Weston, who finally pronounced him fit to appear in the public streets. He accordingly started with his friend, taking the omnibus to the Bank, whence they proceeded to the Docks on foot, saving the other sixpence; and beguiling the journey with main curious arguments and opinions about *ichthyosauri* the Blue Lias Clay.

The inspection of the fossils was most satisfactory, and they were pronounced highly interesting, the more so because several of them were perfectly incomprehensible; and notwithstanding the confined and heated places in which they were stowed, Mr. Grubbe poked about amongst the packing cases, covered with dust and perspiration, and dragging his friend after him, until every available object had been investigated, and they emerged from the hold into the free air.

A fresh treat now awaited him. His friend was attached to everything old equally with himself, and old wine possessed no insignificant share of his affections. With praiseworthy foresight he had provided a lasting order as a crowning finish to their excursion; and having raised Mr. Grubbe's curiosity by mysterious hints of pipes and casks that had long slumbered in cool excavations below the level of the Thames, and wine more generous, oily, and sparkling than ever came into the dealer's hands, they were not long in furnishing themselves with inches of candle in split laths, and following their guide—a priest of Bacchus in high lows and corduroys—into the bowels of the Docks.

How long they lingered therein we are ashamed to state; nor will we tell the world too ruthlessly how many casks were broached by the relentless gimlet; how the wine leaped bright and creaming from the wood; how the glasses held twice the ordinary quantity, and how they were even rinsed out with claret and madeira, which was thrown about amongst the sawdust like water. Neither will we betray the number of samples tasted by the visitors; nor do more than just hint at Mr. Grubbe's slapping the cellarman on the back for a good fellow, and endeavouring to strike up an ancient Bacchanalian melody, sung by Dignum in his young days.

We only know that this subterranean sojourn was protracted to a period we blush to chronicle, delayed, no doubt, by a learned disquisition, poured forth by Mr. Grubbe, upon the homemade wines of Thebes, which ended just as they got to the top of the staircase, and stood once more, blinking and confused, in the glaring sunshine of a July afternoon. And terrible was the effect of the hot atmosphere upon their temperaments before a few minutes had passed. *Whiz-z-z-z-z-z* went then eyes and brains together; the ships flew round and round like the revolving boats at Greenwich fair, and the warehouses heaved and rolled as the billows of the sea.

It was with the greatest difficulty, amidst this general *bouleversement* of surrounding objects, that the two men of science staggered to the gate, and deposited themselves in the first omnibus that passed. They had not particularly inquired in what direction it was going; and, in consequence, alter much travelling, Mr. Grubbe was somewhat surprised to find the vehicle stop in Tottenham-court-road, when he expected to be at the White Horse Cellar. But he was in the humour for treating any mishap that might have occurred with exceeding levity; and finding that the locality suited his friend just as well, even better, than Piccadilly, he wished him goodbye very affectionately, and took advantage of its proximity to pay a visit to his favourite British Museum, partly in the belief that its cool tranquillity would allay his cerebral excitement.

He left his inseparable gingham umbrella—which answered the double purpose of keeping off the rain when open and serving as a portmanteau of collected curiosities when shut—with the porter upon entering; and then turned his steps toward the Egyptian gallery, which was his usual lounge, still cherishing some vague notion that his skull had turned into a bag of hydrogen, so elastic and vivacious was his step.

There were, as usual, a great many people gaping about and asking foolish questions of the attendant; some mixing up the sphynx with the fossils they had seen, and asking if it ever was alive; others feeling rather afraid of going too near the mummies by themselves; and others lost in mental arguments as to whether the colossal list of red granite was a thunderbolt or the hand of a petrified giant; together with a great many ill-conducted little boys, with no veneration for antiquities, who laughed at the different objects as they would have done at any of the wondrous creations in a pantomime.

Heedless of the visitors, Mr. Grubbe was soon lost in mighty speculations upon the mysterious productions by which he was surrounded; and so, continued until the constant shuffling of feet and increasing influx of strangers, whose inane remarks grated upon his learned ears, drove him from the block upon which he was sitting, to some more remote corner of the gallery. Ensconcing himself in a recess behind one of the enormous heads, and screened by a sarcophagus, he fell into a fresh train of intense thought upon hieroglyphics in general, and those of mummies in particular. To this succeeded a confused picture of wine-vaults, pyramids, docks, claret-casks, and megatheria; and finally, overcome by the influence of heat, fatigue, and the tasting-order, he fell last asleep.

How long he slumbered remains to this day a mystery, and probably ever will do so. But when he awoke all was still and quiet as the interior of the, Theban tombs; the gallery was entirely deserted, and the moon was pouring a flood of light through the windows, which fell upon the statues and remains, rendering them still more cold and ghastly.

In an instant the truth broke upon the unhappy antiquary; he had been overlooked when the museum was cleared at seven o'clock, and was locked in—bolted, barred, almost hermetically shut up in the gallery, in the most remote part of the building, with nothing but stony monsters and crumbling mortality for his associates! Chilled to the heart with terror, despair, and the reaction of his previous excitement, he started from his corner with the intention of trying the doors, when his movement was arrested by the chime of a clock. He knew the sound well; it was the bell of St. George's, Bloomsbury, and it proclaimed the hour of twelve. And he was there alone——alone, at midnight, in the Egyptian chamber of the British Museum!

In a frenzy of terror, he rushed towards the large doors, in the hope of finding them open; but they were last closed, and he rattled the handles until the whole building rang with the echoes. Mark! what was that sound? The echo had died away, and was now renewed, although he had desisted from his impotent attempts to gain some mode of egress. it sounded from above, and now came nearer and nearer, louder and louder, like the deadened and regular beat of muffled drums. There were footsteps too—he could plainly distinguish them, in audible progression, coming downstairs.

And now a fearful spectacle met his horrified gaze. The immense marble *scarabaeus* on the floor of the gallery vibrated with incipient animation; then it stretched forth its huge feelers and opened its massy wings, like a newly born insect trying the properties of its novel limbs; and next, with the heavy cumbrous motion of a tortoise, it crept across the floor, throwing back the moonbeams from its polished surface, towards the principal entrance of the gallery. *Tramp, tramp, tramp*—onward came the noise as of a great assembly, the drums still keeping up their monotonous accompaniment, and at last they approached close to the door, which quivered immediately afterwards with three loud knocks upon its panels from without.

As the hapless Mr. Grubbe shrank still further into the recess, the large beetle scuffled nearer to the door, and then, raising one of its hideous feelers, it turned the handle. The gigantic granite first moved by itself towards the entrance, and repeated the signal on the panels; and, at the last blow, a sound like the low rumbling of thunder echoed through the edifice, and the doors flew open, admitting a glare of purple light, that for a few moments blinded the learned intruder, whilst on either side the Memnon and the Sphynx retreated back against the wall, to allow room for the dismal *cortége* that approached.

The whole collection of mummy-cases in the rooms above had given up their inmates, who now glided down the staircase, one after another, to join their ancient compatriots of the gallery below, lifting up the covers of their painted tombs, and stretching forth their pitched and blackened arms to welcome them. And next, the curious monsters with the birds' heads, who, up to this moment, had remained patiently sitting against the side of the room with their hands upon their knees, rose courteously to salute their visitors.

The light which filled the apartment, although proceeding from no visible point, grew brighter and brighter until it assumed the brilliancy of oxyhydrogen, and when the last of the dusty and bandaged guests had arrived, the doors closed violently, and the orgies began. The figures in the pictures became animated and descended from the tablets, being by far the most attractive portion of the company, either male or female, as they were semblances of life, bearing *amphorae* of the choicest wine from the vineyards of Memphis; strange birds in long striped tunics, and stranger creations, whose shapes inherited an attribute of every class of the animal kingdom, acted as attendants, and obsequiously wailed upon the superior deities; whilst the greatest feature of the gallery, the mystic, awe inspiring Memnon, moved in stately progress to the end of the room, and commenced pouring forth that wondrous harmony with which at sunrise and twilight he welcomed his early worshipers.

Then commenced an unearthly *galopade*—a dreary carnival of the dead, to the music of their master, accompanied by the strange sounds of instruments brought by the mummies most inclined to conviviality, from the glass-cases upstairs. But the strangest sight in the whole spectacle was the curious way in which Mr. Grubbe, despite his fears, perceived that they mingled ancient with modern manners, when the dance came to an end.

Some of the animated Egyptians betook themselves to pipes and beer; others brought large aerolites from the different rooms and began to play at ninepins with the inferior household gods of blue glazed clay; one young Memphian even went so far as to thrust an enormous hook, as big as an anchor, through the body of a *scarabaeus*, and then spin him at the end of a rope about the room; and, finally, they wheeled a sarcophagus into the centre of the gallery, and filled it with what Mr. Grubbe's nose told him was excellent mixed punch, which they tippled until the eyes of Memnon twinkled with conviviality, as he snuffed up the goodly aroma; and at length, forgetting his dignity altogether, volunteered to play the *Aurora* waltzes (in compliment of course to his mother) out of his head.

The monumental punch-bowl was directly pushed on one side, and they began to dance again, Mr. Grubbe, getting gradually more and more excited by the music, until, unable to contain himself any longer, he rushed from his recess, and seizing a fair young daughter of the Nile round the waist, was in an instant whirling round in the throng of deities, mummies, hieroglyphics, ibises, and anomalous creations who composed the assembly.

The hours flew along like joyous minutes, and still the unearthly waltz was continued with persisting energy, until Mr. Grubbe's brain became giddy and bewildered. His strength also began to fail in spite of the attractions of his young *Memphienne,* whose soft downy cheeks, roguish kissable lips, and supernaturally-sparkling eyes, had for a time made him forget his age. He requested her to stop in their wild gyrations, but she heeded him not—breathless and exhausted, he was pulled round and round, whilst the Memnonian orchestra played itself louder and louder, until at length, losing all power, he fell down in the midst of the dancers.

Twenty others, who had been twirling onwards, not perceiving their prostrate companion, immediately lost their footing; and, finally, the whole assembly, like so many bent cards, giddy with wine and excitement, bundled one over the other, the unfortunate antiquary being the undermost of the party. In vain he struggled to be free—each moment the pressure of the superincumbent Egyptians increased; until, in a last extremity, unable to breathe, bruised by their legs and arms, and half suffocated with mummy-dust, he gave a few fruitless gasps for air, and then became insensible.

It was broad daylight when he once more opened his eyes; and the motes were dancing in the bright morning sunbeams that darted into the gallery. There were sounds of life and motion too, on every side (although no one had as yet entered the apartment), and the rumble of distant vehicles in the streets. it was some little time before Mr. Grubbe could collect his ideas for his brain was still slightly clouded— his lips, also, were parched, and his eyeballs smarting with the revelry of the night.

But there he still was, in the room, surrounded by his late company, though they had now resumed their usual situations: the Memnon and Sphynx were *vis-à-vis,* and the *scarabaeus* in his customary place, as cold and inanimate as ever; whilst the gigantic fist had once more taken possession of its pedestal, and the gentlemen with the curious heads were sitting with their hands upon their knees in their wonted gravity. But, notwithstanding all this chill reality, the antiquary's mind was in a tumult of excitement. The dim undying magic of ancient Egypt was still in force, unconquered by time or distance. He had been admitted to the orgies of Memnon; he had watched the revelries and manners of the hitherto mysterious race; above all, he had gleaned information for a paper that would bring the Society of Antiquaries at his feet in wondrous veneration!

The doors were, ere long, thrown open, and Mr. Grubbe left the gallery unnoticed. On arriving at Brompton, he found Mrs. Weston in a state of extreme terror and exhaustion, having watched the whole night for her master's return, that worthy gentleman never having passed so long a period from home.

He retired immediately to his study, and laboured until dusk with unceasing industry; and from that period Egypt alone occupied his thoughts. He thought of nothing else by day, and dreamed of that subject only by night. The subject grew beneath his hands and ideas, and what with the circumstances he imagined, and those he dreamed about—for in his labours he ever confounded them together—the work is still unfinished; and he will not give it to the world in an imperfect condition, although his most intimate friends already fear that his application is affecting his brain.

But, when his task is concluded, great will be his triumph: he will have furnished—at least such is his expectation—a key to all the mystic customs of the early Nile; the hidden lore of Memphis will be unravelled to the million; he will walk abroad a thing for men to gaze at and reverence; and his name will go down to posterity in company with Memnon and the Great Pyramid.

These are his own anticipations: his intimate friends have only one hope—that he will be spared from Bedlam sufficiently long to perfect his colossal undertaking; and that on no account will he be induced any more to venture, with a lasting-order, to the Docks.

The Lost Room

It was oppressively warm. The sun had long disappeared, but seemed to have left its vital spirit of heat behind it. The air rested; the leaves of the acacia-trees that shrouded my windows hung plumb-like on their delicate stalks. The smoke of my cigar scarce rose above my head, but hung about me in a pale blue cloud, which I had to dissipate with languid waves of my hand. My shirt was open at the throat, and my chest heaved laboriously in the effort to catch some breaths of fresher air. The noises of the city seemed to be wrapped in slumber, and the shrilling of the mosquitoes was the only sound that broke the stillness.

As I lay with my feet elevated on the back of a chair, wrapped in that peculiar frame of mind in which thought assumes a species of lifeless motion, the strange fancy seized me of making a languid inventory of the principal articles of furniture in my room. It was a task well suited to the mood in which I found myself. Their forms were duskily defined in the dim twilight that floated shadowily through the chamber; it was no labour to note and particularize each, and from the place where I sat I could command a view of all my possessions without even turning my head.

There was, *imprimis*, that ghostly lithograph by Calame. It was a mere black spot on the white wall, but my inner vision scrutinized every detail of the picture. A wild, desolate, midnight heath, with a spectral oak-tree in the centre of the foreground. The wind blows fiercely, and the jagged branches, clothed scantily with ill-grown leaves, are swept to the left continually by its giant force. A formless wrack of clouds streams across the awful sky, and the rain sweeps almost parallel with the horizon. Beyond, the heath stretches off into endless blackness, in the extreme of which either fancy or art has conjured up some undefinable shapes that seem riding into space. At the base of the huge

313

oak stands a shrouded figure. His mantle is wound by the blast in tight folds around his form, and the long cock's feather in his hat is blown upright, till it seems as if it stood on end with fear. His features are not visible, for he has grasped his cloak with both hands, and drawn it from either side across his face. The picture is seemingly objectless. It tells no tale, but there is a weird power about it that haunts one, and it was for that I bought it.

Next to the picture comes the round blot that hangs below it, which I know to be a smoking-cap. It has my coat of arms embroidered on the front, and for that reason I never wear it; though, when properly arranged on my head, with its long blue silken tassel hanging down by my cheek, I believe it becomes me well. I remember the time when it was in the course of manufacture.

I remember the tiny little hands that pushed the coloured silks so nimbly through the cloth that was stretched on the embroidery-frame,—the vast trouble I was put to to get a coloured copy of my armorial bearings for the heraldic work which was to decorate the front of the band,—the pursings up of the little mouth, and the contractions of the young forehead, as their possessor plunged into a profound sea of cogitation touching the way in which the cloud should be represented from which the armed hand, that is my crest, issues,— the heavenly moment when the tiny hands placed it on my head, in a position that I could not bear for more than a few seconds, and I, kinglike, immediately assumed my royal prerogative after the coronation, and instantly levied a tax on my only subject, which was, however, not paid unwillingly. Ah! the cap is there, but the embroiderer has fled; for Atropos was severing the web of life above her head while she was weaving that silken shelter for mine!

How uncouthly the huge piano that occupies the corner at the left of the door looms out in the uncertain twilight! I neither play nor sing, yet I own a piano. It is a comfort to me to look at it, and to feel that the music is there, although I am not able to break the spell that binds it. It is pleasant to know that Bellini and Mozart, Cimarosa, Porpora, Glück, and all such,—or at least their souls,—sleep in that unwieldy case. There lie embalmed, as it were, all operas, *sonatas*, *oratorios*, *notturnos*, marches, songs, and dances, that ever climbed into existence through the four bars that wall in melody. Once I was entirely repaid for the investment of my funds in that instrument which I never use. Blokeeta, the composer, came to see me.

Of course, his instincts urged him as irresistibly to my piano as if some magnetic power lay within it compelling him to approach. He tuned it, he played on it. All night long, until the grey and spectral dawn rose out of the depths of the midnight, he sat and played, and I lay smoking by the window listening. Wild, unearthly, and sometimes insufferably painful, were the improvisations of Blokeeta. The chords of the instrument seemed breaking with anguish. Lost souls shrieked in his dismal preludes; the half-heard utterances of spirits in pain, that groped at inconceivable distances from anything lovely or harmonious, seemed to rise dimly up out of the waves of sound that gathered under his hands.

Melancholy human love wandered out on distant heaths, or beneath dank and gloomy cypresses, murmuring its unanswered sorrow, or hateful gnomes sported and sang in the stagnant swamps, triumphing in unearthly tones over the knight whom they had lured to his death. Such was Blokeeta's night's entertainment; and when he at length closed the piano, and hurried away through the cold morning, he left a memory about the instrument from which I could never escape.

Those snow-shoes that hang in the space between the mirror and the door recall Canadian wanderings,—a long race through the dense forests, over the frozen snow, through whose brittle crust the slender hoofs of the caribou that we were pursuing sank at every step, until the poor creature despairingly turned at bay in a small juniper coppice, and we heartlessly shot him down. And I remember how Gabriel, the *habitant*, and François, the half-breed, cut his throat, and how the hot blood rushed out in a torrent over the snowy soil; and I recall the snow *cabane* that Gabriel built, where we all three slept so warmly; and the great fire that glowed at our feet, painting all kinds of demoniac shapes on the black screen of forest that lay without; and the deer-steaks that we roasted for our breakfast; and the savage drunkenness of Gabriel in the morning, he having been privately drinking out of my brandy-flask all the night long.

That long, haftless dagger that dangles over the mantelpiece-makes my heart swell. I found it, when a boy, in a hoary old castle in which one of my maternal ancestors once lived. That same ancestor—who, by the way, yet lives in history—was a strange old sea-king, who dwelt on the extremest point of the southwestern coast of Ireland. He owned the whole of that fertile island called Inniskeiran, which directly faces Cape Clear, where between them the Atlantic rolls furiously, forming what the fishermen of the place call "the Sound." An awful place in winter is that same Sound. On certain days, no boat can live there for a moment, and Cape Clear is frequently cut off for days from any communication with the main land.

This old sea-king—Sir Florence O'Driscoll by name—passed a stormy life. From the summit of his castle he watched the ocean, and when any richly laden vessels, bound from the south to the industrious Galway merchants, hove in sight, Sir Florence hoisted the sails of his galley, and it went hard with him if he did not tow into harbour ship and crew. In this way, he lived; not a very honest mode of livelihood, certainly, according to our modern ideas, but quite reconcilable with the morals of the time. As may be supposed, Sir Florence got into trouble. Complaints were laid against him at the English court by the plundered merchants, and the Irish Viking set out for London, to plead his own cause before good Queen Bess, as she was called.

He had one powerful recommendation: he was a marvellously handsome man. Not Celtic by descent, but half Spanish, half Danish in blood, he had the great northern stature with the regular features, flashing eyes, and dark hair of the Iberian race. This may account for the fact that his stay at the English court was much longer than was necessary, as also for the tradition, which a local historian mentions, that the English queen evinced a preference for the Irish chieftain, of other nature than that usually shown by monarch to subject.

Previous to his departure, Sir Florence had intrusted the care of his property to an Englishman named Hull. During the long absence of the knight, this person managed to ingratiate himself with the local authorities, and gain their favour so far that they were willing to support him in almost any scheme. After a protracted stay, Sir Florence, pardoned of all his misdeeds, returned to his home. Home no longer. Hull was in possession, and refused to yield an acre of the lands he had so nefariously acquired. It was no use appealing to the law, for its officers were in the opposite interest.

It was no use appealing to the queen, for she had another lover, and had forgotten the poor Irish knight by this time; and so, the Viking passed the best portion of his life in unsuccessful attempts to reclaim his vast estates, and was eventually, in his old age, obliged to content himself with his castle by the sea and the island of Inniskeiran, the only spot of which the usurper was unable to deprive him. So, this old story of my kinsman's fate looms up out of the darkness that enshrouds that haftless dagger hanging on the wall.

It was somewhat after the foregoing fashion that I dreamily made the inventory of my personal property. As I turned my eyes on each object, one after the other,—or the places where they lay, for the room was now so dark that it was almost impossible to see with any distinctness,—a crowd of memories connected with each rose up before me, and, perforce, I had to indulge them. So, I proceeded but slowly, and at last my cigar shortened to a hot and bitter morsel that I could barely hold between my lips, while it seemed to me that the night grew each moment more insufferably oppressive. While I was revolving some impossible means of cooling my wretched body, the cigar stump began to burn my lips. I flung it angrily through the open window, and stooped out to watch it falling. It first lighted on the leaves of the acacia, sending out a spray of red sparkles, then, rolling off, it fell plump on the dark walk in the garden, faintly illuminating for a moment the dusky trees and breathless flowers.

Whether it was the contrast between the red flash of the cigar-stump and the silent darkness of the garden, or whether it was that I detected by the sudden light a faint waving of the leaves, I know not; but something suggested to me that the garden was cool. I will take a turn there, thought I, just as I am; it cannot be warmer than this room, and however still the atmosphere, there is always a feeling of liberty and spaciousness in the open air, that partially supplies one's wants. With this idea running through my head, I arose, lit another cigar, and passed out into the long, intricate corridors that led to the main staircase. As I crossed the threshold of my room, with what a different feeling I should have passed it had I known that I was never to set foot in it again!

I lived in a very large house, in which I occupied two rooms on the second floor. The house was old-fashioned, and all the floors communicated by a huge circular staircase that wound up through the centre of the building, while at every landing long, rambling corridors stretched off into mysterious nooks and corners. This palace of mine was very high, and its resources, in the way of crannies and windings, seemed to be interminable. Nothing seemed to stop anywhere. *Cul-de-sacs* were unknown on the premises. The corridors and passages, like mathematical lines, seemed capable of indefinite extension, and the object of the architect must have been to erect an edifice in which people might go ahead forever.

The whole place was gloomy, not so much because it was large, but because an unearthly nakedness seemed to pervade the structure. The staircases, corridors, halls, and vestibules all partook of a desert-like desolation. There was nothing on the walls to break the sombre monotony of those long vistas of shade. No carvings on the wainscoting, no moulded masks peering down from the simply severe cornices, no marble vases on the landings. There was an eminent dreariness and want of life—so rare in an American establishment—all over the abode. It was Hood's haunted house put in order and newly painted.

The servants, too, were shadowy, and chary of their visits. Bells rang three times before the gloomy chambermaid could be induced to present herself; and the negro waiter, a ghoul-like looking creature from Congo, obeyed the summons only when one's patience was exhausted or one's want satisfied in some other way. When he did come, one felt sorry that he had not stayed away altogether, so sullen and savage did he appear. He moved along the echoless floors with a slow, noiseless shamble, until his dusky figure, advancing from the gloom, seemed like some reluctant *afreet*, compelled by the superior power of his master to disclose himself. When the doors of all the chambers were closed, and no light illuminated the long corridor save the red, unwholesome glare of a small oil lamp on a table at the end, where late lodgers lit their candles, one could not by any possibility conjure up a sadder or more desolate prospect.

Yet the house suited me. Of meditative and sedentary habits, I enjoyed the extreme quiet. There were but few lodgers, from which I infer that the landlord did not drive a very thriving trade; and these, probably oppressed by the sombre spirit of the place, were quiet and ghost-like in their movements. The proprietor I scarcely ever saw. My bills were deposited by unseen hands every month on my table, while I was out walking or riding, and my pecuniary response was intrusted to the attendant *afreet*. On the whole, when the bustling, wideawake spirit of New York is taken into consideration, the sombre, half-vivified character of the house in which I lived was an anomaly that no one appreciated better than I who lived there.

I felt my way down the wide, dark staircase in my pursuit of zephyrs. The garden, as I entered it, did feel somewhat cooler than my own room, and I puffed my cigar along the dim, cypress-shrouded walks with a sensation of comparative relief. It was very dark. The tall-growing flowers that bordered the path were so wrapped in gloom as to present the aspect of solid pyramidal masses, all the details of leaves and blossoms being buried in an embracing darkness, while the trees had lost all form, and seemed like masses of overhanging cloud. It was a place and time to excite the imagination; for in the impenetrable cavities of endless gloom there was room for the most riotous fancies to play at will.

I walked and walked, and the echoes of my footsteps on the un-gravelled and mossy path suggested a double feeling. I felt alone and yet in company at the same time. The solitariness of the place made itself distinct enough in the stillness, broken alone by the hollow re-verberations of my step, while those very reverberations seemed to imbue me with an undefined feeling that I was not alone. I was not, therefore, much startled when I was suddenly accosted from beneath the solid darkness of an immense cypress by a voice saying, "Will you give me a light, sir?"

"Certainly," I replied, trying in vain to distinguish the speaker amidst the impenetrable dark.

Somebody advanced, and I held out my cigar. All I could gather definitively about the individual who thus accosted me was that he must have been of extremely small stature; for I, who am by no means an overgrown man, had to stoop considerably in handing him my ci-gar. The vigorous puff that he gave his own lighted up my Havana for a moment, and I fancied that I caught a glimpse of a pale, weird coun-tenance, immersed in a background of long, wild hair. The flash was, however, so momentary that I could not even say certainly whether this was an actual impression or the mere effort of imagination to embody that which the senses had failed to distinguish.

"Sir, you are out late," said this unknown to me, as he, with half-uttered thanks, handed me back my cigar, for which I had to grope in the gloom.

"Not later than usual," I replied, dryly.

"Hum! you are fond of late wanderings, then?"

"That is just as the fancy seizes me."

"Do you live here?"

"Yes."

"Queer house, isn't it?"

"I have only found it quiet."

"Hum! But you will find it queer, take my word for it." This was earnestly uttered; and I felt at the same time a bony finger laid on my arm, that cut it sharply like a blunted knife.

"I cannot take your word for any such assertion," I replied, rudely, shaking off the bony finger with an irrepressible motion of disgust.

"No offence, no offence," muttered my unseen companion rapidly, in a strange, subdued voice, that would have been shrill had it been louder; "your being angry does not alter the matter. You will find it a queer house. Everybody finds it a queer house. Do you know who live there?"

"I never busy myself, sir, about other people's affairs," I answered sharply, for the individual's manner, combined with my utter uncertainty as to his appearance, oppressed me with an irksome longing to be rid of him.

"O, you don't! Well, I do. I know what they are,—well, well, well!" and as he pronounced the three last words his voice rose with each, until, with the last, it reached a shrill shriek that echoed horribly among the lonely walks. "Do you know what they eat?" he continued.

"No, sir,—nor care."

"O, but you will care. You must care. You shall care. I'll tell you what they are. They are enchanters. They are ghouls. They are cannibals. Did you never remark their eyes, and how they gloated on you when you passed? Did you never remark the food that they served up at your table? Did you never in the dead of night hear muffled and unearthly footsteps gliding along the corridors, and stealthy hands turning the handle of your door? Does not some magnetic influence fold itself continually around you when they pass, and send a thrill through spirit and body, and a cold shiver that no sunshine will chase away? O, you have! You have felt all these things! I know it!"

The earnest rapidity, the subdued tones, the eagerness of accent, with which all this was uttered, impressed me most uncomfortable. It really seemed as if I could recall all those weird occurrences and influences of which he spoke; and I shuddered in spite of myself in the midst of the impenetrable darkness that surrounded me.

"Hum!" said I, assuming, without knowing it, a confidential tone, "may I ask how you know these things?"

"How I know them? Because I am their enemy; because they tremble at my whisper; because I hang upon their track with the perseverance of a bloodhound and the stealthiness of a tiger; because—because—I was *of* them once!"

"Wretch!" I cried excitedly, for involuntarily his eager tones had wrought me up to a high pitch of spasmodic nervousness, "then you mean to say that you—"

As I uttered this word, obeying an uncontrollable impulse, I stretched forth my hand in the direction of the speaker and made a blind clutch. The tips of my fingers seemed to touch a surface as smooth as glass, that glided suddenly from under them. A sharp, angry hiss sounded through the gloom, followed by a whirring noise, as if some projectile passed rapidly by, and the next moment I felt instinctively that I was alone.

A most disagreeable feeling instantly assailed me;—a prophetic instinct that some terrible misfortune menaced me; an eager and overpowering anxiety to get back to my own room without loss of time. I turned and ran blindly along the dark cypress alley, every dusky clump of flowers that rose blackly in the borders making my heart each moment cease to beat. The echoes of my own footsteps seemed to redouble and assume the sounds of unknown pursuers following fast upon my track. The boughs of lilac-bushes and syringas, that here and there stretched partly across the walk, seemed to have been furnished suddenly with hooked hands that sought to grasp me as I flew by, and each moment I expected to behold some awful and impassable barrier fall across my track and wall me up forever.

At length, I reached the wide entrance. With a single leap, I sprang up the four or five steps that formed the stoop, and dashed along the hall, up the wide, echoing stairs, and again along the dim, funereal corridors until I paused, breathless and panting, at the door of my room. Once so far, I stopped for an instant and leaned heavily against one of the panels, panting lustily after my late run. I had, however, scarcely rested my whole weight against the door, when it suddenly gave way, and I staggered in head-foremost. To my utter astonishment the room I had left in profound darkness was now a blaze of light.

So intense was the illumination that, for a few seconds while the pupils of my eyes were contracting under the sudden change, I saw absolutely nothing save the dazzling glare. This fact in itself, coming on me with such utter suddenness, was sufficient to prolong my confusion, and it was not until after several minutes had elapsed that I perceived the room was not only illuminated, but occupied. And such occupants! Amazement at the scene took such possession of me that I was incapable of either moving or uttering a word. All that I could do was to lean against the wall, and stare blankly at the strange picture.

It might have been a scene out of *Faublas*, or Grammont's *Memoirs*, or happened in some palace of Minister Fouque.

Round a large table in the centre of the room, where I had left a student-like litter of books and papers, were seated half a dozen persons. Three were men and three were women. The table was heaped with a prodigality of luxuries. Luscious eastern fruits were piled up in silver filigree vases, through whose meshes their glowing rinds shone in the contrasts of a thousand hues. Small silver dishes that Benvenuto might have designed, filled with succulent and aromatic meats, were distributed upon a cloth of snowy damask. Bottles of every shape, slender ones from the Rhine, stout fellows from Holland, sturdy ones from Spain, and quaint basket-woven flasks from Italy, absolutely littered the board.

Drinking-glasses of every size and hue filled up the interstices, and the thirsty German flagon stood side by side with the aerial bubbles of Venetian glass that rest so lightly on their threadlike stems. An odour of luxury and sensuality floated through the apartment. The lamps that burned in every direction seemed to diffuse a subtle incense on the air, and in a large vase that stood on the floor I saw a mass of magnolias, tuberoses, and jasmines grouped together, stifling each other with their honeyed and heavy fragrance.

The inhabitants of my room seemed beings well suited to so sensual an atmosphere. The women were strangely beautiful, and all were attired in dresses of the most fantastic devices and brilliant hues. Their figures were round, supple, and elastic; their eyes dark and languishing; their lips full, ripe, and of the richest bloom. The three men wore half-masks, so that all I could distinguish were heavy jaws, pointed beards, and brawny throats that rose like massive pillars out of their doublets. All six lay reclining on Roman couches about the table, drinking down the purple wines in large draughts, and tossing back their heads and laughing wildly.

I stood, I suppose, for some three minutes, with my back against the wall staring vacantly at the bacchanal vision, before any of the revellers appeared to notice my presence. At length, without any expression to indicate whether I had been observed from the beginning or not, two of the women arose from their couches, and, approaching, took each a hand and led me to the table. I obeyed their motions mechanically. I sat on a couch between them as they indicated. I unresistingly permitted them to wind their arms about my neck.

"You must drink," said one, pouring out a large glass of red wine, "here is *Clos Vougeot* of a rare vintage; and here," pushing a flask of amber-hued wine before me, "is *Lachryma Christi*."

"You must eat," said the other, drawing the silver dishes toward her. "Here are cutlets stewed with olives, and here are slices of a *filet* stuffed with bruised sweet chestnuts";—and as she spoke, she, without waiting for a reply, proceeded to help me.

The sight of the food recalled to me the warnings I had received in the garden. This sudden effort of memory restored to me my other faculties at the same instant. I sprang to my feet, thrusting the women from me with each hand.

"Demons!" I almost shouted, "I will have none of your accursed food. I know you. You are cannibals, you are ghouls, you are enchanters. Begone, I tell you! Leave my room in peace!"

A shout of laughter from all six was the only effect that my passionate speech produced. The men rolled on their couches, and their half-masks quivered with the convulsions of their mirth. The women shrieked, and tossed the slender wine-glasses wildly aloft, and turned to me and flung themselves on my bosom fairly sobbing with laughter.

"Yes," I continued, as soon as the noisy mirth had subsided, "yes, I say, leave my room instantly! I will have none of your unnatural orgies here!"

"His room!" shrieked the woman on my right.

"His room!" echoed she on my left.

"His room! He calls it his room!" shouted the whole party, as they rolled once more into jocular convulsions.

"How do know you that it is your room?" said one of the men who sat opposite to me, at length, after the laughter had once more somewhat subsided.

"How do I know?" I replied, indignantly. "How do I know my own room? How could I mistake it, pray? There's my furniture—my piano—"

"He calls that a piano!" shouted my neighbours, again in convulsions as I pointed to the corner where my huge piano, sacred to the memory of Blokeeta, used to stand. "O, yes! It is his room. There—there is his piano!"

The peculiar emphasis they laid on the word "piano" caused me to scrutinise the article I was indicating more thoroughly. Up to this time, though utterly amazed at the entrance of these people into my chamber, and connecting them somewhat with the wild stories I had heard in the garden, I still had a sort of indefinite idea that the whole thing was a masquerading freak got up in my absence, and that the bacchanalian orgie I was witnessing was nothing more than a portion of some elaborate hoax of which I was to be the victim. But when my eyes turned to the corner where I had left a huge and cumbrous piano, and beheld a vast and sombre organ lifting its fluted front to the very ceiling, and convinced myself, by a hurried process of memory, that it occupied the very spot in which I had left my own instrument, the little self-possession that I had left forsook me. I gazed around me bewildered.

In like manner, everything was changed. In the place of that old haftless dagger, connected with so many historic associations personal to myself, I beheld a Turkish *yataghan* dangling by its belt of crimson silk, while the jewels in the hilt blazed as the lamplight played upon them. In the spot where hung my cherished smoking-cap, memorial of a buried love, a knightly casque was suspended, on the crest of which a golden dragon stood in the act of springing. That strange lithograph by Calame was no longer a lithograph, but it seemed to me that the portion of the wall which it had covered, of the exact shape and size, had been cut out, and, in place of the picture, a real scene on the same scale, and with real actors, was distinctly visible.

The old oak was there, and the stormy sky was there; but I saw the branches of the oak sway with the tempest, and the clouds drive before the wind. The wanderer in his cloak was gone; but in his place, I beheld a circle of wild figures, men and women, dancing with linked hands around the bole of the great tree, chanting some wild fragment of a song, to which the winds roared an unearthly chorus. The snow-shoes, too, on whose sinewy woof I had sped for many days amidst Canadian wastes, had vanished, and in their place, lay a pair of strange up-curled Turkish slippers, that had, perhaps, been many a time shuffled off at the doors of mosques, beneath the steady blaze of an orient sun.

All was changed. Wherever my eyes turned they missed familiar objects, yet encountered strange representatives. Still, in all the substitutes there seemed to me a reminiscence of what they replaced. They seemed only for a time transmuted into other shapes, and there lingered around them the atmosphere of what they once had been. Thus, I could have sworn the room to have been mine, yet there was nothing in it that I could rightly claim. Everything reminded me of some former possession that it was not. I looked for the acacia at the window, and, lo! long, silken palm-leaves swayed in through the open lattice; yet they had the same motion and the same air of my favourite tree, and seemed to murmur to me, "Though we seem to be palm-leaves, yet are we acacia-leaves; yea, those very ones on which you used to watch the butterflies alight and the rain patter while you smoked and dreamed!" So, in all things; the room was, yet was not, mine; and a sickening consciousness of my utter inability to reconcile its identity with its appearance overwhelmed me, and choked my reason.

"Well, have you determined whether or not this is your room?" asked the girl on my left, proffering me a huge tumbler creaming over with champagne, and laughing wickedly as she spoke.

"It is mine," I answered, doggedly, striking the glass rudely with my hand, and dashing the aromatic wine over the white cloth. "I know that it is mine; and you are jugglers and enchanters who want to drive me mad."

"Hush! hush!" she said, gently, not in the least angered at my rough treatment. "You are excited. Alf shall play something to soothe you."

At her signal, one of the men sat down at the organ. After a short, wild, spasmodic prelude, he began what seemed to me to be a symphony of recollections. Dark and sombre, and all through full of quivering and intense agony, it appeared to recall a dark and dismal night, on a cold reef, around which an unseen bat terribly audible ocean broke with eternal fury. It seemed as if a lonely pair were on the reef, one living, the other dead; one clasping his arms around the tender neck and naked bosom of the other, striving to warm her into life, when his own vitality was being each moment sucked from him by the icy breath of the storm. Here and there a terrible wailing minor key would tremble through the chords like the shriek of sea-birds, or the warning of advancing death.

While the man played I could scarce restrain myself. It seemed to be Blokeeta whom I listened to, and on whom I gazed. That wondrous night of pleasure and pain that I had once passed listening to him seemed to have been taken up again at the spot where it had broken off, and the same hand was continuing it. I stared at the man called Alf. There he sat with his cloak and doublet, and long rapier and mask of black velvet. But there was something in the air of the peaked beard, a familiar mystery in the wild mass of raven hair that fell as if wind-blown over his shoulders, which riveted my memory.

"Blokeeta! Blokeeta!" I shouted, starting up furiously from the couch on which I was lying, and bursting the fair arms that were linked around my neck as if they had been hateful chains,—"Blokeeta! my friend! speak to me, I entreat you! Tell these horrid enchanters to leave me. Say that I hate them. Say that I command them to leave my room."

The man at the organ stirred not in answer to my appeal. He ceased playing, and the dying sound of the last note he had touched faded off into a melancholy moan. The other men and the women burst once more into peals of mocking laughter.

"Why will you persist in calling this your room?" said the woman next me, with a smile meant to be kind, but to me inexpressibly loathsome. "Have we not shown you by the furniture, by the general appearance of the place, that you are mistaken, and that this cannot be your apartment? Rest content, then, with us. You are welcome here, and need no longer trouble yourself about your room."

"Rest content!" I answered, madly; "live with ghosts! eat of awful meats, and see awful sights! Never, never! You have cast some enchantment over the place that has disguised it; but for all that I know it to be my room. You shall leave it!"

"Softly, softly!" said another of the sirens. "Let us settle this amicably. This poor gentleman seems obstinate and inclined to make an uproar. Now we do not want an uproar. We love the night and its quiet; and there is no night that we love so well as that on which the moon is coffined in clouds. Is it not so, my brothers?"

An awful and sinister smile gleamed on the countenances of her unearthly audience, and seemed to glide visibly from underneath their masks.

"Now," she continued, "I have a proposition to make. It would be ridiculous for us to surrender this room simply because this gentleman states that it is his; and yet I feel anxious to gratify, as far as may be fair, his wild assertion of ownership. A room, after all, is not much to us; we can get one easily enough, but still we should be loath to give this apartment up to so imperious a demand. We are willing, however, to *risk* its loss. That is to say,"—turning to me,—"I propose that we play for the room. If you win, we will immediately surrender it to you just as it stands; if, on the contrary, you lose, you shall bind yourself to depart and never molest us again."

Agonised at the ever-darkening mysteries that seemed to thicken around me, and despairing of being able to dissipate them by the mere exercise of my own will, I caught almost gladly at the chance thus presented to me. The idea of my loss or my gain scarce entered into my calculations. All I felt was an indefinite knowledge that I might, in the way proposed, regain, in an instant, that quiet chamber and that peace of mind of which I had so strangely been deprived.

"I agree!" I cried, eagerly; "I agree. Anything to rid myself of such unearthly company!"

The woman touched a small golden bell that stood near her on the table, and it had scarce ceased to tinkle when a negro dwarf entered with a silver tray on which were dice-boxes and dice. A shudder passed over me as I thought in this stunted African I could trace a resemblance to the ghoul-like black servant to whose attendance I had been accustomed.

"Now," said my neighbour, seizing one of the dice-boxes and giving me the other, "the highest wins. Shall I throw first?"

I nodded assent. She rattled the dice, and I felt an inexpressible load lifted from my heart as she threw fifteen.

"It is your turn," she said, with a mocking smile; "but before you throw, I repeat the offer I made you before. Live with us. Be one of us. We will initiate you into our mysteries and enjoyments,—enjoyments of which you can form no idea unless you experience them. Come; it is not too late yet to change your mind. Be with us!"

My reply was a fierce oath, as I rattled the dice with spasmodic nervousness and flung them on the board. They rolled over and over again, and during that brief instant I felt a suspense, the intensity of which I have never known before or since. At last they lay before me. A shout of the same horrible, maddening laughter rang in my ears. I peered in vain at the dice, but my sight was so confused that I could not distinguish the amount of the cast. This lasted for a few moments. Then my sight grew clear, and I sank back almost lifeless with despair as I saw that I had thrown but twelve!

"Lost! lost!" screamed my neighbor, with a wild laugh. "Lost! lost!" shouted the deep voices of the masked men. "Leave us, coward!" they all cried; "you are not fit to be one of us. Remember your promise; leave us!"

Then it seemed as if some unseen power caught me by the shoulders and thrust me toward the door. In vain I resisted. In vain I screamed and shouted for help. In vain I implored them for pity. All the reply I had was those mocking peals of merriment, while, under the invisible influence, I staggered like a drunken man toward the door. As I reached the threshold the organ pealed out a wild, triumphal strain.

The power that impelled me concentrated itself into one vigorous impulse that sent me blindly staggering out into the echoing corridor, and, as the door closed swiftly behind me, I caught one glimpse of the apartment I had left forever. A change passed like a shadow over it. The lamps died out, the siren women and masked men vanished, the flowers, the fruits, the bright silver and bizarre furniture faded swiftly, and I saw again, for the tenth of a second, my own old chamber restored. There was the acacia waving darkly; there was the table littered with books; there was the ghostly lithograph, the dearly beloved smoking-cap, the Canadian snow-shoes, the ancestral dagger. And there, at the piano, organ no longer, sat Blokeeta playing.

The next instant the door closed violently, and I was left standing in the corridor stunned and despairing.

As soon as I had partially recovered my comprehension I rushed madly to the door, with the dim idea of beating it in. My fingers touched a cold and solid wall. There was no door! I felt all along the corridor for many yards on both sides. There was not even a crevice to give me hope. I rushed down stairs shouting madly. No one answered. In the vestibule, I met the negro; I seized him by the collar, and demanded my room. The demon showed his white and awful teeth, which were filed into a saw-like shape, and, extricating himself from my grasp with a sudden jerk, fled down the passage with a gibbering laugh. Nothing but echo answered to my despairing shrieks. The lonely garden resounded with my cries as I strode madly through the dark walks, and the tall funereal cypresses seemed to bury me beneath their heavy shadows. I met no one,—could find no one. I had to bear my sorrow and despair alone.

Since that awful hour I have never found my room. Everywhere I look for it, yet never see it. Shall I ever find it?

My Wife's Tempter

1: A PREDESTINED MARRIAGE

Elsie and I were to be married in less than a week. It was rather a strange match, and I knew that some of our neighbours shook their heads over it and said that no good would come. The way it came to pass was thus.

I loved Elsie Burns for two years, during which time she refused me three times, I could no more help asking her to have me, when the chance offered, than I could help breathing or living. To love her seemed natural to me as existence. I felt no shame, only sorrow, when she rejected me; I felt no shame either when I renewed my suit. The neighbours called me mean-spirited to take up with any girl that had refused me as often as Elsie Burns had done; but what cared I about the neighbours? If it is black weather, and the sun is under a cloud every day for a month, is that any reason why the poor farmer should not hope for the blue sky and the plentiful burst of warm light when the dark month is over? I never entirely lost heart.

Do not, however, mistake me. I did not mope, and moan, and grow pale, after the manner of poetical lovers. No such thing. I went bravely about my business, ate and drank as usual, laughed when the laugh went round, and slept soundly, and woke refreshed. Yet all this time I loved—desperately loved—Elsie Burns. I went wherever I hoped to meet her, but did not haunt her with my attentions. I behaved to her as any friendly young man would have behaved: I met her and parted from her cheerfully. She was a good girl, too, and behaved well. She had me in her power,—how a woman in Elsie's situation could have mortified a man in mine! —but she never took the slightest advantage of it. She danced with me when I asked her, and had no foolish fears of allowing me to see her home of nights, after a ball was over, or of wandering with me through the pleasant New England fields when the wild-flowers made the paths like roads in fairy-land.

On the several disastrous occasions when I presented my suit I did it simply and manfully, telling her that I loved her very much, and would do everything to make her happy, if she would be my wife. I made no fulsome protestations, and did not once allude to suicide. She, on the other hand, calmly and gravely thanked me for my good opinion, but with the same calm gravity rejected me. I used to tell her that I was grieved; that I would not press her; that I would wait and hope for some change in her feelings. She had an esteem for me, she would say, but could not marry me. I never asked her for any reasons. I hold it to be an insult to a woman of sense to demand her reasons on such an occasion. Enough for me that she did not then wish to be my wife; so the old intercourse went on,—she cordial and polite as ever, I never for one moment doubting that the day would come when my roof-tree would shelter her, and we should smile together over our fireside at my long and indefatigable wooing.

I will confess that at times I felt a little jealous,—jealous of a man named Hammond Brake, who lived in our village. He was a weird, saturnine fellow, who made no friends among the young men of the neighbourhood, but who loved to go alone, with his books and his own thoughts for company. He was a studious, and, I believe, a learned young man, and there was no avoiding the fact that he possessed considerable influence over Elsie. She liked to talk with him in corners, or in secluded nooks of the forest, when we all went out blackberry-gathering or picnicking. She read books that he gave her, and whenever a discussion arose relative to any topic higher than those ordinary ones we usually canvassed, Elsie appealed to Brake for his opinion, as a disciple consulting a beloved master. I confess that for a time I feared this man as a rival. A little closer observation, however, convinced me that my suspicions were unfounded. The relation between Elsie and Hammond Brake was purely intellectual. She reverenced his talents and acquirements, but she did not love him. His influence over her, nevertheless, was none the less decided.

In time—as I thought all along—Elsie yielded. I was what was considered a most eligible match, being tolerably rich, and Elsie's parents were most anxious to have me for a son-in-law. I was good-looking and well-educated enough, and the old people, I believe, pertinaciously dinned all my advantages into my little girl's ears. She battled against the marriage for a long time with a strange persistence,—all the more strange because she never alleged the slightest personal dislike to me; but after a vigorous cannonading from her own garrison, (in which, I am proud to say, I did not in any way join,) she hoisted the white flag and surrendered.

I was very happy. I had no fear about being able to gain Elsie's heart. I think—indeed I know—that she had liked me all along, and that her refusals were dictated by other feelings than those of a personal nature. I only guessed as much then. It was some time before I knew all.

As the day approached for our wedding Elsie did not appear at all stricken with woe. The village gossips had not the smallest opportunity for establishing a romance, with a compulsory bride for the heroine. Yet to me it seemed as if there was something strange about her. A vague terror appeared to beset her. Even in her most loving moments, when resting in my arms, she would shrink away from me, and shudder as if some cold wind had suddenly struck upon her. That it was caused by no aversion to me was evident, for she would the moment after, as if to make amends, give me one of those voluntary kisses that are sweeter than all others.

I reflected over this gravely, as was my custom, but could come to no conclusion. I dismissed it as one of those mysteries of maidenhood which it is not given to man to fathom.

The day came at length on which we were to be married,—a glorious autumnal day, on which the sweet season of fruits and flowers seemed to have copied the kings of old, and robed itself in its brightest purple and gold, in order to die with becoming splendour. The little village church was nearly filled with the bridal party and the curious crowd who came to see the persevering lover win his bride. Elsie was calm, and grave, and beautiful. The sober beauty of the autumn itself seemed to tinge her face.

Once only did she show any emotion. When the solemn question was put to her, the answer to which was to decide her destiny, I felt her hand—which was in mine—tremble. As she gasped out a convulsive "Yes," she gave one brief, imploring glance at the gallery on the right. I placed the ring upon her finger, and. looked in the direction in which she gazed. Hammond Brake's dark countenance was visible looking over the railings, and his eyes were bent sternly on Elsie. I turned quickly round to my bride, but her brief emotion, of whatever nature, had vanished. She was looking at me anxiously, and smiling— somewhat sadly—through her maiden's tears.

I kissed her, and whispered a loving word or two in her ear, at which she brightened; and her grave, decorous old father, and quaint, tender-hearted mother, kissed her, and we rode all alone through glories of the autumn woods to our home.

2: THE STRANGE BOOK

The months went by quickly, and we were very happy. I learned that Elsie really loved me, and of my love for her she had proof long ago. I will not say that there was no cloud upon our little horizon. There was one, but it was so small, and appeared so seldom, that I scarcely feared it. The old vague terror seemed still to attack my wife. If I did not know her to be pure as heaven's snow, I would have said it was a *remorse*. At times, she scarcely appeared to hear what I said, so deep would be her reverie. Nor did those moods seem pleasant ones. When rapt in such, her sweet features would contract, as if in a hopeless effort to solve some mysterious problem. A sad pain, as it were, quivered in her white, drooped eyelids.

One thing I particularly remarked: *she spent hours at a time gazing at the west.* There was a small room in our house whose windows, every evening, flamed with the red light of the setting sun. Here Elsie would sit and gaze westward, so motionless and entranced that it seemed as if her soul was going down with the day. Her conduct to me was curiously varied. She apparently loved me very much, yet there were times when she absolutely avoided me. I have seen her strolling through the fields, and left the house with the intention of joining her, but the moment she caught sight of me approaching, she has fled into the neighbouring copse, with so evident a wish to avoid me that it would have been absolutely cruel to follow.

Once or twice the old jealousy of Hammond Brake crossed my mind, but I was obliged to dismiss it as a frivolous suspicion. Nothing in my wife's conduct justified any such theory. Brake visited us once or twice a week,—in fact, when I returned from my business in the village, I used to find him seated in the parlour with Elsie, reading some favourite author, or conversing on some novel literary topic; but there was no disposition to avoid my scrutiny. Brake seemed to come as a matter of right; and the perfect unconsciousness of furnishing any grounds for suspicion with which he acted was a sufficient answer to my mind for any wild doubts that my heart may have suggested.

Still I could not but remark that Brake's visits were in some manner connected with Elsie's melancholy. On the days when he had appeared and departed the gloom seemed to hang more thickly than ever over her head. She sat, on such occasions, all the evening at the western window, silently gazing at the cleft in the hills through which the sun passed to his repose.

At last I made up my mind to speak to her. It seemed to me to be my duty, if she had a sorrow, to partake of it. I approached her on the matter with the most perfect confidence that I had nothing to learn beyond the existence of some girlish grief, which a confession and a few loving kisses would exorcise forever.

"Elsie," I said to her one night, as she sat, according to her custom, gazing westward, like those maidens of the old ballads of chivalry watching for the knights that never came,—"Elsie, what is the matter with you, darling? I have noticed a strange melancholy in you for some time past. Tell me all about it."

She turned quickly round and gazed at me with eyes wide open and face filled with a sudden fear. "Why do you ask me that, Mark?" she answered. "I have nothing to tell."

From the strange, startled manner in which this reply was given, I felt convinced that she had something to tell, and instantly formed a determination to discover what it was. A pang shot through my heart as I thought that the woman whom I held dearer than anything on earth hesitated to trust me with a petty secret.

"Elsie," I said, "don't treat me as if I was a grand inquisitor, with racks and thumb-screws in readiness for you if you prove contumacious. You need not look at me in that frightened way. I'm not an ogre, child. I don't breakfast on nice, cosy little women five months married. Supposing you do owe a bill to the milliner, in Boston,—what does it matter? I'm tolerably rich. How much is it?"

I knew perfectly well that she did not owe any such bill, but it was a mode of testing her. A look of relief passed over her features as I spoke.

"Mark," she said, stroking my hair with her little hand and smiling faintly, "you're a goose. I don't owe any bill to the milliner in Boston, and I have no secret worth knowing. I know I'm a little melancholy at times,—I feel weary; but that is not unnatural, you know, just now, Mark dear,"—kissing me on the lips,—"you must bear with my moods for a little while, until there are three of us, and then I'll be better company."

I knew what she alluded to, but, God help me! I felt sad enough at the moment, though I kissed her back, and ceased to question her. I felt sad, because my instinct told me that she deceived me; and it is very hard to be deceived, even in trifles, by those we love. I left her sitting at her favourite window, and walked out into the fields. I wanted to think.

I remained out until I saw lights in the parlour shining through the dusk evening; then I returned slowly. As I passed the windows,—which were near the ground, our house being cottage-built,—I looked in. Hammond Brake was sitting with my wife. She was sitting in a rocking-chair opposite to him, holding a small volume open on her lap. Brake was talking to her very earnestly, and she was listening to him with an expression I had never before seen on her countenance. Awe, fear, and admiration were all blent together in those dilating eyes. She seemed absorbed, body and soul, in what this man said. I shuddered at the sight.

A vague terror seized upon me; I hastened into the house. As I entered the room, rather suddenly, my wife started and hastily concealed the little volume that lay on her lap in one of her wide pockets. As she did so, a loose leaf escaped from the volume and slowly fluttered to the floor unobserved by either her or her companion. But I had my eye upon it. I felt that it was a clew.

"What new novel or philosophical wonder have you both been poring over?" I asked, quite gayly, stealthily watching at the same time the tell-tale embarrassment under which Elsie was labouring.

Brake, who was not in the least discomposed, replied. "That," said he, "is a secret which must be kept from you. It is an advance copy, and is not to be shown to anyone except your wife."

"Ha!" cried I, "I know what it is. It is your volume of poems that Ticknor is publishing. Well, I can wait until it is regularly for sale."

I knew that Brake had a volume in the hands of the publishing house I mentioned, with a vague promise of publication sometime in the present century. Hammond smiled significantly, but did not reply. He evidently wished to cultivate this supposed impression of mine. Elsie looked relieved, and heaved a deep sigh. I felt more than ever convinced that a secret was beneath all this. So, I drew my chair over the fallen leaf that lay unnoticed on the carpet, and talked and laughed with Hammond Brake gayly, as if nothing was on my mind, while all the time a great load of suspicion lay heavily at my heart.

At length Hammond Brake rose to go. I wished him goodnight, but did not offer to accompany him to the door. My wife supplied this omitted courtesy, as I had expected. The moment I was alone I picked up the book-leaf from the floor. It was *not* the leaf of a volume of poems. Beyond that, however, I learned nothing. It contained a string of paragraphs printed in the Biblical fashion, and the language was Biblical in style. It seemed to be a portion of some religious book. Was it possible that my wife was being converted to the Romish faith? Yes, that was it. Brake was a Jesuit in disguise,—I had heard of such things,—and had stolen into the bosom of my family to plant there his destructive errors. There could be no longer any doubt of it. This was some portion of a Romish book;—some infamous Popish publication. Fool that I was not to see it all before! But there was yet time. I would forbid him the house.

I had just formed this resolution when my wife entered. I put the strange leaf in my pocket and took my hat.

"Why, you are not going out, surely?" cried Elsie, surprised.

"I have a headache," I answered. "I will take a short walk."

Elsie looked at me with a peculiar air of distrust. Her woman's instinct told her that there was something wrong. Before she could question me, however, I had left the room and was walking rapidly on Hammond Brake's track.

He heard the footsteps, and I saw his figure, black against the sky, stop and peer back through the dusk to see who was following him.

"It is I, Brake," I called out. "Stop; I wish to speak with you."

He stopped, and in a minute or so we were walking side by side along the road. My fingers itched at that moment to be on his throat. I commenced the conversation.

"Brake," I said, "I 'm a very plain sort of man, and I never say anything without good reason. What I came after you to tell you is, that I don't wish you to come to my house any more, or to speak with Elsie any farther than the ordinary salutations go. It's no joke. I'm quite in earnest."

Brake started, and, stopping short, faced me suddenly in the road. "What have I done?" he asked. "You surely are too sensible a man to be jealous, Dayton."

"O," I answered, scornfully, "not jealous in the ordinary sense of the word, a bit. But I don't think your company good company for my wife. Brake. If you will have it out of me, I suspect you of being a Roman Catholic, and of trying to convert my wife."

A smile shot across his face, and I saw his sharp, white teeth gleam for an instant in the dusk.

"Well, what if I am a Papist?" he said, with a strange tone of triumph in his voice. "The faith is not criminal. Besides, what proof have you that I was attempting to proselyte your wife?"

"This," said I, pulling the leaf from my pocket,—"this leaf from one of those devilish Papist books you and she were reading this evening. I picked it up from the floor. Proof enough, I think!"

In an instant Brake had snatched the leaf from my hand and torn it into atoms.

"You shall be obeyed," he said. "I will not speak with Elsie as long as she is your wife. Goodnight. So, you think I'm a Papist, Dayton? You're a clever fellow!" And with rather a sneering chuckle he marched on along the road and vanished into the darkness.

3: THE SECRET DISCOVERED

Brake came no more. I said nothing to Elsie about his prohibition, and his name was never mentioned. It seemed strange to me that she should not speak of his absence, and I was very much puzzled by her silence. Her moodiness seemed to have increased, and, what was most remarkable, in proportion as she grew more and more reserved, the intenser were the bursts of affection which she exhibited for me. She would strain me to her bosom and kiss me, as if she and I were about to be parted forever. Then for hours she would remain sitting at her window, silently gazing, with that terrible, wistful gaze of hers, at the west.

I will confess to having watched my wife at this time. I could not help it. That some mystery hung about her I felt convinced. I must fathom it or die. Her honour I never for a moment doubted; yet there seemed to weigh continually upon me the prophecy of some awful domestic calamity. This time the prophecy was not in vain.

About three weeks after I had forbidden Brake my house, I was strolling over my farm in the evening, apparently inspecting my agriculture, but in reality, speculating on that topic which latterly was ever present to me.

There was a little knoll covered with evergreen oaks at the end of the lawn. It was a picturesque spot, for on one side the bank went off into a sheer precipice of about eighty feet in depth, at the bottom of which a pretty pool lay, that in the summer time was fringed with white water-lilies. I had thought of building a summer-house in this spot, and now my steps mechanically directed themselves toward the place. As I approached I heard voices. I stopped and listened eagerly. A few seconds enabled me to ascertain that Hammond Brake and my wife were in the copse talking together. She still followed him, then;

and he, scoundrel that he was, had broken his promise.

A fury seemed to fill my veins as I made this discovery. I felt the impulse strong upon me to rush into the grove, and then and there strangle the villain who was poisoning my peace. But with a powerful effort I restrained myself. It was necessary that I should overhear what was said. I threw myself flat on the grass, and so glided silently into the copse until I was completely within ear-shot. This was what I heard.

My wife was sobbing. "So soon,—so soon? Hammond, give me a little time!"

"I cannot, Elsie. My chief orders me to join him. You must prepare to accompany me."

"No, no!" murmured Elsie. "He loves me so! And I love him. Our child, too,—how can I rob him of our unborn babe?"

"Another sheep for our flock," answered Brake, solemnly. "Elsie, do you forget your oath? Are you one of us, or are you a common hypocrite, who will be of us until the hour of self-sacrifice, and then fly like a coward? Elsie, you must leave tonight."

"Ah! my husband, my husband!" sobbed the unhappy woman.

"You have no husband, woman," cried Brake, harshly. "I promised Dayton not to speak to you as long as you were his wife, but the vow was annulled before it was made. Your husband in God jet awaits you. You will yet be blessed with the true spouse."

"I feel as if I were going to die," cried Elsie. "How can I ever forsake him,—he who was so good to me?"

"Nonsense! no weakness. He is not worthy of you. Go home and prepare for your journey. You know where to meet me. I will have everything ready, and by daybreak there shall be no trace of us left. Beware of permitting your husband to suspect anything. He is not very shrewd at such things,—he thought I was a Jesuit in disguise,—but we had better be careful. Now go. You have been too long here already. Bless you, sister."

A few faint sobs, a rustling of leaves, and I knew that Brake was alone. I rose, and stepped silently into the open space in which he stood. His back was toward me. His arms were lifted high over his head with an exultant gesture, and I could see his profile, as it slightly turned toward me, illuminated with a smile of scornful triumph. I put my hand suddenly on his throat from behind, and flung him on the ground before he could utter a cry.

"Not a word," I said, unclasping a short-bladed knife which I carried; "answer my questions, or, by heaven, I will cut your throat from ear to ear!"

He looked up into my face with an unflinching eye, and set his lips as if resolved to suffer all.

"What are you? Who are you? What object have you in the seduction of my wife?"

He smiled, but was silent.

"Ah! you won't answer. We'll see."

I pressed the knife slowly against his throat. His face contracted spasmodically, but although a thin red thread of blood sprang out along the edge of the blade, Brake remained mute. An idea suddenly seized me. This sort of death had no terrors for him. I would try another. There was the precipice. I was twice as powerful as he was, so I seized him in my arms, and in a moment transported him to the margin of the steep, smooth cliff, the edge of which was garnished with the tough stems of the wild vine. He seemed to feel it was useless to struggle with me, so allowed me passively to roll him over the edge. When he was suspended in the air, I gave him a vine stem to cling to and let him go. He swung at a height of eighty feet, with face upturned and pale. He dared not look down. I seated myself on the edge of the cliff, and with my knife began to cut into the thick vine a foot or two above the place of his grasp. I was correct in my calculation. This terror was too much for him. As he saw the notch in the vine getting deeper and deeper, his determination gave way.

"I'll answer you," he gasped out, gazing at me with starting eyeballs; "what do you ask?"

"What are you?" was my question, as I ceased cutting at the stem.

"A Mormon," was the answer, uttered with a groan. "Take me up. My hands are slipping. Quick!"

"And you wanted my wife to follow you to that infernal Salt Lake City, I suppose?"

"For God's sake, release me! I'll quit the place, never to come back. Do help me up, Dayton,—I'm falling!"

I felt mightily inclined to let the villain drop; but it did not suit my purpose to be hung for murder, so I swung him back again on the sward, where he fell panting and exhausted.

"Will you quit the place tonight?" I said. "You'd better. By Heaven, if you don't, I'll tell all the men in the village, and we'll lynch you, as sure as your name is Brake."

"I'll go,—I'll go," he groaned. "I swear never to trouble you again."

"You ought to be hanged, you villain. Be off!"

338

He slunk away through the trees like a beaten dog; and I went home in a state bordering on despair. I found Elsie crying. She was sitting by the window as of old. I knew now why she gazed so constantly at the west. It was her Mecca. Something in my face, I suppose, told her that I was labouring under great excitement. She rose startled, as soon as I entered the room.

"Elsie," said I, "I am come to take you home."

"Home? Why, I am at home, am I not? What do you mean?"

"No. This is no longer your home. You have deceived me. You are a Mormon. I know all. You have become a convert to that apostle of hell, Brigham Young, and you cannot live with me. I love you still, Elsie, dearly; but—you must go and live with your father."

She saw there was no appeal from my word, and with a face hopeless with despair she arranged her dress and passively went with me.

I live in the same village with my wife, and yet am a widower. She is very penitent, they say; yet I cannot bring myself to believe that one who has allowed the Mormon poison to enter her veins can ever be cured. People say that we shall come together again, but I know better. Mine is not the first hearth that Mormonism has rendered desolate.

The Hasheesh Eater

It was at Damascus that I took my first dose of hasheesh, and laid the foundations of that habit which, through the earlier years of my manhood, imprisoned me like an enchanted palace. It was surely a worthy spot on which to build up such an edifice of hallucination as I did there erect and cement around my soul by the daily use of this weed of insanity. Certainly, no other spot could be so worthy, unless it were Bagdad, the marvellous city of the marvellous *Sultan*, Haroun at Rashid. I need not tell the reasons: everyone can imagine them; every one, at least, who knows what Damascus is: much more everyone who has been there.

It was among shadowy gardens, filled with oriental loungers, and in Saracenic houses, gay as kaleidoscopes with gilding and bright tunings, that I made myself the slave of the hasheesh. It was surrounded by objects so suitable for dream-work, that, by the aid of this wizard of plants, I fabricated that palace of alternating pleasure and torture which was for years my abiding place. In this palace, I sometimes revelled with a joy so immense that I may well call it multitudinous; or I ran and shrieked it through its changeful spaces with an agony which the pen of a demon could not describe suitably; surrounded, chased, over-clouded by all the phantasms of mythology or the Arabian Nights; by every strange, ludicrous, or horrible shape that ever stole into my fancy, from books of romance or tales of spectredom.

It is useless to think of relating, or even mentioning, the visions which, during four or five years passed through my drugged brain. A library would not suffice to describe them all: many, also, were indistinct in their first impressions; and others have so mingled together with time, that I cannot now trace their individual outlines. As the habit grew upon me, too, my memory gradually failed, and a stupor crept over me which dulled the edges of all events, whether dreams or realities. A dull confusion surrounded me at all times, and I dropped down its hateful current, stupid, indifferent, unobserving, and never thoroughly awake except when a fresh dose of the plant stimulated my mind into a brief consciousness of itself and its surroundings.

The habit and its consequences naturally deepened my morbid unsociability of temper, and sunk me still more fixedly in the hermit-like existence which I had chosen. For some years I made no acquaintance with the many European travellers who pass through Syria; and I even, at last, got to avoid the presence of my listless oriental companions—keeping up no intimacy except with those who, like myself, daily wandered through the saharas and oases of hasheesh dreamland. Never before did I so completely give myself up to my besetting sin; for a sin, I now consider it to cast off one's moorings to humanity; to fly from one's fellow-beings and despise, at once, their good will and their censure.

A terrible fever at last came to my relief and saved me by dragging me, as it were, through the waters of death. While the sickness continued, I could not take the hasheesh; and when I recovered, I had so far gained my self-control, that I resolved to fling the habit aside forever. I am ashamed to confess that it was partly the urgings of an old friend which supported me to this pitch of real heroism. He was a young physician from my own city, and we had been companions and often roommate's through school and college, although it was by the merest accident that he met me in Beirut a few days before my seizure. Two months he watched by me, and then perfected his work by getting me on board the steamer for Marseilles, and starting me well homeward. I shall have to speak of him again; but I cannot give his name, further than to call him Doctor Harry, the pet title by which he was known in his own family.

I reached Marseilles, hurried through France, without passing more than a night even at Paris, and sailed for New York in a Havre steamer. In less than a month after I stepped from the broken columns which lie about the landing place of Beirut, I was strolling under the elms of my native city in Connecticut. The spell was broken by this time, and its shackles fallen altogether both from mind and body. I felt no longing after the hasheesh; and the dreary languor which once seemed to demand its restorative energy had disappeared; for my constitution was vigorous, and I was still several years under thirty.

But such chains as I had worn, could not be carried so long without leaving some scars behind them. The old despotism asserted itself yet in horrible dreams, or in painful reveries which were almost as vivid, and as difficult to break as dreams. These temporary illusions generally made use of two subjects, as the scaffolds on which to erect their troublesome cloud-castles: first, the scenery and personages of my old hasheesh visions; second, the incidents of my journey homeward. I was not at all surprised to find myself haunted by *sultans*, Moors, elephants, afreets, rocs, and other monstrosities of the Arabian Nights; but it did seem unreasonable that I should be plagued, in the least degree, by the reminiscences of that wholesome, and, on the whole, pleasant flight from the land of my captivity.

The rapidity and picturesqueness of the transit had impressed themselves on my imagination; and I now journeyed in spirit, night after night, and sometimes day after day, without rest and without goal; hurried on by an endless succession of steamers, diligences and railroad trains, all driven at their utmost speed; beholding oceans of foam, immeasurable snow mountains, cities of many leagues in extents and population, whose multitudes obstructed my passage.

But these illusions, whether sleeping or waking, were faint and mild compared with my old hasheesh paroxysms, and they grew rapidly weaker as time passed onward. The only thing which seriously and persistently annoyed me was an idea that my mind was slightly shaken. I vexed myself with minute self-examinations on this point, and actually consulted a physician as to whether some of my mental processes did not indicate incipient insanity. He replied in the best manner possible: he laughed at me, and forbade-my pursuing those speculations.

All this time I amused myself in society, and even worked pretty faithfully at my legal profession. I shall say nothing of my cases, however, for, like most young lawyers, I had very few of them; all the fewer, doubtless, because long residence abroad had put me back in my studies. But I must speak at some length of my socialities, inasmuch as they soon flung very deep roots in my heart, and mingled themselves there with the poisonous decay of my former habit.

The first family whose acquaintance I renewed, on reaching home, was that of my dear friend, Doctor Harry. His father, the white-headed old doctor, and his dignified, kindly mother, greeted me with a heartiness that was like enthusiasm. I had been a school-fellow of their absent son; and more than that I had very lately seen him; and more still, I spoke of him with warm praise and gratitude. They treated me with as much affection as if it were I who had saved Harry's life, and not Harry who had saved mine. A reception equally cordial was granted me by the doctor's two daughters: Ellen and Ida. Ellen, whom I knew well, was twenty-three years old, and engaged to be married. She was the same lively, nervous, sentimental thing as of old; wore the same long black ringlets, and tossed her head in the same flighty style.

Ida, four years younger than her sister, was almost a stranger to me; for she was a mere child when I first became a *beau*, and had been transferred from the nursery to the boarding-school without attracting my student observation. She was quite a novelty, therefore, a most attractive novelty also—the prettiest, unobtrusive style of woman that ever made an unsought conquest. I was the conquest, not the only conquest that she ever made, indeed; but the only one that she ever deigned to accept. I could not resist the mild blue eyes, the sunny brown hair, the sweet blonde lace, and the dear little coral mouth. She had the dearest little expression in her mouth when she was moved; a pleading, piteous expression that seemed to beg and entreat without a spoken word; an expression that was really infantine, not in silliness, but in an unutterable pathetic innocence. Well, she quite enslaved me, so that in three months I was more her captive than I had ever been to the hasheesh, even in the time of my deepest enthrallment.

I would not, however, offer myself to her until I had written to Doctor Harry, and asked him if he could permit his little sister to become the wife of the hasheesh eater. His reply was not kinder than I expected, but it was more cordial, and fuller of confidence. He knew little, in comparison with myself, of the strength of that old habit; nothing at all of the energy with which it can return upon one of its escaped victims. He was sure that I had broken its bonds; sure, that I never would be exposed to its snares again; sure, that I would resist the temptation were it to come ever so powerful. Yes, he was quite willing that I should marry Ida; he would rejoice to meet me at his home as his brother. I might, if I chose, tell my history to his father, and leave the matter to him; but that was all that honour could demand of me, and even that was not sternly necessary.

I did as Harry directed, and related to the old physician all my dealings with the demon of hasheesh. Like a fine doctor, he was immensely interested in the symptoms, and plunged into speculations as to whether the diabolical plant could not be introduced with advantage into the *materia medica*. No astonishment at my rashness; no horror at my danger; no grave disapproval of my weak wickedness; no particular rejoicing at what I considered my wonderful escape. And when, a few days after, I asked him if he could surrender his child to such a man as I, he laughed heartily, and shook both my hands with an air of the warmest encouragement. I felt guilty at that moment, as well as happy; for it seemed as if I were imposing upon an unsuspecting ignorance, which could not and would not be enlightened.

Nor did Ida say *no* anymore than the others, although she made a piteous little face when I took her hand, and looked as if she thought I had no right to ask her for so much as her whole self. So, I was engaged to Ida, and was happier than all the hasheesh eaters from Cairo to Stamboul.

It was about a month after our engagement, and two months before the time fixed for our marriage, that a box reached us from Smyrna. it contained a quantity of Turkish silks, and other presents from Harry to his sisters, besides the usual variety of *nargeelehs, chibouks, tarbooshes,* scimitars, and so forth, such as young travellers usually pick up in the East. The doctor and I opened the packages, while Ellen, Ida, and their mother skipped about in delight from wonder to wonder. Among the last things came a small wooden box, which Ellen eagerly seized upon, declaring that it contained attar of roses. She tore off the cover, and displayed to my eyes a mass of that well-remembered drug, the terrible hasheesh.

"What is it?" she exclaimed. "Is this attar of roses? No, it isn't. What is it, Edward? Here, you ought to know."

"It is hasheesh," I said, looking at it as it I saw an afreet or a ghoul.

"Well, what is hasheesh? Is it good to eat? Why, what are you staring at it so for? Do you want some? Here, eat a piece. I will if you will."

"Bless me!" exclaimed the doctor, dropping a Persian dagger and coming hastily forward. "Is that the real hasheesh? Bless me, so that is hasheesh, is it? Dear me, I must have a specimen. What is the ordinary dose for an adult, Edward?"

I took out a bit as large as a hazelnut, and held it up before his exes. He received it reverently from my hands, and surveyed it with a prodigious scientific interest.

"Wife," said he, "Ellen, Ida, this is hasheesh. This is an ordinary dose for an adult."

"Well, what is hasheesh?" repeated Ellen, tossing her ringlets as a colt does his mane. "Father! what is it? Did you ever take any, Edward?"

"Yes," mumbled the doctor, examining the lump with microscopic minuteness; "Edward is perfectly acquainted with the nature of the drug; he has made some very interesting experiments with it."

"Oh, take some, Edward," cried Ellen. "Come, that's a good fellow. Here, take this other bit. Let's take a dose all round."

"No, no," said Ida, catching her sister's hand. "Why, you imprudent child! Better learn a little about it before you make its acquaintance. Tell us, Edward, what does it do to people?"

I told them in part what it had done to me; that is, I told them what mighty dreams and illusions it had wrapped around me; but I could not bring myself to narrate before Ida how shamefully I had been its slave. When I had finished my story, Ellen broke forth again; "Oh, Edward, take a piece, I beg of you. I want to see you crazy once. Come, you are sane enough in a general way; and we should all enjoy it so to see you make a fool of yourself for an hour or two."

She put the morsel to my lips and held it there until Ida pushed her hand away, almost indignantly. I looked at my little girl, and, although she said nothing, I saw on her mouth that piteous, pleading expression, which appeared to me enough to move angels or demons. It moved me, but not sufficiently; the smell of the hasheesh seemed to sink into my brain; the thought of the old visions came up like a wave of intoxication. Still I refused; two or three times that afternoon I refused; but in the evening, Ellen handed me the drug again.

"It is the last time," I said to myself; and taking it from her hand I began to prepare it. The doctor stood by, nervous with curiosity, and urged caution; nothing more than caution; that was the whole of his warning. Ida looked at me in her imploring way, but said nothing; for she only suspected, and did not at all comprehend the danger.

I swallowed the drug while they all stood silent around me; and I laughed loudly, with a feeling of crazed triumph, as I perceived the well-remembered savour. My little girl caught my sleeve with a look of extreme terror; the doctor quite as eagerly seized my pulse and drew out his repeater.

"Oh, what fun!" said Ellen. "Do you see anything now, Edward?"

Of course, I saw nothing as yet; for, be it known, that the effect of the hasheesh is not immediate; half an hour or even an hour must elapse before the mind can fully feel its influence. I told them so, and I went on talking in my ordinary style until they thought that I had been jesting with them, and had taken nothing. But forty minutes had not passed before I began to feel the usual symptoms, the sudden nervous thrill, followed by the whirl and prodigious apparent enlargement of the brain. My head expanded wider and wider, revolving with inconceivable rapidity, and enlarging in space with every revolution. it filled the room—the house—the city; it became a world, peopled with the shapes of men and monsters. I spun away into its great vortex, and wandered about its expanses as about a universe. I lost all perception of time and space, and knew no distinction between the realities around me, and the *phantasmata* which sprung in endless succession from my brain. Ida and the others occasionally spoke to me; and once I thought that they kneeled around and worshipped me; while I, from behind a marble altar, responded like a Jupiter. Then night descended, and I heard a voice saying: "Christ is come, and thou art no more a divinity."

The altar disappeared at that instant, and I came back to this present century, and to my proper human form. I was in the doctor's house, standing by a window, and gazing out upon a moonlit street filled with promenading citizens. Beside me was a sofa upon which Ida lay and slept, with her head thrown back, and her throat bared to the faint silvery brilliance which stole through the gauze curtains. I stooped and kissed it passionately; for I had never before seen her asleep, nor so beautiful; and I loved her as dearly in that moment as I had ever done when in full possession of my sanity. As I raised my head, her father opened a door and looked into the room. He started forward when he saw me; then he drew back, and I heard him whisper to himself: "She is safe enough, he will not hurt her."

The moment he closed the door a window opened, and a voice muttered: "Kill her, kill her, and the altar and the adoration shall be yours again;" to which innumerable voices from the floor, and the ceiling and the four walls responded: "Glory, glory in the highest to him who can put himself above man, and to him who fears not the censure of man!"

I drew a knife from my pocket, and opened it instantly; for a mighty persuasion was wrought in me by those promises. "I will kill her," I said to myself, "dearly as I love her; for the gift of Divinity outweighs the love of woman or the wrath of man."

I bent over her and placed the knife to her throat without the least pity or hesitation, so completely had all love, all nobleness, all humanity, been extinguished in me by the abominable demon of hasheesh. But suddenly she awoke, and fixed on me that sweet, piteous, startled look which was so characteristic of her. It made me forget my purpose for one moment, so that, with a lunatic inconsistency, I bent my head

347

and kissed her hand as gently as I had ever done. Then the demoniac whisper, as if to recall my wandering resolution, swept again through the eglantines of the window: "Kill her, kill her, and the altar and the adoration shall be yours again."

She did not seem to hear it; for she stretched out her hands to give me a playful push backwards, while, closing her eyes again, she sank back to renewed slumber. Then, in the height of my drugged insanity, in the cold fury of my possession, I struck the sharp slender blade into her white throat once, and once more, with quick repetition, into her heart.

"Oh, Edward, you have killed me!" she said, and seemed to die with a low moan, not once stirring from her position on the sofa.

I took no further notice of her; I did not see her in fact after the blow; for the smoke of sacrifices rose around me, obscuring the room; and once more I stood in divine elevation above a marble altar. There were giant colonnades on either side, sweeping forward to a monstrous portal, through which I beheld countless sphinxes facing each other adown an interminable avenue of granite. Before me, in the mighty space between the columns, was a multitude of men, all bowing with their faces to the earth, while priests chanted anthems to my praise as the great Osiris.

But suddenly, before I could shake the temple with my nod, I saw one in the image of Christ enter the portal and advance through the crowd to the foot of my altar. it was not Christ the risen and glorified; but the human and crucified Jesus of Nazareth. I knew him by his grave sweetness of countenance; I knew him still better by his wounded hands and bloody vestments. He beckoned me to descend and kneel before him; and when I would have called on my worshipers for aid, I found that they had all vanished; so that I was forced to come down and fall at his pierced feet in helpless condemnation. Then he passed judgment upon me, saying: "Forasmuch as thou hast sought to put thyself above man, all men shall abhor and shun thee."

He disappeared, and when I rose the temple had disappeared also, with every trace of that mighty worship by which I had been for a moment surrounded. Then did my punishment commence; nor did it cease throughout a seeming eternity; for, in order to complete it, time was reversed, and I could live in bygone ages; so that I ran through the whole history of the world, and was avoided with loathing by even-generation, first I stood near the garden of Eden, and saw a hideous man hurrying by it, alone, with a bloody mark on his forehead. "'This is Cain," I said to myself; "this is a wicked murderer, also, and he will be my comrade."

I ran toward him confidently, eagerly, and with an intense longing for companionship; but when he saw me he covered his face and fled away from me, with incomparable swiftness, shrieking: "Save me, O God, from this abominable wretch!"

After that, I hastened wildly over earth, across many countries, and through many successive ages, alone always, avoided always, an object of fear, of horror, of incredible detestation. Everyone that saw me, knew me, and fled from my presence, even to certain death, if that were necessary, to evade my contact. I saw men of Gomorrah rush back into the flames of their perishing city, when they beheld me coming humbly to meet them. Egyptians, who had barely escaped from the Red Sea, leaped again into the foaming waters as I ran toward them along the shore. Everywhere that I went, populations even of mighty cities, scattered from my track, like locusts using in hurried flight before the feet of a camel, The loneliest shipwrecked sailor, on the most savage island of the sea, fled from his hut of reeds, and plunged into untrackcd and serpent-haunted marshes at the sight of my supplicating visage.

Unable to obtain the companionship of men, I at last sought that of wild beasts and reptiles—of the gods of ancient mythology, and the monsters of fairydom; but, all to no purpose. The crocodiles buried themselves in the mid-current of the Nile, as I stealthily approached its banks. I unavailingly chased the terrified speed of tigers and anacondas through the stifling heat of the jungles of Bengal. Memnon arose from his throne, and hid himself in the clouds, when he saw me kneeling at his granite feet. I followed in vain the sublime flight of Odin over the polar snows and ice-islands of both hemispheres.

Satyrs hid from me; dragons and gorgons avoided me. The very ants and insects disappeared from my presence, taking refuge in dead trunks, and in the bowels of the earth. My punishment was constant and fearful—it was greater than I could bear; yet, I bore it for ages. I tried in many ways to escape from it by death; but always unsuccessfully. I sought to fling myself down precipices, but an unseen power drew me back; I endeavoured to drown myself in the sea, but the billows upheld me, like a leather. It was not remorse that prompted me to these attempts at sell-destruction. Remorse, penitence, and every other noble emotion had been swallowed up in mere anguish under the dreadfulness of my punishment. Sometimes I could not believe that all this was a reality, and struggled with wild, but useless ragings to break the dreadful presence of horror.

At other times, I fell convinced of its perfect truth; because I saw that the punishment was exactly suited to the offense, and that it reproved, with astonishing directness, that unsocial and almost misanthropic spirit which I had so long encouraged by my habits of life and temper of thought. Thus, dragging about with me a ghastly immortality, I wandered through miserable year after year, through desolation after desolation, until I stood once more on the deck of the steamer to Marseilles. Now I again performed my journey homeward, passing, as before, through a succession of steamers, railroads, and diligences. But the steamers were empty; for the passengers and sailors leaped overboard at my appearance; and the vessel reeled on unguided, through wild, lonely seas that I knew not.

Just in the same manner, every one fled before me from the railcars; and, through descried plains and valleys, I arrived, at headlong speed, in great cities, as the only passenger. My diligence journeys were performed without companion, or conductor, or postillion, in shattering vehicles, drawn by horses which flew in the very lunacy of fright. Paris was a solitude when I entered it—without man, and without inhabitant, and without beast—silence in its streets, in its galleries, and in its palaces—the sentinels all fled from the gates, and the children from the gardens.

At last I arrived at the entrance of my native city; and now I hoped that in presence of this familiar spot my vision would break; but it did not, and so I paused in a most miserable stupor of despair. It was early dawn, and the sky was yet grey; nor had many people arisen from their sleep. I heard dogs barking in the streets, and birds singing in the orchards; but, as always, neither the one race nor the other ventured near the spot where I stood. I sat down behind a thicket, where I could see the road, but could not be seen from it, and wept for an hour over my terrible misery. It was the first lime[1] that tears bad come to soften my terrible punishment; for, hitherto my anguish had been desperate and sullen, or wild and blasphemous; but now I wept easily, with some feeling of tender penitence, and speechless supplication. I looked wistfully down the street, longing to enter the town, yet dreading to see the universal terror which I knew would spread through the inhabitants the moment I stepped in among them.

At last persons began to pass me; chiefly, I believe, workmen, or market people; but among them were some whose faces I had seen before. I cannot describe the thrill of tremulous, fearful, painful pleasure with which I looked from so near upon these familiar human countenances. How I longed, yet dreaded, to have one of them turn his eyes upon me. At last I said to myself: "These people know of my crime; perhaps they will not fly from me, and will only kill me."

I stepped out suddenly in front of a couple of ruddy countrymen, who were driving a market-cart from the city, and fell on my knees, with my hands uplifted toward their faces, for a moment they stared at me in ghastly horror, then, wheeling their rearing horse, they lashed him into violent flight. I rose in desperation, in fury, and, with the steps of a greyhound, leaped after them through streets now resonant with human footsteps. Oh, the wild terror! oh, the agonised shrieking! oh, the wide confusion! and oh, the swift vanishing of all life which marked my passage! I hastened on, panting, stamping, screaming, foaming in the uttermost extremity of despair and anguish, until I reached the house where my darling had once lived. As I neared the steps, I saw a person whom I knew to be Harry. He did not shriek and fly at my approach, but met me and looked me steadily in the face. His eyes, at first, were full of inquiry; but, in a moment, he seemed to gather the whole truth from my visage; and then, with a terrible tremor of abhorrence, he drew a pistol from his bosom.

"It is right, Harry," I said; "kill me, as I killed her."

But with a quick motion which I could not arrest, he placed the muzzle to his own temples, drew the trigger, and fell a disfigured corpse at my feel. I howled as if I were a wild beast, and sprang over him into the doorway. I saw Ellen and her father and mother flying with uplifted hands out of the other end of the passage. I did not follow them, but turned into the parlour where I had committed my crime; and there to my amazement, I saw Ida lying on the sofa in the same position in which I had left her; her head fallen backward, her eyes closed, her throat hidden by her long hair, and her hands clasped upon her bosom. On the floor lay my knife still open, just as it had fallen. I picked it up and passed my finger over the keen edge of the blade muttering: "Now, I know that all this is real; now I can kill myself, for this is the time and the place to die."

Just as I was placing: the knife to my throat, I saw a sweet smile stealing over Ida's lips. She has become a seraph, I thought, and is smiling to see the eternal glory. But, suddenly, as I looked at her for this last time, she opened her eyes on me, and over her mouth stole that sweet pleading expression which was the outward sign of her gentle spirit.

"Stop, Edward!" she cried, earnestly; and springing up, she caught my hand firmly, although I could feel that her own trembled. In that moment, my horrible dream began to fade from me, and I gazed around no longer utterly blinded by the hazes of the hasheesh demon. She was not harmed, then! No, and I was not her murderer; no, and I had not been the loathing of mankind. Nothing of the whole scene had been real, except her slumber on the sofa, and the knife which I held in my hand.

I flung it fiercely from me; for I thought of what I might have done with it had my madness been only a little more persistent and positive. Then, struck by a sudden thought, half suspicion and half comprehension, I ran to the front doorway. Harry was not, indeed, lying there in his blood; but he was there, nevertheless, upright and in full health; and we exchanged a delighted greeting before the rest of the family could reach him.

"Why, Harry," said the doctor, in the parlour again, "that was a most interesting substance you sent us—that hasheesh. I have made an extraordinary experiment with it upon Edward here. He muttered wonders for an hour or two in my study. He then went to sleep, and I missed him about two minutes ago. I really had no idea that he had come to."

That closing dream of crime and punishment, then, had passed through my brain in less than two minutes; and I had been standing by the sleeping form of my little girl all the time that I seemed to be wandering through that eternity of horror.

"What!" said Harry, "has Edward gone back to the hasheesh again?"

"Yes," I replied; "but I have taken my last dose, my dear fellow. With your permission, doctor, I will pitch that infernal drug into the fire."

"Really," said the doctor, "I—I—don't know. I should like to reserve a few doses for experiments."

"Oh! Don't throw it away," urged Ellen. "It is *such* fun. Edward has been saying *such* queer things."

"Where is it?" asked Harry resolutely. "I will settle that question."

"It is in the fire, brother," replied Ida. "I threw it there half an hour ago."

I raised the little girl's hand to my lips and kissed it; and since then I have taken no other hasheesh than such as that.

Seeing the World

The hall reverberated with plaudits. The *improvisatore* surpassed himself. Scarcely was a subject given to him by the spectators than grand ideas, profound sentiments, clad in majestic verse, rolled from his lips, as it evoked by some magic. The artist did not reflect for an instant. In the twinkling of an eye his newly-born thoughts ran through all the phases of growth, and appeared clothed in the most exact expression. Ingenuity of form, splendour of imagery, harmony of rhythm, all were exhibited at the same moment. But this was a trifle. People gave him two or three subjects at the same time. The *improvisatore* dictated a poem on one, wrote a second, and improvised a third; and each production was, in its way, perfect. The first excited enthusiasm; the second called the tears into the eyes of the listeners; and the third was so humorous that none could restrain their laughter. In the midst of this the *improvisatlore* did not seem to be in the least preoccupied with his subject. He talked and laughed with his neighbours. All the elements of poetical composition seemed to be at his disposal, as the pieces on a chessboard, which he used when he needed them, with the most superb indifference.

At last the attention and admiration of the spectators were exhausted. They were more wearied than the *improvisatore*. He was calm and cold. One could not trace on his countenance the slightest of fatigue; his features, in place of expressing the lofty joy of the poet content with his labour, displayed only the vulgar satisfaction of the conjuror who astonishes a stupid crowd. He listened to the laughter, and watched the tears tremble on the cheeks, with a sort of disdain; he alone neither laughed nor wept; he alone had no belief in his utterances. In the moments of divinest inspiration, he had the air of a faithless priest, whom long habit has familiarised with the mysteries of the temple. The last of the audience had scarcely issued from the apartment when the *improvisatore* flung himself upon the pile of money received at the door, and commenced counting it with the avidity of Harpagon. The sum was large. He had never received so large a one in a single evening, and he was enchanted.

His joy was very pardonable. From his infancy upward poverty, cold and hard, had crushed him in its stony arms. He had not been born amidst songs, but amidst the dolorous sighs of his mother. When his intellect began to awaken, he beheld no rose-gardens in life; his young imagination encountered everywhere the icy smile of indigence. Nature was a little more generous to him than Fate. She gave him the creative faculty, but she condemned him to seek with the sweat of his brow the expression of his poetical conceptions.

The editors and publishers paid him for his poetry prices that would have enabled him to live in comfort, if he was not obliged to spend an eternity of time on the composition of the smallest verse it sometimes occurred, but very rarely, that in a moment of inspiration his intellect—always vailed in clouds—shone out with clearness; but if, on such occasions, this nebulous star showed itself clear and brilliant, it was only for an instant, and the poor poet had to make superhuman efforts to profit by the fleeting light.

Here again the labour recommenced: the expression fled before the words; the words would not come, or, if they did, were the wrong ones; the metre was rebellious; hideous prepositions came at the end of each line, interminable verbs became entangled in a web of substantives, and the rhymes—the accursed rhymes—always appeared in the shape of some barbarous and discordant words. Every verse cost the unhappy poet broken pens, fingernails bitten to the quick, and locks of hair torn from his head in moments of agony. All his efforts were impotent. A thousand times he vowed to abandon poesy, and adopt some honest profession.

But without having all the gifts, he had all the faults of a poet—the innate passion for independence, the incorrigible aversion to manual labour, the habit of awaiting inspiration, the radical want of punctuality. Add to this, the irritability which always accompanies poetic natures, an instinctive tendency to luxury, and an aristocratic craving for distinction. He could neither translate nor work by the page or column; and while his brother authors made considerable sums by compositions that were frequently insignificant, he saw himself universally neglected by editors and publishers. The little that he did receive for works that often cost him years of labour, went to pay usurious interest on money borrowed of the Jews, and poor Cipriano—as the poet was named—found his necessitous condition as hard and cheerless as ever.

In the town in which Cipriano resided lived also a physician named Segelius. Thirty years previously he had earned the reputation of being a skilful and learned practitioner; but he was poor, and had so small a practice, that he resolved to abandon medicine and take to commerce. After remaining a long time in India, he returned to his native country with ingots of gold, and an immense quantity of precious stones. He built a magnificent mansion surrounded by a vast park, and hired numberless servants. His old acquaintances remarked with astonishment that neither the years he had spent, nor the long voyages he had made in tropical countries, had produced the slightest change in him. On the contrary, he appeared more young, more elastic, more sprightly than before. Not less surprising was the fact that the plants of every country in the world grew and prospered in his park, without any care being bestowed on them.

Beyond this Segelius had nothing extraordinary about him. He was a man of good figure and excellent manners, with black moustaches. His clothes were simple, but elegant. He received the best society, but himself scarcely ever went beyond his huge park. He lent money to young men without interest; had a capital cook, the best wines, and liked to remain a long time at table, he went to bed early, and rose late. In fact, he led a superbly aristocratic existence.

Segelius had not entirely abandoned his practice as a physician, yet followed it but seldom, and then with a sort of repugnance, as if he did not wish to be troubled with it. But when he did practice he performed miracles. However grave the disease or the wound, and although the invalid was yielding up his last sigh, Segelius took no pains whatever, and would not even go to see him. After putting two or three questions to the relatives, more as a matter of form than anything else, he took a small bottle from a box, and ordered them to give it to the patient, who, without fail, was as well as ever next morning. Segelius took no pay for these services. His disinterestedness, added to his marvellous good-nature, would have drawn patients to him from every corner of the earth, if he had not imposed on the invalids the most singular and fantastic conditions.

For instance, to throw a certain sum of money into the sea; to perform some very disagreeable task; to burn one's house, etc. Rumour increased the singularity of these actions, and prevented even the most despairing invalids from coming to him. it was remarked that since a certain time no one had come to consult him; and it was further noticed, that if any of his patients did not comply with the conditions of his prescriptions, they infallibly died. The same happened, people said, to those who went to law with him, spoke evil of him, or displeased him.

It was natural after this that Segelius should have a great number of enemies. The physicians and apothecaries were, of course, his bitterest foes, and denied his right to make use of secret remedies; the most natural deaths were attributed to his poisons. They did not stop even there. They hinted suspiciously at the origin of his great fortune, and accused him of all species of crime. These public clamours obliged the police to visit his house, and institute a rigorous search. His servants were taken aside and interrogated. Segelius favoured the inquisition, left the field free to his inquisitors, whom he scarcely honoured with a glance, and retired smiling disdainfully at their attempts.

Their search was, indeed, vain. Nothing was discovered in the house but vases of gold, pipes ornamented with diamonds, delightfully luxurious beds and lounges, exquisite tables, and secret *boudoirs* filled up with perfumed furniture, and concealing harmonious instruments. In short, the doctor's house enclosed all the comforts and luxuries of life, but nothing more; nothing that could awaken the suspicions of justice. His correspondence revealed naught beyond his many relations with the bankers and chief merchants in every quarter of the globe. Some Arabian manuscripts, and packets of papers covered with writing in cipher excited at last some suspicion, but on examination they proved to be nothing more than commercial letters, as the doctor had before stated. Finally, this inquiry justified the doctor on every point, and recoiled upon the heads of his enemies, every one of whom met shortly after with some misfortune.

It was to this man, strange and mysterious, that Cipriano, in a paroxysm of despair, came one day to solicit aid.

"Doctor," said he, casting himself on his knees, "relieve the most unfortunate man in the world. Nature has given me the passion for poesy, but refused me the boon of words and the faculty of expressing my thoughts. I think deeply, but when I wish to speak words fail me. If I wish to write, it is still worse. My sufferings are more horrible, I swear to you, than any you have ever alleviated. O God, can it be that it is you who have cast a spell over me, and condemned me to this eternal pain?"

"Son of Adam," said the doctor—this was his phrase in his gayer moments—"Son of Adam, behold the privilege of thy race! Thou canst obtain nothing but by the sweat of the brow! It is destiny. Nevertheless," he added, after a moment's pause, "I can give thee a remedy for thy fate; but on one condition."

"I will consent to all that you wish, doctor, rather than die a thousand deaths every day."

"What they say of me, then, in the town does not frighten you?"

"No, doctor, because I can be in no worse plight than that in which you see me."

The doctor smiled.

"I will be frank with you," continued Cipriano. "It is not alone the love of poesy, nor the love of glory that has brought me to you. I nurse another sentiment more tender than either. Could I be but assured of facility of composition, I would be able to earn a living, and Charlotte would be mine. You understand me, doctor."

"That's what I like," cried Segelius; "I love nothing better than frankness. Evil lights alone on those who play a double game. You are, I see, a man true and open, and you merit a reward. I consent willingly to grant your prayer, and give you the faculty of producing without labour; but my first condition is, that the gift shall always remain with you."

"You mock me, Doctor Segelius."

"Not at all. I am also a frank man, and conceal nothing from those who have confidence in me. Listen, and take good heed of what I say. The faculty I give you will become a part of yourself; will grow, live, and die with you. You consent?"

"Can you doubt it?"

"Very good. My second condition is, that you will see everything, know everything, and comprehend everything. Do you accept?"

"You certainly jest, doctor. I know not how to thank you. In place of one faculty, you give me four. Why should I not accept?"

"But understand me well. *You will see, you will know, and you will comprehend everything.*"

"You are the most generous of men. Doctor Segelius."

"You accept then?"

"Certainly. Do you want a written engagement?"

"It is not needed. Your word suffices. A promise cannot be torn like a piece of paper. Know that in this world nothing is lost, nothing perishes."

At these words Segelius placed his hand on the head of the poet, and another on his heart, and pronounced the following words—in a solemn voice:

"Receive from the mysterious sphere's the gift of knowing all things; of reading everything in the world, of speaking and writing nobly, in a gay or serious vein, in verse or prose, for heat or for cold, in sleeping and waking, on wood and on sand, in joy as in pain, and in every language of the earth."

Segelius then put a manuscript in the poet's hand and dismissed him.

When Cipriano was gone, the doctor burst into a fit of laughter, and cried,

"Pepe! my cloak of frieze!"

And, as in *Freyschutz,* all the panels of the library replied by a dia-bolical echo, "*Ahou! Ahou!*"

Cipriano imagined these words to be an order given by Segelius to his *valet de chambre,* and was astonished that so elegant a man as the doctor would wear so common a garment. He peeped through the keyhole of the door and beheld a singular occurrence.

All the books in the library were in motion, from one of the man-uscripts the figure 8 came out, I from another the letter *aleph,* from a third the Greek A, and so through all. At last the room was filled with animated figures and letters, that bowed and straightened them-selves, and again closed themselves convulsively; dancing, leaping on their deformed feet, and falling on the floor. The commas, the periods, the marks of accentuation, glided through the midst of the band, like the infusoria seen through a solar microscope; and an old Chaldean volume beat time to the infernal dance with such vigour that the window-panes trembled with fear. Cipriano fled.

When he was somewhat more calm, he opened the manuscript which Segelius had given him. it was a huge roll covered with un-known characters. But scarcely had Cipriano cast his eyes, illumined with superior light, upon the paper than he understood the mysteri-ous writing. There all the forces of nature were enumerated—the sys-tematic life of the crystal, the fantastic will of the poet, the magnetic oscillations of the globe, the passions of the infusoria, the nervous laws of language, the capricious wanderings of rivers. Everything appeared to him arranged in mathematical progression—things of the mind as those of the heart. Cipriano beheld creation naked, and the lofty mystery of the conception and birth of thoughts seemed to him commonplace and easy.

There existed for him a miraculous bridge, cast across the abyss that separates thought from expression—he spoke in verse.

We have seen at the commencement oi this narrative the prodigious success which Cipriano enjoyed in his *role* of *improvisatore*. The first time that he tested this astonishing faculty he returned home with a full purse and a gay heart, but a little fatigued. Having taken a glass of water to appease his thirst, he suddenly started while he was carrying it to his lips. He looked at it. The tumbler did not contain water, but was full of something horrible and revolting. Two gases in a perpetual struggle were filled with myriads of microscopic insects that swam in them. Cipriano emptied his glass and filled another. There was the same odious mixture. He ran to the stream from which the water had been brought. A far off he beheld its waves pure and silvery, rolling calmly; but when he drew near, there was the same frightful fluid, full of busy animalcules.

The unhappy *improvisatore* shivered, and his blood seemed to freeze. In his despair, he flung himself on the grass, and sought to forget his sufferings in sleep. Scarcely had he lain down when he heard grinding noises, blows, hisses, as it thousands of hammers were striking on an anvil, as if iron hoofs trampled upon a stone pavement, as if steel files were tearing some hard and polished surface. He rose and looked around him. The moon lit the garden. The shadow of the railings fell in dark bands across the foliage of the shrubs. All was calm and silent. He lay down again, and the noise recommenced. He could not sleep, and passed the night without closing his eyes.

In the morning Cipriano ran to Charlotte's house, to confide to her his joy and grief, and to find repose by her side. Charlotte, who had heard of his success, awaited him with impatience. She was elegantly dressed, with bows of red ribbon in her beautiful fair hair, and from time to time she admired herself in her mirror, with innocent *coquetry*. Cipriano entered, ran toward Charlotte, holding out his hand smilingly, but suddenly he stopped and gazed at her with eyes of terror.

He beheld—what? Through the garments and the flesh, he saw the triangular artery called the heart beating in the young girl's bosom. He saw the blood coursing up to the roots of the hair, and forming the delicate blush upon the cheeks that he had loved so much. Wretched man! In those eyes, so beautiful and full of love he found nothing more than a species of *camera obscura*, made of a reticulated membrane and a drop of liquid. In that graceful walk, he saw only the play of ingenious mechanism. Alas! Charlotte was no longer an angel upon earth for him, and the object of his purest hopes. She was nothing more in his eyes than an anatomical preparation. Cipriano fled with terror.

Not far from this was a portrait of the Madonna to which Cipriano had often had recourse in his hours of suffering and despair, and whose radiant face had always ravished and soothed him. He fell on his knees before the holy picture and prayed. Scarcely had he lifted his eyes in adoration than all disappeared. There was no longer a picture before the penetrating eyes of the *improvisatore,* but a piece of canvas and a blotch of colours; the work of the artist seemed nothing more than a chemical amalgam.

Who can tell how Cipriano suffered? Sight, taste, smell, hearing—all the senses had acquired in him a frightful acuteness. An insect, a grain of dust, that did not exist to the rest of mankind, was to him a cause of anguish and suffering. The flapping of the wing of a butterfly almost deafened him. *He saw everything— comprehended everything.* But between him and mankind there was an abyss always. Nothing in the world of nature harmonised with him.

When he wished to seek forgetfulness in the perusal of some great poetical work, or in burying himself in historical studies, or in employing his intellect in the subtleties of some system of philosophy, all was in vain. His tongue babbled the words, but his mind saw other things.

Beneath the varnish of poetical expression, he discovered all the artifices of the poet. In the consoling truths, in the eternal progress that history deduces from events, he saw nothing but an arbitrary arrangement of facts. The invention of a system of philosophy was nothing in his eyes but the desire of saying something new. For him there was no more music; the majestic harmonies of Haydn and Mozart struck him as only physical phenomena, as peculiar vibrations of the molecules of air. When he was among his relatives and intimate friends he read the evil thoughts in their hearts, and the criminal designs that each nourished against the other.

Cipriano went mad. He left his country, and sought to fly from himself, travelling through distant lands, but always, as of old, *seeing everything—knowing everything.*

He still retained the fatal gift of poesy. If the cruel faculty of seeing and knowing all slumbered for an instant, the passion for verse replaced it, and the *stanzas* rolled from his lips like water from a fountain. With what bitter regret he recalled that time of sweet suffering, when inspiration came to him seldom, or objects appeared to him under a doubtful form, waveringly and in slow succession. Today he sees all—all simultaneously in a melancholy nudity. Then, from another world, a buzzing swarm of poetic inspirations descends incessantly on his head.

For many years Cipriano wandered from country to country, and necessity obliged him often to have recourse to the fatal gift of Segelius. This procured him all the luxuries of life—all the material enjoyments. But each one of those joys contained a poison the sting of which was more acute after each success. At last he resolved to use this accursed faculty no more; to stifle it, to crush it, even if it were at the price of starvation and death. But it was too late. In this savage struggle against himself Cipriano gave way. His reason trembled. The delicate links that united the mysterious elements of thought and sentiment were broken. Sentiment remained to him no longer, nor ideas; only vertigos of sensibility, fragments of thoughts, that he clad still in confused words that he himself did not understand. Misery and hunger had crushed his frame. He wandered for a long time, living on public charity, and not knowing himself whither be went.

I saw him once, when, in my capacity of American engineer on a Russian railroad, I travelled through the *Steppes*. He was living in the house of a Russian gentleman of small means, where he played the part of the old court fool. He wore a *caftan* of thick cloth, belted round the waist with a band of red leather. He babbled verses incessantly, in an incomprehensible language composed of all the idioms of the earth. He related his story to me himself, and complained bitterly of his poverty; but above all, his sorest affliction was that of not being comprehended, and being beaten every time that he, in one of his poetic inspirations, not having any paper, wrote his verses on the walls and tables. That, however, which pained him more than all was the fact that the family and servants laughed at the only happy memory which the fatal gifts of Segelius had not destroyed—his first verses to Charlotte.

The Golden Ingot

I had just retired to rest, with my eyes almost blind with the study of a new work on physiology by M. Brown-Sequard, when the night-bell was pulled violently.

It was winter, and I confess I grumbled as I rose and went down stairs to open the door. Twice that week I had been aroused long after midnight for the most trivial causes. Once, to attend upon the son and heir of a wealthy family, who had cut his thumb with a penknife, which, it seems, he insisted on taking to bed with him; and once, to restore a young gentleman to consciousness, who had been found by his horrified parent stretched insensible on the staircase. Diachylon in the one case and ammonia in the other, were all that my patients required; and I had a faint suspicion that the present summons was perhaps occasioned by no case more necessitous than those I have quoted. I was too young in my profession, however, to neglect opportunities. It is only when a physician rises to a very large practice that he can afford to be inconsiderate. I was on the first step of the ladder, so I humbly opened my door.

A woman was standing ankle-deep in the snow that lay upon the stoop. I caught but a dim glimpse of her form, for the night was cloudy; but I could hear her teeth rattling like castanets, and, as the sharp wind blew her clothes close to her form, I could discern from the sharpness of the outlines that she was very scantily supplied with raiment.

"Come in, come in, my good woman," I said hastily, for the wind seemed to catch eagerly at the opportunity of making itself at home in my hall, and was rapidly forcing an entrance through the half-open door. "Come in, you can tell me all you have to communicate inside."

She slipped in like a ghost, and I closed the door. While I was striking a light in my office, I could hear her teeth still clicking, out in the dark hall, till it seemed as if some skeleton was chattering. As soon as I obtained a light I begged her to enter the room, and, without occupying myself particularly about her appearance, asked her abruptly what her business was.

"My father has met with a severe accident," she said, "and requires instant surgical aid. I entreat you to come to him immediately."

The freshness and the melody of her voice startled me. Such voices rarely if ever issue from any but beautiful forms. I looked at her attentively, but, owing to a nondescript species of shawl in which her head was wrapped, I could discern nothing beyond what seemed to be a pale, thin face, and large eyes. Her dress was lamentable. An old silk, of a colour now unrecognisable, clung to her figure in those limp folds which are so eloquent of misery. The creases where it had been folded were worn nearly through, and the edges of the skirt had decayed into a species of irregular fringe, which was clotted and discoloured with mud. Her shoes—which were but half concealed by this scanty garment—were shapeless and soft with moisture. Her hands were hidden under the ends of the shawl which covered her head and hung down over a bust, the outlines of which, although angular, seemed to possess grace. Poverty, when partially shrouded, seldom fails to interest: witness the statue of the Veiled Beggar, by Monti.

"In what manner was your father hurt?" I asked, in a tone considerably softened from the one in which I put my first question.

"He blew himself up, sir, and is terribly wounded."

"Ah! He is in some factory then?"

"No, sir, he is a chemist."

"A chemist? Why, he is a brother professional. Wait an instant and I will slip on my coat and go with you. Do you live far from here?"

"In the Seventh Avenue, not more than two blocks from the end of this street."

"So much the better. We will be with him in a few minutes. Did you leave anyone in attendance on him?"

"No, sir. He will allow no one but myself to enter his laboratory. And, injured as he is, I could not induce him to quit it."

"Indeed! He is engaged in some great research, perhaps? I have known such cases."

We were passing under a lamp-post, and the woman suddenly turned and glared at me with a look of such wild terror that for an instant I involuntarily glanced round me under the impression that some terrible peril, unseen by me, was menacing us both.

"Don't—don't ask me any questions," she said breathlessly. "He will tell you all. But do, O, do hasten! Good God! he may be dead by this time!"

I made no reply, but allowed her to grasp my hand, which she did with a bony, nervous clutch, and endeavoured with some difficulty to keep pace with the long strides—I might well call them bounds, for they seemed the springs of a wild animal rather than the paces of a young girl—with which she covered the ground. Not a word more was uttered until we stopped before a shabby, old-fashioned tenement-house in the Seventh Avenue, not far above Twenty-Third Street. She pushed the door open with a convulsive pressure, and, still retaining hold of my hand, literally dragged me upstairs to what seemed to be a back off-shoot from the main building, as high, perhaps, as the fourth story. In a moment more, I found myself in a moderate-sized chamber, lit by a single lamp. In one corner, stretched motionless on a wretched pallet-bed, I beheld what I supposed to be the figure of my patient.

"He is there," said the girl; "go to him. See if he is dead,—I dare not look."

I made my way as well as I could through the numberless dilapidated chemical instruments with which the room was littered. A French chafing-dish supported on an iron tripod had been overturned, and was lying across the floor, while the charcoal, still warm, was scattered around in various directions. Crucibles, alembics, and retorts were confusedly piled in various corners, and on a small table I saw distributed in separate bottles a number of mineral and metallic substances, which I recognized as antimony, mercury, plumbago, arsenic, borax, etc. It was veritably the apartment of a poor chemist.

All the apparatus had the air of being second-hand. There was no lustre of exquisitely annealed glass and highly polished metals, such as dazzles one in the laboratory of the prosperous analyst. The makeshifts of poverty were everywhere visible. The crucibles were broken, or gallipots were used instead of crucibles. The coloured tests were not in the usual transparent vials, but were placed in ordinary black bottles. There is nothing more melancholy than to behold science or art in distress. A threadbare scholar, a tattered book, or a battered violin is a mute appeal to our sympathy.

I approached the wretched pallet-bed on which the victim of chemistry was lying. He breathed heavily, and had his head turned toward the wall. I lifted his arm gently to arouse his attention. "How goes it, my poor friend?" I asked him. "Where are you hurt?"

In a moment, as if startled by the sound of my voice, he sprang up in his bed, and cowered against the wall like a wild animal driven to bay. "Who are you? I don't know you. Who brought you here? You are a stranger. How dare you come into my private rooms to spy upon me?"

And as he uttered this rapidly, with a frightful nervous energy, I beheld a pale distorted face, draped with long grey hair, glaring at me with a mingled expression of fury and terror.

"I am no spy," I answered mildly. "I heard that you had met with an accident, and have come to cure you. I am Doctor Luxor, and here is my card."

The old man took the card, and scanned it eagerly. "You are a physician?" he inquired distrustfully.

"And surgeon also."

"You are bound by oath not to reveal the secrets of your patients."

"Undoubtedly."

"I am afraid that I am hurt," he continued faintly, half sinking back in the bed.

I seized the opportunity to make a brief examination of his body. I found that the arms, a part of the chest, and a part of the face were terribly scorched; but it seemed to me that there was nothing to be apprehended but pain.

"You will not reveal anything that you may learn here?" said the old man, feebly fixing his eyes on my face while I was applying a soothing ointment to the burns. "You will promise me?"

I nodded assent.

"Then I will trust you. Cure me,—I will pay you well."

I could scarce help smiling. If Lorenzo de' Medici, conscious of millions of *ducats* in his coffers, had been addressing some leech of the period, he could not have spoken with a loftier air than this inhabitant of the fourth storey of a tenement-house in the Seventh Avenue.

"You must keep quiet," I answered. "Let nothing irritate you. I will leave a composing draught with your daughter, which she will give you immediately. I will see you in the morning. You will be well in a week."

"Thank God!" came in a murmur from a dusk corner near the door. I turned, and beheld the dim outline of the girl, standing with clasped hands in the gloom of the dim chamber.

"My daughter!" screamed the old man, once more leaping up in the bed with renewed vitality. "You have seen her, then? When?

where? O, may a thousand cur—"

"Father! father! Anything,—anything but that. Don't, don't curse me!" And the poor girl, rushing in, flung herself sobbing on her knees beside his pallet.

"Ah, brigand! you are there, are you? Sir," said he, turning to me, "I am the most unhappy man in the world. Talk of Sisyphus rolling the ever-recoiling stone,—of Prometheus gnawed by the vulture since the birth of time. The fables yet live. There is my rock, forever crushing me back! there is my eternal vulture, feeding upon my heart! There! there! there!" And, with an awful gesture of malediction and hatred, he pointed with his wounded hand, swathed and shapeless with bandages, at the cowering, sobbing, wordless woman by his side.

I was too much horror-stricken to attempt even to soothe him. The anger of blood against blood has an electric power which paralyzes bystanders.

"Listen to me, sir," he continued, "while I skin this painted viper. I have your oath; you will not reveal. I am an alchemist, sir. Since I was twenty-two years old, I have pursued the wonderful and subtle secret. Yes, to unfold the mysterious Rose guarded with such terrible thorns; to decipher the wondrous Table of Emerald; to accomplish the mystic nuptials of the Red King and the White Queen; to marry them soul to soul and body to body for ever and ever, in the exact proportions of land and water,—such has been my sublime aim, such has been the splendid feat that I have accomplished."

I recognised at a glance, in this incomprehensible *farrago*, the *argot* of the true alchemist. Ripley, Flamel, and others have supplied the world, in their works, with the melancholy spectacle of a scientific Bedlam.

"Two years since," continued the poor man, growing more and more excited with every word that he uttered,—"two years since, I succeeded in solving the great problem,—in transmuting the baser metals into gold. None but myself, that girl, and God knows the privations I had suffered up to that time. Food, clothing, air, exercise, everything but shelter, was sacrificed toward the one great end. Success at last crowned my labours. That which Nicholas Flamel did in 1382, that which George Ripley did at Rhodes in 1460, that which Alexander Sethon and Michael Scudivogius did in the seventeenth century, I did in 1856. I made gold! I said to myself, 'I will astonish New York more than Flamel did Paris.' He was a poor copyist, and suddenly launched into magnificence.

"I had scarce a rag to my back: I would rival the Medicis. I made gold every day. I toiled night and morning; for I must tell you that I never was able to make more than a certain quantity at a time, and that by a process almost entirely dissimilar to those hinted at in those books of alchemy I had hitherto consulted. But I had no doubt that facility would come with experience, and that erelong I should be able to eclipse in wealth the richest sovereigns of the earth.

"So, I toiled on. Day after day I gave to this girl here what gold I succeeded in fabricating, telling her to store it away after supplying our necessities. I was astonished to perceive that we lived as poorly as ever. I reflected, however, that it was perhaps a commendable piece of prudence on the part of my daughter. Doubtless, I said, she argues that the less we spend the sooner we shall accumulate a capital wherewith to live at ease; so, thinking her course a wise one, I did not reproach her with her niggardliness, but toiled on amid want, with closed lips.

"The gold which I fabricated was, as I said before, of an invariable size, namely, a little ingot worth perhaps thirty or forty-five dollars. In two years, I calculated that I had made five hundred of these ingots, which, rated at an average of thirty dollars apiece, would amount to the gross sum of fifteen thousand dollars. After deducting our slight expenses for two years, we ought to have nearly fourteen thousand dollars left. It was time, I thought, to indemnify myself for my years of suffering, and surround my child and myself with such' moderate comforts as our means allowed. I went to my daughter and explained to her that I desired to make an encroachment upon our little hoard.

"To my utter amazement, she burst into tears, and told me that she had not got a dollar,—that all of our wealth had been stolen from her. Almost overwhelmed by this new misfortune, I in vain endeavoured to discover from her in what manner our savings had been plundered. She could afford me no explanation beyond what I might gather from an abundance of sobs and a copious flow of tears.

"It was a bitter blow. Doctor, but *nil desperandum* was my motto, so I went to work at my crucible again, with redoubled energy, and made an ingot nearly every second day. I determined this time to put them in some secure place myself; but the very first day I set my apparatus in order for the projection, the girl Marian—that is my daughter's name—came weeping to me and implored me to allow her to take care of our treasure. I refused, decisively, saying that, having found her already incapable of filling the trust, I could place no faith in her again. But she persisted, clung to my neck, threatened to abandon me, in short used so many of the bad but irresistible arguments known to women, that I had not the heart to refuse her. She has since that time continued to take the ingots.

"Yet you behold," continued the old alchemist, casting an inexpressibly mournful glance around the wretched apartment, "the way we live. Our food is insufficient and of bad quality; we never buy clothes; the rent of this hole is a mere nothing. What am I to think of the wretched girl who plunges me into this misery? Is she a miser, think you? or a female gamester? or—or—does she squander it riotously in places I know not of? Doctor, Doctor! do not blame me if I heap imprecations on her head, for I have suffered bitterly!" The poor man here closed his eyes and sank back groaning on his bed.

This singular narrative excited in me the strangest emotions. I glanced at the girl Marian, who had been a patient listener to these horrible accusations of cupidity, and never did I behold a more angelic air of resignation than beamed over her countenance. It was impossible that anyone with those pure, limpid eyes, that calm, broad forehead, that childlike mouth, could be such a monster of avarice or deceit as the old man represented. The truth was plain enough: the alchemist was mad,—what alchemist was there ever who was not?—and his insanity had taken this terrible shape. I felt an inexpressible pity move my heart for this poor girl, whose youth was burdened with such an awful sorrow.

"What is your name?" I asked the old man, taking his tremulous, fevered hand in mine.

"William Blakelock," he answered. "I come of an old Saxon stock, sir, that bred true men and women in former days. God! how did it ever come to pass that such a one as that girl ever sprung from our line?" The glance of loathing and contempt that he cast at her made me shudder.

"May you not be mistaken in your daughter?" I said, very mildly. "Delusions with regard to alchemy are, or have been, very common—"

"What, sir?" cried the old man, bounding in his bed. "What? Do you doubt that gold can be made? Do you know, sir, that M. C. Théodore Tiffereau made gold at Paris, in the year 1854, in the presence of M. Levol, the assayer of the Imperial Mint, and the result of the experiments was read before the Academy of Sciences on the sixteenth of October of the same year? But stay; you shall have better proof yet. I will pay you with one of my ingots, and you shall attend me until I am well. Get me an ingot!"

This last command was addressed to Marian, who was still kneeling close to her father's bedside. I observed her with some curiosity as this mandate was issued. She became very pale, clasped her hands convulsively, but neither moved nor made any reply.

"Get me an ingot, I say!" reiterated the alchemist, passionately.

She fixed her large eyes imploringly upon him. Her lips quivered, and two huge tears rolled slowly down her white cheeks.

"Obey me, wretched girl," cried the old man in an agitated voice, "or I swear, by all that I reverence in heaven and earth, that I will lay my curse upon you forever!"

I felt for an instant that I ought perhaps to interfere, and spare the girl the anguish that she was so evidently suffering; but a powerful curiosity to see how this strange scene would terminate withheld me.

The last threat of her father, uttered as it was with a terrible vehemence, seemed to appal Marian. She rose with a sudden leap, as if a serpent had stung her, and, rushing into an inner apartment, returned with a small object in her hand, which she placed in mine, and then flung herself in a chair in a distant corner of the room, weeping bitterly.

"You see—you see," said the old man sarcastically, "how reluctantly she parts with it. Take it, sir; it is yours."

It was a small bar of metal. I examined it carefully, poised it in my hand,—the colour, weight, everything, announced that it really was gold.

"You doubt its genuineness, perhaps," continued the alchemist. "There are acids on yonder table,—test it."

I confess that I *did* doubt its genuineness; but after I had acted upon the old man's suggestion, all further suspicion was rendered impossible. It was gold of the highest purity. I was astounded. Was then, after all, this man's tale a truth? Was his daughter, that fair, angelic-looking creature, a demon of avarice, or a slave to worse passions? I felt bewildered. I had never met with anything so incomprehensible. I looked from father to daughter in the blankest amazement. I suppose that my countenance betrayed my astonishment, for the old man said, "I perceive that you are surprised. Well, that is natural. You had a right to think me mad until I proved myself sane."

"But, Mr. Blakelock," I said, "I really cannot take this gold. I have no right to it. I cannot in justice charge so large a fee."

"Take it,—take it," he answered impatiently; "your fee will amount to that before I am well. Beside," he added mysteriously, "I wish to secure your friendship. I wish that you should protect me from her,"— and he pointed his poor, bandaged, hand at Marian.

My eye followed his gesture, and I caught the glance that replied,— a glance of horror, distrust, despair. The beautiful face was distorted into positive ugliness.

"It's all true," I thought; "she is the demon that her father represents her."

I now rose to go. This domestic tragedy sickened me. This treachery of blood against blood was too horrible to witness. I wrote a prescription for the old man, left directions as to the renewal of the dressings upon his burns, and, bidding him goodnight, hastened towards the door.

While I was fumbling on the dark, crazy landing for the staircase, I felt a hand laid on my arm.

"Doctor," whispered a voice that I recognised as Marian Blakelock's, "Doctor, have you any compassion in your heart?"

"I hope so," I answered, shortly, shaking off her hand,—her touch filled me with loathing.

"Hush! don't talk so loud. If you have any pity in your nature, give me back, I entreat of you, that gold ingot which my father gave you this evening."

"Great heaven!" said I, "can it be possible that so fair a woman can be such a mercenary, shameless wretch?"

"Ah! you know not,—I cannot tell you! Do not judge me harshly. I call God to witness that I am not what you deem me. Some day or other you will know. But," she added, interrupting herself, "the ingot,—where is it? I must have it. My life depends on your giving it to me."

"Take it, impostor!" I cried, placing it in her hand, that closed on it with a horrible eagerness. "I never intended to keep it. Gold made under the same roof that covers such as you must be accursed."

So saying, heedless of the nervous effort she made to detain me, I stumbled down the stairs and walked hastily home.

The next morning, while I was in my office, smoking my matutinal cigar, and speculating over the singular character of my acquaintances of last night, the door opened, and Marian Blakelock entered. She had the same look of terror that I had observed the evening before, and she panted as if she had been running fast.

"Father has got out of bed," she gasped out, "and insists on going on with his alchemy. Will it kill him?"

"Not exactly," I answered, coldly. "It were better that he kept quiet, so as to avoid the chance of inflammation. However, you need not be alarmed; his burns are not at all dangerous, although painful."

"Thank God! thank God!" she cried, in the most impassioned accents; and, before I was aware of what she was doing, she seized my hand and kissed it.

"There, that will do," I said, withdrawing my hand; "you are under no obligations to me. You had better go back to your father."

"I can't go," she answered. "You despise me,—is it not so?"

I made no reply.

"You think me a monster,—a criminal. When you went home last night, you were wonder-struck that so vile a creature as I should have so fair a face."

"You embarrass me, madam," I said, in a most chilling tone. "Pray relieve me from this unpleasant position."

"Wait! I cannot bear that you should think ill of me. You are good and kind, and I desire to possess your esteem. You little know how I love my father."

I could not restrain a bitter smile.

"You do not believe that? Well, I will convince you. I have had a hard struggle all last night with myself, but am now resolved. This life of deceit must continue no longer. Will you hear my vindication?"

I assented. The wonderful melody of her voice and the purity of her features were charming me once more. I half believed in her innocence already.

"My father has told you a portion of his history. But he did not tell you that his continued failures in his search after the secret of metallic transmutation nearly killed him. Two years ago, he was on the verge of the grave, working every day at his mad pursuit, and every day growing weaker and more emaciated. I saw that if his mind was not relieved in some way he would die. The thought was madness to me, for I loved him,—I love him still, as a daughter never loved a father before. During all these years of poverty I had supported the house with my needle; it was hard work, but I did it,—I do it still!"

"What?" I cried, startled, "does not—"

"Patience. Hear me out. My father was dying of disappointment. I must save him. By incredible exertions, working night and day, I saved about thirty-five dollars in notes. These I exchanged for gold, and one day, when my father was not looking, I cast them into the crucible in which he was making one of his vain attempts at transmutation. God, I am sure, will pardon the deception. I never anticipated the misery it would lead to.

"I never beheld anything like the joy of my poor father, when, after emptying his crucible, he found a deposit of pure gold at the bottom. He wept, and danced, and sang, and built such castles in the air, that my brain was dizzy to hear him. He gave me the ingot to keep, and went to work at his alchemy with renewed vigour. The same thing occurred. He always found the same quantity of gold in his crucible. I alone knew the secret. He was happy, poor man, for nearly two years, in the belief that he was amassing a fortune. I all the while plied my needle for our daily bread.

"When he asked me for his savings, the first stroke fell upon me. Then it was that I recognised the folly of my conduct. I could give him no money. I never had any,—while he believed that I had fourteen thousand dollars. My heart was nearly broken when I found that he had conceived the most injurious suspicions against me. Yet I could not blame him. I could give no account of the treasure I had permitted him to believe was in my possession. I must suffer the penalty of my fault, for to undeceive him would be, I felt, to kill him. I remained silent then, and suffered.

"You know the rest. You now know why it was that I was reluctant to give you that ingot,—why it was that I degraded myself so far as to ask it back. It was the only means I had of continuing a deception on which I believed my father's life depended. But that delusion has been dispelled. I can live this life of hypocrisy no longer. I cannot exist, and hear my father, whom I love so, wither me daily with his curses. I will undeceive him this very day. Will you come with me, for I fear the effect on his enfeebled frame?"

"Willingly," I answered, taking her by the hand; "and I think that no absolute danger need be apprehended. Now, Marian," I added, "let me ask forgiveness for having even for a moment wounded so noble a heart. You are truly as great a martyr as any of those whose sufferings the Church perpetuates in altar-pieces,"

"I knew you would do me justice when you knew all," she sobbed, pressing my hand; "but come. I am on fire. Let us hasten to my father, and break this terror to him."

When we reached the old alchemist's room, we found him busily engaged over a crucible which was placed on a small furnace, and in which some indescribable mixture was boiling. He looked up as we entered.

"No fear of me, Doctor," he said, with a ghastly smile, "no fear. I must not allow a little physical pain to interrupt my great work, you know. By the way, you are just in time. In a few moments, the marriage of the Red King and White Queen will be accomplished, as George Ripley calls the great act, in his book entitled *The Twelve Gates*. Yes, Doctor, in less than ten minutes you will see me make pure, red, shining gold! "And the poor old man smiled triumphantly, and stirred his foolish mixture with a long rod, which he held with difficulty in his bandaged hands. It was a grievous sight for a man of any feeling to witness.

"Father," said Marian, in a low, broken voice, advancing a little toward the poor old dupe, "I want your forgiveness."

"Ah, hypocrite! for what? Are you going to give me back my gold?"

"No, father, but for the deception that I have been practising on you for two years—"

"I knew it! I knew it!" shouted the old man, with a radiant countenance. "She has concealed my fourteen thousand dollars all this time, and now comes to restore them. I will forgive her. Where are they, Marian?"

"Father,—it must come out. You never made any gold. It was I who saved up thirty-five dollars, and I used to slip them into your crucible when your back was turned,—and I did it only because I saw that you were dying of disappointment. It was wrong, I know,—but, father, I meant well. You'll forgive me, won't you?" And the poor girl advanced a step towards the alchemist.

He grew deathly pale, and staggered as if about to fall. The next instant, though, he recovered himself, and burst into a horrible sardonic laugh. Then he said, in tones full of the bitterest irony, "A conspiracy, is if? Well done. Doctor! You think to reconcile me with this wretched girl by trumping up this story, that I have been for two years a dupe of her filial piety. It's clumsy, Doctor, and is a total failure. Try again."

"But I assure you, Mr. Blakelock," I said as earnestly as I could, "I believe your daughter's statements to be perfectly true. You will find it to be so, as she has got the ingot in her possession which so often deceived you into the belief that you made gold, and you will certainly find that no transmutation has taken place in your crucible."

"Doctor," said the old man, in tones of the most settled conviction, "you are a fool. That girl has wheedled you. In less than a minute I will turn you out a piece of gold, purer than any the earth produces. Will that convince you?"

"That will convince me," I answered. By a gesture I imposed silence on Marian, who was about to speak. I thought it better to allow the old man to be his own undeceiver,—and we awaited the coming crisis.

The old man, still smiling with anticipated triumph, kept bending eagerly over his crucible, stirring the mixture with his rod, and muttering to himself all the time. "Now," I heard him say, "it changes. There,—there's the scum. And now the green and bronze shades flit across it. O, the beautiful green! the precursor of the golden-red hue, that tells of the end attained! Ah! now the golden-red is coming— slowly—slowly! It deepens, it shines, it is dazzling! Ah, I have it!" So saying, he caught up his crucible in a chemist's tongs, and bore it slowly toward the table on which stood a brass vessel.

"Now, incredulous Doctor!" he cried, "come and be convinced"; and immediately began carefully pouring the contents of the crucible into the brass vessel. When the crucible was quite empty, he turned it up, and called me again. "Come, Doctor, come and be convinced. See for yourself."

"See first if there is any gold in your crucible," I answered, without moving.

He laughed, shook his head derisively, and looked into the crucible. In a moment, he grew pale as death.

"Nothing!" he cried. "O, a jest! a jest! There must be gold somewhere. Marian!"

"The gold is here, father," said Marian, drawing the ingot from her pocket; "it is all we ever had."

"Ah!" shrieked the poor old man, as he let the empty crucible fall, and staggered toward the ingot which Marian held out to him. He made three steps, and then fell on his face. Marian rushed toward him, and tried to lift him, but could not. I put her aside gently, and placed my hand on his heart.

"Marian," said I, "it is perhaps better as it is. He is dead!"

The Bohemian

I was launched into the world when I reached twenty-one, at which epoch I found myself in possession of health, strength, physical beauty, and boundless ambition., I was poor. My father had been an unsuccessful operator in Wall Street;—had passed through the various vicissitudes of fortune common to his profession, and ended by being left a widower, with barely enough to live upon and to give me a collegiate education. As I was aware of the strenuous exertions he had made to accomplish this last, how he had pinched himself in a thousand ways to endow me with intellectual capital, I immediately felt, on leaving college, the necessity of burdening him no longer. The desire for riches entirely possessed me. I had no dream but wealth. Like those poor wretches so lately starving on the Darien Isthmus, who used to beguile their hunger with imaginary banquets, I consoled my pangs of present poverty with visions of boundless treasure.

A friend of mine, who was paying-teller in one of our New York banks, once took me into the vaults when he was engaged in depositing his specie, and as I beheld the golden coins falling in yellow streams from his hands, a strange madness seemed to possess me. I became from that moment a prey to a morbid disorder, which, if we had a psychological pathology, might be classed as the *mania aurabilis*. I literally saw gold,—nothing but gold. Walking in the country my eyes involuntarily sought the ground, as if hoping to pierce the sod and discover some hidden treasure.

Coming home late at night, through the silent New York streets, every stray piece of mud or loose fragment of paper that lay upon the sidewalk was carefully scanned; for, in spite of my better reason, I cherished the vague hope that some time or other I should light upon a splendid treasure, which, for want of a better claimant, would remain mine. It seemed, in short, as if one of those gold gnomes of the Hartz

Mountains had taken possession of me and ruled me like a master. I dreamed such dreams as would cast Sinbad's valley of diamonds into the shade. The very sunlight itself never shone upon me but the wish crossed my brain that I could solidify its splendid beams and coin them into "eagles."

I was by profession a lawyer. Like the rest of my fraternity I had my little office, a small room on the fourth story in Nassau Street, with magnificent painted tin labels announcing my rank and title all the way up the stairs. Despite the fact that I had many of these labels fixed to the walls, and in every available corner, my legal threshold was virgin. No client gladdened my sight. Many and many a time my heart beat as I heard heavy footsteps ascending the stairs, but the half-dawning hope of employment was speedily crushed. They always stopped on the floor below, where a disgusting conveyancer, with a large practice, had put up his shingle. So I passed day after day alone with my Code and Blackstone, and my Chitty, writing articles for the magazines on legal-looking paper,—so that in case a client entered he might imagine I was engaged at my profession,—by which I earned a scanty and precarious subsistence.

I was, of course, at this period in love. That a young man should be very ambitious, very poor, and very unhappy, and not in love, would be too glaring a contradiction of the usual course of worldly destinies. I was, therefore, entirely and hopelessly in love. My life was divided between two passions,—the desire of becoming wealthy, and my love for Annie Deane.

Annie was an author's daughter. Need I add, after this statement, that she was as poor as myself? This was the only point in my theory of the conquest of wealth on which I contradicted myself. To be consistent, I should have devoted myself to some of those young ladies, about whom it is whispered, before you are introduced, that "she will have a hundred and fifty thousand dollars." But though I had made up my mind to devote my life to the acquisition of wealth, and though I verily believe I might have parted with my soul for the same end, I had yet too much of the natural man in my composition to sacrifice my heart.

Annie Deane was, however, such a girl as to make this infraction of my theory of life less remarkable. She was, indeed, marvellously beautiful. Not of that insipid style of beauty which one sees in Greek statues and London annuals. Her nose did not form a grand line with her forehead. Her mouth would scarcely have been claimed by Cupid as his bow; but then, her upper lip was so short, and the teeth within so pearly, the brow was so white and full, and the throat so round, slender, and pliant! and when, above all this, a pair of wondrous dark-grey eyes reigned in supreme and tender beauty, I felt that a portion of the wealth of my life had already been acquired, in gaining the love of Annie Deane.

Our love affair ran as smoothly as if the old adage never existed;—probably for the reason that there was no goal in sight, for we were altogether too poor to dream of marriage as yet, and there did not seem very much probability of my achieving the success necessary to the fulfilment of our schemes. Annie's constitutional delicacy, however, was a source of some uneasiness to me. She evidently possessed a very highly strung nervous organisation, and was to the extremest degree what might be termed impressionable. The slightest change in the weather affected her strangely. Certain atmospheres appeared to possess an influence over her for better or for worse; but it was in connection with social instincts, so to speak, that the peculiarities of her organism were so strikingly developed.

These instincts, for I cannot call them anything else, guided her altogether in her choice of acquaintance. She was accustomed to de-clare that, by merely touching a person's hand, she became conscious of liking or aversion. Upon the entrance of certain persons into a room where she was, even if she had never seen them before, her frame would shrink and shiver like a dying flower, and she would not recover until they had left the apartment. For these strange affections, she could not herself account, and they on more than one occasion were the source of very bitter annoyances to herself and her parents.

Well, things were in this state when one day, in the early part of June, I was sitting alone in my little office. The beginning of a story which I was writing lay upon the table. The title was elaborately writ-ten at the top of the page, but it seemed as if I had stuck in the middle of the second paragraph. In the first,—for it was an historical tale after the most approved model,—I had described the month, the time of day, and the setting sun. In the second, I introduced my three horse-men, who were riding slowly down a hill. The nose of the first and elder horseman, however, upset me. I could not for the life of me determine whether it was to be aquiline or Roman.

While I was debating this important point, and swaying between a multitude of suggestions, there came a sharp, decisive knock at my door. I think, if the knock had come upon the nose about which I was thinking, or on my own, I should scarcely have been more surprised. "A client!" I cried to myself. "Huzza! the gods have at last laid on a pipe from Pactolus for my especial benefit." In reality, between ourselves, I did not say anything half so good; but the exclamation, as I have written it, will convey some idea of the vague exultation that filled my soul when I heard that knock.

"Come in! "I cried, when I had reached down a Chitty and concealed my story under a second-hand brief which I had borrowed from a friend in the profession. "Come in" and I arranged myself in a studious and absorbed attitude.

The door opened and my visitor entered. I had a sort of instinct that he was no client, from the first moment. Rich men—and who but a rich man goes to law—may sometimes be seedy in their attire, but it is always a peculiar and respectable seediness. The air of wealth is visible, I know not by what magic, beneath the most threadbare coat. You see at a glance that the man who wears it might, if he chose, be clad in fine linen. The seediness of the poor man is, on the other hand, equally unmistakable. You seem to discern instantly that his coat is poor from necessity. My visitor, it was easy to perceive, was of this latter class. My hopes of profit sank at the sight of his pale, unshaven face, his old, shapeless boots, his shabby Kossuth hat, his over-coat shining with long wear, which, though buttoned, I could see no longer merited its name, for it was plain that no other coat lurked beneath it. Withal, this man had an air of conscious power as he entered. You could see that he had nothing in his pockets, but then he looked as if he had much in his brain.

He saluted me with a sort of careless respect as he entered. I bowed in return, and offered him the other chair. I had but two.

"Can I do anything for you, sir?" I inquired blandly, still clinging to the hope of clientage.

"Yes," said he, shortly; "I never make purposeless visits."

"Hem! If you will be so kind as to state your case,"—for his rudeness rather shook my faith in his poverty,—"I will give it my best attention."

"I've no doubt of that, Mr. Cranstoun," he replied, "for you are as much interested in it as I am."

"Indeed! "I exclaimed, not without some surprise and much interest at this sudden disclosure. "To whom have I the honour of speaking, then?"

"My name is Philip Brann."

"Brann?—Brann? A resident of this city?"

"No. I am by birth an Englishman, but I never reside anywhere."

"O, you are a commercial agent, then, perhaps?"

"I am a Bohemian."

"A what?"

"A Bohemian," he repeated, coolly removing the papers with which I had concealed my magazine story, and glancing over the commencement. "You see my habits are easy."

"I see it perfectly, sir," I answered.

"When I say that I am a Bohemian, I do not wish you to understand that I am a Zingaro. I don't steal chickens, tell fortunes, or live in a camp. I am a social Bohemian, and fly at higher game."

"But what has all this got to do with me?" I asked, sharply; for I was not a little provoked at the disappointment I experienced in the fellow's not having turned out to be a client.

"Much. It is necessary that you should know something about me before you do that which you will do."

"O, I am to do something, then?"

"Certainly. Have you read Henri Murger's *Scènes de la Vie de Bohème?*"

"Yes."

"Well, then, you can comprehend my life. I am clever, learned, witty, and tolerably good-looking. I can write brilliant magazine articles,"—here his eye rested contemptuously on my historical tale,—"I can paint pictures, and, what is more, sell the pictures I paint. I can compose songs, make comedies, and captivate women."

"On my word, sir, you have a choice of professions," I said, sarcastically; for the scorn with which the Bohemian had eyed my story offended me.

"That's it," he answered; "I don't want a profession. I could make plenty of money if I chose to work, but I don't choose to work. I will never work. I have a contempt for labour."

"Probably you despise money equally," I replied, with a sneer.

"No, I don't. To acquire money without trouble is the great object of my life, as to acquire it in any way or by any means is the great object of yours."

"And pray, sir, how do you know that I have any such object?" I asked, in a haughty tone.

"O, I know it. You dream only of wealth. You intend to try and obtain it by industry. You will never succeed."

"Your prophecies, sir, are more dogmatical than pleasant."

"Don't be angry," he replied, smiling at my frowns. "You shall be wealthy. I can show you the road to wealth. We will follow it together!"

The sublime assurance of this man astounded me. His glance, penetrating and vivid, seemed to pierce into my very heart. A strange and uncontrollable interest in him and his plans filled my breast. I burned to know more.

"What is your proposal?" I asked, severely; for a thought at the moment flashed across me that some unlawful scheme might be the aim of this singular being.

"You need not be alarmed," he answered, as if reading my thoughts. "The road I wish to lead you is an honest one. I am too wise a man ever to become a criminal.

"Then, Mr. Philip Brann, if you will explain your plans I shall feel more assured on that point."

"Well, in the first place," he began, crossing his legs and taking a cigar out of a bundle that lay in one of the pigeon-holes of my desk, "in the first place, you must introduce me to the young lady to whom you are engaged, Miss Annie Deane."

"Sir!" I exclaimed, starting to my feet, and quivering with indignation at such a proposal; "what do you mean'? Do you think it likely that I would introduce to a young lady in whom I am interested a man whom I never saw before today, and who has voluntarily confessed to being a vagabond? Sir, in spite of your universal acquirements, I think Providence forgot to endow you with sense."

"I'll trouble you for one of those matches. Thank you. So, you refuse to introduce me! I knew you would. But I also know that ten minutes from this time you will be very glad to do it. Look at my eyes!"

The oddity of this request, and the calm assurance with which it was made, were too much for me. In spite of my anger, I burst into a fit of loud laughter. He waited patiently until my mirth had subsided.

"You need not laugh," he resumed; "I am perfectly serious. Look at my eyes attentively, and tell me if you see anything strange in them."

At such a proposition from any other man, I should have taken for granted that he was mocking me, and kicked him downstairs. This Bohemian, however, had an earnestness of manner that staggered me. I became serious, and I did look at his eyes.

They were certainly very singular eyes,—the most singular eyes that I had ever beheld. They were long, grey, and of a very deep hue.

Their steadiness was wonderful. They never moved. One might fancy that they were gazing into the depths of one of those Italian lakes, on an evening when the waters are so calm as to seem solid. But it was the interior of these organs—if I may so speak—that was so marvellous. As I gazed, I seemed to behold strange things passing in the deep grey distance which seemed to stretch infinitely away. I could have sworn that I saw figures moving, and landscapes wonderfully real. My gaze seemed to be fastened to his by some inscrutable power; and the outer world, gradually passing off like a cloud, left me literally living in that phantom region which I beheld in those mysterious eyes.

I was aroused from this curious lethargy by the Bohemian's voice. It seemed to me at first as if muffled by distance, and sounded drowsily in my ear. I made a powerful effort and recalled my senses, which seemed to be wandering in some far-off place.

"You are more easily affected than I imagined," remarked Brann, as I stared heavily at him with a half-stupefied air.

"What have you done? What is this lethargy that I feel upon me?" I stammered out.

"Ah! you believe now," replied Brann, coldly; "I thought you would. Did you observe nothing strange in my eyes?"

"Yes. I saw landscapes, and figures, and many strange things. I almost thought I could distinguish Miss—Miss—Deane!"

"Well, it is not improbable. People can behold whatever they wish in my eyes."

"But will you not explain? I no longer doubt the fact that you are possessed of extraordinary powers, but I must know more of you. Why do you wish to be introduced to Miss Deane?"

"Listen to me, Cranstoun," answered the Bohemian, placing his hand on my shoulder; "I do not wish you to enter into any blindfold compact. I will explain all my views to you; for, though I have learned to trust no man, I know you cannot avail yourself of any information I may give you without my assistance."

"So much the better," said I; "for then you will not suspect me."

"As you have seen," continued the Bohemian, "I possess some remarkable powers. The origin, the causes of these endowments, I do not care to investigate. The scientific men of France and Germany have wearied themselves in reducing the psychological phenomena of which I am a practical illustration to a system. They have failed. An arbitrary nomenclature, and a few interesting and suggestive experiments made by Reichenbach, are all the results of years of the intellectual toil of our greatest minds. As you will have guessed by this time, I am what is vulgarly called 'a mesmerist.' I can throw people into trances, deaden the nervous susceptibilities, and do a thousand things by which, if I chose to turn exhibitor, I could realize a fortune. But, while possessing those qualities which exhibit merely a commonplace superiority of psychical force, and which are generally to be found in men of a highly sympathetic organization, I yet can boast of unique powers such as I have never known to be granted to another being besides myself What these powers are I have now no need to inform you. You will very soon behold them practically illustrated.

"Now, to come to my object. Like you, I am ambitious; but I have, unlike you, a constitutional objection to labour. It is sacrilege to expect men with minds like yours and mine to work. Why should we,—who are expressly and evidently created by nature to enjoy,— why should we, with our delicate tastes, our refined susceptibilities, our highly wrought organizations, spend our lives in ministering to the enjoyment of others? In short, my friend, I do not wish to row the boat in the great voyage of life. I prefer sitting at the stern, with purple awnings and ivory couches around me, and my hand upon the golden helm. I wish to achieve fortune at a single stroke. With your assistance, I can do it. You will join me!"

"Under certain conditions."

I was not yet entirely carried away by the earnest eloquence of this strange being.

"I will grant what conditions you like," he continued, fervently. "Above all, I will set your mind at rest by swearing to you, whatever may be my power, never in any way to interfere between you and the young girl whom you love. I will respect her as I would a sister."

This last promise cleared away many of my doubts. The history which this man gave of himself, and the calm manner with which he asserted his wondrous power over women, I confess, rendered me somewhat cautious about introducing him to Annie. His air was, however, now so frank and manly, he seemed to be so entirely absorbed by his one idea of wealth, that I had no hesitation in declaring to him that I accepted his strange proposals.

"Good! "he exclaimed. "You are, I see, a man of resolution. We shall succeed. I will now let you into my plans. Your *fiancée*, Miss Annie Deane, is a *clairvoyante* of the first water. I saw her the other day at the Academy of Design. I stood near her as she examined a picture, and my physiognomical and psychological knowledge enabled me to ascertain beyond a doubt that her organization was the most nervous and sympathetic I had ever met. It is to her pure and piercing instincts that we shall owe our success."

Without regarding my gestures of astonishment and alarm, he continued:—

"You must know that this so-called science of mesmerism is in its infancy. Its professors are, for the most part, incapables; its pupils, credulous fools. As a proof of this, endeavour to recall, if you can, any authentic instance in which this science has been put to any practical use. Have these mesmeric professors and their instruments ever been able to predict or foresee the rise of stocks, the course of political events, the approaches of disaster? Never, my friend, save in the novels of Alexandre Dumas and Sir Edward Bulwer Lytton. The reason of this is very simple. The professors were limited in their power, and the *somnambules* limited in their susceptibilities. When two such people as Miss Deane and myself labour together, everything is possible!"

"O, I see! You propose to operate in the stocks. My dear sir, you are mad. Where is the money?"

"Bah! who said anything about operating in stocks? That involves labour and an office. I can afford neither. No, Cranstoun, we will take a shorter road to wealth than that. A few hours' exertion is all we need to make us *millionaires*."

"For heaven's sake explain! I am wearied with curiosity deferred."

"It is thus. This island and its vicinity abound in concealed treasure. Much was deposited by the early Dutch settlers during their wars with the Indians. Captain Kidd and other buccaneers have made numberless *caches* containing their splendid spoils, which a violent death prevented their ever reclaiming. Poor Poe, you know, who was a Bohemian, like myself, made a story on the tradition, but, poor fellow! *he* only dug up his treasure on paper. There was also a considerable quantity of plate, jewels, and coin concealed by the inhabitants of New York and the neighbourhood during the war with England. You may wonder at my asserting this so confidently. Let it suffice for you that I know it to be so. It is my intention to discover some of this treasure."

Having calmly made this announcement, he folded his arms and gazed at me with the air of a god prepared to receive the ovations of his worshippers.

"How is this to be accomplished?" I inquired, earnestly, for I had begun to put implicit faith in this man, who seemed equally gifted and audacious.

"There are two ways by which we can arrive at our desires. The first is by the command of that power common to *somnambules*, who, having their faculties concentrated on a certain object during the magnetic trance, become possessed of the power of inwardly beholding and verbally describing it, as well as the locality where it is situated. The other is peculiar to myself, and, as you have seen, consists in rendering my eyes a species of camera-obscura to the *clairvoyante*, in which she vividly perceives all that we would desire. This mode I have greater faith in than in any other, and I believe that our success will be found there."

"How is it," I inquired, "that you have not before put this wondrous power to a like use? Why did you not enrich yourself long since through this means?"

"Because I have never been able to find a *somnambule* sufficiently impressionable to be reliable in her evidence. I have tried many, but they have all deceived me. You confess to having beheld certain shadowy forms in my eyes, but you could not define them distinctly. The reason is simply that your magnetic organization is not perfect. This faculty of mine, which has so much astonished you, is nothing new. It is employed by the Egyptians, who use a small glass mirror where I use my eyes. The testimony of M. Leon Laborde, who practised the art himself, Lord Prudhoe, and a host of other witnesses, have recorded their experience of the truth of the science which I preach. However, I need discourse no further on it. I will prove to you its verity. Now that you have questioned me sufficiently, will you introduce me to your lady-love, Mr. Henry Cranstoun?"

"And will you promise me, Mr. Philip Brann, on your honour as a man, that you will respect my relations with that lady?"

"I promise, upon my honour."

"Then I yield. When shall it be?"

"Tonight. I hate delays."

"This evening, then, I will meet you at the Astor House, and we will go together to Mr. Deane's house."

That night, accompanied by my new friend, the Bohemian, I knocked at the door of Mr. Deane's house, in Amity Place. A modest neighbourhood, fit for a man who earned his living by writing novels for cheap publishers, and correspondence for Sunday newspapers. Annie was, as usual, in the sitting-room on the first floor, and the lamps had not yet been lighted, so that the apartment seemed filled with a dull gloom as we entered.

"Annie dear," said I, as she ran to meet me, "let me present to you my particular friend, Mr. Philip Brann, whom I have brought with me for a special purpose, which I will presently explain."

She did not reply.

Piqued by this strange silence, and feeling distressed about the Bohemian, who stood calmly upright, with a faint smile on his lips, I repeated my introduction rather sharply.

"Annie," I reiterated, "you could not have heard me. I am anxious to introduce to you my friend, Mr. Brann."

"I heard you," she answered, in a low voice, catching at my coat as if to support herself, "but I feel very ill."

"Good heavens! What's the matter, darling? Let me get you a glass of wine, or water."

"Do not be alarmed," said the Bohemian, arresting my meditated rush to the door, "I understand Miss Deane's indisposition thoroughly. If she will permit me, I will relieve her at once."

A low murmur of assent seemed to break involuntarily from Annie's lips. The Bohemian led her calmly to an armchair near the window, held her hands in his for a few moments, and spoke a few words to her in a low tone. In less than a minute she declared herself quite recovered.

"It was you who caused my illness," she said to him, in a tone whose vivacity contrasted strangely with her previous languor. "I felt your presence in the room like a terrible electrical shock."

"And I have cured what I caused," answered the Bohemian; "you are very sensitive to magnetic impressions. So much the better."

"Why so much the better?" she asked anxiously.

"Mr. Cranstoun will explain," replied Brann, carelessly; and, with a slight bow, he moved to another part of the dusky room, leaving Annie and myself together.

"Who is this Mr. Brann, Henry?" asked Annie, as soon as the Bohemian was out of earshot. "His presence affects me strangely."

"He is a strange person, who possesses wonderful powers," I answered; "he is going to be of great service to us, Annie."

"Indeed! how so?"

I then related to her what had passed between the Bohemian and myself at my office, and explained his object in coming hither on this evening. I painted in glowing colours the magnificent future that opened for her and myself, if his scheme should prove successful, and ended by entreating her, for my sake, to afford the Bohemian every facility for arriving at the goal of his desires.

As I finished, I discovered that Annie was trembling violently. I caught her hand in mine. It was icy cold, and quivered with a sort of agitated and intermittent tremor,

"O Henry!" she exclaimed, "I feel a singular presentiment that seems to warn me against this thing. Let us rest content in our poverty. Have a true heart, and learn to labour and to wait. You will be rich in time; and then we will live happily together, secure in the consciousness that our means have been acquired by honest industry. I fear those secret treasure seekings."

"What nonsense!" I cried; "these are a timid girl's fears. It would be folly to pine patiently for years in poverty, when we can achieve wealth at a stroke. The sooner we are rich, the sooner we shall be united, and to postpone that moment would be to make me almost doubt your love. Let us try this man's power. There will be nothing lost if he fails."

"Do with me as you will, Henry," she answered, "I will obey you in all things; only I cannot help feeling a vague terror that seems to forebode misfortune."

I laughed and bade her be of good cheer, and rang for lights in order that the experiment might be commenced at once. We three were alone. Mrs. Deane was on a visit at Philadelphia; Mr. Deane was occupied with his literary labours in another room, so that we had everything necessary to insure the quiet which the Bohemian insisted should reign during his experiments.

The Bohemian did not magnetize in the common way, with passes and manipulations. He sat a little in the shade, with his back to the strong glare of the chandeliers, while Annie sat opposite to him, looking full in his face. I sat at a little distance, at a small table, with a pencil and note-book, with which I was preparing to register such revelations as our *clairvoyante* should make.

The Bohemian commenced operations by engaging Miss Deane in a light and desultory conversation. He seemed conversant with all the topics of the town, and talked of the opera, and the annual exhibition at the Academy of Design, as glibly as if he had never done anything but cultivate small talk. Imperceptibly but rapidly, however, he gradually led the conversation to money matters. From these he glided into a dissertation on the advantages of wealth, touched on the topic of celebrated misers, thence slid smoothly into a discourse on concealed treasures, about which he spoke in so eloquent and impressive a manner as to completely fascinate both his hearers.

Then it was that I observed a singular change take place in Annie Deane's countenance. Hitherto pale and somewhat listless, as if suffering from mental depression, she suddenly became illumined as if by an inward fire. A rosy flush mounted to her white cheeks; her lips, eagerly parted as if drinking in some intoxicating atmosphere, were ruddy with a supernatural health, and her eyes dilated as they gazed upon the Bohemian with a piercing intensity.

The latter ceased to speak, and after a moment's silence he said, gently, "Miss Deane, do you see?"

"I see!" she murmured, without altering the fixity of her gaze for an instant.

"Mark well what you observe," continued the Bohemian; "describe it with all possible accuracy." Then, turning to me, he said rapidly, "Take care and note everything."

"I see," pursued Annie, speaking in a measured monotone and gazing into the Bohemian's eyes while she waved her hand gently as if keeping time to the rhythm of her words,—"I see a sad and mournful island on which the ocean beats forever. The sandy ridges are crowned with manes of bitter grass that wave and wave sorrowfully in the wind. No trees or shrubs are rooted in that salt and sterile soil. The burning breath of the Atlantic has seared the surface and made it always barren: The surf, that whitens on the shore, drifts like a shower of snow across its bleak and storm-blown plains. It is the home of the sea-gull and the crane."

"It is called Coney Island?" the Bohemian half inquired, half asserted.

"It is the name," pursued the seeress, but in so even a tone that one would scarce imagine she had heard the question. She then continued to speak as before, still keeping up that gentle oscillation of her hand, which, in spite of my reason, seemed to me to have something terrible in its monotony.

"I see the spot," she continued, "where what you love lies buried. My gaze pierces through the shifting soil until it finds the gold that burns in the gloom. And there are jewels, too, of regal size and priceless value, hidden so deeply in the barren sand! No sunlight has reached them for many years, but they burn for me as if they were set in the glory of an eternal day!"

"Describe the spot accurately!" cried the Bohemian, in a commanding tone, making for the first time a supremely imperative gesture.

"There is a spot upon that lonely island," the seeress continued, in the unimpassioned monotone that seemed more awful than the thunder of an army, "where three huge, sandy ridges meet. At the junction of these three ridges a stake of locust-wood is driven deeply down. When by the sun it is six o'clock, a shadow falls westward on the sand. Where this shadow ends, the treasure lies."

"Can you draw?" asked the Bohemian.

"She cannot," I answered hastily. The Bohemian raised his hand to enjoin silence.

"I can draw *now*," the seeress replied firmly, never for an instant removing her eyes from the Bohemian's.

"Will you draw the locality you describe, if I give you the materials?" pursued the magnetizer.

"I will."

Brann drew a sheet of Bristol-board and a pencil from his pocket, and presented them to her in silence. She took them, and, still keeping her eyes immovably fixed on those of the magnetizer, began sketching rapidly. I was thunderstruck. Annie, I knew, had never made even the rudest sketch before.

"It is done!" she said, after a few minutes' silence, handing the Bristol-board back to the Bohemian. Moved by an inexpressible curiosity, I rose and looked over his shoulder. It was wonderful! There was a masterly sketch of such a locality as she described executed on the paper. But its vividness, its desolation, its evident truth, were so singularly given that I could scarcely believe my senses. I could almost hear the storms of the Atlantic howling over the barren sands.

"There is something wanting yet," said the Bohemian, handing the sketch back to her, and smiling at my amazement.

"I know it," she remarked, calmly. Then, giving a few rapid strokes with her pencil, she handed it to him once more.

The points of the compass had been added in the upper right-hand corner of the drawing. Nothing more was needed to establish the perfect accuracy of the sketch.

"This is truly wonderful!" I could not help exclaiming.

"It is finished," cried the Bohemian, exultingly, and dashing his handkerchief two or three times across Annie's face. Under this new influence her countenance underwent a rapid change. Her eyes, a moment before dilated to their utmost capabilities, now suddenly became dull, and the eyelids drooped heavily over them. Her form, that during the previous scene had been rigidly erect and strung to its highest point of tension, seemed to collapse like one of those strips of gold-leaf that electricians experiment with, when the subtle fluid has ceased to course through its pores. Without uttering a word, and before the Bohemian or myself could stir, she sank like a corpse on the floor.

"Wretch!" I cried, rushing forward, "what have you done?"

"Secured the object of our joint ambition," replied the fellow, with that imperturbable calmness that so distinguished him. "Do not be alarmed at this fainting fit, my friend. Exhaustion is always the consequence of such violent psychological phenomena. Miss Deane will be perfectly recovered by tomorrow evening, and by that time we shall have returned, *millionaires.*"

"I will not leave her until she is recovered," I answered sullenly, while I tried to restore the dear girl to consciousness.

"Yes, but you will," asserted Brann, lighting his cigar as coolly as if nothing very particular had happened. "By dawn tomorrow, you and I will have embarked for Coney Island."

"You cold-blooded savage!" I cried passionately, "will you assist me to restore your victim to consciousness? If you do not, by heaven, I will blow your brains out!"

"What with'? The fire-shovel?" he answered with a laugh. Then, carelessly approaching, he took Annie's hands in his, and blew with his mouth gently upon her forehead. The effect was almost instantaneous. Her eyes gradually unclosed, and she made a feeble effort to sustain herself.

"Call the housekeeper," said the Bohemian, "have Miss Deane conducted to bed, and by tomorrow evening all will be tranquil."

I obeyed his directions almost mechanically, little dreaming how bitterly his words would be realised. Yes, truly! All *would* be tranquil by tomorrow evening!

I sat up all night with Brann. I did not leave Mr. Deane's until a late hour, when I saw Annie apparently wrapped in a peaceful slumber, and betook myself to a low tavern that remained open all night, where the Bohemian awaited me. There we arranged our plan. We were to take a boat at the Battery, at the earliest glimpse of dawn; then, provided with a spade and shovel, a pocket compass, and a valise in which to transport our treasure, we were to row down to our destination. I was feverish and troubled. The strange scene I had witnessed, and the singular adventure that awaited, seemed in combination to have set my brain on fire. My temples throbbed; the cold perspiration stood upon my forehead, and it was in vain that I allowed myself to join the Bohemian in the huge draughts of brandy which he continually gulped down, and which seemed to produce little or no effect on his iron frame. How madly, how terribly, I longed for the dawn!

At last the hour came. We took our implements in a carriage down to the Battery, hired a boat, and in a short time were out in the stream pulling lustily down the foggy harbour. The exercise of rowing seemed to afford me some relief. I pulled madly at my oar, until the sweat rolled in huge drops from my brow, and hung in trembling beads on the curls of my hair. After a long and wearisome pull, we landed on the island at the most secluded spot we could find, taking particular care that it was completely sheltered from the view of the solitary hotel, where doubtless inquisitive idlers would be found. After beaching our boat carefully, we struck toward the centre of the island, Brann seeming to possess some wonderful instinct for the discovery of localities, for almost without any trouble he walked nearly straight to the spot we were in search of.

"This is the place," said he, dropping the valise which he carried. "Here are the three ridges, and the locust stake, lying exactly due north. Let us see what the true time is."

So saying, he unlocked the valise and drew forth a small sextant, with which he proceeded to take an observation. I could not help admiring the genius of this man, who seemed to think of and foresee everything. After a few moments engaged in making calculations on the back of a letter, he informed me that exactly twenty-one minutes would elapse before the shadow of the locust-stake would fall on the precise spot indicated by the seeress. "Just time enough," said he, "to enjoy a cigar."

Never did twenty-one minutes appear so long to a human being as these did to me. There was nothing in the landscape to arrest my attention. All was a wild waste of sand, on which a few patches of salt grass waved mournfully. My heart beat until I could hear its pulsations. A thousand times I thought that my strength must give way beneath the weight of my emotions, and that death would overtake me ere I had realized my dreams. I was obliged at length to dip my handkerchief in a marshy pool that was near me, and bind it about my burning temples.

At length, the shadow from the locust log fell upon the enchanted spot. Brann and myself seized the spades wildly, and dug with the fury of ghouls who were rooting up their loathsome repast. The light sand flew in heaps on all sides. The sweat rolled from our bodies. The hole grew deeper and deeper!

At last—O heavens!—a metallic sound! My spade struck some hollow, sonorous substance. My limbs fairly shook as I flung myself into the pit, and scraped the sand away with my nails. I laughed like a madman, and burrowed like a mole. The Bohemian, always calm, with a few strokes of his shovel laid bare an old iron pot with a loose lid. In an instant, this was smashed with a frantic blow of my fist, and my hands were buried in a heap of shining gold! Red, glittering coins,—bracelets that seemed to glow like the stars in heaven,—goblets, rings, jewels, in countless profusion,—flashed before my eyes for an instant like the sparkles of an aurora. Then came a sudden darkness—and I remember no more!

How long I lay in this unconscious state I know not. It seemed to me that I was aroused by a sensation similar to that of having water poured upon me, and it was some moments before I could summon up sufficient strength to raise myself on one elbow. I looked bewilderedly around: I was alone! I then strove to remember something that I seemed to have forgotten, when my eye fell on the hole in the sand, on the edge of which I found I was lying. A dull-red gleam as of gold seemed to glimmer from out the bottom.

This talismanic sight restored to me everything,—my memory and my strength. I sprang to my feet: I gazed around. The Bohemian was nowhere visible. Had he fled with the treasure? My heart failed me for a moment at the thought; but no! there lay the treasure gleaming still in the depths of the hole, with a dull-red light, like the distant glare of hell. I looked at the sun; he had sunk low in the horizon, and the dews already falling had, with the damp sea-air, chilled me to the bone. While I was brushing the moisture from my coat, wondering at this strange conduct of the Bohemian, my eye caught sight of a slip of paper pinned upon my sleeve. I tore it off eagerly. It contained these words:—

"I leave you. I am honest though I am selfish, and have divided with you the treasure which you have helped me to gain. You are now rich, but it may be that you will not be happy. Return to the city, but return in doubt.

"The Bohemian."

What terrible enigma was this that the last sentence of this note enshrouded'? what veiled mystery was it that rose before my inward vision in shapeless horror? I knew not. I could not guess, but a fore-boding of some unknown and overwhelming disaster rushed instantly upon me, and seemed to crush my soul. Was it Annie, or was it my father? One thing was certain, there was no time to be lost in penetrating the riddle. I seized the valise, which the Bohemian had charitably left me,—how he bore away his own share of the treasure I know not,—and poured the gold and jewels into it with trembling hands. Then, scarce able to travel with the weight of the treasure, I staggered toward the beach, where we had left the boat. She was gone. Without wasting an instant, I made my way as rapidly as I could to the distant pier, where a thin stream of white smoke informed me that the steamer for New York was waiting for the bathers. I reached her just as she was about to start, and, staggering to an obscure corner, sorrowfully sat down upon my treasure.

With what different feelings from those which I anticipated was I returning to the city. My dream of wealth had been realised beyond my wildest hopes. All that I had thought necessary to yield me the purest happiness was mine, and yet there was not a more miserable wretch in existence. Those fatal words, "Return to the city, but return in doubt!" were ever before me. O, how I counted every stroke of the engine that impelled me to the city!

There was a poor, blind, humpbacked fiddler on board, who played all along the way. He played execrably, and his music made my flesh creep. As we neared the city he came round with his hat soliciting alms. In my recklessness, I tumbled all the money I had in my pockets into his hands. I never shall forget the look of joy that flashed over his poor old seared and sightless face at the touch of these few dollars.

"Good heavens!" groaned, "here am I, sitting on the wealth of a kingdom, which is all mine, and dying of despair; while this old wretch has extracted from five dollars enough of happiness to make a saint envious!"

Then my thoughts wandered back to Annie and the Bohemian, and there always floated before me in the air the agonising words, "Return to the city, but return in doubt!"

The instant I reached the pier, I dashed through the crowd with my valise, and, jumping into the first carriage I met, promised a liberal bounty to the driver if he would drive me to Amity Place in the shortest possible space of time. Stimulated by this, we flew through the streets, and in a few moments, I was standing at Mr. Deane's door. Even then it seemed to me as if a dark cloud hung over that house, above all others in the city. I rang; but my hand had scarcely left the bell-handle when the door opened, and Doctor Lott, the family physician, appeared on the threshold. He looked grave and sad.

"We were expecting you, Mr. Cranstoun," he said, very mournfully.

"Has—has anything—happened?" I stammered, catching at the railings for support.

"Hush! come in." And the kind doctor took me by the arm and led me like a child into the parlour.

"Doctor, for heaven's sake, tell me what is the matter. I know something has happened. Is Annie dead? O, my brain will burst unless you end this suspense!"

"No,—not dead. But tell me, Mr. Cranstoun, has Miss Deane experienced any uncommon excitement lately?"

"Yes—yes—last night!" I groaned wildly, "she was mesmerised by a wretch. O, fool that I was to suffer it!"

"Ah! that explains all," answered the doctor. Then he took my hand gently in his. "Prepare yourself, Mr. Cranstoun," he continued, with deep pity in his voice, "prepare yourself for a terrible shock."

"She is dead, then!" I murmured. "Is she not?"

"She is. She died this morning, of over-excitement, of the cause of which I was ignorant until now. Calm yourself, my dear sir. She expired blessing you."

I tore myself from his grasp, and rushed upstairs. The door of her room was open, and, in spite of myself, my agitated tramp softened to a stealthy footfall as I entered. There were two figures in the room. One was an old man, who knelt by the bedside of my lost love, sobbing bitterly. It was her father. The other lay upon the bed, with marble face, crossed hands, and sealed eyelids. All was tranquil and serene in the chamber of death. Even the sobbings of the father, though bitter, were muffled and subdued. And she lay on the couch, with closed eyes, the calmest of all! O, the seeress now saw more than earthly science could show her!

I felt, as I knelt by her father and kissed her cold hand in the agony of my heart, that I was justly punished.

Below stairs, in the valise, lay the treasure I had gained. Here, in her grave-clothes, lay the treasure I had lost.

The Dragon Fang Possessed by the Conjurer Piou-Lu

CHAPTER OF THE MIRACULOUS DRAGON FANG

"Come, men and women, and little people of Tchingtou, come and listen. The small and ignoble person who annoys you by his presence is the miserable conjurer known as Piou-Lu. Everything that can possibly be desired he can give you ;—charms to heal dissensions in your noble and illustrious families;—spells by which beautiful little people without style may become learned Bachelors, and reign high in the palaces of literary composition;—Supernatural red pills, with which you can cure your elegant and renowned diseases;—wonderful incantations, by which the assassins of any members of your shining and virtuous families can be discovered and made to yield compensation, or be brought under the just eye of the Brother of the Sun. What is it that you want? This mean little conjurer, who now addresses you, can supply all your charming and refreshing desires; for he is known everywhere as Piou-Lu, the possessor of the ever-renowned and miraculous Dragon Fang!"

There was a little, dry laugh, and a murmur among the crowd of idlers that surrounded the stage erected by Piou-Lu in front of the Hotel of the Thirty-Two Virtues. Fifth-class Mandarins looked at fourth-class *mandarins* and smiled, as much as to say, "We who are educated men know what to think of this fellow." But the fourth-class *mandarins* looked haughtily at the fifth-class, as if they had no business to smile at their superiors. The crowd, however, composed as it was principally of small traders, barbers, porcelain-tinkers, and country people, gazed with open mouths upon the conjurer, who, clad in a radiant garment of many colours, strutted proudly up and down upon his temporary stage.

"What is a Dragon Fang, ingenious and well-educated conjurer?" at last inquired Wei-chang-tze, a solemn-looking *mandarin* of the third class, who was adorned with a sapphire button, and a one-eyed peacock's feather. "What is a Dragon Fang?"

"Is it possible," asked Piou-Lu, "that the wise and illustrious son of virtue, the Mandarin Wei-chang-tze, does not know what a Dragon Fang is?" and the conjurer pricked up his ears at the Mandarin, as a hare at a barking dog.

"Of course, of course," said the Mandarin Wei-chang-tze, looking rather ashamed of his having betrayed such ignorance, "one does not pass his examinations for nothing. I merely wished that you should explain to those ignorant people here what a Dragon Fang is; that was why I asked."

"I thought that the Soul of Wisdom must have known," said Piou-Lu, triumphantly, looking as if he believed firmly in the knowledge of Wei-chang-tze. "The noble commands of Wei-chang-tze shall be obeyed. You all know," said he, looking round upon the people, "that there are three great and powerful Dragons inhabiting the universe. Lung, or the Dragon of the Sky; Li, or the Dragon of the Sea; and Kiau, or the Dragon of the Marshes. All these Dragons are wise, strong, and terrible. They are wondrously formed, and can take any shape that pleases them. Well, good people, a great many moons ago, in the season of spiked grain, I was following the profession of a barber in the mean and unmentionable town of Siho, when one morning, as I was sitting in my shop waiting for customers, I heard a great noise of tam-tams, and a princely *palanquin* stopped before my door.

"I hastened, of course to observe the honourable Rites toward this newcomer, but before I could reach the street a *mandarin*, splendidly attired, descended from the *palanquin*. The ball on his cap was of a stone and colour that I had never seen before, and three feathers of some unknown bird hung down behind his head-dress. He held his hand to his jaw, and walked into my house with a lordly step. I was greatly confused, for I knew not what rank he was of, and felt puzzled how to address him. He put an end to my embarrassment.

"'I am in the house of Piou-Lu, the barber,' he said, in a haughty voice that sounded like the roll of a copper drum amidst the hills.

"'That disgraceful and ill-conditioned person stands before you,' I replied, bowing as low as I could.

"'It is well,' said he, seating himself in my operating-chair, while two of his attendants fanned him. 'Piou-Lu, I have the toothache!'

"'Does your lordship,' said I, 'wish that I should remove your noble and illustrious pain?'

"'You must draw my tooth,' said he. 'Woe to you if you draw the wrong one!'

"'It is too much honour,' I replied; 'but I will make my abominable and ill-conducted instruments entice your lordship's beautiful tooth out of your high-born jaw with much rapidity.'

"So, I got my big pincers, and my opium-bottle, and opened the strange *mandarin's* mouth. Ah! it was then that my low-born and despicable heart descended into my bowels. I should have dropped my pincers from sheer fright if they had not caught by their hooked ends in my wide sleeve. The *mandarin's* mouth was all on fire inside. As he breathed, the flames rolled up and down his throat, like the flames that gather on the Yellow Grass Plains in the season of Much Heat. His palate glowed like red-hot copper, and his tongue was like a brass stew-pan that had been on the salt-fire for thirty days. But it was his teeth that affrighted me most. They were a serpent's teeth. They were long, and curved inward, and seemed to be made of transparent crystal, in the centre of which small tongues of orange-coloured fire leaped up and down out of some cavity in the gums.

"'Well, dilatory barber,' said the *mandarin*, in a horrible tone, while I stood pale and trembling before him, 'why don't you draw my tooth? Hasten, or I will have you sliced lengthwise and fried in the sun.'

"'O, my lord!' said I, terrified at this threat, 'I fear that my vicious and unendurable pincers are not sufficiently strong.'

"'Slave!' answered he in a voice of thunder, 'if you do not fulfil my desires, you will not see another moon rise.'

"I saw that I should be killed anyway, so I might as well make the attempt. I made a dart with my pincers at the first tooth that came, closed them firmly on the crystal fang, and began to pull with all my strength. The *mandarin* bellowed like an ox of Thibet. The flames rolled from his throat in such volumes that I thought they would singe my eyebrows. His two attendants and his four *palanquin*-bearers put their arms round my waist to help me to pull, and there we tugged for three or four minutes, until at last I heard a report as loud as nine thousand nine hundred and ninety-nine fire-crackers. The attendants, the *palanquin*-bearers, and myself all fell flat on the floor, and the crystal fang glittered between the jaws of the pincers.

"The *mandarin* was smiling pleasantly as I got up from the floor. 'Piou-Lu,' said he, 'you had a narrow escape. You have removed my toothache, but had you failed, you would have perished miserably; for I am the Dragon Lung, who rules the sky and the heavenly bodies, and I am as powerful as I am wise. Take as a reward the Dragon Fang which you drew from my jaw. You will find it a magical charm with which you can work miracles. Honour your parents, observe the Rites, and live in peace.'

"So saying, he breathed a whole cloud of fire and smoke from his throat, that filled my poor and despicable mansion. The light dazzled and the smoke suffocated me, and when I recovered my sight and breath the Dragon Lung, the attendants, the *palanquin*, and the four bearers had all departed, how and whither I knew not. Thus, was it, elegant and refined people of Tching-tou, that this small and evilminded person who stands before you became possessed of the wonderful Dragon Fang, with which he can work miracles."

This story, delivered as it was with much graceful and dramatic gesticulation, and a volubility that seemed almost supernatural, had its effect upon the crowd, and a poor little tailor, named Hang-pou, who was known to be always in debt, was heard to say that he wished he had the Dragon-Fang, wherewith to work miracles with his creditors. But the *mandarins*, blue, crystal, and gilt, smiled contemptuously, and said to themselves, "We who are learned men know how to esteem these things."

The Mandarin Wei-chang-tze, however, seemed to be of an inquiring disposition, and evinced a desire to continue his investigations.

"Supremely visited conjurer," said he to Piou-Lu, "your story is indeed wonderful. To have been visited by the Dragon Lung must have been truly refreshing and enchanting. Though not in the least doubting your marvellous relation, I am sure this virtuous assemblage would like to see some proof of the miraculous power of your Dragon Fang."

The crowd gave an immediate assent to this sentiment by pressing closer to the platform on which Piou-Lu strutted, and exclaiming with one voice, "The lofty *mandarin* says wisely. We would like to behold."

Piou-Lu did not seem in the slightest degree disconcerted. His narrow black eyes glistened like the dark edges of the seeds of the water-melon, and he looked haughtily around him.

"Is there any one of you who would like to have a miracle performed, and of what nature?" he asked, with a triumphant wave of his arms.

"I would like to see my debts paid," murmured the little tailor,

Hang-pou.

"Hang-pou," replied the conjurer, "this unworthy personage is not going to pay your debts. Go home and sit in your shop, and drink no more rice-wine, and your debts will be paid; for labour is the Dragon Fang that works miracles for idle tailors!"

There was a laugh through the crowd at this sally, because Hang-pou was well known to be fond of intoxicating drinks, and spent more of his time in the street than on his shop-board.

"Would either of you like to be changed into a camel?" continued Piou-Lu. "Say the word, and there shall not be a finer beast in all Thibet!"

No one, however, seemed to be particularly anxious to experience this transformation. Perhaps it was because it was warm weather, and camels bear heavy burdens.

"I will change the whole honourable assemblage into turkey-buzzards, if it only agrees," continued the conjurer; "or I will make the Lake Tung come up into the town in the shape of a water-melon, and then burst and overflow everything."

"But we should all be drowned!" exclaimed Hang-pou, who was cowardly as well as intemperate.

"That's true," said Piou-Lu, "but then you need not fear your creditors,"—and he gave such a dart of his long arm at the poor little tailor, that the wretched man thought he was going to claw him up and change him into some frightful animal.

"Well, since this illustrious assembly will not have turkey-buzzards or camels, this weak-minded, ill-shapen personage must work a miracle on himself," said Piou-Lu, descending from his platform into the street, and bringing with him a little three-legged stool made of bamboo rods.

The crowd retreated as he approached, and even the solemn Wei-chang-tze seemed rather afraid of this miraculous conjurer. Piou-Lu placed the bamboo stool firmly on the ground, and then mounted upon it.

"Elegant and symmetrical bamboo stool," he said, lifting his arms, and exhibiting something in his hand that seemed like a piece of polished jade-stone,—"elegant and symmetrical bamboo stool, the justly despised conjurer, named Piou-Lu, entreats that you will immediately grow tall, in the name of the Dragon Lung!"

Truly the stool began to grow, in the presence of the astonished crowd. The three legs of bamboo lengthened and lengthened with great rapidity, bearing Piou-Lu high up into the air. As he ascended he bowed gracefully to the open-mouthed assembly.

"It is delightful!" he cried; "the air up here is so fresh! I smell the tea-winds from Fuh-kien. I can see the spot where the heavens and the earth cease to run parallel. I hear the gongs of Pekin, and listen to the lowing of the herds in Thibet. Who would not have an elegant bamboo stool that knew how to grow?"

By this time Piou-Lu had risen to an enormous height. The legs of the slender tripod on which he was mounted seemed like silkworm's threads, so thin were they compared with their length. The crowd began to tremble for Piou-Lu.

"Will he never stop?" said a *mandarin* with a gilt ball, named Lin.

"O, yes!" shouted Piou-Lu from the dizzy height of his bamboo stool. "O, yes! this ugly little person will immediately stop. Elegant stool, the poor conjurer entreats you to stop growing; but he also begs that you will afford some satisfaction to this beautifying assemblage down below, who have honoured you with their inspection."

The bamboo stool, with the utmost complaisance, ceased to lengthen out its attenuated limbs, but on the moment experienced another change as terrifying to the crowd. The three legs began to approach each other rapidly, and before the eye could very well follow their motions had blended mysteriously and inexplicably into one, the stool still retaining a miraculous equilibrium. Immediately this single stem began to thicken most marvellously, and instead of the dark shining skin of a bamboo stick, it seemed gradually to be encased in overlapping rings of a rough bark.

Meanwhile a faint rustling noise continued overhead, and when the crowd, attracted by the sound, looked up, instead of the flat disk of cane-work on which Piou-Lu had so wondrously ascended, they beheld a cabbage-shaped mass of green, which shot forth every moment long, pointed satiny leaves of the tenderest green, and the most graceful shape imaginable. But where was Piou-Lu? Some fancied that in the yellow crown that topped the cabbage-shaped bud of this strange tree they could see the tip of his cap, and distinguish his black, roguish eyes, but that may have been all fancy; and they were quickly diverted from their search for the conjurer by a shower of red, pulpy fruits, that began to fall with great rapidity from the miraculous tree. Of course, there was a scramble, in which the *mandarins* themselves did not disdain to join; and the crimson fruits—the like of which no one in Tching-tou had ever seen before—proved delightfully sweet and palatable to the taste.

"That's right! That's right! perfectly bred and very polite people," cried a shrill voice while they were all scrambling for the crimson fruits; "pick fruit while it is fresh, and tea while it is tender. For the sun wilts, and the chills toughen, and the bluest plum blooms only for a day."

Everybody looked up, and lo! there was Piou-Lu, as large as life, strutting upon the stage, waving a large green fan in his hand. While the crowd was yet considering this wonderful reappearance of the conjurer, there was heard a very great outcry at the end of the street, and a tall thin man in a coarse blue gown came running up at full speed.

"Where are my plums, sons of thieves?" he cried, almost breathless with haste. "Alas! alas! I am completely ruined. My wife will perish miserably for want of food, and my sons will inherit nothing but empty baskets at my death! Where are my plums?"

"Who is it that dares to address the virtuous and well-disposed people of Tching-tou after this fashion?" demanded the Mandarin Lin, in a haughty voice, as he confronted the newcomer.

The poor man, seeing the gilt ball, became immediately very humble, and bowed several times to the *mandarin*.

"O, my lord! "said he, "I am an incapable and undeserving plum-seller, named Liho. I was just now sitting at my stall in a neighbouring street selling five cash worth of plums to a customer, when suddenly all the plums rose out of my baskets as if they had the wings of hawks, and flew through the air over the tops of the houses in this direction. Thinking myself the sport of demons, I ran after them, hoping to catch them, and—Ah! there are my plums," he cried, suddenly interrupting himself, and making a dart at some of the crimson fruits that the tailor Hang held in his hand, intending to carry them home to his wife.

"These your plums!" screamed Hang, defending his treasure vigorously. "Mole that you are, did you ever see scarlet plums?"

"This man is stricken by Heaven," said Piou-Lu, gravely. "He is a fool who hides his plums and then thinks that they fly away. Let some-one shake his gown."

A porcelain-cobbler who stood near the fruiterer immediately seized the long blue robe and gave it a lusty pull, when, to the wonder of everybody, thousands of the most beautiful plums fell out, as from a tree shaken by the winds of autumn. At this moment, a great gust of wind arose in the street, and a pillar of dust mounted up to the very top of the strange tree, that still stood waving its long satiny leaves languidly above the house-tops. For an instant everyone was blinded, and when the dust had subsided so as to permit the people to use their eyes again the wonderful tree had completely vanished, and all that could be seen was a little bamboo stool flying along the road, where it was blown by the storm. The poor fruiterer, Liho, stood aghast, looking at the plums, in which he stood knee-deep.

The *mandarin*, addressing him, said sternly, "Let us hear no more such folly from Liho, otherwise he will get twenty strokes of the stick."

"Gather your plums, Liho," said Piou-Lu kindly, "and think this one of your fortunate days; for he who runs after his losses with open mouth does not always overtake them."

And as the conjurer descended from his platform it did not escape the sharp eyes of the little tailor Hang that Piou-Lu exchanged a mysterious signal with the Mandarin Wei-chang-tze.

THE CHAPTER OF THE SHADOW OF THE DUCK.

It was close on nightfall when Piou-Lu stopped before Wei-chang-tze's house. The lanterns were already lit, and the porter dozed in a bamboo chair so soundly, that Piou-Lu entered the porch and passed the screen without awaking him. The inner room was dimly lighted by some horn lanterns elegantly painted with hunting scenes; but despite the obscurity the conjurer could discover Wei-chang-tze seated at the farther end of the apartment on an inclined couch covered with blue and yellow satin.

Along the corridor that led to the women's apartments the shadows lay thick; but Piou-Lu fancied he could hear the pattering of little feet upon the matted floor, and see the twinkle of curious eyes illuminating the solemn darkness. Yet, after all, he may have been mistaken, for the corridor opened on a garden wealthy in the rarest flowers, and he may have conceived the silver dripping of the fountain to be the pattering of dainty feet, and have mistaken the moonlight shining on the moist leaves of the lotus for the sparkle of women's eyes.

"Has Piou-Lu arrived in my dwelling?" asked Wei-chang-tze from the dim corner in which he lay.

"That ignoble and wrath-deserving personage bows his head before you," answered Piou-Lu, advancing and saluting the *mandarin* in accordance with the laws of the *Book of Rites.*

"I hope that you performed your journey hither in great safety and peace of mind," said Wei-chang-tze, gracefully motioning to the conjurer to seat himself on a small blue sofa that stood at a little distance.

"When so mean an individual as Piou-Lu is honoured by the request of the noble Wei-chang-tze, good fortune must attend him. How could it be otherwise?" replied Piou-Lu, seating himself not on the small blue sofa, but on the satin one which was partly occupied by the *mandarin* himself.

"Piou-Lu did not send in his name, as the Rites direct," said Wei-chang-tze, looking rather disgusted by this impertinent freedom on the part of the conjurer.

"The elegant porter that adorns the noble porch of Wei-chang-tze was fast asleep," answered Piou-Lu, "and Piou-Lu knew that the great *mandarin* expected him with impatience."

"Yes," said Wei-chang-tze; "I am oppressed by a thousand demons; devils sleep in my hair, and my ears are overflowing with evil spirit; I cannot rest at night, and feel no pleasure in the day. Therefore, was it that I wished to see you, in hopes that you would, by amusing the demon that inhabits my stomach, induce him to depart."

"I will endeavour to delight the respectable demon who lodges in your stomach with my unworthy conjurations," replied Piou-Lu. "But first I must go into the garden to gather flowers."

"Go," said Wei-chang-tze. "The moon shines, and you will see there very many rare and beautiful plants that are beloved by my daughter Wu."

"The moonlight itself cannot shine brighter on the lilies than the glances of your lordship's daughter," said the conjurer, bowing and proceeding to the garden.

Ah! what a garden it was that Piou-Lu now entered! The walls that surrounded it were lofty, and built of a rosy stone brought from the mountains of Mantchouria. This wall, on whose inner face flowery designs and triumphal processions were sculptured at regular intervals; sustained the long and richly laden shoots of the white magnolia, which spread its large snowy chalices in myriads over the surface.

Tamarisks and palms sprang up in various parts of the grounds, like dark columns supporting the silvery sky; while the tender and mournful willow drooped its delicate limbs over numberless fishponds, whose waters seemed to repose peacefully in the bosom of the emerald turf. The air was distracted with innumerable perfumes, each more fragrant than the other. The blue convolvulus, the crimson *ipomea*, the prodigal azaleas, the spotted tiger-lilies, the timid and half-hidden jasmine, all poured forth, during the day and night, streams of perfume from the inexhaustible fountains of their chalices. The heavy odours of the tube-rose floated languidly through the leaves, as a rich-ly-plumaged bird would float through summer air, borne down by his own splendour.

The blue lotus slept on the smooth waves of the fishponds in sub-lime repose. There seemed an odour of enchantment over the entire place. The flowers whispered their secrets in the perfumed silence; the inmost heart of every blossom was unclosed at that mystic hour; all the magic and mystery of plants floated abroad, and the garden seemed filled with the breath of a thousand spells. But amidst the lilies and lotuses, amidst the scented roses and the drooping convolvuli, there moved a flower fairer than all.

"I am here," whispered a low voice, and a dusky figure came glid-ing toward Piou-Lu, as he stood by the fountain.

"Ah!" said the conjurer, in a tender tone, far different from the shrill one in which he addressed the crowd opposite the Hotel of the Thirty-Two Virtues. "The garden is now complete. Wu, the Rose of Completed Beauty, has blossomed on the night."

"Let Piou-Lu shelter her under his mantle from the cold winds of evening, and bear her company for a little while, for she has grown up under a lonely wall," said Wu, laying her little hand gently on the conjurer's arm, and nestling up to his side as a bird nestles into the fallen leaves warmed by the sun.

"She can lie there but a little while," answered Piou-Lu, folding the *mandarin's* daughter in a passionate embrace, "for Wei-chang-tze awaits the coming of Piou-Lu impatiently, in order to have a conjura-tion with a devil that inhabits his stomach."

"Alas!" said Wu, sadly, "why do you not seek some other and more distinguished employment than that of a conjurer? Why do you not seek distinction in the Palace of Literary Composition, and obtain a style? Then we need not meet in secret, and you might without fear demand my hand from my father."

Piou-Lu smiled, almost scornfully. He seemed to gain an inch in stature, and looked around him with an air of command.

"The marble from which the statue is to be carved must lie in the quarry until the workman finds it," he answered, "and the hour of my destiny has not yet arrived."

"Well, we must wait, I suppose," said Wu, with a sigh. "Meantime, Piou-Lu, I love you."

"The hour will come sooner than you think," said Piou-Lu, returning her caress; "and now go, for the *mandarin* waits."

Wu glided away through the gloom to her own apartment, while the conjurer passed rapidly through the garden and gathered the blossoms of certain flowers as he went. He seemed to linger with a strange delight over the buds bathed in the moonlight and the dew; their perfume ascended into his nostrils like incense, and he breathed it with a voluptuous pleasure.

"Now let the demon tremble in the noble stomach of Wei-chang-tze," said Piou-Lu, as he re-entered the hall of reception laden with flowers. "This ill-favoured personage will make such conjurations as shall delight the soul of the elegant and well-born *mandarin*, and cause his illustrious persecutor to fly terrified."

Piou-Lu then stripped off the petals from many of the flowers, and gathered them in a heap on the floor. The mass of leaves was indeed variegated. The red of the *quamoclit*, the blue of the convolvulus, the tender pink of the camellia, the waxen white of the magnolia, were all mingled together like the thousand hues in the Scarfs of Felicity. Having built this confused mass of petals in the shape of a pyramid, Piou-Lu unwound a scarf from his waist and flung it over the heap. He then drew the piece of jade-stone from his pocket, and said,—

"This personage of outrageous presence desires that what will be may be shown to the lofty Mandarin Weichang-tze."

As he pronounced these words, he twitched the scarf away with a rapid jerk, and lo! the flower-leaves were gone, and in their place stood a beautiful mandarin duck, in whose gorgeous plumage one might trace the brilliant hues of the flowers. Piou-Lu now approached the duck, caught it up with one hand, while with the other he drew a sharp knife from his girdle and severed the bird's head from its body at a single stroke. To the great astonishment of Wei-chang-tze, the body and dismembered head of the bird vanished the moment the knife had passed through the neck; but at the same instant a duck, resembling it in every respect, escaped from the conjurer's hands and flew across the room. When I say that this duck resembled the other in every respect, I mean only in shape, size, and colours. For the rest, it was no bodily duck. It was impalpable and transparent, and even when it flew it made no noise with its wings.

"This is indeed wonderful!" said Wei-chang-tze. "Let the marvellous conjurer explain."

"The duck formed out of flowers was a duck pure in body and

in spirit, most lofty *mandarin*," said Piou-Lu, "and when it died under the knife, I ordered its soul to pass into its shadow, which can never be killed. Hence the shadow of the duck has all the colours as well as the intelligence of the real duck that gave it birth."

"And to what end has the very wise Piou-Lu created this beautiful duck-shadow?" asked the *mandarin*.

"The cultivated Wei-chang-tze shall immediately behold," answered the conjurer, drawing from his wide sleeve a piece of rock-salt and flinging it to the farther end of the room. He had hardly done this when a terrific sound, between a bark and a howl, issued from the dim corner into which he had cast the rock-salt, and immediately a large grey wolf issued wonderfully from out of the twilight, and rushed with savage fangs upon the shadow of the beautiful duck.

"Why, it is a wolf from the forests of Mantchouria! "exclaimed Wei-chang-tze, rather alarmed at this frightful apparition. "This is no shadow, but a living and bloodthirsty beast."

"Let my lord observe and have no fear," said Piou-Lu, tranquilly.

The wolf seemed rather confounded when, on making a snap at the beautiful duck, his sharp fangs met no resistance, while the bird flew with wonderful venom straight at his fiery eyes. He growled, and snapped, and tore with his claws at the agile shadow that fluttered around and over him, but all to no purpose. As well might the hound leap at the reflection of the deer in the pool where he drinks. The shadow of the beautiful duck seemed all the while to possess some strange, deadly influence over the savage wolf. His growls grew fainter and fainter, and his red and flaming eyes seemed to drop blood. His limbs quivered all over, and the rough hairs of his coat stood on end with terror and pain,—the shadow of the beautiful duck never ceasing all the time to fly straight at his eyes.

"The wolf is dying!" exclaimed Wei-chang-tze.

"He will die,—die like a dog," said Piou-Lu, in a tone of savage triumph.

And presently, as he predicted, the wolf gave two or three faint howls, turned himself round in a circle as if making a bed to sleep on, and then laid down and died. The shadow of the beautiful duck seemed now to be radiant with glory. It shook its bright wings, that were lovely and transparent as a rainbow, and, mounting on the dead body of the wolf, sat in majesty upon his grim and shaggy throne.

"And what means this strange exhibition, learned and wise conjurer?" asked Wei-chang-tze, with a sorely troubled air.

"I will tell you," said Piou-Lu, suddenly dropping his respectful and ceremonious language, and lifting his hand with an air of supreme power. "The *mandarin* duck, elegant, faithful, and courageous, is an emblem of the dynasty of Ming, that true Chinese race that ruled so splendidly in this land before the invaders usurped the throne. The cowardly and savage wolf is a symbol of the Mantchou Tartar robbers who slew our liberties, shaved our heads, and enchained our people. The time has now arrived when the duck has recovered its splendour and its courage, and is going to kill the wolf; for the wolf cannot bite it, as it works like a shadow in the twilight and mystery of secret association. This you know, Wei-chang-tze, as well as I."

"I have indeed heard of a rebel Chinese named Tién-té, who has raised a flame in our peaceful land, and who, proclaiming himself a lineal descendant of the dynasty of Ming, seeks to dethrone our wise and heavenly sovereign, Hién-foung."

"Lie not to me, Wei-chang-tze, for I know your inmost thoughts. Chinese as you are, I know that you hate the Tartar in your heart, but you are afraid to say so for fear of losing your head."

The *mandarin* was so stupefied at this audacious address that he could not reply, while the conjurer continued: "I come to make you an offer. Join the forces of the heaven-descended Emperor Tién-té. Join with him in expelling this tyrannical Tartar race from the Central Kingdom, and driving them back again to their cold hills and barren deserts. Fly with me to the Imperial camp, and bring with you your daughter Wu, the Golden Heart of the Lily, and I promise you the command of one third of the Imperial forces, and the Presidency of the College of Ceremonies."

"And who are you, who dare to ask of Wei-chang-tze to bestow on you his nobly-born daughter?" said Wei-chang-tze, starting in a rage from his couch.

"I!" replied Piou-Lu, shaking his conjurer's gown from his shoulders and displaying a splendid garment of yellow satin, on the breast of which was emblazoned the Imperial Dragon,—"I am your Emperor, Tién-té?"

"Ha!" screamed a shrill voice behind him at this moment, "here he is. The elegant and noble rebel for whose head our worthy Emperor has offered a reward of ten thousand silver tales. Here he is. Catch! beautiful and noble *mandarins*, catch him! and I will pay my creditors with the head-money."

Piou-Lu turned, and beheld the little tailor Hang-pou, at whose back were a whole file of soldiers and a number of *mandarins*. Wei-chang-tze shuddered, for in this compromise of his character he knew that his death was written if he fell into the Imperial hands.

THE CHAPTER OF "ALL IS OVER"

"Stately and temperate tailor," said Piou-Lu, calmly, "why do you wish to arrest me?"

"Ho! because I will get a reward, and I want to pay my debts," said Hang-pou, grinning spitefully.

"A reward for me, the miserable and marrowless conjurer, Piou-Lu! O, elegant cutter of summer gowns, your well-educated brains are not at home!"

"O, we know you well enough, mighty conjurer. You are none other than the contumacious rebel, Tién-té, who dares to claim the throne held by the wise and merciful Hién-Foung; and we will bear you to the court of Pekin in chains, so that you may wither in the light of his terrible eyes."

"You think you will get a reward of ten thousand silver *tales* for my head?" said Piou-Lu.

"Certainly," replied the little tailor, rubbing his hands with glee,— "certainly. His Unmatched and Isolated Majesty has promised it, and the Brother of the Sun never lies."

"Listen, inventive closer of symmetrical seams! Listen, and I will tell you what will become of your ten thousand silver *tales*. There is a long avenue leading to the Imperial treasury, and at every second step is an open hand. When the ten thousand *tales* are poured out, the first hand grasps a half, the second hand an eighth of the remaining half, the third hand grasps a fourth of the rest, and when the money-bags get down a little lower, all the hands grasp together; so that when the bags reach the little tailor Hang-pou, who stands stamping his feet very far down indeed, they are entirely empty; for Tartar robbers surround the throne, and a Tartar usurper sits upon it, and the great Chinese nation toils in its rice-fields to gild their palaces, and fill their *seraglios*, and for all they give get neither justice nor mercy.

" But I, Tién-té, the Heavenly Emperor of this Central Land, will ordain it otherwise, and hurl the false Dragon from his throne; for it is written in the *Book of Prognostics*, a copy of which was brought to me on the wings of a yellow serpent, that the dynasty of Han shall rule once more, and the Tartar wolves perish miserably out of the Land of Flowers."

"This is treason against the Light of the Universe, our most gracious Emperor," said the Mandarin Lin. "You shall have seventy times seven pounds of cold iron put upon your neck for these blasphemies, and I will promise you that many bamboo splinters shall be driven up under your rebellious nails."

"Let our ears be no longer filled with these atrocious utterances!" cried Hang-pou. "brave and splendid *mandarins*, order your terrifying tigers to arrest this depraved rebel, in order that we may hasten with him to Pekin."

"Before you throw the chains of sorrow around my neck, tailor of celestial inspirations," said Piou-Lu, with calm mockery,—"before the terrible weight of your just hand falls upon me, I pray you, if you would oblige me, to look at that duck." So saying, Piou-Lu pointed to where the shadow of the duck was sitting on the body of the wolf.

"O, what a beautiful duck!" cried Hang-pou, with glistening eyes, and clapping his hands. "Let us try and catch him!"

"It is indeed a majestic duck," said Mandarin Lin, gravely stroking his moustache. "I am favourable to his capture."

"You will wait until we catch the duck, illustrious rebel!" said Hang-pou to Piou-Lu, very innocently, never turning his eyes from the duck, to which they seemed to be glued by some singular spell of attraction.

"I will talk with the Mandarin Wei-chang-tze while you put your noble manoeuvres into motion," answered Piou-Lu.

"Now let us steal upon the duck," said Hang-pou. "Handsomely-formed duck, we entreat of you to remain as quiet as possible, in order that we may grasp you in our hands."

Then, as if actuated by a single impulse, the entire crowd, with the exception of Wei-chang-tze and Piou-Lu, moved toward the duck. The *mandarins* stepped on tiptoe, with bent bodies, and little black eyes glistening with eagerness; Hang-pou crawled on his belly like a serpent; and the soldiers, casting aside their bows and shields, crept, with their hands upon their sides, toward the beautiful bird. The duck remained perfectly quiet, its variegated wings shining like painted tale, and its neck lustrous as the court robe of a first-class *mandarin*. The crowd scarcely breathed, so intense was their eagerness to capture the duck; and they moved slowly forward, gradually surrounding it.

Hang-pou was the first to make a clutch at the bird, but he was very much astonished to find his hand closing on empty air, while the duck remained seated on the wolf, as still as a picture.

"Miserable tailor!" cried Mandarin Liu, "your hand is a sieve, with meshes wide enough to strain elephants. How can you catch the beautiful duck? Behold me!" and Mandarin Lin made a rapid and well-calculated dive at the duck. To the wonderment of everyone except Piou-Lu and Wei-chang-tze, the duck seemed to ooze through his fingers, and, escaping, flew away to the other end of the room.

"If my hand is a sieve," said Hang-pou, "it is evident that the noble *mandarin's* hand is not a wall of beaten copper, for it lets ducks fly through with wonderful ease."

"It is a depraved and abominable duck, of criminal parentage," said Mandarin Lin, in a terrible rage; "and I vow, by the whiskers of the Dragon, that I will catch it and burn it on a spit."

"O, yes! "cried the entire crowd,—*Mandarins*, soldiers, and the little tailor,—all now attracted to the chase of the duck by a power that they could no longer resist. "O, yes! we will most assuredly capture this little duck, and, depriving him of his feathers, punish him on a spit that is exceedingly hot."

So, the chase commenced. Here and there, from one corner to the other, up the walls, on the altar of the household gods,—in short, in every possible portion of the large room, did the *mandarins*, the little tailor, and the soldiers pursue the shadow of the beautiful duck. Never was seen such a duck. It seemed to be in twenty places at a time. One moment Mandarin Lin would throw himself bodily on the bird, in hopes of crushing it, and would call out triumphantly that now indeed he had the duck; but the words would be hardly out of his mouth when a loud shout from the rest of the party would disabuse his mind, and, turning, he would behold the duck marching proudly down the centre of the floor.

Another time a soldier would declare that he had the duck in his breeches pocket; but while his neighbours were carefully probing that recess the duck would be seen calmly emerging from his right-hand sleeve. One time Hang-Pou sat down suddenly on the mouth of a large china jar, and resolutely refused to stir, declaring that he had seen the duck enter the jar, and that he was determined to sit upon the mouth until the demon of a duck was starved to death.

But even while uttering his heroic determination, his mouth was seen to open very wide, and, to the astonishment of all, the duck flew out. In an instant, the whole crowd was after him again; Mandarin Hy-le tumbled over Mandarin Ching-tze, and 'Mandarin Lin nearly drove his head through Hang-pou's stomach. The unhappy wretches began now to perspire and grow faint with fatigue. but the longer the chase went on the hotter it grew. There was no rest for any of them. From corner to corner, from side to side,—now in one direction, now in another,—no matter whither the duck flew, they were compelled to follow. Their faces streamed, and their legs seemed ready to sink under them. Their eyeballs were ready to start out of their heads, and they had the air of government couriers who had travelled five hundred *li* in eleven days. They were nearly dead.

"Those men will surely perish, illustrious claimant of the throne," said Wei-chang-tze, gazing with astonishment at this mad chase.

"Let them perish!" said the conjurer; "so will perish all the enemies of the Celestial sovereign, Tién-té. Wei-chang-tze, once more, do you accept my offer'? If you remain here, you will be sent to Pekin in chains; if you come with me, I will gird your waist with the scarf of Perpetual Delight. We want wise men like you to guide our armies, and—"

"And the illustrious Tién-té loves the *mandarin's* daughter," said Wei-chang-tze, roguishly finishing the sentence. "Light of the Universe and Son of Heaven, Wei-chang-tze is your slave!"

Piou-Lu—for I still call him by his conjurer's name—gave a low whistle, and, obedient to the summons, Wu's delicate shape came gliding from the corridor toward her lover, with the dainty step of a young fawn going to the fountain.

"Wu," said Piou-Lu, "the marble is carved, and the hour is come."

"My father, then, has consented?" said Wu, looking timidly at her father.

"When the Emperor of the Central Land condescends to woo, what father dare refuse?" said Wei-chang-tze.

"Emperor!" said Wu, opening her black eyes with wonder. "My Piou-Lu an Emperor!"

"I am indeed the son of the Dragon," said Piou-Lu, folding her to his breast, "and you shall sit upon a throne of ivory and gold."

"And I thought you were only a conjurer!" murmured Wu, hiding her head in his yellow gown.

"But how are we to leave this place?" asked Wei-chang-tze, looking alarmed. "The guard will seize us if they get knowledge of your presence."

"We shall be at my castle in the mountains of Tse-Hing, near the Kouéï-Lin, in less than a minute," answered Piou-Lu; "for to the possessor of the Dragon Fang all things are possible,"

Even as he spoke the ground began to slide from under their feet with wonderful rapidity, leaving them motionless and upright. Houses, walls, gardens, fields, all passed by them with the swiftness of a dream, until, in a few seconds, they found themselves in the mountain castle of Tién-té, where they were welcomed with a splendid hospitality. Wu became the favourite wife of the adventurous Emperor, and Wei-chang-tze one of his most famous generals.

The day after these events some Tartar soldiers entered Wei-chang-tze's house to search for the *mandarin*, when, in the reception-hall, they were confounded at finding a number of men lying dead upon the floor, while in the midst sat a beautiful duck, that immediately on their entrance flew out through a window, and was seen no more. The dead men were soon recognized, and it was the opinion of the people of Tching-tou that Wei-chang-tze had poisoned all the soldiers and *mandarins*, and then fled. The tailor, Hang-pou, being among the corpses, was found to have given his creditors the slip forever.

Victory still sits on the banner of Tién-té, and he will, without doubt, by the time that the tea is again fit to gather, sit upon the ancient throne of his ancestors.

Everything is now gracefully concluded.

The Child That Loved a Grave

Far away in the deep heart of a lonely country there was an old solitary churchyard. People were no longer buried there, for it had fulfilled its mission long, long ago, and its rank grass now fed a few vagrant goats that clambered over its ruined wall and roamed through the sad wilderness of graves. It was bordered all round with willows and gloomy expresses; and the rusty iron gate, seldom or ever opened, shrieked when the wind stirred it on its hinges as if some lost soul, condemned to wander in that desolate place forever, was shaking its bars and wailing at the terrible imprisonment.

In this churchyard, there was one grave unlike all the rest. The stone which stood at the head bore no name, but instead the curious device, rudely sculptured, of a sun uprising out of the sea. The grave was very small and covered with a thick growth of dock and nettle, and one might tell by its size that it was that of a little child.

Not far from the old churchyard a young boy lived with his parents in a dreary cottage; he was a dreamy, dark-eyed boy, who never played with the children of the neighbourhood, but loved to wander in the fields and lie by the banks of rivers, watching the leaves fall and the waters ripple, and the lilies sway their white heads on the bosom of the current. It was no wonder that his life was solitary and sad, for his parents were wild, wicked people who drank and quarrelled all day and all night, and the noises of their quarrels were heard in calm summer nights by the neighbours that lived in the village under the brow of the hill.

The boy was terrified at all this hideous strife, and his young soul shrank within him when he heard the oaths and the blows echoing through the dreary cottage, so he used to fly out into the fields where everything looked so calm and pure, and talk with the lilies in a low voice as if they were his friends.

In this way, he came to haunt the old churchyard, roaming through its half-buried headstones, and spelling out upon them the names of people that had gone from earth years and years ago. The little grave, nameless and neglected however, attracted him more than all others. The strange device of the sun uprising out of the sea was to him a perpetual source of mystery and wonder; and so, whether by day or night, when the fury of his parents drove him from his home, he used to wander there and lie amidst the thick grass and think who was buried beneath it.

In time, his love for the little grave grew so great that he adorned it after his childish fashion. He cleared away the docks and the nettles and the mulleins that grew so sombrely above it, and clipped the grass until it grew thick and soft as the carpet of heaven. Then he brought primroses from the green banks of dewy lanes where the hawthorn rained its white flowers, and red poppies from the cornfields, and blue-bells from the shadowy heart of the forest, and planted them around the grave. With the supple twigs of the silver osier he hedged it round with a little simple fence, and scraped the creeping mosses from the grey headstone until the little grave looked as if it might have been the grave of a good fairy.

Then he was content. All the long summer days he would lie upon it with his arms clasping its swelling mound, while the soft wind with wavering will would come and play about him and timidly lift his hair. From the hillside, he heard the shouts of the village boys at play, and sometimes one of them would come and ask him to join in their sports; but he would look at him with his calm, dark eyes and gently answer no; and the boy, awed and flushed, would steal back to his companions and speak in whispers about the child that loved a grave.

In truth, he loved the little grave better than all play. The stillness of the churchyard, the scent of the wild flowers, the golden checkers of the sunlight falling through the trees and playing over the grass were all delights to him. He would lie on his back for hours gazing up at the summer sky and watching the while clouds sailing across it, and wondering if they were the souls of good people sailing home to heaven. But when the black thunder-clouds came up bulging with passionate tears, and bursting with sound and fire, he would think of his bad parents at home, and, turning to the grave, lay his little cheek against it as if it were a brother.

So, the summer went passing into autumn. The trees grew sad and shivered as the time approached when the fierce wind would strip them of their cloaks, and the rains and the storms bullet their naked limbs. The primroses grew pale and withered, but in their last moments seemed to look up at the child smilingly, as if to say, "Do not weep for us. We will come again next year." But the sadness of the season came over him as the winter approached, and he often wet the little grave with his tears, and kissed the grey headstone, as one kisses a friend that is about to depart for years.

One evening toward the close of autumn, when the woods looked brown and grim, and the wind as it came over the hills had a fierce, wicked growl, the child heard, as he was sitting by the grave, the shriek of the old gate swinging upon its rusty hinges, and looking up he saw a strange procession enter. There were five men. Two bore between them what seemed to be a long box covered with black cloth, two more carried spades in their hands, while the fifth, a tall stern-faced man clad in a long cloak, walked at their head. As the child saw these men pass to and fro through the graveyard, stumbling over half-buried headstones, or stooping down and examining half-effaced inscriptions, his little heart almost ceased to beat, and he shrank behind the grey stone with the strange device in mortal terror.

The men walked to and fro, with the tall one at their head, searching steadily in the long grass, and occasionally pausing to consult. At last the leader turned and walked toward the little grave, and stooping down gazed at the grey stone. The moon had just risen, and its light fell on the quaint sculpture of the sun rising out of the sea. The tall man then beckoned to his companions. "I have found it," he said; "it is here." With that the four men came along, and all five stood by the grave. The child behind the stone could no longer breathe.

The two men bearing the long box laid it down in the grass, and taking off the black cloth, the child saw a little coffin of shining ebony covered with silver ornaments, and on the lid, wrought in silver, was the device of a sun uprising out of the sea, and the moon shone over all.

"Now to work!" said the tall man; and straightway the two that held the spades plunged them into the little grave. The child thought his heart would break; and, no longer able to restrain himself, he flung his body across the mound, and cried out to the strange leader.

"Oh, Sir!" he cried, sobbing, "do not touch my little grave! it is all I have to love in the world. Do not touch it; for all day long, I lie here with my arms about it, and it seems like my brother. I tend it, and keep the grass short and thick, and I promise you, if you will leave it to me, that next year I will plant about it the finest flowers in the meadows."

"Tush, child, you are a fool!" answered the stern-faced man. "This is a sacred duty that I have to perform. He who is buried here was a child like you; but he was of royal blood, and his ancestors dwelt in palaces. it is not meet that bones like his should rest in common soil. Across the sea a grand mausoleum awaits them, and I have come to take them with me and lay them in vaults of porphyry and marble, take him away, men, and to your work!"

So, the men dragged the child from the grave by main force, and laid him nearby in the grass, sobbing as if his heart would break; and then they dug up the grave. Through his tears he saw the small white bones gathered up and put in the ebony coffin, and heard the lid shut down, and saw the men shovel back the earth into the empty grave, and he felt as if they were robbers. Then they look up the coffin and retraced then steps. The gate shrieked once more on its hinges, and the child was alone.

He returned home silent, and tearless, and white as any ghost. When he went to his little bed he called his father, and told him he was going to die, and asked him to have him buried in the little grave that had a grey headstone with a sun rising out of the sea carved upon it. The father laughed, and told him to go to sleep; but when morning came the child was dead!

They buried him where he wished; and when the sod was patted smooth, and the funeral procession departed, that nigh a new star came out in heaven and watched above the grave.

The Diamond Lens

1: THE BENDING OF THE TWIG.

From a very early period of my life the entire bent of my inclinations had been towards microscopic investigations. When I was not more than ten years old, a distant relative of our family, hoping to astonish my inexperience, constructed a simple microscope for me, by drilling in a disk of copper a small hole, in which a drop of pure water was sustained by capillary attraction. This very primitive apparatus, magnifying some fifty diameters, presented, it is true, only indistinct and imperfect forms, but still sufficiently wonderful to work up my imagination to a preternatural state of excitement.

Seeing me so interested in this rude instrument, my cousin explained to me all that he knew about the principles of the microscope, related to me a few of the wonders which had been accomplished through its agency, and ended by promising to send me one regularly constructed, immediately on his return to the city. I counted the days, the hours, the minutes, that intervened between that promise and his departure.

Meantime I was not idle. Every transparent substance that bore the remotest resemblance to a lens I eagerly seized upon, and employed in vain attempts to realise that instrument, the theory of whose construction I as yet only vaguely comprehended. All panes of glass containing those oblate spheroidal knots familiarly known as "bull's-eyes" were ruthlessly destroyed, in the hope of obtaining lenses of marvellous power. I even went so far as to extract the crystalline humour from the eyes of fishes and animals, and endeavoured to press it into the microscopic service. I plead guilty to having stolen the glasses from my Aunt Agatha's spectacles, with a dim idea of grinding them into lenses of wondrous magnifying properties,—in which attempt it is scarcely necessary to say that I totally failed.

At last the promised instrument came. It was of that order known as Field's simple microscope, and had cost perhaps about fifteen dollars. As far as educational purposes went, a better apparatus could not have been selected. Accompanying it was a small treatise on the microscope,—its history, uses, and discoveries. I comprehended then for the first time the *Arabian Nights' Entertainments.* The dull veil of ordinary existence that hung across the world seemed suddenly to roll away, and to lay bare a land of enchantments. I felt towards my companions as the seer might feel towards the ordinary masses of men. I held conversations with nature in a tongue which they could not understand. I was in daily communication with living wonders, such as they never imagined in their wildest visions.

I penetrated beyond the external portal of things, and roamed through the sanctuaries. Where they beheld only a drop of rain slowly rolling down the window-glass, I saw a universe of beings animated with all the passions common to physical life, and convulsing their minute sphere with struggles as fierce and protracted as those of men. In the common spots of mould, which my mother, good housekeeper that she was, fiercely scooped away from her jam pots, there abode for me, under the name of mildew, enchanted gardens, filled with dells and avenues of the densest foliage and most astonishing verdure, while from the fantastic boughs of these microscopic forests hung strange fruits glittering with green, and silver, and gold.

It was no scientific thirst that at this time filled my mind. It was the pure enjoyment of a poet to whom a world of wonders has been disclosed. I talked of my solitary pleasures to none. Alone with my microscope, I dimmed my sight, day after day and night after night, poring over the marvels which it unfolded to me. I was like one who, having discovered the ancient Eden still existing in all its primitive glory, should resolve to enjoy it in solitude, and never betray to mortal the secret of its locality. The rod of my life was bent at this moment. I destined myself to be a microscopist.

Of course, like every novice, I fancied myself a discoverer. I was ignorant at the time of the thousands of acute intellects engaged in the same pursuit as myself, and with the advantage of instruments a thousand times more powerful than mine. The names of Leeuwenhoek, Williamson, Spencer, Ehrenberg, Schultz, Dujardin, Schact, and Schleiden were then entirely unknown to me, or if known, I was ignorant of their patient and wonderful researches. In every fresh specimen of cryptogamia which I placed beneath my instrument I believed that I discovered wonders of which the world was as yet ignorant. I remember well the thrill of delight and admiration that shot through me the first time that I discovered the common wheel animalcule (*Rotifera vulgaris*) expanding and contracting its flexible spokes, and seemingly rotating through the water. Alas! as I grew older, and obtained some works treating of my favourite study, I found that I was only on the threshold of a science to the investigation of which some of the greatest men of the age were devoting their lives and intellects.

As I grew up, my parents, who saw but little likelihood of anything practical resulting from the examination of bits of moss and drops of water through a brass tube and a piece of glass, were anxious that I should choose a profession. It was their desire that I should enter the counting-house of my uncle, Ethan Blake, a prosperous merchant, who carried on business in New York. This suggestion I decisively combated. I had no taste for trade; I should only make a failure; in short, I refused to become a merchant.

But it was necessary for me to select some pursuit. My parents were staid New England people, who insisted on the necessity of labour; and therefore, although, thanks to the bequest of my poor Aunt Agatha, I should, on coming of age, inherit a small fortune sufficient to place me above want, it was decided that, instead of waiting for this, I should act the nobler part, and employ the intervening years in rendering myself independent.

After much cogitation, I complied with the wishes of my family, and selected a profession. I determined to study medicine at the New York Academy. This disposition of my future suited me. A removal from my relatives would enable me to dispose of my time as I pleased without fear of detection. As long as I paid my Academy fees, I might shirk attending the lectures if I chose; and, as I never had the remotest intention of standing an examination, there was no danger of my being "plucked." Besides, a metropolis was the place for me. There I could obtain excellent instruments, the newest publications, intimacy with men of pursuits kindred with my own,—in short, all things necessary to insure a profitable devotion of my life to my beloved science. I had an abundance of money, few desires that were not bounded by my illuminating mirror on one side and my object-glass on the other; what, therefore, was to prevent my becoming an illustrious investigator of the veiled worlds! It was with the most buoyant hope that I left my New England home and established myself in New York.

2: The Longing of a Man of Science.

My first step, of course, was to find suitable apartments. These I obtained, after a couple of days' search, in Fourth Avenue; a very pretty second-floor unfurnished, containing sitting-room, bedroom, and a smaller apartment which I intended to fit up as a laboratory. I furnished my lodgings simply, but rather elegantly, and then devoted all my energies to the adornment of the temple of my worship. I visited Pike, the celebrated optician, and passed in review his splendid collection of microscopes,—Field's Compound, Hingham's, Spencer's, Nachet's Binocular, (that founded on the principles of the stereoscope,) and at length fixed upon that form known as Spencer's Trunnion Microscope, as combining the greatest number of improvements with an almost perfect freedom from tremor.

Along with this I purchased every possible accessory,—draw-tubes, micrometers, a *camera-lucida*, lever-stage, chromatic condensers, white cloud illuminators, prisms, parabolic condensers, polarising apparatus, forceps, aquatic boxes, fishing-tubes, with a host of other articles, all of which would have been useful in the hands of an experienced microscopist, but, as I afterwards discovered, were not of the slightest present value to me. It takes years of practice to know how to use a complicated microscope. The optician looked suspiciously at me as I made these wholesale purchases. He evidently was uncertain whether to set me down as some scientific celebrity or a madman. I think he inclined to the latter belief I suppose I was mad. Every great genius is mad upon the subject in which he is greatest. The unsuccessful madman is disgraced and called a lunatic.

Mad or not, I set myself to work with a zeal which few scientific students have ever equalled. I had everything to learn relative to the delicate study upon which I had embarked,—a study involving the most earnest patience, the most rigid analytic powers, the steadiest hand, the most untiring eye, the most refined and subtle manipulation.

For a long time, half my apparatus lay inactively on the shelves of my laboratory, which was now most amply furnished with every possible contrivance for facilitating my investigations. The fact was that I did not know how to use some of my scientific implements,—never having been taught microscopies,—and those whose use I understood theoretically were of little avail, until by practice I could attain the necessary delicacy of handling. Still, such was the fury of my ambition, such the untiring perseverance of my experiments, that, difficult of credit as it may be, in the course of one year I became theoretically and practically an accomplished microscopist.

During this period of my labours, in which I submitted specimens of every substance that came under my observation to the action of my lenses, I became a discoverer,—in a small way, it is true, for I was very young, but still a discoverer. It was I who destroyed Ehrenberg's theory that the *Volvox globator* was an animal, and proved that his "monads" with stomachs and eyes were merely phases of the formation of a vegetable cell, and were, when they reached their mature state, incapable of the act of conjugation, or any true generative act, without which no organism rising to any stage of life higher than vegetable can be said to be complete. It was I who resolved the singular problem of rotation in the cells and hairs of plants into ciliary attraction, in spite of the assertions of Mr. Wenham and others, that my explanation was the result of an optical illusion.

But notwithstanding these discoveries, laboriously and painfully made as they were, I felt horribly dissatisfied. At every step, I found myself stopped by the imperfections of my instruments. Like all active microscopists, I gave my imagination full play. Indeed, it is a common complaint against many such, that they supply the defects of their instruments with the creations of their brains. I imagined depths beyond depths in nature which the limited power of my lenses prohibited me from exploring. I lay awake at night constructing imaginary microscopes of immeasurable power, with which I seemed to pierce through all the envelopes of matter down to its original atom.

How I cursed those imperfect mediums which necessity through ignorance compelled me to use! How I longed to discover the secret of some perfect lens, whose magnifying power should be limited only by the resolvability of the object, and which at the same time should be free from spherical and chromatic aberrations, in short from all the obstacles over which the poor microscopist finds himself continually stumbling! I felt convinced that the simple microscope, composed of a single lens of such vast yet perfect power was possible of construction. To attempt to bring the compound microscope up to such a pitch would have been commencing at the wrong end; this latter being simply a partially successful endeavour to remedy those very defects of the simple instrument, which, if conquered, would leave nothing to be desired.

It was in this mood of mind that I became a constructive microscopist. After another year passed in this new pursuit, experimenting on every imaginable substance,—glass, gems, flints, crystals, artificial crystals formed of the alloy of various vitreous materials,—in short, having constructed as many varieties of lenses as Argus had eyes, I found myself precisely where I started, with nothing gained save an extensive knowledge of glass-making. I was almost dead with despair. My parents were surprised at my apparent want of progress in my medical studies, (I had not attended one lecture since my arrival in the city,) and the expenses of my mad pursuit had been so great as to embarrass me very seriously.

I was in this frame of mind one day, experimenting in my laboratory on a small diamond,—that stone, from its great refracting power, having always occupied my attention more than any other,—when a young Frenchman, who lived on the floor above me, and who was in the habit of occasionally visiting me, entered the room.

I think that Jules Simon was a Jew. He had many traits of the Hebrew character: a love of jewellery, of dress, and of good living. There was something mysterious about him. He always had something to sell, and yet went into excellent society. When I say sell, I should perhaps have said peddle; for his operations were generally confined to the disposal of single articles,—a picture, for instance, or a rare carving in ivory, or a pair of duelling-pistols, or the dress of a Mexican *caballero*. When I was first furnishing my rooms, he paid me a visit, which ended in my purchasing an antique silver lamp, which he assured me was a Cellini,—it was handsome enough even for that,—and some other knickknacks for my sitting-room.

Why Simon should pursue this petty trade I never could imagine. He apparently had plenty of money, and had the *entrée* of the best houses in the city,—taking care, however, I suppose, to drive no bargains within the enchanted circle of the Upper Ten. I came at length to the conclusion that this peddling was but a mask to cover some greater object, and even went so far as to believe my young acquaintance to be implicated in the slave-trade. That, however, was none of my affair.

On the present occasion, Simon entered my room in a state of considerable excitement.

"*Ah! mon ami!*" he cried, before I could even offer him the ordinary salutation, "it has occurred to me to be the witness of the most astonishing things in the world. I promenade myself to the house of Madame —— How does the little animal—*le renard*—name himself in the Latin?"

"Vulpes," I answered.

"Ah! yes,—Vulpes. I promenade myself to the house of Madame Vulpes."

"The spirit medium?"

"Yes, the great medium. Great heavens! what a woman! I write on a slip of paper many of questions concerning affairs the most secret,—affairs that conceal themselves in the abysses of my heart the most profound; and behold! by example! what occurs? This devil of a woman makes me replies the most truthful to all of them. She talks to me of things that I do not love to talk of to myself What am I to think? I am fixed to the earth!"

"Am I to understand you, M. Simon, that this Mrs. Vulpes replied to questions secretly written by you, which questions related to events known only to yourself?"

"Ah! more than that, more than that," he answered, with an air of some alarm. "She related to me things—But," he added, after a pause, and suddenly changing his manner, "why occupy ourselves with these follies? It was all the biology, without doubt. It goes without saying that it has not my credence.—But why are we here, *mon ami?* It has occurred to me to discover the most beautiful thing as you can imagine,—a vase with green lizards on it, composed by the great Bernard Palissy. It is in my apartment; let us mount. I go to show it to you."

I followed Simon mechanically; but my thoughts were far from Palissy and his enamelled ware, although I, like him, was seeking in the dark a great discovery. This casual mention of the spiritualist, Madame Vulpes, set me on a new track. What if this spiritualism should be really a great fact? What if, through communication with more subtle organisms than my own, I could reach at a single bound the goal, which perhaps a life of agonizing mental toil would never enable me to attain?

While purchasing the Palissy vase from my friend Simon, I was mentally arranging a visit to Madame Vulpes.

3: THE SPIRIT OF LEEUWENHOEK

Two evenings after this, thanks to an arrangement by letter and the promise of an ample fee, I found Madame Vulpes awaiting me at her residence alone. She was a coarse-featured woman, with keen and rather cruel dark eyes, and an exceedingly sensual expression about her mouth and under jaw. She received me in perfect silence, in an apartment on the ground floor, very sparely furnished. In the centre of the room, close to where Mrs. Vulpes sat, there was a common round mahogany table. If I had come for the purpose of sweeping her chimney, the woman could not have looked more indifferent to my appearance. There was no attempt to inspire the visitor with awe. Everything bore a simple and practical aspect. This intercourse with the spiritual world was evidently as familiar an occupation with Mrs. Vulpes as eating her dinner or riding in an omnibus.

"You come for a communication, Mr. Linley?" said the medium, in a dry, business-like tone of voice.

"By appointment,—yes."

"What sort of communication do you want?—a written one?"

"Yes,—I wish for a written one."

"From any particular spirit?"

"Yes."

"Have you ever known this spirit on this earth?"

"Never. He died long before I was born. I wish merely to obtain from him some information which he ought to be able to give better than any other."

"Will you seat yourself at the table, Mr. Linley," said the medium, "and place your hands upon it?"

I obeyed,—Mrs. Vulpes being seated opposite to me, with her hands also on the table. We remained thus for about a minute and a half, when a violent succession of raps came on the table, on the back of my chair, on the floor immediately under my feet, and even on the windowpanes. Mrs. Vulpes smiled composedly.

"They are very strong tonight," she remarked. "You are fortunate." She then continued, "Will the spirits communicate with this gentleman?"

Vigorous affirmative.

"Will the particular spirit he desires to speak with communicate?"

A very confused rapping followed this question.

"I know what they mean," said Mrs. Vulpes, addressing herself to me; "they wish you to write down the name of the particular spirit that you desire to converse with. Is that so?" she added, speaking to her invisible guests.

That it was so was evident from the numerous affirmatory responses. While this was going on, I tore a slip from my pocket-book, and scribbled a name, under the table.

"Will this spirit communicate in writing with this gentleman?" asked the medium once more.

426

After a moment's pause, her hand seemed to be seized with a violent tremor, shaking so forcibly that the table vibrated. She said that a spirit had seized her hand and would write. I handed her some sheets of paper that were on the table, and a pencil. The latter she held loosely in her hand, which presently began to move over the paper with a singular and seemingly involuntary motion. After a few moments had elapsed, she handed me the paper, on which I found written, in a large, uncultivated hand, the words, "He is not here, but has been sent for." A pause of a minute or so now ensued, during which Mrs. Vulpes remained perfectly silent, but the raps continued at regular intervals. When the short period I mention had elapsed, the hand of the medium was again seized with its convulsive tremor, and she wrote, under this strange influence, a few words on the paper, which she handed to me. They were as follows:—

"I am here. Question me.

"Leeuwenhoek."

I was astounded. The name was identical with that I had written beneath the table, and carefully kept concealed. Neither was it at all probable that an uncultivated woman like Mrs. Vulpes should know even the name of the great father of microscopies. It may have been biology; but this theory was soon doomed to be destroyed. I wrote on my slip—still concealing it from Mrs. Vulpes—a series of questions, which, to avoid tediousness, I shall place with the responses, in the order in which they occurred:—

I.—Can the microscope be brought to perfection?

Spirit.—Yes.

I.—Am I destined to accomplish this great task?

Spirit.—You are.

I.—I wish to know how to proceed to attain this end. For the love which you bear to science, help me!

Spirit.—A diamond of one hundred and forty carats, submitted to electro-magnetic currents for a long period, will experience a rearrangement of its atoms *inter se*, and from that stone you will form the universal lens.

I.—Will great discoveries result from the use of such a lens?

Spirit.—So great that all that has gone before is as nothing.

I.—But the refractive power of the diamond is so immense, that the image will be formed within the lens. How is that difficulty to be surmounted?

Spirit.—Pierce the lens through its axis, and the difficulty is obviated. The image will be formed in the pierced space, which will itself serve as a tube to look through. Now I am called. Goodnight.

I cannot at all describe the effect that these extraordinary communications had upon me. I felt completely bewildered. No biological theory could account for the *discovery* of the lens. The medium might, by means of biological *rapport* with my mind, have gone so far as to read my questions, and reply to them coherently. But biology could not enable her to discover that magnetic currents would so alter the crystals of the diamond as to remedy its previous defects, and admit of its being polished into a perfect lens. Some such theory may have passed through my head, it is true; but if so, I had forgotten it.

In my excited condition of mind there was no course left but to become a convert, and it was in a state of the most painful nervous exaltation that I left the medium's house that evening. She accompanied me to the door, hoping that I was satisfied. The raps followed us as we went through the hall, sounding on the balusters, the flooring, and even the lintels of the door. I hastily expressed my satisfaction, and escaped hurriedly into the cool night air. I walked home with but one thought possessing me,—how to obtain a diamond of the immense size required. My entire means multiplied a hundred times over would have been inadequate to its purchase. Besides, such stones are rare, and become historical. I could find such only in the regalia of Eastern or European monarchs.

4: THE EYE OF MORNING

There was a light in Simon's room as I entered my house. A vague impulse urged me to visit him. As I opened the door of his sitting-room unannounced, he was bending, with his back toward me, over a carcel lamp, apparently engaged in minutely examining some object which he held in his hands. As I entered, he started suddenly, thrust his hand into his breast pocket, and turned to me with a face crimson with confusion.

"What!" I cried, "poring over the miniature of some fair lady? Well, don't blush so much; I won't ask to see it."

Simon laughed awkwardly enough, but made none of the negative protestations usual on such occasions. He asked me to take a seat.

"Simon," said I, "I have just come from Madame Vulpes."

This time Simon turned as white as a sheet, and seemed stupefied, as if a sudden electric shock had smitten him. He babbled some incoherent words, and went hastily to a small closet where he usually kept

428

his liquors. Although astonished at his emotion, I was too preoccupied with my own idea to pay much attention to anything else.

"You say truly when you call Madame Vulpes a devil of a woman," I continued. "Simon, she told me wonderful things tonight, or rather was the means of telling me wonderful things. Ah! if I could only get a diamond that weighed one hundred and forty carats! "

Scarcely had the sigh with which I uttered this desire died upon my lips, when Simon, with the aspect of a wild beast, glared at me savagely, and, rushing to the mantelpiece, where some foreign weapons hung on the wall, caught up a Malay *creese*, and brandished it furiously before him.

"No!" he cried in French, into which he always broke when excited. "No! you shall not have it! You are perfidious! You have consulted with that demon, and desire my treasure! But I will die first! Me! I am brave! You cannot make me fear!"

All this, uttered in a loud voice trembling with excitement, astounded me. I saw at a glance that I had accidentally trodden upon the edges of Simon's secret, whatever it was. It was necessary to reassure him.

"My dear Simon," I said, "I am entirely at a loss to know what you mean. I went to Madame Vulpes to consult with her on a scientific problem, to the solution of which I discovered that a diamond of the size I just mentioned was necessary. You were never alluded to during the evening, nor, so far as I was concerned, even thought of. What can be the meaning of this outburst? If you happen to have a set of valuable diamonds in your possession, you need fear nothing from me. The diamond which I require you could not possess; or, if you did possess it, you would not be living here."

Something in my tone must have completely reassured him; for his expression immediately changed to a sort of constrained merriment, combined, however, with a certain suspicious attention to my movements. He laughed, and said that I must bear with him; that he was at certain moments subject to a species of vertigo, which betrayed itself in incoherent speeches, and that the attacks passed off as rapidly as they came. He put his weapon aside while making this explanation, and endeavoured, with some success, to assume a more cheerful air.

All this did not impose on me in the least. I was too much accustomed to analytical labours to be baffled by so flimsy a veil. I determined to probe the mystery to the bottom.

"Simon," I said, gayly, "let us forget all this over a bottle of Burgundy. I have a case of Lausseure's *Clos Vougeot* downstairs, fragrant with the odours and ruddy with the sunlight of the Côte d'Or. Let us have up a couple of bottles. What say you?"

"With all my heart," answered Simon, smilingly.

I produced the wine and we seated ourselves to drink. It was of a famous vintage, that of 1848, a year when war and wine throve together,—and its pure but powerful juice seemed to impart renewed vitality to the system. By the time we had half-finished the second bottle, Simon's head, which I knew was a weak one, had begun to yield, while I remained calm as ever, only that every draught seemed to send a flush of vigour through my limbs. Simon's utterance became more and more indistinct. He took to singing French *chansons* of a not very moral tendency. I rose suddenly from the table just at the conclusion of one of those incoherent verses, and, fixing my eyes on him with a quiet smile, said: "Simon, I have deceived you. I learned your secret this evening. You may as well be frank with me. Mrs. Vulpes, or rather one of her spirits, told me all."

He started with horror. His intoxication seemed for the moment to fade away, and he made a movement towards the weapon that he had a short time before laid down. I stopped him with my hand.

"Monster!" he cried, passionately, "I am ruined! What shall I do? You shall never have it! I swear by my mother!"

"I don't want it," I said; "rest secure, but be frank with me. Tell me all about it."

The drunkenness began to return. He protested with maudlin earnestness that I was entirely mistaken,—that I was intoxicated; then asked me to swear eternal secrecy, and promised to disclose the mystery to me. I pledged myself, of course, to all. With an uneasy look in his eyes, and hands unsteady with drink and nervousness, he drew a small case from his breast and opened it. Heavens! How the mild lamp-light was shivered into a thousand prismatic arrows, as it fell upon a vast rose-diamond that glittered in the case! I was no judge of diamonds, but I saw at a glance that this was a gem of rare size and purity. I looked at Simon with wonder, and—must I confess it?—with envy. How could he have obtained this treasure?

In reply to my questions, I could just gather from his drunken statements (of which, I fancy, half the incoherence was affected) that he had been superintending a gang of slaves engaged in diamond-washing in Brazil; that he had seen one of them secrete a diamond, but, instead of informing his employers, had quietly watched the negro

430

until he saw him bury his treasure; that he had dug it up and fled with it, but that as yet he was afraid to attempt to dispose of it publicly,—so valuable a gem being almost certain to attract too much attention to its owner's antecedents,—and he had not been able to discover any of those obscure channels by which such matters are conveyed away safely. He added, that, in accordance with oriental practice, he had named his diamond with the fanciful title of "The Eye of Morning."

While Simon was relating this to me, I regarded the great diamond attentively. Never had I beheld anything so beautiful. All the glories of light, ever imagined or described, seemed to pulsate in its crystalline chambers. Its weight, as I learned from Simon, was exactly one hundred and forty carats. Here was an amazing coincidence. The hand of destiny seemed in it. On the very evening when the spirit of Leeuwenhoek communicates to me the great secret of the microscope, the priceless means which he directs me to employ start up within my easy reach! I determined, with the most perfect deliberation, to possess myself of Simon's diamond.

I sat opposite to him while he nodded over his glass, and calmly revolved the whole affair. I did not for an instant contemplate so foolish an act as a common theft, which would of course be discovered, or at least necessitate flight and concealment, all of which must interfere with my scientific plans. There was but one step to be taken,—to kill Simon. After all, what was the life of a little peddling Jew, in comparison with the interests of science? Human beings are taken every day from the condemned prisons to be experimented on by surgeons. This man, Simon, was by his own confession a criminal, a robber, and I believed on my soul a murderer. He deserved death quite as much as any felon condemned by the laws: why should I not, like government, contrive that his punishment should contribute to the progress of human knowledge?

The means for accomplishing everything I desired lay within my reach. There stood upon the mantel-piece a bottle half full of French laudanum. Simon was so occupied with his diamond, which I had just restored to him, that it was an affair of no difficulty to drug his glass. In a quarter of an hour he was in a profound sleep.

I now opened his waistcoat, took the diamond from the inner pocket in which he had placed it, and removed him to the bed, on which I laid him so that his feet hung down over the edge. I had possessed myself of the Malay *creese*, which I held in my right hand, while with the other I discovered as accurately as I could by pulsation the exact locality of the heart. It was essential that all the aspects of his death should lead to the surmise of self-murder. I calculated the exact angle at which it was probable that the weapon, if levelled by Simon's own hand, would enter his breast; then with one powerful blow I thrust it up to the hilt in the very spot which I desired to penetrate.

A convulsive thrill ran through Simon's limbs. I heard a smothered sound issue from his throat, precisely like the bursting of a large air-bubble, sent up by a diver, when it reaches the surface of the water; he turned half round on his side, and, as if to assist my plans more effectually, his right hand, moved by some mere spasmodic impulse, clasped the handle of the *creese*, which it remained holding with extraordinary muscular tenacity. Beyond this there was no apparent struggle. The laudanum, I presume, paralyzed the usual nervous action. He must have died instantly.

There was yet something to be done. To make it certain that all suspicion of the act should be diverted from any inhabitant of the house to Simon himself, it was necessary that the door should be found in the morning *locked on the inside*. How to do this, and afterwards escape myself? Not by the window; that was a physical impossibility. Besides, I was determined that the windows *also* should be found bolted. The solution was simple enough. I descended softly to my own room for a peculiar instrument which I had used for holding small slippery substances, such as minute spheres of glass, etc. This instrument was nothing more than a long slender hand-vice, with a very powerful grip, and a considerable leverage, which last was accidentally owing to the shape of the handle.

Nothing was simpler than, when the key was in the lock, to seize the end of its stem in this vice, through the keyhole, from the outside, and so lock the door. Previously, however, to doing this, I burned a number of papers on Simon's hearth. Suicides almost always burn papers before they destroy themselves. I also emptied some more laudanum into Simon's glass,—having first removed from it all traces of wine,—cleaned the other wine-glass, and brought the bottles away with me. If traces of two persons drinking had been found in the room, the question naturally would have arisen, Who was the second?

Besides, the wine-bottles might have been identified as belonging to me. The laudanum I poured out to account for its presence in his stomach, in case of a *post-mortem* examination. The theory naturally would be, that he first intended to poison himself, but, after swallowing a little of the drug, was either disgusted with its taste, or changed his mind from other motives, and chose the dagger. These arrangements made, I walked out, leaving the gas burning, locked the door with my vice, and went to bed.

Simon's death was not discovered until nearly three in the afternoon. The servant, astonished at seeing the gas burning,—the light streaming on the dark landing from under the door,—peeped through the keyhole and saw Simon on the bed. She gave the alarm. The door was burst open, and the neighbourhood was in a fever of excitement.

Everyone in the house was arrested, myself included. There was an inquest; but no clew to his death beyond that of suicide could be obtained. Curiously enough, he had made several speeches to his friends the preceding week, that seemed to point to self-destruction. One gentleman swore that Simon had said in his presence that "he was tired of life." His landlord affirmed that Simon, when paying him his last month's rent, remarked that "he should not pay him rent much longer." All the other evidence corresponded,—the door locked inside, the position of the corpse, the burnt papers. As I anticipated, no one knew of the possession of the diamond by Simon, so that no motive was suggested for his murder. The jury, after a prolonged examination, brought in the usual verdict, and the neighbourhood once more settled down into its accustomed quiet.

5: ANIMULA

The three months succeeding Simon's catastrophe I devoted night and day to my diamond lens. I had constructed a vast galvanic battery, composed of nearly two thousand pairs of plates,—a higher power I dared not use, lest the diamond should be calcined. By means of this enormous engine I was enabled to send a powerful current of electricity continually through my great diamond, which it seemed to me gained in lustre every day.

At the expiration of a month I commenced the grinding and polishing of the lens, a work of intense toil and exquisite delicacy. The great density of the stone, and the care required to be taken with the curvatures of the surfaces of the lens, rendered the labour the severest and most harassing that I had yet undergone.

At last the eventful moment came; the lens was completed. I stood trembling on the threshold of new worlds. I had the realization of Alexander's famous wish before me. The lens lay on the table, ready to be placed upon its platform. My hand fairly shook as I enveloped a drop of water with a thin coating of oil of turpentine, preparatory to its examination,—a process necessary in order to prevent the rapid evaporation of the water. I now placed the drop on a thin slip of glass under the lens, and throwing upon it, by the combined aid of a prism and a mirror, a powerful stream of light, I approached my eye to the minute hole drilled through the axis of the lens. For an instant, I saw nothing save what seemed to be an illuminated chaos, a vast luminous abyss. A pure white light, cloudless and serene, and seemingly limitless as space itself, was my first impression. Gently, and with the greatest care, I depressed the lens a few hair's-breadths. The wondrous illumination still continued, but as the lens approached the object a scene of indescribable beauty was unfolded to my view.

I seemed to gaze upon a vast space, the limits of which extended far beyond my vision. An atmosphere of magical luminousness permeated the entire field of view. I was amazed to see no trace of *animalculous* life. Not a living thing, apparently, inhabited that dazzling expanse. I comprehended instantly that, by the wondrous power of my lens, I had penetrated beyond, the grosser particles of aqueous matter, beyond the realms of *infusoria* and *protozoa*, down to the original gaseous globule, into whose luminous interior I was gazing, as into an almost boundless dome filled with a supernatural radiance.

It was, however, no brilliant void into which I looked. On every side, I beheld beautiful inorganic forms, of unknown texture, and coloured with the most enchanting hues. These forms presented the appearance of what might be called, for want of a more specific definition, foliated clouds of the highest rarity; that is, they undulated and broke into vegetable formations, and were tinged with splendours compared with which the gilding of our autumn woodlands is as dross compared with gold. Far away into the illimitable distance stretched long avenues of these gaseous forests, dimly transparent, and painted with prismatic hues of unimaginable brilliancy.

The pendent branches waved along the fluid glades until every vista seemed to break through half-lucent ranks of many-colored drooping silken pennons. What seemed to be either fruits or flowers, pied with a thousand hues, lustrous and ever varying, bubbled from the crowns of this fairy foliage. No hills, no lakes, no rivers, no forms animate or inanimate, were to be seen, save those vast auroral copses that floated serenely in the luminous stillness, with leaves and fruits and flowers gleaming with unknown fires, unrealizable by mere imagination.

How strange, I thought, that this sphere should be thus condemned to solitude! I had hoped, at least, to discover some new form of animal life,—perhaps of a lower class than any with which we are at present acquainted, but still, some living organism. I found my newly discovered world, if I may so speak, a beautiful chromatic desert.

While I was speculating on the singular arrangements of the internal economy of Nature, with which she so frequently splinters into atoms our most compact theories, I thought I beheld a form moving slowly through the glades of one of the prismatic forests. I looked more attentively, and found that I was not mistaken. Words cannot depict the anxiety with which I awaited the nearer approach of this mysterious object. Was it merely some inanimate substance, held in suspense in the attenuated atmosphere of the globule? or was it an animal endowed with vitality and motion? It approached, flitting behind the gauzy, coloured veils of cloud-foliage, for seconds dimly revealed, then vanishing. At last the violet pennons that trailed nearest to me vibrated; they were gently pushed aside, and the form floated out into the broad light.

It was a female human shape. When I say human, I mean it possessed the outlines of humanity,—but there the analogy ends. Its adorable beauty lifted it illimitable heights beyond the loveliest daughter of Adam.

I cannot, I dare not, attempt to inventory the charms of this divine revelation of perfect beauty. Those eyes of mystic violet, dewy and serene, evade my words. Her long, lustrous hair following her glorious head in a golden wake, like the track sown in heaven by a falling star, seems to quench my most burning phrases with its splendours. If all the bees of Hybla nestled upon my lips, they would still sing but hoarsely the wondrous harmonies of outline that enclosed her form.

She swept out from between the rainbow-curtains of the cloud-trees into the broad sea of light that lay beyond. Her motions were those of some graceful naiad, cleaving, by a mere effort of her will, the clear, unruffled waters that fill the chambers of the sea. She floated forth with the serene grace of a frail bubble ascending through the still atmosphere of a June day. The perfect roundness of her limbs formed suave and enchanting curves. It was like listening to the most spiritual symphony of Beethoven the divine, to watch the harmonious flow of lines. This, indeed, was a pleasure cheaply purchased at any price. What cared I, if I had waded to the portal of this wonder through another's blood? I would have given my own to enjoy one such moment of intoxication and delight.

Breathless with gazing on this lovely wonder, and forgetful for an instant of everything save her presence, I withdrew my eye from the microscope eagerly,—alas! As my gaze fell on the thin slide that lay beneath my instrument, the bright light from mirror and from prism sparkled on a colourless drop of water! There, in that tiny bead of dew, this beautiful being was forever imprisoned. The planet Neptune was not more distant from me than she. I hastened once more to apply my eye to the microscope.

Animula (let me now call her by that dear name which I subsequently bestowed on her) had changed her position. She had again approached the wondrous forest, and was gazing earnestly upwards. Presently one of the trees—as I must call them—unfolded a long ciliary process, with which it seized one of the gleaming fruits that glittered on its summit, and, sweeping slowly down, held it within reach of Animula. The sylph took it in her delicate hand and began to eat. My attention was so entirely absorbed by her, that I could not apply myself to the task of determining whether this singular plant was or was not instinct with volition.

I watched her, as she made her repast, with the most profound attention. The suppleness of her motions sent a thrill of delight through my frame; my heart beat madly as she turned her beautiful eyes in the direction of the spot in which I stood. What would I not have given to have had the power to precipitate myself into that luminous ocean, and float with her through those groves of purple and gold! While I was thus breathlessly following her every movement, she suddenly started, seemed to listen for a moment, and then cleaving the brilliant ether in which she was floating, like a flash of light, pierced through the opaline forest, and disappeared.

Instantly a series of the most singular sensations attacked me. It seemed as if I had suddenly gone blind. The luminous sphere was still before me, but my daylight had vanished. What caused this sudden disappearance? Had she a lover or a husband? Yes, that was the solution! Some signal from a happy fellow-being had vibrated through the avenues of the forest, and she had obeyed the summons.

The agony of my sensations, as I arrived at this conclusion, startled me. I tried to reject the conviction that my reason forced upon me. I battled against the fatal conclusion,—but in vain. It was so. I had no escape from it. I loved an animalcule!

It is true that, thanks to the marvellous power of my microscope, she appeared of human proportions. Instead of presenting the revolting aspect of the coarser creatures, that live and struggle and die, in the more easily resolvable portions of the water-drop, she was fair and delicate and of surpassing beauty. But of what account was all that? Every time that my eye was withdrawn from the instrument, it fell on a miserable drop of water, within which, I must be content to know, dwelt all that could make my life lovely.

Could she but see me once! Could I for one moment pierce the mystical walls that so inexorably rose to separate us, and whisper all that filled my soul, I might consent to be satisfied for the rest of my life with the knowledge of her remote sympathy. It would be something to have established even the faintest personal link to bind us together,—to know that at times, when roaming through those enchanted glades, she might think of the wonderful stranger, who had broken the monotony of her life with his presence, and left a gentle memory in her heart!

But it could not be. No invention of which human intellect was capable could break down the barriers that nature had erected. I might feast my soul upon her wondrous beauty, yet she must always remain ignorant of the adoring eyes that day and night gazed upon her, and, even when closed, beheld her in dreams. With a bitter cry of anguish, I fled from the room, and, flinging myself on my bed, sobbed myself to sleep like a child.

6: The Spilling of the Cup

I arose the next morning almost at daybreak, and rushed to my microscope. I trembled as I sought the luminous world in miniature that contained my all. Animula was there. I had left the gas-lamp, surrounded by its moderators, burning, when I went to bed the night before. I found the sylph bathing, as it were, with an expression of pleasure animating her features, in the brilliant light which surrounded her. She tossed her lustrous golden hair over her shoulders with innocent *coquetry*.

She lay at full length in the transparent medium, in which she supported herself with ease, and gambolled with the enchanting grace that the nymph Salmacis might have exhibited when she sought to conquer the modest Hermaphroditus. I tried an experiment to satisfy myself if her powers of reflection were developed. I lessened the lamp-light considerably. By the dim light that remained, I could see an expression of pain flit across her face. She looked upward suddenly, and her brows contracted. I flooded the stage of the microscope again with a full stream of light, and her whole expression changed. She sprang

437

forward like some substance deprived of all weight. Her eyes sparkled and her lips moved. Ah! if science had only the means of conducting and reduplicating sounds, as it does the rays of light, what carols of happiness would then have entranced my ears! what jubilant hymns to Adonais would have thrilled the illumined air!

I now comprehended how it was that the Count de Gabalis peopled his mystic world with sylphs,—beautiful beings whose breath of life was lambent fire, and who sported forever in regions of purest ether and purest light. The Rosicrucian had anticipated the wonder that I had practically realized.

How long this worship of my strange divinity went on thus I scarcely know. I lost all note of time. All day from early dawn, and far into the night, I was to be found peering through that wonderful lens. I saw no one, went nowhere, and scarce allowed myself sufficient time for my meals. My whole life was absorbed in contemplation as rapt as that of any of the Romish saints. Every hour that I gazed upon the divine form strengthened my passion,—a passion that was always overshadowed by the maddening conviction, that, although I could gaze on her at will, she never, never could behold me!

At length, I grew so pale and emaciated, from want of rest, and continual brooding over my insane love and its cruel conditions, that I determined to make some effort to wean myself from it. "Come," I said, "this is at best but a fantasy. Your imagination has bestowed on Animula charms which in reality she does not possess. Seclusion from female society has produced this morbid condition of mind. Compare her with the beautiful women of your own world, and this false enchantment will vanish."

I looked over the newspapers by chance. There I beheld the advertisement of a celebrated *danseuse* who appeared nightly at Niblo's. The Signorina Caradolce had the reputation of being the most beautiful as well as the most graceful woman in the world. I instantly dressed and went to the theatre.

The curtain drew up. The usual semicircle of fairies in white muslin were standing on the right toe around the enamelled flower-bank, of green canvas, on which the belated prince was sleeping. Suddenly a flute is heard. The fairies start. The trees open, the fairies all stand on the left toe, and the queen enters. It was the *signorina*. She bounded forward amid thunders of applause, and, lighting on one foot, remained poised in air. Heavens! was this the great enchantress that had drawn monarchs at her chariot-wheels? Those heavy muscular limbs, those thick ankles, those cavernous eyes, that stereotyped smile, those crudely painted cheeks! Where were the vermeil blooms, the liquid expressive eyes, the harmonious limbs of Animula?

The *signorina* danced. What gross, discordant movements! The play of her limbs was all false and artificial. Her bounds were painful athletic efforts; her poses were angular and distressed the eye. I could bear it no longer; with an exclamation of disgust that drew every eye upon me, I rose from my seat in the very middle of the *signorina's pas-de-fascination,* and abruptly quitted the house.

I hastened home to feast my eyes once more on the lovely form of my sylph, I felt that henceforth to combat this passion would be impossible. I applied my eye to the lens. Animula was there,—but what could have happened? Some terrible change seemed to have taken place during my absence. Some secret grief seemed to cloud the lovely features of her I gazed upon. Her face had grown thin and haggard; her limbs trailed heavily; the wondrous lustre of her golden hair had faded. She was ill! —ill, and I could not assist her! I believe at that moment I would have gladly forfeited all claims to my human birthright, if I could only have been dwarfed to the size of an animalcule, and permitted to console her from whom fate had forever divided me.

I racked my brain for the solution of this mystery. What was it that afflicted the sylph? She seemed to suffer intense pain. Her features contracted, and she even writhed, as if with some internal agony. The wondrous forests appeared also to have lost half their beauty. Their hues were dim and in some places faded away altogether. I watched Animula for hours with a breaking heart, and she seemed absolutely to wither away under my very eye.

Suddenly I remembered that I had not looked at the water-drop for several days. In fact, I hated to see it; for it reminded me of the natural barrier between Animula and myself. I hurriedly looked down on the stage of the microscope. The slide was still there,—but, great heavens! the water-drop had vanished! The awful truth burst upon me; it had evaporated, until it had become so minute as to be invisible to the naked eye; I had been gazing on its last atom, the one that contained Animula,—and she was dying!

I rushed again to the front of the lens, and looked through. Alas! the last agony had seized her. The rainbow-hued forests had all melted away, and Animula lay struggling feebly in what seemed to be a spot of dim light. Ah! the sight was horrible: the limbs once so round and lovely shrivelling up into nothings; the eyes—those eyes that shone like heaven.—being quenched into black dust; the lustrous golden hair now lank and discoloured. The last throe came. I beheld that final struggle of the blackening form—and I fainted.

When I awoke out of a trance of many hours, I found myself lying amid the wreck of my instrument, myself as shattered in mind and body as it. I crawled feebly to my bed, from which I did not rise for months.

They say now that I am mad; but they are mistaken. I am poor, for I have neither the heart nor the will to work; all my money is spent, and I live on charity. Young men's associations that love a joke invite me to lecture on Optics before them, for which they pay me, and laugh at me while I lecture. "Linley, the mad microscopist," is the name I go by. I suppose that I talk incoherently while I lecture. Who could talk sense when his brain is haunted by such ghastly memories, while ever and *anon* among the shapes of death I behold the radiant form of my lost Animula!

The Comet and I

1

I was walking down Broadway on last Tuesday night—alter having taken dinner with a sick friend—and on looking up at the clear blue sky, sown with such myriads of silver stars, I became filled with disgust at my ignorance of the noble science of astronomy. There were constellations distributed generally on all sides of me, and aristocratic stars of the first magnitude, and eccentric stars, remarkable for some peculiarity of form or habit, as Horace Greeley is remarkable for his boots, and yet I did not know the name of one of them. The Great Bear, Orion, Sirius, the Southern Cross, the Plough, and all the rest of them, might have been right over my head without my knowing anything at all about it. The fact is, that, with all due deference to astronomers, whenever any of these constellations were pointed out to me by some friend who was just learning the use of the globes, I never could detect the slightest similarity between them and the objects after which they were named.

"I know so little about astronomy," I muttered to myself, "that I must certainly write a book about it."

At this moment, I found myself opposite the New York Hospital, where the patient man with the long brass telescope is always ready, for a small remuneration, to sweep the sidereal heavens. While I was gazing upon this forlorn astronomer, and wondering whether a first-class star paid him as well as Miss Heron must have paid her enterprising New York manager, the idea of the comet, which is so soon to smash into us, crossed my mind.

"By Jove!" thought I, "I'll have a look for him. Who knows but he may be within sight? So that, having a little warning of his coming, I may go into New Jersey in order to be out of the way."

I suppose I must have given utterance to these thoughts aloud, for just as I was putting my hand in my pocket to feel if I had the necessary coin to entitle me to a peep through the telescope, I felt a tap on my shoulder, and, turning round, saw a queer, rubicund-looking little old man standing beside me. He was dressed in an odd flame-coloured suit, a red cap, and I declare most solemnly that I beheld, protruding from underneath his Raglan, a long, fan-shaped tail. This last, though, seemed more phantasmal than real; for when I tried to tread on it my foot passed as through vapor.

"Well, Sir! what do you want?" I demanded, angrily; for I felt annoyed at being tapped on the shoulder by so ridiculous a personage.

"Put up your money," answered the stranger; "don't spend it foolishly!"

"I'll spend my money if I like, Sir!" I replied, with dignity. "Besides, I wish to see if there is any sign of Charles the Twelfth's comet, which is expected every day."

"It won't be here till the evening of the eighteenth of June," said the stranger.

I own the preciseness and confidence of his assertion struck me as being remarkable.

"Pray, Sir, how do you know this so positively?" I demanded, with a half sneer.

"How do I know it? Because I am the Comet! Stay, here's my card." And so, saying, he pulled a steel card-case out of his pocket, and presented me with a small square of linen, on which was printed:

THE COMET
Of Charles, the Twelfth
At Home.
Thursday, 18th June, 1837.

"I hope I shall have the pleasure of seeing you on that evening," continued the Comet, with an air of elegant politeness, such as a *marquis* of the time of Louis XIV, would have exhibited in inviting me to a grand *fête*. "My cards, as you perceive, are of linen. The reason is, that I have them made of asbestos in order to insure their being incombustible. Otherwise they would take fire in my pocket."

I now remarked that the card was warm!

"Then you are really going to destroy the world on the day mentioned?" I said, inquiringly, feeling a decidedly uncomfortable feeling in my heart and throat.

"Not at all," answered the Comet. "My devastation will be only partial. I have come to cleanse rather than to destroy. Purification by fire is what will be accomplished by my advent; and I will, as it were, cauterise all the sores of the world."

"But what brings you on in advance of your arrival—if you will excuse the apparent Hibernicism?" I asked.

"Ah! simply in order to know where to strike. I wish to see for myself. For instance, I don't want to run amuck through New York, killing blindly. I wish to gain such information as will enable me to extirpate nuisances, and leave uninjured whatever I find good and pure."

"Heaven protect us!" I ejaculated. "Then New York is a total ruin."

"Not so—not so!" repealed the Comet. "Let me see for myself. You can assist me. I know you; you are the Man about Town, and you can guide me through this labyrinth. If you will give me the information that I want, I will give you a ticket of safety, insuring your preservation from any of the effects of my visit."

"It's a bargain!" I cried, much relieved in my mind by this proposition. "Let us take a drink on it."

The bar-room that we entered was one of the most splendid in Broadway. Its walls were hung with seductive coloured prints; its ceiling was frescoed with loose designs, while the bar itself glittered with a magnificently-decorated machinery for the distribution of poisoned liquor. A thick cloud of tobacco-smoke floated through the room; the click of billiard-balls jarred sharply from the farther end; and the place was swarming with knots of youth—few of them more than twenty years—whose flushed faces were dimly lit by heavy, dissipated eyes, and whose pale lips were jaded with drink and smoke, and blasphemous with constant oaths.

"Here," said I, as the Comet and myself quaffed our lager-bier—a drink to which my erratic friend seemed to take very kindly—"here is one of a class of places of amusement which I think we might dispense with. It is not because young men spend their dollars here that I object to it. It is because across that bar something more than money is taken. Youth, and health, and vigour; innocence, good feeling, and refinement; all senses of social decency pass across that counter invisibly night after night, and their owners go on none the wiser for their loss, until, in some hour of self-examination, they awake to the consciousness of all that they have squandered."

The Comet nodded his head approvingly, and taking out a black notebook, traced some memoranda on it with his finger, which left a glittering mark like phosphorus. We then went out into the town.

"Where are we now:'" asked the Comet, after we had walked some time, stopping suddenly under the facade of a large building.

"This is the celebrated Wall Street," I answered; "the paradise of adventurers. Sweep it, my dear Comet, from top to bottom. Don't leave a trace of it. A single fragment of it, if left floating around, will, like the polypus, become an independent settlement, and grow to its original size. It is here that speculation fattens as a bubble grows, swelling and swelling, until suddenly, *piff! paff!* the thing bursts, and all that remains is a little dirty water. This is the great central habitation where a colony of spiders have fixed their abode, and from which they spread their nets over the whole city. Unlike the ordinary spider, they rarely fight among themselves, and generously assist each other when in distress. It is against the poor outside insects that their machinations are chiefly directed. There is a fraternity of brigandage among these brokers that forbids them devouring each other; but woe to him who, belonging not to their band, ventures with full pockets into their domain. Here many lofty hopes have died. Here many honourable shields have been stained forever. Here is what may be considered the great centre of the floating capital of New York. Yet there is not a prison in the city that has not had its ranks of malefactors recruitedflrom the Board of Brokers."

Out came the Comet's note-book, and down went a memorandum fatal to Wall Street. Heaven help the Exchange on the 18th of June!

"What order of architecture does that building belong to?" asked the Comet, as we were passing the City Hall, a short time after.

"That," said I, "is what is commonly called the Dutch Corinthian. That noble edifice, of which our city is so proud, is the Hotel de Ville of New York; in other words, the City Hall. You should see it, my dear Comet, on the 4th of July, when the front is decorated with an imposing effigy of the Father of his Country, and ten thousand dollars' worth of firecrackers testify the patriotic enthusiasm of our newly-imported citizens. There is a fine field for a sweep of your tail in the corridors of that edifice, most noble Comet! Street-contractors that don't do their work; Mayors that make a job of politics; policemen that are appointed because they are good shoulder-hitters at primary elections; together with a thousand corruptions which I have no time to name. Make a note, most noble Comet!"

"That tall, rickety building, but of which I see a crazed-looking man in a white hat and old boots issuing, what is that?"

"That is the office of the *Rostrum,* the great philanthropical journal of America, which, like the Baron Spolasco, or any other gentleman of his kidney, earns a living by being eccentric. Everything is determinedly turned topsy-turvy by the *employés* of that paper. They want to make men of women, and women of men. Their trowsers are always too short and their hair too long. They employ Russians to write their English, and musicians to instruct the public on politics. They keep a parson who reviews then profane literature, and a layman who writes sermons on popped corn. They attack everybody, and bellow like the Bulls of Bashan if they are attacked in turn. They profess to be intensely democratic, and their building is a sort of *caravanserai* for foreign noblemen who bivouac among the desks and exchanges. They have their line eyes, like Mrs. Jellyby, always fixed on Africa, and do not see the civic sores that fester at their very feet. In short, their eccentricities and 'isms' are as wide as the brims of their hats, and, like them, shut them off from the light of heaven!"

"I guess we'll let the *Rostrum* building stand," said the Comet. "It is a harmless institution, and affords the public amusement. I like to see a comic newspaper thrive."

From the Park we passed upward, and I pointed out many shams to the Comet, which he promised to attend to on the 18th of June, he said that he would most particularly wait upon the Central Park Commission, on Coroner Connery, on Mr. Russ, and on the gentleman who has been promising the public a catalogue of the books in the Astor Library ever since that institution opened.

We were now opposite to the Cooper Institute, and while I was explaining to my friend the Comet that this noble gift to the people should be held sacred, not alone on account of the amiable donor, but for the benefit which the rising generation would derive from it, I suddenly heard a whizzing noise in the air. I looked up, and behold the Comet was shooting away into space like a rocket, leaving a long, luminous wake after him. He kissed his hand and smiled to me as he soared upward.

"Oh crikey!" cried a little boy behind me, "ain't that a jolly rocket!" and I saw a number of people look aloft. They all saw only a firework. I alone knew it was the Comet.

2

I am horribly disappointed! The tiger who misses his spring; the young lady who, hoping for a proposal from a certain swain for her own hand, receives one for her younger sister; the salmon-fisher, at the moment that the rod straightens with a jerk, and he knows that "he is gone."—all these are but faint types of the agonising disappointment I experienced when I found that the Comet did not strike the earth.

The case, I submit, was very hard. I had met, as I conceived, a well-bred, gentlemanly Comet—a Comet of his word—who made me certain promises, in which I blindly believed, and on the faith of which I made certain arrangements. The apparent sincerity with which he spoke of his impingement on the earth, did not allow me room for a doubt. He seemed calm and self-assured—and now, after all this, he has not come! The earth still revolves in its accustomed orbit; the City Hall—I regret still more to say—still lifts its proud chimney-pots over the adjacent buildings!

But the predicament in which this breach of faith on the part of the Comet has placed me is very lamentable. When I was assured at that memorable interview related in a previous "Man About Town," that such a body was really about to visit us, I immediately commenced to reflect on certain consequences which must inevitably result from such a catastrophe.

"If the earth is smashed up," I thought, "debt must certainly be abolished; therefore, I have nothing to fear from that infuriated class of acquaintances known to me as creditors. Likewise, if there is a general collision to take place in the course of a week or so, I see no crime in running still farther into debt. Before the bills can by any possibility become due, debtor and creditor will be involved in common ruin. *Dum vivimus vivamus!*—'*A short life and a merry one!*' as Epictetus says in his *Enchiridion*. Let us, without delay, run into debt!"

Accordingly, I proceeded on the most approved principles. For the last fortnight, I have exhausted every pleasure. Dinners, suppers, horses, clothes, jewellery, cards. What boots I ordered! what entrancing coats! What seraphic waistcoats! My convivial parties have been the talk of the town. My friends and myself have exhausted the supply of several of the finest wines that come to this market. The epicures of the city wander wildly from restaurant to restaurant calling in vain for *Vieux Ceps,* for *Clos Vougeot,* for *St. Peray.* "It is all gone!" reply the proprietors. "'The Man About Town' has drunk it all up!" I bought a yacht; purchased a picture-gallery and a library; gave a thousand dollars for a gold dressing-case, mounted with turquoises (there were a pair of dress boot-hooks in it made of amber, that took my fancy); ordered twenty thousand cigars, at a hundred and twenty-five dollars a thousand—in short, indulged in all the luxury of buying.

What is the consequence? The Comet has not kept his word, and I am besieged. My bell is going all day, and creditors are ten deep round my door. Tailors' boys, bending under loads of trousers and waistcoats, are continually coming to my room, with long bills in their hands, and departing threatening and unpaid. I cannot go into a single respectable restaurant without being dunned for dinners, suppers, and breakfasts obtained during the brief period of my luxury. As I walk down Broadway ravenous tradespeople spring at me, and demand their money. I have had enough of executions served on me to paper my walls with. Sheriffs' officers assail me before I rise in the morning with legal documents, the terrors of which are quadrupled in magnitude from my not understanding them.

I am growing thin and pale. My life is forever rendered wretched by this ungentlemanly conduct of the Comet. If the wealthy and respectable firm of publishers with whom I am connected do not immediately advance me twenty thousand dollars on account of literary matter to be hereafter furnished, I see no resource left me but to take Prussic acid, or go back with General Walker to Nicaragua.

I sometimes wonder why it was that the Comet did not come. I am afraid he was disgusted at the disparaging manner in which out scientific man spoke of him in the *Weekly*. If I thought that this was really the case, I would challenge our scientific man.

What am I to do?

Oh, faithless Comet!

The Crystal Bell

It was a country tavern, and I sat in the bar-room for lack of something better to do. Heaven knows there was little enough to amuse one in that dreary temple of Bacchus. There were five newspapers, the newest a month old, lying on the table—I knew every advertisement in them. There was a picture of the favourite Presidential candidate hanging over the fireplace, which, if it at all resembled the gentleman in question, entitled him to a glass-case in Barnum's Museum rather than to a chair in the White House. A book for registering name's lay on a sort of desk in the corner, but since my arrival the pages, though dated, were destitute of a single name. Apple-jack, bad gin, and blazing brandy in bottles of eccentric colours, filled a glass press behind a counter, which was called by courtesy a bar; and behind this stood a wooden image called by courtesy a landlord.

When a man has no books, and no acquaintances at a country tavern, he is apt to fall back on the landlord. I have met in my time very amusing landlords—landlords who could talk about fishing, and shooting, and politics, and perhaps retail to you some of the gossip of the neighbourhood; for it is wonderful how a man in the strait in which I was, will find amusement in the doings of people he knows nothing about. But the landlord of the Hominy House was not to be relied upon in such an emergency. you were not to take any such liberties with him, Sir, let me tell you. He took you into his house, as it were, under protest. He gave you a bed with an air that seemed to say he regretted doing it, but still he did not like to refuse; and you ate your dinner before him in fear and trembling, lest he should reconsider his hospitality and order you out of the house.

Whether it was a natural inflexibility of joints, or whether it was a high sense of personal dignity, I do not know; but certainly, General Dubbley, the landlord of the Hominy House, in the village of Hopskotch, New Jersey, was the most dignified man I ever saw. The halo which he threw round a glass of whisky and water was perfectly wonderful. you might have imagined you were drinking "green seal" to judge by the lofty expression of his countenance as he handed you the bottle. At the dinner-table he fairly awed the appetite out of one; and I shall never, as long as I live, forget the thunder-cloud which gathered on his brow, when, one day, I unluckily asked to be helped to soup twice. When Lafayette passed through Hopskotch, General Dubbley was one of the committee that received him.

I did not know him at that period, not having been born, but I have formed a theory that from this epoch may be dated his tremendous dignity. Whether this interview with the French patriot had anything to do with turning the General's hair green, I cannot say; but it is, nevertheless, a fact that he was remarkable for possessing a lock of bright verdant olive on either side of his head. This eccentricity of colour, I presume, must remain forever a mystery.

As I was saying, I sat in the bar-room. General Dubbley stood behind the bar counting the contents of the till with Olympian dignity. Quarter-dollars seemed to become thunderbolts in his hands. I was very weary. Weary of Hopskotch, weary of Dubbley, weary of the Presidential candidate over the mantelpiece, who seemed to have been born with a patch of strawberries on each check; weary of the old newspapers; weary of everything, in fact, except the memory of my dear Annie to whom I was engaged, and on whose account, I had left New York and immured myself, in mid-winter, at the Hominy House, in order, before our marriage, to settle some matters connected with my property, which lay near Hopskotch. I yawned in the very teeth of General Dubbley.

The door opened ere my teeth closed again, and a man entered, and, shaking off the snow that lay in thick flakes on his coat, advanced to the wood fire that blazed and crackled on the broad hearth, and spread out his hands to the cheering warmth. He was a very seedy-looking man. He had but one coat on—an old, threadbare evening coat—which was tenderly buttoned across a chest which seemed afraid to breathe too lustily lest it should burst the frail buttons. His shoes were old and soaked, looking as if he had found them after they had been boiled for soup by Lieutenant Strain and his companions on the Isthmus. His trowsers were also wet, and very scanty, and shrank from contact with his shoes as it they had been as sensitively constituted as the mimosa. Poor fellow! he looked as if he had not had a dinner in his stomach, or a cent in his pocket for a very long time.

As he entered, the General raised his head from the till and looked at him severely. I saw the poor man shrink a little, but presently he seemed to muster up sufficient courage to go up to the bar.

"Can I have a bed here tonight?" he asked, in a timid voice.

"Full, Sir, full!" said the General, frowning until his old eyebrows fairly creaked; "besides, we seldom have accommodation for strangers."

The poor man gave a glance at his threadbare coat, and smiled. But, oh! how sad the smile was! Patient, but very sorrowful!

"It is a very bad night," said the stranger, pleadingly; "and I am not particular as to where I sleep. Anywhere would do for me."

Unphilosophical stranger! A worse method than a confession of heedlessness of comfort could not have been adopted to win the General's favour. If he had blustered up to the bar and shouted for a bed of rose-leaves with every leaf ironed out, the majestic Dubbley might have overlooked the seedy coat; but not to care where he slept! that settled him.

"Sorry, Sir, but can't accommodate you;" and with this brief intimation the Jove of Hopskotch commenced once more to make quarter-dollars look like thunder-bolts.

The stranger sighed; looked wistfully at the bright fire; gave another hopeless glance at the wooden Dubbley, and then moved slowly to the door. It was more than I could stand. Olympus had no terrors for me at the moment.

"Stay!" I cried, advancing from the obscure corner in which 1 had been seated; "stay, Sir, for a moment. This weather is too inclement for any human being to wander in at night. I have not the pleasure of knowing who you are, but there are two beds in my room, and I esteem it my duty to offer you one of them. Pray accept it."

I almost lost the murmured thanks with which the seedy man accepted this impetuous offer, in the consideration of General Dubbley's countenance. I don't think I ever beheld such a picture of astounded dignity. My heart sank after my speech was fairly out; for really, I expected nothing more than to be turned out myself; and, what is more, I believe that I would have gone. To my surprise, however, the General took another tone.

"If Mr. Massy was willing to proffer such indiscriminate hospitality," he said, "*he* was perfectly satisfied."

For the first time, the truth burst upon me that the General was not so awful as he looked, and that by the aid of a little resolution he might even be reduced to the position of a landlord. I plucked up courage from this supposed discovery, and having opened the breach, pushed on.

"I want some supper, General Dubbley," said I, peremptorily.

"Sir, you have had your supper," answered the General, clutching madly at the last rag of his importance that was being torn so ruthlessly from him.

"No matter; I wish to sup again. I sometimes sup frequently during an evening."

I was reckless with victory, and began to talk wildly.

"You shall be served, Sir."

And the General abdicated his thunderbolts and disappeared into the kitchen. I had conquered. A hand was laid very gently on me, and the stranger now spoke audibly to me for the first time.

"I am very, very much obliged to you," he said, "for all this kindness; but if in getting this supper you put yourself to inconvenience on my account, may I beg that you will countermand it?"

"Not at all," I replied, diplomatically; "but as you have reminded me of it, perhaps you will favour me by supping with me—that is; if you have not supped?"

"I have not dined," said the stranger, with a feeble smile. "I see through your kind *ruse*," he added; "and to a gentleman who can act so feelingly as you have done, I have little shame in confessing that if I have not dined, it was because I had no money."

"Come, come!" said I, trying to bluster away those confounded tears that always *will* get in my eyes when I hear such things, "Come, we will have a jolly good supper together; and then we will talk of business matters afterward. Let us sit by the fire until it is ready, and, meanwhile, drink this."

So saying, I invaded the General's Olympian domains, and pouring out a stiff horn of applejack, forced it upon my new friend. it did him good, I am certain, for I saw the dim eyes brighten and the thin cheek flush; and it was not the firelight that did it, cheery as it was.

I never met a more delightful man than this seedy stranger. He had been everywhere, seen everything, done everything, knew everybody. He was a finished scholar, an original critic, a delightful singer, an epitome of wit. He so fascinated me, that we sat up in my room until almost twelve—an unearthly hour in Hopskotch, where the people go to roost with the chickens—and it never once entered into my head to ask him who he was, what he was called, or how it was that he was wandering about in the snow without any money. I even went to bed without locking my door, or putting my watch under my pillow.

It was the grey dawn of the morning when someone sitting on my bedside awoke me suddenly. I startled upright in an instant, and beheld my friend. He was completely dressed, and in the dim light seemed like a departing ghost. For a moment, in the incoherence of my ideas, I had a confused idea that he was about to rob me, and seized him instinctively by the arm.

"Don't be alarmed," he said, with a smile. "I intended to awake you, and before I went—for I am going immediately—I wished to thank you for your extreme kindness to me. God bless you for it! I have but little to offer you in the way of return, but what I have is yours. Here is a crystal bell," and he drew a tiny glass bell from his pocket, a thing like a child's toy. "It was forged in distant lands, where the sun makes the rocks vocal, and its maker sang over it in the furnace the spells known only to the children of the East. It is the touchstone of truth. Whoever utters a falsehood to him who bears it about, that moment the crystal bell will vibrate. Scoff at the story now, if you will, but try the talisman—it will never betray you. Farewell!"

And laying the little bell upon the counterpane, before I could sufficiently collect my scattered senses he glided to the door and went out, closing it softly after him.

I took up the bell mechanically, and examined it. it was entirely formed of what seemed to be the purest crystal. The tongue was also of crystal, but flexible as the finest watch-spring. I tried to ring it, but although the ball at the end of the pendant tongue visibly struck the clear sides of the bell, it did not emit the slightest sound. I tried it again and again, and always with the same result.

I got up and looked for my watch. It was safe. My pockets were untouched; my drawers intact. My seedy friend, therefore, was not an impostor. Again, I returned to the mysterious bell, and agitated its crystal tongue in vain. Not even a muffled tinkling was to be drawn from it. Had the pendulum been a leather it could not have been more silent.

All day long I felt wretchedly uncomfortable with the crystal bell in my pocket. I scarcely answered the sneering inquiries after my seedy friend with which General Dubbley assailed me. I scarcely took the trouble to inform him that I had not been robbed. I was indifferent to the display which he made of his counting his spoons in my presence.

The last words of my mysterious guest continually rang in my ears—"Whoever utters a falsehood to him who bears it, that moment the crystal bell will vibrate."

Annie Gray! sweet truthful, pure-eyed Annie Gray! why was it that your face continually rose up before me whenever I touched the-magic bell? Whenever I drew it forth, and looked through its crystal walls, why was it that your fair countenance seemed dimly visible within, but clouded with some horrible shadow? And when I thought of you, why did the name of that hateful Aubyn always flicker in big letters before my mind's eye?

I suffered positive torture. Here was I, engaged to be married to one of the sweetest girls in New York, beloved by her to my heart's content, and rich enough to satisfy her every wish, when in comes a stranger, who puts what he calls a talisman for testing truth into my hands, and straightway I begin to doubt the dear girl whom I had never doubted before. Did she really love me, or was it only for my wealth that she became mine? Did she not rather prefer that horrible Harry Aubyn, who danced so well, and who talked so charmingly about nothing? The more I tried to conquer this abominable fantasy of jealousy the more positive it became, until at last I had worked myself into such a fever of excitement that I could bear suspense no longer. Yes! I would instantly hurry to New York and test this wondrous gift! it was folly—madness; I knew that well enough, but still I would test it—test it all the more willingly, for I had such faith in Annie. But why did she encourage that empty dandy, Harry Aubyn?

In less than two hours I was in New York, ringing madly at Annie Gray's door.

As I entered the drawing-room hastily, out walked Mr. Aubyn. We saluted coldly, but I could have strangled him at the moment, if such things were permissible in this century. I must have been rather pale and disordered-looking, for I had scarce entered the room when Annie's first words were,

"Oh, Gerald! has anything happened?"

Dear girl! how could any but a madman doubt that anxious, fond look—that quivering lip? I kissed her forehead, and reassured her.

"Annie, dear, why do you have that Mr. Aubyn here in my absence! You know I don't like him."

"Why, Gerald, I really can't help if he calls. I don't care about his visits. I assure you; but I cannot be rude to him, I have known him so long."

Gracious heavens! was it fancy? or did I hear a faint, crystalline tinkling in my pocket! A cold shiver ran through my frame; but I endeavoured to dissemble my agony, and, with a forced smile, went on.

"So, you don't like him really, you little puss! Come now, confess that at one time you did care a little—a very little—for Aubyn, your old playmate?"

"Why, what ails you, Gerald? You look so queer. I assure you, I never cared anything for Harry Aubyn."

Tinkle! tinkle! tinkle! in my pocket. I felt the blood rush to my head; it was a Niagara of emotion, but I subdued it.

"And you love your poor Gerald, then, better than anybody else; better even than the old school-fellow you have known so long?"

"What a fool you are, Gerald! of course I do," and she kissed me gently on the forehead.

Tinkle! tinkle! tinkle! in my pocket. Plain, clear, distinct. Every vibration of the crystal bell thrilled through my frame. If the bells of every cathedral, headed by Tom of Lincoln, had pealed altogether at my ear they could not have moved me half so much as that sharp, shrill crystal tintinnabulation from that horrible bell. I could bear it no longer.

"Traitress! I shouted, flinging away the tender arms that wound around my neck. "Hypocrite! I despise you! Yes, madam, the eyes of your dupe were opened in time. You shall not laugh at the credulous Gerald Massy."

"Gerald! are you mad?"

"Not quite; though a week after our marriage I would have been, impostor that you are! But I know you. Know that you don't love me. Know that you have lied to me three times within this last half hour." She tried to embrace me; but I flung her off. She wrung her hands, and the big tears rolled over her cheeks, and her gentle head was bent, as if stricken with some great blow. She acted her part excellently well.

"What can you mean, Gerald? I have never deceived you in thought or word. If you have proofs of my hypocrisy advance them, but do not storm me down with assertions."

"My proofs are here!" I cried, holding up the bell triumphantly—the triumph of despair. "Here! look on this talisman, falsest of women, and tremble!"

"But, Gerald, are you sane? I see nothing but this bell."

"And this bell, as you call it, has told me within the last half hour that you are a worthless woman."

One tigress-like leap, and she caught it from my hand. With flaming eyes, she held it aloft, and then dashed it on the ground. A crash, like the bursting of a thousand hand-grenades—thundering of cathedral bells, that seemed to shake the world; and, looking up, I saw General Dubbley standing over me in a dignified altitude.

"Mr. Massy," said he, "the dinner-bell has been ringing these ten minutes; but you appear to have been sleeping so soundly that you have not heard it. Dinner waits."

And so, it was a dream. No seedy friend—no talisman—no falsehood in sweet Annie Gray. I rubbed my eyes and went into dinner; but as I ate my soup under the awful eye of the General, I confess I regretted the non-reality of that portion of my dream in which I had subdued the Thunderer of the tavern.

I never told Annie Gray that I had ever doubted her even in a dream, until we had been a month married.

The King of Nodland and His Dwarf

Chapter 1: Some Little Account of Nodland

Far away in the wide tracts of the southern seas lies a country called Nodland. If any of my readers are geographically inclined, I fear that I shall he quite unable to answer the usual question as to latitude and longitude. But when I say that its shores were lashed by the waves of the Pacific Ocean, I settle its position quite as definitely as the objects of this little story require. Nodland was a strange but beautiful country. The soil is rich and fertile, and the land sometimes rose into soft, green hills, with their summits crowned with fragrant trees, whose blossoms never faded. In other districts, the surface of the soil was dotted all over with numberless small lakes, belted round and hidden from the world by tall sombre trees, until they looked like myriads of beautiful blue eyes, shaded by their long, dark lashes.

Then were some portions, too, covered with wild, savage forests, where the panther and hyena roared their lives away, and splendid birds with wings of gold and azure fluttered amid the trees, until it seemed as if the blue stars and yellow sunbeams had come down from heaven to make a holiday among those lonely woods. Yet withal this beauty there was a lifelessness around the land. The air seemed heavy with sleep; the tall corn-stalks in the field, and the orange trees on the sunny slopes, bowed their heads and nodded drowsily. The very wind was lazy, and seemed to blow only on compulsion.

The inhabitants of Nodland shared in this universal torpor. Sleep appeared to be the greet object of existence, and sleep they did all through the day, and far into the night. Life with them had but two alternations—from the bed to the table; from the table to the bed. In this way, a Nodlander was very happy. He had a king who was not worse than the general run of monarchs; the soil was fruitful, and a good nap was always to be had at will. Possessing these things, he wished for nothing more. In such a drowsy state of society, it may be supposed that the people were not much given to work.

A Nodlander would as soon have thought of committing suicide as digging a hole, or planting a carrot A potato furrow would have been a Rubicon impossible to get over, and all the corn in Nodland might have rotted in its fullness, ere one sheaf of it would have fallen before the scythe of those destined to consume it. Now though the soil of Nodland was fertile, it was not sufficiently generous to produce, unaided, all that was requisite for the support of so lazy a nation. It was necessary to plough, manure and sow it with the requisite seed, and as it was quite out of the question that this could be done by the Nodlanders, it was equally obvious that somebody else must be got who would do it, otherwise the consequences to the nation at large might be excessively unpleasant This was the great principle on which the constitution of Nodland turned too lazy to labour themselves, the Nodlanders must have people to labour for them. But where were these to be had?

Once every year, in the early spring, when the winter-hidden flowers were bursting joyously up through the soil, to meet their old friend the sunshine, the people of Nodland cast off for a brief while the constitutional lethargy which enchained them, and donned the sword and buckler of the warrior. They formed themselves into a great army, and like most lazy people they were brave when they were thoroughly aroused and marched with much martial pomp across the borders of their own kingdom into the heart of the neighbouring country.

This country was inhabited by a peaceful and industrious race called the Cock-Crow Indians, who, amid the fertile valleys of their lofty hills, cultivated the soil and lived a life of pastoral innocence. They knew little of the use of warlike weapons, and though they were brave, were unhappily defenceless. The Nodlanders therefore found them an easy conquest It was in vain that they fled to the summits of their mountains, and hurled huge crags upon the heads of the invaders; it was in vain that they sought refuge in the dark caverns among the rocks, and shot their feeble arrows from thence against the foe: their simple strategy was of no avail, when opposed to the art of the more cultivated Nodlander, and every year brought sorrow and desolation amid the steep hills of the Cock-Crows.

The captives which the Nodlanders brought back from these expeditions served to supply all their agricultural wants, and fill the industrial gap which their own indolence left unoccupied. The unhappy

Cock-Crows were sold by the government as slaves, and the honest mountaineers found themselves reduced from the proud independence of their alpine farms, to the degrading drudgery of tilling the soil for their ungrateful tyrants. Historians who relate these facts, state that it was a piteous sight to behold the army of Nodland returning from one of these recruiting expeditions with a long and melancholy rank of captives in its train. None but the most stalwart Cock-Crows were selected as slaves, and it frequently happened that whole families were dependent upon the labour of these youths for subsistence.

What then could be more heart-rending than to see aged mothers, helpless fathers, and tender sisters weeping bitterly as they saw their only support torn from them? What a terrible sight to behold a wife convulsed with an agony of grief, at the prospect of losing her husband, in the very dawn of wedded happiness! Along the road for many a mile, even to the very borders of Nodland, the army would be accompanied by crowds of lamenting and despairing relatives, weeping and invoking curses upon the heads of those who had wrecked the happiness of their country, and scattered the ashes of desolation upon their hearth.

Once reached the limits that separated the two countries, the train of mourners stayed their steps, and then, after a moment of brief agony, those that they loved best in the world were torn from their gaze and borne off into slavery. Then the unhappy destiny of the Cock-Crow captives commenced. Some tilled the soil from morn till night; some breathed the heavy air of towns, where they manufactured goods; others subdued their free mountain step into the hushed and stealthy tread of the trained domestic. All were employed, but it was not the free, unshackled toil which strengthens soul and body. They were slaves, and they knew it; and that knowledge made even the lightest task of their servitude seem heavy, and poisoned their every enjoyment

Thus, did the Nodlanders supply their necessities, and force others to do for them what they were too lazy to do for themselves. And having accomplished this inroad upon their quiet neighbours, and carried sorrow and desolation into a thousand peaceful homes, they relapsed into their usual lethargic state, until the returning spring warned them again that the time was come when it was necessary that they should recruit their slave ranks.

King Slumberous of Nodland was a great king. History proclaims the fact, and it must be true; besides, it would have been very unsuitable if he had not been, for Nodland was a great country. King

Slumberous's claims to distinction were many and well founded. He never taxed the people, except when he was in need of money. He spent the public funds right royally, and gave the people occasional glimpses of his august person with unparalleled condescension. He made war upon a grand scale, and was never known to retire from the field without leaving a mountain of corpses behind him. Most of those, to be sure, were his own soldiers; but that mattered little: they lost their lives, but the nation gained a battle, and who would cavil at such an exchange?

He built the finest palaces in the world, and it did the people's hearts good to go on a fine summer's evening, between nap-times, and look at the outside of these gorgeous edifices. The Nodlanders would slap their pockets at the sight, and cry proudly, "Bless King Slumberous! I helped to build him that palace, and I'm as proud of it as if it was my own. How kind of him, to be sure, to allow us to come and look at it every day!"

King Slumberous did the nation credit by the way in which he entertained foreign potentates when they paid him a visit. Entertainments of the most magnificent description enlivened the palace night and day. Gorgeous *fêtes*, wondrous illuminations, and delightful hunting excursions occupied the royal leisure, that is waking moments, and the delighted people cried, "Bless our good King Slumberous for showing us all these beautiful things!" There were some discontented spirits in Nodland, who said that the king was a humbug, and that the people were taxed tyrannically; but they were low, demagogical fellows, and no one paid any attention to them. There was one thing, however, which above all endeared the monarch to his subjects. King Slumberous was beyond all question the heaviest sleeper in the kingdom. This stamped him at once as a remarkable man, and the people would have done anything for a sovereign who could sleep fifty-six hours on a stretch

It may be supposed that with these somniferous habits, King Slumberous had little time or inclination to attend to the affairs of state. But while the gracious monarch snored and dreamed, there was one man in his kingdom who was always wide awake—a man who, though born to the usual drowsy inheritance of his countrymen, had by training so far conquered his nature as to require scarcely any sleep at all. This ever-watchful individual was the Lord Incubus, prime minister to King Slumberous, and the most hated man in all Nodland.

Lord Incubus was a dwarf; probably the most successful epitome of ugliness that nature ever published. With a swarthy and misshapen countenance, and long spidery arms, he seemed to be a combination of the beetle and the monkey, and possessed all the malicious cunning of the one, with the repulsive loathsomeness of the other. Even his ability was distorted. He was exceedingly clever, but it was a very unpleasant kind of talent No man could devise a new and oppressive impost better than he. No one could cook up the public accounts into a plausible shape, or even popular indignation by some apparently liberal, but really worthless concession, more successful than he. When nature bestowed upon him the faculty of telling a lie better than any other man in the kingdom, when she made him cruel, unscrupulous, and dishonest, she seemed to have designed him for a prime minister, and her end was fully answered.

Incubus managed the affairs of state, as Slumberous gently nodded in an intermittent slumber; but while conducting money from the pockets of the people into the royal treasury, he had a little private syphon off the main tube, which terminated in a certain strong box in the minister's own palace. The people did not like Lord Incubus; they feared him much and hated him more. Popular perception was sufficiently acute to perceive that good King Slumberous had little hand in the oppressive system of taxation with which they were overwhelmed. They also saw pretty clearly that Incubus was making a good profit out of the concern, and murmurs of indignation arose through the land against the dwarf minister. The brooding spirit was shortly brought to a head by a movement on the part of Incubus, which shook the constitution of Nodland to its foundation.

It had been a long time a matter of grave deliberation with Incubus and his ministers, as to what was the best means of imposing a fresh tax upon the people. Imposts already existed upon every available article in the kingdom, and there was a serious need of money in the royal treasury, it became a question of vital importance how it was to be raised. Many and grave were the councils held upon the matter. The ministers racked their brains in order to discover some commodity as yet untaxed, but in vain, and the royal treasury stood a very fair chance of being bankrupt. At length, a young Secretary of State (whose fortune was made by this one suggestion) hit upon a bright idea.

It is a well-known fact that the inhabitants of Nodland are distinguished by a wonderful passion for high heels to their shoes. No Nodlander of any position whatever would condescend to appear in public unless his heels were removed at least four inches from the surface of the earth. Fashionable people wet still farther, and elevated themselves to five, and sometimes even six inches, and to such a pitch was this fashionable eccentricity carried, that at the coronation of King Slumberous one of the ladies attached to the court was severely hurt, in consequence of her having the misfortune, to get a fall off her heels. Now the young Secretary argued very properly, and with much discrimination, that as the Nodlanders would almost as soon lose their heads as their heels, heels were a legitimate object for taxation.

"The more necessary a thing is," said he "the more it ought to be taxed. Superfluities can be dispensed with, but if you want to be sure of a man's money, tax something that he cannot possibly do without."

This proposition met with great applause, and the tax was finally resolved on. The ministers, however, did not include in their calculations the popular indignation which so sweeping a measure would excite; and when it was proclaimed that all persons wishing to wear heels above one inch in height must pay a tax for every inch by which they exceeded the proposed standard, all Nodland was aroused. A spirit of anarchy, which had been for some time past brooding in the breasts of certain demagogues, now seized the occasion to break out in full force, and the country flamed with rebellion. Meetings were held, and banners flaunted with the devices of "Down with Incubus!" "High heels for ever!" and one represented pictorially a great giant, allegorical of public opinion, crushing the dwarf minister beneath a heel of Titanic proportions.

Strangely enough, the leader of all this anarchical confusion was not a Nodlander by birth. He was a native of a neighbouring island on the coast called Broga, and having been expelled from his own country for his misconduct, he sought the friendly shelter of Nodland, which was always open to the stranger. The first return he made for this hospitality was to stir up ill-feeling and disunion through the land that he lived in. He possessed a certain species of vulgar, brazen eloquence, that was very effective with a particular class. His effrontery was dauntless, and his conscience, from systematic stretching, had become so large that it was capable of embracing any set of opinions from which the most profit was to be derived. He blustered largely about an article he called "patriotism", but which in reality meant self-interest; he was, in short, one of those bold, bad men who was sufficiently elevated above his own low class to be regarded by them as a leader, but who was too far beneath any other to be looked on in the light of anything but an unpleasant pest.

This man was called Ivned. Ivned seized the opportunity offered by the heel-tax, with great avidity. He talked largely about the interests of his country, forgetting that he was not even a citizen by adoption, and with his unscrupulous speeches, and impudent attacks on the government, raised a flame in the land which it took a long time to extinguish. King Slumberous grew alarmed at this unusual demonstration from his subjects; and when one day a sacrilegious wretch, supposed to be in the pay of Ivned, flung a rotten egg full in the face of the gracious monarch, when he was engaged in taking the air, he remonstrated seriously with Incubus as to his policy in taxing so necessary a portion of a Nodlander's person as his heels. The dwarf promised to calm the tumults, but refused to abolish the tax. He must have money, he said, and money could only come from the people. The riots meantime grew more serious; monster meetings were held throughout the land, and the nation seemed on the eve of a convulsion.

Ivned was in high spirits, for there was nothing in which he delighted so much as anarchy and confusion. At this juncture, Incubus put in practice one of those expedients for which he was celebrated. He caused it to be publicly announced, that in consequence of the consideration which his Majesty King Slumberous had for the opinions of his people, the odious heel-tax would be abolished. The people were in ecstasies. Incubus was a god, the preserver of the nation, and Slumberous was the greatest king that ever reigned. Votes of thanks were resolved on all over the country to the dwarf premier, and a grand banquet was given to him by the citizens of the metropolis. Ivned was overwhelmed with confusion, for in the general excitement no one would listen to his insidious speeches. But amid this popular phrensy, no one observed the birth of a little edict which slipped into the world immediately on the heels of the proclamation repealing the tax.

Astounded by the magnitude of the concession, the people were blinded to everything else; and it was only when they awoke from their dream that they discovered that they had all the while been quietly submitting to a similar impost, if possible more oppressive than the heel-tax. It was nothing less than a duty levied upon everybody who wore their own hair. The Nodlanders, being rather a vain people, scarcely liked to disfigure themselves with wigs, and the people began to murmur. But the reaction which Incubus had calculated on was taking place. The people had exhausted their indignation in the previous riots, and a general apathy overspread them. Even Ivned could not get an audience, and in a few months the tax was paid as willingly as any other. Thus, the royal treasury was filled, the feuds between the citizens and the government were healed, and the people were sold.

I have given this little history of the events that happened in Nodland previous to the opening of my story. It is dry and tedious, but was necessary in order to understand perfectly what follows.

Chapter 2 The Way to Build a Palace

It was noon. A dead silence reigned in the king's chamber, while he himself slumbered amid billows of down. Two Cock-Crow slaves waved fans made from the feathers of the *grochayo* noiselessly above his head, and a cool breeze, perfumed in passing through the flower-clad lattices, wandered through the room It was a luxurious apartment. The floor was paved with a peculiar granite of a delicate purple colour, and susceptible of the highest polish. The walls were lined with slender pillars, carved and stained in imitation of palm trees, from whose lofty crowns long pendent leaves of green satin waved in the fragrant breeze. In the centre of the hall an elegant fountain threw a silver stream of water into the air, that fell back again in light showers upon the rich lilies and sleepy water plants that were twined around the basin's edge

A low, subdued, murmuring music wandered fitfully through the place, this was produced by a species of water-organ which was concealed beneath the fountain. Graduated streams of water trickled upon sonorous plates of metal, and produced a series of mournful but soothing sounds. At one end of this luxurious apartment, King Slumberous lay sleeping. He did not snore. An air of calm, torpid enjoyment, glassed over his smooth features. His breathing was low and regular, and he lay in an attitude of conspicuous ease. He knew how to sleep. At the other end of the room, perched on a high stool, with no back to lean against, or no cushion to repose on, sat the restless Incubus, His Majesty's Prime Minister.

The small black eyes of the dwarf were fixed with a glittering uneasiness upon the form of the sleeping king He fidgeted on his stool, and endeavoured to make a necklace of his long, thin legs, and twisted his misshapen form into every imaginable attitude. He was evidently suffering all the pangs of impatience, and grunted occasionally very intelligible signs of his dissatisfaction. At last, as if his patience was completely exhausted, he suddenly sprang like a squirrel off his high stool, and alit with a tremendous clatter on the granite pavement. The Cock-Crow slaves, startled at the sound, let their fans fall; the music of the water-organ was drowned in the rude echoes that reverberated through the hall; the down pillows that encircled royalty were suddenly disturbed, and King Slumberous awoke. He raised himself on his couch, and rubbing his eyes like any other man, demanded what the—no, no—simply, "what *was* the matter?"

Incubus advanced and made a profound obeisance to the king.

"Ah! Incubus, is that you?" said His Majesty, drowsily; "what do you want?"

"Money, your Majesty," replied the dwarf laconically

"Money? impossible! What has become of the last hundred thousand bloodrops, (Nodland currency), which came in from the tax on ringlets?"

"Spent, your Majesty; every ounce of it—spent."

"Hum! is there nothing in the treasury then?"

"Yes, your Majesty, there is one thing."

"What is that?"

"Invention When everything else has fled from the treasury box, invention, like hope, remains at the bottom."

"What! a new tax, Incubus? Do you think they'll stand it?"

"Oh! they'll make a noise about it, and hold meetings, and probably attempt to assassinate your Majesty; but they'll pay it—oh! They'll pay it in the end."

King Slumberous wriggled a little among his down pillows at this allusion of the dwarf to his life being imperilled, but it did not make much impression on him apparently, for he laughed in a drowsy kind way, and said.

"Well, let us have a new tax, Incubus; I leave it all to you, only let me have enough of money to build my new palace;" and he lay back seemingly with a strong intention of going off to sleep again.

"It is easy to say, let us have a tax," said the dwarf impressively; "but what are we to tax?"

"Oh! anything-—everything—something that the people can't do without."

"All the necessaries in the kingdom are taxed to the utmost."

"Then we must bring something into fashion, and when the people come to want it we will tax it."

"Your Majesty is ingenious," said the dwarf with a sneer; "but the people are cunning."

"It's a very hard case," said the king, mournfully, "that a man has nothing left in his kingdom on which he can raise a little ready money. Couldn't we put a tax upon life, Incubus? couldn't we make the people pay for the privilege of existing?"

"We might do that, certainly, your Majesty, but what if the people refused to pay?"

"Kill them!"

"True! if they will not pay the tax, we kill them. But recollect that when we kill them, they are not bound to pay the tax. The idea is ingenious, your Majesty, but I am afraid it is not practicable."

"What are we to do?" asked the king, sitting up amid his pillows with an air of ludicrous bewilderment. "We can't get on without money, you know, Incubus, There's the Prince of Fungi, whom I have invited to a great hunting party next week, and we must have funds, or we shall be positively disgraced. Incubus, you must raise the money or lose your head."

"But, your Majesty—"

"I have said it; I give you an hour for reflection. Meanwhile, I will enjoy that of which, thank Heaven, no tax can deprive me—sleep!"

The dwarf made three bounds as the king uttered these words, and at the third his head almost touched the pendants that hung down from the lofty ceiling.

"Are you mad, Incubus! Are you distracted? asked the king, angry at this apparently disrespectful conduct

"Yes, with joy, your Majesty; mad with sheer joy! I have found a tax, I have found such a beautiful impost."

"Ah! let us hear it; what is this tax? Come, I am all impatience, Incubus."

"You let it slip yourself, your Majesty, not a moment since. We will instantly lay a tax on sleep."

"What! on sleep? tax a Nodlander's slumbers? Oh! Incubus, it will never do; it would be too tyrannous. They could not exist without it."

"They can have it by paying for it."

"But they will rebel, Incubus!"

"Oh, your Majesty, leave that to me. I'll manage them, I warrant you."

"But really, Incubus, such cruelty!"

"Recollect the palace, and the Prince of Fungi, your Majesty: we must have money."

"True, true," muttered the king; "we must have money. Well, Incubus, I leave it all to you; but be gentle, be gentle. Certainly, when one comes to think of it, sleep is worth paying for."

Two minutes after this the king was fast asleep.

Incubus laughed a low, silent, malicious laugh, as he left the royal chamber, and betook himself to the office of the Secretary of State.

"There is but one man," he muttered to himself, "who is at all to be feared. We must muzzle Ivned."

The next morning Nodland was in commotion. A royal edict had been published during the night, and which was found at daybreak in all conspicuous places, to the effect, that inasmuch as it was the sovereign will and pleasure of his gracious Majesty King Slumberous the First, that his well-beloved subjects should be subject to a certain tax, duty and impost, which was to be levied on sleep. The edict, after some further preamble, went on to say, that the maximum of sleep to be allowed to each individual was four hours. All transgression of these limits was to be taxed as a luxury, according to a scale which was therein laid down. It may be imagined what the sensation must have been in a place like Nodland, where every man consumed at least fourteen hours out of the twenty-four in slumber. Every city in the land convened public meetings as soon as the oppressive edict was made known. Speakers ranted on platforms, and patriots began to make money.

Ivned was in his glory He wrote diatribes against the king. He foamed at the mouth in public with virtuous indignation. There was no word so foul, that he hesitated to fling it at the government. He denounced Incubus as a public pest, and all monarchs as hereditary evils. "What," he would cry at some public meeting, flinging his arms aloft with frenzy, "deprive us of our natural rights? contravene the immutable and wise designs of Providence? Base and bloody tyranny! wretched and besotted king! wicked and distorted minister! The seasons change. To the summer succeeds the winter, and earth veils in rest the quickness of her bosom; she recruits her strength with a three months slumber, but we are not to rest, save by Act of Parliament! Our sleep must be legal, or not at all. For aught we know, our dreams may be contraband! Fellow-citizens, shall we suffer this? Shall we be trampled underfoot, and have our slumbers measured out to us with an ell wand? No! rather let our sacred constitution perish, than have it made the hobbyhorse of such tyrants."

In this way, and with such addresses as these, Ivned raised a flame through the land. Some people, to be sure, said that, not being a Nodlander born, he had no earthly right to talk; nay, that he even did not require the quantity of sleep which a Nodlander required. But the mass of the people did not care who spoke, if his discourse was well seasoned with popular blasphemy and sedition. The state of the country grew alarming; revolt menaced the government on every side. But Incubus was inexorable. He appointed officers under the late act, and styled them sleep-wardens. It was the duty of these men to enforce the payment of the tax, and see that no person in their district enjoyed more sleep than the law allowed, without paying for it. Offices were established in every townland to grant certificates of sleep, to those who chose to buy them, and these places were thronged from morning till night with a crowd of discontented, murmuring citizens, who, although they were plotting treason against the State, preferred buying their certificate in the interval, to being martyrs to the cause of independence. Rebellion was brooding. A vast scheme to dethrone King Slumberous, murder the dwarf minister, and establish an elective monarchy, was on foot. Of course, Ivned was at head of it, and hoped, no doubt, to win the suffrages of the people, and be elected king. The day was fixed for the first demonstration, and the drowsy King Slumberous stood, without knowing it, on the edge of a volcano.

The evening before the day appointed for the breaking out of the rebellion a strange sight met the eyes of the bewildered Nodlanders. It was nothing less than a bulletin in the Court Journal, announcing that Signor Ivned had, by the gracious will of His Majesty been appointed to the office of Lord Chamberlain. The people could not believe their eyesight. They hastened to Ivned's house, but that gentleman sent them word that he was too busy to see them just then, but if they had any complaint to make, they might put it in the form of a petition. His disappointed adherents went away muttering threats of vengeance. The whole conspiracy was paralyzed at a blow. Ivned was no longer there to stir the sediment of public wrongs, and it began to settle down. The day appointed for the revolution arrived.

A few undecided groups of people were seen in the public squares. One or two enthusiasts endeavoured to address the crowds, but were promptly arrested, and the conspirators, seeing that it was useless to proceed with the affair after the treachery of Ivned, went back to their homes in silence. Thus, was the great sleep-tax established. Henceforth Nodlanders slept according to law; the king built his palace and entertained the Prince of Fungi, and Lord Incubus added another blossom to the crown of public hate which he already wore.

Chapter 3. A Hunting Expedition by the Lake of Dreams

It was a glorious autumn morning; the tall shadowy trees that belted round the dark Lake of Dreams were gemmed here and there with spots of ruby and gold; the small, white clouds floated in the clear blue sky like sleeping sea-birds. The wood-wind murmured to the wave-wind an invitation to forsake the monotonous lake, and come and play among the leaves.

The Lake of Dreams, usually so silent and solitary, on this morning seemed to have actively cast off its gloomy torpor. Bugle notes rang through the rocks and the forest. The deep bay of the hounds echoed through the sonorous aisles of trees, and horsemen gaily attired flashed through the green vistas of the woods. King Slumberous gave a great hunting party that day to his guest and neighbour, the Prince of Fungi

In the middle of a large green circle, which had been artificially cut in the forest for the accommodation of royalty, stood King Slumberous and his suite, accompanied by the Prince of Fungi Ivned was there too, gorgeously dressed, but bearing the vulgar impress of the plebeian on his countenance, and which all his splendour of attire could not disguise. Incubus was there, perched on the top of a tall horse, and looking more like a wood-gnome who had dropped from the branches above upon the saddle, than anything human. The dwarf's principal amusement was plaguing Ivned with allusions to his low origin, and unexpected rise in the world, the topic of all others which wounded the Lord Chamberlain most deeply.

The rest of the group was composed of the young nobility of the court, and no less than five of King Slumberous's wives were present in *palanquins* to see the hunt. The rivalry between these ladies amused the court not a little. Their palanquins were borne on the shoulders of Cock-Crow slaves, and it was a great point with each of them to endeavour to have her *palanquin* held a few inches higher from the ground than the rest Accordingly, the poor Cock-Crows were forced by the rival owners to hold the heavy vehicles as high above their heads as was possible, and even then, each lady might be seen leaning out, and striking her slaves on the head with little sticks, in order to force them to lift her half an inch higher.

"May I never sleep again," said King Slumberous impatiently, "if we have not been here over half an hour without finding even a wild boar. This will never do."

"Here is a tame one, your Majesty," replied Incubus, pointing to Ivned, who looked as if he could swallow the dwarf, horse and all.

"He does not look active enough to promise good sport," said the king, laughing heartily at the dwarf's old wit

"How should he be active?" said Incubus with a sneer; "he has been used the greater part of his life to lying in the mire."

Ivned grew as red as the fallen leaves around him, at this bitter allusion to his birth. He raised himself in his stirrups, elevated his right arm, and assumed the menacing attitude he was once so famous for, when he rose to reply to some assailant at the demagogical meetings. But suddenly remembering where he was, and his altered position, he let his arm drop, and glancing maliciously over the dwarfs deformed person, said:

"Whether I lay in the mire, or whether I led the people, I always left a better impression than you could make, Lord Incubus."

"Ha! you have it there, Incubus," said the Prince of Fungi, who always thought it necessary to explain other people's jokes. "He alludes to your being so ill-made."

"And I," said Incubus, darting a glance full of malice at Ivned, "alluded to his being so ill-begotten."

"Ha! you have it now, Signer Ivned," said the prince; "he means that you are low-born."

"Better that, your Highness, than—"

What this retort would have been was never known, for just at this moment a loud cry broke from a thicket close by, and everybody's attention was instantly drawn to the place from which it proceeded.

"Let us see what all this is," said King Slumberous, spurring his horse into the thicket; "it sounded like the snarl of a hyena."

The rest of the party forced their way after the king, and as they plunged deeper and deeper into the wood, the cries became louder, and were apparently mingled with the low, ferocious growl of hounds at combat. Full of curiosity, the king and his suite hurried on, as fast as the thick brushwood would allow, and bursting through a thick screen of low trees, found themselves suddenly the spectators of a very curious scene.

In the centre of a small glade, two huge hounds belonging to the royal pack were engaged in fierce combat with a beautiful leopard. The latter, though attacked on both sides, defended itself with equal dexterity and courage. Its eyes gleamed like the wood-flames at night, and its white teeth were flecked with the blood of its assailants. It used its long, graceful tail as a weapon of defence, and dealt the hounds heavy blows with it whenever they came within its reach. Its attitudes were so full of grace, its bounds so supple and elegant, and its courage so indomitable, that the king could not restrain an exclamation of admiration,

"Hold off! hold off!" he cried to the hounds; "where is our master of the hunt? We must have that leopard alive. He is a beautiful creature."

The hounds, awed by the king's voice, ceased, their attacks, and drew off to a little distance, where, with bleeding flanks, they stood and glared at their enemy. The leopard, as soon as he found himself free, glanced disdainfully at the crowd of spectators, and walked slowly towards the edge of the thicket.

"Why, look, brother," cried the Prince of Fungi, pointing to him as be retreated, "what an extraordinary circumstance! he has a steel collar round his neck. He must be a tame beast."

"So, he has, by Somnus!" cried the king. "Let us follow him. I must have him for my menagerie."

The leopard, when he saw himself pursued by the king, turned round and showed his teeth as if expecting an attack; but finding that the king stopped too, he again went his way towards the thicket. When he arrived at the edge, he stopped at what seemed to be a heap of dead leaves, and smelled carefully all round. He then lay down.

"I see a man!" cried Incubus; "I see a man half covered with leaves, near to where the leopard is lying. The beast has killed somebody."

"If he has, he shall suffer for it." said the king, dismounting. Then, drawing his sword, he cautiously approached the spot indicated by the dwarf. The leopard did not move, and as the king drew nearer he saw that the animal was lying with his head resting on the chest of a man whose form was half concealed in the dry leaven, he never took his eye off of the king for a moment, and was ready in an instant to act on either the offensive or defensive. The king gazed curiously at the man thus strangely guarded, and then beckoned to some of his suite to come closer.

"The man is asleep," said he, as Incubus cautiously drew near.

"What! a man asleep in the royal forest?" cried the dwarf. "We must see whether he has got his certificate."

So saying, the dwarf stooped down, and flung a small pebble at the sleeping man, who awoke with a sudden start, and gazed round with a bewildered air at finding himself in the centre of so brilliant a throng of people.

"What is your name; and what do you here?" asked Incubus, in a tone of authority

The man—or rather youth, for he did not seem more than nineteen years of age—stared in astonishment for a few moments, and said in a weak voice.

"I was faint with travel, and lay down to sleep. Pina, here, promised to watch over me while I slumbered, but she has betrayed her trust;" and he looked reproachfully at the leopard, which still lay in the same position. The animal, as if it understood its master, gave a low moan, and turned its large eyes pleadingly towards him. "What ails thee, Pina?" he continued, laying his hand gently on its head; "what ails thee? Do not grieve; I am not angry with thee; but stay—what is this? Oh! how did this happen to thee, dear Pina?"

This exclamation was the result of a slight movement on the part of Pina, thereby disclosing a maimed and shattered leg, which easily accounted for her apparent breach of trust. The youth seemed as much grieved as if it had been his own limb that had been wounded, and hung over his pet with an air of touching grief.

"The animal defended you bravely," said the king. "It was in a combat with two of my bloodhounds that she received that wound."

"Poor, faithful Pina!" muttered the youth.

"But you have not answered for yourself," persisted Incubus, who smelled a mystery as a beagle would a hare "What do you here; and what is your name?"

"I am called Zoy," said the youth suddenly.

"Zoy! why, that must be a Cock-Crow name. Are you one of that nation?'

"I am."

"Whose slave, are you?"

"I am no man's slave!' and the youth looked at Incubus with a proud glance.

"A Cock-Crow in Nodland, and not a slave? By my faith, this is strange. Where is your sleep-certificate?"

"What certificate? I have none."

"Do you not know that any man sleeping without a certificate is liable to be imprisoned for life? at least according to the act passed by His Gracious Majesty the King here;" and Incubus nodded at King Slumberous as he spoke.

The youth caught at the word

"Is this the king?" he asked eagerly, and quite forgetting poor Pina's wounded leg in his anxiety to learn.

"I am the king," said His Majesty; "what want you?"

"Justice! your Majesty, justice!" cried the youth, throwing himself at the king's feet. "I ask for justice."

"A downright insult to the king's prime minister," said Ivned to the Prince of Fungi, in a tone loud enough for Incubus to hear it.

"Ha! there's at you, Incubus," cried the prince, explaining as usual; "he means that while you are at the head of affairs, there is little use in asking for such a thing."

"In what way have you been aggrieved, young man?" asked the king gently

"I had a bride, your Majesty, a dear bride, the only creature in life I cared for, except Pina there, we lived together in a little cottage in our own country, we were very happy and knew no care; I hunted for our living, and we had plenty of venison drying over our chimney, and Pina—poor Pina there, used to hunt down a deer or two for us whenever we were out of meat."

Pina waved her tufted tail gently, as if she took some pleasure in these reminiscences of her sporting exploits.

"Well, your Majesty, we were very happy, as I say, until one day we saw a great army coming up the mountain, and a bugle was blown, and I saw my neighbours hurrying away to hide themselves, and then I knew that the Nodlanders were on us. Well, I caught up my bride in my arms, and tried to escape to a cavern hard by, where I might remain concealed, but I was intercepted by twenty or thirty soldiers, who fell upon me; and though Pina there and I fought hard, we were overpowered and both left for dead, and when I recovered my senses I found my bride gone—torn from me—torn off into slavery, she that had never soiled her hands with work in her life! Oh! your Majesty! give me back my bride, give me justice, or let me work by her side. It is a cruel, cruel system!" and the youth wept bitterly

"My friend!" said King Slumberous solemnly, "the Cock-Crow question is one that we never discuss. What was your bride's name?"

"She was called Lereena, your Majesty; but she would be easily known by her beauty."

"Lereena!" exclaimed Incubus starting; "that was her name then?"

"Yes! Lereena. Oh! do you know anything of her, sir? is she still alive?"

"No, no, the name merely struck me as being a strange one, that is all. I know nothing of her, I assure you. Your Majesty had better send this fellow to prison, for being without his sleep certificate," whispered the dwarf in a low voice to the king, "The example is worth making."

"I leave all these things to you, Incubus," replied the king; then turning to Zoy: "You will have to be a slave, young man. It is the law. But I will cause inquiries to be made after Lereena, and if she can be discovered, you shall be placed in the same household."

"Heaven bless your Majesty!" cried poor Zoy, as much delighted as if he received a court appointment instead of being doomed to captivity. "I will work better than any Cock-Crow in Nodland, if I am near my Lereena."

"Your leopard there?"

"Poor Pina!" said Zoy, turning tenderly to her, "she has broken her leg. Your Majesty will let her remain with me—will you not? She is the only one now that loves me."

"Pina shall be cared for," answered the king, "but she cannot remain with you. She shall be attached to the palace. My favourite wife wants a pet, and this beautiful leopard will be sure to please her. Incubus, attach this young man to your body of slaves; and, in the interval, institute inquiries about his bride Lereena."

"But, your Majesty! I have not room," and the dwarf looked anything but pleased at this arrangement

"I have said it," rejoined the king, with oriental significance.

Zoy, when he heard that Pina was to be separated from him, turned sadly away, and large tears rolled down his smooth, youthful cheeks. He stooped down and kissed the wounded animal, while his chest might be seen heaving with suppressed sobs.

"Pina," he whispered, as if he fancied that she was imbued with intelligence equal to his own; "Pina, you will be free, when I am in captivity; make use of your liberty, Pina, as I would make use of mine, if I had it Seek out our Lereena!"

Pina raised her large, soft eyes to his face, as if she fully understood what he said, and accepted the task which he had assigned to her

Incubus, who, for some reason best known to himself, did not appear at all obliged to King Slumberous for giving Zoy to him as a slave, but was of course obliged to obey the royal mandate, gave his new acquisition in charge to two of his attendants, with whispered directions that the moment they reached his palace, they were to confine the youth in the eastern dungeon, and on no account to allow him to be seen by anyone about his residence. So Zoy, after making a profound obeisance to the king, and giving a farewell glance at poor Pina, whose broken leg the huntsman was binding up, set off for the dwarf's palace between his two ferocious-looking guards.

Then the bugle sounded once more; the hounds bayed through the deep woods, the king mounted his horse, Incubus commenced his verbal attacks on Ivned, while the Prince of Fungi continued his explanations, and the whole cavalcade swept from the scene, leaving the spot, which was a moment before brilliant with golden trappings and waving plumes, to its original silence. And the leaves that dared not fall before in the presence of majesty, now rained down in brown myriads from the boughs; the wild birds peeped forth from their coverts, lost in wonder at the strange beings who had just disturbed their solitude, and the timid heart of the hidden deer regained its usual pulse, as it heard the frightful voice of man no longer.

Chapter 4: Lereena

The palace of the dwarf minister was situated in the suburb. A more delightful spot can scarcely be imagined. Beautiful grounds extended about the house, which was built of the finest red and white marble. Fountains hidden among the trees sent a soothing murmur through the shadowy walks with which the place was traversed, and all through the domain were scattered the most luxurious apparatus for slumber that the ingenuity of a people who made sleep the principal object of their existence could contrive. Sometimes it was a swing which hung from the summit of some sturdy oak, and which oscillated gently with the breeze that played among the branches. Another was a cool grotto, where couches of moss and fragrant herbs invited the indolent and the weary to a perfumed repose. Or it might be a delicious arbour cunningly contrived, in the very heart of some great tree, screened round by faintly rustling leaves, and guarded by sentinel birds of a peculiar species, that were fond of such trees, and who, sitting motionless among the boughs, emitted all day long a low, stream-like note, like an Aeolian harp played beneath the waves

The interior of the palace was not less enchanting. Fountains played in the centre of the rooms, each of which opened into a conservatory devoted to the culture of a certain species of plant. Beautiful birds, tamed and highly trained, flew among the graceful leaves and blossoms, and every possible description of couch was scattered through the apartments.

It was evening. The sun was setting above the dark crests of a grove of chestnuts, and pouring his blood-red beams through the lofty window of stained glass which decorated one end of a room in the palace called "the Chamber of Poppies." Through this room a heavy narcotic odour diffused itself from an adjoining conservatory, which was filled with every species of soporific plant—an odour that merely soothed the nerves, or produced complete slumber, according as certain glass valves which formed a means of atmospheric communication were cither closed or open. A fountain of delicate pink water played in the centre of the chamber, and its spray, lit by the crimson light of the sunbeams, assumed an aspect of prismatic splendour. Here, reclining on cushions of green velvet whose pile was so high that it resembled moss more than any artificial fabric, reposed Lord Incubus.

At his feet, with a species of ivory *mandolin* in her hand, reclined a young girl of the most exquisite beauty. Her features were regular, and her complexion pale; and with eyes of the most lustrous darkness she combined the rare beauty of tresses that seemed like a mass of spider-webs dyed in liquid sunlight.

She was looking very sad and melancholy. Her *mandolin* lay in a listless hand, and she gazed at the sun that was sinking below the treetops as if she wished that she could die with it.

"Lereena!" said Incubus, gazing at her with a hideous leer of affection, "you look sad and melancholy. This must not be, or I shall cease to love you!" and the misshapen wretch laughed as if that would be one of the greatest of misfortunes.

The girl cast a glance of ineffable loathing at him, and sighed deeply.

"Ah! you sigh, Lereena!" the dwarf continued. "What is this secret grief? Are you lamenting the absent Pina? or, perhaps, it is the handsome Zoy for whom you are pining?"

Lereena started.

"Tina—Zoy!" she exclaimed earnestly; "where did you learn those names? Do you know aught about them? Oh, tell me, for pity's sake, tell me about my husband!"

"What charming conjugal affection!" cried Incubus, with affected enthusiasm "What a pity that so faithful a pair should have been ever separated!"

"And my dear faithful Pina! Oh, if she were here, none would dare confine or insult me. She would avenge every dastardly glance;" and as she uttered these words she dashed her *mandolin* passionately on the marble pavement, where it shivered into a thousand fragments.

"How beautiful she looks in a passion!" murmured the dwarf to himself, in a tone of sneering admiration. "I like her beauty even better than when it is in repose."

"What do you know about my Zoy?" cried Lereena, turning round suddenly and casting a fierce glance at her companion. "You have by this mention of these names roused all that was brooding in my heart; take care that it does not overflow and sweep you into the nothing from which you should never have emerged."

If Lereena imagined that by this violence she was going to over-awe Incubus, she was sadly mistaken. The dwarf was far too cool and self-possessed ever to feel absolute fear. He was brave on philosophical principles, because he knew that fear incapacitated one from taking proper care of one's self. So, when Lereena stood before him, with flashing eye and advanced foot, and one hand grasping a small dagger that hung at her girdle, he only laughed and emitted the species of sound that one would use to an irritated cat.

"Be quiet, Lereena, will you?" he said contemptuously. "Sit down there; I have something to say to you."

Lereena bit her lip, but obeyed him.

"Now," continued Incubus, settling himself amid his pillows, "as you have imagined, I do know something about your handsome Zoy, and your dear faithful Pina. In fact, I may say, I know a good deal about them."

Lereena's eyes flashed, and she looked for an instant as if she was about to spring on him. She restrained herself, however, and contented herself with tearing the red and blue beads off of her slippers.

"I know," went on the dwarf, "that Zoy is in prison, and will perhaps remain there for life."

"Zoy in prison! oh, what has he done?"

"Simply this. He came on a wild-goose chase in search of you. He was found slumbering in the royal forest without a sleep certificate, and you know that the punishment for that, in a Cock-Crow, is imprisonment for life"

This was a pure invention of the dwarf's, for Zoy was at that moment working in the farmyard, and there was no such punishment attached to sleeping without a certificate—a fine was all that the law exacted in such cases. But the falsehood had its full effect on poor

Lereena, and she covered her face with her hands and wept bitterly.

"Now," continued Incubus, his eyes twinkling with pleasure at the sight of such grief, "I will restore Zoy to liberty, and also take dear, faithful Pina out of the nasty, filthy menagerie where she is confined in company with a wolf and three owls."

"You will!" cried Lereena, overcome with joy.

"Oh, I will bless you on one condition," said the dwarf in a solemn tone. "You know that I have long tried to win your love."

"Wretch!" cried Lereena, starting from him as one does from a snake when one's feet are bare.

"The time is now come. You are my slave; I bought you. Well, I want you to be something dearer to me. Love me, Lereena, and Zoy shall be free tonight, and Pina shall again gambol at your side and be at once your plaything and protector."

"And forget my husband, my beautiful Zoy? No, no, my Lord Incubus. You have it in your power to make me draw water and hew wood, but to make me love you is beyond your will!"

"You will not consent, then?"

"Never! never! never!"

"You will think better of it If you do not, fair Lereena, you will feel my vengeance. I leave you here to think over my offer. I will return in half an hour, and if you still refuse, why, we shall see."

And with a horrid laugh the dwarf skipped up from his cushions, and locking the door behind him, was gone before Lereena could gather breath to reply.

The moment the monster was out of sight, all the pride that had supported her gave way. She buried her head among the cushions and wept bitterly. Almost unwillingly, her fancy went back to the times when she lived a pure, happy life with her Zoy, among the mountains. She thought of the anxious watches she spent when he was out hunting the deer with Pina, and wild infantine joy when he returned laden with spoil. Her pleasures were few, but each one was so fresh and unpalling that they were worth a whole year of city joys; and all this pure delicious freedom had been in a single day violently exchanged for the basest slavery. It was no wonder that poor Lereena should twist her fingers in her beautiful silken hair, and writhe among the cushions like one in the agonies of death.

She lay in a sort of stupor, the consequence of intense excitement. A low murmur rang through the room, and shaped itself into a melody. Lereena scarce listened at first, but presently it seemed to fall more definitely on her ear. She raised herself from amid the soft pillows, and the following words were heard in a sort of whisper-song, with an accompaniment so aerial and spiritual that one might imagine it some angel playing upon a lyre whose strings were sunbeams:

Lereena, Lereena, the finger of dawn
Has opened the lids of the night,
And I must be gone to the hills where the fawn
Flies along like some vapoury sprite.
But e'er I depart
There's a voice at my heart,
Which whispers to me soft and low—
Lereena, Lereena,
Like scent of verbena,
Will your kiss be to me ere I go?
Lereena!
My queen, ah!
You'll give me a kiss ere I go!

Lereena, Lereena, the flame dripping Sun
Is kissing the lips of the sky;
The white mists fling down, to each mountainous crown,
Moist kisses; why not you and I?
I'm off to the hill
Where the vapours are chill;
I'll want something warm 'midst the snow,
Then Lereena, Lereena,
My sweet little queen, ah!
You'll give me a kiss ere I go—
Lereena,
Sweet queen, ah!
Give one little kiss ere I go!"

"Zoy! Zoy! my own Zoy!" cried Lereena passionately, as the low notes of the last phrase died away. "Oh! come to me! speak to me!"

The doors that separated the conservatory from the room in which she was, opened gently, and amid a stream of narcotic perfume, which flowed from the plants with which it was filled, young Zoy glided into the arms of his bride After the first passionate caresses had exhausted themselves, and they found words to speak, Lereena asked the youth how he had escaped from prison.

"Prison!" echoed Zoy. "I was in no prison, save for the first three days after my apprehension in the forest. I have been working in the farmyard for the last month."

"What a dreadful liar that wretch Incubus is!" cried Lereena; "he told me that you were in prison, and would be condemned to confinement for life in consequence of being found asleep in the forest without a certificate; and he offered to have you released, if—if—I would love him."

"The monster!" said Zoy, grinding his teeth; "he will rue this. I have something to tell you about Incubus You know a man of the name of Ivned."

"The Lord Chamberlain?"

"The same. Well, Ivned has received intelligence that Incubus intends to disgrace him with the king and deprive him of his office. Now he intends to be beforehand with the dwarf. A vast conspiracy is on foot, of which he is the head, to remodel the constitution, appoint new ministers, do away with the oppressive taxation, and liberate our countrymen, the unhappy Cock-Crows. The first step will be taken this evening. The dwarf must die."

"I would plead for his life, Zoy; but while he lives, we can never hope for happiness. Let him die. But we must be cautious. He will return here in a few minutes, to learn my answer to his infamous proposal. He must not find you here, or you are lost. By the way, how did you find me?"

"Ivned led me here. The dwarf is about to return, you say So much the better. You must keep him in conversation, Lereena."

"Zoy! you surely would not—here, in my presence? Besides, if you fail, you will be executed."

"I will run no risk, Lereena; the execution of the plan is confided to one who is irresponsible to human law."

A low whistle sounded outside in the conservatory, and with a farewell embrace, Zoy glided hastily through the door leading to his retreat, almost at the same moment that Incubus entered by another.

"Ha! my fair Lereena," exclaimed Incubus, advancing joyously, rubbing his hands; "you look as bright as a May morning—a fair augury for my hopes. Come; you have reflected, and will listen to reason?" So saying, he endeavoured to pass his hand round her waist.

"Unhand me, monster!" she exclaimed, struggling to escape from his grasp, "unhand me, or you will rue it."

"Come, this is childishness," said Incubus, gnashing his teeth with fury. "I will not be baffled—by Heaven, I will not;" and he wound his long nervous arms around her like a cord.

"Help, help!" cried Lereena, rendered utterly powerless by the sinewy grasp of her assailant.

"Hush!" cried the dwarf; "you will be heard."

At this moment, a strange sound rang through the room; the glass in the conservatory was heard to break, and a swift rushing, like that of an embodied storm, succeeded. Lereena turned her eyes for an instant in the direction of the sound, and to her she saw speeding with great bounds through the twilight, a huge animal, with glaring eyes, and tail that swept around like a pine branch tossed in the tempest. Two leaps more, and the ferocious animal had fastened its claws firmly between the shoulders of the dwarf.

"My God! what is this?" cried Incubus, as he found this unexpected burden on his shoulders, and loosing his grasp of Lereena, he staggered back, making furious efforts to free himself from his new assailant. Lereena, in the confusion of the moment, fancying that her last hour was come, veiled her face, and sank upon her knees. Meanwhile, the struggle between the dwarf and the leopard continued. Incubus, though deformed, was muscular, sinewy, and wonderfully active, and now fought more like a wild beast than a human being. The leopard still retained its original position between his shoulders, striving to drive its powerful white fangs into his vertebrae, while Incubus rolled on the floor, and twisted his body round and round in the attempt to strangle his indomitable antagonist.

They rolled about inextricably mingled, and every now and then the dwarf's long legs or thin arms would be tossed aloft in the air, in the frantic attempt to grasp some vital part of the animal. Then the leopard would lash its tail, and taking a deeper hold with its talons, bury its fangs into the dwarf's sinewy neck. All this took place in perfect silence, broken now and then by a hoarse, guttural cry of despair and agony from Incubus, which the leopard would answer with a short impatient growl, as if he was enraged that the struggle should be so protracted. At length, the dwarf's strength seemed to be exhausted; his wild contortions ceased, and he lay motionless on the floor with the leopard crouched upon his body. He was not yet dead: for a second or two all sound of combat ceased, and in the silence might be heard his heavy, stertorous breathing

The leopard then suddenly raised his head, and seemed for an instant about to forsake his prey, but the next instant his wide jaws opened, an agonized shriek burst from the dwarf—a dull sound, like the cracking of rotten wood, was heard. Incubus's body was suddenly contracted into a lump, by some powerful action of the muscles—then it quivered, straightened out again, and all was still.

The leopard lingered for a moment, raised his head, and looked steadfastly at the body, then leaped with a graceful swinging bound on to the floor, and coming to where Lereena knelt, crouched itself at her feet.

The door of the conservatory opened cautiously, and two men entered with a stealthy step. One was Zoy, the other Ivned.

"It is all over," said Ivned, pointing to the dwarf's body, which lay in a heap on the floor. "The monster will offend society no longer."

"We must lose no time," answered Zoy; "where is Lereena?"

"There she is," replied Ivned, "kneeling at the base of that pillar, with the leopard crouched at her feet."

"Lereena!" cried Zoy, "rejoice with us; our enemy is dead. See! our dear Pina has avenged us both."

But Lereena did not reply, and when Zoy hastened up to her and unfastened the folds of her veil, he discovered that she had fainted. A few drops of the icy water in the fountain, sprinkled upon her forehead, soon brought her to, and all her fears vanished when she recognised in the fierce animal, that she saw bounding through the gloom, her faithful and affectionate Pina.

Ivned now explained that there was no time to lose. In the death of the dwarf, the first step had been taken, and it was necessary to follow it up immediately. The conspirators were assembled in a large body outside Incubus's palace, and only awaited the signal from Ivned to march on the king's residence and demand the restitution of their rights and the abolishment of the sleep-tax. So, without any more delay, Lereena, Zoy, and the demagogue hastened from the palace, followed by Pina, whose jaws were still smeared with the blood of the dwarf, and joined the multitude outside.

Here Ivned made one of his violent speeches against the tyranny of the government; pledged himself to head the people when they went to demand their privileges from the king, and in the conclusion, threw out an indefinite, but sufficiently tangible hint, that now as the dwarf-premier was dead, owing to an *accidental* encounter with a wild animal that had escaped from the king's menagerie, the best thing the King could do would be to place him, Ivned, in his place, and the best thing that the people could do was to insist upon its being done. As there were a great many allusions in this speech to the greatness of Nodland and Nodlanders in general, the people applauded; hut when Ivned alluded to the enfranchisement of the Cock-Crows, a deadly silence fell over the multitude. Man looked at man, as if each feared the other They cast their eyes upon the ground, put their hands in their pockets, and pursed up their lips into little funnels, but not a word was spoken As King Slumberous truly said, "the Cock-Crow question was never discussed in Nodland."

Ivned, when he saw this, turned to Zoy and Lereena, who stood near him, and shrugging his shoulders, whispered something in their ears; whatever it was, it had the effect of producing their immediate departure.

"Come!" said Zoy to his young bride, "let us fly from this accursed country while there is yet time; we should never be anything but slaves here, while if we go far in among the hills of our own dear land, we will live poor, unmolested and free. Leave Ivned to mingle in the stormy whirlpool of politics; the day will perhaps come, when he will be glad to exchange his tedious honours for our peaceful obscurity."

So, saying, the Cock-Crow, followed by his bride and Pina, stole unobserved through the crowd while it was palpitating under the influence of some fiery sentence of Ivned's, and taking immediately to the fields, struck out for the borders of the Cock-Crow country

CHAPTER 5: THE END OF THE DEMAGOGUE

It was a bright morning in spring, the wind blew freshly down the deep ravines, and the eagles that hung in the light-blue atmosphere, swung to and fro upon its currents. A little cottage stood nestled on the side of the hill, into a piece of green pasture, which was shaded gently off into in-closures, filled with springing corn. A waterfall on one side flashed through the foliage of some live oaks that backed the house, while on the other a small patch, evidently sacred to Vertumnus, blushed with all the flowers that spring could call up from the half-awakened earth,

Outside the door of the cottage, and basking in the morning sunbeams, lay a beautiful leopard stretched at full length, while a ruddy bronze-skinned youth was standing close by, leaning on a spear. Presently a young girl issued from the cottage, with a leathern belt in her hand, to which were attached hooks to which the huntsman attached the slaughtered game; this she fastened around the waist of the youth, and then twining her arms around his neck, leaned against him, and turned her eyes lovingly upon his youthful face. It was a charming picture of young, unsatisfied love—she nestling in close to him as if she would work her way into his heart, and he enjoying the luxurious pleasure of such gentle demonstrations, without at the same time forfeiting the peculiar dignity of his sex.

"At what hour will you return, dear Zoy?" asked the girl in a low tone, that expressed something more than the question.

"Oh! I shall not be long, Lereena. If Pina there is not too lazy, we shall have a fat deer in less than an hour."

Pina gave a slight switch of her tail, as if to show that there was yet a portion of animal energy in her that had not evaporated in the hot sunshine.

"Who is that ascending the hill, dear Zoy?" asked Lereena, pointing to the distant figure of a man, who was slowly coming up the ravine. "I never see a stranger, that fear does not riot in my heart, lest it may be those horrid Nodlanders who have come to bear us into slavery."

"Fear not!" said Zoy, grasping his spear with a savage glance. "You will die by my hand, Lereena, before another manacle binds your arm."

"There is something familiar in the appearance of this stranger!" said Lereena, scanning the approaching individual rather anxiously; "but he appears very faint and weary, and his clothes are in tatters. Go to him, Zoy, and help him with your arm; he is weak."

"Why?" cried Zoy, rushing down to meet the stranger, "it is Ivned! what can have brought him here?"

Pina opened one eye on the strength of all this hubbub, but seeing only her master and an old tattered beggar, she wisely concluded that any active measures on her part would be out of place, and closing it again resumed her slumbers.

It was Ivned. But how changed from the brisk favourite of fortune, whom Zoy had left leading a whole nation! He was thin and grey. His eye, once so bold and unquellable, was now sunken and unsteady. His gait was feeble and tottering; his clothes were in tatters, and it would have been indeed impossible to recognize in him the daring, reckless demagogue, for whom no task was too difficult and no assertion too impudent.

"Ah!" said he, when in the evening he was seated at the fire in Zoy's cottage, "I forswear politics for ever. When you fled from Nodland I was in a fair way to greatness. I made the king submit to my terms. The sleep-tax was abolished, and every *burgher* and mechanic in the nation was my friend. Trade improved, because everybody was more attentive than when they had to pay for their sleep. That commodity being taxed, people thought that they were extravagant if they did not take the value of their money; the consequence was, they slept the full legal allowance, which was several hours more than they used to sleep before. But under my administration all this was reformed, and the commerce of Nodland recovered from its lethargy I found the king a feeble man, and I ruled him judiciously. I made him do exactly what I liked, but those measures were always for the good of the people. I consequently became a popular favourite, and when the king and I drove out together, twice as many people cried, 'Long life to Ivned, as to King Slumberous."

"Hum!" said Zoy, in rather a disapproving tone.

"Well, one day I made a covert sneer at the king, which I never intended he should see, and which he never would have seen if it had not been for the Prince of Fungi, who explained the satire to him after his usual manner. The joke was a severe one, and His Majesty never forgave me. But a short time afterwards I was accused of high treason, and of entering into a plot to dethrone the king, and place myself in his stead. I was innocent, but I was imprisoned. However, by the aid of some gold, I effected my escape, and here I am in this delightful rural retreat of yours, among a new people where all is innocence, and who only want a scientific constitution to be perfect. I shall be very happy here, I know."

"I think not," said Zoy gravely, "if your happiness lies, as it did once, in political turmoil and endless quarrel. Listen to me, Ivned: We are an innocent people, we Cock-Crows; we have retired up into these hills which are beyond the reach of the Nodlanders, and we intend to retain our purity. We want no brawling demagogues here; we have no politics, therefore we want no politicians. If you cannot live in peace, and must have excitement and dissension, return to Nodland or to your native island. Your speeches here will not be listened to, and your appeals against tyranny will go for nothing, for everyone is free. But if you are content to settle down as one of us; to hunt the deer, instead of pursuing popular opinion; to cultivate muscle instead of cunning, and to change your political baton into a huntsman's spear, then we will give you the welcome of a man, and you shall be honoured among us."

"You are very kind," said Ivned bitterly, "but I will not trespass upon the hospitality of a country that prescribes rules to its guest. I will return to Nodland, where a scaffold or a throne awaits me: either is preferable to your pastoral obscurity."

So, saying, Ivned arose, and shaking the dust from off his feet, passed out of the house. Zoy made no effort to detain him, but turning to Lereena, he kissed her, and said, "I am sorry, but perhaps it is as well. He could not live in peace, and our country is better without him He is a dangerous man."

And the husband and wife again embraced; and Pina waved her tail gently, until she found that she was waving it into the fire and burning it, when she got up and went growling to the other end of the room; and the deer hung from the rafters; and the noise of the waterfall at the back stole soothingly in through the half-opened window; and all was still and peaceful; and amid this peace, with the hope that it never was disturbed, we leave Zoy and Lereena.

A Legend of Barlagh Cave

Some hundred years ago there lived upon the shores of this lake a young maiden named Aileen. She was beautiful, and of noble and generous disposition. Nigh to her father's home resided a youth called Connor, handsome as Apollo, and brave as Achilles. Aileen loved this youth, but was not loved in return; his affections were cast upon another maiden, worthy of love certainly, but not possessing one-half the charms of Aileen. The latter pined on in secret grief. Each day that she saw Connor go down to his boat and sail out to sea, a tide of blood would rush from her heart, and leave her almost fainting with excess of passion. She watched him when he sought the hills with his gun upon his shoulder, and her eyes traced him up the steep mountain paths with a sick yet loving gaze.

But, oh! what untold agony that maiden suffered when, in the glorious summer evenings, as the sun was sinking in a golden sea, and the grey twilight was creeping like a fox from the hills, she beholds Connor and his betrothed wandering along the fragrant beach, with twining arms and touching cheeks. Then the gorgeous clouds that floated in the western sky, those airy unsubstantial shapes of splendour, seemed to her distempered fancy to change into faces that stared at her with fierce mockery, while the azure heavens glowered upon her with myriads of sneering eyes. The low wind, as it wandered along the beach, sounded in her ear like derisive laughter. The very sea-birds that whirled above the calm surface of the lake, seemed to shriek wildly to her tales of anguish and despair.

As time wore on, so much the deeper did her vain love eat into her soul and inflame her brain. Connor knew not this. He knew not that the hollow eyes and pale cheek which now never deserted Aileen, were all the fruits of love for him. When he met her, he was kind and gentle to the suffering girl—never dreaming that each soft word he uttered planted a fresh arrow in her torn bosom. Nay, once even he saved her from an imminent danger, and bore her in his arms to her father's cottage, when, if he had but known the despair that racked her heart, he would have left her to perish rather than restore her to a life which was nothing but one long calendar of anguish.

At last, the passion that burned within her became too great to be concealed. She determined to make known to Connor her devouring secret. Before doing so, however, she thought she would consult the Spirit of the Hill, who dwelt in a vast breezy cave, on the summit of Cunna Conma, and endeavoured to discover from him some means of winning Connor to her side. One starry night, when the summer dews were falling like a gentle rain, and nought living was on foot save the fox and the wild cat, Aileen left her restless bed, and stealing softly from the house, took the wild and rugged path that led to the summit of the mountain. As she trod that broken and uncertain footway, strange fancies haunted her. The tall dark pines that fringed the narrow path seemed instinct with a sombre life, and nodded and whispered to each other gloomily.

Indistinct and shadowy shapes rushed wildly through the thick brushwood, and chuckling laughter echoed through the trees. There was not an old grey stone that raised itself from out the coppice, which did not take the form and aspect of some terrible and unearthly thing. Aileen walked, surrounded by a mist of horrors. At length, she reached the summit of the mountain, and wended her steps to the cave where dwelt the Spirit of the Hill. Large grey clouds continually veiled the entrance of this solemn place, and within, the plaintive winds chanted all night and day their mountain hymns. Aileen stood upon the rocky threshold, and with a bold and fearless voice, called upon the Spirit. A long, hollow moan, that sounded like the voice of some vanished year, replied to her summons.

"Spirit of the Hill!" she cried, "I summon thee to answer me. How shall I attain either happiness or death? Tell me, thou unseen being, how to win Connor or to die!"

A moment's pause, and then the answer came from the depths of the cave in tones like those of the tempest in a forest

"Seek the cave of Barlagh tomorrow eve," said the hollow voice of the Spirit, "and there wilt thou find rest"

"'Thanks, thanks!" cried Aileen, as the murmurs died away along the hill. "Tomorrow, then, I shall perhaps rest in Connor's arms."

She trod the downward path that night with a lighter step than she had known for months; and, happy in the belief that Heaven had at last taken pity on her hopeless love, she sought her bed, and sank lightly into slumber.

The evening sun was sinking into an amber sea, when Aileen, full of hope, sought this cave of Barlagh. As she urged her little boat through the rapids with a steady hand, her heart beat wildly in her bosom, and delightful visions full of bliss and love floated between her and the gorgeous sky. That destiny would lead Connor to the cave, and that there, through the intervention of the Spirit of the Hill, he would reward her attachment by a return of the passion, Aileen felt quite assured. No shadow of misfortune clouded her soul. No forbidding angel stood between her and the paradise of her imagination. The foaming waves of the rapids soon brought her little skiff abreast of the cavern's mouth, and sweeping round the rocky corner, she was about to enter, when a blue pigeon flew wildly out and almost skimmed her face. She started, and had scarcely time to utter an ejaculation of surprise, when a loud report rang through the echoing chambers of the cavern, and she fell back in the stern-sheets, with her life-blood welling from her bosom.

Another second, and a boat shot out rapidly from the dusky cave, and Connor, who stood in the prow with his gun still smoking in his hand, beheld with horror the form of the bleeding girl. He jumped wildly into her boat, and lifting her in his arms, tried in vain to arrest the flight of her ebbing soul. Then there, with that solemn cave-temple rising grandly above her head, and none to look upon her agony save *Him* and the golden sun—there, in that hour of mortal trial, with the last energies of life quivering and flickering upon her lips, did Aileen pour into Connor's ear the history of her despairing love. She told him of her long days of misery and sorrow, of her sleepless nights, of her sick and wretched soul. She told him how deep, how ungovernable, was her love for him, and how she strove in vain to conquer it, but could not. She related how she had sought the Spirit of the Hill, and what reply he had given.

"He was right!" she said faintly, for her voice was growing weaker each moment, and the shades of death were creeping across her pale face. "The Spirit was right. I am dying in your arms, Connor; and is not that finding rest?"

Sadly, and sorrowfully did Connor hang over the dying girl. Pained by her sad history, wrung with despair at having been the innocent cause of her death, nought but the remembrance that he had someone to live for prevented him from terminating his existence with his own hand. But he knew that there were longing eyes and anxious hearts which awaited his return, and he refrained. Aileen was now speechless, and the coldness of death was chilling her frame. Yet still her dying eyes sought his, and her white lips moved and told him, though he heard no sound, that her heart was uttering a fond farewell. This lasted but a few moments. When the last sunbeam had ceased to cast its golden shadow on the heavens and the ocean, her spirit fled.

The Wonderful Adventures of Mr. Papplewick

1

Mr. Papplewick kept a hardware store in Maiden lane. He was a man of grave demeanour, and was much respected by his neighbours, both for the probity of his conduct and the sobriety of his manners. He was well to do in the world, and was more than usually blessed in the domestic relations of life, as he had the happiness to possess an affectionate spouse and two lovely children. This social felicity which he had enjoyed uninterruptedly for eleven years was, however, soon to be shivered, and the very ties which once constituted his entire enjoyment were about to add keener pangs to his misery.

One day, after dining with a friend, Mr. Papplewick felt a little unwell, and happening to mention this to an old lady who was just then paying a visit to his wife, she immediately advised him to send to the next apothecary for some Magnesian Pills, which medicine, she said, was an infallible specific for all dyspeptic affections. Having great faith in the old lady's knowledge in all matters relating to the healing art, Mr. Papplewick did as she recommended, and at once despatched the female servant, Bridget, to the nearest apothecary's, with directions to get him a small box of the Magnesian Pills.

Now, Bridget misunderstanding the directions given to her, went to the apothecary and asked him for a box of *Magnetic Pills,* which she brought to Mr, Papplewick, who, without considering the label, swallowed as many of them as he considered would constitute a dose. Now these pills, as their nature indicates, possess the terrible power of rendering whoever swallows them magnetic in the highest degree, and were intended by the inventor to be used solely for the destruction of rats and mice, which vermin on devouring the pills find themselves (owing to the magnetic power) suddenly attracted to the nearest steel rat trap, where they meet the usual fate of their race. The wondrous powers of these pills had never yet been tried on a human being, until Mr. Papplewick became the unhappy victim of the inventor's well-meant science.

Immediately after he had swallowed the fatal potion, he felt a sort of cold vibration run through his veins, and his extremities became like ice and seemed to move independent of his will. The next moment he observed that a strange vitality appeared to have infused itself into several articles of furniture in the room. The fire-irons suddenly began to move slowly from their places within the fender, and advance towards him. Terrified at what he believed to be some diabolical sorcery, Mr. Papplewick retreated rapidly into a corner of the room, where he remained a picture of terror. But all attempt at escape seemed vain. The fire-irons followed him with increasing speed, and he now saw several other metallic articles in his vicinity gradually putting themselves into motion and advancing in the same direction as their companions.

Firmly believing that he was a victim to some deep-laid scheme of the Evil One, Mr. Papplewick shouted loudly for assistance and began to utter his prayers lustily, but just at this moment the fire-irons having approached more nearly, suddenly flew up in the most wonderful manner and attached themselves to his person, while all the metal furniture of the apartment was rushing rapidly towards him, preparatory to following their example. It was then, for the first time, that the terrible truth burst upon him, that since the moment he had swallowed the pills he had become a *living magnet!* He rushed towards the table, through much incommoded by the strange additions the last minute had made to his person, and taking up the box read upon the label in large letters,

LYONS' MAGNETIC PILLS!

"Gracious Heaven!" he cried, "I am doomed for the rest of my existence, to be nothing more than a human loadstone. Why was I ever born to have such a fate pursue me? Better, a thousand times better, that I had perished before these eyes had ever opened upon the light of day!"

Overpowered with this terrible prospect, he sank with a groan into a rocking chair that was near, and covering his face with his hands continued to inveigh against Providence which had so wantonly persecuted him. "What have I ever done" said he, "that I should be thus punished? I have never wronged a neighbour—neither have I forsaken a friend when he wanted my assistance. I have been a faithful husband, an indulgent father, and a conscientious employer. I owe not any man, and out of my superfluous wealth I have given largely to the poor. But in spite of all this, Heaven has cursed me with a misfortune which is of too terrible a nature to be visited on the worst of sinners."

In this way did the unhappy man rail against Providence and with sighs and tears contemplate the horrible future which stretched out so drearily before his mental vision. He was aroused from these bitter reflections by the opening of the door, and his wife, who had been attracted by his cries for help, entered and approached him. As soon as she beheld the condition in which he was, she was struck with the most profound grief and astonishment.

"Good God!" she exclaimed, "what sight is this I behold? Speak, Hezekiah, speak, and in mercy to me explain the meaning of this frightful mystery."

"Alas! Jemima," he replied, "Your Hezekiah no longer belongs to himself or you. He is an outcast from society; a curse to himself and a burden to his friends."

So, saying, he related to the weeping Jemima the history of the strange events which had befallen him, telling her how he had swallowed the wrong pills in mistake, and how in consequence he had been immediately transformed into a human magnet, with the power of attracting every metallic substance which came within his sphere. "And now, dear Jemima, I have told you all"— he concluded, pointing to the fire shovel which had attached itself to his nose—"You have a magnet for a husband, and behold the result."

Though nearly overwhelmed by this astounding misfortune, Mrs. Papplewick still maintained that presence of mind which, in cases of sudden difficulty, renders woman so superior to man. She instantly began to revolve in her mind whether there was not some means of ridding her husband of this unhappy attribute, and at last came to the resolution of taking him without further loss of time to a celebrated foreign physician, who possessed a great reputation for dealing successfully with uncommon cases. She proposed it to her husband, who having implicit confidence in his wife's judgment, instantly prepared to accompany her.

A new and unforeseen difficulty however arose. On making an attempt to rise from the rocking chair into which he had flung himself in his first paroxysm of grief, he found himself held back by an irresistible power. The chair was unhappily constructed of iron, and the magnetic power now inherent in his body gaining strength by contact with the metal, became so powerful that he found he must either remain always where he then was, or carry the chair along with him in its present position. The latter, from its weight, was impossible, and all his efforts to extricate himself proved unavailing

He was again sinking into a state of utter despondency, and calling on death to release him from his sufferings, when the quick intellect of Mrs, Papplewick suggested a remedy. She sent out instantly and hired a number of strong labourers. A powerful machine was then introduced through the window, like the cranes used on wharves, and the chair in which Mr. Papplewick was imprisoned was firmly screwed to the floor. A rope was now passed through a pulley at the end of the machine, and fastened strongly under Mr. Papplewick's shoulders. The other end of the rope was held by six powerful men who pulled at it with all their might.

The operation was highly painful to Mr. Papplewick, because being clung to the chair at one end and dragged towards the ceiling at the other, his body naturally became gradually elongated and his joints cracked horribly. He endured it all, however, without a murmur, and after some minutes hard pulling he had the satisfaction of finding himself gradually lifted out of the chair, and then suddenly propelled against the ceiling with considerable violence. A cry of joy burst from his wife's lips at the success of her experiment, but her enthusiasm was considerably damaged when on his being lowered she perceived that her husband, who had always been a man of very ordinary stature, had been considerably lengthened in the process of extrication, and from being rather short and stout had grown to be exceedingly tall and proportionately slender Happy, however, at loosing him from bondage under any circumstances, she embraced him affectionately and sent for a carriage to convey him to the foreign physician's—taking, however, the precaution to oil his body all over, so that in case he stuck to any of the iron work of the vehicle the slippery surface would render his release less difficult.

2

The foreign physician lived at the upper end of Broadway, close to the New York Hotel. He was a very famous man and had a great number of grand titles prefixed to his name, all of which he declared had been conferred on him by the principal potentates of Europe for distinguished services he had rendered them in extreme cases. Mrs. Papplewick had great faith in him on account of a certain wonderful cure he was said to have performed on a poor boy with distorted limbs. The youth came to Dr. Baron Splashassco (such was the physician's name) in order to have his legs straightened. The Baron declared the cure to be quite possible, and having obtained the usual fee, he ordered the boy to keep his legs in boiling water until the misshapen bones softened, when nothing was easier than to remould the legs into a symmetrical form The poor boy, unfortunately for the interest of science, lacked the moral courage necessary to enable him to undergo the operation "But," as Mrs. Papplewick afterwards said, 'there can he no doubt but that the boy would have been cured, if he only did what the doctor told him."

By a lucky chance the baron was at home when Mr. and Mrs Papplewick arrived—he met them at the door with a respectful inclination of the head and ushered them into his private study, the walls of which were decorated with the portraits of celebrated cripples he had cured, one picture representing the unfortunates in a state of unnatural distortion, the other portraying them restored to a symmetrical form by the wondrous art of the Physician.

When Mrs. Papplewick had fully described the unhappy events which had brought them, and explained the terrible destiny which pursued her husband, she paused with intense anxiety for the baron's reply. That gentleman, however, did not seem to have any intention of speaking. At first Mrs. Papplewick imagined that he was ruminating profoundly over her husband's case, but presently perceiving his eyes directed scrutinisingly towards her hands she instantly recollected that it was the invariable custom of this great physician to receive his fee in advance, and he was now, no doubt, waiting to have the established usage complied with. Producing her purse, she at once handed him a note for fifty dollars, and it was wonderful to see the effect which the transfer had on the hitherto grave countenance of the baron. He lost all his lugubrious aspect, and proceeded with much animation to examine Mr. Papplewick.

"This is a strange case indeed," said he, as soon as he had completed his investigation, "there is only one similar case on record, and that occurred at St. Petersburgh, in Russia. The man was an officer in one of the Cossack regiments, and the magnetic disease attacked him very suddenly. The first intimation he had of it was one day on parade,

495

when the lances of his men suddenly escaped from their grasp, and flying towards him with the velocity of an arrow, pierced his heart with a hundred wounds."

Mr. Papplewick groaned audibly.

"There is but one mode of treating this malady," continued the Baron, "and that is unhappily a severe one. The magnetic power has by this infused itself into our friend's blood, and of this infected blood it will be absolutely necessary to drain him ere we can hope to rid him of the disease. As soon as his veins are thoroughly exhausted of all sanguine matter they contain, we can easily refill them with the blood of some young healthy animal—a lamb for instance."

At this horrible picture of what was before him, Mr Papplewick's brain whirled. He saw himself stretched on a board wounded with a hundred lancets, and counting the tickings of the Doctor's watch as his tide of life ebbed slowly away. Then he saw people holding a nasty bleeding quadruped, from whose impure veins his were supplied with an unnatural circulation. Who knows then, but that with the blood he may imbibe the habits of the animal—and ever after bleat or bray through the world. Oh! it was too much. His brain grew hot as fire, and with a wild shriek he rushed from the room into the street. He sped down Broadway like a mad man. There was but little fear of his friends' recognising him, as his figure had become greatly elongated in his extrication from the rocking chair, and the wild terror now painted in his features rendered such a chance still more improbable.

For a long time, he wandered about not knowing where to go, and industriously avoiding every place where he might appear to meet those he knew. His distress of mind was terrible, and he thought with anguish upon the happiness of the home from which a cruel destiny had driven him. He was likewise much annoyed in his passage through the streets, by the numerous bits of old iron and broken horse shoes scattered about, all of which would instantly attach themselves to his person and cause considerable trouble in the removal. At the corner of Fulton street, and only a few doors from the *Lantern* office, while he was in the act of detaching a piece of rusty hoop which had clung to his leg, a gentleman accosted him, attracted no doubt by the singularity of his movements. The gentleman spoke so kindly that Papplewick felt irresistibly attracted to him, and it was not long before he unbosomed himself to the stranger, giving him a detail of all his misfortunes. His new acquaintance seemed greatly interested in his sad history, and evinced a strong desire to assist and comfort him.

"Come!" said the benevolent stranger, "thou can'st not wander about the streets all night—come with me, my house is near and right gladly will I give thee shelter; we will treat thee well and make thee as one of the family."

Touched to the heart by this disinterested offer, Papplewick gladly accepted it, and his smooth-spoken acquaintance bidding him follow led the way to his abode.

It seemed a strange house to Mr. Papplewick. It was very large, and covered outside with paintings There was a band playing on the balcony, and crowds of people were continually passing in and out. On remarking this, the stranger replied that owing to his being a public man he had a great many visitors Pushing through the crowd, the stranger led Papplewick up a private staircase into a large room in which were some half dozen persons of very singular aspect There was a boy so enormously tall that his head nearly touched the ceiling—there was an old withered man not more than three feet in height, who was sitting on the mantle-piece, while at the farther end of the room was what appeared to be a large bath, in which was swimming some animal with a human head and the tail of a fish. The stranger now bid Papplewick remain where he was, and promising to be back presently he left the room.

Papplewick's reflections were anything but pleasant in the curious company in which he found himself, and he wondered seriously at the strange taste of his new friend, who could fill his house with such a number of monstrosities. While he was thus cogitating upon this and his own melancholy prospects, a door at the farther end of the room was thrown open and a crowd of people entered eagerly. Papplewick was surprised to find himself almost immediately the object of their undivided attention. They walked around him and stared at him, until he began to feel both indignant and uncomfortable, and he actually saw one man sketching him on the leaf of his tablets.

Several little boys present annoyed him greatly by presenting penknives at his person, and crying out with delight when they stuck to him. Totally at a loss to imagine what was the reason of all this curiosity, Papplewick began to wish heartily for the return of the stranger. Just then two gentlemen entered, who came up to him and regarded him with great attention. After a little time one of them opened a small packet and taking a handful of iron filings out of it, threw them towards Papplewick, to whose person they immediately adhered. Both the gentlemen cried "how very singular! what a curious phenomenon!" and Papplewick, full of indignation was about to resent so unprovoked an insult, when his eye fell on a bill which one of them carried in his hand. There, to his horror, he saw in large letters—

BARNUM'S MUSEUM
MR. PAPPLEWICK,
THE HUMAN MAGNET?!!
ADMISSION 25 CENTS.

Overpowered at this discovery he sank into a chair. All was now clear to him. His hospitable friend was no other than the Arch-Speculator himself, and for the future he was to be exhibited at 25 cents a head, in company with a giant, a dwarf and a mermaid.

3

As soon as Mr Papplewick had recovered from the stupor into which his appalling discovery had thrown him, he burst into the most bitter reproaches against his false friend who, under the guise of hospitality, had converted him into a degrading exhibition.

"Oh! my Jemima," he cried in heartbroken accents, "how foolish was I ever to leave your affectionate bosom to wander madly through the world a prey to the designing, and an object of pity to none, Heaven is my witness that if I ever again find myself by your side, no misfortune, however great, shall tempt me to abandon it, for there is no pang which cannot be alleviated by the tender cares of those that love us."

While he was thus bitterly inveighing against his destiny, the giant approached him and endeavoured to console him in his own rough fashion.

"Bless you!" said he, "it's nothing when you're used to it; at first I didn't like it but as little as you, but now I take it all easy and the people may stare as much as they like for all that I care. So, cheer up old fellow, there's no use in being down in the mouth about it. It isn't every man whose figure is a fortune to him like yours and mine."

Papplewick made no reply to this well-meant address, but to groan bitterly and rock himself to and fro in his chair; while he was indulging in these sombre reflections, he heard a noise behind him and turning round, to his horror discovered that the mermaid had got out of her bath and was making advances towards him of a character not to be mistaken. Completely upset by this new discovery, he sprang from his chair and rushed violently towards the door, which before he had reached it opened inwards and the Arch-Speculator, accompanied by two gentlemen, stood before him.

"Save me, save me!" gasped Papplewick, seizing the speculator by the arms.

"What's the matter? what has happened?" demanded his friend.

"Th-th-at thing th-th-e-re wanted to kiss me," stammered Papplewick, pointing to the mermaid who was floundering back to her bath in a great hurry.

"Oh! is that all," they exclaimed, and the three gentlemen fell to laughing violently at Mr. Papplewick's distress. The Arch-Speculator then took him on one side and told him that the two gentlemen whom he saw with him were celebrated philosophers, who had been attracted by the strange magnetic phenomenon which he, Mr. Papplewick's person, exhibited. That they had made a proposal to him relative to Mr. Papplewick, which he trusted, for the interest of science and for the sake of the world at large, that gentleman would not hesitate to accept. This was nothing less than that Mr. Papplewick should undertake a voyage of discovery to the North Pole—the magnetic power which was inherent in his system fitting him peculiarly for such a task.

At the bare mention of this proposition, Mr. Papplewick's heart sank within him, and he saw himself undergoing all the perils of an Arctic winter, blocked up in the ice, hunted by Polar bears and probably in the end reduced to the extremity of subsisting for weeks together upon a pair of boots. In vain, however, did he decline this honourable but dangerous office. The scientific gentlemen talked so much and so loudly, and painted in such a lively manner the immortality which would encompass his name in case of success, that Papplewick's resolution melted before their arguments as snow before a kitchen fire, and it was not long until home, Jemima, children and all were forgotten in the gorgeous and golden dreams of Fame. As soon as his consent to the expedition had been obtained, the scientific gentlemen immediately undertook to put it into instant execution.

A liberal merchant volunteered the use of one of his condemned ships for the voyage, and a promise of liberal payment soon secured the services of an active and valuable crew. As to Mr. Papplewick, he spent all the time previous to his departure in preparing for the exigencies of his undertaking. Tailors measured him for Polar suits, Navy

Contractors presented him with casks of preserved meats that could not be smelt farther than half a mile, and a celebrated Chemist bestowed on him a box of life preserving pills, one of which was sufficient to sustain existence for a month without the aid of any other nourishment. All arrangements having been completed, Mr. Papplewick arrayed himself in a nautical suit, purchased a telescope with a leather sling, put on a yachting hat and prepared for his departure. Previous to this, however, he had an affecting interview with his wife and children, which was of too harrowing a nature to inflict upon the reader.

At ten o'clock, on a fine April morning, Mr. Papplewick sailed in the schooner *Bam*, amid the acclamations of the assembled multitude, which he gracefully acknowledged from the poop, bowing and waving his little hat repeatedly.

Despite the perils he was about to encounter, and the agony of parting from his country and relatives, Mr. Papplewick did not feel so well since the fatal hour when he imbibed the magnetic dose. He was growing accustomed to his fate, the novelty was wearing off and with it much of the anguish, and nothing now filled his mind but magnificent visions of glory Sebastian Cabot, Vespucius, Columbus, Cortez, all sank into insignificance before the illustrious Papplewick, who, single handed, was about to solve the great mystery of the world and drag away with daring hand the icy veil with which it was shrouded by the spells of nature? Papplewick indicated the greatness of the thoughts that were passing through his soul by standing treat that night to all the crew, which liberality elevated him considerably in the opinions of the sailors, and towards the end of the evening he was on such good terms with them that he was heard to pronounce them to be "cabilalset of fellows." Thus, passed Papplewick's first night at sea.

Days, weeks went by and the weather became colder and colder. The *Bam* though an old vessel was a fast sailer, and every day enormous icebergs might be seen floating by with a look of placid but mighty majesty. The crew being chosen almost at hazard were mutinous and reckless, and the days and nights were spent in carousal and debauch. Several times the captain was observed to look at the compass with a strange and puzzled air, and he took many solar and lunar observations but still seemed to be at fault. The first mate was heard likewise to declare that something extraordinary must be the matter with the needle, or their charts must be false, as they could not determine the ship's position by the usual course.

This state of things continued for several days until the crew, which had hitherto left the vessel very much to herself, began to gather in knots on the forecastle, and whisper and point at Mr. Papplewick mysteriously. Papplewick never dreaming of any machinations against his safety, was standing one evening on the quarter deck watching the numberless icebergs which surrounded the ship on all sides, and which glowed in the light of the setting sun like mountains of opal. As he was dreaming of his future glory and wondering who would write his life, the captain stepped up to him and begged to speak with him. He then told him that the crew had declared that Mr. Papplewick's magnetic power had caused such a variation in the needle, that the ship had lost its bearings and that they were not safe as long as he remained on board. They had, therefore come to the resolution of disposing of him as a second Jonah, and throwing him into the sea.

Horrified at this termination to his expedition, Mr. Papplewick threw himself upon his knees before the captain and begged for mercy. But the crew rushed forward in a body, and regardless of his tears and entreaties they were preparing to throw him over the side, when an appalling cry issued from the captain's lips. Everybody turned and looked at the ship's bow, where his finger was pointed. There, hastening towards the vessel with a smooth and awful rapidity, they beheld a vast mountain of ice whose cold summits glowing with reflected fire, towered far above the mast. Every heart grew still. Papplewick was forgotten. Not a cry was heard, but every man stood face to face with death.

On came the giant of ice, his chilly breath swept across the pale faces of the crowd, and they heard the waves rippling around his sharp and jagged base. Majestically, swiftly, noiselessly it swept on to the devoted vessel, the very incarnation of silent but resistless power—then came a grating sound, every one shut his teeth and held his breath—then a dull soft crash, the frail timbers of the vessel split asunder like water, there was a sound of swelling waves and the schooner swaled downwards with a sickening motion Every soul on board looked to heaven for the last time and beheld a tall glittering spire of ice, that seemed to reach to and pierce the skies, then the planks sank beneath their feet. The iceberg moved majestically on, and there was not a trace of the *Bam* upon the ocean!

4

Engulphed in the foaming surge, hollow, gurgling sounds swelled in Papplewick's ears, and a horrible sense of suffocation pressed, like a load of iron, on his chest. He struck out wildly in all directions, but still seemed to sink downwards with a swift and easy motion. Flashes of many coloured fires danced before his eyes, and by a strange mental operation, a continuous vision of his entire life from childhood up to the present hour flitted before him like a panorama, and impressed him with all the vivid sensations of reality. Then a black mist came over all—his breath was suspended; he could feel the blood rushing through his brain with the noise of some vast waterfall, and the same instant consciousness entirely forsook him.

When Mr. Papplewick recovered his senses, the sun was shining brightly, and gilding with the most gorgeous hues a host of lofty icebergs that floated on every side. He looked around for the schooner, but there was no sign to tell that she ever had been—not even a broken plank or a hencoop floated on the waves. Next, his thoughts naturally reverted to himself, and what was his astonishment at finding that he was self-supported in the water, and floated there as buoyantly as a piece of cork. Though entirely at a loss to account for this singular phenomenon, (unless it was that his magnetic powers had, through some mysterious operation of nature, diminished his specific gravity,) he nevertheless felt considerably reassured by the discovery that he was, at all events insured from the chance of being drowned.

But as he looked around him and saw the cold icebergs floating gradually onwards, without a trace of vegetation upon their glittering spires, and as his eyes wandered over the trackless fields of ice that stretched away in the distance, without a single living thing to break the awful desolation, the conviction flashed upon him that although he might not drown, still there was every possibility of being starved. The prospect of so horrible a fate made him exceedingly melancholy, and as he was inwardly bemoaning his situation, he suddenly recollected his life-preserving pills which the great chemist had given him previous to his departure in the ill-fated *Bam*. Trembling with eagerness, he anxiously sought, in all his pockets, and, to his great and inexpressible joy, discovered the invaluable box which contained the treasure, carefully stowed away in an inner one.

He opened the box and counted the pills. There were exactly twelve, and as each pill was capable of sustaining existence for a month, he calculated on being able to subsist for one year, before the expiration of which it was more than probable that some vessel, bound on a polar expedition, would pick him up. Strange to say, Papplewick did not experience the cold generally so keenly felt by voyagers in these regions. It would seem as if his frame, on becoming magnetic, had also acquired a singular power of retaining caloric. On the whole, therefore, Mr. Papplewick was rather comfortable under such adverse circumstances, and having discovered a little pocket pistol, which was filled with the best *eau de rie* in the left-hand pocket of his nautical jacket, he paid such marked attention to it that, in a short time, he rather began to like the ice, and absolutely went so far as to ask one of the tallest icebergs "if it would take a drink?" Night, or rather twilight, closed in, and Mr. Papplewick, to use the language of poetry, "*slept, like a bird upon the waters.*"

Next morning, he was awakened by strange, hoarse cries and gruntings, and a great splashing in the water; lifting up his head from the billow, (which served him as a pillow,) he was astonished to find himself close to the sharp edges of a large iceberg, on the smooth edges of which a number of strange hairy animals, with fierce black eyes and long tusks, were grunting hoarsely, and floundering about in a state of great excitement. They looked so very large and savage that Mr. Papplewick began to get seriously alarmed at his position, and guessing from their appearance, which much resembled the woodcuts of the seal in the book on natural history which he read at school, that they belonged to the same tribe, though infinitely larger and more dangerous looking; he wished himself anywhere but where he was, as he had a vivid recollection of a passage which stated that:

"Animals of the seal tribe, when they catch hold of a man's limb with their powerful jaws, never relinquish their hold until they hear the bones crack; on which account, the fishermen that hunt them fill their trousers with cinders which of course, on being bitten, crack easily, and deceive the seal, so far as to induce him to let go, when he is immediately knocked on the head."

These reminiscences of his early studies were not at all calculated to allay Papplewick's apprehensions, and he already imagined he felt his *tibia* breaking beneath the remorseless jaws of the savage animals.

"I wonder what it is?" ejaculated Papplewick to himself, as he saw one of the animals, an immense fellow, covered with long grey hair, advancing towards him with a peculiarly awkward motion.

"I'm a walrus," replied the hairy individual.

Papplewick nearly jumped out of the sea with astonishment at hearing the animal answer him distinctly. He thought he must be dreaming. "A what?" he demanded with staring eyes.

"A walrus," repeated the grey-haired old fellow, "you're a very ig-norant old dog not to know what we are. I thought everybody had heard of us, now that so many ships come out here looking for the North Pole, and then go home and write a parcel of lies about our attacking boats and killing sailors, and what not. However, I'm very glad to see you. It was getting very dull here, and your society will be an advantage."

Papplewick thanked the walrus for his hospitality, and to say the truth, he was very much rejoiced to find that he was not going to be eaten. Still, he could not help thinking it very odd that a walrus should talk such good English, and he sighed as he thought that if he was spared to return to his own country, this part of his story would certainly never be believed.

"Now," said the walrus, "you'd better get out of the sea, and come in here, for I see that you aren't used to much swimming. We've got a nice, comfortable cave in this iceberg, and there are some capital whale-calf steaks for dinner today."

So, saying, with the assistance of the rest of the walruses, the old fel-low, landed Papplewick safely on the iceberg.

"By the way," said this old walrus, who appeared to be the chief of the party, as soon as Papplewick was settled comfortably, "By the way, how is Sir John Parry?"

Papplewick had never heard of Sir John Parry, but fancying, from this question that he must be some polar voyager, he answered at haz-ard that he was "very well."

"And my old friend Ross—I hope he's all right?"

Papplewick replied, confidently, that he was "quite right."

"I remember, as well as if it was only yesterday," continued the walrus, "when old Ross knocked this left eye of mine out. I had been fishing all day, and was rather tired, when I saw Ross coming towards me in a small boat; so, I thought that I would rest myself a little, if he would let me. Accordingly, I swam up to the boat, and was going to hold on by my tusks, when one of the sailors cried out that I was trying to upset the boat—an act that I would not have been guilty of for the world; but Sir John Ross, who was then rather a young man, got up in the stern-sheets the moment he heard the cry, and draw-ing a pistol from his belt, fired at me, and wounded me in the left eye. I don't blame him for it," continued the walrus mildly, "for he acted under a false impression, but I have lost the sight of that eye ever since."

Just as the walrus had concluded his tale, Papplewick heard a peculiar cry uttered, and the old grey beard, starting up, said—

"Our dinner is ready. Come with me, and I will show you the way to our cave."

So saying, the walrus, followed by his comrades, jumped into the water, and directing Papplewick to lay hold of his long fur, swam rapidly along the shores of the iceberg. After proceeding for about five minutes, the walrus told Papplewick to hold on fast, and then suddenly dived. The latter thought at first that the walrus was playing him false, and that this was a stratagem to suffocate him; but after a few seconds submission, he felt himself rising; and on reaching the surface of the water, a most singular scene met his view. They were at the entrance of a large Gothic arch, which led into a vast grotto of ice, at the farther end of which were congregated round a large fire about a hundred and fifty walruses, of all sizes and ages. They appeared to be enjoying themselves very pleasantly, and the young ones were playing a variety of antics, which, from their unwieldy forms, appeared doubly comical.

"This, you perceive, is our cave," said walrus to Papplewick, "and I can assure you we are tolerably comfortable here. The only drawback upon our residence is that frequently that portion of the iceberg which is below water, and which is, of course, the heavier end, is continually melting away from the higher temperature of the sea, until, at last, the upper portion becomes the heavier, when the entire iceberg turns over; the ends are reversed, and, of course, we are obliged, on such occasions, to seek another cave. But come. The whale calf steaks are nearly done, and it is time that we eat something."

As soon as Papplewick's companion was perceived by the rest of the walruses, they set up a great cry of applause, and it was evident by the way in which he was welcomed, that he was a walrus of considerable dignity.

Notwithstanding the delicacy of the whale-calf steaks, Papplewick did not eat much of them. He was lost in amazement at the state of civilization to which walruses had arrived. He listened, too, with great interest to their stories about encounters with white bears, which savage animals they considered to be their most deadly enemies, and several of their skins were hanging in the grotto as trophies of the courage of the walruses.

While this conversation was going on, Papplewick, who was much wearied with all that he had lately undergone fell into a deep slumber, in which we will for the present leave him.

5

When Papplewick awoke it was broad daylight, and the cavern was deserted, the walruses having departed on a fishing excursion. While our hero was ruminating on the strange events which had befallen him lately, and cogitating whether it was possible to enlist his friend the walrus in his scheme for the discovery of the North Pole, his attention was attracted by a low growl, proceeding from a remote corner of the cavern. Thinking that the walrus had, perhaps, returned, he advanced in the direction from whence the sound proceeded, and as the light was somewhat obscure, he saw nothing, until he suddenly discovered himself face to face with an enormous white bear, who was eagerly sniffing up the foetid odour of last night's feast, which still lingered in the cavern.

On seeing Papplewick, the bear, who doubtless had never expected to light on such a dainty morsel, opened his terrible jaws, that seemed like a real cavern, hedged round with pillars of glittering ivory. Papplewick started back, horrified at this appalling sight, and, almost mechanically thrusting his hand into his pocket, drew forth his snuffbox; and as the hungry animal was just in the act of springing upon him, threw the entire of its pungent contents into his face. The next instant the ponderous icicles that hung from the roof were shivered by a succession of the most stentorian sneezes, and Papplewick, taking advantage of Bruin's discomfiture, and without having the courtesy even to offer him a pocket handkerchief, fled swiftly up a narrow passage which was near, and seemed to lead in an upward direction.

After proceeding for some time, slipping upon the icy path, mounting over huge frozen flocks, and squeezing through narrow crevices, Papplewick emerged into the open air upon a ledge of ice, which jutted from the main body of the Berg, and overhung the sea. It was a glorious Polar summer's day. The sunbeams played brilliantly upon the lofty spires of the Berg, until it seemed like a cathedral, built of splendid jewels; and a whole army of detached masses of ice floated solemnly on the calm waters. While Papplewick was enjoying the beautiful prospect, and watching the evolutions of the icebergs, he heard a loud crackling noise above his head, and before he could turn to see what it proceeded from, a large fragment of ice, which had been loosened by the heat of the sun, slid down rapidly, and catching the ledge on which Papplewick was standing, toppled inwards, fairly enclosing that gentleman in a solid prison of ice, through whose semi-transparent walls his figure was dimly visible.

Our hero had now become so inured to extraordinary and unforeseen casualties, that he had ceased to be astonished at them; and so far, conquered the fear natural to his nature, as to bear with a considerable degree of philosophy even the most distressing calamities. When he found himself, therefore, suddenly immured in this transparent dungeon, he resigned himself to his fate, and with the more equanimity when he reflected, that having the life-preserving pills in his possession, he could not starve for at least a twelvemonth. Besides, he trusted to an accidental thaw releasing him before then. Deliverance, however, came sooner than he expected. After he had been several hours imprisoned, he heard a peculiar whistle, which he recognised as the property of his friend the walrus.

Presently that worthy individual scrambled up on the ledge, and uttered an exclamation of joy at seeing Papplewick, for whom he had conceived a great affection. Perceiving the dilemma in which his friend was, the walrus made signs expressive of sympathy, (because the ice interrupted all sound,) and telegraphing, in this way, that he would soon return, he plunged into the water. In about half an hour he returned, accompanied by a herd of walruses, and three strange animals. These were evidently not amphibious animals, for they staid in the water while the walrus was making his arrangements on the ice-berg for Papplewick's deliverance.

All these animals had some strange appendage to their noses. One had a long ivory saw, with sharp teeth, projecting from his snout; another's nose terminated in a gigantic spear of black polished bone; while the third bore before him a sort of ivory javelin, which grew just above his upper lip. Papplewick thought he had seen pictures of the saw-fish, and the narwhal, or sea unicorn, in natural histories, which much resembled the new arrivals; but these latter were so much larger in size, that they could only be a gigantic variety of the species. Now, by order of the walrus, the saw-fish raised himself out of the water, and commenced sawing away the wall of ice which surrounded Papplewick, while the narwhal and sword-fish dug away with their ivory spears, until large splinters of the ice flew about, like chips of marble beneath the stone-cutter's chisel. In a very short space of time the ice wall was completely sawn through, and separated into two pieces, both of which fell with a great splash into the sea, and Papplewick once more emerged into the free air.

As soon as this was fully accomplished, the walrus dismissed the saw-fish and his companions, having ordered them to be rewarded with a considerable gratuity of bear's liver for their services, Papplewick and he then proceeded in triumph to the cave, where they had a great feast in honour of the former gentleman's deliverance.

Towards evening the walrus produced some pipes, made out of a narwhal's tusk, and tobacco, which had been found in a vessel deserted by some Polar voyagers, and asking Papplewick whether he ever blew a cloud, he lit one himself, and the two friends retired to a quiet corner of the cave, to enjoy a smoke.

Finding the walrus in an amiable humour, Papplewick thought this a good opportunity to broach his favourite scheme of the North Pole discovery to his friend He accordingly asked him whether he had ever been there?

At this question, the walrus looked very mysterious, indeed, and appeared anxious to evade any reply; but Papplewick pressing it on him, he said—

"You are now treading on dangerous ground. The sights and scenes that exist at the North Pole are mysteries, to which no man has ever yet been admitted; but as I have conceived a regard for you, I will, if you are willing to brave the danger consequent upon the attempt, take you tonight to a grand meeting of the Dodos, the wisest birds in the world. They have deserted the surface of the earth, and it is thought by men that the race is extinct; but they live many miles northward, in a subterranean cave, heated with volcanic fire. They will, perhaps, gratify your curiosity; and if the Chief Dodo takes a fancy to you, we will try and get him to introduce you to the Living Loadstones."

At the mention of the Living Loadstones, Papplewick's heart bounded with joy, for he felt that they must have some connection with the great mystery which he was seeking to solve. He found it was in vain, however, to question the walrus any further on the subject, that individual preserving a profound silence on the topic, so that Papplewick was fain to content himself with listening to the walrus' stories of Sir John Ross and Captain Parry, and waited very patiently until the time should arrive for his introduction to the Dodos.

When night fell in the walrus, having finished his pipe, asked Papplewick whether he was ready to go, as the Dodos were already assembled. Our hero prepared himself for the expedition with the greatest alacrity, and the walrus, taking from a pouch made of the skin of a sea serpent, a small fragment of some brown substance, told Papplewick to swallow it He obeyed the command, and had scarcely put it to his lips than he became totally insensible

When he recovered his recollection, he found himself in a lofty chamber, the roof of which seemed to be lost in distance. Large spiral jets of fire spouted up through apertures in the floor at regular distances, illuminating the chamber to its remotest corners. The walls were formed of solid rock, against which hung files of every newspaper which was ever published. There Papplewick could discern the familiar features of the *New York Herald*, the *Tribune*, and the *Lantern*. At the upper end of this subterranean chamber sat a number of grave-looking unwieldy birds, with large bills, which our hero conjectured could be none other than the famous Dodos. Every Dodo had a book or newspaper in its claw, and on a sort of dais in the centre sat one Dodo, larger and wiser looking than any of the rest. This bird was intently perusing a late number of the *Lantern*, and, by the frequent shaking of his short wings, Papplewick could see that the pungent wit of that periodical was not lost upon him.

The walrus, who was close by, now whispered to Papplewick, and the pair advanced towards the Chief Dodo, making respectful obeisances. That grave dignitary, as soon as he perceived them, arose, and greeted the walrus very warmly, acknowledging Papplewick's salutation with a condescending smile. After the usual preliminaries of conversation, the Dodo, turning to Papplewick, said—

"What a bad accident that was on the Erie railroad the other day!"

Papplewick stared.

The Dodo, seeing his confusion, continued—

"Ah! no doubt you have not heard of it, as you have been some time from home; but I get all the daily papers here. The account is in yesterday's *Herald*. Would you like to see it?"

Papplewick, whose mind was intent only on one object, declined respectfully; but could not help wondering how the Dodo got the newspapers so soon.

"My friend, the walrus," resumed the Dodo, "tells me you are anxious to be introduced to the Living Loadstones."

"I am, indeed, very desirous to meet with them," replied Papplewick.

"They are strange persons," said the Dodo, "and are not over fond of strangers. They are also very dangerous at times. However, if your curiosity is strong enough to overcome your fear, I will introduce you to them tomorrow."

Papplewick thanked the Dodo with a grateful heart

"Now," said the Dodo, "you are about to see the trial of one of our body. We are very exclusive, and are bound by certain laws never to visit the upper earth, where we once endured so much persecution from hunters, under the penalty of death. A young Dodo, not more than three hundred years old, has been detected not alone in a breach of this law, but we have also discovered that he has married an albatross, whom he visits very frequently on the surface of the earth. For this offence, he is to be tried this night, and, if convicted, he must die."

It seemed then to Papplewick that the Chief Dodo, and all the other Dodos, suddenly changed into big unwieldy judges, clothed in black and white feathers. And the Chief Dodo took his seat upon the highest bench, while the others sat round him. Two rather shabbily feathered Dodos then dragged forward the prisoner, who appeared to be sinking with terror. His feathers were all brushed up the wrong way, and there were heavy fetters upon his legs. The Chief Dodo then recapitulated the charge brought against him, and asked him what he had to say in his defence? The poor fellow acknowledged his guilt, but pleaded his extreme youth as a reason for his punishment being mitigated. The Chief Dodo, after having consulted with his brother judges, put on a cap made of the skin of a black albatross, and proceeded to pass sentence of death upon the prisoner, commenting at the same time severely upon the degradation he had brought upon the race of Dodos by intermarrying with an Albatross. After the awful sentence had been pronounced, and the court had resumed their seats, the two jailor Dodos took the fetters off of the prisoner's legs, and left him panting with terror in the centre of the cave.

The Chief Justice then gave a signal, by striking the tusk of a narwhal against the skull of a whale; and, as the gong-like sound rolled along the cave, Papplewick beheld the jets of fire that sported up through the floor, suddenly leave their places, and advance towards the unhappy Dodo prisoner. In vain did he flap his short wings, and run round the cave, seeking to escape. The fountains of fire encompassed him in every direction, casting upon him spouts of lurid flame, until his feathers were scorched to cinders, and he sank gasping on the floor. Then all the fires suddenly rushed together, and formed a belt of flame around his expiring body. Papplewick heard a faint shriek, a hissing crackling sound; and then what with the foetid odour of burnt feathers, and the sickness consequent on beholding such a death, he fell back from his seat, and swooned away.

Eight Poems

THE GHOST

I is the ghost of Stevey Fizzlegig,
If you'll believe me,
Who died for love of Sukey Swizzleswig,
It did so grieve me:
For nobody did never see,
In my life's time, that day when she
Did say, "For Stevey Fizzlegig
I keres a single ha'penny".
Chorus. Oh! Oh! Oh!

To Fag-lane, near the sign o' th' Morniment,
If you'll believe me,
To tell my love, oft'times, forlorn I went,
Which much did grieve me:
For there this Sukey Swizzleswig
Baked faggots, maws and hogs-feet sells,
Jest oppersite Bess Frowzy's shed,
Who in it cat's and dog's meat sells.
Chorus. Oh! Oh! Oh!

I could not work at all, through loving so,
If you'll believe me,
Yet she prefarred one they calls cussing Joe,
Which much did grieve me,
'Cause he duz treat her oftentimes,
And her out on a Sunday take;
And (though he'd better mind his work)
With her oft does St. Monday make.
Chorus. Oh! Oh! Oh!

Says I, "Through Joe your scorn you throws at me",
If you'll believe me;
At them words she turns up her nose at me;
How that did grieve me!
But, when I sed "I doubts he in
A sartin place oft stops a gap",
She calls me sniv'ling cull, and then
Gave each of these here chops a slap.

Chorus. Oh! Oh! Oh!

Through this, when to my room upstairs I goes,
If you'll believe me,
Says I, "How full of thoughts and cares I grows,
Which much does grieve me."
And then, as I'd no chair, I fetched
My master's little darter's stool,
And cried cause Suk had sarved me so,
While I did off my garters pull.

Chorus. Oh! Oh! Oh!

First, that they wouldn't eas'ly break I tries,
If you'll believe me;
Next, one end of 'em round my neck I ties,
And that did grieve me:
The stool I then did mount, and to
A joist tied t'other end of 'em,
Then kicked the stool away, and swung
Like our cuckoo-clock pendulum.

Chorus. Oh! Oh! Oh!

E'en when intarred she called me snotty fool,
If you'll believe me,
Because my love was fur too hot to cool,
And which did grieve me:
But, as I knows they're in the dark
In Suk's back room, I'll whiz through air,
And in revenge I'll frighten 'em
Until they sweat, nay, p — — , through fear.

Chorus. Oh! Oh! Oh!

THE LOST STEAMSHIP

"Ho, there! Fisherman, hold your hand!
Tell me what is that far away,—
There, where over the isle of sand
Hangs the mist-cloud sullen and grey?
See! it rocks with a ghastly life,
Rising and rolling through clouds of spray,
Right in the midst of the breakers' strife,—
Tell me what is it, Fisherman, pray?"

"That, good sir, was a steamer stout
As ever paddled around Cape Race;
And many's the wild and stormy bout
She had with the winds, in that self-same place;
But her time was come; and at ten o'clock
Last night she struck on that lonesome shore;
And her sides were gnawed by the hidden rock,
And at dawn this morning she was no more."

"Come, as you seem to know, good man,
The terrible fate of this gallant ship,
Tell me about her all that you can;
And here's my flask to moisten your lip.
Tell me how many she had aboard,—
Wives, and husbands, and lovers true,—
How did it fare with her human hoard?
Lost she many, or lost she few?"

"Master, I may not drink of your flask,
Already too moist I feel my lip;
But I'm ready to do what else you ask,
And spin you my yarn about the ship:
'Twas ten o'clock, as I said, last night,
When she struck the breakers, and went ashore;
And scarce had broken the morning's light
Than she sank in twelve feet of water or more.

"But long ere this they knew her doom,
And the captain called all hands to prayer;
And solemnly over the ocean's boom
Their orisons wailed on the troublous air.
And round about the vessel there rose
Tall plumes of spray as white as snow,

Like angels in their ascension clothes,
Waiting for those who prayed below.

"So, these three hundred people clung
As well as they could to spar and rope;
With a word of prayer upon every tongue,
Nor on any face a glimmer of hope
But there was no blubbering weak and wild,—
Of tearful faces I saw but one,
A rough old salt, who cried like a child,
And not for himself, but the captain s son.

"The captain stood on the quarter-deck,
Firm, but pale, with trumpet in hand;
Sometimes he looked at the breaking wreck,
Sometimes he sadly looked to land.
And often he smiled to cheer the crew—
But, Lord! the smile was terribly grim—
Till over the quarter a huge sea flew;
And that was the last they saw of him.

"I saw one young fellow with his bride,
Standing amidships upon the wreck;
His face was white as the boiling tide,
And she was clinging about his neck.
And I saw them try to say goodbye,
But neither could hear the other speak;
So, they floated away through the sea to die—
Shoulder to shoulder, and cheek to cheek.

"And there was a child, but eight at best,
Who went his way in a sea she shipped;
All the while holding upon his breast
A little pet parrot whose wings were clipped.
And as the boy and the bird went by,
Swinging away on a tall wave's crest,
They were gripped by a man, with a drowning cry,
And together the three went down to rest.

"And so, the crew went one by one,
Some with gladness, and few with fear;
Cold and hardship such work had done
That few seemed frightened when death was near.
Thus every soul on board went down,—

Sailor and passenger, little and great;
The last that sank was a man of my town,
A capital swimmer,—the second mate."

"Now, lonely Fisherman, who are you
That say you saw this terrible wreck?
How do I know what you say is true,
When every mortal was swept from the deck?
Where were you in that hour of death?
How did you learn what you relate?"
His answer came in an under-breath,—
"Master, I was the second mate!"

THE DEMON OF THE GIBBET

There was no west, there was no east,
No star abroad for eye to see;
And Norman spurred his jaded beast
Hard by the terrible gallows-tree.
"O Norman, haste across this waste—
For something seems to follow me!"
"Cheer up, dear Maud, for, thanked be God,
We nigh have passed the gallows-tree!"
He kissed her lip; then—spur and whip!
And fast they fled across the lea!
But vain the heel and rowel steel,—
For something leaped from the gallows-tree!
"Give me your cloak, your knightly cloak,
That wrapped you oft beyond the sea;
The wind is bold, my bones are old,
And I am cold on the gallows-tree."
"O holy God! O dearest Maud,
Quick, quick, some prayers,—the best that be!
A bony hand my neck has spanned,
And tears my knightly cloak from me!"
"Give me your wine,—the red, red wine,
That in the flask hangs by your knee!
Ten summers burst on me accurst,
And I'm athirst on the gallows-tree."
"O Maud, my life! my loving wife!
Have you no prayer to set us free?
My belt unclasps,—a demon grasps

517

And drags my wine-flask from my knee!"
"Give me your bride, your bonnie bride,
That left her nest with you to flee!
O, she hath flown to be my own,
For I'm alone on the gallows-tree!"
"Cling closer, Maud, and trust in God!
Cling close!—Ah, heaven, she slips from me!"—
A prayer, a groan, and he alone
Rode on that night from the gallows-tree.

The Shadow by the Tree

There grows in pleasant Manordene
As fair an elm as ever grew;
Its limbs are tough. its leaves are green;
Its rugged bark is healthy too.
But though it is a noble sight
For all that act an honest part,
To me it is the blackest blight
That ever withered up a heart

Long, long ago, when I was young,
There lay, where now that fair elm stands,
A darksome pool where dank weeds clung,
And nightshade trailed its deadly bands.
The water-lilies, green and wide,
Spread halfway o'er its blackened face;
No ripple ever roughed its tide.
No wild bird lurked about the place.

One summer's eve, a fair girl stooped
To pluck a lily on the brink,
When two rough arms were round her looped;
She had no time to pray or think:
A muffled shriek—a heavy swing—
The water-lilies rose and fell.
What hand had done this horrid thing
I dare not say—I will not tell.

But from that hour an iron fate
Compelled me to the lonely pond;
From morning time to even late
I had no pleasant aim beyond.
I hovered round the swampy edge,

I gazed until I lost my breath;
It seemed alway as if the sedge
Was filled with stagnant shapes of death.

And lo! that sombre swamp in time
Became to me a place of dread.
The heavy plants smelt sick with crime;
The loathsome weeds—the stagnant bed,
The dark, dark waters of the place,
That turned the very sunshine black,
And in whose mirror my white face
Shone like a villain's on the rack.

The neighbours thought me crazed outright,
And pointed at me in my walk:
I went, a strange, distracted wight,
That muttered fiercely in his talk.
And when the boys and girls anear
Made holiday upon the green,
A listener would be sure to hear
About the Lord of Manordene.

And thus, it passed, until I fell,
Oh! deadly sick with wandering there;
Then, thought I, 'twould be full as well
Blot out this source of dark despair.
But as its depths contained a sight
Unsuited to the honest day,
I dug an outlet one dark night,
And drained the waters all away.

Then, then with hard, unceasing toil
I worked until my fingers bled;
I shovelled in the healthy soil,
And strove to fill the vacant bed.
But when some lily, crushed by me,
Would gleam from out the creviced sod,
I'd start and fancy it was *she*
With pale hand pointing up to God!

I filled it in—I smoothed it o'er;
I trampled on it with my feet:
I never took such pains before
To make a spot of earth look sweet

I scattered grass seeds round and round;
I brought primroses from the lea,
And in the centre of the mound
I planted deep, a young elm tree.

I was at peace for many a day;
Thrice seven summers shone for me;
I saw the hawthorn on the spray,
I smelled the cowslips on the lea.
The ripened grass obeyed the scythe,
The crimson hips with winter came,
While I had heart as gay and blithe
As any peasant loon could claim.

And lo! the elm meantime grew great;
Green grew the turf that I had laid;
And often round that place of Fate
My gentle, fair-haired Alice played.
Oh! she was innocent and fair,
With soul like summer heavens clear;
I thought no wicked thing would dare
Approach the spot while she was near.

But, like a swallow to its nest,
Comes back the deathless curse of crime:
Had man an adamantine breast,
'Twould worm through to his heart in time!
That I was free, I did believe;
I proudly vaunted I was free;
Yet in one quiet summer s eve
Came back that deadly curse to me!

My wife sat in the elm tree's shade,
And read a book upon her knee;
My fair-haired Alice round us played,
And sang with sweet unconscious glee;
She sang, like some young throstle wild,
An unconnected, wayward hymn;
When lo! between my wife and child,
There loomed a shadow huge and dim!

It thrust itself between the pair,
It clasped them in its deadly bound;
It mowed and flickered here and there,

And played fantastics on the ground.
It dwindled to a narrow spot;
It towered among the branches high;
Then grew so great as if 'twould blot
With one vast veil the evening sky.

I could not breathe, I could not speak;
My heart, like dazzled bird, lay still.
I felt the shadow on my cheek,
And wondered had it power to kill
But still it flickered here and there;
The hideous wanton came and fled,
 Until, in my intense despair,
I wished the whole wide world was dead.

I hurried both my treasures home,
And strove to talk in accents gay;
But the bright smile would feebly come:
My mirth chased others' mirth away.
All, all were heavy with the blight,
The shadow would not be defied;
And in the middle of that night
My gentle, fair-haired Alice died.

Then day and night, and night and day,
I roamed around that haunted tree;
And, with its dark, disgusting play,
The shadow came and sat by me:
It played until my brain grew hot;
It sat until my heart grew chill.
Oh! had it but one mortal spot,
I had the hand and nerve to kill.

And every day I wander there,
To face the shadow on the mound;
But wisdom sometimes helps despair—
I'll meet it on its own dread ground!
Let shade with shade for victory fight,
From human bonds and fetters free;
 Oh! yes, by Heaven, this very night
Will see *two* Shadows by the Tree!

MADNESS

It came by slow degrees across my brain;
A shadow stealing on a summer sea;
A little cloud, but pregnant with a storm,
And deepening, deepening, deepening as it came.
Lo! then my soul most suddenly grew large:
It seemed a gloomy palace where a court
Was held of wandering and troubled thoughts,
That came and went, and came and went again;
And yet they never seemed one half to fill
Its sick and dreary vastness. None had shape,
But yet possessed a certain clouded form—
An indistinct identity which puzzled
My nerveless brain. Faint memories of childhood
Came trooping in with noise and bustling joy;
And having traversed every winding stair,
And ransacked every well-remembered nook,
They took a tearless farewell and departed.
Then came a dream of strong though stripling love
With deep low murmurs on its lips it came,
Sighing fond names, and talking rich, ripe words,
That tell like melting peaches from its tongue.
Throughout the vastness of my soul it wandered,
Seeking in vain for some sweet company.
It peeped into my brain; then, with a shudder
At something that it saw there, turned and fled.
Then rushed a throng of Manhood's fiery pleasures;
Lofty desires and great ambitious hopes;
Cares that, once born, seemed ever breeding more;
Griefs that, like snails, left slimy tracks behind,
And went as slowly; bad deeds that, for shame,
Carried red blushes blazoned on their shields.
On came they, trooping through the portals wide,
A motley army; mingling songs and sighs
With shouts that echoed through the lofty vault
Of what was once a soul. On, on they came,
Making my spirit tremble with their tread.
Then suddenly each noisy tongue grew hushed;
They seemed to veil their heads as smit with fear,
And, flinging on the air a wild farewell,

They fled, and left me gazing on. The Terror!
Oh! seemed it then as if a mighty fosse
Gaped 'twixt my spirit and the world without
I felt like some lone house, (if such could feel,)
Deserted, naked, and for ever void;
While in the charnel chambers of my soul
Distorted fantasies, like dungeon rats,
Grew bold in solitude, and peeping out,
Thrilled every nerve with loathsome rioting.
Thought, healthy Thought, had fled away, and I
Was face to face with Madness!

THE SEWING BIRD

1

A chimney's shadow, flung by the sun
As it sank in the west when the day was done.
Silent and dark as the noiseless bat
Crept through the room where the work-girl sat,
Where she sat all day at her poor pine table,
Working, as long as her hands were able.
On shirt and collar and chemisette.
On gowns of silk and on veils of net.
Till her busy fingers seemed to be
A skeleton kind of machinery.
The table was strewn with threads of silk,
With pearly buttons that shone like milk.
With gaudy stuffs of a thousand dyes.
And beads that gleamed in the gloom like eyes;
While in the midst of these beautiful things
Glimmered a Sewing Bird's silver wings.
But the blankets that lay on her bed were poor,
And cracks were plain in the crazy door.
The roof was low and the floor was old.
And the work-girl shivered as if a-cold;
And to judge by the veins in her wan white hand,
She did not live on the fat of the land.

2

Now when the shadow crept through the room,
Filling the place with a cheerless gloom,
So that the weary work was stopped,

Her thin, mechanical hands she dropped,
And gazed at the wall so bare and bald,
Where the shadowy feet of the twilight crawled.
If at that moment she dreamed at all,
Or peopled with visions the cold, white wall.
She thought perhaps of that one bright day,
In the month of June or the month of May,
When, rich with the savings of many a week.
She felt fresh winds blow over her cheek,
As, with friends as poor and lowly as she.
She caught her first glimpse of the calm, blue sea,
Or roamed by copses or sunny lea,
And learned how bright the world could be.
But I doubt if the poor are rich in dreams,
Or build fine castles by golden streams;
For want, like frost-bite, kills the grain
That Fancy sows in the teeming brain,
And it is not every dreamy stare
That is filling with fairies the twilight air.

3

Yet still she sat, and, it may be, dreamed—
I hope so—until there suddenly seemed
To sweep through the room a rustle of wings.
With a tinkling as if of silver rings,
And then a low and a soaring song,
That every instant grew more strong.
She looked at wall and window and floor,
She peered through the gloom at the crazy door;
Nothing was visible anywhere,
Yet still the song was thrilling the air;
Then she turned her eyes to the table of pine,
And saw something shiver and dimly shine;
And lo! from the midst of the shreds of silk.
And the pearly buttons that shone like milk,
There came the song of the silver rings,
And the gleam and flutter of shining wings;
As up from the table the Sewing Bird sprang.
While singing it soared, and soaring it sang:—
"Follow me up and follow me down.
Hither and thither, through all the town;

For there are lessons that must he taught,
And there are changes that must he wrought,
And there are wrongs that the world shall know,—
So, follow, follow, where'er I go!"

4

Then the work-girl rose from her rickety chair.
And opened the door that led on the stair,
While swift overhead the Sewing Bird flew,
And carolled and fluttered as if it knew
That it led her spirit in threads as strong
As the chains of love or the poet's song;
While ever there rang through the corridor hollow
The silvery strain of *"Follow! Follow!"*

5

So down the avenue of Broadway,
Where the lamplight shone like an amber day,
The Sewing Bird led the maiden along,
To the airy tune of its fairy song.
They came to a palace ornate and tall,
With marble pillars and marble wall,
And windows of glass so large and clear
That the panes seemed lucid as atmosphere.
The work-girl stopped as the crowd went by,
And gazed through the windows with wistful eye;
For the walls were splendid with paint and gold,
The couches were fit for the Sybarites old.
And the floor was soft with the Brussels woof,
And flowery frescos ran over the roof.
While a delicate radiance from globes of glass
Fell soft as sunlight upon the grass.

6

Who are the princes—the work-girl thought—
That dwell in this palace by Genii wrought?
She looked, and beheld some dozen or ten
Young and excessively nice young men;
Their faces were beardless, rosy, and fair,
An astonishing curl was in their hair,
Their feet were squeezed into shiny boots.
Their nails were pink, and white at the roots.

Their hands were as taper, their limbs as fine.
As an Arab maiden's in Palestine;
Their waistcoats were miracles to behold,
Ribbed with velvet and flecked with gold;
And perfect rivers of watch-chain ran
Over the breast of each nice young man.
But you could not see in a single face
Of courage or manhood the faintest trace;
Through every feature the sentiment ran,
"If you please, I would rather not be a man!"
One of them sat in an easy chair.
With smirking, impudent, indolent air,
Blandly explaining, with smile serene,
The merits of Cantator's sewing-machine;
While others lounged through the gorgeous room.
Diffusing the odours of Lubin's perfume,
Or gossiping over the last new play,
Or their "spree" last week—and "Wasn't it gay?"
But the crowd at the windows thought them sublime
And wished that they had such an easy time.
As the work-girl gazed at this splendid array
Of Cantator's youths on show in Broadway,
She gathered her shawl round her wasted form.
While her breath congealed on the window-panes warm.
And sighed, "Ah me! ah me! ah me!
This is the place where I should be!"

7

Then the Sewing Bird swelled his silvery throat.
And trilled through the air his crystalline note:—
"Follow me up and follow me down,
Hither and thither, through all the town;
For there are still more splendid marts,
That never will warm the work-girl' hearts,
And the lesson is still to be fully learned
How woman's pittance by man is earned!"

8

'Twas a vast, majestic dry-goods store,
Into whose portals from every shore
Came cashmeres, satins, and silks, and shawls,

To flood the counters and fill the halls:
There Paris sent its delicate gloves,
With mantles, "Such beauties!" and bonnets, "Such loves!"
And China yielded from primitive looms
Its silks shot over with changeable blooms.
While India's golden tissues blent
With camel' s-hair from the Syrian's tent.
At each counter was something,—not man, not boy,—
A sort of effeminate hobbledehoy,
And over the laces it simpered and smiled.
And blandly each feminine idiot beguiled
With "Charmingest fashion!" and "Isn't it sweet?"
"Just allow me to show you—remarkably neat!"
"No pattern is like it—on honour—in town,
Just becomes your complexion,—shall I put it down?"
And its frippery fingers went dabbling through tapes,
And its glozing discourse was of trimmings and capes,
And to see its expressionless eyes you'd have thought
That its soul, like its tapes, had been long ago bought.
As the work-girl gazed on this muscleless crew.
Who were doing the things she was suited to do,
She sighed, "Ah me! ah me! ah me!
This is the place where I should be!"
9

Then the Sewing Bird swelled his silvery throat,
And uttered a piercing, reverberant note:—
"Follow me here, and follow me there,
Out through the free-blowing mountain air,
Up to the heart of the healthy hill,
Deep in the heart of the backwoods still;
For the lesson still remains for you —
To show you the labour that men should do."
10

Up in a wild Californian hill,
Where the torrents swept with a mighty will,
And the grandeur of nature filled the air,
And the cliffs were lofty, rugged, and bare.
Some thousands of lusty fellows she saw
Obeying the first great natural law.

From the mountain's side, they had scooped the earth
Down to the veins where the gold had birth.
And the mighty pits they had girdled about
With ramparts massive, and wide, and stout;
And they curbed the torrents, and swept them round
Wheresoever they willed, through virgin ground.
They rocked huge cradles the livelong day.
And shovelled the heavy, tenacious clay,
And grasped the nugget of gleaming ore.
The sinew of commerce on every shore.
Their beards were rough and their eyes were bright,
For their labour was healthy, their hearts were light;
And the kings and princes of distant lands
Blessed the work of their stalwart hands.
Then high o'er the shovel's and pickaxe's clang
Loudly the song of the Sewing Bird rang:—
"*See, see, see, see!*
This is the place where men should be!"
And he soared once more through the boundless air,
While the work-girl followed him, wondering where.

11

She saw a region of mighty woods
Stretching away for millions of roods;
The odorous cedar and pine-tree tall,
And the live oak, the grandest among them all,
And the solemn hemlock, massive and grim.
Claiming broad space for each mighty limb.
Then she heard the clang of the woodman's axe
Booming along through the lumber-tracks.
And she heard the crack of the yielding trunk,
As deeper and deeper the keen axe sunk,
And the swishing fall—the sonorous thrill—
And the following stillness, more than still.
Then, moving among the avenues dim,
She saw the lumbermen, giant of limb;
The frankness of heaven was in each face.
And their forms were grand with untutored grace;
Their laugh was hearty, their blow was strong,
And sweet as the wood-notes their working song,
As they hewed the limbs from the giant tree,

And stripped off his leafy mystery;
They breathed the air with elastic lungs.
They trolled their ditties with mirthful tongues,
And to see it would do a citizen good.
With what unction, they relished their homely food;
For their hunger was keen as their trenchant axe.
And their jokes as broad as their brawny backs.
Then the Sewing Bird sang, again and again,
As he soared o'er the sonorous woods of Maine,
"*See, see, see, see!*
This is the place where men should be!"
And he floated once more through the azure air,
And the work-girl followed him, wondering where.

12

Vast plateaus of loamy land she saw,
Quickening with life in the early thaw.
The pulse of the waking spring she heard.
And the broken trills of the gladdened bird.
And the teams afield with their heavy plod
As they dragged the share through the juicy sod.
Through the crisp, clear air she heard the voice
Of sturdy ploughmen and farmer-boys.
And a busy din from the farmyards rang.
And she heard the spades in the furrows clang.
Then a sudden change swept over the scene,
As the summer sun with a light serene
Smiled upon cottage and field and fold.
And reddened the harvests of waving gold.
Then down through the golden sea there came
The mowers swarthy and stout of frame;
And the cradle-scythe in their hands they swung
Till the hiss of the blade through the grain-fields rung,
As they cut their way with a mighty motion.
Like sharp-prowed ships in a yellow ocean.
Then the Sewing Bird sang like a mellow horn,
As it soared o'er Ohio's land of corn,
"*See, see, see, see!*
This is the place where men should be!"

13

The work-girl sat in her attic room,
Cold and silent, and wrapped in gloom;
There was no longer a glimmer of day,
And the Sewing Bird still on the table lay.
The voice was silent that once had sung,
And silent forever the silver tongue;
But she pondered long on the strange decree
That she, wherever she turned, must see
Men in the places where women should be!

Sir Brasil's Falcon

The hunt was o'er. The last thin bugle-note
Had stole away among the friendly trees,
Declining gently on its weary way,
And dying in their arms. The exhausted hounds
Besmeared with wild-boar's blood lay down, and licked
Their sanguine coats; or, growling, strove to scare
With lazy paw the floating globes of flies
That buzzed around them lured with scent of gore.
The horses, bridle-tethered to the trees,
With flanks thin drawn, where lay the hardened sweat
In glistening furrows, champed the cruel bit,
Or nibbled at the leaves. Beneath the shade
Of a great chestnut that obscured the sun
The hunters, gathered in a little group,
Talked of the chase; and pleasant stories ran
Of perils, magnified with sportsman's boasts,
And huge leaps taken in the heat of chase.
Then hearty laughs at some green youth's mishap
Went round the circle like a jocund ring
Of sparkling merriment. The men were gay
In joyance of rude strength. Their eyes were bold;
Their white teeth glistened through their nut-brown beard;
Like foam-beads in dark ale. Their skins were tanned
By honest wind and sun, and every limb
Was large and fit for use. These men were rough
As prickly-pear or pomegranate, but they
Were ripe, and honest-fruited at the core.
Then in each pause a silver bowl went round,

Filled with red wine, and every hunter drank,
'Health to St. Hubert, our good patron saint!'
And passed the wine bowl on, until it came
To where Sir Brasil sat. And he outspoke,
'You know, my friends, I live not to drink wine,
Since that sad day when in the Holy Land
The *Emir* made me quaff my brother's blood
Disguised as wine. I cannot join your revel.
Pardon me, comrades, I will seek some stream.
Hid in the twilight of this leafy glade.
And drink your healths in a more homely draught.'
Then rose he 'mid good-natured jeers and smiles
At such faint-heartedness in belted knight.
And, yielding in return mock courtesies,
He leashed his favourite falcon to his wrist.
And, girding on his sword, straight took his way,
Along the silent glades.

                There was no water
In all the summer woods. The insatiate sun
Had drunk all up, and robbed each secret spring,
Save the round beads of dew that nestling dwelt
Deep in the bottom of the foxglove's bells.
There was no water. Beds of vanished streams
Mocked him with memories of lucid waves.
That rose and fell before his fancy's eye
In glassy splendour. As the soothing wind
Stole softly o'er the leaves, it gave low tones,
That sounded in Sir Brasil's sharpened ear
Like distant ripplings of a pleasant stream;
But there was none. The umbered soil was dry,
And the hare rustled through parched, crisping grass.
Sir Brasil sighed: his brow was hot,—his tongue
Beat dry against his teeth. His upmost thought
Was water,—water, clear, and bright, and cool!
A storm-cock flew across the glade; his beak
Was red with berries of the mountain ash,
That had lain hidden from the bygone frost
Deep in some cranny of the gaping earth.
Then quoth Sir Brasil, 'I will follow him,
For I have heard that birds do fly to springs,

As sands of steel to magnets.' So, he struck
A bee's line through the woods, and followed him.
Thick grew the brambles, for there was no path
For dainty feet; but gnarled roots of oak
Pushed earth aside and twined in curving cords
Like snakes at play. Pale wild-flowers grew in crowds,
Like captive fays, o'er whom the giant trees
Kept watch and ward. Through the green canopy
That stretched o'erhead, stray, vagrant sunbeams stole,
Turning with fairy power the withered leaves
To evanescent gold. Lizards, with skins
Like *lapis-lazuli,* peeped with glittering eyes
Between the crevices of mouldering trees.
The hum of bees 'round many a trunk foretold
The heavy honeycomb that lay within,
Concealed with cunning passages and doors
Of deftly-woven moss. The bright jay chattered,
And the bold robin gazed with mute surprise
On the strange shape whose daring seemed to make
The woods his own, while on Sir Brasil went,
Stumbling o'er roots, embraced by brambly arms,
And leaving fragments of his rich attire
Fluttering on thorny boughs, that many a day
Held in great awe the timid woodland birds.
The sun grew low. It was three hours beyond
The middle day, when, lo! Sir Brasil stepped
With hooded falcon leashed upon his wrist,
Cloak torn in shreds, and plume that hung awry,
Beyond the limit of the lonely wood,
And found himself upon the rugged brink
Of a dried water-course. It was a dank
And dismal place. The broad, misshapen trees
Were bare anatomies, with scarce a leaf
To clothe their withered bones. Huge, fleshy weeds
Grew in black groups along the ragged edge
Of a tall, beetling cliff, whose steep face sloped
With slabs of rock, adown whose pallid sides
The thin, white moss spread like a leprosy.
Along the base of this pale cliff there ran
The channel of some fitful winter stream

Long fled. The smooth, round pebbles paved
The empty bed, and all the secret rocks
Lay bare and dry. Some there were quaintly holed,
And eaten through by the soft, toothless weaves,
And some were strangely carved, and smoothly hewn,
With watery chisels, into phantasm forms.
There was no stream. No. limpid water went
With trickling step along the stony course.
The ousel had forsook the place, and sought
Another stream to dipple with its wings.
The heron stood no longer by the brink.
The azure of the halcyon flashed no more
From bank to bank. The tall brown-tufted reeds.
That sung so softly to the evening wind,
Had withered all, and lay in matted heaps
Upon the arid earth. Sir Brasil sighed,
'There is no water here, I am athirst.
O, I would give a broad piece for one drop
To cool my parching throat!' As said he this,
The sunlight flashed upon some glittering point
That shone like diamond. Hastening forward, he
Beheld from out the crevice of a rock
A sluggish flow, that trickled drop by drop,
Of dark, green water. So reluctantly
It oozed through the fissure, that it seemed
Like the last lifeblood of a river-god
Ebbing in lingering drops from out his heart!
'My faith!' Sir Brasil said, 'though not as clear
As wave of Castaly or Hippocrene,
Thou art right welcome,—for my throat is dry.
And I am faint with thirst; and thou, poor bird,
Shalt share my luck, and quaff this scanty spring.'
So saying to the falcon on his wrist.
He loosed its leashes and unlaced its hood,
And let its bold eye gaze abroad again
Upon the sunny world. The joyous bird
Gave one far skyward glance; another swept
The wide horizon round, then preening all
His plumes, and ruffling them toward the sun,
He pecked the knight with a love-softened beak,

And nestled to his arm.

                                  Then Brasil straight
Unloosed a silken belt from which there swung
A golden bugle. Taking it, he stopped
The jewelled mouthpiece with a plug of moss;
Then, stooping, held the inverted bell beneath
The slowly falling stream. With toil and pain
He gathered each slow drop, and watched them rise
By hair's-breadth after hair's-breadth, till he saw
The dear draught level with the golden rim;
Then joyously he raised it to his lips,
And cried, 'Here's to thee, goddess of the stream!
Locked in the heart of this cold rock. Alone,
Forsaken by the fickle waves that made
The current of thy life, thou art most desolate,
And weep'st all day those trickling drops, which are
Thy tears. In them I pledge me to thy grief!'
But as he raised the golden bugle up
Toward his lips, the falcon with swift stroke
Of his long pinion dashed it from his hand,
And all the precious draught ran waste on earth.
Sir Brasil frowned. 'How now, bold bird?' he cried,
'Thou dost not know how toilsomely I filled
That scanty measure, or thou never wouldst
Have wasted it. Next time take better heed.
Or thou wilt rue it.' Once again Sir Brasil
With weary hand and long delay filled up
The golden measure, and as he did raise
It to his lips, the falcon with one stroke
Of his swift pinion dashed it to the earth.
Sir Brasil swore, 'Now by the sacred cup
Which Christ did drink of, I will wring thy neck,
Thou foolish bird, an thou do that again!'
A third time did he stoop, and, horn in hand,
Bend his broad back to catch the sluggish stream;
A third time did he raise the bugle up
Toward his lips; a third time with swift wing
The falcon dashed the measure from his hand.
Then flashed Sir Brasil's eye with humid fire,
Quivered his thin-drawn lip, and paled his cheek,

And with an ungloved hand he smote the bird
Full in the throat. It fluttered on his wrist,
And drew its jesses taut; with panting strength
Spread out its arrowy wings convulsively,
As if 'twould flee right sunward from black death.
Then drew them close. The silver Milan bells,

★★★★★★

Note:—Milan bells. The tinkling bells that were fastened to the falcon's legs came from this city. It was necessary that their tone should be sonorous and shrill, and they were graduated in a rising scale of semitones.

★★★★★★

That quivered on its legs, rattled a chime
Of mortal melody that smote the sky.
Its old domain. Its curved beak opened wide,
Agape for air. Its large, round, golden eye
Turned one long look of sad, reproachful love
Full on Sir Brasil; then, with a faint gasp,
That stifling burst from its choked, swollen throat.
It fluttering fell. The silken jesses slipped;
Its proud head bent in death's last agony;
And, tumbling from his wrist, it gasped and died!
The stern knight bit his lip as he looked down;
He loved the bird, but had a hasty hand.
And hastier temper. 'Well-a-day!' he said,
'The bird was mulish and deserved its fate.
Yet would I had not killed it!' Then he took
With mournful hand his bugle, and a sigh
Fluttered between his lips, like some sad bird
From prison flying blindly. 'Well!' he said,
''T is weary work filling these sluggish draughts;
Each takes an hour at least. I'll to the source
Of this thin stream, and ravish it with lips
As eager as e'er pressed the Sabine maid.
When Roman youth grew hot. I'll dip my horn,
And raise it diamond-dripping from the wave,
And as I drink, the abundant stream shall well
Over the brim, and trickle down my beard,
Like morning dew. I'll quaff with thirsty joy.
And when I've drank I'll fling the lucid lees

535

On the dry leaves, and arid flowers, that they
May share the moist delight!' And with these words
He sought the secret windings of the stream,
And followed them.

                Starkly the falcon lay;
The dry leaves rattled with a stealthy sound;
The beetle hummed, the insects in the grass
Made silver whisperings; the mouse crept out
From underneath the sod, and, timid, gazed
On the proud foe that lay so stiff and strange.
Half fearing stratagem, it dared not move.
But pricked its ears, and oped its glittering eyes
Enchained with wonder, till a lizard slim
Darted from out the grass, and boldly brushed
The falcon's lifeless wing. Then did the mouse
Believe its foe was dead. Then did it play
Around the corpse, and gaze into its eyes.
Those large, round golden eyes, that from the clouds
Could pierce the crouching vermin of the earth
With overhanging death!

                  The dry leaves fell;
The water dropped; the insects in the grass
Hummed their sharp songs that sounded in the ear
Like tiny silver tinklings. In the midst
Of all this fair monotony of life
Lay the dead falcon!

                With much weary toil
Sir Brasil traced the windings of the stream,
Through rock defiles, as wild as sculptured dreams
Where naked horrors frowned. Through oozy swamps
Coated with marish oil in which the sun
Made slimy rainbows; through forsaken beds
Of ancient streams; o'er massive boulder stones,
Humped with old age, and coated with grey moss;
O'er trunks of rotting trees that in the night
Lit with pale splendour the dark paths around,
And slept in light; o'er sharp volcanic soil
That crackled 'neath the tread; o'er naked plains,
Where the sad wind could find not even a stone

To whet its breath on, but went babbling round
With dull, blunt edge,—Sir Brasil took his way
With weary foot, and tongue that often wagged
In sanctimonious oath. A full, slow hour
Had passed, and e'en the knight, though faint with thirst,
Was nigh to turn upon his steps and wend
Back through the woods, when, lo! like sapphires seen
Through the smoke-curling clouds of maiden's hair,
Gleamed something blue. It twisted as it shone,
And glanced in distance like an azure spray.
As speeds the Arab after five days' thirst
To the green oasis,—that desert's teat
At which its children suck,—so Brasil sped,
And nerved his flagging limbs to reach the spot
So distant and so dear.
                            'At last!' he cried,
'At last, at last, the water glads my sight!
O, I will lave, and drink, and lave again,
Until my very bones the moisture feel.
And half my blood is water!' And he ran
Like a young deer; but as he nearer came,
A poisonous vapor seemed to load the air.
And foul mephitic clouds that clogged each sense
Hovered oppressively with leaden wings.
Sir Brasil staggered on. The poisoned air
Smote on his brain like an invisible sword,
And clove his consciousness. He raved, and reeled,
And threw his arms aloft, and tried to pray,
And spoke pet words to his dead falcon, as
It were alive; then suddenly he seemed
With one great effort to regain himself,
And onward strode.
                        But as he neared the place
Whence shot the sapphire gleam, a horrid sight
Burst on his view. Lo! coiling on a mound
A huge, green serpent lay. Tier upon tier
Of emerald scales that glistered into blue
Swept upwards in grand spirals. His great head
Lay open-jawed, and hanging o'er the brink

Of a steep rock, while slavering from his mouth
A stream of distilled poison, green and rank,
Trickled in sluggish drops, that at the base
Gathered themselves into an oily stream,
And flowed away.

                  Sir Brasil's heart grew sick;
For now he saw what he would fain have drunk,
And what the falcon wasted, was the venom
That slavered from the serpent on the rock.
And, filtering through some secret stony way,
Welled out below in green and sluggish drops
Of withering poison. Now like a fierce wind
Remorse howled through his soul, and hunted thought
Fled from its scorching breath. His nature swung
Naked and desolate as a gibbet corpse
From which the flesh drops piecemeal. He did feel
That death should fly him, as a ghost of guilt
More horrid than himself. He felt that God
Held not within his arsenal of curses
One great enough for him; that earth's green skin
Crept, as he trode, as shudders human flesh
When loathsome beings touch it. He grew white
As the swamp-lily, and upon his cheek
Stood beads of dew, round and distinct as those
That morning winds brush from the shivering trees.
His strong frame shook; short sobbings dry and fierce
Rang in his throat, and on his swelling chest
The silken doublet rose and fell amain,
Like bellying sail that labours with the wind.
He tore his long, fair curls, and cast them down
And stamped upon them, whilst he cursed himself
For his deep cruelty. to so fair a bird.
Then he took counsel with himself, and thought
If it were good to turn his dagger in
And sheathe it in his heart; but, lo! within
His soul a spirit rose—like those that flit
From out deep fountains in the even-time
To warn us of dark ills—and spread a mist
Betwixt him and the thought of foul self-murder.
Straightway he turned, and said unto himself,

'The guilty, by the avenging will of God,
Are dragged by secret force toward the spot
Where lie their victims. I will hasten back
To where my dead bird lies by the steep bank.
And mark each footstep with a moan, as monks
Mark rosaries with prayers.'—So saying went,
With ashen cheek, slow step, and muttering lips.
Straight to the spot where the dead falcon lay.
A little while he stood regarding it
With a drear wistful look; then, stooping down,
He smoothed its ruffled plumage with his hand,
Closed its round, staring eyes, and gently folded
Its stiffened wings along its breast; then broke
Into a lamentation wild.

                       'O bird,
My soul is darkened in thy death! strong grief
Winds like a snake about my heart, and crushes it
In its chill clasp. I never yet did feel
Such bitter wrath against mine own right hand
As I do now. To think that this fond hand.
On which so oft thou lovingly hast sat.
Should turn against thee, and with one foul blow
Dash all thy life away! O, 'twas a deed
Becoming some vile lackey, whose coarse wrath
Is blinded by thick blood; but not a knight.
Whose blood was filtered through three thousand years,
And to cross swords with whom might surely make
The foe a gentleman! I mind me well
The day we came together. Thou wert young,
Scarce fledged, and with thy talons yet ungrown;
But there was courage in thee, and one day,
When thou didst see a heron in the sky.
Thou beat'st thy breast against the window-pane,
And all the falcon sparkled in thine eyes!
Then 't was my pride to deck thee splendidly.
Thy silver bells, wrought in old Milan's town,
Were shrill as whistle, and the ascending tones
Were modulated cunningly. Thy hood
Of purple cramoise, worked with threads of gold,
Came from that maiden's hand whom I do prize

Beyond all other women. Then thy food
Was dainty in its kind, as thou hadst been
The merlin of an emperor. I did love thee;
All proves that I did love thee; and I would
Have chopped this right hand from its arm before
It should have hurt thee wittingly; but I
Am hot, and when thy persevering wing
Stretched between me and death, it angered me,
And I—I—O, I cannot think of it,
Except I curse myself, and wish myself
Accursed by God and man!

                            O, never more
Will thy silk jesses twine around my wrist!
No more will we two wander in the dawn.
When the wild-flowers are necklaced all with dew,
And the wet grass pulses with morning life.
To watch a sedge of herons by the stream.
Or listen for the bittern's lonely boom
Rising from out the reeds! No more, no more,
When the game springs from out the sedgy pool
And soars aloft, shall I tear off thy hood.
Unloose thy jesses, and then launch thee forth
Upon the deadly race. I ne'er shall see
Thee rise in airy spirals to the clouds.
While the wide heron labours far below,
Till when almost a speck, with sudden swoop,
Like a live thunderbolt, thou dashest down
Full on the foe, and, striking at his heart,
Fall'st fastened to thy victim!

                              How tell
The maiden fair who worked thy purple hood
And loved to stroke thy feathers i' the sun,—
How shall I tell my crime? Why, she would loathe me,
And wave me from her sight with crushing look,
And shut me from her heart. I should be held
By all good knights, and ladies fair, a dastard
Who raised his hand against a loving bird,
And killed it for its love. I cannot home!
The first quest I should hear would be, "Where is

Thy falcon, Brasil?" and could I reply,
"Three times it saved my life, fair dame.
Therefore, I slew it." O, no home for me!
Here in this lonely glade I'll lay me down
Close to my murdered bird—and then—and then
Let what will come.

                The shades of evening fell,
The invisible dews dropped spirit-like on earth;
The woods were silent, and, when the white moon
Came riding o'er their tops, she sadly saw
The knight beside the falcon.

The Enchanted Titan

1

Curse you! O, a hundred thousand curses
Weigh upon your soul, you black enchanter!
Could I pour them like the coins from purses,
I would utter such a pile instanter
As would crush you to a bloody pulp.
But my rage I fain am forced to gulp;
Anathemas are vain against cold iron,
Nor can I swear this magic box asunder,
Where I've been stifling since the days of Chiron,
Fretting on tempered bolts, and hurling muffled thunder.

2

Through the chinks I see the dim green waters
Filled with sunshine, or with moonlight hazy;
Through them swim the oceanic daughters,
Beautiful enough to drive me crazy.
The fishes gaze at me with sphery eyes,
And seem to say, with cold-blooded surprise.
What Titan is it, that's so barred and bolted,
Caged like a rat in some infernal cellar?
Why even Enceladus, when the dog revolted,
Was not so hardly treated by the Cloud-Compeller!

3

And all, forsooth, because I loved his daughter!
Loved that child of spells and incantation;
Love her now, beneath this dreary water.

Love her through eternal tribulation!
I wonder if her lips lament me still,
In her enchanted castle on the hill 1
Or has she yielded to that damned magician,
And with my pygmy rival weakly wedded?
Jove! the torment of this bare suspicion
Preying forever on my heart, and like the Hydra headed!

4

O bitter day, when spells, like snakes uprearing,
Enwrapped my limbs, and, muscular as pliant.
Pinioned my struggling arms, until despairing
I lay upon the earth, a captured giant!
Then came the horror of this iron box,—
The closing of its huge enchanted locks;
Then the cursed wizard to the windy summit
Of the tall cape a coffered prisoner bore me,
And flung me off, until, like seaman's plummet,
I sank, and the drear ocean closed forever o'er me!

www.ingramcontent.com/pod-product-compliance
Lightning Source LLC
Chambersburg PA
CBHW030922020726
47498CB00001B/75